THOMAS HARDY

THE EXCLUDED AND COLLABORATIVE STORIES

THOMAS HARDY

The Excluded and Collaborative Stories

Edited by
PAMELA DALZIEL

CLARENDON PRESS · OXFORD
1992

Oxford University Press, Walton Street, Oxford OX2 6DP
Oxford   New York   Toronto
Delhi   Bombay   Calcutta   Madras   Karachi
Petaling Jaya   Singapore   Hong Kong   Tokyo
Nairobi   Dar es Salaam   Cape Town
Melbourne   Auckland
and associated companies in
Berlin   Ibadan

Oxford is a trade mark of Oxford University Press

Published in the United States
by Oxford University Press, New York

British Library Cataloguing in Publication Data
Data available

Library of Congress Cataloging-in-Publication Data
Hardy, Thomas, 1840–1928.
Thomas Hardy, the excluded and collaborative stories / edited by
Pamela Dalziel.
Includes bibliographical references.
I. Dalziel, Pamela. II. Title.
PR4742.D35   1992
823'.8—dc20   91–36082
ISBN 0–19–812245–4

Typeset by BP Integraphics Ltd., Bath
Printed and bound in
Great Britain by Bookcraft Ltd.
Midsomer Norton, Bath

ACKNOWLEDGEMENTS

I wish to thank the Trustees of the Estate of the late Miss E. A. Dugdale for permission to publish 'The Unconquerable' and to quote from Florence Hardy's letters, and Sir Christopher Cockerell for permission to quote from his father's diaries and letters. I also thank the following private owners and public institutions for allowing me access to materials in their collections: Mr Frederick B. Adams; Bowdoin College, Brunswick, Maine; British Library; University of California at Los Angeles; Colby College Library, Waterville, Maine; Dorset County Museum; Gillingham Local History Society; Mr David Holmes; Dr James Jesty; Mr and Mrs T. W. Jesty; King's College, Cambridge; Brotherton Collection, University of Leeds; John Rylands University Library of Manchester; Professor Michael Millgate; National Library of Scotland; Albert A. and Henry W. Berg Collection, Astor, Lenox and Tilden Foundations, New York Public Library; Bodleian Library, University of Oxford; Morris Parrish Collection, Princeton University; Robert H. Taylor Collection, Princeton University; Signet Library, Edinburgh; Harry Ransom Humanities Research Center, University of Texas at Austin; Thomas Fisher Library, University of Toronto; Wiltshire Record Office; Beinecke Library, Yale University.

I am grateful to the editors of the *Papers of the Bibliographical Society of America*, the *Review of English Studies*, and the *Thomas Hardy Journal* for permission to reprint material from articles of mine which first appeared in their pages, and I am happy to acknowledge the financial support of the Commonwealth Scholarship Association and the Social Sciences and Humanities Research Council of Canada during my four years at Merton College, Oxford.

During the writing of the D.Phil. thesis on which this edition is based it was my privilege to have as supervisors Professor John Bayley, Dr J. D. Fleeman, and Professor D. F. McKenzie; to them I owe an enormous debt for their wise counsel and unwavering faith in this project and in me. Others who graciously assisted me with advice and answers to queries include: Dr Iain G. Brown, Dr J. Fraser Cocks, III, Professor Peter Davison, Professor Simon Gatrell, Mr and

Mrs T. W. Jesty, Professor Dale Kramer, Mrs Patricia Ingham, Mr R. N. R. Peers, and Mr John Pinnock.

For personal support of various kinds I am deeply grateful to Dr Yolande Chan, Ms Carol Westpfahl, the people of St Andrew's, Oxford, and my family. I also owe very special debts to Mr and Mrs Frederick B. Adams, both for access to indispensable documents and for the extraordinary kindness and generosity which alone made my work on this material possible, to Mr and Mrs T. W. Jesty for their warm hospitality and friendship, and, above all, to Professor Michael Millgate, at once the sternest of critics and the most generous of scholars, mentors, and friends.

Pamela Dalziel

December 1990

CONTENTS

REFERENCES AND ABBREVIATIONS

Unless otherwise indicated, references are to the Clarendon editions of *The Woodlanders* (ed. Dale Kramer, 1981) and *Tess of the d'Urbervilles* (ed. Juliet Grindle and Simon Gatrell, 1983) and to the Macmillan Wessex Edition (1912–13) of all of Hardy's other fiction collected during his lifetime. Shakespearean references are to the volume and page number of the 1856 Bell and Daldy edition owned by Hardy, but for ease of reference the corresponding act, scene, and line numbers from the Houghton Mifflin *Riverside Shakespeare* (ed. G. Blakemore Evans, 1974) have been included in parentheses.

For each story the sigla used in the variants are identified in the Note on the Text. The following abbreviations are used throughout:

EH	Emma Hardy
FEH	Florence Emily Hardy
FH	Florence Henniker
TH	Thomas Hardy
TN	Textual Notes
Adams	Frederick B. Adams collection
Beinecke	Richard Little Purdy Collection, Beinecke Library, Yale University
BL	British Library
DCM	Dorset County Museum
Biography	Michael Millgate, *Thomas Hardy: A Biography* (Oxford: Oxford University Press, 1982)
CL	*The Collected Letters of Thomas Hardy*, ed. Richard Little Purdy and Michael Millgate (7 vols.; Oxford: Clarendon Press, 1978–88)
Life	*The Life and Work of Thomas Hardy*, ed. Michael Millgate (London: Macmillan, 1984)
PN	*The Personal Notebooks of Thomas Hardy*, ed. Richard H. Taylor (London: Macmillan, 1979)
Purdy	Richard Little Purdy, *Thomas Hardy: A Bibliographical Study* (Oxford: Clarendon Press, 1954; rev. edn., 1978)

EDITORIAL INTRODUCTION

This edition brings together for the first time those stories of Thomas Hardy's which were excluded from the collective volumes published during his lifetime: 'How I Built Myself a House', 'Destiny and a Blue Cloak', 'The Thieves Who Couldn't Help Sneezing', 'An Indiscretion in the Life of an Heiress', 'Our Exploits at West Poley', 'Old Mrs Chundle', and 'The Doctor's Legend'. Also collected here are Hardy's collaborative stories, 'The Spectre of the Real', 'Blue Jimmy: The Horse Stealer', and 'The Unconquerable', the first written in collaboration with Florence Henniker, the latter two with Florence Dugdale. Although these works occupy significant, if sometimes minor, positions within Hardy's career as a writer of fiction, none of them has received serious editorial treatment in the past or currently exists in any kind of reliable published edition. For the most part they have also been ignored or lightly passed over by critics and biographers, and such discussion as they have aroused has generally been based on false (because unexamined) assumptions. This edition seeks to eliminate some of these deficiencies in Hardy scholarship.

The act of bringing together these ten stories perhaps suggests a coherence they do not in fact possess. Each story is an individual work, meriting treatment as such, and its unique conditions of composition and publication (or non-publication) have been carefully considered, in so far as they are now recoverable, when making editorial decisions. At the same time, those decisions have been based on a general policy which, as the title of this volume suggests, is both author-centric and—in relation to the collaborative stories—Hardy-centric. While it is clearly necessary, as Jerome J. McGann and D. F. McKenzie have demonstrated,[1] to recognize that the process of

[1] See, e.g., Jerome J. McGann, *A Critique of Modern Textual Criticism* (Chicago: University of Chicago Press, 1983); 'The Monks and the Giants: Textual and Bibliographical Studies and the Interpretation of Literary Works', in McGann (ed.), *Textual Criticism and Literary Interpretation* (Chicago: University of Chicago Press, 1985); 'Interpretation, Meaning, and Textual Criticism: A Homily', *Text*, 3 (1987), 55–62; and D. F. McKenzie, 'Typography and Meaning: The Case of William Congreve', in Giles Barber and Bernhard Fabian (eds.), *Buch und Buchhandel in Europa im achtzehnten Jahrhundert* (Wolfenbütteler Schriften zur Geschichte des Buchwesens, 4; Hamburg: Ernst Hanswedell, 1981); *Bibliography and the Sociology of Texts* (London: British Library, 1986).

textual production with its attendant editorial and compositorial collaboration (desired or undesired) is an inevitable and determining cultural phenomenon, it has seemed essential to emphasize the authorial function and responsibility in editing a collection held together only by the common (co-)authorship of the stories and concerned primarily with Hardy's creative process as exemplified in both original composition and revision. In any case, not all of the stories could be approached as products of their publication conditions, since not all were published.

That Hardy did not willingly submit his work to the vagaries of the production process emerges clearly from his holograph note on the typescript used as setting copy for 'The Spectre of the Real': '*To the printer*: Insert all *accents* & hyphens, & punctuate precisely as in copy. T.H.'[2] This injunction was not sufficient to prevent numerous variants being introduced into the proofs, but the fact that Hardy left most of these 'uncorrected' seems to constitute a merely passive endorsement rather than an expression of active preference. In this edition, then, the consistent aim has been to remove identifiable errors or intrusions on the part of amanuenses, typists, editors, and compositors and so recover, as far as possible, Hardy's own 'intentions' for each text.[3]

The question of which authorial 'intentions' to privilege—first, final, or something in between—is less problematic for the stories collected here than for any of Hardy's other fiction, precisely because they were not included in the Macmillan Wessex Edition which Hardy painstakingly prepared in his early seventies and thereafter considered 'definitive'.[4] Indeed, none of these stories was revised by

---

[2] Adams. Similar directions appear on the page proofs for the 1901 'sixpenny' edition of *Far from the Madding Crowd* (Signet Library, Edinburgh), and on the MS of *Poems of the Past and the Present* (Bodleian Library).

[3] The concept of authorial intention—final or otherwise—continues to be a controversial one. Notable discussions of the problem include: Hershel Parker, 'Melville and the Concept of "Author's Final Intentions"', *Proof*, 1 (1971), 156–68; James Thorpe, *Principles of Textual Criticism* (San Marino: Huntington Library, 1972); G. Thomas Tanselle, 'The Editorial Problem of Final Authorial Intention', *Studies in Bibliography*, 29 (1976), 167–211; Steven Mailloux, 'Textual Scholarship and "Author's Final Intention"', in *Interpretive Conventions: The Reader in the Study of American Fiction* (Ithaca: Cornell University Press, 1982); James McLaverty, 'The Concept of Authorial Intention in Textual Criticism', *Library*, 6th ser., 6 (June 1984), 121–38; and Hans Walter Gabler, 'The Text as Process and the Problem of Intentionality', *Text*, 3 (1987), 107–16.

[4] See, e.g., *CL* iv. 217, 227, 228. The first twenty vols. of the Wessex Edition were published at the rate of two per month in 1912–13, the remaining four at irregular intervals concluding (posthumously) in 1931.

Hardy subsequent to its first publication, a fact which renders it unnecessary to engage with the vexed issue of subsequent authorial revision in later years—the question of whether or not authors (to use Hershel Parker's terminology) fail to 're-enter' the original creative process and thus violate the integrity of their work, producing 'maimed' texts.[5] At the same time, the exclusion of these stories from the Wessex Edition points up the particular need for them to be edited critically:[6] of all Hardy's fiction they alone are not available in the edition which, irrespective of its limitations, is certainly authoritative.[7]

In view, then, of the limited number of authorized editions of these stories, it is relatively straightforward to establish editorial procedures which privilege Hardy's intentions, in so far as they are now recoverable. For the stories which survive only in a single authoritative printing ('How I Built Myself a House',[8] 'Destiny', 'Thieves', and 'Exploits') or only in a single manuscript or typescript ('Old Mrs Chundle' and 'The Unconquerable'), that text has necessarily been

---

[5] The most comprehensive statement of Parker's position is *Flawed Texts and Verbal Icons: Literary Authority in American Fiction* (Evanston, Ill.: Northwestern University Press, 1984). In *Hardy the Creator: A Textual Biography* (Oxford: Clarendon Press, 1988), Simon Gatrell maintains a much more conservative position than Parker's but does demonstrate that many of TH's late revisions fundamentally alter the direction of the novels.

[6] The limitations of the modern editions of the uncollected stories are discussed in Pamela Dalziel, 'A Critical Edition of Thomas Hardy's Uncollected Stories', D. Phil. thesis (University of Oxford, 1989), 17ff. The thesis also includes lists of sample errors.

[7] Because of its indisputable authority, the Wessex Edition has become the textual crux for most editors of TH's fiction. The debate centres on the choice of copy-text: critics who favour the Wessex Edition maintain that TH's close revision of the text indicates his active acceptance of its pointing and styling, while those (essentially following Greg–Bowers (see n. 9)) who opt for the MS not only argue that such acceptance is passive rather than active but that the MS punctuation is itself both distinctive and deliberate. See Simon Gatrell, 'Hardy, House-Style, and the Aesthetics of Punctuation', in Anne Smith (ed.), *The Novels of Thomas Hardy* (London: Vision, 1979); Philip Gaskell, *From Writer to Reader: Studies in Editorial Method* (Oxford: Clarendon Press, 1978); Robert C. Schweik and Michael Piret, 'Editing Hardy', *Browning Institute Studies*, 9 (1981), 15–41; Dale Kramer, 'Editing Hardy's Novels', in Norman Page (ed.), *Thomas Hardy Annual No. 5* (London: Macmillan, 1987); Gatrell, *Hardy the Creator*; and the editorial introductions to *The Woodlanders*, ed. Dale Kramer (Oxford: Clarendon Press, 1981); *Tess of the d'Urbervilles*, ed. Juliet Grindle and Simon Gatrell (Oxford: Clarendon Press, 1983); *Jude the Obscure*, ed. Patricia Ingham (Oxford: Oxford University Press, 1985); and *A Pair of Blue Eyes*, ed. Alan Manford (Oxford: Oxford University Press, 1985).

[8] 'How I Built Myself a House' in fact survives in two printings authorized by Hardy, but the later one does not introduce a single variant.

used as copy-text. For 'Indiscretion', published simultaneously in England and the United States, the copy-text is the edition apparently set from corrected proofs; for 'The Doctor's Legend' and 'Blue Jimmy' it is, respectively, the manuscript written out by Emma Hardy and the magazine proofs, both corrected by Hardy, the only other surviving textual witness in each case being the authorized, but clearly not authorially revised, periodical printing. With 'Spectre' the Hardy-centricity of the editorial policy becomes evident: the earliest surviving textual witness is used as copy-text and virtually all the subsequent revisions made by Hardy on the later typescript and on the magazine proofs are incorporated, while the largely bowdlerizing revisions introduced by Florence Henniker in her collective volume are excluded.

The thrust of the editorial policy for the stories in this volume has thus been towards the production of 'ideal first editions', and the texts presented here can perhaps be so categorized. Because of the paucity of surviving textual witnesses, however, it is a policy not fundamentally inconsistent with a Greg–Bowersian approach,[9] with the necessary proviso that in the collaborative texts it is only *Hardy's* authorial intentions which are being privileged.

For the stories which survive only in printed texts, emendations of wording have been introduced only when the compositorial reading is clearly erroneous and when the correction can be shown to fulfil the double criterion of supplying the sense required by the context and revealing the manner in which the corruption arose.

---

[9] Based on W. W. Greg's seminal essay, 'The Rationale of Copy-Text', *Studies in Bibliography*, 3 (1950–1), 19–36, and on Fredson Bowers's numerous endorsements and elaborations of that rationale both in his general discussions of editing and in his own critical editions. See, e.g., Bowers, *Textual and Literary Criticism* (Cambridge: Cambridge University Press, 1959); 'Textual Criticism', in *The Aims and Methods of Scholarship in Modern Languages and Literatures* (New York: Modern Language Association of America, 1963); *Bibliography and Textual Criticism* (Oxford: Clarendon Press, 1964); and 'Some Principles for Scholarly Editions of Nineteenth-Century American Authors', *Studies in Bibliography*, 17 (1964), 223–8. Bowers has been associated with numerous editions but the most influential in terms of the history of textual criticism are probably the Cambridge Dekker and the Ohio State Hawthorne. In recent years G. Thomas Tanselle has been the most prominent defender and continuator of the Greg–Bowers position: see, e.g., 'Greg's Theory of Copy-Text and the Editing of American Literature', *Studies in Bibliography*, 28 (1975), 167–229; 'Recent Editorial Discussion and the Central Questions of Editing', *Studies in Bibliography*, 34 (1981), 23–65; and 'Historicism and Critical Editing', *Studies in Bibliography*, 39 (1986), 1–46.

No attempt has been made to 'recreate' the missing manuscript: pointing uncharacteristic of Hardy may be recognizable but, given the inconsistencies in his own practice, gestures towards 'correction' would inevitably introduce still more non-authorial readings. Even in the case of Hardy's hyphenation practice, which to some extent could be statistically determined, emendation would still only be based on probability: there are literally hundreds of examples— such as the spellings 'bakehouse' and 'bake-house' within the space of a page in the manuscript of *The Woodlanders*[10]—which testify to his irregular usage. Because of this inconsistency—also exemplified in the profusion of such alternative spellings as Oh/O, further/farther, inquire/enquire, awhile/a while, and so forth—to impose any kind of regular system would amount, as Hershel Parker has convincingly argued in 'Regularizing Accidentals: The Latest Form of Infidelity', to a form of unnecessary modernization.[11]

A case can be made, however, for emendations of accidentals which serve to restore demonstrable rather than probable authorial usage. To follow strictly the copy-texts of the stories which survive only in US printings ('Destiny' and 'Exploits') would surely be to succumb to the 'tyranny of the copy-text', reproduce spellings Hardy never used, and pointlessly disturb the reading experience.[12] Hardy himself, although characteristically tolerant of such changes when encountered at the proof stage, can in no sense be said to have preferred them: when discussing a proposed *édition de luxe* of his works which was to be produced in the United States but also distributed in Britain he sought reassurance that the spelling would not be American.[13] Emendation is not always straightforward, however, since Hardy did use some forms usually thought of as American. Most obvious is his preference for '-ize' rather than '-ise' endings, demonstrated not only by his manuscript practice but also by his alterations of '-ise' to '-ize' in transcripts and

---

[10] fos. 95–6 (DCM).

[11] *Proof*, 3 (1973), 1–20; see also Joseph Moldenhauer's comments in his edition of *The Maine Woods* (Princeton: Princeton University Press, 1972), 399–400, on not regularizing copy-text pointing and styling to the statistically dominant forms in Thoreau's MSS.

[12] Cf. Harrison Hayford, Hershel Parker, and G. Thomas Tanselle's rationale for emending British spellings in the copy-text of *Typee* (Evanston: Northwestern University Press; Chicago: Newberry Library, 1968), 320.

[13] To Frederick Macmillan, 12 Oct. 1910 (*CL* iv. 124).

proofs[14] and by his instructions to printers.[15] It could even be argued that Hardy's intentions might be best honoured by emending the '-ise' words in the copy-texts which are English printings, but his practice was again inconsistent: 'surprize/d' and 'surprise/d' alternate in the 'For Conscience' Sake' manuscript, 'criticizing' and 'criticising' appear in a single paragraph of a 1921 letter, and so forth.[16] Hence the copy-text spellings of '-ize/-ise' words, and also of 'grey/gray' (both of which Hardy used), have been retained, even while all other US forms have been altered to conform with standard British usage.

Single quotation marks in printed copy-texts have also been emended. In his manuscripts Hardy invariably used double quotation marks for dialogue and there seems no justification for preserving demonstrably non-authorial features even when they affect only the formal presentation of the text. Manuscript ampersands have been expanded and, in accordance with Hardy's normal practice, periods after 'Mr', 'Mrs', and 'Dr' in printed copy-texts have been removed. He seems to have been much less consistent with respect to the abbreviation of 'Saint', and here the copy-text forms have been followed.

Such obvious errors as misspellings, omitted full stops and quotation marks, and so forth, have been corrected. The only 'regularization' involves the placing of punctuation marks in relation to closing quotation marks. Hardy did not always use pointing to set passages of dialogue off from the identification of the speaker,[17] but when he did do so his normal practice was to place it before the quotation marks; dashes indicating interrupted or unfinished sentences are also so placed. Those occasional instances where the quotation marks precede the punctuation have therefore been emended.[18] Less straightforward emendations of punctuation—for the most part in texts

---

[14] To give just two out of dozens of examples: 'idiotised' in EH's transcription of 'The Doctor's Legend' (p. 412) and 'sympathise' in the proofs of 'The Son's Veto' (*Life's Little Ironies* proofs, col. 6; DCM).

[15] E.g. on the MS of *Poems of the Past and the Present* (Bodleian Library) and the page proofs for the 1901 'sixpenny' edition of *Far from the Madding Crowd* (Signet Library, Edinburgh).

[16] 'For Conscience' Sake' MS, fos. 6, 10, 11, 15, 22 (John Rylands University Library of Manchester); *CL* vi. 77.

[17] See, e.g., pp. 228. 27, 234. 29, 235. 20, and Kramer, 'The Edited Text', in *The Woodlanders*, 55.

[18] Punctuation ambiguously placed below the quotation marks in EH's transcription of 'The Doctor's Legend' has been silently moved to the left.

which survive only in printed witnesses not read in proof by Hardy—
are discussed in the textual notes. Silent emendations are confined to
matters of styling. Story titles and section headings are standardized,
as is the capitalization of the first words of opening paragraphs, and
ellipses are reduced to the conventional three points. Also unrecorded
are differences in type-size and spacing, mechanical corrections
(typists' overstrikes, for example), slips of the pen corrected in the
process of transcription, and reinscriptions of imperfectly typed
letters and words. Punctuation redundancies resulting from typing
errors or Hardy's oversight during revision do not figure in the variants lists but are mentioned in the textual notes.

   In order to facilitate the examination of editorial emendations, all
alterations of copy-text wording, pointing, and spelling are signalled
in the variants lists by the presence of a dagger (†). The siglum '*Ed.*'
indicates that the emendation does not occur in any surviving textual
witness. Variants in wording, preceded by line numbers, are recorded
at the foot of each page. Punctuation and styling variants and typographical (or transcriptional) errors are listed at the back of the
volume; references are to page and line numbers. Superscript numbers distinguish among multiple occurrences of a word within a single
line. The presence of an asterisk indicates that the lemma does not
appear in the edited text and can be found in the wording variants.
Swung dashes are used to represent identical words, carets to indicate
missing punctuation.

   All variants are listed in *reverse* chronological order and each is
followed by the siglum of the earliest text in which it occurred, the same
reading appearing in all subsequent texts unless otherwise indicated.
Readings marked '*p*' were written in pencil, those marked '*p&i*' first in
pencil, then in ink. Layers of revision are indicated by '*MS(1)*'—or
'*TS(1)*'—'*MS(2)*', and so forth, '*MS(1)*' being the earliest layer. All
variant readings appearing earlier than the last reading are deletions
(or erasures if written in pencil) and all appearing later than the first
are additions unless otherwise indicated. Thus in the following
example Hardy initially wrote 'flowers. The', then altered the full stop
to a semi-colon and wrote above the line '& on this incident, trivial as it
was, hung much afterwards of concern to the house & lineage of the
Squire. It seems that', and finally added 'that was' before 'afterwards':

flowers ... seems that the *MS(3)TH*] ... much afterwards ... *MS(2)TH*]
flowers. The *MS(1)*

The lemma here includes 'flowers' in order to permit the display of a punctuation change which only makes sense within the context of the revised wording. Sometimes an initial unaltered word also appears in the lemma to indicate or clarify the location. In the first of the following examples 'away' has been deleted; in the second 'the' has been added to a line containing another 'the':

went *MS(2)TH*] went away *MS(1)*
chose the *MS(2)TH*] chose *MS(1)*

Uncertain readings are enclosed in angle brackets. Material added to expand rather than to replace an earlier reading is marked '[*added*]'. A revision which occurs in the same line as an earlier reading is marked '[*altered in same line*]'; a deletion not representing a complete earlier version is signified by '[*not continued*]'. An isolated plus sign concluding a listing of variants (for example, '*2TS* +')[19] indicates that in the interests of clarity 'major' and 'minor' revisions to the same passage have been presented separately, and that the immediately following listings need to be read in conjunction with the preceding entry.

Variants in printed texts are recorded in essentially the same way, though in the absence of holograph corrections the terminology necessarily differs. Added material, for example, is indicated by '[*not in —*]'. Moreover, since there is no need to indicate deletions, lemmata which could technically be reduced to a single word in frequent use have been expanded for ease of reference, as in the following:

was what] is what
success that] success

Punctuation which concludes wording variants is recorded only if it is part of the emendation (i.e. if the original mark has been deleted and another, even if of the same kind, has been added), or if its omission would be potentially misleading owing to the length of the variants. For example:

looked disturbed, *MS(2)TH*] turned pale, *MS(1)*
turned,] returned
as the darkness ... building,] the rector's pulpit candles shone to the remotest nooks of the building as the darkness deepened during the progress of the sermon,

[19] Where there is no space between the lemma and the plus sign (e.g. '*2TS*+') the plus sign indicates that the same reading recurs in all subsequent texts.

Alterations made by Thomas Hardy, Emma Hardy, and Florence Henniker are marked '*TH*', '*EH*', and '*FH*', respectively. In the case of deletions and changes of punctuation the hand often cannot be positively identified, but the context and the nature of the revision in combination with other factors (the shade of ink or the neatness of the pen-stroke, for example) provide a relatively reliable guide. In general it has been assumed that Hardy did most of the revising of the pointing as he did of the wording; doubtful instances are marked '*TH?*'. Corrections apparently made by typists are marked '*TS(2)*' rather than '*TS(2)TH*'.

It should be noted that the lemma is quoted from the edited text, and may therefore incorporate 'automatic' editorial emendations not present in the text indicated by the siglum. This is particularly noticeable, and potentially misleading, when copy-text quotation marks have been altered, since the variant readings have not been 'regularized' but are recorded as they appear. Thus in the following example the revised manuscript actually reads 'Squire",' and the reading is included not because of the quotation marks but because of the upper-case 's' and the placing of the comma:

Squire', *MS(2)TH*] ~,' *IN*] squire", *MS(1)*

Note, too, that, since differences in the use of quotation marks are described as a group rather than individually recorded, separate entries have not been included for readings which do not differ in some other respect. For example, the US edition of *In Scarlet and Grey* uses single quotation marks throughout, and therefore reads ' 'I' even though the reading is recorded:

"I *1TS, SGa*] ∧I *SG*

Compound words hyphenated at the end of the line in the edited text are hyphenated in the copy-text. Discrepant end-line hyphenations in other textual witnesses are not recorded unless they are clearly variants. For example, neither 'day-/light' nor 'drawing-/room' is recorded because the copy-text reads 'daylight' and 'drawing-room', but 'rain-/spots', set from 'rain spots', is included. Compound words hyphenated at the end of the line in the copy-texts are recorded in a separate list and appear in the edited texts in the form Hardy most frequently used.

How I Built Myself a House

INTRODUCTION

In 1880 Emma Hardy began a list of her husband's works with '*How I built myself a House*—A short sketch—Chambers' Journal May 1864—or 65. Only two or three pages'.[1] The story was in fact published in March 1865, almost three years after Hardy had left Dorset for London in order to pursue his architectural career. Shortly after his arrival in April 1862 he had found employment as an assistant architect in Arthur Blomfield's office, where for the next five years he performed his duties with considerable competence, if not with particular enthusiasm.[2] Although he considered the work 'monotonous and mechanical', it was not arduous, leaving him with sufficient time and energy to pursue other interests—even during office hours.[3] One of his young colleagues at Blomfield's later recalled that Hardy was much given to talking about 'literature & the writers of that time', an activity also mentioned in the autobiographical *Life*:

he used to deliver short addresses or talks on poets and poetry to Blomfield's pupils and assistants on afternoons when there was not much to be done, or at all events when not much was done. There is no tradition of what Blomfield thought of this method of passing office hours instead of making architectural plans.[4]

On such an afternoon Hardy doubtless read out 'How I Built Myself a House'—a 'humorous trifle', as he described it in *Life*, 'written to amuse the pupils of Blomfield'[5]—before sending it to the London office of *Chambers's Journal*. Received between 25 November and

---

[1] DCM; the date can be inferred from EH's last item, '*The Fellow Townsmen*' [*sic*] (published Apr. 1880). TH revised the list—presumably in late 1880 or early 1881, since his added entry for *A Laodicean* refers only to the first month of the serialization (Dec. 1880)—and in including 'An Essay on Brick & Terra Cotta Architecture' relegated 'How I Built Myself a House' to second place.

[2] *Biography*, 75, 81, 92, 97; *Life*, 49.   [3] *Life*, 49.

[4] W. O. Milne to C. J. Blomfield, 23 May 1911 (Adams); *Life*, 49.

[5] *Life*, 49–50.

10 December 1864,[6] the story was 'accepted at once'[7] and published anonymously as the leading contribution in the 18 March 1865 issue. The receipt, dated 'London, May 3rd, 1865' and signed by Hardy, reads: 'Received from Messrs W. & R. Chambers the sum of Three pounds 15/— being payment in full for writing How I built myself a house for publication in Chambers Journal, and any other of their works.'[8]

In 1863 Hardy had begun to train himself for a possible new career as an art critic or some kind of literary journalist[9]—ambitions which presumably would have been encouraged by the story's acceptance. But, in spite of the statement (in the manuscript of the biographical article Hardy prepared for the Boston *Literary World* in 1878) that 'fiction thence forward became his hobby',[10] there is no evidence that he submitted for publication any other prose during this period. He did, however, consciously attempt to establish himself as a poet— reading and studying others' work, as well as making his own experiments with diction, rhythm, and form[11] —though apparently not, at this point, with any expectation of making a living as a writer.

In the published version of the *Literary World* article the acceptance of 'How I Built Myself a House' is no longer said to have made fiction Hardy's 'hobby', but to have 'determined' his career.[12] The revision, presumably authorial, anticipates a remark in *Life*: 'It may have been the acceptance of this *jeu d'esprit* that turned his mind in the direction of prose'.[13] The *Chambers's* publication not only brought Hardy his first literary earnings but also forced him to recognize that fiction was more placeable—and certainly more lucrative—than poetry. According to *Life*, he had begun to send poems to magazines by 1866,[14] but all were rejected and, with a characteristic lack of self-confidence, he essentially abandoned verse, at least as a potential source of income, for the next thirty years. Although he continued to

---

[6] Chambers 'Authors' Book' (National Library of Scotland, Dep. 341/292). Submissions were apparently not recorded daily; the batch including TH's story is dated 10 Dec., the preceding one 25 Nov.

[7] MS of *Literary World* article (Bowdoin College, Brunswick, Maine); although in EH's hand, it has been revised by TH and was undoubtedly written by him (see *Biography*, 195, and Purdy, 295).

[8] National Library of Scotland, Dep. 341/332.   [9] *Biography*, 81, 86–7.

[10] See n. 7.

[11] *Biography*, 87–9; *Life*, 49.

[12] 'Thomas Hardy', *Literary World* (Aug. 1878), 46.

[13] *Life*, 50.   [14] Ibid. 49.

write poetry during the latter half of the decade[15]—and, indeed, to some extent throughout his career—with the composition in 1867 of his first novel, *The Poor Man and the Lady*, he can be said to have 'seriously take[n] up prose'.[16]

Towards the end of his life Hardy spoke disparagingly of 'How I Built Myself a House', not only referring to it in *Life* as a 'humorous trifle', but also rejecting Paul Lemperly's 2 December 1909 request to republish it (presumably in a limited edition) on the grounds that: 'The idea does not commend itself to me, the sketch being unrepresentative, & having arisen out of an incident that had no connection with my literary pursuits at the time.'[17] It is true that the story is 'unrepresentative' and that in 1864–5 Hardy's literary interests were predominantly poetic; on the other hand, the implication that it was not worth reprinting—explicitly stated in his 27 June 1924 letter to C. E. S. Chambers ('I should have included it in my miscellaneous works if I had not thought it too trifling')—is somewhat undercut by his subsequent claim not to 'mind at all' if it were included in the issue of *Chambers's Journal* marking the diamond jubilee of its original publication.[18] And printed it was in the first issue for 1925 (published 6 December 1924), along with a new poem, 'A Bird-scene at a Rural Dwelling', and preceded by several laudatory paragraphs headed, ' " 'TIS SIXTY YEARS SINCE." | THOMAS HARDY AND *CHAMBERS'S JOURNAL*. | 1865. OUR GREATEST CONTRIBUTOR. 1925.'

The story had in fact been reprinted 'by courtesy of the owners of the copyright, Messrs. W. & R. Chambers, Ltd.',[19] though without Hardy's authorization,[20] twice already—in the *Review of Reviews* (May 1922) and the *First Edition and Book Collector* (July–August 1924). Ernest Brennecke subsequently included it in his entirely unauthorized *Life and Art* (New York: Greenberg, 1925), which Hardy described as 'an olla podrida', a volume 'ingeniously made up of articles, &c., all copyright in England, but having been mostly printed before 1891, not copyright in America, together with letters to the papers, & other raked up scraps'.[21] After Hardy's death, too, the story was published in the *Book League Monthly* (December 1928) and,

---

[15] *Biography*, 108.   [16] *Life*, 50.   [17] Ibid. 49; *CL* iv. 70.
[18] *CL* vi. 261; 1 Aug. 1924, *CL* vi. 267.
[19] *Review of Reviews* (May 1922), 512; C. E. S. Chambers to TH, 1 July 1924 (DCM).
[20] TH to Chambers, 27 June, 5 July 1924 (*CL* vi. 261, 263).
[21] To Borlase Childs, 18 Apr. 1925 (*CL* vi. 322).

more recently, in Harold Orel's edition, *Thomas Hardy's Personal Writings* (Lawrence: University of Kansas Press, 1966). The interest that such a history reflects is no doubt primarily attributable to the simple fact that 'How I Built Myself a House' is Hardy's first published story. None the less, it is not without independent attractions, particularly its shrewd humour and deft handling of viewpoint. Its resemblance to the 'typical' *Chambers's* contribution of the 1860s in tone, length, and subject-matter[22] can be linked with Hardy's remark to Leslie Stephen nine years later when writing *Far from the Madding Crowd*: 'Perhaps I may have higher aims some day ... but for the present circumstances lead me to wish merely to be considered a good hand at a serial'.[23] As is demonstrated by his willingness to act on the suggestions of early readers— notably Alexander Macmillan, John Morley, and George Meredith[24]—Hardy was eager to write what the public wanted: 'How I Built Myself a House' is a self-conscious exercise in a conventional mode; its style is unabashedly Dickensian[25]—especially in such comic scenes as the exchange between architect and clerk or the scaffold-climbing—while its satire is often Thackerayan. Hardy had not yet adopted the advice of his early mentor Horace Moule ('you must in the end write *your own* style, unless you w^d be a mere imitator')[26] and was very much writing under the shadow of his famous Victorian predecessors. Even so, the style does suggest competence and assurance, while the story itself prefigures Hardy's subsequent fiction in various ways. Michael Millgate's remark that 'How I Built Myself a House' 'seems wholly out of key with Hardy's later work' in 'almost every respect'—its 'satirical archness', 'use of a dramatised first-person point of view', and 'adoption of a specifically urban and middle-class persona'[27]—is for the most part true. But there are exceptions, most notably, it would seem, the lost first novel,

[22] Cf. the selections in Robert Chambers, *Essays Familiar and Humorous (Reprinted from 'Chambers's Journal')*, 2nd ser. (London and Edinburgh: W. & R. Chambers [1866]).

[23] [18 Feb. 1874?], *CL* i. 28.

[24] See pp. 14, 72, and 76, and Charles Morgan, *The House of Macmillan (1843–1943)* (London: Macmillan, 1943), 87 ff.

[25] Remarked by Robert Gittings, *Young Thomas Hardy* (London: Heinemann, 1975), 77.

[26] 2 July 1863 (DCM).

[27] Michael Millgate, *Thomas Hardy: His Career as a Novelist* (London: The Bodley Head, 1971), 18.

The Poor Man and the Lady: Morley, one of the very few to read that manuscript, remarked on its 'cleverness & hard sarcasm'; it is said to have been told '*By the Poor Man*';[28] and the protagonist becomes a (perhaps marginalized) member of the urban middle class (see p. 71). Moreover, the novel's original subtitle was '*A Story with no plot*'.[29] According to Morley, 'the thing [hung] too loosely together',[30] and the same could be said of the essentially anecdotal 'How I Built Myself a House'—frequently, and not inappropriately, referred to as a 'sketch' both by Hardy and by others.[31]

It was only with *Desperate Remedies* that Hardy, acting on Meredith's advice, deliberately sought to create a 'complicated "plot"'[32]—going too far, however, in the opposite direction, as he was also to do in his second short story, 'Destiny and a Blue Cloak'. There is, in fact, little resemblance between 'How I Built Myself a House' and *Desperate Remedies*, Hardy's earliest surviving fictional works, though architecture does figure in both, Mr Penny being succeeded by numerous architects in the later novel, and the farcical scaffold-climbing episode giving place to the dramatic fall from the scaffolding around the church spire. The use of architects and architectural scenes—compare, too, 'Fellow-Townsmen' and *A Laodicean*—reflects Hardy's tendency throughout his career to write for the most part about familiar things. His experience of house-building at this time was, however, only that of an architect not that of a prospective owner (though the story appears to have prophetically foreshadowed some of the difficulties in building Max Gate)[33] and there is little resemblance—at least externally—between him and his protagonist-narrator, a 'typical' middle-class client. It is therefore by no means the least interesting aspect of the story that it should be one of the few surviving prose examples—the only others being 'Our Exploits

---

[28] Macmillan 'Reviews of Manuscripts', i (BL Add. MS 55931), 63; *Life*, 58.

[29] *Life*, 58.

[30] Macmillan 'Reviews of Manuscripts', i. 62.

[31] *CL* iii. 260, iv. 69, v. 94; EH's two lists of TH's works (DCM); *Biography*, 87; Purdy, 293. Although discussed in Kristin Brady, *The Short Stories of Thomas Hardy: Tales of Past and Present* (London: Macmillan, 1982), it is omitted from the New Wessex editions of both *Old Mrs Chundle and Other Stories* (London: Macmillan, 1977) and *Collected Short Stories* (London: Macmillan, 1988), and included under the heading 'Reminiscences and Personal Views' in *Thomas Hardy's Personal Writings*, ed. Orel. Note that TH's distinction between 'sketch' and 'story' is essentially evaluative rather than ontological (see p. 28).

[32] *Life*, 64.   [33] *Biography*, 257.

at West Poley', 'A Tryst at an Ancient Earthwork', and 'Alicia's Diary'—of Hardy's sustained use of a fully dramatized and clearly non-authorial first-person narrator. Moreover, as Kristin Brady remarks, the story anticipates Hardy's subsequent work 'in its perception that life is intrinsically unsatisfactory'[34]—if not bitterly so. In a similarly light-hearted way the protagonist-narrator—taken advantage of by his wife, the architect, the foreman, the builder, and the surveyor—can be said to prefigure those numerous Hardyan figures who 'feel the painful sting of ... modern mankind, the disproportion between the desire for serenity and the power of obtaining it'.[35]

BIBLIOGRAPHICAL DESCRIPTIONS

Periodical Publication

Chambers's Journal of Popular Literature, Science, and Art, 4th ser. (18 Mar. 1865)
The double-columned text begins on p. [161] and concludes in col. 1 of p. 164. The title, heading col. 1, reads:
HOW I BUILT MYSELF A HOUSE.
No mention is made of the author's name.

Chambers's Journal, 7th ser., 15 (6 Dec. 1924)
The double-columned text appears on pp. 2–5. The title reads:
HOW I BUILT MYSELF A HOUSE. | By THOMAS HARDY. |
[Reprinted from *Chambers's Journal* for March 18, 1865.]

NOTE ON THE TEXT

The copy-text is the 18 March 1865 *Chambers's Journal* text, which was also the basis for the other four printings during TH's lifetime. Of the four, only the 6 December 1924 *Chambers's Journal* printing was authorized by TH[1] and the reset text does not vary in a single reading from the original. The only recorded variants, then, are editorial emendations of the copy-text and neither lemmata nor variants are followed by sigla.

[34] Brady, *Short Stories*, 159.
[35] TH, rev. of *Poems of Rural Life in the Dorset Dialect*, by William Barnes, *New Quarterly Magazine* (Oct. 1879), 472.
[1] Although the variant readings in the other three texts lack authorial authority, they are significant in relation to the story's textual history and can be found in Pamela Dalziel, 'A Critical Edition of Thomas Hardy's Uncollected Stories', D. Phil. thesis (University of Oxford, 1989), 53 ff.

HOW I BUILT MYSELF A HOUSE

My wife Sophia, myself, and the beginning of a happy line, formerly
lived in the suburbs of London, in the sort of house called a Highly-
Desirable Semi-detached Villa. But in reality our residence was the
very opposite of what we wished it to be. We had no room for our
5 friends when they visited us, and we were obliged to keep our coals
out of doors in a heap against the back-wall. If we managed to squeeze
a few acquaintances round our table to dinner, there was very great
difficulty in serving it; and on such occasions the maid, for want of
sideboard room, would take to putting the dishes in the staircase, or
10 on stools and chairs in the passage, so that if anybody else came after
we had sat down, he usually went away again, disgusted at seeing the
remains of what we had already got through standing in these places,
and perhaps the celery waiting in a corner hard by. It was therefore
only natural that on wet days, chimney-sweepings, and those
15 cleaning times when chairs may be seen with their legs upwards, a tub
blocking a doorway, and yourself walking about edgeways among the
things, we called the villa hard names, and that we resolved to escape
from it as soon as it would be politic, in a monetary sense, to carry out
a notion which had long been in our minds.
20 This notion was to build a house of our own a little further out of
town than where we had hitherto lived. The new residence was to be
right and proper in every respect. It was to be of some mysterious size
and proportion, which would make us both peculiarly happy ever
afterwards—that had always been a settled thing. It was neither to
25 cost too much nor too little, but just enough to fitly inaugurate the
new happiness. Its situation was to be in a healthy spot, on a stratum of
dry gravel, about ninety feet above the springs. There were to be trees
to the north, and a pretty view to the south. It was also to be easily
accessible by rail.
30 Eighteen months ago, a third baby being our latest blessing, we
began to put the above-mentioned ideas into practice. As the house
itself, rather than its position, is what I wish particularly to speak of, I
will not dwell upon the innumerable difficulties that were to be

overcome before a suitable spot could be found. Maps marked out in little pink and green oblongs clinging to a winding road, became as familiar to my eyes as my own hand. I learned, too, all about the coloured plans of Land to be Let for Building Purposes, which are exhibited at railway stations and in agents' windows—that sketches 5 of cabbages in rows, or artistically irregular, meant large trees that would afford a cooling shade when they had been planted and had grown up—that patches of blue showed fishponds and fountains; and that a wide straight road to the edge of the map was the way to the station, a corner of which was occasionally shown, as if it would come 10 within a convenient distance, disguise the fact as the owners might.

After a considerable time had been spent in these studies, I began to see that some of our intentions in the matter of site must be given up. The trees to the north went first. After a short struggle, they were followed by the ninety feet above the springs. Sophia, with all wifely 15 tenacity, stuck to the pretty view long after I was beaten about the gravel subsoil. In the end, we decided upon a place imagined to be rather convenient, and rather healthy, but possessing no other advantage worth mentioning. I took it on a lease for the established period, ninety-nine years. 20

We next thought about an architect. A friend of mine, who sometimes sends a paper on art and science to the magazines, strongly recommended a Mr Penny, a gentleman whom he considered to have architectural talent of every kind, but if he was a trifle more skilful in any one branch of his profession than in another, 25 it was in designing excellent houses for families of moderate means. I at once proposed to Sophia that we should think over some arrangement of rooms which would be likely to suit us, and then call upon the architect, that he might put our plan into proper shape.

I made my sketch, and my wife made hers. Her drawing and dining 30 rooms were very large, nearly twice the size of mine, though her doors and windows showed sound judgment. We soon found that there was no such thing as fitting our ideas together, do what we would. When we had come to no conclusion at all, we called at Mr Penny's office. I began telling him my business, upon which he took a sheet of 35 foolscap, and made numerous imposing notes, with large brackets and dashes to them. Sitting there with him in his office, surrounded by rolls of paper, circles, squares, triangles, compasses, and many other of the inventions which have been sought out by men from time to

time, and perceiving that all these were the realities which had been
faintly shadowed forth to me by Euclid some years before, it is no
wonder that I became a puppet in his hands. He settled everything in
a miraculous way. We were told the only possible size we could have
5 the rooms, the only way we should be allowed to go upstairs, and the
exact quantity of wine we might order at once, so as to fit the wine-
cellar he had in his head. His professional opinions, propelled by his
facts, seemed to float into my mind whether I wished to receive them
or not. I thought at the time that Sophia, from her silence, was in the
10 same helpless state; but she has since told me it was quite otherwise,
and that she was only a little tired.

I had been very anxious all along that the stipulated cost, eighteen
hundred pounds, should not be exceeded, and I impressed this again
upon Mr Penny.

15 "I will give you an approximate estimate for the sort of thing we are
thinking of," he said. "Linem." (This was the clerk.)

"Did you speak, sir?"

"Forty-nine by fifty-four by twenty-eight, twice fourteen by thirty-
one by eleven, and several small items which we will call one hundred
20 and sixty."

"Eighty-two thousand four hundred—"

"But eighteen hundred at the very outside," I began, "is what—"

"Feet, my dear sir—feet, cubic feet," said Mr Penny. "Put it down
at sixpence a foot, Linem, remainders not an object."

25 "Two thousand two hundred pounds." This was too much.

"Well, try it at something less, leaving out all below hundreds,
Linem."

"About eighteen hundred and seventy pounds."

"Very satisfactory, in my opinion," said Mr Penny turning to me.
30 "What do you think?"

"You are so particular, John," interrupted my wife. "I am sure it is
exceedingly moderate: elegance and extreme cheapness never do go
together."

(It may be here remarked that Sophia never calls me "my dear"
35 before strangers. She considers that, like the ancient practice in
besieged cities of throwing loaves over the walls, it really denotes a
want rather than an abundance of them within.)

I did not trouble the architect any further, and we rose to leave.

"Be sure you make a nice conservatory, Mr Penny," said my wife;

"something that has character about it. If it could only be in the
Chinese style, with beautiful ornaments at the corners, like Mrs
Smith's, only better," she continued, turning to me with a glance in
which a broken tenth commandment might have been seen.

"Some sketches shall be forwarded, which I think will suit you,"   5
answered Mr Penny pleasantly, looking as if he had possessed for
some years a complete guide to the minds of all people who intended
to build.

It is needless to go through the whole history of the plan-making.
A builder had been chosen, and the house marked out, when we   10
went down to the place one morning to see how the foundations
looked.

It is a strange fact, that a person's new house drawn in outline on
the ground where it is to stand, looks ridiculously and
inconveniently small. The notion it gives one is, that any portion of 15
one's after-life spent within such boundaries must of necessity be
rendered wretched on account of bruises daily received by running
against the partitions, doorposts, and fireplaces. In my case, the
lines showing sitting-rooms seemed to denote cells; the kitchen
looked as if it might develop into a large box; whilst the study   20
appeared to consist chiefly of a fireplace and a door. We were told
that houses always looked so; but Sophia's disgust at the sight of
such a diminutive drawing-room was not to be lessened by any
scientific reasoning. Six feet longer—four feet then—three it must
be, she argued, and the room was accordingly lengthened. I felt   25
rather relieved when at last I got her off the ground, and on the road
home.

The building gradually crept upwards, and put forth chimneys.
We were standing beside it one day, looking at the men at work on
the top, when the builder's foreman came towards us.   30

"Being your own house, sir, and as we are finishing the last
chimney, you would perhaps like to go up," he said.

"I am sure I should much, if I were a man," was my wife's
observation to me. "The landscape must appear so lovely from that
height."   35

This remark placed me in something of a dilemma, for it must be
confessed that I am not given to climbing. The sight of cliffs, roofs,
scaffoldings, and elevated places in general, which have no sides to
keep people from slipping off, always causes me to feel how infinitely

preferable a position at the bottom is to a position at the top of them. But as my house was by no means lofty, and it was but for once, I said I would go up.

My knees felt a good deal in the way as I ascended the ladder; but
5   that was not so disagreeable as the thrill which passed through me as I followed my guide along two narrow planks, one bending beneath each foot. However, having once started, I kept on, and next climbed another ladder, thin and weak-looking, and not tied at the top. I could not help thinking, as I viewed the horizon between the steps,
10 what a shocking thing it would be if any part should break; and to get rid of the thought, I adopted the device of mentally criticising the leading articles in that morning's *Times;* but as the plan did not answer, I tried to fancy that, though strangely enough it seemed otherwise, I was only four feet from the ground. This was a failure too;
15 and just as I had commenced upon an idea that great quantities of feather-beds were spread below, I reached the top scaffold.

"Rather high," I said to the foreman, trying, but failing to appear unconcerned.

"Well, no," he answered; "nothing to what it is sometimes (I'll just
20 trouble you not to step upon the end of that plank there, as it will turn over); though you may as well fall from here as from the top of the Monument for the matter of life being quite extinct when they pick you up," he continued, looking around at the weather and the crops, as it were.

25 Then a workman, with a load of bricks, stamped along the boards, and overturned them at my feet, causing me to shake up and down like the little servant-men behind private cabs. I asked, in trepidation, if the bricks were not dangerously heavy, thinking of a newspaper paragraph headed "Frightful Accident from an
30 Overloaded Scaffold."

"Just what I was going to say. Dan has certainly too many there," answered the man. "But it won't break down if we walk without springing, and don't sneeze, though the mortar-boy's hooping-cough was strong enough in my poor brother Jim's case," he continued
35 abstractedly, as if he himself possessed several necks, and could afford to break one or two.

My wife was picking daisies a little distance off, apparently in a state of complete indifference as to whether I was on the scaffold, at the foot of it, or in St George's Hospital; so I roused myself for a descent, and tried the small ladder. I cannot accurately say how I did get down; but during that performance, my body seemed perforated by holes, through which breezes blew in all directions. As I got nearer the earth, they went away. It may be supposed that my wife's notion of the height differed considerably from my own, and she inquired 5 particularly for the landscape, which I had quite forgotten; but the discovery of that fact did not cause me to break a resolution not to trouble my chimneys again.

Beyond a continual anxiety and frequent journeyings along the sides of a triangle, of which the old house, the new house, and the 10 architect's office were the corners, nothing worth mentioning happened till the building was nearly finished. Sophia's ardour in the business, which at the beginning was so intense, had nearly burned itself out, so I was left pretty much to myself in getting over the later difficulties. Amongst them was the question of a porch. I had often 15 been annoyed whilst waiting outside a door on a wet day at being exposed to the wind and rain, and it was my favourite notion that I would have a model porch whenever I should build a house. Thus it was very vexing to recollect, just as the workmen were finishing off, that I had never mentioned the subject to Mr Penny, and that he had 20 not suggested anything about one to me.

"A porch or no porch is entirely a matter of personal feeling and taste," was his remark, in answer to a complaint from me; "so, of course, I did not put one without its being mentioned. But it happens that in this case it would be an improvement—a feature, in fact. 25 There is this objection, that the roof will close up the window of the little place on the landing; but we may get ventilation by making an opening higher up, if you don't mind a trifling darkness, or rather gloom."

My first thought was that this might tend to reduce myself and 30 family to a state of chronic melancholy; but remembering there were reflectors advertised to throw sunlight into any nook almost, I agreed to the inconvenience, for the sake of the porch, though I found afterwards that the gloom was for all time, the patent reflector, naturally enough, sending its spot of light against the opposite wall, 35 where it was not wanted, and leaving none about the landing, where it was.

In getting a house built for a specified sum by contract with a builder, there is a certain pit-fall into which unwary people are sure to

step—this accident is technically termed "getting into extras." It is evident that the only way to get out again without making a town-talk about yourself, is to pay the builder a large sum of money over and above the contract amount—the value of course of the extras. In the
5 present case, I knew very well that the perceptible additions would have to be paid for. Common sense, and Mr Penny himself perhaps, should have told me a little more distinctly that I must pay if I said "yes" to questions whether I preferred one window a trifle larger than it was originally intended, another a trifle smaller, second thoughts as
10 to where a doorway should be, and so on. Then came a host of things "not included"—a sink in the scullery, a rain-water tank and a pump, a trap-door into the roof, a scraper, a weather-cock and four letters, ventilators in the nursery, same in the kitchen, all of which worked vigorously enough, but the wrong way; patent remarkable bell-pulls;
15 a royal letters extraordinary kitchen-range, which it would cost exactly threepence three-farthings to keep a fire in for twelve hours, and yet cook any joint in any way, warm up what was left yesterday, boil the vegetables, and do the ironing. But not keeping a strict account of all these expenses, and thinking myself safe in Mr Penny's
20 hands from any enormous increase, I was astounded to find that the additions altogether came to some hundreds of pounds. I could almost go through the worry of building another house, to show how carefully I would avoid getting into extras again.

Then they have to be wound up. A surveyor is called in from
25 somewhere, and, by a fiction, his heart's desire is supposed to be that you shall not be overcharged one halfpenny by the builder for the additions. The builder names a certain sum as the value of a portion—say double its worth, the surveyor then names a sum, about half its true value. They then fight it out by word of mouth, and
30 gradually bringing their valuations nearer and nearer together, at last meet in the middle. All my accounts underwent this operation.

A Families-removing van carried our furniture and effects to the new building without giving us much trouble; but a number of vexing little incidents occurred on our settling down, which I should have
35 felt more deeply had not a sort of Martinmas summer of Sophia's interest in the affair now set in, and lightened them considerably. Smoke was one of our nuisances. On lighting the study-fire, every particle of smoke came curling into the room. In our trouble, we sent for the architect, who immediately asked if we had tried the plan of

opening the register to cure it. We had not, but we did so, and the smoke ascended at once. The last thing I remember was Sophia jumping up one night and frightening me out of my senses with the exclamation: "O that builder! Not a single bar of any sort is there to the nursery-windows. John, some day those poor little children will   5 tumble out in their innocence—how should they know better?—and be dashed to pieces. Why *did* you put the nursery on the second floor?" And you may be sure that some bars were put up the very next morning.

Destiny and a Blue Cloak

INTRODUCTION

On 12 September 1874 Hardy wrote to Louis Jennings, the editor of the *New-York Times*: 'I forward to-day the MS. of a short story called "Destiny and a Blue Cloak" which I have written for the *New York Times* at the request of Mr J. H. Fyfe, Saville [*sic*] Club, on terms probably known to yourself.'[1] The letter is written from 4 Celbridge Place, the London lodgings to which Hardy had returned from Bockhampton in mid-July after completing the final instalment of *Far from the Madding Crowd*.[2] The novel had been appearing in both England and the United States since January,[3] and its immediate success had evidently led the *New-York Times* editor to seek a contribution through the paper's London agent, James Hamilton Fyfe. That Jennings himself admired Hardy's work is suggested by the conclusion of Hardy's letter: 'I beg to express my gratification of your appreciation of my writings ...'

Just because Hardy claimed to have written the story specifically for the *New-York Times* does not necessarily mean that he had in fact done so. Compare, for example, his remarks on 'The Doctor's Legend' (see pp. 237–8). Millgate thinks that 'Destiny' was 'probably written earlier [than 1874]',[4] but gives no grounds for this assumption, though he does emphasize that Hardy was very much in the shadow of Hooper Tolbort—to some extent the 'original' of Oswald Winwood—during the late 1850s and early 1860s. A brilliant linguist, Tolbort was encouraged to sit the Oxford Middle Class and Indian Civil Service examinations by his former schoolmaster, William Barnes, and by Horace Moule, arguably the most significant—in both intellectual and emotional terms—of Hardy's male friends. Tolbort took first place in both examinations, in 1859 and 1862 respectively, and Hardy was later to recall Moule's telling him of the latter success and producing 'a copy of the *Times*, where our friend's

---

[1] *CL* i. 31.   [2] *Life*, 103.   [3] Purdy, 14.   [4] *Biography*, 71

name stood at the head of the list, followed by 200 of lower rank'.[5] (So in 'Destiny' Agatha opens *The Times* to find that Oswald, similarly educated at an 'obscure little academy', was 'first on the list ... while underneath came public school and college men in shoals'.) Evidently intimidated by Tolbort as a young man, and jealous of his favour with Moule,[6] Hardy always retained a vivid memory of his examination success—to the point of mentioning it in *Life*[7] more than fifty years later.

There thus seems no need to associate 'Destiny' with a period earlier than 1874 simply because of its incorporation of Tolbort material. More to the point in arguing for a pre-1874 composition date is that in terms of literary development the story seems in its relative crudity of structure and language an odd successor to *Far from the Madding Crowd*—but so, for that matter, does *The Hand of Ethelberta*, and periods of recession were to be not at all uncommon in Hardy's career.[8] His turning to the *Noble Dames* stories after *Tess* is only one instance of his responding to the completion of a major work and subsequent mental exhaustion by writing something less ambitious and less consistently sustained.

There are, in fact, no clear grounds for doubting Hardy's claim to have produced 'Destiny' specifically for the *New-York Times*. Writing in 1927 to the collector Howard Bliss, Florence Hardy—probably working from her husband's draft—described 'Destiny' as 'a flimsy little story written offhand as a pot-boiler'.[9] Having recently given up his architectural career and accepted the increased financial responsibilities of marriage, Hardy in 1874 was still to some extent willing to sacrifice 'higher aims' in the interests of 'keep[ing] base life afoot'.[10] It would therefore not be surprising for him first to have accepted Fyfe's (presumably not ungenerous) offer, and only then to have turned his attention to the question of how the commitment was

[5] 'The Late Mr. T. W. H. Tolbort, B.C.S.', *Dorset County Chronicle*, 16 Aug. 1883, 10.

[6] As Millgate (*Biography*, 71) remarks, TH recognized that he himself 'seemed to Moule the less promising of his two protégés': 'At the time when Moule was urging Tolbort on to spectacular examination successes he was counselling Hardy to concentrate on his architectural career rather than persist with the study of Greek plays.'

[7] *Life*, 168.

[8] The most obvious example is, of course, the period following the publication of *The Return of the Native* when TH wrote *The Trumpet-Major*, *A Laodicean*, and *Two on a Tower*.

[9] Undated typescript (Beinecke) of replies to queries relating mainly to the MS of *The Woodlanders*, purchased by Bliss in Dec. 1924.

[10] *CL* i. 28; *Life*, 105.

to be fulfilled. That 'Destiny' was indeed rather hastily put together can perhaps be inferred by the date of the covering letter to Jennings—12 September 1874—just five days before Hardy's wedding. In *Life* Hardy recalled that in view of the impending marriage the last few chapters of *Far from the Madding Crowd* had 'been done at a gallop'—all the instalments had in fact been produced under considerable pressure—'hurriedly corrected', and sent off 'early in August'.[11] It therefore seems reasonable to assume[12] that 'Destiny' was written in the interval between posting the *Far from the Madding Crowd* manuscript and 12 September.

The content of the story also suggests that it belongs to the period between *Far from the Madding Crowd* and *The Hand of Ethelberta*. The description of Lovill 'lifting his fingers privately, to express amazement on a small scale' is almost a direct quotation of Henery Fray's response to Bathsheba's unexpected gift of ten shillings.[13] More to the point, perhaps, is the extended example of self-plagiarism embodied in *The Hand of Ethelberta*.[14] Although the comic caricature of the foolish and doting aged admirer in 'Destiny' is transformed in the novel into an altogether more sinister figure, the external resemblance between Lovill and Mountclere is marked: both are 'really and fairly old—sixty-five years of age at least' (p. 36)[15]—yet cling to the things of youth; both are perpetually and somewhat absurdly merry, punctuating their speech with 'hee-hee' (a characteristic shared by another elderly suitor, Heddegan in 'A Mere Interlude'). The two men are also physically similar in their feebleness—both prefer walking with a cane—and stooped posture: as Lovill beneath Agatha's window straightens his back 'nearly to a perpendicular' and then 'yet an inch taller', so Mountclere on noticing Ethelberta straightens himself 'to ten years younger' (*HE* 16). And Agatha's snappish prediction about the old man's arm not being able to support her is realized in the novel when Ethelberta, accepting Mountclere's gallantly offered arm, finds both her strength and her

---

[11] *Life*, 103; *Biography*, 156, 160.

[12] As does Kristin Brady (*The Short Stories of Thomas Hardy: Tales of Past and Present* (London: Macmillan, 1982), 161).

[13] 'Fray ... lifted his eyebrows and fingers to express amazement on a small scale' (*Far from the Madding Crowd*, 88; the reading is identical in the 1874 serialization).

[14] First remarked by Carl J. Weber, *Hardy of Wessex: His Life and Literary Career* (1940; rev. edn., London: Routledge & Kegan Paul, 1965), 98.

[15] Cf. *The Hand of Ethelberta*, *Cornhill*, 33 (1876), 9, 16; the page numbers of subsequent quotations (all from vol. 33) appear in the text preceded by *HE*.

ingenuity heavily taxed in her endeavour 'to appear as the supported and not the supporter' (*HE* 19).

But it is the accounts of the two escape attempts which are most strikingly similar—sufficiently so to suggest that when writing the novel Hardy had in front of him the passage from 'Destiny', or perhaps a notebook entry for a possible plot from which the story originally derived.

The basic elements are the same in both: the overheard plans for flight to the nearest railway station, the anticipated time (be it for departure or for receiving a note of instructions), the mistaken identity of the 'accomplice', the woman's increasing puzzlement at his silence, the unexpected stop, and the consequent revelation—accompanied by the elderly lover's characteristic 'hee-hee' and the bride's horrified dismay.

Moreover, Lovill's insistence that 'it was a pleasant jest on this auspicious morn' and that 'there was nothing he had enjoyed all his life so much as a practical joke which did no harm' anticipates Mountclere's response: 'A very pleasant joke ... And no more than was to be expected on this merry happy day of our lives. Nobody enjoys a good jest more than I do: I always enjoyed a jest—hee-hee!' (*HE* 630).

The two women, stoically accepting defeat, can likewise be paired: Agatha, though 'nearly slain' by Frances's revelation, refuses to 'flinch in the presence of her adversary'; Ethelberta, equally overwhelmed by the presence of Mountclere, walks 'as by a miracle, but she would walk. She would have died rather than not have walked then' (*HE* 631).

It has been argued that the marked similarities between the two works deterred Hardy from including 'Destiny' in his collected volumes[16]—as, indeed, Florence Hardy suggested (again presumably reflecting her husband's views) in response to a query from Bliss.[17] The available evidence tends to suggest, however, that the self-plagiarism was ultimately less significant than Hardy's own negative assessment of the story.[18] Although included in the list of works written out by Emma Hardy in 1880, it was even then disparagingly categorized—along with 'How I Built Myself a House' and

[16] E.g. Weber, *Hardy of Wessex*, 98; Purdy, 294; F. B. Pinion, *A Hardy Companion: A Guide to the Works of Thomas Hardy and their Background* (London: Macmillan, 1968; rev. edn., 1976), 61.

[17] The typescript (see n. 9) reads: '["Destiny"] came just before "The Hand of Ethelberta", some situations in it being embodied in the [novel], which was probably why he did not reprint it.'

[18] As Brady (*Short Stories*, 162) argues.

'The Impulsive Lady of Croome Castle' (an early version of 'The Duchess of Hamptonshire')—as a 'sketch', implicitly distinct from an artistically superior 'story'.[19] In 1917 Florence Hardy told Sydney Cockerell: 'My husband hoped that "Destiny & a Blue Cloak" had quite passed into oblivion. . . . I must confess that I think it one of the worst things he ever did.'[20] Ten years later, in response to Richard Purdy's request for permission to publish a limited edition of the story, she wrote that her husband 'would prefer not to have it reprinted', considering it 'an impromptu of a trivial kind and of no literary value'.[21]

After Hardy's death the story was, however, included (along with 'The Doctor's Legend') in Carl J. Weber's *Revenge is Sweet: Two Short Stories by Thomas Hardy*, published in 1940 by the Colby College Library, Waterville, Maine, in a limited issue of twenty-five copies and in a trade issue.[22] More recently, the story has been collected in the Macmillan New Wessex Edition of both *Old Mrs Chundle and Other Stories* (1977) and *Collected Short Stores* (1988), edited by F. B. Pinion.[23]

No major literary claims can be made for the story and certainly its extreme intricacy of plotting tends to obscure any more serious concerns, including its criticism of the social marginalization of women.[24] But the story is, in any case, not without interest merely as an example of the kind of contrived and sensational plot to which Hardy resorted when creatively exhausted or financially pressured. The 'Hardyan' plot elements are obvious: the mistaken identity, the secret engagement, the departure in search of financial betterment, the stealthy exchange of letters, the fatefully delayed return, and, above all, the climactic and ruthlessly ironic mistiming. 'Destiny' is, then, a

---

[19] DCM. 'The Impulsive Lady of Croome Castle' is in fact referred to as a 'mere sketch'; with the exception of 'Thieves', annotated 'Child's story', the other short stories included in the list ('Indiscretion', 'The Distracted Young Preacher', and 'Fellow-Townsmen') are not described.
[20] 10 Nov. 1917 (Beinecke).   [21] 2 Nov. 1927 (Beinecke).
[22] Referred to on the verso of the title-leaf as the 'SECOND PRINTING'; there was also a 'THIRD PRINTING' published by the Colby Chapter of Phi Beta Kappa in March 1940.
[23] *Collected Short Stories*, however, acknowledges Pinion only as the author of the notes, but the same type-setting film was apparently used to produce the texts of both volumes.
[24] See Pamela Dalziel, 'Hapless "Destiny"': An Uncollected Story of Marginalized Lives', *Thomas Hardy Journal* (forthcoming).

significant precursor not only of *The Hand of Ethelberta* but also of those numerous novels, stories, and poems of Hardy's which turn upon one of life's little (or larger) ironies.

BIBLIOGRAPHICAL DESCRIPTION

Periodical Publication

New-York Times, 4 Oct. 1874
The text appears on p. 2, cols. 1–7, and p. 3, cols. 1–2. The title (in col. 1) reads:
WRITTEN EXPRESSLY FOR THE NEW-YORK TIMES. | *DESTINY AND A BLUE CLOAK* | [*French rule 13mm.*] | BY THOMAS HARDY, | *Author of "Far from the Madding Crowd," "A Pair of Blue Eyes," &c.*

NOTE ON THE TEXT

The copy-text is the sole surviving authoritative text, the 4 October 1874 *New-York Times* printing (*NYT*). Since the only variants are editorial emendations of the copy-text, lemmata and recorded variants are not followed by sigla.

DESTINY AND A BLUE CLOAK

I

"Good morning, Miss Lovill!" said the young man, in the free manner usual with him toward pretty and inexperienced country girls.

5   Agatha Pollin—the maiden addressed—instantly perceived how the mistake had arisen. Miss Lovill was the owner of a blue autumn wrapper, exceptionally gay for a village; and Agatha, in a spirit of emulation rather than originality, had purchased a similarly enviable article for herself, which she wore to-day for the first time. It may be
10 mentioned that the two young women had ridden together from their homes to Maiden-Newton on this foggy September morning, Agatha prolonging her journey thence to Weymouth by train, and leaving her acquaintance at the former place. The remark was made to her on Weymouth esplanade.

15 Agatha was now about to reply very naturally, "I am not Miss Lovill," and she went so far as to turn up her face to him for the purpose, when he added, "I've been hoping to meet you. I have heard of your—well, I must say it—beauty, long ago, though I only came to Beaminster yesterday."

20 Agatha bowed—her contradiction hung back—and they walked slowly along the esplanade together without speaking another word after the above point-blank remark of his. It was evident that her new friend could never have seen either herself or Miss Lovill except from a distance.

25 And Agatha trembled as well as bowed. This Miss Lovill— Frances Lovill—was of great and long renown as the beauty of Cloton village, near Beaminster. She was five and twenty and fully developed, while Agatha was only the niece of the miller of the same place, just nineteen, and of no repute as yet for comeliness, though she
30 undoubtedly could boast of much. Now, were the speaker, Oswald Winwood, to be told that he had not lighted upon the true Helen, he would instantly apologize for his mistake and leave her side, a contingency of no great matter but for one curious emotional

circumstance—Agatha had already lost her heart to him. Only in secret had she acquired this interest in Winwood—by hearing much report of his talent and by watching him several times from a window; but she loved none the less in that she had discovered that Miss Lovill's desire to meet and talk with the same intellectual luminary 5 was in a fair way of approaching the intensity of her own. We are never unbiased appraisers, even in love, and rivalry usually operates as a stimulant to esteem even while it is acting as an obstacle to opportunity. So it had been with Agatha in her talk to Miss Lovill that morning concerning Oswald Winwood. 10

The Weymouth season was almost at an end, and but few loungers were to be seen on the parades, particularly at this early hour. Agatha looked over the iridescent sea, from which the veil of mist was slowly rising, at the white cliffs on the left, now just beginning to gleam in a weak sunlight, at the one solitary yacht in the midst, and still delayed 15 her explanation. Her companion went on:

"The mist is vanishing, look, and I think it will be fine, after all. Shall you stay in Weymouth the whole day?"

"No. I am going to Portland by the twelve o'clock steam-boat. But I return here again at six to go home by the seven o'clock train." 20

"I go to Maiden Newton by the same train, and then to Beaminster by the carrier."

"So do I."

"Not, I suppose, to walk from Beaminster to Cloton at that time in the evening?" 25

"I shall be met by somebody—but it is only a mile, you know."

That is how it all began; the continuation it is not necessary to detail at length. Both being somewhat young and impulsive, social forms were not scrupulously attended to. She discovered him to be on board the steamer as it ploughed the emerald waves of Weymouth 30 Bay, although he had wished her a formal good-bye at the pier. He had altered his mind, he said, and thought that he would come to Portland, too. They returned by the same boat, walked the velvet sands till the train started, and entered a carriage together.

All this time, in the midst of her happiness, Agatha's conscience 35 was sombre with guiltiness at not having yet told him of his mistake. It was true that he had not more than once or twice called her by Miss Lovill's name since the first greeting in the morning; but he certainly was still under the impression that she was Frances Lovill. Yet she

perceived that though he had been led to her by another's name, it was her own proper person that he was so rapidly getting to love, and Agatha's feminine insight suggested blissfully to her that the face belonging to the name would after this encounter have no power to
5 drag him away from the face of the day's romance.

They reached Maiden-Newton at dusk, and went to the inn door, where stood the old-fashioned hooded van which was to take them to Beaminster. It was on the point of starting, and when they had mounted in front the old man at once drove up the long hill leading
10 out of the village.

"This has been a charming experience to me, Miss Lovill," Oswald said, as they sat side by side. "Accidental meetings have a way of making themselves pleasant when contrived ones quite fail to do it."

15 It was absolutely necessary to confess this time, though all her bliss were at once destroyed.

"I am not really Miss Lovill!" she faltered.

"What! not the young lady—and are you really not Frances Lovill?" he exclaimed, in surprise.

20 "O forgive me, Mr Winwood! I have wanted so to tell you of your mistake; indeed I have, all day—but I couldn't—and it is so wicked and wrong of me! I am only poor Agatha Pollin, at the mill."

"But why couldn't you tell me?"

"Because I was afraid that if I did you would go away from me and
25 not care for me any more, and I l-l-love you so dearly!"

The carrier being on foot beside the horse, the van being so dark, and Oswald's feelings being rather warm, he could not for his life avoid kissing her there and then.

"Well," he said, "it doesn't matter; you are yourself anyhow. It is
30 you I like, and nobody else in the world—not the name. But, you know, I was really looking for Miss Lovill this morning. I saw the back of her head yesterday, and I have often heard how very good-looking she is. Ah! suppose you had been she. I wonder—"

He did not complete the sentence. The driver mounted again,
35 touched the horse with the whip, and they jogged on.

"You forgive me?" she said.

"Entirely—absolutely—the reason justified everything. How strange that you should have been caring deeply for me, and I ignorant of it all the time!"

They descended into Beaminster and alighted, Oswald handing her down. They had not moved from the spot when another female figure also alighted, dropped her fare into the carrier's hand, and glided away.

"Who is that?" said Oswald to the carrier. "Why, I thought we were the only passengers!"

"What?" said the carrier, who was rather stupid.

"Who is that woman?"

"Miss Lovill, of Cloton. She altered her mind about staying at Beaminster, and is come home again."

"Oh!" said Agatha, almost sinking to the earth. "She has heard it all. What shall I do, what shall I do?"

"Never mind it a bit," said Oswald.

II

The mill stood beside the village high-road, from which it was separated by the stream, the latter forming also the boundary of the mill garden, orchard, and paddock on that side. A visitor crossed a little wood bridge embedded in oozy, aquatic growths, and found himself in a space where usually stood a waggon laden with sacks, surrounded by a number of bright-feathered fowls.

It was now, however, just dusk, but the mill was not closed, a stripe of light stretching as usual from the open door across the front, across the river, across the road, into the hedge beyond. On the bridge, which was aside from the line of light, a young man and girl stood talking together. Soon they moved a little way apart, and then it was apparent that their right hands were joined. In receding one from the other they began to swing their arms gently backward and forward between them.

"Come a little way up the lane, Agatha, since it is the last time," he said. "I don't like parting here. You know your uncle does not object."

"He doesn't object because he knows nothing to object to," she whispered. And they both then contemplated the fine, stalwart figure of the said uncle, who could be seen moving about inside the mill, illuminated by the candle, and circumscribed by a faint halo of flour, and hindered by the whirr of the mill from hearing anything so gentle as lovers' talk.

Oswald had not relinquished her hand, and, submitting herself to a bondage she appeared to love better than freedom, Agatha followed him across the bridge, and they went down the lane engaged in the low, sad talk common to all such cases, interspersed with remarks
5 peculiar to their own.

"It is nothing so fearful to contemplate," he said. "Many live there for years in a state of rude health, and return home in the same happy condition. So shall I."

"I hope you will."
10 "But aren't you glad I am going? It is better to do well in India than badly here. Say you are glad, dearest; it will fortify me when I am gone."

"I am glad," she murmured faintly. "I mean I am glad in my mind. I don't think that in my heart I am glad."
15 "Thanks to Macaulay, of honoured memory, I have as good a chance as the best of them!" he said, with ardour. "What a great thing competitive examination is; it will put good men in good places, and make inferior men move lower down; all bureaucratic jobbery will be swept away."
20 "What's bureaucratic, Oswald?"

"Oh! that's what they call it, you know. It is—well, I don't exactly know what it is. I know this, that it is the name of what I hate, and that it isn't competitive examination."

"At any rate it is a very bad thing," she said, conclusively.
25 "Very bad, indeed; you may take my word for that."

Then the parting scene began, in the dark, under the heavy-headed trees which shut out sky and stars. "And since I shall be in London till the Spring," he remarked, "the parting doesn't seem so bad—so all at once. Perhaps you may come to London before the Spring,
30 Agatha."

"I may; but I don't think I shall."

"We must hope on all the same. Then there will be the examination, and then I shall know my fate."

"I hope you'll fail!—there, I've said it; I couldn't help it, Oswald!"
35 she exclaimed, bursting out crying. "You would come home again then!"

"How can you be so disheartening and wicked, Agatha! I—I didn't expect—"

"No, no; I don't wish it; I wish you to be best, top, very very best!"

she said. "I didn't mean the other; indeed, dear Oswald, I didn't. And will you be sure to come to me when you are rich? Sure to come?" "If I'm on this earth I'll come home and marry you." And then followed the good-bye.

III

In the Spring came the examination. One morning a newspaper directed by Oswald was placed in her hands, and she opened it to find it was a copy of the *Times*. In the middle of the sheet, in the most conspicuous place, in the excellent neighbourhood of the leading articles, was a list of names, and the first on the list was Oswald Winwood. Attached to his name, as showing where he was educated, was the simple title of some obscure little academy, while underneath came public school and college men in shoals. Such a case occurs sometimes, and it occurred then.

How Agatha clapped her hands! for her selfish wish to have him in England at any price, even that of failure, had been but a paroxysm of the wretched parting, and was now quite extinct. Circumstances combined to hinder another meeting between them before his departure, and, accordingly, making up her mind to the inevitable in a way which would have done honour to an older head, she fixed her mental vision on that sunlit future—far away, yet always nearing— and contemplated its probabilities with a firm hope.

At length he had arrived in India, and now Agatha had only to work and wait; and the former made the latter more easy. In her spare hours she would wander about the river brinks and into the coppices, and there weave thoughts of him by processes that young women understand so well. She kept a diary, and in this, since there were few events to chronicle in her daily life, she sketched the changes of the landscape, noted the arrival and departure of birds of passage, the times of storms and foul weather—all which information, being mixed up with her life and taking colour from it, she sent as scraps in her letters to him, deriving most of her enjoyment in contemplating his.

Oswald, on his part, corresponded very regularly. Knowing the days of the Indian mail, she would go at such times to meet the post-man in early morning, and to her unvarying inquiry, "A letter for me?" it was seldom, indeed, that there came a disappointing answer. Thus the season passed, and Oswald told her he should be a judge some day, with many other details, which, in her mind, were viewed chiefly in their bearing on the grand consummation—that he was to come home and marry her.

Meanwhile, as the girl grew older and more womanly, the woman
5   whose name she had once stolen for a day grew more of an old maid, and showed symptoms of fading. One day Agatha's uncle, who, though still a handsome man in the prime of his life, was a widower with four children, to whom she acted the part of eldest sister, told Agatha that Frances Lovill was about to become his second wife.
10   "Well!" said Agatha, and thought, "What an end for a beauty!"

And yet it was all reasonable enough, notwithstanding that Miss Lovill might have looked a little higher. Agatha knew that this step would produce great alterations in the small household of Cloton Mill, and the idea of having as aunt and ruler the woman to whom she
15   was in some sense indebted for a lover, affected Agatha with a slight thrill of dread. Yet nothing had ever been spoken between the two women to show that Frances had heard, much less resented, the explanation in the van on that night of the return from Weymouth.

IV

20   On a certain day old farmer Lovill called. He was of the same family as Frances, though their relationship was distant. A considerable business in corn had been done from time to time between miller and farmer, but the latter had seldom called at Pollin's house. He was a bachelor, or he would probably never have appeared in this history,
25   and he was mostly full of a boyish merriment rare in one of his years. To-day his business with the miller had been so imperative as to bring him in person, and it was evident from their talk in the mill that the matter was payment. Perhaps ten minutes had been spent in serious converse when the old farmer turned away from the door, and,
30   without saying good-morning, went toward the bridge. This was unusual for a man of his temperament.

He was an old man—really and fairly old—sixty-five years of age at least. He was not exactly feeble, but he found a stick useful when walking in a high wind. His eyes were not yet bleared, but in their
35   corners was occasionally a moisture like majolica glaze—entirely absent in youth. His face was not shrivelled, but there were unmistakable puckers in some places. And hence the old gentleman,

unmarried, substantial, and cheery as he was, was not doted on by the young girls of Cloton as he had been by their mothers in former time. Each year his breast impended a little further over his toes, and his chin a little further over his breast, and in proportion as he turned down his nose to earth did pretty females turn up theirs at 5 him. They might have liked him as a friend had he not shown the abnormal wish to be regarded as a lover. To Agatha Pollin this aged youth was positively distasteful.

It happened that at the hour of Mr Lovill's visit Agatha was bending over the pool at the mill head, sousing some white fabric in 10 the water. She was quite unconscious of the farmer's presence near her, and continued dipping and rinsing in the idlest phase possible to industry, until she remained quite still, holding the article under the water, and looking at her own reflection within it. The river, though gliding slowly, was yet so smooth that to the old man on the 15 bridge she existed in duplicate—the pouting mouth, the little nose, the frizzed hair, the bit of blue ribbon, as they existed over the surface, being but a degree more distinct than the same features beneath.

"What a pretty maid!" said the old man to himself. He walked up 20 the margin of the stream, and stood beside her.

"Oh!" said Agatha, starting with surprise. In her flurry she relinquished the article she had been rinsing, which slowly turned over and sank deeper, and made toward the hatch of the mill-wheel.

"There—it will get into the wheel, and be torn to pieces!" she 25 exclaimed.

"I'll fish it out with my stick, my dear," said Farmer Lovill, and kneeling cautiously down he began hooking and crooking with all his might. "What thing is it—of much value?"

"Yes; it is my best one!" she said involuntarily. 30

"It—what is the it?"

"Only something—a piece of linen." Just then the farmer hooked the endangered article, and dragging it out, held it high on his walking-stick—dripping, but safe.

"Why, it is a chemise!" he said. 35

The girl looked red, and instead of taking it from the end of the stick, turned away.

"Hee-hee!" laughed the ancient man. "Well, my dear, there's nothing to be ashamed of that I can see in owning to such a necessary and innocent article of clothing. There, I'll put it on the grass for you, and you shall take it when I am gone."

Then Farmer Lovill retired, lifting his fingers privately, to express amazement on a small scale, and murmuring, "What a nice young
5 thing! Well, to be sure. Yes, a nice child—young woman rather; indeed, a marriageable woman, come to that; of course she is."

The doting old person thought of the young one all this day in a way that the young one did not think of him. He thought so much about her, that in the evening, instead of going to bed, he hobbled
10 privately out by the back door into the moonlight, crossed a field or two, and stood in the lane, looking at the mill—not more in the hope of getting a glimpse of the attractive girl inside than for the pleasure of realizing that she was there.

A light moved within, came nearer, and ascended. The staircase
15 window was large, and he saw his goddess going up with a candle in her hand. This was indeed worth coming for. He feared he was seen by her as well, yet hoped otherwise in the interests of his passion, for she came and drew down the window blind, completely shutting out his gaze. The light vanished from this part, and reappeared in a
20 window a little further on.

The lover drew nearer; this, then, was her bedroom. He rested vigorously upon his stick, and straightening his back nearly to a perpendicular, turned up his amorous face.

She came to the window, paused, then opened it.
25 "Bess its deary-eary heart! it is going to speak to me!" said the old man, moistening his lips, resting still more desperately upon his stick, and straightening himself yet an inch taller. "She saw me then!"

Agatha, however, made no sign; she was bent on a far different purpose. In a box on her window-sill was a row of mignonette, which
30 had been sadly neglected since her lover's departure, and she began to water it, as if inspired by a sudden recollection of its condition. She poured from her water-jug slowly along the plants, and then, to her astonishment, discerned her elderly friend below.

"A rude old thing!" she murmured.
35 Directing the spout of the jug over the edge of the box, and looking in another direction that it might appear to be an accident, she allowed the stream to spatter down upon her admirer's face, neck, and shoulders, causing him to beat a quick retreat. Then Agatha serenely closed the window, and drew down that blind also.

"Ah! she did not see me; it was evident she did not, and I was mistaken!" said the trembling farmer, hastily wiping his face, and mopping out the rills trickling down within his shirt-collar as far as he could get at them, which was by no means to their termination. "A pretty creature, and so innocent, too! Watering her flowers; how I 5 like a girl who is fond of flowers! I wish she had spoken, and I wish I was younger. Yes, I know what I'd do with the little mouse!" And the old gentleman tapped emotionally upon the ground with his stick.

V 10

"Agatha, I suppose you have heard the news from somebody else by this time?" said her Uncle Humphrey some two or three weeks later. "I mean what Farmer Lovill has been talking to me about."

"No, indeed," said Agatha.

"He wants to marry ye if you be willing." 15

"O, I never!" said Agatha with dismay. "That old man!"

"Old? He's hale and hearty; and, what's more, a man very well to do. He'll make you a comfortable home, and dress ye up like a doll, and I'm sure you'll like that, or you baint a woman of woman born."

"But it *can't be*, uncle!—other reasons—" 20

"What reasons?"

"Why, I've promised Oswald Winwood—years ago!"

"Promised Oswald Winwood years ago, have you?"

"Yes; surely you know it, Uncle Humphrey. And we write to one another regularly." 25

"Well, I can just call to mind that ye are always scribbling and getting letters from somewhere. Let me see—where is he now? I quite forget."

"In India still. Is it possible that you don't know about him, and what a great man he's getting? There are paragraphs about him in 30 our paper very often. The last was about some translation from Hindostani that he'd been making. And he's coming home for me."

"I very much question it. Lovill will marry you at once, he says."

"Indeed, he will not."

"Well, I don't want to force you to do anything against your will, 35 Agatha, but this is how the matter stands. You know I am a little behindhand in my dealings with Lovill—nothing serious, you know, if he gives me time—but I want to be free of him quite in order to go to Australia.''

''Australia!''

''Yes. There's nothing to be done here. I don't know what business
5 is coming to—can't think. But never mind that; this is the point: if you will marry Farmer Lovill, he offers to clear off the debt, and there will no longer be any delay about my own marriage; in short, away I can go. I mean to, and there's an end on't.''

''What, and leave me at home alone?''

10 ''Yes, but a married woman, of course. You see the children are getting big now. John is twelve and Nathaniel ten, and the girls are growing fast, and when I am married again I shall hardly want you to keep house for me—in fact, I must reduce our family as much as possible. So that if you could bring your mind to think of Farmer
15 Lovill as a husband, why, 'twould be a great relief to me after having the trouble and expense of bringing you up. If I can in that way edge out of Lovill's debt I shall have a nice bit of money in hand.''

''But Oswald will be richer even than Mr Lovill,'' said Agatha, through her tears.

20 ''Yes, yes. But Oswald is not here, nor is he likely to be. How silly you be.''

''But he will come, and soon, with his eleven hundred a year and all.''

''I wish to Heaven he would. I'm sure he might have you.''

25 ''Now, you promise that, uncle, don't you?'' she said, brightening. ''If he comes with plenty of money before you want to leave, he shall marry me, and nobody else.''

''Ay, if he comes. But, Agatha, no nonsense. Just think of what I've been telling you. And at any rate be civil to Farmer Lovill. If this man
30 Winwood were here and asked for ye, and married ye, that would be a very different thing. I do mind now that I saw something about him and his doings in the papers; but he's a fine gentleman by this time, and won't think of stooping to a girl like you. So you'd better take the one who is ready; old men's darlings fare very well as the world goes.
35 We shall be off in nine months, mind, that I've settled. And you must be a married woman afore that time, and wish us good-bye upon your husband's arm.''

''That old arm couldn't support me.''

''And if you don't agree to have him, you'll take a couple of hundred pounds out of my pocket; you'll ruin my chances altogether—that's the long and the short of it."

Saying which the gloury man turned his back upon her, and his footsteps became drowned in the rumble of the mill.

VI

Nothing so definite was said to her again on the matter for some time. The old yeoman hovered round her, but, knowing the result of the interview between Agatha and her uncle, he forbore to endanger his suit by precipitancy. But one afternoon he could not avoid saying, "Aggie, when may I speak to you upon a serious subject?"

"Next week," she replied, instantly.

He had not been prepared for such a ready answer, and it startled him almost as much as it pleased him. Had he known the cause of it his emotions might have been different. Agatha, with all the womanly strategy she was capable of, had written post-haste to Oswald after the conversation with her uncle, and told him of the dilemma. At the end of the present week his answer, if he replied with his customary punctuality, would be sure to come. Fortified with his letter she thought she could meet the old man. Oswald she did not doubt.

Nor had she any reason to. The letter came prompt to the day. It was short, tender, and to the point. Events had shaped themselves so fortunately that he was able to say he would return and marry her before the time named for the family's departure for Queensland.

She danced about for joy. But there was a postscript to the effect that she might as well keep this promise a secret for the present, if she conveniently could, that his intention might not become a public talk in Cloton. Agatha knew that he was a rising and aristocratic young man, and saw at once how proper this was.

So she met Mr Lovill with a simple flat refusal, at which her uncle was extremely angry, and her disclosure to him afterward of the arrival of the letter went but a little way in pacifying him. Farmer Lovill would put in upon him for the debt, he said, unless she could manage to please him for a short time.

"I don't want to please him," said Agatha. "It is wrong to encourage him if I don't mean it."

"Will you behave toward him as the Parson advises you?"

The Parson! That was a new idea, and, from her uncle, unexpected.

"I will agree to what Mr Davids advises about my mere daily behaviour before Oswald comes, but nothing more," she said. "That is, I will if you know for certain that he's a good man, who fears God and keeps the commandments."

5 "Mr Davids fears God, for sartin, for he never ventures to name Him outside the pulpit; and as for the commandments, 'tis knowed how he swore at the church-restorers for taking them away from the chancel."

"Uncle, you always jest when I am serious."

10 "Well, well! at any rate his advice on a matter of this sort is good."

"How is it you think of referring me to him?" she asked, in perplexity; "you so often speak slightingly of him."

"Oh—well," said Humphrey, with a faintly perceptible desire to parry the question, "I have spoken roughly about him once now and 15 then; but perhaps I was wrong. Will ye go?"

"Yes, I don't mind," she said, languidly.

When she reached the Vicar's study Agatha began her story with reserve, and said nothing about the correspondence with Oswald; yet an intense longing to find a friend and confidant led her to indulge in 20 more feeling than she had intended, and as a finale she wept. The genial incumbent, however, remained quite cool, the secret being that his heart was involved a little in another direction—one, perhaps, not quite in harmony with Agatha's interests—of which more anon.

"So the difficulty is," he said to her, "how to behave in this trying 25 time of waiting for Mr Winwood, that you may please parties all round and give offence to none."

"Yes, Sir, that's it," sobbed Agatha, wondering how he could have realized her position so readily. "And uncle wants to go to Australia."

"One thing is certain," said the Vicar; "you must not hurt the 30 feelings of Mr Lovill. Wonderfully sensitive man—a man I respect much as a godly doer."

"Do you, Sir?"

"I do. His earnestness is remarkable."

"Yes, in courting."

35 "The cue is: treat Mr Lovill gently—gently as a babe! Love opposed, especially an old man's, gets all the stronger. It is your policy to give him seeming encouragement, and so let his feelings expend themselves and die away."

"How am I to? To advise is so easy."

"Not by acting untruthfully, of course. You say your lover is sure to come back before your uncle leaves England."

"I know he will."

"Then pacify old Mr Lovill in this way: Tell him you'll marry him when your uncle wants to go, if Winwood doesn't come for you before 5 that time. That will quite content Mr Lovill, for he doesn't in the least expect Oswald to return, and you'll see that his persecution will cease at once."

"Yes; I'll agree to it," said Agatha promptly.

Mr Davids had refrained from adding that neither did he expect 10 Oswald to come, and hence his advice. Agatha on her part too refrained from stating the good reasons she had for the contrary expectation, and hence her assent. Without the last letter perhaps even her faith would hardly have been bold enough to allow this palpable driving of her into a corner. 15

"It would be as well to write Mr Lovill a little note, saying you agree to what I have advised," said the Parson evasively.

"I don't like writing."

"There's no harm. 'If Mr Winwood doesn't come I'll marry you,' &c. Poor Mr Lovill will be content, thinking Oswald will not come; 20 you will be content, knowing he will come; your uncle will be content, being indifferent which of two rich men has you and relieves him of his difficulties. Then, if it's the will of Providence, you'll be left in peace. Here's a pen and ink; you can do it at once."

Thus tempted, Agatha wrote the note with a trembling hand. It 25 really did seem upon the whole a nicely strategic thing to do in her present environed situation. Mr Davids took the note with the air of a man who did not wish to take it in the least, and placed it on the mantle-piece.

"I'll send it down to him by one of the children," said Aggy, 30 looking wistfully at her note with a little feeling that she should like to have it back again.

"Oh, no, it is not necessary," said her pleasant adviser. He had rung the bell; the servant now came, and the note was sent off in a trice. 35

When Agatha got into the open air again her confidence returned, and it was with a mischievous sense of enjoyment that she considered how she was duping her persecutors by keeping secret Oswald's intention of a speedy return. If they only knew what a firm foundation

she had for her belief in what they all deemed but an improbable contingency, what a life they would lead her; how the old man would worry her uncle for payment, and what general confusion there would be. Mr Davids' advice was very shrewd, she thought, and she was
5 glad she had called upon him.

Old Lovill came that very afternoon. He was delighted, and danced a few bars of a hornpipe in entering the room. So lively was the antique boy that Agatha was rather alarmed at her own temerity when she considered what was the basis of his gaiety; wishing she
10 could get from him some such writing as he had got from her, that the words of her promise might not in any way be tampered with, or the conditions ignored.

"I only accept you conditionally, mind," she anxiously said. "That is distinctly understood."

15 "Yes, yes," said the yeoman. "I am not so young as I was, little dear, and beggars musn't be choosers. With my ra-ta-ta—say, dear, shall it be the first of November?"

"It will really never be."

"But if he doesn't come, it shall be the first of November?"

20 She slightly nodded her head.

"Clk!—I think she likes me!" said the old man aside to Aggy's uncle, which aside was distinctly heard by Aggy.

One of the younger children was in the room, drawing idly on a slate. Agatha at this moment took the slate from the child, and
25 scribbled something on it.

"Now you must please me by just writing your name here," she said in a voice of playful indifference.

"What is it?" said Lovill, looking over and reading. " 'If Oswald Winwood comes to marry Agatha Pollin before November, I agree to
30 give her up to him without objection.' Well, that is cool for a young lady under six feet, upon my word—hee-hee!" He passed the slate to the miller, who read the writing and passed it back again.

"Sign—just in courtesy," she coaxed.

"I don't see why—"

35 "I do it to test your faith in me; and now I find you have none. Don't you think I should have rubbed it out instantly? Ah, perhaps I can be obstinate too!"

He wrote his name then. "Now I have done it, and shown my faith," he said, and at once raised his fingers as if to rub it out again.

But with hands that moved like lightning she snatched up the slate, flew up stairs, locked it in her box, and came down again.

"Souls of men—that's sharp practice," said the old gentleman.

"Oh, it is only a whim—a mere memorandum," said she. "You had my promise, but I had not yours."

"Ise wants my slate," cried the child.

"I'll buy you a new one, dear," said Agatha, and soothed her.

When she had left the room old Lovill spoke to her uncle somewhat uneasily of the event, which, childish as it had been, discomposed him for the moment.

"Oh, that's nothing," said Miller Pollin assuringly; "only play—only play. She's a mere child in nater, even now, and she did it only to tease ye. Why, she overheard your whisper that you thought she liked ye, and that was her playful way of punishing ye for your confidence. You'll have to put up with these worries, farmer. Considering the difference in your ages, she is sure to play pranks. You'll get to like 'em in time."

"Ay, ay, faith, so I shall! I was always a Turk for sprees!—eh, Pollin? hee-hee!" And the suitor was merry again.

VII

Her life was certainly much pleasanter now. The old man treated her well, and was almost silent on the subject nearest his heart. She was obliged to be very stealthy in receiving letters from Oswald, and on this account was bound to meet the postman, let the weather be what it would. These transactions were easily kept secret from people out of the house, but it was a most difficult task to hide her movements from her uncle. And one day brought utter failure.

"How's this—out already, Agatha?" he said, meeting her in the lane at dawn on a foggy morning. She was actually reading a letter just received, and there was no disguising the truth.

"I've been for a letter from Oswald."

"Well, but that won't do. Since he don't come for ye, ye must think no more about him."

"But he's coming in six weeks. He tells me all about it in this very letter."

"What—really to marry you?" said her uncle incredulously.

"Yes, certainly."

"But I hear that he's wonderfully well off."

"Of course he is; that's why he's coming. He'll agree in a moment to be your surety for the debt to Mr Lovill."

"Has he said so?"

5   "Not yet; but he will."

"I'll believe it when I see him and he tells me so. It is very odd, if he means so much, that he hev never wrote a line to me."

"We thought—you would force me to have the other at once if he wrote to you," she murmured.

10   "Not I, if he comes rich. But it is rather a cock-and-bull story, and since he didn't make up his mind before now, I can't say I be much in his favour. Agatha, you had better not say a word to Mr Lovill about these letters; it will make things deuced unpleasant if he hears of such goings on. You are to reckon yourself bound by your word. Oswald

15   won't hold water, I'm afeard. But I'll be fair. If he do come, proves his income, marries ye willy-nilly, I'll let it be, and the old man and I must do as we can. But barring that—you keep your promise to the letter."

"That's what it will be, uncle. Oswald will come."

20   "Write you must not. Lovill will smell it out, and he'll be sharper than you will like. 'Tis not to be supposed that you are to send love-letters to one man as if nothing was going to happen between ye and another man. The first of November is drawing nearer every day. And be sure and keep this a secret from Lovill for your own

25   sake."

The more clearly that Agatha began to perceive the entire contrast of expectation as to issue between herself and the other party to the covenant, the more alarmed she became. She had not anticipated such a narrowing of courses as had occurred. A malign influence

30   seemed to be at work without any visible human agency. The critical time drew nearer, and, though no ostensible preparation for the wedding was made, it was evident to all that Lovill was painting and papering his house for somebody's reception. He made a lawn where there had existed a nook of refuse; he bought furniture for a woman's

35   room. The greatest horror was that he insisted upon her taking his arm one day, and there being no help for it she assented, though her distaste was unutterable. She felt the skinny arm through his sleeve, saw over the wry shoulders, looked upon the knobby feet, and shuddered. What if Oswald should not come; the time for her uncle's

departure was really getting near. When she reached home she ran up to her bedroom.

On recovering from her dreads a little, Agatha looked from the window. The deaf lad John, who assisted in the mill, was quietly glancing toward her, and a gleam of friendship passed over his kindly face as he caught sight of her form. This reminded her that she had, after all, some sort of friend close at hand. The lad knew pretty well how events stood in Agatha's life, and he was always ready to do on her part whatever lay in his power. Agatha felt stronger, and resolved to bear up.

VIII

Heavens! how anxious she was! It actually wanted only ten days to the first of November, and no new letter had come from Oswald.

Her uncle was married, and Frances was in the house, and the preliminary steps for emigration to Queensland had been taken. Agatha surreptitiously obtained newspapers, scanned the Indian shipping news till her eyes ached, but all to no purpose, for she knew nothing either of route or vessel by which Oswald would return. He had mentioned nothing more than the month of his coming, and she had no way of making that single scrap of information the vehicle for obtaining more.

"In ten days, Agatha," said the old farmer. "There is to be no show or fuss of any kind; the wedding will be quite private, in consideration of your feelings and wishes. We'll go to church as if we were taking a morning walk, and nobody will be there to disturb you. Tweedledee!" He held up his arm and crossed it with his walking-stick, as if he were playing the fiddle, at the same time cutting a caper.

"He will come, and then I shan't be able to marry you, even th-th-though I may wish to ever so much," she faltered, shivering. "I have promised him, and I *must* have him, you know, and you have agreed to let me."

"Yes, yes," said Farmer Lovill, pleasantly. "But that's a misfortune you need not fear at all, my dear; he won't come at this late day and compel you to marry him in spite of your attachment to me. But, ah—it is only a joke to tease me, you little rogue! Your uncle says so."

"Agatha, come, cheer up, and think no more of that fellow," said her uncle when they chanced to be alone together. " 'Tis ridiculous, you know. We always knew he wouldn't come."

The day passed. The sixth morning came, the noon, the evening. The fifth day came and vanished. Still no sound of Oswald. His
5 friends now lived in London, and there was not a soul in the parish, save herself, that he corresponded with, or one to whom she could apply in such a delicate matter as this.

It was the evening before her wedding-day, and she was standing alone in the gloom of her bedchamber looking out on the plot in front
10 of the mill. She saw a white figure moving below, and knew him to be the deaf miller lad, her friend. A sudden impulse animated Agatha. She had been making desperate attempts during the last two days to like the old man, and, since Oswald did not come, to marry him without further resistance, for the sheer good of the family of her
15 uncle, to whom she was indeed indebted for much; but had only got so far in her efforts as not to positively hate him. Now rebelliousness came unsought. The lad knew her case, and upon this fact she acted. Gliding down stairs, she beckoned to him, and, as they stood together in the stream of light from the open mill door, she communicated her
20 directions, partly by signs, partly by writing, for it was difficult to speak to him without being heard all over the premises.

He looked in her face with a glance of confederacy, and said that he understood it all. Upon this they parted.

The old man was at her house that evening, and when she
25 withdrew wished her good-bye "for the present" with a dozen smiles of meaning. Agatha had retired early, leaving him still there, and when she reached her room, instead of looking at the new dress she was supposed to be going to wear on the morrow, busied herself in making up a small bundle of ordinary articles of clothing. Then she
30 extinguished her light, lay down upon the bed without undressing, and waited for a preconcerted time.

In what seemed to her the dead of night, but which she concluded must be the time agreed upon—half-past five—there was a slight noise as of gravel being thrown against her window. Agatha jumped
35 up, put on her bonnet and cloak, took up her bundle, and went down stairs without a light. At the bottom she slipped on her boots, and passed amid the chirping crickets to the door. It was unbarred. Her uncle, then, had risen, as she had half expected, and it necessitated a little more caution. The morning was dark as a cavern, not a star

being visible; but knowing the bearings well, she went cautiously and in silence to the mill door. A faint light shone from inside, and the form of the mill-cart appeared without, the horse ready harnessed to it. Agatha did not see John for the moment, but concluded that he was in the mill with her uncle, who had just at this minute started the wheel for the day. She at once slipped into the vehicle and under the tilt, pulling some empty sacks over, as it had been previously agreed that she should do, to avoid the risk of discovery. After a few minutes of suspense she heard John coming from under the wall, where he had apparently been standing and watching her safely in, and mounting in front, away he drove at a walking pace.

Her scheme had been based upon the following particulars of mill business: Thrice a week it was the regular custom for John and another young man to start early in the morning, each with a horse and covered cart, and go in different directions to customers a few miles off, the carts being laden overnight. All that she had asked John to do this morning was to take her with him to a railway station about ten miles distant, where she might safely wait for an up train.

How will John act on returning—what will he say—how will he excuse himself? she thought as they jogged along. "John!" she said, meaning to ask him about these things; but he did not hear, and she was too confused and weary after her wakeful night to be able to think consecutively on any subject. But the relief of finding that her uncle did not look into the cart caused a delicious lull in her, and while listlessly watching the dark gray sky through the triangular opening between the curtains at the fore part of the tilt, and John's elbow projecting from the folds of one of them, showing where he was sitting on the outside, she fell asleep.

She awoke after a short interval—everything was just the same— jog, jog, on they went; there was the dim slit between the curtains in front, and, after slightly wondering that John had not troubled himself to see that she was comfortable, she dozed again. Thus Agatha remained until she had a clear consciousness of the stopping of the cart. It aroused her, and looking at once through a small opening at the back, she perceived in the dim dawn that they were turning right about; in another moment the horse was proceeding on the way back again.

"John, what are you doing?" she exclaimed, jumping up, and pulling aside the curtain which parted them.

John did not turn.

"How fearfully deaf he is!" she thought, "and how odd he looks behind, and he hangs forward as if he were asleep. His hair is snow-white with flour; does he never clean it, then?" She crept across the
5 sacks, and slapped him on the shoulder. John turned then.

"Hee-hee, my dear!" said the blithe old gentleman; and the moisture of his aged eye glistened in the dawning light, as he turned and looked into her horrified face. "It is all right; I am John, and I have given ye a nice morning's airing to refresh ye for the uncommon
10 duties of to-day; and now we are going back for the ceremony—hee-hee!"

He wore a miller's smock-frock on this interesting occasion, and had been enabled to play the part of John in the episode by taking the second cart and horse and anticipating by an hour the real John in
15 calling her.

Agatha sank backward. How on earth had he discovered the scheme of escape so readily; he, an old and by no means suspicious man? But what mattered a solution! Hope was crushed, and her rebellion was at an end. Agatha was awakened from thought by
20 another stopping of the horse, and they were again at the mill-door.

She dimly recognized her uncle's voice speaking in anger to her when the old farmer handed her out of the vehicle, and heard the farmer reply, merrily, that girls would be girls and have their freaks, that it didn't matter, and that it was a pleasant jest on this auspicious
25 morn. For himself, there was nothing he had enjoyed all his life so much as a practical joke which did no harm. Then she had a sensation of being told to go into the house, have some food, and dress for her marriage with Mr Lovill, as she had promised to do on that day.

All this she did, and at eleven o'clock became the wife of the old
30 man.

When Agatha was putting on her bonnet in the dusk that evening, for she would not illuminate her ghastly face by a candle, a rustling came against the door. Agatha turned. Her uncle's wife, Frances, was looking into the room, and Agatha could just discern upon her aunt's
35 form the blue cloak which had ruled her destiny.

The sight was almost more than she could bear. If, as seemed likely, this effect was intended, the trick was certainly successful. Frances did not speak a word.

Then Agatha said in quiet irony, and with no evidence whatever of regret, sadness, or surprise at what the act revealed: "And so you told Mr Lovill of my flight this morning, and set him on the track? It would be amusing to know how you found out my plan, for he never could have done it by himself, poor old darling."

"Oh, I was a witness of your arrangement with John last night— that was all, my dear," said her aunt pleasantly. "I mentioned it then to Mr Lovill, and helped him to his joke of hindering you.... You remember the van, Agatha, and how you made use of my name on that occasion, years ago, now?"

"Yes, and did you hear our talk that night? I always fancied otherwise."

"I heard it all. It was fun to you; what do you think it was to me—fun, too?—to lose the man I longed for, and to become the wife of a man I care not an atom about?"

"Ah, no. And how you struggled to get him away from me, dear aunt!"

"And have done it, too."

"Not you, exactly. The Parson and fate."

"Parson Davids kindly persuaded you, because I kindly persuaded him, and persuaded your uncle to send you to him. Mr Davids is an old admirer of mine. Now do you see a wheel within a wheel, Agatha?"

Calmness was almost insupportable by Agatha now, but she managed to say: "Of course you have kept back letters from Oswald to me?"

"No, I have not done that," said Frances. "But I told Oswald, who landed at Southampton last night, and called here in great haste at seven this morning, that you had gone out for an early drive with the man you were to marry to-day, and that it might cause confusion if he remained. He looked very pale, and went away again at once to catch the next London train, saying something about having been prevented by a severe illness from sailing at the time he had promised and intended for the last twelvemonth."

The bride, though nearly slain by the news, would not flinch in the presence of her adversary. Stilling her quivering flesh, she said smiling: "That information is deeply interesting, but does not concern me at all, for I am my husband's darling now, you know, and I wouldn't make the dear man jealous for the world." And she glided down stairs to the chaise.

The Thieves Who Couldn't Help Sneezing

INTRODUCTION

On 5 March 1876, as the serialization of *The Hand of Ethelberta* was nearing completion, Hardy wrote to George Smith, the publisher: 'I do not wish to attempt any more original writing of any length for a few months, until I can learn the best line to take for the future'.[1] By the end of the year he had decided on a story he subsequently described as 'dealing with remote country life, somewhat of the nature of "Far from the Madding Crowd"'[2]—what was to become *The Return of the Native*. None the less, he was in many ways still 'feeling his way to a method',[3] as is demonstrated by the variety in kind and variability in quality of his work during the next few years (see p. 157). Nor was he quite established financially: he received only £440 for the English serial and volume rights of *The Return of the Native*—in comparison with £700 for *The Hand of Ethelberta*[4]—and was eager to exploit such supplementary sources of income as the publication of cheap one-volume editions[5] and the sale of continental rights.[6] It is, therefore, not too surprising that, in the midst of writing *The Return of the Native*, he should agree to supply a story for a children's Christmas annual.

Father Christmas, published at the office of the *Illustrated London News*, ran for twenty-two years, beginning in 1877 with the issue containing Hardy's 'The Thieves Who Couldn't Help Sneezing'. The first three numbers were edited by 'N. D'Anvers', actually Nancy R. E. Meugens, a prolific if undistinguished writer of works varied in subject and kind, but for the most part addressed to a juvenile audience; no less than three pieces by her—two short stories and a play, *The Snow Queen*, described as 'Founded on the German of Hans Anderson'—appeared in the 1877 issue. Although precedence was given to

[1] *CL* i. 43.   [2] To John Blackwood, 13 Feb. 1877 (*CL* i. 47).
[3] Prefatory Note, *Desperate Remedies*, p. vii.
[4] *Biography*, 169, 188, 197; moreover, the arrangements for the volume publication of *The Return of the Native* were not made until Sept. 1878.
[5] *A Pair of Blue Eyes* (Henry S. King), *Far from the Madding Crowd* (Smith, Elder), and *The Hand of Ethelberta* (Smith, Elder) appeared in 1877.
[6] *Far from the Madding Crowd* was sold to Tauchnitz in 1877 (*Biography*, 189).

Hardy's story, which begins on the first page immediately after the opening Christmas poem, 'The Little Messenger', the writer of a promotional paragraph in the *Illustrated London News: Christmas Number* was less deferential, specifically mentioning only the editor, 'Miss D'Anvers, whose contributions to literature, for youth especially, are well known', and Austin Dobson, the author of the 'charming piece of verse, entitled "Little Blue Ribbons["]'[7] (in truth an embarrassingly bad poem). In the preceding regular number of the *Illustrated London News* Hardy's name was mentioned, though only as one of several. The paragraph, which nicely sums up both the annual's contents and the responses anticipated from its readers, is worth quoting at length:

A new claimant, entitled "Father Christmas: Our Little Ones' Budget," is announced to appear shortly. It comes with weighty claims on the favour of the rising generation, being crowded with amusing tales, songs, riddles, and acrostics, by its fair editor, Miss N. D'Anvers, Austin Dobson, Thomas Hardy, W. H. G. Kingston, Reginald Gatty, and other writers of note in this special field of literature. Among its numerous illustrations there are three printed in colours, the principal of which, a chromolithograph, entitled "A Merry Christmas," represents a blooming young lady, just entered into her teens, tracing the appropriate greeting in snow. It is safe to prognosticate that many a youth will take possession of this picture, and keep it safe locked in his desk to snatch furtive glances at the damsel, or hang it in his bedroom where he may contemplate her charms the first thing on rising and the last on going to bed. This interesting collection of stories and pictures for the young will be published at the office of the *Illustrated London News*, 198, Strand; and, judging from the bill of fare, and the names of the skilled artists engaged in setting forth the entertainment, there can be no doubt that it will be keenly relished by boys and girls.[8]

The *Christmas Number* paragraph—quite possibly written by the same person, of course—also makes much of the 'three pictures printed in colours, one of which is a chromolithograph of a fascinating little belle, who has just entered her teens, and who, if alive, would break many a boy's heart'.[9] (As this picture is missing from the Bodleian copy[10] of the annual, one wonders if her charms were sufficient to overrule the scruples of a Victorian librarian!) This emphasis on

<hr>

[7] *Illustrated London News*, 12 Dec. 1877, 34. [8] Ibid. 8 Dec. 1877, 543.

[9] Ibid. 12 Dec. 1877, 34.

[10] The only other known copy of the 1877 issue of this extremely rare annual is in the Beinecke.

illustration anticipates a direction *Father Christmas* was increasingly to take: whereas the first three numbers, edited by Meugens, were essentially short-story papers, the complete listing of contents in the advertisement for the 1877 issue gave way in 1878 and 1879 to the announcement of the titles of the coloured pictures,[11] while the 1880 number contained only one long story but sixteen large colour illustrations in addition to the chromolithograph. By 1889 the subtitle had become 'The Children's Casket of Pictures' and the text (mainly verse) had all but disappeared.

In 1877, however, fiction was the dominant feature of *Father Christmas* and 'The Thieves Who Couldn't Help Sneezing' was thus an appropriate contribution. Presumably Meugens solicited the story, for it is unlikely that Hardy—though willing to experiment with various types of fiction, especially if potentially lucrative—would independently have decided to write a piece for children or even have known of the annual's projected existence. That she should have sought out Hardy even though he had not previously written anything for children is doubtless primarily attributable to a desire for a celebrated contributor. She may also have been acquainted with him already: his earliest surviving letter to her (13 July 1877) is addressed to 'My dear Madam' and mentions Roger Smith, an architect for whom Hardy had worked in 1872 and the author of the preface to Meugens's *Elementary History of Art*, published in 1874.[12]

On 13 July 1877, having previously agreed to supply something for *Father Christmas*, Hardy provided Meugens with further particulars:

That you may know at once the space available for other contributors to your Christmas number I will undertake that my tale shall consist of 1200 words, which according to your calculation will be about two pages of the publication. This I hope to be able to send you in the course of two or three weeks.[13]

On 20 October Hardy sent Meugens the corrected proof of 'Thieves'—which indeed ran to just over two of the annual's pages, though amounting in fact to 2,600 words—and said that his terms for the story would be nine pounds.[14] *Father Christmas* was duly published in early December[15] and, as Meugens evidently told Hardy,[16] was

[11] *Illustrated London News*, 12 Dec. 1877, 2; 21 Dec. 1878, 574; 13 Dec. 1879, 542.
[12] *CL* i. 50.   [13] Ibid.   [14] Ibid. i. 51.
[15] *Illustrated London News*, 12 Dec. 1877, 2.
[16] On 31 Jan. 1878 he wrote: 'I am glad to hear of the success of Father Christmas' (*CL* i. 52).

well received—sufficiently so to justify the appearance the following year not only of a new number but also of the original number to which he had contributed. The advertisement for the 1878 number included the following announcement: 'FATHER CHRISTMAS FOR 1877. In consequence of the great demand for copies of last year's FATHER CHRISTMAS, it has been reprinted, and a few copies are now on sale.'[17]

In spite of the annual's success, 'Thieves' as an independent story seems to have attracted little attention, either at the time of its first publication or since. Presumably Hardy himself in his later years thought that the story was less than memorable—he may of course have literally forgotten it—since he neither collected it nor mentioned it in *Life*. The story in fact remained obscure—at least to the extent of not being mentioned in either A. P. Webb's *A Bibliography of the Works of Thomas Hardy, 1865–1915* (London: Frank Hollings, 1916) or the bibliography by John Lane appended to the second edition of Lionel Johnson's *The Art of Thomas Hardy* (London: John Lane, The Bodley Head, 1923)—until 1942 when Weber arranged for it to be printed in a small volume, one hundred copies of which were published by Colby College Library. The story was also included in *Old Mrs Chundle and Other Stories*, but not in *Collected Short Stories*.

Hardy's opinion of 'Thieves' appears to have altered over the years. Certainly at the beginning of his career he was not ashamed to acknowledge it, adding in his own hand the title, publication details, and annotation 'Child's story' to the list of works drawn up by Emma Hardy in 1880.[18] And, though it may be slight, the story is by no means uninteresting in terms of its relation to traditional forms of children's literature. The opening words are not 'Once upon a time', nor even 'Any years ago', as Brady claims[19]—the *Father Christmas* illustrator has perhaps too cleverly incorporated the initial 'M' of 'Many' into a sketch of the sneezing thieves—but they do invoke the world of fairy-tale: 'Many years ago, when oak-trees now past their prime were about as large as elderly gentlemen's walking-sticks, there lived in Wessex a yeoman's son, whose name was Hubert.'

---

[17] *Illustrated London News*, 21 Dec. 1878, 574; repr. 28 Dec. 1878, 598. No copy of the reprinted 1877 number is known to survive.

[18] DCM; in view of the pejorative use of 'sketch' in this list and elsewhere, it also seems significant that 'Thieves' was classified as a 'story'.

[19] Kristin Brady, *The Short Stories of Thomas Hardy: Tales of Past and Present* (London: Macmillan, 1982), 163.

Romance expectations are created by the formulaic structure (—— years ago, there lived in —— a ——'s son, whose name was ——) and by the relative unspecificity of time and place. Although 'Wessex', effectively introduced by Hardy in *Far from the Madding Crowd* (1874), was by 1877 already gaining acceptance as a regional designation,[20] it still carried associations of ancient and somewhat vaguely defined kingdoms, and even the identification in the second paragraph of the Vale of Blackmoor (or Blackmore, as Hardy here spells it) does little to dispel the impression that the story could be taking place in any 'thickly wooded' and 'somewhat lonely district'. In truth the role of the Vale of Blackmoor as a specific location is negligible in 'Thieves', even though it was to be so vividly depicted more than a decade later in *Tess* and even though Hardy in 1877 was actually living there, in Sturminster Newton. That setting should be so little exploited in the story seems especially surprising in view of its dominance in *The Return of the Native*, on which Hardy was currently working, but perhaps therein lies the explanation: not only were his main creative energies focused intensely on a non-local region—specifically Bockhampton and the heath—but the story itself was one which deliberately sought to create an impression of indefiniteness.

It seems indeed impossible to identify with any confidence the period at which Hardy imagined the action of 'Thieves' as taking place. He refers to past visits to the house of the story by 'Queen Elizabeth and King Charles successively', but it does not in fact appear that the Vale of Blackmoor was ever visited by Elizabeth or by either Charles I or Charles II. Elizabeth never went to Dorset; Charles I seems to have gone only in order to hunt on Cranborne Chase; while Charles II spent nineteen days hidden in a manor-house in south-west Dorset after his defeat at the battle of Worcester in 1651. Since the house of the story is identified largely in terms of royal visitations that seem never to have occurred, there are similar difficulties in the way of suggesting a plausible 'original', although Sherborne Castle, at the western extremity of the Vale, is certainly a possibility: it answers broadly to the description given in the story, once belonged to Queen Elizabeth, and was used by Hardy later in his career as the setting for 'Anna, Lady Baxby' in *A Group of Noble Dames*. 'Short's Gibbet' appears to have been an invented name and place—although gibbets were common enough in the countryside

[20] See *Biography*, 181.

throughout the eighteenth century[21]—but it is certainly relevant that the Vale of Blackmoor should be described as being for the most part 'thickly wooded'. As the Forest of the White Hart, much of the Vale had in medieval and Tudor times been a royal hunting forest, but it was enclosed and disforested during the course of the seventeenth century, and especially during the reign of Charles I. In his review of William Barnes's *Poems of Rural Life in the Dorset Dialect*, written within two years of the publication of 'Thieves', Hardy spoke of the Vale of Blackmoor as having remained densely wooded down to 'comparatively recent times',[22] an unfathomable phrase that none the less leaves open the possibility of accepting, for want of better evidence, the late seventeenth- or early eighteenth-century dating suggested by the reference to the period when snuff-boxes were 'becoming common among young and old throughout the country'. It might not be far from the truth to suspect that Hardy wrote quickly and with only the vaguest sense of historical period, using the miscellaneous references to past time, to 'Sir Simon' the 'Baronet', to the battlemented 'mansion', and to royal visitors simply as available means of enhancing the story's modest narrative pretensions. His main purpose, in any case, as is made clear by the conventionally fabular opening and the portentous allusion to the slow growth of oak-trees, was to suggest a time sufficiently remote, hence sufficiently mysterious and unknown, to render acceptable the occurrence of exceptional events. Hubert's adventures are certainly less than common and the narrative does conform to archetypal romance patterns, culminating in recognition and resolution, but at the same time the story, like virtually all of Hardy's fiction, remains firmly grounded in the credible. If 'Thieves' reads like a fable, the fabulous itself none the less remains obstinately, and characteristically, absent.

BIBLIOGRAPHICAL DESCRIPTION

Periodical Publication

Father Christmas: Our Little Ones' Budget, [Dec.] 1877
The double-columned text appears on pp. [1]–3. The title (in col. 1) reads:

[21] See, e.g., *CL* v. 269.
[22] Rev. of *Poems of Rural Life in the Dorset Dialect*, by William Barnes, *New Quarterly Magazine* (Oct. 1879), 470; precisely the same sentence occurs in *Tess* (20).

THE THIEVES WHO COULDN'T HELP SNEEZING. | BY
THOMAS HARDY.

NOTE ON THE TEXT

The copy-text is the sole surviving authoritative text, the 1877 *Father
Christmas* printing.

THE THIEVES WHO COULDN'T HELP
SNEEZING

Many years ago, when oak-trees now past their prime were about as
large as elderly gentlemen's walking-sticks, there lived in Wessex a
yeoman's son, whose name was Hubert. He was about fourteen years
of age, and was as remarkable for his candour and lightness of heart as
for his physical courage, of which, indeed, he was a little vain. 5
One cold Christmas Eve his father, having no other help at hand,
sent him on an important errand to a small town several miles from
home. He travelled on horseback, and was detained by the business
till a late hour of the evening. At last, however, it was completed; he
returned to the inn, the horse was saddled, and he started on his way. 10
His journey homeward lay through the Vale of Blackmore, a fertile
but somewhat lonely district, with heavy clay roads and crooked
lanes. In those days, too, a great part of it was thickly wooded.

It must have been about nine o'clock when, riding along amid the
overhanging trees upon his stout-legged cob Jerry, and singing a 15
Christmas carol, to be in harmony with the season, Hubert fancied
that he heard a noise among the boughs. This recalled to his mind
that the spot he was traversing bore an evil name. Men had been
waylaid there. He looked at Jerry, and wished he had been of any
other colour than light grey; for on this account the docile animal's 20
form was visible even here in the dense shade. "What do I care?" he
said aloud, after a few minutes of reflection. "Jerry's legs are too
nimble to allow any highwayman to come near me."

"Ha! ha! indeed," was said in a deep voice; and the next moment a
man darted from the thicket on his right hand, another man from the 25
thicket on his left hand, and another from a tree-trunk a few yards
ahead. Hubert's bridle was seized, he was pulled from his horse, and
although he struck out with all his might, as a brave boy would
naturally do, he was overpowered. His arms were tied behind him, his
legs bound tightly together, and he was thrown into the ditch. The 30
robbers, whose faces he could now dimly perceive to be artificially
blackened, at once departed, leading off the horse.

As soon as Hubert had a little recovered himself, he found that by great exertion he was able to extricate his legs from the cord; but, in spite of every endeavour, his arms remained bound as fast as before. All, therefore, that he could do was to rise to his feet and proceed on
5   his way with his arms behind him, and trust to chance for getting them unfastened. He knew that it would be impossible to reach home on foot that night, and in such a condition; but he walked on. Owing to the confusion which this attack caused in his brain, he lost his way, and would have been inclined to lie down and rest till morning among
10 the dead leaves had he not known the danger of sleeping without wrappers in a frost so severe. So he wandered further onwards, his arms wrung and numbed by the cord which pinioned him, and his heart aching for the loss of poor Jerry, who never had been known to kick, or bite, or show a single vicious habit. He was not a little glad
15 when he discerned through the trees a distant light. Towards this he made his way, and presently found himself in front of a large mansion with flanking wings, gables, and towers, the battlements and chimneys showing their shapes against the stars.

All was silent; but the door stood wide open, it being from this door
20 that the light shone which had attracted him. On entering he found himself in a vast apartment arranged as a dining-hall, and brilliantly illuminated. The walls were covered with a great deal of dark wainscoting, formed into moulded panels, carvings, closet-doors, and the usual fittings of a house of that kind. But what drew his attention
25 most was the large table in the midst of the hall, upon which was spread a sumptuous supper, as yet untouched. Chairs were placed around, and it appeared as if something had occurred to interrupt the meal just at the time when all were ready to begin.

Even had Hubert been so inclined, he could not have eaten in his
30 helpless state, unless by dipping his mouth into the dishes, like a pig or cow. He wished first to obtain assistance; and was about to penetrate further into the house for that purpose when he heard hasty footsteps in the porch and the words, "Be quick!" uttered in the deep voice which had reached him when he was dragged from the horse.
35 There was only just time for him to dart under the table before three men entered the dining-hall. Peeping from beneath the hanging edges of the tablecloth, he perceived that their faces, too, were blackened, which at once removed any remaining doubts he may have felt that these were the same thieves.

"Now, then," said the first—the man with the deep voice—"let us hide ourselves. They will all be back again in a minute. That was a good trick to get them out of the house—eh?"

"Yes. You well imitated the cries of a man in distress," said the second.

"Excellently," said the third.

"But they will soon find out that it was a false alarm. Come, where shall we hide? It must be some place we can stay in for two or three hours, till all are in bed and asleep. Ah! I have it. Come this way! I have learnt that the further closet is not opened once in a twelvemonth; it will serve our purpose exactly."

The speaker advanced into a corridor which led from the hall. Creeping a little farther forward, Hubert could discern that the closet stood at the end, facing the dining-hall. The thieves entered it, and closed the door. Hardly breathing, Hubert glided forward, to learn a little more of their intention, if possible; and, coming close, he could hear the robbers whispering about the different rooms where the jewels, plate, and other valuables of the house were kept, which they plainly meant to steal.

They had not been long in hiding when a gay chattering of ladies and gentlemen was audible on the terrace without. Hubert felt that it would not do to be caught prowling about the house, unless he wished to be taken for a robber himself; and he slipped softly back to the hall, out at the door, and stood in a dark corner of the porch, where he could see everything without being himself seen. In a moment or two a whole troop of personages came gliding past him into the house. There were an elderly gentleman and lady, eight or nine young ladies, as many young men, besides half-a-dozen men-servants and maids. The mansion had apparently been quite emptied of its occupants.

"Now, children and young people, we will resume our meal," said the old gentleman. "What the noise could have been I cannot understand. I never felt so certain in my life that there was a person being murdered outside my door."

Then the ladies began saying how frightened they had been, and how they had expected an adventure, and how it had ended in nothing after all.

"Wait a while," said Hubert to himself. "You'll have adventure enough by-and-by, ladies."

It appeared that the young men and women were married sons and daughters of the old couple, who had come that day to spend Christmas with their parents.

The door was then closed, Hubert being left outside in the porch. He thought this a proper moment for asking their assistance; and, since he was unable to knock with his hands, began boldly to kick the door.

"Hullo! What disturbance are you making here?" said a footman who opened it; and, seizing Hubert by the shoulder, he pulled him into the dining-hall. "Here's a strange boy I have found making a noise in the porch, Sir Simon."

Everybody turned.

"Bring him forward," said Sir Simon, the old gentleman before mentioned. "What were you doing there, my boy?"

"Why, his arms are tied!" said one of the ladies.

"Poor fellow!" said another.

Hubert at once began to explain that he had been waylaid on his journey home, robbed of his horse, and mercilessly left in this condition by the thieves.

"Only to think of it!" exclaimed Sir Simon.

"That's a likely story," said one of the gentleman-guests, incredulously.

"Doubtful, hey?" asked Sir Simon.

"Perhaps he's a robber himself," suggested a lady.

"There is a curiously wild wicked look about him, certainly, now that I examine him closely," said the old mother.

Hubert blushed with shame; and, instead of continuing his story, and relating that robbers were concealed in the house, he doggedly held his tongue, and half resolved to let them find out their danger for themselves.

"Well, untie him," said Sir Simon. "Come, since it is Christmas Eve, we'll treat him well. Here, my lad; sit down in that empty seat at the bottom of the table, and make as good a meal as you can. When you have had your fill we will listen to more particulars of your story."

The feast then proceeded; and Hubert, now at liberty, was not at all sorry to join in. The more they eat and drank the merrier did the company become; the wine flowed freely, the logs flared up the chimney, the ladies laughed at the gentlemen's stories; in short, all went as noisily and as happily as a Christmas gathering in old times possibly could do.

Hubert, in spite of his hurt feelings at their doubts of his honesty, could not help being warmed both in mind and in body by the good cheer, the scene, and the example of hilarity set by his neighbours. At last he laughed as heartily at their stories and repartees as the old Baronet, Sir Simon, himself. When the meal was almost over one of the sons, who had drunk a little too much wine, after the manner of men in that century, said to Hubert, "Well, my boy, how are you? Can you take a pinch of snuff?" He held out one of the snuff-boxes which were then becoming common among young and old throughout the country.

"Thank you," said Hubert, accepting a pinch.

"Tell the ladies who you are, what you are made of, and what you can do," the young man continued, slapping Hubert upon the shoulder.

"Certainly," said our hero, drawing himself up, and thinking it best to put a bold face on the matter. "I am a travelling magician."

"Indeed!"

"What shall we hear next?"

"Can you call up spirits from the vasty deep, young wizard?"

"I can conjure up a tempest in a cupboard," Hubert replied.

"Ha—ha!" said the old Baronet, pleasantly rubbing his hands. "We must see this performance. Girls, don't go away: here's something to be seen."

"Not dangerous, I hope?" said the old lady.

Hubert rose from the table. "Hand me your snuff-box, please," he said to the young man who had made free with him. "And now," he continued, "without the least noise, follow me. If any of you speak it will break the spell."

They promised obedience. He entered the corridor, and, taking off his shoes, went on tiptoe to the closet door, the guests advancing in a silent group at a little distance behind him. Hubert next placed a stool in front of the door, and, by standing upon it, was tall enough to reach to the top. He then, just as noiselessly, poured all the snuff from the box along the upper edge of the door, and, with a few short puffs of breath, blew the snuff through the chink into the interior of the closet. He held up his finger to the assembly, that they might be silent.

"Dear me, what's that?" said the old lady, after a minute or two had elapsed.

A suppressed sneeze had come from inside the closet.

Hubert held up his finger again.

5 "How very singular," whispered Sir Simon. "This is most interesting."

Hubert took advantage of the moment to gently slide the bolt of the closet door into its place. "More snuff," he said, calmly.

"More snuff," said Sir Simon. Two or three gentlemen passed their
10 boxes, and the contents were blown in at the top of the closet. Another sneeze, not quite so well suppressed as the first, was heard: then another, which seemed to say that it would not be suppressed under any circumstances whatever. At length there arose a perfect storm of sneezes.

15 "Excellent, excellent for one so young!" said Sir Simon. "I am much interested in this trick of throwing the voice—called, I believe, ventriloquism."

"More snuff," said Hubert.

"More snuff," said Sir Simon. Sir Simon's man brought a large jar
20 of the best scented Scotch.

Hubert once more charged the upper chink of the closet, and blew the snuff into the interior, as before. Again he charged, and again, emptying the whole contents of the jar. The tumult of sneezes became really extraordinary to listen to—there was no cessation. It was like
25 wind, rain, and sea battling in a hurricane.

"I believe there are men inside, and that it is no trick at all!" exclaimed Sir Simon, the truth flashing on him.

"There are," said Hubert. "They are come to rob the house; and they are the same who stole my horse."

30 The sneezes changed to spasmodic groans. One of the thieves, hearing Hubert's voice, cried, "Oh! mercy! mercy! let us out of this!"

"Where's my horse?" said Hubert.

"Tied to the tree in the hollow behind Short's Gibbet. Mercy! mercy! let us out, or we shall die of suffocation!"

35 All the Christmas guests now perceived that this was no longer sport, but serious earnest. Guns and cudgels were procured; all the men-servants were called in, and arranged in position outside the closet. At a signal Hubert withdrew the bolt, and stood on the defensive. But the three robbers, far from attacking them, were found

crouching in the corner, gasping for breath. They made no resistance; and, being pinioned, were placed in an out-house till the morning.

Hubert now gave the remainder of his story to the assembled company, and was profusely thanked for the services he had rendered. Sir Simon pressed him to stay over the night, and accept the use of the best bed-room the house afforded, which had been occupied by Queen Elizabeth and King Charles successively when on their visits to this part of the country. But Hubert declined, being anxious to find his horse Jerry, and to test the truth of the robbers' statements concerning him.

Several of the guests accompanied Hubert to the spot behind the gibbet, alluded to by the thieves as where Jerry was hidden. When they reached the knoll and looked over, behold! there the horse stood, uninjured, and quite unconcerned. At sight of Hubert he neighed joyfully; and nothing could exceed Hubert's gladness at finding him. He mounted, wished his friends "Good-night!" and cantered off in the direction they pointed out as his nearest way, reaching home safely about four o'clock in the morning.

An Indiscretion in the Life of an Heiress

INTRODUCTION

On 14 January 1878 Francis Hueffer, then editor of the *New Quarterly Magazine*, wrote to Hardy to solicit a story for delivery by 10 March.[1] Hardy was apparently glad to accept the offer but could not—or at any rate did not—submit a contribution by the specified date. Instead, a June deadline must have been negotiated, for on the 4th of that month Hardy wrote: 'I have been able to get through the story a few days sooner than I expected, & send it to you by book-post.'[2] Less than a month earlier, on 9 May, he had written:

I will endeavour to make the story cover at least 40 pages—& it may possibly be longer; but I mention that length in case the subject I have thought of may not safely bear extension further. Of course if it should naturally work out to a greater length I will not curtail it.[3]

The story in question was 'An Indiscretion in the Life of an Heiress', and in the end it ran to some sixty-four *New Quarterly* pages. In agreeing to write a long story—essentially a novella—Hardy was no doubt influenced by the expectation that the increased wordage would mean increased remuneration[4] not only from the *New Quarterly* but also from a US magazine. He had, however, very little time to negotiate US serial rights, since he had undertaken to submit in June a story which he was still referring to as unwritten on 9 May and, in the absence of an international copyright agreement between Great Britain and the United States, the sole advantage to a US magazine (or publisher) in purchasing an English author's work lay in being able to obtain advance copy and thereby anticipate the likely piracies. This time constraint—and perhaps also Hardy's relative unfamiliarity with US publishers and their trade practices—

---

[1] DCM.   [2] *CL* i. 57.   [3] Ibid. vii. 91.

[4] TH's move from Dorset to London in March—doubtless one of the reasons for his inability to meet Hueffer's original deadline—had meant a substantial rise in household expenses and he was eager to find new sources of literary income, especially since he expected relatively little in monetary terms from *The Return of the Native* (see p. 52).

presumably determined his decision not to make a direct approach to any US magazine but to place the story through his first US publisher, Henry Holt, who had previously undertaken a similar commission with regard to 'The Fire at Tranter Sweatley's'.[5] Writing to Hardy on 8 June, Holt said that Harper & Brothers had agreed to pay £20 for the right to print the story in their *Weekly* and that he would himself probably bring it out later in a little volume and give Hardy 10 per cent of the retail price, the same commission as he was currently paying on the novels, five of which had already appeared in his Leisure Hour Series.[6] Since Holt never in fact published 'Indiscretion' as a separate volume, even though he continued to publish Hardy's new novels for another eight years, and since *Harper's Weekly* spread the story over no less than five instalments, Hardy can scarcely have been overjoyed at his transatlantic remuneration on this occasion.

He had, however, supplied copy in time for the story to appear in the July 1878 issue of the *New Quarterly* and to begin in the 29 June issue of *Harper's Weekly*—subsequent instalments appearing in the issues of 6, 13, 20, and 27 July. Given that the manuscript was not posted to the *New Quarterly* until 4 June—at which point Hardy asked for the proofs to be sent to him as soon as possible[7]—it is obvious that the final stages of his work on the story must have been completed with great rapidity and that these circumstances must be relevant in some way to the existence of extensive differences between the English and US texts. In the introduction to his edition of 'Indiscretion', Terry Coleman is presumably right in assuming that Harper & Brothers were supplied with proofs of the *New Quarterly* printing— Hardy seems never to have sent a duplicate manuscript in such circumstances—but he is on much weaker ground in arguing that 'the numerous changes must have been made either by Hardy on the English proof [as sent to *Harper's*], or by the American sub-editors'.[8] Although editors are notorious for generating non-authorial readings, it seems in this instance extravagant to hold them responsible for the more than 350 verbal divergences between the two texts, some only a word or two in length, others, especially in the radically different first chapter, considerably more extensive, and almost all of

[5] *CL* i. 40.   [6] DCM; and see *CL* i. 58.   [7] *CL* i. 57.

[8] Coleman, Introduction to *An Indiscretion in the Life of an Heiress* (London: Hutchinson, 1976), 17.

them overlooked by Coleman.[9] Coleman's theory that some of the changes might have been made by Hardy himself on the proof sheets before posting them to New York is not convincing either: since copy for *Harper's* would have had to be sent well before the date at which proofs needed to be returned to the *New Quarterly*, it seems improbable, to say the least, that Hardy would have revised the US text and not the English. There is certainly nothing to suggest that he was deliberately creating two versions, as he was to do, for example, in the bowdlerized English and (relatively) unbowdlerized US serializations of *Tess*.[10] Moreover, virtually all the *New Quarterly* readings can be characterized as stylistically or structurally superior to those of *Harper's*—as Coleman himself implicitly acknowledges by choosing to print the English version.

The *New Quarterly* text, then, is surely the later, more heavily revised text, Hardy having evidently sent Harper & Brothers copy in the form of duplicate proofs,[11] as he was currently doing with *The Return of the Native*,[12] but without having had or taken time to revise them—except, perhaps, in the most cursory fashion. The *Harper's* text is thus one stage closer to the manuscript, hence of particular interest in light of the fact that 'Indiscretion', as Hardy told Frederick Macmillan thirty-five years after its original publication, was 'a sort of patchwork of the remains of "The Poor Man & the Lady" ',[13] his first, unpublished, and now lost novel. Clearly, it was the availability of

[9] Coleman (ibid. 18) mentions six, two of which are cited in illustration of the 'other tiny changes'.

[10] Juliet Grindle and Simon Gatrell, Introduction to *Tess of the d'Urbervilles* (Oxford: Clarendon Press, 1983), 37–40.

[11] This is also Purdy's opinion (274).   [12] *CL* i. 54.

[13] 4 Oct. 1913, *CL* iv. 306. George Douglas ('Thomas Hardy. Some Recollections and Reflections', *Hibbert Journal*, 26 (Apr. 1928), 392) was apparently the first to remark in print about the relationship between the published story and TH's lost novel, and many have since reinforced and expanded his suggestion. The most extensive discussions can be found in William R. Rutland, *Thomas Hardy: A Study of his Writings and their Background* (Oxford: Basil Blackwell, 1938), 111 ff., and Pamela Dalziel, 'A Critical Edition of Thomas Hardy's Uncollected Stories', D. Phil. thesis (University of Oxford, 1989), 152 ff. See also Carl J. Weber, Introduction to *An Indiscretion in the Life of an Heiress* (Baltimore: Johns Hopkins Press, 1935); Sylvia Niemeier, '*An Indiscretion and The Poor Man*', M.A. thesis (University of Toronto, 1944); Evelyn Hardy, *Thomas Hardy: A Critical Biography* (London: Hogarth Press, 1954), 89 ff.; Purdy, 275–6; Michael Millgate, *Thomas Hardy: His Career as a Novelist* (London: The Bodley Head, 1971), 20, 364; Lawrence Jones, 'The Music Scenes in "The Poor Man and the Lady", "Desperate Remedies" and "An Indiscretion in the Life of an Heiress" ', *Notes and Queries*, 24 (1977), 32–4; and Simon Gatrell, *Hardy the Creator: A Textual Biography* (Oxford: Clarendon Press, 1988), 12–14.

this body of unpublished material—already drawn upon for *Desperate Remedies*, *Under the Greenwood Tree*, and *A Pair of Blue Eyes*—that had determined his willingness to promise the *New Quarterly* early delivery of so extensive a contribution at a time when he was already busy with various other tasks, from the composition of 'The Impulsive Lady of Croome Castle' to the correction of the proofs for *The Return of the Native*.[14]

Hardy had begun writing *The Poor Man and the Lady* in the late summer of 1867, shortly after leaving Blomfield's London office to resume employment with the Dorchester architect John Hicks.[15] On 25 July of the following year the completed manuscript, divided into two parts and totalling 440 pages, was dispatched to Alexander Macmillan.[16] Received on 27 July and forwarded the same day to John Morley, then Macmillan's principal reader of fiction manuscripts, it was returned to the office a week later, accompanied by a report sufficiently favourable to induce Macmillan to ask to see it himself.[17] Morley's report and Macmillan's comments in his 10 August letter to Hardy[18] are the only surviving first-hand responses to *Poor Man* and, in the absence of a manuscript, remain the most reliable sources of information for Hardy's unpublished first novel. The other sources—Hardy's own remarks in *Life*, Gosse's synopsis apparently based on a conversation with Hardy, the *Human Shows* poem 'A Poor Man and a Lady', and 'Indiscretion' itself—are by no means to be disregarded, but their individual limitations do need to be recognized.

The freedom with which Hardy treated material incorporated into *Life*—letters, memoranda, notes, and even the facts themselves[19]—calls into question all the unverifiable statements in the work, as, to some extent, does his not having composed it until late in his eighth decade. On the other hand, he did still possess

---

[14] *Biography*, 194–5; during the first half of 1878 TH was also writing some 'Napoleonic' ballads and correcting the Tauchnitz edition of *Far from the Madding Crowd*.

[15] *Life*, 58.

[16] *CL* i. 7; Macmillan 'Record of Manuscripts', i. 1866–71 (BL Add. MS 56016), fo. 7^v.

[17] Macmillan 'Record of Manuscripts', fo. 7^v; part I of the MS was sent on 6 Aug., part II on 8 Aug.

[18] References to Morley's report (Macmillan 'Reviews of Manuscripts', i (BL Add. MS 55931), 62–3) and Macmillan's letter (DCM) are identified in the text as Morley and Macmillan respectively.

[19] Millgate, *Life*, pp. xiv–xvi, xxv–xxvi.

Macmillan's letter at that time, as well as a bound fragment of the original manuscript (see p. 81), and the few details related to *Poor Man* that are in fact provided in *Life* can probably be accepted with only minor reservations.

Somewhat more suspect is Gosse's 'T. Hardy and "The Poor Man"', originally written as a kind of diary record for 25 April 1915.[20] Purdy, only aware of the published version ('Thomas Hardy's Lost Novel', *Sunday Times*, 22 Jan. 1928), described Gosse's recollections as 'remarkably circumstantial and to be accepted with caution',[21] and it is certainly true that the references in the *Sunday Times* article to the date when Hardy narrated these particulars as both 1921 and 'an earlier occasion [than 1920]'—and, indeed, the differences between the printed text and manuscript[22]—do not inspire particular confidence. However, as Millgate points out, Gosse was certainly with Hardy on 25 April 1915, and his account of *Poor Man* does not significantly contradict the other sources.[23] Its failure to provide a conclusion (see p. 79) also suggests that Hardy refused to be pressured by Gosse into 'remembering' what was in fact forgotten. At the same time, his inability to recollect is a reminder that Hardy was attempting to reconstruct the plot from memory at the age of seventy-four, forty-two years and more after writing the novel and the early works which drew heavily upon it. The potential for error, elaboration, or downright invention—either Hardy's or Gosse's—certainly exists, and, even if as a general outline the account seems reliable enough, it cannot be regarded as accurate in all its details. For the purposes of this discussion, however, the synopsis—the only extended description of the plot to survive—is quoted without articulated reservations when it does not conflict with other sources of information.

Of similarly questionable reliability, though for different reasons, is 'A Poor Man and a Lady'. In a published note to the poem Hardy said that it 'was intended to preserve an episode in the story of "The Poor Man and the Lady," written in 1868, and, like these lines, in the first person; but never printed, and ultimately destroyed.'[24] The poem is

---

[20] Brotherton Collection, University of Leeds, GOSSE, MSS, D-5, B4499:1/2-B4500:1; subsequent references to Gosse's account are simply identified as such in the text.

[21] Purdy, 275.

[22] The MS narrative is not contradicted, but it is tidied up and slightly expanded.

[23] *Biography*, 109.

[24] *Human Shows, Far Phantasies, Songs, and Trifles* (London: Macmillan, 1925), 197.

none the less a distinct creative work, published nearly sixty years after the novel's composition. In 'preserving' an element from *Poor Man* Hardy was presumably not unduly concerned about its original details and he may well have reshaped them—like the notes, events, and memories which so often provided the initial impetus for his poetic creativity—to fit the thematic and stylistic needs of the poem.

Nor, finally, can 'Indiscretion' itself be used as an infallible indicator of the lost novel's content, substantial modifications again having been necessitated by the change in form. But it is at least written in prose, even if in the third rather than the first person (see p. 14), and passages from *Poor Man* were undoubtedly incorporated into it with only minimal alteration.

In comparing 'Indiscretion' with *Poor Man*, in so far as the latter can plausibly be reconstructed from these various sources, the differences are no less interesting than the similarities. Both use a rural setting, presumably Dorset, for their opening episodes and focus on the love affair between a young man in humble circumstances and the 'beautiful and spirited' daughter and heiress of the local squire (Gosse).[25] Egbert Mayne, the schoolteacher protagonist of 'Indiscretion', differs from his prototype, however, in that he is the son of 'a painter of good family' and 'a small farmer's daughter', while Will Strong of *Poor Man* is 'the son of peasants working on the [squire's] estate' (Gosse). Both men have been educated, Egbert at his parents' expense at 'a good school' and Will by the patronage of 'the people of the great house', who subsequently arrange for him to be trained as an architect (Gosse). Egbert, like the narrator of 'A Poor Man and a Lady', a 'striver with deeds to do, | And little enough to do them with',[26] seeks fame and fortune through literary work in London; Will is sent to London—out of reach of the squire's daughter—where he successfully pursues his architectural career (Gosse). In view of the autobiographical elements in much of Hardy's early fiction, it seems significant that his own abandonment of architecture for literature

[25] Rutland's comparison (*Thomas Hardy*, 114 ff.) of 'Indiscretion' with Macmillan's letter and the published version of Gosse's synopsis, though considerably less developed, inevitably overlaps at times with the following account, but neither points of agreement nor of difference have been individually recorded.

[26] *The Complete Poetical Works of Thomas Hardy*, ed. Samuel Hynes, iii (Oxford: Clarendon Press, 1985), 112; cf. Mayne's reflection: 'He would have to engage in a more active career.' Subsequent references to the poem are simply identified as such in the text.

should be echoed in the alteration of the protagonist's profession. In 1935 Florence Hardy told Purdy that the schoolmaster in 'Indiscretion' was unmistakably based on the author himself,[27] as, indeed, is suggested by the nearly synonymous surnames—'hardy', 'strong', 'main'.[28] The decision to make Egbert a writer, however, was presumably an attempt to render him less like the architects Stephen Smith in *A Pair of Blue Eyes* and Edward Springrove in *Desperate Remedies*.

Perhaps, too, Hardy had taken to heart Macmillan's criticism that *Poor Man* lacked the '*modesty of nature* of fact': 'King Cophetua & the beggar maid make a pretty tale in an old ballad; but make a story in which the Duke of Edinburgh takes in lawful wedlock even a private gentlemans [*sic*] daughter! ... Given your characters, could it happen in the present day?' The difference in social position does appear to have been reduced in 'Indiscretion': Geraldine, unlike the 'lady' of *Poor Man*, is never described as a 'great' heiress (Gosse); her father has become simply Squire Foy Allenville instead of the Hon. Foy Allancourt (Macmillan); and Will's peasant parents survive only in the reference to Egbert's mother's peasant *ancestry*. Nor is Egbert beholden to the squire for past patronage. Moreover, in the *Harper's* text—the surviving witness closest to the manuscript of *Poor Man*—Egbert is convinced that Geraldine speaks without inhibition because she considers him to be 'an innocent nobody', while in the *New Quarterly* text he becomes, rather more substantially, 'a person' on whom she can try out her ideas. Similarly, Egbert's reference to himself as a man 'of no social standing' is altered in the later text to read 'of his unequal history'.

The revisions made to the *New Quarterly* text also embody—in keeping with the change of title between novel and story—an attempt to move away from the issue of the poor man's worship of the lady to that of the lady's indiscretion. Not that Egbert ceases to adore Geraldine 'as one from above the sky' or, indeed, to give her 'great pleasure' in so doing. But the essentially passive object of Egbert's love in the early chapters of the *Harper's* text is not present in the *New Quarterly*. The narrator's remark that Geraldine was 'not in love herself' is altered to not 'quite' in love, while Egbert's reflection that 'she certainly had encouraged him' is no longer qualified ('or, at any rate,

---

[27] *Biography*, 112.
[28] First remarked on by Weber (Introduction to *Indiscretion*, 18).

had not discouraged him') but said to be 'only too true'. In the opening scene she returns his glance, albeit unknown to him, several times—in the *Harper's* text she merely looks at him once at the conclusion of the service—and in the fourth chapter direct reference is made to her 'indiscreet interest in him' being 'still further' kindled by his devotion. Even more explicit is the added passage introducing her second visit to the school: 'when a passionate liking for his society was creeping over the reckless though pure girl, slowly, insidiously, and surely, like ripeness over fruit, she further committed herself by coming alone to the school.'

Other revisions incorporated in the *New Quarterly* text also accentuate her thoughtless impulsiveness. She is no longer simply 'young and impressionable' but 'unreflecting and impressionable', and the sounding of her father as to the possibility of making an unequal match is now described as 'this new imprudence of hers'. Even the newspaper account of the elopement focuses on her recklessness: her father is left alone 'to mourn the young lady's rashness' rather than 'to mourn her loss'.

But it is circumstance as well as character which precipitates the heiress's indiscretion. In both versions of the story—and presumably also in *Poor Man*—emphasis is placed on Geraldine's 'false notions of the world'. Egbert recognizes that 'she was a girl nursed up like an exotic, with no real experience', and 'had as yet seen little or no society', as is later corroborated by her own letter: 'We were but a girl and a boy at the time of our meetings at Tollamore. What was our knowledge? A list of other people's words. What was our wisdom? None at all.' Nor at seventeen has Geraldine, 'residing in a great house with no companion but an undemonstrative father', had any experience of passionate love. Trapped like so many Victorian heroines—and women—in a life which 'dragged on as uneventfully as that of one in gaol', with little more to alleviate the boredom than an occasional local function (such as the stone-laying ceremony) or a visit to the village school, she is naturally susceptible to the attentions of an intelligent young man of 'cultivated manner' and a 'distracting order of beauty'.

Geraldine's responsiveness is rendered still more inevitable in the revised *New Quarterly* text by the introduction of the sensational threshing-machine episode.[29] Egbert, having prevented her from

[29] Purdy (274) was the first to remark on the two different accounts of the lovers' meeting.

being caught in the machine and 'whirled round the wheel as a mangled carcase', becomes a romantic figure for her, the heroic rescuer who has saved her from a 'ghastly death'. Hardy knew that the very intensity of a life-and-death situation could in itself create or precipitate a bond—as in *A Pair of Blue Eyes*, for instance, where the mutual avowal of love follows the cliff-hanging scene—and he capitalized on this emotive potential, introducing references to the lovers' dramatic meeting not only to explain such responses as Geraldine's unease during her first visit to the school or her desire to prevent the eviction of Egbert's grandfather but also, to a great extent, to account for her being interested in Egbert in the first place. Egbert himself acknowledges, 'It was my saving her from the threshing-machine that began it.'

In the *Harper's* version—as, apparently, in *Poor Man*—there is no such romantic stimulus for Geraldine's fascination, simply a comparatively brief description of the first meeting:

It was the second Sunday after Christmas, and he had lately come there to teach. This was the second time in his life that he had set eyes on the only daughter and heiress of the family at Tollamore House; the first was when he arrived, a week earlier, and had been obliged to take up his quarters in the mansion, because the school-house was not quite ready. She had spoken very kindly to him—almost with imprudent kindness; and his gaze at her during the church service was the result of their acquaintance.

Though clearly not a direct borrowing, the passage does echo the lost novel in referring to the heiress's 'family'—Geraldine, unlike her precursor, has only one surviving parent—and in emphasizing her initial (and initiating) 'imprudent kindness', since in *Poor Man* it is Miss Allancourt who first takes 'a romantic interest' in Will (Gosse). Their meeting indoors, too, is consistent with the squire's patronage of Will, which would have provided ample opportunity for an encounter at the manor-house. That Will did first see her indoors is also implied by the description—presumably adapted from *Poor Man*[30]—of Geraldine wearing 'the same dress that she had worn when they first met on the previous Christmas, and her hair . . . loose, as at that time', since she would almost certainly not have worn her hair loose when outdoors.

[30] In *Under the Greenwood Tree*, a work also heavily dependent upon *Poor Man*, Dick first sees Fancy on Christmas Eve with her hair about her shoulders. So, too, in *A Pair of Blue Eyes*, Elfride's hair is loose when she meets Stephen.

In revising 'Indiscretion' Hardy perhaps felt that the *Harper's* account of the lovers' meeting was too perfunctory, and the introduction of the threshing-machine episode certainly increased the credibility of Geraldine's interest in the young schoolmaster. Moreover, the unrevised version of the story was problematic, as Hardy probably realized, in that it conflicted with the later narrative: not only does Egbert never live in the schoolhouse but he could have stayed with his grandfather that first week as well as later.[31] The *New Quarterly* text, however, is not consistent either, for it still refers to the time when Egbert 'lived at the school' and, indeed, to the lovers' meeting at Christmas and presumably indoors rather than at harvest-time outdoors.

Hardy was always capable of such inconsistencies, especially when he was producing something in a hurry—compare, for example, 'Exploits'—or substantially revising an earlier version, but their incidence in 'Indiscretion' does seem uncharacteristically high: many remarks, if not blatantly contradictory, are at the very least incongruous. For example, when insisting upon his family's respectability Egbert mentions only that his father was 'a painter of no mean power, and a gentleman by education', not—what would have been more to the point—that his father was 'of good family' and that he himself, 'sent away from home at an early age to a good school', has had a gentleman's education. Similarly, Egbert is said to be Geraldine's master in literature 'thanks to his tastes', without reference to his superior education: but the remark is in fact more applicable to Will's background, since he, like Hardy, was educated locally and then attached to an architect's office (Gosse). A similarly incongruous note is struck by Egbert's statement after the squire's plan for enlarging the park has been reintroduced: 'we shall go now . . . and make room for newer people'. Not only would the departure of Egbert and his grandfather in no sense make room for others—the plan was to tear down the house and give the farm to a current tenant—but Egbert was in any case only a temporary inhabitant, living in the farmhouse simply 'in order that the old man . . . might have the benefit of his society during the long winter evenings'. Egbert's comment— like Geraldine's 'Say that you forgive me for thinking he and yourself had better leave'—probably appeared in some form in

---

[31] Coleman (Introduction to *Indiscretion*, 19) makes this point.

Poor Man, from which the threatened eviction episode was certainly derived.[32]

The numerous inconsistencies, then, can to a great extent be attributed to the difficulty of creating a coherent, independent story out of the manuscript of a full-length novel. Inevitably there would have been problems of organization and integration: episodes were doubtless rearranged, locations altered, chronologies muddled. In one chapter it is said that the lovers' meetings took place 'without any pretence of accident', in the next that 'much sophistry lay in their definition of "accidental" [meetings] at this season'. The reworking of the material has also created an anachronism: according to the chronology of 'Indiscretion' the date of Geraldine's second visit to the school is late May or early June,[33] yet at the time that the children are dismissed night is approaching and it is 'almost dark in the room'.

That Hardy deliberately sought to revise his material in the process of taking it from *Poor Man*—thereby further increasing the difficulty of producing a consistent narrative—is also apparent in the moderation of the virulent satire which the novel is said to have contained. Once again, he was probably influenced by the readers' comments on the *Poor Man*: according to *Life*, Meredith warned him 'not to "nail his colours to the mast" so definitely',[34] while Macmillan's letter insisted that his 'chastisement would fall harmless from its very excess'. 'Indiscretion' certainly has little of the 'cynical description' and 'hard sarcasm' Morley remarked upon in *Poor Man*, and what social criticism remains is frequently rendered still less emphatic in the revised version—presumably to prevent its being criticized as 'exaggerated & untrue' (Macmillan).[35] Thus in the *New Quarterly* 'utterly', 'at once', and 'purest' do not appear in Egbert's

---

[32] The striking verbal parallels in the scenes depicting the manipulative use of squirearchical power and its consequences in 'Indiscretion' and *Desperate Remedies* indicate that both were based on a common source (see Dalziel, 'Thomas Hardy's Uncollected Stories', 172 ff.).

[33] The earliest possible date is 24 May, since the visit takes place on a Tuesday after 17 May 1864 (see p. 100 and *Biography*, 118). It is also curious that Broadford should be threshing corn some weeks *before* August (pp. 107, 112).

[34] *Life*, 62.

[35] The charge of exaggeration may also have influenced such revisions as the alteration of 'many' to 'some' in the description of the schoolchildren going off in the pelting rain, 'many for a walk of more than two miles', and the omission of the sentence describing Egbert's zealousness in London: 'At first he had unflinchingly worked sixteen hours a day; but finding this to be a mistaken policy, he reduced the number to thirteen.'

reflection upon the anomaly that 'the habits of men should be so utterly subversive of the law of nature as to indicate that he was not at once worthy to marry a woman whose own purest instincts said that he was worthy'. So, too, in the revised text a world in which such divisions can exist is described merely as 'troublesome' rather than 'wretched'.

The diminution in 'Indiscretion' of what Hardy later defined as the 'socialistic, not to say revolutionary', tendency of the writing in *Poor Man*[36] is of course to some extent the consequence of circumscribing the original narrative in order to focus primarily on the love plot. The story echoes the novel in its two-part division and presumably also in its basic structure—Part I, set in Dorset, chronicling the development of the love relationship, and Part II marking the move to London, though concluding in Dorset.[37] But much has been omitted: 'the opening pictures of the Christmas Eve in the tranters [*sic*] house' (Morley); the scene in Rotten Row, the conversations in the drawing-rooms and ballrooms about the working classes, and the retraction of the Palace of Hobbies Company's award (Macmillan); Will's radical public speech (Macmillan and Gosse); the confrontation with Mrs Allancourt (Gosse); and the visit to an architect's kept mistress.[38] With the exception of the Christmas Eve scenes—subsequently adapted for *Under the Greenwood Tree*—these episodes were all set in London and were later characterized in *Life* as 'a sweeping dramatic satire of the squirearchy and nobility, London society, the vulgarity of the middle class, modern Christianity, church restoration, and political and domestic morals in general'.[39]

Much of this material probably had little directly to do with the love plot, but Will's diatribe condemning the landed classes was evidently used as the initial means of breaking off the lovers' relations: Miss Allancourt, happening to drive by in her carriage when he is addressing a crowd in Trafalgar Square, stops to listen and is 'greatly offended' by his radicalism (Gosse). She subsequently meets him at a concert (as Geraldine does Egbert), becomes reconciled

---

[36] *Life*, 63.

[37] The Dorset–London–Dorset structure coincides with Gosse's account and all Morley's page references to cynical or sarcastic passages in the *Poor Man* MS (280, 333–52, 338, 358–9) are to the latter half—the examples mentioned by Macmillan would suggest the London-dominated half—of the 440-page manuscript. TH (*Life*, 63) maintained that the novel's most important scenes were set in London.

[38] *Life*, 63.   [39] Ibid. 62–3.

with him, and asks him to call on her openly, but the visit is disastrous:

> Unfortunately the Lady was out, and her mother received him, with great anger and arrogance. He lost his temper, and they both became so excited that the Mother fainted away. He found some water, and flung it over her face, with the result that the rouge ran on her cheeks. On coming to, she discovered this, with redoubled rage, and the Squire himself coming in, a footman turned the architect out at the front door. (Gosse)

Hardy probably showed good judgement in leaving this comic, even farcical, episode out of 'Indiscretion', although—like the Trafalgar Square scene—it was perhaps in any case inseparable from Will's radicalism and the specifically political plot of *Poor Man*.

To accommodate such omissions the love plot in 'Indiscretion' has evidently been simplified. No specific event leads Geraldine to break off relations with Egbert: forbidden to seek out, correspond with, or receive him,[40] she drifts gradually away, immerses herself in the distractions of society—compare 'A Poor Man and a Lady', where the lovers' union becomes 'Less grave' in the woman's eyes during her 'town campaigns'—and, 'to satisfy [her] friends', agrees to marry Lord Bretton. A similar sequence of events—albeit set in the country—presumably occurred in *Poor Man*, but not until after the confrontation with Mrs Allancourt: the family returns to Dorset, 'no more letters [are] passed', and in 'the course of time' Will hears of the engagement from his relations (Gosse). (In the poem, as in 'Indiscretion', he sees the announcement in the 'current news-sheets'.)

Scenes which Hardy wanted to incorporate from *Poor Man* he simply modified in accordance with the new plot requirements. In the novel the meeting at the concert is accidental and leads to reconciliation:

> A short time afterwards [i.e. after the rupture occasioned by Will's radical speech] ... there was given a concert, at which the Lady happened to be seated alone at the last row of the expensive places, and the architect immediately behind her in the front row of the cheap places. Both were extremely moved by the emotion of the music, and as she chanced to put her hand on the back of her seat, he took it in his, and held it till the end of the performance. They walked away together, and all their affection was renewed. (Gosse)

---

[40] Since in 'Indiscretion' Geraldine never has received Egbert, the reference is probably a survival from *Poor Man*. TH perhaps recognized the incongruity as the phrase does not appear in the revised *New Quarterly* text.

In 'Indiscretion' it is the standing for the 'Hallelujah Chorus' which enables the lovers to hold hands, and, more significantly, it is by Egbert's contrivance that they attend the same concert. His being both metaphorically and literally roped off from her (a red cord divides the area where he is sitting 'from stalls of a somewhat superior kind') points up the unbridgeable gap between them—somewhat ironically so in this instance, since his seat allocation was in fact determined by ticket availability and not by financial constraints. He would have purchased a place in her row had one been free, but circumstances inexorably ensure that they are separated. Nor do they walk away together as in *Poor Man*: she leaves through one doorway, he through the other.

Some details—for example, of the lovers' meeting in the church—have been altered to a degree that renders the various versions almost impossible to reconcile, but it is the scarcity rather than the irreconcilability of information that makes it difficult to determine whether or not in *Poor Man* Miss Allancourt actually married either Will Strong or 'the heir of [the] great neighbouring landowner' (Gosse). Attempting to outline the plot in 1915, Hardy 'racked his brain to recollect, but in vain: he could not tell at all' (Gosse). Macmillan's letter, emphasizing the unnaturalness of a hypothetical story in which the Duke of Edinburgh 'takes in lawful wedlock' even a private gentleman's daughter, implies that, as in 'Indiscretion', the unequal match does take place. Certainly the summoning of Egbert to Geraldine's bedside at the doctor's insistence seems to have been derived from *Poor Man*, since Macmillan refers to the squire having 'so far broken through the prejudices of his class as to send for Strong in the hope of saving his daughters [*sic*] life'.

It is in any case sufficiently clear from Macmillan's comments that the daughter subsequently dies: 'Is it conceivable that any man however base & soul corrupted would do as you make The Hon Foy Allancourt do at the close, accept an estimate for his daughters [*sic*] tomb—*because it cost him nothing?*' Moreover, her death, like Geraldine's, is caused by some kind of haemorrhage.[41] In response to a query from Hardy when finishing off *Poor Man*, George Brereton Sharpe, a distant relation and former physician, wrote that 'Hemorrage [*sic*] of the lungs' would be the best way to dispose of the

---

[41] In the revised *New Quarterly* text the specific reference to the nature of Geraldine's illness has been removed, 'attack' replacing 'hemorrhage'.

heroine quickly and unexpectedly while at the same time allowing her to retain possession of her faculties to the very end.[42] This convenient mode of death was subsequently exploited not only in 'Indiscretion' but also in *Desperate Remedies*. Miss Aldclyffe's attack, like Geraldine's, is related by one of the servants:

she complained of fulness ... in the chest.... [On hearing] that Manston had killed himself in gaol—she shrieked—broke a blood-vessel—and fell upon the floor.... They say she is sure to get over it ... She has suffered from it before.[43]

Compare 'Indiscretion':

I felt a fulness on my chest ...

[Directly Miss Allenville] saw her father it gave her such a turn that she fainted and burst a blood-vessel, and fell upon the floor.... [W]e are afraid she won't live over it. She has suffered from it before.

The description of Geraldine's last moments—'Everything was so still that her weak act of trying to live seemed a silent wrestling with all the powers of the universe'—also figures in *Desperate Remedies*,[44] while for both characters it is 'another effusion' which brings on death.[45]

Such parallel passages—of which there are a great many more[46]— suggest the remarkable degree to which 'Indiscretion' uses material from *Poor Man* already drawn upon during the writing of *Desperate Remedies*. A similar demonstration—again emphasizing the debt to this common source—could be offered of the striking verbal similarities between 'Indiscretion' and Hardy's next two novels, *Under the Greenwood Tree* and *A Pair of Blue Eyes*.[47] All three novels were of course published before the story appeared, but it is by no means clear that this extensive and—one might have thought—potentially embarrassing reuse of publicly used material was in fact the determining factor in Hardy's decision to exclude 'Indiscretion' from his collective

---

[42] 21 Jan. 1868 (Dorset County Library).

[43] *Desperate Remedies* (London: Tinsley Bros., 1871) iii. 247; subsequent references are also to the three-volume first edition.

[44] Ibid. 248; the sentence in the novel is expanded but follows essentially the same structure and wording. Rutland (*Thomas Hardy*, 130–1) was the first to note this parallel.

[45] *Desperate Remedies*, iii. 259.

[46] See Dalziel, 'Thomas Hardy's Uncollected Stories', 165 ff.

[47] Ibid. 175 ff.

volumes. The similarities, though numerous, are not blatantly obvious, and it is conceivable that they were not even recognized by Hardy himself when he hurriedly put the story together in 1878, five years after the last of the novels clearly related to *Poor Man* appeared in volume form. Hardy's own explanation for the story's non-collection is in fact quite convincing. It could appropriately have been included in *A Changed Man*, and on 30 September 1913, as the arrangements for that volume were being finalized, Frederick Macmillan forwarded to Hardy a letter from the manager of the *Burlington Magazine* which praised 'Indiscretion' as 'a delightful story'.[48] Responding on 4 October, Hardy pointed out, apparently for the first time, the story's debt to *Poor Man*, but then concluded:

I have not included The "Indiscretion" in the new volume because the point & force of the original story was abstracted from this pale shadow of it, & I thought I might find it amusing in my old age to endeavour to restore the original from the modification, aided by my memory & a fragment still in existence of "The P.M. & Lady"—merely a few pages.[49]

When discussing the lost novel a year and a half later, Hardy led Gosse to believe that the surviving fragment consisted only of '4 or 5 pages' from 'the least interesting part of the book' (Gosse). Hardy may simply have made a rather vague reference, as in *Life*, to 'a few unimportant leaves',[50] allowing Gosse to jump to an inaccurate conclusion about their actual number, for in fact they were sufficiently numerous to justify binding, as Sydney Cockerell later recalled: 'Hardy showed me in the latter half of 1916 a good portion of the MS. of *The Poor Man and the Lady* and I undertook to get it handsomely bound in blue morocco. This I did at a cost of two pounds and he seemed very pleased.'[51] The volume arrived at Max Gate on 10 February 1917 and was presented by Hardy to his wife in commemoration of their wedding three years previously.[52] Writing to Cockerell a year later, however, Florence Hardy said:

I have given back to T.H. the beautifully bound "Poor Man & the Lady" as he says he wants to feel himself at liberty to do what he likes with it. I am *quite sure* that it is the exquisite binding alone when [*sic*] prevents him from burning it—as he feels now his early MSS. had been better destroyed.[53]

[48] *CL* iv. 306.   [49] Ibid.   [50] *Life*, 64.
[51] Letter to Rutland (Rutland, *Thomas Hardy*, 113); later still, Cockerell wrote to Purdy: 'I should guess there were about 80 leaves' (29 Jan. 1943; Millgate collection).
[52] FEH to Cockerell, 10 Feb. 1917 (Beinecke).   [53] 2 Feb. 1918 (Beinecke).

Hardy subsequently did burn the bound fragment,[54] and of course he never undertook the proposed reconstruction of the novel, perhaps more an attractive idea of the moment than a seriously considered enterprise, and one which would have been extraordinarily difficult to carry out, given the dispersal and essential transformation of so much of the original material in the early works. Hardy may in any case have decided that a reconstruction would not be worthwhile, especially at a time when he was far more concerned to remain active as a poet than as a writer of prose. He had apparently admitted to Gosse that *Poor Man* 'was very crude',[55] and the novel was perhaps more impressive absent than present: with the destruction of the manuscript some of Hardy's more extravagant claims—his insistence, for example, that *Poor Man* 'was the most original thing (for its date) that [he] ever wrote'[56]—could not effectively be challenged.

The non-appearance of a reconstructed version of *Poor Man* did not, however, lead to the production of a new edition of 'Indiscretion'. The story was in fact reprinted only once during Hardy's lifetime—presumably without his authorization or even knowledge[57]—in the Boston periodical *Littell's Living Age*, 5 and 12 October 1878, less than four months after its original simultaneous English and US publication. In 1929, after Hardy's death, Paul Lemperly sought permission to have it privately printed, but his request, like the similar one he had made in respect of 'How I Built Myself a House' twenty years earlier, was denied. Cockerell subsequently insisted that as literary executors both he and Hardy's widow had felt that 'it would be a mistake' to reprint the story;[58] Florence Hardy's own 21 May 1930 letter to Lemperly, however, suggests that the decision was essentially Cockerell's: 'I could not, I believe, give permission without his assent also, & he is *very strongly* opposed to the publication of

[54] *Life*, 64; Rutland, *Thomas Hardy*, 113.

[55] Gosse, 'Thomas Hardy's Lost Novel', *Sunday Times*, 22 Jan. 1928.

[56] To Clodd, 5 Dec. 1910 (*CL* iv. 130); cf. *Life*, 66, 111.

[57] Coleman's claim (Introduction to *Indiscretion*, 5) that the story was sold is highly improbable in light of the absence of US copyright protection for British authors. *Littell's Living Age* appears in fact to have survived by pirating material from British magazines: the two issues containing 'Indiscretion' (set from the *New Quarterly* text) also included works from *Blackwood's*, the *Contemporary Review*, the *Cornhill*, *Fraser's*, the *Gentleman's Magazine*, *Macmillan's*, the *Nineteenth Century*, the *Pall Mall Gazette*, and the *Spectator*.

[58] Cockerell, 'Early Hardy Stories', letter to the *Times Literary Supplement*, 14 Mar. 1935, 160.

any early short stories by my husband— He was exceedingly angry about the re-publication of "Old Mrs Chundle".'[59] Given the violence of that disagreement over 'Old Mrs Chundle', culminating in January 1929 with her promise to leave similar decisions to Cockerell in future (see pp. 216 ff.), it is perhaps not surprising that, when the question of reprinting 'Indiscretion' arose later that same year, she should have allowed Cockerell to have his way.

By 1934, however, when Florence Hardy was again approached about republishing 'Indiscretion', she had become completely estranged from Cockerell and had been effectively acting as sole literary executor for some time.[60] She therefore made an entirely independent decision to have one hundred copies privately printed at the Curwen Press, Plaistow. As she told Howard Bliss, 'I thought I would ... do it as I liked—so that I could give copies to friends.'[61] To Daniel Macmillan she insisted that her edition was an attempt to forestall Carl J. Weber's, which was in fact published by the Johns Hopkins University Press in 1935:

These Americans kept writing to me, & asked my permission to publish the story. Feeling certain, from their letter, that they intended to print it with or without my permission, I hastily printed it myself—or rather had it printed with the help of Mr Desmond Flower who is the son of an old friend, & understands printing & binding.... This, however, has not prevented the book from being published in America—but I hope mine is the first edition.[62]

Ready for distribution on 5 October 1934, Florence Hardy's privately printed edition did indeed precede Weber's, as Flower pointed out in his letter to *The Times*[63] after the American edition was announced on 1 March 1935.

It was only through publication of Flower's letter that Cockerell learned of the private printing, and he immediately remonstrated with Florence Hardy:

[59] Colby College Library, Waterville, Maine.

[60] On 20 Mar. 1934 FEH wrote to H. Geikie at Macmillan & Co.: 'I thought Sir Sydney Cockerell's duties as co literary-executor had lapsed since I had not heard from him for nearly three years' (BL Add. MS 54926).

[61] 9 Oct. 1934 (Morris Parrish Collection, Princeton University).

[62] 6 Mar. 1935 (BL Add. MS 54926); FEH explained her decision to Bliss in similar terms (9 Oct. 1934 and 28 Mar. 1935; Morris Parrish Collection, Princeton University).

[63] Published 4 Mar. 1935.

Considering that your husband appointed me one of his literary executors I think that I ought to have been consulted before the printing of *An Indiscretion in the Life of an Heiress*; quite apart from the fact that you solemnly promised, after that unfortunate American publication [of 'Old Mrs Chundle'], that you would never do such a thing again without seeking my views.[64]

He also publicly disassociated himself from the edition in his letter to the *Times Literary Supplement*, published on 14 March:

As one of the literary executors of Thomas Hardy, the other being Mrs. Hardy, I desire to state that I was not consulted about the printing of a limited edition of "An Indiscretion["] ... Nor have I seen a copy, but I read it some years ago in an American magazine of 1878, and came to the conclusion that Hardy had some reason for not reprinting it and that it would be a mistake to do so. This was also Mrs. Hardy's opinion in 1929...[65]

The breach between Florence Hardy and Cockerell was perhaps already irremediable, but with the publication of this letter any possibility of reconciliation finally evaporated. Two years later Florence Hardy wrote to Lemperly:

That printing, by me, of "An Indiscretion" was an unfortunate step indeed. You may know that Sydney Cockerell ... wrote a violent letter to the Times Literary Supplement attacking me—to the amazement of even his own friends. This made it quite impossible for me ever to have anything to do with him again ...[66]

Certainly there were those who did not think that Florence Hardy's decision was 'an unfortunate step'. Shortly after her edition appeared James Barrie, insisting that she had done 'the right and proper thing', said of the story: 'It is as haunting with an unearthly charm as his more famous works. I cannot think that if I had seen it on its first quiet appearance I could have failed to know that another great one was arising. One can't be sure, but at any rate it could have come from no other pen.'[67] What Hardy himself would have thought about the

[64] 4 Mar. 1935 (quoted by Wilfrid Blunt, *Cockerell* (London: Hamish Hamilton, 1964), 222).

[65] Cockerell, 'Early Hardy Stories'. Perhaps because he had not yet made the connection between 'Indiscretion' and the story he had read years earlier, Cockerell had been less absolute in his private letter to FEH: 'I have not seen this publication, or even heard of it until this morning's announcement in *The Times*, and it may be something of the printing of which your husband would have approved' (quoted by Blunt, *Cockerell*, 222).

[66] 7 Mar. 1937 (Colby College Library, Waterville, Maine).

[67] To FEH, 4 Nov. 1934 (Morris Parrish Collection, Princeton University).

edition cannot be determined. That he might have reprinted the story in his lifetime if he had not contemplated a reconstruction of *Poor Man* is suggested by his 4 October 1913 letter to Frederick Macmillan; on the other hand, that he would have approved of the separate volume publication of what he undoubtedly considered a minor work seems highly unlikely.[68] When told that Gosse intended to write down the particulars he had related concerning *Poor Man*, Hardy apparently said: 'Oh! very well ... they may be amusing some day; but it is hunting very small deer!'[69]

Presumably 'Indiscretion' would have been still more firmly relegated to the 'small deer' category, but it has in fact received substantially more attention than any of Hardy's other uncollected stories. Coleman's volume edition, published by Hutchinson in 1976 and reprinted in paperback in 1985, is still in print and the story is also included in Pinion's *Old Mrs Chundle and Other Stories*. Clearly 'Indiscretion' is central to an understanding not only of the relationships among Hardy's early works but also—as recent criticism has demonstrated—of the essential continuity of his thinking on social issues throughout his fiction-writing career: if the late novels are the most obviously radical of his works, there is none the less little doubt that 'Indiscretion'—even in its revised form—similarly questions both the conventional class and gender ideologies and the narrative structures which support them.[70]

BIBLIOGRAPHICAL DESCRIPTIONS

Periodical Publication

Harper's Weekly, 29 June–27 July 1878 (5 instalments)

29 June, 514, cols. 1–4; 515, cols. 1–2: chapters I–IV of part I. Heading the first two columns is:

AN INDISCRETION IN THE LIFE OF AN HEIRESS. | By THOMAS HARDY, | AUTHOR OF "FAR FROM THE MADDING CROWD," "THE RETURN OF THE NATIVE," ETC. | [*rule 51 mm.*]

---

[68] Cf. TH's attitude to 'How I Built Myself a House'.

[69] Gosse, 'Thomas Hardy's Lost Novel'.

[70] See Penny Boumelha, *Thomas Hardy and Women: Sexual Ideology and Narrative Form* (Brighton: Harvester, 1982), 35 ff.; Pamela Dalziel, 'Hardy's Unforgotten "Indiscretion": The Centrality of an Uncollected Work', *Review of English Studies* (forthcoming); Patricia Ingham, *Thomas Hardy* (London: Harvester Wheatsheaf, 1989), 48 ff.

6 July, 530, cols. 1–4; 531, cols. 1–2: chapters V–VII of part I. The title (in col. 1) reads:

An Indiscretion in the Life of an Heiress. | By THOMAS HARDY, | AUTHOR OF "FAR FROM THE MADDING CROWD," | "THE RETURN OF THE NATIVE," ETC. | [*French rule 22.5 mm.*]

13 July, 554, cols. 1–4; 555, cols. 1–2: chapter VIII of part I and chapters I–II of part II. The title appears in the same form as on 6 July.

20 July, 574, cols. 1–4; 575, cols. 1–3: chapters III–V of part II. The title appears in the same form as on 6 and 13 July.

27 July, 594, cols. 1–4; 595, col. 1: chapters VI–VII of part II. The title appears in the same form as on 6, 13, and 20 July.

New Quarterly Magazine, 10 (July 1878)
The text appears on pp. [315]–378; the title reads:

AN INDISCRETION IN THE LIFE | OF AN HEIRESS.
Hardy's name appears at the conclusion of the text.

NOTE ON THE TEXT

The copy-text is the July 1878 *New Quarterly Magazine* printing (*NQM*). The only other authoritative text is the *Harper's Weekly* printing (*HW*), set from the uncorrected *New Quarterly* proofs, or possibly, though not probably, from a duplicate manuscript. In either case *HW* represents an earlier, unrevised, and, as far as TH was concerned, essentially unfinished version. In terms of its pointing and styling *HW* also has marginally less authority than *NQM*, which was set from TH's manuscript and corrected by him in proof.

In the variants lists the source of the lemma is *NQM* and that of the recorded variant is *HW* unless otherwise specified.

AN INDISCRETION IN THE LIFE OF AN HEIRESS

PART I

CHAPTER I

> When I would pray and think, I think and pray
> To several subjects: heaven hath my empty words;
> Whilst my invention, hearing not my tongue,   5
> Anchors on Isabel.

The congregation in Tollamore Church were singing the evening hymn, the people gently swaying backwards and forwards like trees in a soft breeze. The heads of the village children, who sat in the gallery, were inclined to one side as they uttered their shrill notes, their eyes   10
listlessly tracing some crack in the old walls, or following the movement of a distant bough or bird, with features rapt almost to painfulness.

In front of the children stood a thoughtful young man, who was plainly enough the schoolmaster; and his gaze was fixed on a remote part of the aisle beneath him. When the singing was over, and all had   15
sat down for the sermon, his eyes still remained in the same place. There was some excuse for their direction, for it was in a straight line forwards; but their fixity was only to be explained by some object before them. This was a square pew, containing one solitary sitter. But that sitter was a young lady, and a very sweet lady was she.   20

Afternoon service in Tollamore parish was later than in many others in that neighbourhood; and as the darkness deepened during the progress of the sermon, the rector's pulpit-candles shone to the remotest nooks of the building, till at length they became the sole lights of the congregation. The lady was the single person besides the   25

13 who was [*not in HW*]   15–16 had sat] sat   17 direction, for]
direction, since   19 This was] This was simply   19 solitary sitter] sitter only
20 young [*not in HW*]   20 a very] such a   22–4 as the darkness . . .
building,] the rector's pulpit candles shone to the remotest nooks of the building as the
darkness deepened during the progress of the sermon,   25 single] only

preacher whose face was turned westwards, the pew that she occupied
being the only one in the church in which the seat ran all round. She
reclined in her corner, her bonnet and dark dress growing by degrees
invisible, and at last only her upturned face could be discerned, a
5 solitary white spot against the black surface of the wainscot. Over her
head rose a vast marble monument, erected to the memory of her
ancestors, male and female; for she was one of high standing in that
parish. The design consisted of a winged skull and two cherubim,
supporting a pair of tall Corinthian columns, between which spread a
10 broad slab, containing the roll of ancient names, lineages, and deeds,
and surmounted by a pediment, with the crest of the family at its apex.

As the youthful schoolmaster gazed, and all these details became
dimmer, her face was modified in his fancy, till it seemed almost to
resemble the carved marble skull immediately above her head. The
15 thought was unpleasant enough to arouse him from his half-dreamy
state, and he entered on rational considerations of what a vast gulf lay
between that lady and himself, what a troublesome world it was to live
in where such divisions could exist, and how painful was the evil when a
man of his unequal history was possessed of a keen susceptibility.

20 Now a close observer, who should have happened to be near the large
pew, might have noticed before the light got low that the interested gaze
of the young man had been returned from time to time by the young
lady, although he, towards whom her glances were directed, did not
perceive the fact. It would have been guessed that something in the past
25 was common to both, notwithstanding their difference in social
standing. What that was may be related in a few words.

One day in the previous week there had been some excitement in
the parish on account of the introduction upon the farm of a steam

---

1 pew that] pew   3 bonnet and [*not in HW*]   10 ancient [*not in HW*]
14 her head] it   15 half-dreamy] half-dreaming   16 entered ...
considerations of] considered   17 troublesome] wretched   19 his
unequal ... susceptibility.] no social standing was given a keen susceptibility of
temperament.   20–90. 3 Now ... itself. Only once more] That afternoon an emotion,
which composed the young man's sole motive power through many following years,
first arose and established itself in his breast. It was the second Sunday after Christmas,
and he had lately come there to teach. This was the second time in his life that he had
set eyes on the only daughter and heiress of the family at Tollamore House; the first was
when he arrived, a week earlier, and had been obliged to take up his quarters in the
mansion, because the school-house was not quite ready. She had spoken very kindly to
him—almost with imprudent kindness; and his gaze at her during the church service
was the result of their acquaintance. ¶ Only once

threshing-machine for the first time, the date of these events being some thirty years ago. The machine had been hired by a farmer who was a relative of the schoolmaster's, and when it was set going all the people round about came to see it work. It was fixed in the corner of a field near the main road, and in the afternoon a passing carriage stopped outside the hedge. The steps were let down, and Miss Geraldine Allenville, the young woman whom we have seen sitting in the church pew, came through the gate of the field towards the engine. At that hour most of the villagers had been to the spot, had gratified their curiosity, and afterwards gone home again; so that there were only now left standing beside the engine the engine-man, the farmer, and the young schoolmaster, who had come like the rest. The labourers were at the other part of the machine, under the cornstack some distance off.

The girl looked with interest at the whizzing wheels, asked questions of the old farmer, and remained in conversation with him for some time, the schoolmaster standing a few paces distant, and looking more or less towards her. Suddenly the expression of his face changed to one of horror; he was by her side in a moment, and, seizing hold of her, he swung her round by the arm to a distance of several feet.

In speaking to the farmer she had inadvertently stepped backwards, and had drawn so near to the band which ran from the engine to the drum of the thresher that in another moment her dress must have been caught, and she would have been whirled round the wheel as a mangled carcase. As soon as the meaning of the young man's act was understood by her she turned deadly pale and nearly fainted. When she was well enough to walk, the two men led her to the carriage, which had been standing outside the hedge all the time.

"You have saved me from a ghastly death!" the agitated girl murmured to the schoolmaster. "Oh! I can never forget it!" and then she sank into the carriage and was driven away.

On account of this the schoolmaster had been invited to Tollamore House to explain the incident to the Squire, the young lady's only living parent. Mr Allenville thanked her preserver, inquired the history of his late father, a painter of good family, but unfortunate and improvident; and finally told his visitor that, if he were fond of study, the library of the house was at his service. Geraldine herself had spoken very impulsively to the young man—almost, indeed, with imprudent warmth—and his tender interest in her during the church service was the result of the sympathy she had shown.

And thus did an emotion, which became this man's sole motive power through many following years, first arise and establish itself. Only once more did she lift her eyes to where he sat, and it was when they all stood up before leaving. This time he noticed the glance. Her
5   look of recognition led his feelings onward yet another stage. Admiration grew to be attachment; he even wished that he might own her, not exactly as a wife, but as a being superior to himself—in the sense in which a servant may be said to own a master. He would have cared to possess her in order to exhibit her glories to the world, and he
10 scarcely even thought of her ever loving him.

There were two other stages in his course of love, but they were not reached till some time after to-day. The first was a change from this proud desire to a longing to cherish. The last stage, later still, was when her very defects became rallying-points for defence, when every
15 one of his senses became special pleaders for her; and that not through blindness, but from a tender inability to do aught else than defend her against all the world.

CHAPTER II

She was active, stirring, all fire—
20   Could not rest, could not tire—
Never in all the world such an one!
And here was plenty to be done,
And she that could do it, great or small,
She was to do nothing at all.

25 Five mornings later the same young man was looking out of the window of Tollamore village school in a fixed and absent manner. The weather was exceptionally mild, though scarcely to the degree which would have justified his airy situation at such a month of the year. A hazy light spread through the air, the landscape on which his eyes were resting
30 being enlivened and lit up by the spirit of an unseen sun rather than by its direct rays. Every sound could be heard for miles. There was a great crowing of cocks, bleating of sheep, and cawing of rooks, which

4 This time he noticed the glance. [*not in HW*]   5 recognition] inward recognition   6 attachment . . . that he] attachment, and he wished he 7–8 being . . . in which] superior to himself, as   9 possess her] possess her chiefly   9–10 world . . . her ever] world; for at that time he did not think much about her   12 after to-day] later   14–15 every one of his] all the

proceeded from all points of the compass, rising and falling as the origin of each sound was near or far away. There were also audible the voices of people in the village, interspersed with hearty laughs, the bell of a distant flock of sheep, a robin close at hand, vehicles in the neighbouring roads and lanes. One of these latter noises grew 5 gradually more distinct, and proved itself to be rapidly nearing the school. The listener blushed as he heard it.

"Suppose it should be!" he said to himself.

He had said the same thing at every such noise that he had heard during the foregoing week, and had been mistaken in his hope. But 10 this time a certain carriage did appear in answer to his expectation. He came from the window hastily; and in a minute a footman knocked and opened the school door.

"Miss Allenville wishes to speak to you, Mr Mayne."

The schoolmaster went to the porch—he was a very young man to 15 be called a schoolmaster—his heart beating with excitement.

"Good morning," she said, with a confident yet girlish smile. "My father expects me to inquire into the school arrangements, and I wish to do so on my own account as well. May I come in?"

She entered as she spoke, telling the coachman to drive to the 20 village on some errand, and call for her in half an hour.

Mayne could have wished that she had not been so thoroughly free from all apparent consciousness of the event of the previous week, of the fact that he was considerably more of a man than the small persons by whom the apartment was mainly filled, and that he was as 25 nearly as possible at her own level in age, as wide in sympathies, and possibly more inflammable in heart. But he soon found that a sort of fear to entrust her voice with the subject of that link between them was what restrained her. When he had explained a few details of routine she moved away from him round the school. 30

He turned and looked at her as she stood among the children. To his eyes her beauty was indescribable. Before he had met her he had scarcely believed that any woman in the world could be so lovely. The clear, deep eyes, full of all tender expressions; the fresh, subtly-curved cheek, changing its tones of red with the fluctuation of each thought; 35

7 listener] young man   13 school] school-room   15 he was...
man] what a young man he was   23-4 of the event...fact] that they had met
before;   25 filled, and] filled;   27-9 heart....restrained her.] heart; but he
was not in a position to remark upon such matters as those.   29 explained]
explained to her

the ripe tint of her delicate mouth, and the indefinable line where lip met lip; the noble bend of her neck, the wavy lengths of her dark brown hair, the soft motions of her bosom when she breathed, the light fall of her little feet, the elegant contrivances of her attire, all struck him as
5 something he had dreamed of and was not actually seeing. Geraldine Allenville was, in truth, very beautiful; she was a girl such as his eyes had never elsewhere beheld; and her presence here before his face kept up a sharp struggle of sweet and bitter within him.

He had thought at first that the flush on her face was caused by the
10 fresh air of the morning; but, as it quickly changed to a lesser hue, it occurred to Mayne that it might after all have arisen from shyness at meeting him after her narrow escape. Be that as it might, their conversation, which at first consisted of bald sentences, divided by wide intervals of time, became more frequent, and at last continuous.
15 He was painfully soon convinced that her tongue would never have run so easily as it did had it not been that she thought him a person on whom she could vent her ideas without reflection or punctiliousness—a thought, perhaps, expressed to herself by such words as, "I will say what I like to him, for he is only our schoolmaster."
20   "And you have chosen to keep a school," she went on, with a shade of mischievousness in her tone, looking at him as if she thought that, had she been a man capable of saving people's lives, she would have done something much better than teaching. She was so young as to habitually think thus of other persons' courses.
25   "No," he said, simply; "I don't choose to keep a school in the sense you mean, choosing it from a host of pursuits, all equally possible."
  "How came you here, then?"
  "I fear more by chance than by aim."
  "Then you are not very ambitious?"
30   "I have my ambitions, such as they are."
  "I thought so. Everybody has nowadays. But it is a better thing not to be too ambitious, *I* think."
  "If we value ease of mind, and take an economist's view of our term of life, it may be a better thing."
35   Having been tempted, by his unexpectedly cultivated manner of

11 Mayne] him   11 after all] possibly   12 after her narrow escape
[*not in HW*]   13 consisted of] consisted in   15 would never] never would
16 a person] an innocent nobody   22 a man...lives,] in his place,   23 than
teaching [*not in HW*]   29 ambitious?"] ambitious," she said, gayly.

speaking, to say more than she had meant to say, she found it embarrassing either to break off or to say more, and in her doubt she stooped to kiss a little girl.

"Although I spoke lightly of ambition," she observed, without turning to him, "and said that easy happiness was worth most, I   5 could defend ambition very well, and in the only pleasant way."

"And that way?"

"On the broad ground of the loveliness of any dream about future triumphs. In looking back there is a pleasure in contemplating a time when some attractive thing of the future appeared possible, even   10 though it never came to pass."

Mayne was puzzled to hear her talk in this tone of maturity. That such questions of success and failure should have occupied his own mind seemed natural, for they had been forced upon him by the difficulties he had encountered in his pursuit of a career. He was not   15 just then aware how very unpractical the knowledge of this sage lady of seventeen really was; that it was merely caught up by intercommunication with people of culture and experience, who talked before her of their theories and beliefs till she insensibly acquired their tongue.   20

The carriage was heard coming up the road. Mayne gave her the list of the children, their ages, and other particulars which she had called for, and she turned to go out. Not a word had been said about the incident by the threshing-machine, though each one could see that it was constantly in the other's thoughts. The roll of the wheels may or   25 may not have reminded her of her position in relation to him. She said, bowing, and in a somewhat more distant tone: "We shall all be glad to learn that our schoolmaster is so—nice; such a philosopher." But, rather surprised at her own cruelty in uttering the latter words, she added one of the sweetest laughs that ever came from lips, and said, in   30 gentlest tones, "Good morning; I shall *always* remember what you did for me. Oh! it makes me sick to think of that moment. I came on purpose to thank you again, but I could not say it till now!"

Mayne's heart, which had felt the rebuff, came round to her with a rush; he could have almost forgiven her for physically wounding him   35 if she had asked him in such a tone not to notice it. He watched her out

7 way] way, madam   10 appeared] seemed   19 talked] had talked
19 insensibly] had insensibly   23–5 Not...thoughts. [*not in HW*]   29 words]
words satirically   30–3 said...till now!"] said "Good-morning" in gentlest tones.

of sight, thinking in rather a melancholy mood how time would absorb all her beauty, as the growing distance between them absorbed her form. He then went in, and endeavoured to recall every word that he had said to her, troubling and racking his mind to the
5 utmost of his ability about his imagined faults of manner. He remembered that he had used the indicative mood instead of the proper subjunctive in a certain phrase. He had given her to understand that an old idea he had made use of was his own, and so on through other particulars, each of which was an item of misery.
10 The place and the manner of her sitting were defined by the position of her chair, and by the books, maps, and prints scattered round it. Her "I shall always remember," he repeated to himself, aye, a hundred times; and though he knew the plain import of the words, he could not help toying with them, looking at them from all points,
15 and investing them with extraordinary meanings.

CHAPTER III

But what is this? I turn about
And find a trouble in thine eye.

Egbert Mayne, though at present filling the office of village
20 schoolmaster, had been intended for a less narrow path. His position at this time was entirely owing to the death of his father in embarrassed circumstances two years before. Mr Mayne had been a landscape and animal painter, and had settled in the village in early manhood, where he set about improving his prospects by marrying a
25 small farmer's daughter. The son had been sent away from home at an early age to a good school, and had returned at seventeen to enter upon some professional life or other. But his father's health was at this time declining, and when the painter died, a year and a half later, nothing had been done for Egbert. He was now living with his
30 maternal grandfather, Richard Broadford, the farmer, who was a tenant of Squire Allenville's. Egbert's ideas did not incline to painting, but he had ambitious notions of adopting a literary profession, or entering the Church, or doing something congenial to

7† subjunctive *HW*] subjective *NQM*   12 "I ... remember,"] "good-morning"
13 plain] commonplace   18 And find] I find   22 circumstances...
Mayne] circumstances. The father   23–4 in early manhood] years before
25 son] lad   28 the painter] he

his tastes whenever he could set about it. But first it was necessary to read, mark, learn, and look around him; and, a master being temporarily required for the school until such time as it should be placed under Government inspection, he stepped in and made use of the occupation as a stop-gap for a while.

He lived in his grandfather's farmhouse, walking backwards and forwards to the school every day, in order that the old man, who would otherwise be living quite alone, might have the benefit of his society during the long winter evenings. Egbert was much attached to his grandfather, and so, indeed, were all who knew him. The old farmer's amiable disposition and kindliness of heart, while they had hindered him from enriching himself one shilling during the course of a long and laborious life, had also kept him clear of every arrow of antagonism. The house in which he lived was the same that he had been born in, and was almost a part of himself. It had been built by his father's father; but on the dropping of the lives for which it was held, some twenty years earlier, it had lapsed to the Squire.

Richard Broadford was not, however, dispossessed: after his father's death the family had continued as before in the house and farm, but as yearly tenants. It was much to Broadford's delight, for his pain at the thought of parting from those old sticks and stones of his ancestors, before it had been known if the tenure could be continued, was real and great.

On the evening of the day on which Miss Allenville called at the school Egbert returned to the farmhouse as usual. He found his grandfather sitting with his hands on his knees, and showing by his countenance that something had happened to disturb him greatly. Egbert looked at him inquiringly, and with some misgiving.

"I have got to go at last, Egbert," he said, in a tone intended to be stoical, but far from it. "He is my enemy after all."

"Who?" said Mayne.

"The Squire. He's going to take seventy acres of neighbour Greenman's farm to enlarge the park; and Greenman's acreage is to be made up to him, and more, by throwing my farm in with his. Yes, that's what the Squire is going to have done. ... Well, I thought to have died here; but 'tisn't to be."

He looked as helpless as a child, for age had weakened him. Egbert

7 in order [*not in HW*]   10 so, indeed,] indeed so   11–12 had hindered]
kept   14 same] same one

endeavoured to cheer him a little, and vexed as the young man was, he thought there might yet be some means of tiding over this difficulty. "Mr Allenville wants seventy acres more in his park, does he?" he echoed mechanically. "Why can't it be taken entirely out of Greenman's farm? His is big enough, Heaven knows; and your hundred acres might be left you in peace."

"Well mayest say so! Oh, it is because he is tired of seeing old-fashioned farming like mine. He likes the young generation's system best, I suppose."

"If I had only known this this afternoon," Egbert said.

"You could have done nothing."

"Perhaps not." Egbert was, however, thinking that he would have mentioned the matter to his visitor, and told her such circumstances as would have enlisted her sympathies in the case.

"I thought it would come to this," said old Richard, vehemently. "The present Squire Allenville has never been any real friend to me. It was only through his wife that I have stayed here so long. If it hadn't been for her, we should have gone the very year that my poor father died, and the house fell into hand. I wish we had now. You see, now she's dead, there's nobody to counteract him in his schemes; and so I am to be swept away."

They talked on thus, and by bed-time the old man was in better spirits. But the subject did not cease to occupy Egbert's mind, and that anxiously. Were the house and farm which his grandfather had occupied so long to be taken away, Egbert knew it would affect his life to a degree out of all proportion to the seriousness of the event. The transplanting of old people is like the transplanting of old trees; a twelvemonth usually sees them wither and die away.

The next day proved that his anticipations were likely to be correct, his grandfather being so disturbed that he could scarcely eat or drink. The remainder of the week passed in just the same way. Nothing now occupied Egbert's mind but a longing to see Miss Allenville. To see her would be bliss; to ask her if anything could be done by which his grandfather might retain the farm and premises would be nothing but duty. His hope of good results from the course was based on the knowledge that Allenville, cold and hard as he was, had some considerable affection for or pride in his daughter, and that thus she might influence him.

1 and vexed] for, vexed   9 system ... suppose."] steam and uproar."
14 in the case [*not in HW*]   19 hand] his hand

It was not likely that she would call at the school for a week or two at least, and Mayne therefore tried to meet with her elsewhere. One morning early he was returning from the remote hamlet of Hawksgate, on the further side of the parish, and the nearest way to the school was across the park. He read as he walked, as was customary with him,   5 though at present his thoughts wandered incessantly. The path took him through a shrubbery running close up to a remote wing of the mansion. Nobody seemed to be stirring in that quarter, till, turning an angle, he saw Geraldine's own graceful figure close at hand, robed in fur, and standing at ease outside an open French casement.   10

She was startled by his sudden appearance, but her face soon betrayed a sympathetic remembrance of him. Egbert scarcely knew whether to stop or to walk on, when, casting her eyes upon his book, she said, "Don't let me interrupt your reading."

"I am glad to have—" he stammered, and for the moment could   15 get no farther. His nervousness encouraged her to continue.

"What are you reading?" she said.

The book was, as may possibly be supposed by those who know the mood inspired by hopeless attachments, "Childe Harold's Pilgrimage," a poem which at that date had never been surpassed in   20 congeniality to the minds of young persons in the full fever of virulent love. He was rather reluctant to let her know this; but as the inquiry afforded him an opening for conversation he held out the book, and her eye glanced over the page.

"Oh, thank you," she said hastily, "I ought not to have asked   25 that—only I am interested always in books. Is your grandfather quite well, Mr Mayne? I saw him yesterday, and thought he seemed to be not in such good health as usual."

"His mind is disturbed," said Egbert.

"Indeed, why is that?"   30

"It is on account of his having to leave the farm. He is old, and was born in that house."

"Ah, yes, I have heard something of that," she said with a slightly regretful look. "Mr Allenville has decided to enlarge the park. Born in the house was he?"   35

"Yes. His grandfather built it. May I ask your opinion on the point, Miss Allenville? Don't you think it would be possible to enlarge the park without taking my grandfather's farm? Greenman has already five hundred acres."

She was perplexed how to reply, and evading the question said, "Your grandfather much wishes to stay?"

5   "He does, intensely—more than you can believe or think. But he will not ask to be let remain. I dread the effect of leaving upon him. If it were possible to contrive that he should not be turned out I should be grateful indeed."

"I—I will do all I can that things may remain as they are," she said 10 with a deepened colour. "In fact, I am almost certain that he will not have to go, since it is so painful to him," she added in the sanguine tones of a child. "My father could not have known that his mind was so bent on staying."

Here the conversation ended, and Egbert went on with a lightened 15 heart. Whether his pleasure arose entirely from having done his grandfather a good turn, or from the mere sensation of having been near her, he himself could hardly have determined.

CHAPTER IV

Oh, for my sake, do you with fortune chide,
20   The guilty goddess of my harmful deed
That did not better for my life provide.

Now commenced a period during which Egbert Mayne's emotions burnt in a more unreasoning and wilder worship than at any other time in his life. The great condition of idealisation in love was present 25 here, that of an association in which, through difference in rank, the petty human elements that enter so largely into life are kept entirely out of sight, and there is hardly awakened in the man's mind a thought that they appertain to her at all.

He deviated frequently from his daily track to the spot where the 30 last meeting had been, till, on the fourth morning after, he saw her there again; but she let him pass that time with a bare recognition. Two days later the carriage drove down the lane to the village as he was walking away. When they met she told the coachman to stop.

"I am glad to tell you that your grandfather may be perfectly easy 35 about the house and farm," she said; as if she took unfeigned

19–21 Oh ... provide.] "Then flashed the living lightning from her eyes."
23 burnt] burst   24 in his life] of his life

pleasure in saying it. "The question of altering the park is postponed indefinitely. I have resisted it: I could do no less for one who did so much for me."

"Thank you very warmly," said Egbert so earnestly, that she blushed crimson as the carriage rolled away.

The spring drew on, and he saw and spoke with her several times. In truth he walked abroad much more than had been usual with him formerly, searching in all directions for her form. Had she not been unreflecting and impressionable—had not her life dragged on as uneventfully as that of one in gaol, through her residing in a great house with no companion but an undemonstrative father; and, above all, had not Egbert been a singularly engaging young man of that distracting order of beauty which grows upon the feminine gazer with every glance, this tender waylaying would have made little difference to anybody. But such was not the case. In return for Egbert's presence of mind at the threshing she had done him a kindness, and the pleasure that she took in the act shed an added interest upon the object of it. Thus, on both sides it had happened that a deed of solicitude casually performed gave each doer a sense of proprietorship in its recipient, and a wish still further to establish that position by other deeds of the same sort.

To still further kindle Geraldine's indiscreet interest in him, Egbert's devotion became perceptible ere long even to her inexperienced eyes; and it was like a new world to the young girl. At first she was almost frightened at the novelty of the thing. Then the fascination of the discovery caused her ready, receptive heart to palpitate in an ungovernable manner whenever he came near her. She was not quite in love herself, but she was so moved by the circumstance of her deliverer being in love, that she could think of nothing else. His appearing at odd places startled her; and yet she rather liked that kind of startling. Too often her eyes rested on his face; too often her thoughts surrounded his figure and dwelt on his conversation.

2–3 resisted ... me."] persuaded my father that it will not be desirable to do it at present." 8–9 she not been unreflecting] they not both been young 12 engaging] attractive 15–16 In return ... done him] She had done Egbert 17 pleasure that] pleasure 17 act] act for its own sake 17 added [*not in HW*] 18–19 Thus ... doer] Moreover, it often happens that one deed of kindness casually performed gives 20 still further to] to still further 22–3 To ... Egbert's] In addition to this, Egbert's wild 24 the young girl] Geraldine 26 ready,] ready and 28 quite [*not in HW*] 29 her deliverer] his

One day, when they met on a bridge, they did not part till after a long and interesting conversation on books, in which many opinions of Mayne's (crude and unformed enough, it must be owned) that happened to take her fancy, set her glowing with ardour to unfold her
5 own.

After any such meeting as this, Egbert would go home and think for hours of her little remarks and movements. The day and minute of every accidental rencounter became registered in his mind with the indelibility of ink. Years afterwards he could recall at a moment's
10 notice that he saw her at eleven o'clock on the third of April, a Sunday; at four on Tuesday, the twelfth; at a quarter to six on Thursday, the twenty-eighth; that on the ninth it rained at a quarter past two, when she was walking up the avenue; that on the seventeenth the grass was rather too wet for a lady's feet; and other calendrical and
15 meteorological facts of no value whatever either to science or history.

On a Tuesday evening, when they had had several conversations out of doors, and when a passionate liking for his society was creeping over the reckless though pure girl, slowly, insidiously, and surely, like ripeness over fruit, she further committed herself by coming alone to
20 the school. A heavy rain had threatened to fall all the afternoon, and just as she entered it began. School hours were at that moment over, but he waited a few moments before dismissing the children, to see if the storm would clear up. After looking round at the classes, and making sundry inquiries of the little ones in the usual manner of
25 ladies who patronise a school, she came up to him.

"I listened outside before I came in. It was a great pleasure to hear the voices—three classes reading at three paces." She continued with a laugh: "There was a rough treble voice bowling easily along, an ambling sweet voice earnest about fishes in the sea, and a shrill voice
30 spelling out letter by letter. Then there was a shuffling of feet—then you sang. It seemed quite a little poem."

"Yes," Egbert said. "But perhaps, like many poems, it was hard prose to the originators."

She remained thinking, and Mayne looked out at the weather.
35 Judging from the sky and wind that there was no likelihood of a

---

4 take her fancy,] be akin to Geraldine's   14 other] numerous other
15 value whatever] great value   17–19 and when . . . alone] she came
21 moment] time   26 in. It] in," she said. "It   32 said] murmured
34 Mayne] Egbert

change that night, he proceeded to let the children go. Miss Allenville assisted in wrapping up as many of them as possible in the old coats and other apparel which Egbert kept by him for the purpose. But she touched both clothes and children rather gingerly, and as if she did not much like the contact.

Egbert's sentiments towards her that evening were vehement and curious. Much as he loved her, his liking for the peasantry about him—his mother's ancestry—caused him sometimes a twinge of self-reproach for thinking of her so exclusively, and nearly forgetting all his old acquaintance, neighbours, and his grandfather's familiar friends, with their rough but honest ways. To further complicate his feelings to-night there was the sight, on the one hand, of the young lady with her warm rich dress and glowing future, and on the other of the weak little boys and girls—some only five years old, and none more than twelve, going off in their different directions in the pelting rain, some for a walk of more than two miles, with the certainty of being drenched to the skin, and with no change of clothes when they reached their home. He watched the rain spots thickening upon the faded frocks, worn-out tippets, yellow straw hats and bonnets, and coarse pinafores of his unprotected little flock as they walked down the path, and was thereby reminded of the hopelessness of his attachment, by perceiving how much more nearly akin was his lot to theirs than to hers.

Miss Allenville, too, was looking at the children, and unfortunately she chanced to say, as they toddled off, "Poor little wretches!"

A sort of despairing irritation at her remoteness from his plane, as implied by her pitying the children so unmercifully, impelled him to remark, "Say poor little *children*, madam."

She was silent—awkwardly silent.

"I suppose I must walk home," she said, when about half a minute had passed. "Nobody knows where I am, and the carriage may not find me for hours."

"I'll go for the carriage," said Egbert readily.

But he did not move. While she had been speaking, there had grown up in him a conviction that these opportunities of seeing her would soon necessarily cease. She would get older, and would perceive the incorrectness of being on intimate terms with him merely

5

10

15

20

25

30

35

6 Egbert's] Mayne's   6–7 vehement and curious] curious and changeful
9 her] Geraldine   10 neighbours] his neighbors   15 some] many
17 with no] no   17 home] homes   20 thereby [*not in HW*]   36 intimate]
friendly   36–102. 1 merely ... danger [*not in HW*]

because he had snatched her from danger. He would have to engage in
a more active career, and go away. Such ideas brought on an irresistible
climax to an intense and long-felt desire. He had just reached that point
in the action of passion upon mind at which it masters judgment.

5   It was almost dark in the room, by reason of the heavy clouds and
the nearness of the night. But the fire had just flamed up brightly in
the grate, and it threw her face and form into ruddy relief against the
grey wall behind.

Suddenly rushing towards her, he seized her hand before she
10   comprehended his intention, kissed it tenderly, and clasped her in his
arms. Her soft body yielded like wool under his embrace. As suddenly
releasing her he turned, and went back to the other end of the room.

Egbert's feeling as he retired was that he had committed a crime.
The madness of the action was apparent to him almost before it was
15   completed. There seemed not a single thing left for him to do, but to
go into life-long banishment for such sacrilege. He faced round and
regarded her. Her features were not visible enough to judge of their
expression. All that he could discern through the dimness and his
own agitation was that for some time she remained quite motionless.
20   Her state was probably one of suspension; as with Ulysses before
Melanthus, she may have—

> Entertained a breast
> That in the strife of all extremes did rest.

In one, two, or five minutes—neither of them ever knew exactly how
25   long—apparently without the motion of a limb, she glided noiselessly
to the door and vanished.

Egbert leant himself against the wall, almost distracted. He could
see absolutely no limit to the harm that he had done by his wild and
unreasoning folly. "Am I a man to thus ill-treat the loveliest girl that
30   ever was born? Sweet injured creature—how she will hate me!"
These were some of the expressions that he murmured in the twilight
of that lonely room.

Then he said that she certainly had encouraged him, which,
unfortunately for her, was only too true. She had seen that he was
35   always in search of her, and she did not put herself out of his way. He

2 career...away.] career.   12 turned,] returned   13 Egbert's...
was] It seemed to Mayne, as he retired,   18 All that] All   20 probably
[*not in HW*]   20 as with] like   21 may have— [*not in HW*]   28 harm
that] harm   33–4 which ... true.] or, at any rate, had not discouraged him.

was sure that she liked him to admire her. "Yet, no," he murmured, "I will not excuse myself at all."

The night passed away miserably. One conviction by degrees overruled all the rest in his mind—that if she knew precisely how pure had been his longing towards her, she could not think badly of him. 5 His reflections resulted in a resolve to get an interview with her, and make his defence and explanation in full. The decision come to, his impatience could scarcely preserve him from rushing to Tollamore House that very daybreak, and trying to get into her presence, though it was the likeliest of suppositions that she would never see him. 10

Every spare minute of the following days he hovered round the house, in hope of getting a glimpse of her; but not once did she make herself visible. He delayed taking the extreme step of calling, till the hour came when he could delay no longer. On a certain day he rang the bell with a mild air, and disguised his feelings by looking as if he 15 wished to speak to her merely on copy-books, slates, and other school matters, the school being professedly her hobby. He was told that Miss Allenville had gone on a visit to some relatives thirty-five miles off, and that she would probably not return for a month.

As there was no help for it, Egbert settled down to wait as he best 20 could, not without many misgivings lest his rash action, which a prompt explanation might have toned down and excused, would now be the cause of a total estrangement between them, so that nothing would restore him to the place he had formerly held in her estimation. That she had ever seriously loved him he did not hope or dream; but it 25 was intense pain to him to be out of her favour.

CHAPTER V

So I soberly laid my last plan
To extinguish the man,
Round his creep-hole, with never a break 30
Ran my fires for his sake;
Over head did my thunder combine
With my underground mine:

---

5 towards] to touch   12 getting] obtaining   20 Egbert] Mayne
21 his rash] an   23 cause of] means of causing   23–4 so...would] till
nothing could   25 had ever...him] loved him, after all this,   25 but]
and yet

Till I looked from my labour content
To enjoy the event.
When sudden—how think ye the end?

A week after the crisis mentioned above, it was secretly whispered to
Egbert's grandfather that the park enlargement scheme was after all
to be proceeded with; that Miss Allenville was extremely anxious to
have it put in hand as soon as possible. Farmer Broadford's farm was
to be added to Greenman's, as originally intended, and the old house
that Broadford lived in was to be pulled down as an encumbrance.

"It is she this time!" murmured Egbert, gloomily. "Then I did
offend her, and mortify her; and she is resentful."

The excitement of his grandfather again caused him much alarm,
and even remorse. Such was the responsiveness of the farmer's
physical to his mental state that in the course of a week his usual
health failed, and his gloominess of mind was followed by dimness of
sight and giddiness. By much persuasion Egbert induced him to stay
at home for a day or two; but indoors he was the most restless of
creatures, through not being able to engage in the pursuits to which
he had been accustomed from his boyhood. He walked up and down,
looking wistfully out of the window, shifting the positions of books
and chairs, and putting them back again, opening his desk and
shutting it after a vacant look at the papers, saying he should never
get settled in another farm at his time of life, and evincing all the
symptoms of nervousness and excitability.

Meanwhile Egbert anxiously awaited Miss Allenville's return,
more resolved than ever to obtain audience of her, and beg her not to
visit upon an unoffending old man the consequences of a young one's
folly. Any retaliation upon himself he would accept willingly, and
own to be well deserved.

At length, by making off-hand inquiries (for he dared not ask
directly for her again) he learnt that she was to be at home on the
Thursday. The following Friday and Saturday he kept a sharp look-
out; and, when lingering in the park for at least the tenth time in that
half-week, a sudden rise in the ground revealed her coming along the
path.

Egbert stayed his advance, in order that, if she really objected to
see him, she might easily strike off into a side path or turn back.

23 time of life] age

She did not accept the alternatives, but came straight on to where he lingered, averting her face waywardly as she approached. When she was within a few steps of him he could see that the trimmings of her dress trembled like leaves. He cleared his dry throat to speak.

"Miss Allenville," he said, humbly taking off his hat, "I should be glad to say one word to you, if I may."

She looked at him for just one moment, but said nothing; and he could see that the expression of her face was flushed, and her mood skittish. The place they were standing in was a remote nook, hidden by the trunks and boughs, so that he could afford to give her plenty of time, for there was no fear of their being observed or overheard. Indeed, knowing that she often walked that way, Egbert had previously surveyed the spot and thought it suitable for the occasion, much as Wellington antecedently surveyed the field of Waterloo.

Here the young man began his pleading speech to her. He dilated upon his sensations when first he saw her; and as he became warmed by his oratory he spoke of all his inmost perturbations on her account without the slightest reserve. He related with much natural eloquence how he had tried over and over again not to love her, and how he had loved her in spite of that trying; of his intention never to reveal his passion, till their situation on that rainy evening prompted the impulse which ended in that irreverent action of his; and earnestly asked her to forgive him—not for his feelings, since they were his own to commend or blame—but for the way in which he testified of them to one so cultivated and so beautiful.

Egbert was flushed and excited by the time that he reached this point in his tale.

Her eyes were fixed on the grass; and then a tear stole quietly from its corner, and wandered down her cheek. She tried to say something, but her usually adroit tongue was unequal to the task. Ultimately she glanced at him, and murmured, "I forgive you;" but so inaudibly, that he only recognised the words by their shape upon her lips.

She looked not much more than a child now, and Egbert thought with sadness that her tear and her words were perhaps but the result, the one of a transitory sympathy, the other of a desire to escape. They stood silent for some seconds, and the dressing-bell of the house

---

11 overheard] heard   12 Egbert] Mayne   15 pleading] apologetic
28 quietly] gently   36 seconds, and] seconds, and then

began ringing. Turning slowly away without another word she hastened out of his sight.

When Egbert reached home some of his grandfather's old friends were gathered there, sympathising with him on the removal he would 5 have to submit to if report spoke truly. Their sympathy was rather more for him to bear than their indifference; and as Egbert looked at the old man's bent figure, and at the expression of his face, denoting a wish to sink under the earth, out of sight and out of trouble, he was greatly depressed, and he said inwardly, "What a fool I was to ask 10 forgiveness of a woman who can torture my only relative like this! Why do I feel her to be glorious? Oh that I had never seen her!"

The next day was Sunday, and his grandfather being too unwell to go out, Egbert went to the evening service alone. When it was over, the rector detained him in the churchyard to say a few words about 15 the next week's undertakings. This was soon done, and Egbert turned back to leave the now empty churchyard. Passing the porch he saw Miss Allenville coming out of the door.

Egbert said nothing, for he knew not what to say; but she spoke. "Ah, Mr Mayne, how beautiful the west sky looks! It is the finest 20 sunset we have had this spring."

"It is very beautiful," he replied, without looking westward a single degree. "Miss Allenville," he said reproachfully, "you might just have thought whether, for the sake of reaching one guilty person, it was worth while to deeply wound an old man."

25 "I do not allow you to say that," she answered with proud quickness. "Still, I will listen just this once."

"Are you glad you asserted your superiority to me by putting in motion again that scheme for turning him out?"

"I merely left off hindering it," she said.

30 "Well, we shall go now," continued Egbert, "and make room for newer people. I hope you forgive what caused it all."

"You talk in that strain to make me feel regrets; and you think that because you are read in a few books you may say or do anything."

"No, no. That's unfair."

35 "I will try to alter it—that your grandfather may not leave. Say that you forgive me for thinking he and yourself had better leave—as I

1 slowly] quickly	3 Egbert] Mayne	7 and at] and
15 Egbert] Mayne	29 merely...it,"] hardly know,"	34 That's]
Indeed that's		

forgive you for what you did. But remember, nothing of that sort ever again."

"Forgive you? Oh, Miss Allenville!" said he in a wild whisper, "I wish you had sinned a hundred times as much, that I might show how readily I can forgive all."

She had looked as if she would have held out her hand; but, for some reason or other, directly he had spoken with emotion it was not so well for him as when he had spoken to wound her. She passed on silently, and entered the private gate to the house.

A day or two after this, about three o'clock in the afternoon, and whilst Egbert was giving a lesson in geography, a lad burst into the school with the tidings that Farmer Broadford had fallen from a corn-stack they were threshing, and hurt himself severely.

The boy had borrowed a horse to come with, and Mayne at once made him gallop off with it for a doctor. Dismissing the children, the young man ran home full of forebodings. He found his relative in a chair, held up by two of his labouring-men. He was put to bed, and seeing how pale he was, Egbert gave him a little wine, and bathed the parts which had been bruised by the fall.

Egbert had at first been the more troubled at the event through believing that his grandfather's fall was the result of his low spirits and mental uneasiness; and he blamed himself for letting so infirm a man go out upon the farm till quite recovered. But it turned out that the actual cause of the accident was the breaking of the ladder that he had been standing on. When the surgeon had seen him he said that the external bruises were mere trifles; but that the shock had been great, and had produced internal injuries highly dangerous to a man in that stage of life.

His grandson was of opinion in later years that the fall only hastened by a few months a dissolution which would soon have taken place under any circumstances, from the natural decay of the old man's constitution. His pulse grew feeble and his voice weak, but he continued in a comparatively firm state of mind for some days, during which he talked to Egbert a great deal.

Egbert trusted that the illness would soon pass away; his anxiety

1-2 But ... again."] It was perhaps narrow-minded to do as I have done." 11 burst] rushed   13 corn-stack] corn-stack that   15 with it [*not in HW*]   21 fall was] fall had been   23 till] till he was   24 ladder that] ladder   25 standing on] standing upon

for his grandfather was great. When he was gone not one of the family would be left but himself. But in spite of hope the younger man perceived that death was really at hand. And now arose a question. It was certainly a time to make confidences, if they were ever to be
5   made; should he, then, tell his grandfather, who knew the Allenvilles so well, of his love for Geraldine? At one moment it seemed duty; at another it seemed a graceful act, to say the least.

Yet Egbert might never have uttered a word but for a remark of his grandfather's which led up to the very point. He was speaking of the
10 farm and of the Squire, and thence he went on to the daughter.

"She, too," he said, "seems to have that reckless spirit which was in her mother's family, and ruined her mother's father at the gaming table, though she's too young to show much of it yet."

"I hope not," said Egbert fervently.

15 "Why? What be the Allenvilles to you—not that I wish the girl harm?"

"I think she is the very best being in the world. I—love her deeply."

His grandfather's eyes were set on the wall. "Well, well, my poor
20 boy," came softly from his mouth. "What made ye think of loving her? Ye may as well love a mountain, for any return you'll ever get. Do she know of it?"

"She guesses it. It was my saving her from the threshing-machine that began it."

25 "And she checks you?"

"Well—no."

"Egbert," he said after a silence, "I am grieved, for it can but end in pain. Mind, she's an inexperienced girl. She never thinks of what trouble she may get herself into with her father and with her friends.
30 And mind this, my lad, as another reason for dropping it; however honourable your love may be, you'll never get credit for your honour. Nothing you can do will ever root out the notion of people that where the man is poor and the woman is high-born he's a scamp and she's an angel."

35 "She's very good."

"She's thoughtless, or she'd never encourage you. You must try not to see her."

23–4 it....began it."] it."   25 you] ye   36 encourage you]
encourage ye

"I will never put myself in her way again."

The subject was mentioned no more then. The next day the worn-out old farmer died, and his last request to Egbert was that he would do nothing to tempt Geraldine Allenville to think of him further.

CHAPTER VI

Hath misery made thee blind
To the fond workings of a woman's mind?
And must I say—albeit my heart rebel
With all that woman feels but should not tell;
Because, despite thy faults, that heart is moved—
It feared thee, thank'd thee, pitied, madden'd, loved?

It was in the evening of the day after Farmer Broadford's death that Egbert first sat down in the house alone. The bandy-legged little man who had acted as his grandfather's groom of the chambers and stables simultaneously had gone into the village. The candles were not yet lighted, and Mayne abstractedly watched upon the pale wall the latter rays of sunset slowly changing into the white shine of a moon a few days old. The ancient family clock had stopped for want of winding, and the intense silence that prevailed seemed more like the bodily presence of some quality than the mere absence of sound.

He was thinking how many were the indifferent expressions which he had used towards the poor body lying cold upstairs—the only relation he had latterly had upon earth—which might as well have been left unsaid; of how far he had been from practically attempting to do what in theory he called best—to make the most of every pulse of natural affection; that he had never heeded or particularly inquired the meaning of the different pieces of advice which the kind old man had tendered from time to time; that he had never even thought of asking for any details of his grandfather's history.

His musings turned upon Geraldine. He had promised to seek her no more, and he would keep his promise. Her interest in him might only be that of an exceedingly romantic and freakish soul, awakened but through "lack of other idleness," and because sound sense suggested to her that it was a thing dangerous to do; for it seemed that she was ever and only moved by the superior of two antagonistic forces. She had as yet seen little or no society, she was only seventeen;

and hence it was possible that a week of the town and fashion into which she would soon be initiated might blot out his very existence from her memory.

He was sitting with his back to the window, meditating in this
5 minor key, when a shadow darkened the opposite moonlit wall. Egbert started. There was a gentle tap at the door; and he opened it to behold the well-known form of the lady in his mind.

"Mr Mayne, are you alone?" she whispered, full of agitation.

"Quite alone, excepting my poor grandfather's body upstairs," he
10 answered, as agitated as she.

Then out it all came. "I couldn't help coming—I hope—oh, I do so pray—that it was not through me that he died. Was it I, indeed, who killed him? They say it was the effect of the news that he was to leave the farm. I would have done anything to hinder his being turned out
15 had I only reflected! And now he is dead. It was so cruel to an old man like him; and now you have nobody in the world to care for you, have you, Egbert—except me?"

The ice was wholly broken. He took her hand in both his own and began to assure her that her alarm was grounded on nothing
20 whatever. And yet he was almost reluctant to assure her out of so sweet a state. And when he had said over and over again that his grandfather's fall had nothing to do with his mental condition, that the utmost result of her hasty proceeding was a sadness of spirit in him, she still persisted, as is the custom of women, in holding to that
25 most painful possibility as the most likely, simply because it wounded her most. It was a long while before she would be convinced of her own innocence, but he maintained it firmly, and she finally believed.

They sat down together, restraint having quite died out between them. The fine-lady portion of her existence, of which there was never
30 much, was in abeyance, and they spoke and acted simply as a young man and woman who were beset by common troubles, and who had like hopes and fears.

"And you will never blame me again for what I did?" said Egbert.

"I never blamed you much," she murmured with arch simplicity.
35 "Why should it be wrong for me to be honest with you now, and tell everything you want to know?"

Mayne was silent. That was a difficult question for a conscientious

8 Mr Mayne] Egbert   14–15 have done ... reflected!] not have done any
thing tending to turn him out for all the world, had I only known.

man to answer. Here was he nearly twenty-one years of age, and with some experience of life, while she was a girl nursed up like an exotic, with no real experience, and but little over seventeen—though from the fineness of her figure she looked more womanly than she really was. It plainly had not crossed her young mind that she was on the verge of committing the most horrible social sin—that of loving beneath her, and owning that she so loved. Two years thence she might see the imprudence of her conduct, and blame him for having led her on. Ought he not, then, considering his grandfather's words, to say that it was wrong for her to be honest; that she should forget him, and fix her mind on matters appertaining to her order? He could not do it—he let her drift sweetly on.

"I think more of you than of anybody in the whole world," he replied. "And you will allow me to, will you not?—let me always keep you in my heart, and almost worship you?"

"That would be wrong. But you may think of me, if you like to, very much; it will give me great pleasure. I don't think my father thinks of me at all—or anybody, except you. I said the other day I would never think of you again, but I have done it, a good many times. It is all through being obliged to care for somebody whether you will or no."

"And you will go on thinking of me?"

"I will do anything to—oblige you."

Egbert, on the impulse of the moment, bent over her and raised her little hand to his lips. He reverenced her too much to think of kissing her cheek. She knew this, and was thrilled through with the delight of being adored as one from above the sky.

Up to this day of its existence their affection had been a battle, a species of antagonism wherein his heart and the girl's had faced each other, and been anxious to do honour to their respective parts. But now it was a truce and a settlement, in which each one took up the other's utmost weakness, and was careless of concealing his and her own.

Surely, sitting there as they sat then, a more unreasoning condition of mind as to how this unequal conjunction would end never existed. They swam along through the passing moments, not a thought of

2 exotic] exotic at home   3 real [*not in HW*]   3 little over seventeen—]
seventeen her last birthday,   5 her young] the young   11 order] station
12 not do it—he] not. He   17 father] papa   18 said] thought
21 go ... me?"] think of me a little too?"   26 as one ... sky [*not in HW*]
29† been *HW*] being *NQM*

duty on either side, not a further thought on his but that she was the dayspring of his life, that he would die for her a hundred times; superadded to which was a shapeless uneasiness that she would in some manner slip away from him. The solemnity of the event that had
5   just happened would have shown up to him any ungenerous feeling in strong colours—and he had reason afterwards to examine the epoch narrowly; but it only seemed to demonstrate how instinctive and uncalculating was the love that worked within him.

It was almost time for her to leave. She held up her watch to the
10   moonlight. Five minutes more she would stay; then three minutes, and no longer. "Now I am going," she said. "Do you forgive me entirely?"

"How shall I say 'Yes' without assuming that there was something to forgive?"

15   "Say 'Yes.' It is sweeter to fancy I am forgiven than to think I have not sinned."

With this she went to the door. Egbert accompanied her through the wood, and across a portion of the park, till they were about a hundred yards from the house, when he was forced to bid her farewell.

20   The old man was buried on the following Sunday. During several weeks afterwards Egbert's sole consolation under his loss was in thinking of Geraldine, for they did not meet in private again till some time had elapsed. The ultimate issue of this absorption in her did not concern him at all: it seemed to be in keeping with the system of his
25   existence now that he should have an utterly inscrutable to-morrow.

CHAPTER VII

> Come forward, some great marshal, and organise equality in society.

The month of August came round, and Miss Allenville was to lay the
30   foundation-stone of a tower or beacon which her father was about to erect on the highest hill of his estate, to the memory of his brother, the General. It was arranged that the school children should sing at the ceremony. Accordingly, at the hour fixed, Egbert was on the spot; a crowd of villagers had also arrived, and carriages were visible in the

---

5 any] an   7 seemed] served   8 uncalculating] objectless
33 ceremony. Accordingly] ceremony, and accordingly

distance, wending their way towards the scene. When they had drawn up alongside and the visitors alighted, the master-mason appeared nervous.

"Mr Mayne," he said to Egbert, "you had better do what's to be done for the lady. I shall speak too loud, or too soft, or handle things wrong. Do you attend upon her, and I'll lower the stone."

Several ladies and gentlemen now gathered round, and presently Miss Allenville stood in position for her office, supported on one side by her father, a hard-featured man of five-and-forty, and some friends who were visiting at the house; and on the other by the school children, who began singing a song in keeping with the occasion. When this was done, Geraldine laid down the sealed bottle with its enclosed memorandum, which had been prepared for the purpose, and taking a trowel from her father's hand, dabbled confusedly in the mortar, accidentally smearing it over the handle of the trowel.

"Lower the stone," said Egbert, who stood close by, to the mason at the winch; and the stone began to descend.

The dainty-handed young woman was looking as if she would give anything to be relieved of the dirty trowel; but Egbert, the only one who observed this, was guiding the stone with both hands into its place, and could not receive the tool of her. Every moment increased her perplexity.

"Take it, take it, will you?" she impatiently whispered to him, blushing with a consciousness that people began to perceive her awkward handling.

"I must just finish this first," he said.

She was resigned in an instant. The stone settled down upon its base, when Egbert at once took the trowel, and her father came up and wiped her glove. Egbert then handed her the mallet.

"What must I do with this thing?" she whispered entreatingly, holding the mallet as if it might bite her.

"Tap with it, madam," said he.

She did as directed, and murmured the form of words which she had been told to repeat.

"Thank you," she said softly when all was done, restored to herself by the consciousness that she had performed the last part gracefully.

---

1 had drawn] drew   10 school] school-master and   15 trowel] towel   21 of her] from her   26 just [*not in HW*]

Without lifting her eyes she added, "It was thoughtful of you to remember that I shouldn't know, and to stand by to tell me."

Her friends now moved away, but before she had joined them Egbert said, chiefly for the pleasure of speaking to her: "The tower, when it is built, will be seen many miles off."

"Yes," she replied in a discreet tone, for many eyes were upon her. "The view is very extensive." She glanced round upon the whole landscape stretched out before her, in the extreme distance of which was visible the town of Westcombe.

"How long does it take to go to Westcombe across this way?" she asked of him while they were bringing up the carriage.

"About two hours," he said.

"Two hours—so long as that, does it? How far is it away?"

"Eight miles."

"Two hours to drive eight miles—who ever heard of such a thing!"

"I thought you meant walking."

"Ah, yes; but one hardly means walking without expressly stating it."

"Well, it seems just the other way to me—that walking is meant unless you say driving."

That was the whole of their conversation. The remarks had been simple and trivial, but they brought a similar thought into the minds of both of them. On her part it spread a sudden gloom over her face, and it made him feel dead at heart. It was that horrid thought of their differing habits and of those contrasting positions which could not be reconciled.

Indeed, this perception of their disparity weighed more and more heavily upon him as the days went on. There was no doubt about their being lovers, though scarcely recognised by themselves as such; and, in spite of Geraldine's warm and unreflecting impulses, a sense of how little Egbert was accustomed to what is called society, and the polite forms which constant usage had made almost nature with her, would rise on occasion, and rob her of many an otherwise pleasant minute. When any little occurrence had brought this into more prominence than usual, Egbert would go away, wander about the lanes, and be kept awake a great part of the night by the distress of mind such a recognition brought upon him. How their intimacy

23 sudden [*not in HW*] 27 and more [*not in HW*] 34 minute]
hour

would end, in what uneasiness, yearning, and misery, he could not guess. As for picturing a future of happiness with her by his side there was not ground enough upon which to rest the momentary imagination of it. Thus they mutually oppressed each other even while they loved. 5

In addition to this anxiety was another; what would be thought of their romance by her father, if he were to find it out? It was impossible to tell him, for nothing could come of that but Egbert's dismissal and Geraldine's seclusion; and how could these be borne?

He looked round anxiously for some means of deliverance. There 10 were two things to be thought of, the saving of her dignity, and the saving of his and her happiness. That to accomplish the first he ought voluntarily to leave the village before their attachment got known, and never seek her again, was what he sometimes felt; but the idea brought such misery along with it that it died out under 15 contemplation.

He determined at all events to put the case clearly before her, to heroically set forth at their next meeting the true bearings of their position, which she plainly did not realise to the full as yet. It had never entered her mind that the link between them might be observed 20 by the curious, and instantly talked of. Yes, it was his duty to warn her, even though by so doing he would be heaping coals of fire on his own head. For by acting upon his hint she would be lost to him, and the charm that lay in her false notions of the world be for ever destroyed. 25

That they would ultimately be found out, and Geraldine be lowered in local estimation, was, indeed, almost inevitable. There was one grain of satisfaction only among this mass of distresses. Whatever should become public, only the fashionable side of her character could be depreciated; the natural woman, the specimen of 30 English girlhood that he loved, no one could impugn or harm.

Meetings had latterly taken place between them without any pretence of accident, and these were facilitated in an amazing manner by the duty imposed upon her of visiting the school as the representative of her father. At her very next appearance he told her 35 all he thought. It was when the children had left the room for the quarter of an hour's airing that he gave them in the middle of the morning.

28 grain] atom   30 natural [*not in HW*]

She was quite hurt at being treated with justice, and a crowd of tears came into her sorrowful eyes. She had never thought of half that he feared, and almost questioned his kindness in enlightening her.

"Perhaps you are right," she murmured, with the merest motion of
5   lip. "Yes, it is sadly true. Should our conduct become known, nobody will judge us fairly. 'She was a wild, weak girl,' they will say."

"To care for such a man—a village youth. They will even suppress the fact that his father was a painter of no mean power, and a gentleman by education, little as it would redeem us; and justify their
10   doing so by reflecting that in adding to the contrast they improve the tale:

> And calumny meanwhile shall feed on us
> As worms devour the dead: what we have done
> None shall dare vouch, though it be truly known.

15   And they will continue, 'He was an artful fellow to win a girl's affections in that way—one of the mere scum of the earth,' they'll say."

"Don't, don't make it so bad!" she implored, weeping outright. "They cannot go so far. Human nature is not so wicked and blind.
20   And they *dare* not speak so disrespectfully of me, or of any one I choose to favour." A slight haughtiness was apparent in these words. "But, oh, don't let us talk of it—it makes the time miserable."

However, she had been warned. But the difficulty which presented itself to her mind was, after all, but a small portion of the whole. It
25   was how should they meet together without causing a convulsion in neighbouring society. His was more radical and complex. The only natural drift of love was towards marriage. But how could he picture, at any length of years ahead, her in a cottage as his wife, or himself in a mansion as her husband? He in the one case, she in the other, were
30   alike painfully incredible.

But time had flown, and he conducted her to the door. "Good-bye, Egbert," she said tenderly.

"Good-bye, dear, dear madam," he answered; and she was gone.

Geraldine had never hinted to him to call her by her Christian
35   name, and finding that she did not particularly wish it he did not care to do so. "Madam" was as good a name as any other for her, and by

adhering to it and using it at the warmest moments it seemed to change its nature from that of a mere title to a soft pet sound. He often wondered in after days at the strange condition of a girl's heart which could allow so much in reality, and at the same time permit the existence of a little barrier such as that; how the keen intelligent mind of woman could be ever so slightly hoodwinked by a sound. Yet, perhaps, it was womanlike, after all, and she may have caught at it as the only straw within reach of that dignity or pride of birth which was drowning in her impetuous affection.

CHAPTER VIII

The world and its ways have a certain worth,
And to press a point while these oppose
Were a simple policy: best wait,
And we lose no friends, and gain no foes.

The inborn necessity of ransacking the future for a germ of hope led Egbert Mayne to dwell for longer and longer periods on the at first rejected possibility of winning and having her. And apart from any thought of marriage, he knew that Geraldine was sometimes a trifle vexed that their experiences contained so little in common—that he had never dressed for dinner, or made use of a carriage in his life; even though in literature he was her master, thanks to his tastes.

For the first time he seriously contemplated a visionary scheme which had been several times cursorily glanced at; a scheme almost as visionary as any ever entertained by a man not yet blinded to the limits of the possible. Lighted on by impulse, it was not taken up without long calculation, and it was one in which every link was reasoned out as carefully and as clearly as his powers would permit. But the idea that he would be able to carry it through was an assumption which, had he bestowed upon it one-hundredth part of the thought spent on the details of its working, he would have thrown aside as unfeasible.

To give up the school, to go to London or elsewhere, and there to try to rise to her level by years of sheer exertion, was the substance of this scheme. However his lady's heart might be grieved by his

9 impetuous] indiscreet   22 time] time now   30 its working] working it   34 this scheme] the scheme

apparent desertion, he would go. A knowledge of life and of men must be acquired, and that could never be done by thinking at home.

Egbert's abstract love for the gigantic task was but small; but there was absolutely no other honest road to her sphere. That the habits of
5   men should be so subversive of the law of nature as to indicate that he was not worthy to marry a woman whose own instincts said that he was worthy, was a great anomaly, he thought, with some rebelliousness; but this did not upset the fact or remove the difficulty.

He told his fair mistress at their next accidental meeting (much
10   sophistry lay in their definition of "accidental" at this season) that he had determined to leave Tollamore. Mentally she exulted at his spirit, but her heart despaired. He solemnly assured her that it would be much better for them both in the end; and she became submissive, and entirely agreed with him. Then she seemed to acquire a sort of
15   superior insight by virtue of her superior rank, and murmured, "You will expand your mind, and get to despise me for all this, and for my want of pride in being so easily won; and it will end unhappily."

Her imagination so affected her that she could not hinder the tears from falling. Nothing was more effective in checking his despair than
20   the sight of her despairing, and he immediately put on a more hopeful tone.

"No," he said, taking her by the hand, "I shall rise, and become so learned and so famous that—." He did not like to say plainly that he really hoped to win her as his wife, but it is very probable that she
25   guessed his meaning nearly enough.

"You have some secret resources!" she exclaimed. "Some help is promised you in this ambitious plan."

It was most painful to him to have to tell her the truth after this sanguine expectation, and how uncertain and unaided his plans were.
30   However, he cheered her with the words, "Wait and see." But he himself had many misgivings when her sweet face was turned away.

Upon this plan he acted at once. Nothing of moment occurred during the autumn, and the time for his departure gradually came near. The sale of his grandfather's effects having taken place, and
35   notice having been given at the school, there was very little else for him to do in the way of preparation, for there was no family to be

---

4 her sphere] the sphere   5 subversive] utterly subversive   6 worthy]
at once worthy   6 instincts] purest instincts   34–5 The sale . . . notice]
Notice

consulted, no household to be removed. On the last day of teaching, when the afternoon lessons were over, he bade farewell to the school children. The younger ones cried, not from any particular reflection on the loss they would sustain, but simply because their hearts were tender to any announcement couched in solemn terms. The elder children sincerely regretted Egbert, as an acquaintance who had not filled the post of schoolmaster so long as to be quite spoilt as a human being.

On the morning of departure he rose at half-past three, for Tollamore was a remote nook of a remote district, and it was necessary to start early, his plan being to go by packet from Melport. The candle-flame had a sad and yellow look when it was brought into his bedroom by Nathan Brown, one of his grandfather's old labourers, at whose house he had taken a temporary lodging, and who had agreed to awake him and assist his departure. Few things will take away a man's confidence in an impulsive scheme more than being called up by candlelight upon a chilly morning to commence working it out. But when Egbert heard Nathan's great feet stamping spiritedly about the floor downstairs, in earnest preparation of breakfast, he overcame his weakness and bustled out of bed.

They breakfasted together, Nathan drinking the hot tea with rattling sips, and Egbert thinking as he looked at him that Nathan had never appeared so desirable a man to have about him as now when he was about to give him up.

"Well, good mornen, Mistur Mayne," Nathan said, as he opened the door to let Egbert out. "And mind this, sir; if they use ye bad up there, th'lt always find a hole to put thy head into at Nathan Brown's, I'll warrant as much."

Egbert stepped from the door, and struck across to the manor-house. The morning was dark, and the raw wind made him shiver till walking warmed him. "Good heavens, here's an undertaking!" he sometimes thought. Old trees seemed to look at him through the gloom, as they rocked uneasily to and fro; and now and then a dreary drop of rain beat upon his face as he went on. The dead leaves in the ditches, which could be heard but not seen, shifted their positions with a troubled rustle, and flew at intervals with a little rap against his walking-stick and hat. He was glad to reach the north stile, and

14 temporary [*not in HW*]   31 an undertaking] a crazy undertaking

get into the park, where, with an anxious pulse, he passed beneath the creaking limes.

"Will she wake soon enough; will she be forgetful, and sleep over the time?" He had asked himself this many times since he rose that 5 morning, and still beset by the inquiry, he drew near to the mansion.

Her bedroom was in the north wing, facing towards the church, and on turning the brow of the hill a faint light in the window reassured him. Taking a few little stones from the path he threw them upon the sill, as they had agreed, and she instantly opened the 10 window, and said softly, "The butler sleeps on the ground floor on this side, go to the bow-window in the shrubbery."

He went round among the bushes to the place mentioned, which was entirely sheltered from the wind. She soon appeared, bearing in her hand a wax taper, so small that it scarcely gave more light than a 15 glowworm. She wore the same dress that she had worn when they first met on the previous Christmas, and her hair was loose, as at that time. Indeed, she looked throughout much as she had looked then, except that her bright eyes were red, as Egbert could see well enough.

"I have something for you," she said softly as she opened the 20 window. "How much time is there?"

"Half-an-hour only, dearest."

She began a sigh, but checked it, at the same time holding out a packet to him.

"Here are fifty pounds," she whispered. "It will be useful to you 25 now, and more shall follow."

Egbert felt how impossible it was to accept this. "No, my dear one," he said, "I cannot."

"I don't require it, Egbert. I wish you to have it; I have plenty. Come, do take it." But seeing that he continued firm on this point she 30 reluctantly gave in, saying that she would keep it for him.

"I fear so much that papa suspects me," she said. "And if so, it was my own fault, and all owing to a conversation I began with him without thinking beforehand that it would be dangerous."

"What did you say?"

35 "I said," she whispered, " 'Suppose a man should love me very much, would you mind my being acquainted with him if he were a very worthy man?' 'That depends upon his rank and circumstances,' he said. 'Suppose,' I said, 'that in addition to his goodness he had

26 Egbert] Mayne   30 saying that] saying

much learning, and had made his name famous in the world, but was not altogether rich?' I think I showed too much earnestness, and I wished that I could have recalled my words. 'When the time comes I will tell you,' he said, 'and don't speak or think of these matters again.'"

In consequence of this new imprudence of hers Egbert doubted if it would be right to correspond with her. He said nothing about it then, but it added a new shade to the parting.

"I think your decision a good and noble one," she murmured, smiling hopefully. "And you will come back some day a wondrous man of the world, talking of vast Schemes, radical Errors, and saying such words as the 'Backbone of Society,' the 'Tendency of Modern Thought,' and other things like that. When papa says to you, 'My Lord the Chancellor,' you will answer him with 'A tall man, with a deep-toned voice—I know him well.' When he says, 'Such and such were Lord Hatton's words, I think,' you will answer, 'No, they were Lord Tyrrell's; I was present on the occasion'; and so on in that way. You must get to talk authoritatively about vintages and their dates, and to know all about epicureanism, idleness, and fashion; and so you will beat him with his own weapons, for he knows nothing of these things. He will criticise you; then he will be nettled; then he will admire you."

Egbert kissed her hand devotedly, and held it long.

"If you cannot in the least succeed," she added, "I shall never think the less of you. The truly great stand on no middling ledge; they are either famous or unknown."

Egbert moved slowly away amongst the laurestines. Holding the light above her bright head she smiled upon him, as if it were unknown to her that she wept at the same time.

He left the park precincts, and followed the turnpike road to Melport. In spite of the misery of parting he felt relieved of a certain oppressiveness, now that his presence at Tollamore could no longer bring disgrace upon her. The threatening rain passed off by the time that he reached the ridge dividing the inland districts from the coast. It began to get light, but his journey was still very lonely. Ultimately the yellow shore-line of pebbles grew visible, and the distant horizon of water, spreading like a grey upland against the sky, till he could soon hear the measured flounce of the waves.

6 this new ... Egbert] this, Mayne　　20 nothing [*not in HW*]

He entered the town at sunrise, just as the lamps were extinguished, and went to a tavern to breakfast. At half-past eight o'clock the boat steamed out of the harbour and reached London after a passage of five-and-forty hours.

5

PART II

CHAPTER I

He, like a captain who beleaguers round
Some strong-built castle on a rising ground,
Views all the approaches with observing eyes;
10 This and that other part in vain he tries,
And more on industry than force relies.

Since Egbert Mayne's situation is not altogether a new and unprecedented one, there will be no necessity for detailing in all its minuteness his attempt to scale the steeps of Fame. For 15 notwithstanding the fact that few, comparatively, have reached the top, the lower tracts of that troublesome incline have been trodden by as numerous a company as any allegorical spot in the world.

The reader must then imagine five years to have elapsed, during which rather formidable slice of human life Egbert had been 20 constantly striving. It had been drive, drive from month to month; no rest, nothing but effort. He had progressed from newspaper work to criticism, from criticism to independent composition of a mild order, from the latter to the publication of a book which nobody ever heard of, and from this to the production of a work of really sterling merit, 25 which appeared anonymously. Though he did not set society in a blaze, or even in a smoke, thereby, he certainly caused a good many people to talk about him, and to be curious as to his name.

The luminousness of nature which had been sufficient to attract the attention and heart of Geraldine Allenville had, indeed, meant much. 30 That there had been power enough in the presence, speech, mind, and tone of the poor painter's son to fascinate a girl of Geraldine's station was of itself a ground for the presumption that he might do a work in

14 attempt] attempts   14–15 For notwithstanding] Notwithstanding
16 tracts] areas   26 caused] did cause   27 him . . . name.] him.

the world if he chose. The attachment to her was just the stimulus which such a constitution as his required, and it had at first acted admirably upon him. Afterwards the case was scarcely so happy.

He had investigated manners and customs no less than literature; and for awhile the experience was exciting enough. But several habits which he had at one time condemned in the ambitious classes now became his own. His original fondness for art, literature, and science was getting quenched by his slowly increasing habit of looking upon each and all of these as machinery wherewith to effect a purpose.

A new feeling began to animate all his studies. He had not the old interest in them for their own sakes, but a breathless interest in them as factors in the game of sink or swim. He entered picture galleries, not, as formerly, because it was his humour to dream pleasantly over the images therein expressed, but to be able to talk on demand about painters and their peculiarities. He examined Correggio to criticise his flesh shades; Angelico, to speak technically of the pink faces of his saints; Murillo, to say fastidiously that there was a certain silliness in the look of his old men; Rubens for his sensuous women; Turner for his Turneresqueness. Romney was greater than Reynolds because Lady Hamilton had been his model, and thereby hung a tale. Bonozzi Gozzoli was better worth study than Raffaelle, since the former's name was a learned sound to utter, and all knowledge got up about him would tell.

Whether an intense love for a woman, and that woman Geraldine, was a justifiable reason for this desire to shine it is not easy to say.

However, as has been stated, Egbert worked like a slave in these causes, and at the end of five full years was repaid with certain public applause, though, unfortunately, not with much public money. But this he hoped might come soon.

Regarding his love for Geraldine, the most noteworthy fact to be recorded of the period was that all correspondence with her had ceased. In spite of their fear of her father, letters had passed frequently between them on his first leaving home, and had been continued with ardour for some considerable time. The reason of its

2 constitution] nature   3 scarcely so happy. ¶] different. ¶ At first he had unflinchingly worked sixteen hours a day; but finding this to be a mistaken policy, he reduced the number to thirteen.   10 began to animate] animated   13 not, as formerly,] not   14 images therein expressed] fancies expressed in works of art   14–15 on demand ... peculiarities.] about them on demand.   20 had been] was   21 since] because   27 causes] courses

close will be perceived in the following note, which he received from her two years before the date of the present chapter:—

"Tollamore House.

"MY DEAR EGBERT,

5   "How shall I tell you what has happened! and yet how can I keep silence when sooner or later you must know all?

"My father has discovered what we feel for each other. He took me into his room and made me promise never to write to you, or seek you, or receive a letter from you. I promised in haste, for I was frightened and excited, and now
10 he trusts me—I wish he did not—for he knows I would not be mean enough to lie. So don't write, poor Egbert, or expect to hear from miserable me. We must try to hope; yet it is a long dreary thing to do. But I *will* hope, and not be beaten. How could I help promising, Egbert, when he compelled me? He is my father. I cannot think what we shall do under it all. It is cruel of life to be
15 like this towards us when we have done no wrong.

     *   *   *   *   *   *

"We are going abroad for a long time. I think it is because of you and me, but I don't know. He does not tell me where we shall go. Just as if a place like Europe could make me forget you. He doesn't know what's in me, and how I
20 can think about you and cry at nights—he cannot. If he did, he must see how silly the plan is.

"Remember that you go to church on Sunday mornings, for then I think that perhaps we are reading in the same place at the same moment; and we are sometimes, no doubt. Last Sunday, when we came to this in the Psalms,
25 'And he shall be like a tree planted by the waterside that will bring forth his fruit in due season: his leaf also shall not wither; and look, whatsoever he doeth, it shall prosper,' I thought, 'That's Egbert in London.' I know you were reading that same verse in your church—I felt that you said it with us. Then I looked up to your old nook under the tower arch. It was a misery to see
30 the wood and the stone just as good as ever, and you not there. It is not only that you are gone at these times, but a heavy creature—blankness—seems to stand in your place.

"But how can I tell you of these thoughts now that I am to write no more? Yet we will hope, and hope. Remember this, that should anything serious
35 happen, I will break the bond and write. Obligation would end then. Good-bye for a time. I cannot put into words what I would finish with. Good-bye, good-bye.   "G. A.

---

2 two...chapter:—] at that time.   8 receive] receive you, or receive
17 you and me] me and you   25–6 his fruit] its fruit   30 the stone] stone
35 Obligation] Obligations

"P.S. Might we not write just one line at very wide intervals? It is too much never to write at all."

On receiving this letter Egbert felt that he could not honourably keep up a regular correspondence with her. But a determination to break it off would have been more than he could have adhered to if he had not been strengthened by the hope that he might soon be able to give a plausible reason for renewing it. He sent her a line, bidding her to expect the best results from the prohibition, which, he was sure, would not be for long. Meanwhile, should she think it not wrong to send a line at very wide intervals, he would promptly reply.

But she was apparently too conscientious to do so, for nothing had reached him since. Yet she was as continually in his thought and heart as before. He felt more misgivings than he had chosen to tell her of on the ultimate effect of the prohibition, but could do nothing to remove it. And then he had learnt that Miss Allenville and her father had gone to Paris, as the commencement of a sojourn abroad.

These circumstances had burdened him with long hours of depression, till he had resolved to throw his whole strength into a production which should either give him a fair start towards fame, or make him clearly understand that there was no hope in that direction for such as he. He had begun the attempt, and ended it, and the consequences were fortunate to an unexpected degree.

CHAPTER II

Towards the loadstar of my one desire
I flitted like a dizzy moth, whose flight
Is as a dead leaf's in the owlet light.

Mayne's book having been launched into the world and well received, he found time to emerge from the seclusion he had maintained for several months, and to look into life again.

One warm, fashionable day, between five and six o'clock, he was walking along Piccadilly, absent-minded and unobservant, when an equipage approached whose appearance thrilled him through. It was the Allenville landau, newly-painted up. Egbert felt almost as if he

6 might] must   13 misgivings] misgiving   13 her [*not in HW*]
17 burdened him with] given him   33 landau] barouche

had been going into battle; and whether he should stand forth visibly before her or keep in the background seemed a question of life or death.

5 He waited in unobserved retirement, which it was not difficult to do, his aspect having much altered since the old times. Coachman, footman, and carriage advanced, in graceful unity of glide, like a swan. Then he beheld her, Geraldine, after two years of silence, five years of waiting, and nearly three years of separation; for although he had seen her two or three times in town after he had taken up his residence there, they had not once met since the year preceding her departure for the Continent.

She came opposite, now passively looking round, then actively glancing at something which interested her. Egbert trembled a little, or perhaps a great deal, at sight of her. But she passed on, and the back of the carriage hid her from his view.

So much of the boy was left in him still that he could scarcely withhold himself from rushing after her, and jumping into the carriage. She had appeared to be well and blooming, and an instinctive vexation that their long separation had produced no perceptible effect upon her, speedily gave way before a more generous sense of gratification at her well-being. Still, had it been possible, he would have been glad to see some sign upon her face that she yet remembered him.

This sudden discovery that they were in town after their years of travel stirred his lassitude into excitement. He went back to his chambers to meditate upon his next step. A trembling on Geraldine's account was disturbing him. She had probably been in London ever since the beginning of the season, but she had not given him a sign to signify that she was so near; and but for this accidental glimpse of her he might have gone on for months without knowing that she had returned from abroad.

Whether she was leading a dull or an exciting life Egbert had no means of knowing. That night after night the arms of interesting young men rested upon her waist and whirled her round the ball-room he could not bear to think. That she frequented gatherings and

2 life or] life and   7 beheld] saw   21–2 had it...face] he would have
been glad to see, had it been possible, some sign upon her   24–5 after...stirred]
stirred all   25 went] went at once   26 A trembling] An uneasy
trembling   29 this accidental] the accidental

assemblies of all sorts he calmly owned as very probable, for she was her father's only daughter, and likely to be made much of. That she had not written a line to him since their return was still the grievous point.

"If I had only risen one or two steps further," he thought, "how boldly would I seek her out. But only to have published one successful book in all these years—such grounds are slight indeed."

For several succeeding days he did nothing but look about the Park, and the streets, and the neighbourhood of Chevron Square, where their town-house stood, in the hope of seeing her again; but in vain. There were moments when his distress that she might possibly be indifferent about him and his affairs was unbearable. He fully resolved that he would on some early occasion communicate with her, and know the worst. Years of work remained to be done before he could think of appearing before her father; but he had reached a sort of half-way stage at which some assurance from herself that his track was a hopeful one was positively needed to keep him firm.

Egbert still kept on the look-out for her at every public place; but nearly a month passed, and she did not appear again. One Sunday evening, when he had been wandering near Chevron Square, and looking at her windows from a distance, he returned past her house after dusk. The rooms were lighted, but the windows were still open, and as he strolled along he heard notes from a piano within. They were the accompaniment to an air from the *Messiah*, though no singer's voice was audible. Egbert readily imagined who the player might be, for the *Messiah* was an oratorio which Geraldine often used to wax eloquent upon in days gone by. He had not walked far when he remembered that there was to be an exceptionally fine performance of that stirring composition during the following week, and it instantly occurred to him that Geraldine's mind was running on the same event, and that she intended to be one of the audience.

He resolved upon doing something at a venture. The next morning he went to the ticket-office, and boldly asked for a place as near as possible to those taken in the name of Allenville.

"There is no vacant one in any of those rows," the office-keeper said,

5

10

15

20

25

30

35

---

6 would I] I would   8 succeeding [*not in HW*]   10 their town-house]
the town house   16 herself] her   18 on the] a   23 within]
within the house

"but you can have one very near their number on the other side of the division."

Egbert was astonished that for once in his life he had made a lucky hit. He booked his place, and returned home.

The evening arrived, and he went early. On taking his seat he found himself at the left-hand end of a series of benches, and close to a red cord, which divided the group of seats he had entered from stalls of a somewhat superior kind. He was passing the time in looking at the extent of orchestra space, and other things, when he saw two ladies and a gentleman enter and sit down in the stalls diagonally before his own, and on the other side of the division. It delighted and agitated him to find that one of the three was Geraldine; her two companions he did not know.

"Policy, don't desert me now," he thought; and immediately sat in such a way that unless she turned round to a very unlikely position she would not see him.

There was a certain half-pleasant misery in sitting behind her thus as a possibly despised lover. To-night, at any rate, there would be sights and sounds common to both of them, though they should not communicate to the extent of a word. Even now he could hear the rustle of her garments as she settled down in her seat, and the faint murmur of words that passed between her and her friends.

Never, in the many times that he had listened to that rush of harmonies, had they affected him as they did then; and it was no wonder, considering what an influence upon his own life had been and still was exercised by Geraldine, and that she now sat there before him. The varying strains shook and bent him to themselves as a rippling brook shakes and bends a shadow. The music did not show its power by attracting his attention to its subject; it rather dropped its own libretto and took up in place of that the poem of his life and love.

There was Geraldine still. They were singing the chorus "Lift up your heads," and he found a new impulse of thought in him. It was towards determination. Should every member of her family be against him he would win her in spite of them. He could now see that Geraldine was moved equally with himself by the tones which entered her ears.

"Why do the nations so furiously rage together" filled him with a gnawing thrill, and so changed him to its spirit that he believed he was capable of suffering in silence for his whole lifetime, and of never appearing before her unless she gave a sign.

The audience stood up, and the "Hallelujah Chorus" began. The deafening harmonies flying from this group and from that seemed to absorb all the love and poetry that his life had produced, to pour it upon that one moment, and upon her who stood so close at hand. "I will force Geraldine to be mine," he thought. "I will make that heart ache of love for me." The chorus continued, and her form trembled under its influence. Egbert was for seeking her the next morning and knowing what his chances were, without waiting for further results. The chorus and the personality of Geraldine still filled the atmosphere. "I will seek her to-night—as soon as we get out of this place," he said. The storm of sound now reached its climax, and Geraldine's power was proportionately increased. He would give anything for a glance this minute—to look into her eyes, she into his. "If I can but touch her hand, and get one word from her, I will," he murmured.

He shifted his position somewhat and saw her face. Tears were in her eyes, and her lips were slightly parted. Stretching a little nearer he whispered, "My love!"

Geraldine turned her wet eyes upon him, almost as if she had not been surprised, but had been forewarned by her previous emotion. With the peculiar quickness of grasp that she always showed under sudden circumstances, she had realised the position at a glance.

"Oh, Egbert!" she said; and her countenance flagged as if she would have fainted.

"Give me your hand," he whispered.

She placed her hand in his, under the cord, which it was easy to do without observation; and he held it tight.

"Mine, as before?" he asked.

"Yours now as then," said she.

They were like frail and sorry wrecks upon that sea of symphony, and remained in silent abandonment to the time, till the strains approached their close.

"Can you meet me to-night?" said Egbert.

11 was] was at once   15 storm of sound] harmony   30 under the cord, [*not in HW*]   32 asked] asked, eagerly

She was half frightened at the request, and said, "Where?"

"At your own front door, at twelve o'clock." He then was at once obliged to gently withdraw himself, for the chorus was ended, and the people were sitting down.

5   The remainder was soon over, and it was time to leave. Egbert watched her and her party out of the house, and, turning to the other doorway, went out likewise.

CHAPTER III

Bright reason will mock thee,
10   Like the sun from a wintry sky.

When he reached his chambers he sat down and literally did nothing but watch the hand of the mantel-clock minute by minute, till it marked half-past eleven, scarcely removing his eyes. Then going again into the street he called a cab, and was driven down Park Lane
15   and on to the corner of Chevron Square. Here he alighted, and went round to the number occupied by the Allenvilles.

A lamp stood nearly opposite the doorway, and by receding into the gloom to the railing of the square he could see whatever went on in the porch of the house. The lamps over the doorways were nearly all
20   extinguished, and everything about this part was silent and deserted, except at a house on the opposite side of the square, where a ball was going on. But nothing of that concerned Egbert: his eyes had sought out and remained fixed upon Mr Allenville's front door, in momentary expectation of seeing it gently open.

25   The dark wood of the door showed a keen and distinct edge upon the pale stone of the porch floor. It must have been about two minutes before the hour he had named when he fancied he saw a slight movement at that point, as of something slipped out from under the door.

30   "It is but fancy," he said to himself.

He turned his eyes away, and turned them back again. Some object certainly seemed to have been thrust under the door. At this moment the four quarters of midnight began to strike, and then the hour.

2–3 o'clock. ... withdraw] o'clock," he answered, and gently withdrew
15 on to] to   19 doorways] doorway   28 of something] if something were

Egbert could remain still no longer, and he went into the porch. A note had been slipped under the door from inside.

He took it to the lamp, turned it over, and saw that it was directed only with initials,—"To E. M." Egbert tore it open and glanced upon the page. With a shiver of disappointment he read these words in her   5
handwriting:—

"It was when under the influence of much emotion, kindled in me by the power of the music, that I half assented to a meeting with you to-night; and I believe that you also were excited when you asked for one. After some quiet reflection I have decided that it will be much better for us both if we do not see   10
each other.

"You will, I know, judge me fairly in this. You have by this time learnt what life is; what particular positions, accidental though they may be, ask, nay, imperatively exact from us. If you say 'not imperatively,' you cannot speak from knowledge of the world.   15

"To be woven and tied in with the world by blood, acquaintance, tradition, and external habit, is to a woman to be utterly at the beck of that world's customs. In youth we do not see this. You and I did not see it. We were but a girl and a boy at the time of our meetings at Tollamore. What was our knowledge? A list of other people's words. What was our wisdom? None at   20
all.

"It is well for you now to remember that I am not the unsophisticated girl I was when you first knew me. For better or for worse I have become complicated, exclusive, and practised. A woman who can speak, or laugh, or dance, or sing before any number of men with perfect composure may be no   25
sinner, but she is not what I was once. She is what I am now. She is not the girl you loved. That woman is not here.

"I wish to write kindly to you, as to one for whom, in spite of the unavoidable division between our paths, I must always entertain a heartfelt respect. Is it, after this, out of place in me to remind you how contrasting are   30
all our associations, how inharmonious our times and seasons? Could anything ever overpower this incongruity?

"But I must write plainly, and, though it may grieve you now, it will produce ultimately the truest ease. This is my meaning. If I could accept your addresses without an entire loss of position I would do so; but, since this   35
cannot be, we must forget each other.

"Believe me to be, with wishes and prayers for your happiness,

"Your sincere friend,
"G. A."

22 girl] girl that   29 must] shall   32 ever [*not in HW*]

Egbert could neither go home nor stay still; he walked off rapidly in any direction for the sole sake of vehement motion. His first impulse was to get into darkness. He went towards Kensington; thence threaded across to the Uxbridge Road, thence to Kensal Green,
5   where he turned into a lane and followed it to Kilburn, and the hill beyond, at which spot he halted and looked over the vast haze of light extending to the length and breadth of London. Turning back and wandering among some fields by a way he could never afterwards recollect, sometimes sitting down, sometimes leaning on a stile, he
10 lingered on until the sun had risen. He then slowly walked again towards London, and, feeling by this time very weary, he entered the first refreshment-house that he came to, and attempted to eat something. Having sat for some time over this meal without doing much more than taste it, he arose and set out for the street in which he
15 lived. Once in his own rooms he lay down upon the couch and fell asleep.

When he awoke it was four o'clock. Egbert then dressed and went out, partook of a light meal at his club at the dismal hour between luncheon and dinner, and cursorily glanced over the papers and
20 reviews. Among the first things that he saw were eulogistic notices of his own book in three different reviews, each the most prominent and weighty of its class. Two of them, at least, would, he knew, find their way to the drawing-room of the Allenvilles, for they were among the periodicals which the Squire regularly patronised.
25   Next, in a weekly review he read the subjoined note:—

"The authorship of the book —— ——, about which conjecture has lately been so much exercised, is now ascribed to Mr Egbert Mayne, whose first attempt in that kind we noticed in these pages some eighteen months ago."

He took up a daily paper, and presently lighted on the following
30 paragraph:—

"It is announced that a marriage is arranged between Lord Bretton, of Tosthill Park, and Geraldine, only daughter of Foy Allenville, Esq., of Tollamore House, Wessex."

Egbert arose and went towards home. Arrived there he met the
35 postman at the door, and received from him a small note. The young man mechanically glanced at the direction.

23 Allenvilles] Allenvilles, if they had not done so already   29 took] then
took   31 is arranged] will shortly be celebrated

"From her," he mentally exclaimed. "What does it—"
This was what the letter contained:—

"Twelve o'clock.

"I have just learnt that the anonymous author of the book in which the
world has been so interested during the past two months, and which I have   5
read, is none other than yourself. Accept my congratulations. It seems almost
madness in me to address you now. But I could not do otherwise on receipt of
this news, and after writing my last letter. Let your knowledge of my nature
prevent your misconstruing my motives in writing thus on the spur of the
moment. I need scarcely add, please keep it a secret for ever. I am not morally   10
afraid, but other lives, hopes, and objects than mine have to be considered.
"The announcement of the marriage is premature, to say the least. I would
tell you more, but dare not.

"G. A."

The conjunction of all this intelligence produced in Egbert's heart a   15
stillness which was some time in getting aroused to excitement. His
emotion was formless. He knew not what point to take hold of and
survey his position from; and, though his faculties grew clearer with
the passage of time, he failed in resolving on a course with any
deliberateness. No sooner had he thought, "I will never see her again   20
for my pride's sake," than he said, "Why not see her? she is a woman;
she may love me yet."
He went downstairs and out of the house, and walked by way of the
Park towards Chevron Square.
Probably nobody will rightly appreciate Mayne's wild behaviour   25
at this juncture, unless, which is very unlikely, he has been in a
somewhat similar position himself. It may always appear to cool
critics, even if they are generous enough to make allowances for his
feelings, as visionary and weak in the extreme. Yet it was scarcely to
be expected, after the mental and emotional strain that he had   30
undergone during the preceding five years, that he should have acted
much otherwise.
He rang the bell and asked to see Mr Allenville. He, perhaps
fortunately, was not at home. "Miss Allenville, then," said Mayne.
"She is just driving out," said the footman dubiously.   35
Egbert then noticed for the first time that the carriage was at the

2 was what] is what   15 intelligence] news   19 failed in] failed on
26 unless…unlikely,] unless   27 always [*not in HW*]   29–30 to be
expected] possible   32 much [*not in HW*]

door, and almost as soon as the words were spoken Geraldine came downstairs.

"The madness of hoping to call that finished creature, wife!" he thought.

5 Geraldine recognised him, and looked perplexed.

"One word, Miss Allenville," he murmured.

She assented, and he followed her into the adjoining room.

"I have come," said Egbert. "I know it is hasty of me; but I must hear my doom from your own lips. Five years ago you spurred me on 10 to ambition. I have followed but too closely the plan I then marked out, for I have hoped all along for a reward. What am I to think? Have you indeed left off feeling what you once felt for me?"

"I cannot speak of it now," she said hurriedly. "I told you in my letter as much as I dared. Believe me I cannot speak—in the way you 15 wish. I will always be your friend."

"And is this the end? Oh, my God!"

"And we shall hope to see you to dinner some day, now you are famous," she continued, pale as ashes. "But I—cannot be with you as we once were. I was such a child at that time, you know."

20 "Geraldine, is this all I get after this lapse of time and heat of labour?"

"I am not my own mistress—I have my father to please," she faintly murmured. "I must please him. There is no help for this. Go from me—do go!"

25 Egbert turned and went, for he felt that he had no longer a place beside her.

CHAPTER IV

> Then I said in my heart, "As it happeneth to the fool, so it
> happeneth even to me; and why was I then more wise?"

30 Mayne was in rather an ailing state for several days after the above-mentioned event. Yet the lethean stagnation which usually comes with the realisation that all is over allowed him to take some deep sleeps, to which he had latterly been a stranger.

The hours went by, and he did the best he could to dismiss his

---

30 Mayne] Mayne, not being physically the strongest of men,

regrets for Geraldine. He was assisted to the very little success that he attained in this by reflecting how different a woman she must have become from her old sweet self of five or six years ago.

"But how paltry is my success now she has vanished!" he said. "What is it worth? What object have I in following it up after this?" It rather startled him to see that the root of his desire for celebrity having been Geraldine, he now was a man who had no further motive in moving on. Town life had for some time been depressing to him. He began to doubt whether he could ever be happy in the course of existence that he had followed through these later years. The perpetual strain, the lack of that quiet to which he had been accustomed in early life, the absence of all personal interest in things around him, was telling upon his health of body and of mind.

Then revived the wish which had for some time been smouldering in his secret heart—to leave off, for the present, at least, his efforts for distinction; to retire for a few months to his old country nook, and there to meditate on his next course.

To set about this was curiously awkward to him. He had planned methods of retrogression in case of defeat through want of ability, want of means, or lack of opportunity; but to retreat because his appetite for advance had gone off was what he had never before thought of.

His reflections turned upon the old home of his mother's family. He knew exactly how Tollamore appeared at that time of year. The trees with their half-ripe apples, the bees and butterflies lazy from the heat; the haymaking over, the harvest not begun, the people lively and always out of doors. He would visit the spot, and call upon some old and half-forgotten friends of his grandfather in an adjoining parish.

Two days later he left town. The fine weather, his escape from that intricate web of effort in which he had been bound these five years, the sensation that nobody in the world had any claims upon him, imparted some buoyancy to his mind; and it was in a serene if sad spirit that he entered Tollamore Vale, and smelt his native air.

He did not at once proceed to the village, but stopped at Fairland, the parish next adjoining. It was now evening, and he called upon

1 success that] success   3 five or [*not in HW*]   17 meditate on] meditate upon   25 butterflies] the butterflies   28 half-forgotten] half-forgotten and cheery   28 parish] parish to keep down this horrible gloom 30 effort] thought

some of the old cottagers whom he knew. Time had set a mark upon them all since he had last been there. Middle-aged men were a little more round-shouldered, their wives had taken to spectacles, young people had grown up out of recognition, and old men had passed into 5 second childhood.

Egbert found here, as he had expected, precisely such a lodging as a hermit would desire. It was in an ivy-covered detached house which had been partly furnished for a tenant who had never come, and it was kept clean by an old woman living in a cottage near. She offered 10 to wait upon Egbert whilst he remained there, coming in the morning and leaving in the afternoon, thus giving him the house to himself during the latter part of the day.

When it grew dusk he went out, wishing to ramble for a little time. The gibbous moon rose on his right, the stars showed themselves 15 sleepily one by one, and the far distance turned to a mysterious ocean of grey. He instinctively directed his steps towards Tollamore, and when there towards the school. It looked very little changed since the year in which he had had the memorable meetings with her there, excepting that the creepers had grown higher.

20 He went on towards the Park. Here was the place whereon he had used to await her coming—he could be sure of the spot to a foot. There was the turn of the hill around which she had appeared. The sentimental effect of the scenes upon him was far greater than he had expected, so great that he wished he had never been so reckless as to 25 come here. "But this is folly," he thought. "The betrothed of Lord Bretton is a woman of the world in whose thoughts, hopes, and habits I have no further interest or share."

In the lane he heard the church-bells ringing out their five notes, and meeting a shepherd Egbert asked him what was going on.

30 "Practising," he said, in an uninterested voice. "'Tis against young Miss's wedding, that their hands may be thoroughly in by the day for't."

He presently came to where his grandfather's old house had stood. It was pulled down, the ground it covered having become a shabby, 35 irregular spot, half grown over with trailing plants. The garden had been grassed down, but the old appletrees still remained, their trunks and stems being now sheeted on one side with moonlight. He entertained himself by guessing where the front door of the house had

20 whereon] in which   23 scenes] scene

been, at which Geraldine had entered on the memorable evening when she came to him full of grief and pity, and a tacit avowal of love was made on each side. Where they had sat together was now but a heap of broken rubbish half covered with grass. Near this melancholy spot was the cottage once inhabited by Nathan Brown. But Nathan   5
was dead now, and his wife and family had gone elsewhere.

Finding the effect of memory to be otherwise than cheerful, Mayne hastened from the familiar spot, and went on to the parish of Fairland in which he had taken his lodging.

It soon became whispered in the neighbourhood that Miss   10
Allenville's wedding was to take place on the 17th of October. Egbert heard few particulars of the matter beyond the date, though it is possible that he might have known more if he had tried. He preferred to fortify himself by dipping deeply into the few books he had brought with him; but the most obvious plan of escaping his   15
thoughts, that of a rapid change of scene by travel, he was unaccountably loth to adopt. He felt that he could not stay long in this district; yet an indescribable fascination held him on day after day, till the date of the marriage was close at hand.

CHAPTER V   20

How all the other passions fleet to air,
As doubtful thoughts, and rash-embraced despair
And shudd'ring fear, and green-eyed jealousy!

On the eve of the wedding the people told Mayne that arches and festoons of late summer-flowers and evergreens had been put up   25
across the path between the church porch at Tollamore and the private gate to the Squire's lawn, for the procession of bride and bridesmaids. Before it got dark several villagers went on foot to the church to look at and admire these decorations. Egbert had determined to see the ceremony over. It would do him good, he   30
thought, to be witness of the sacrifice.

Hence he, too, went along the path to Tollamore to inspect the preparations. It was dusk by the time that he reached the churchyard,

4–6 Near … elsewhere. [*not in HW*]   7 Mayne] he   8 familiar [*not in HW*]   24 Mayne] Egbert   25 summer-flowers] flowers   33 time that] time

and he entered it boldly, letting the gate fall together with a loud slam, as if he were a man whom nothing troubled. He looked at the half-completed bowers of green, and passed on into the church, never having entered it since he first left Tollamore.

5 He was standing by the chancel-arch, and observing the quantity of flowers which had been placed around the spot, when he heard the creaking of a gate on its hinges. Two figures entered the church, and Egbert stepped behind a canopied tomb.

The persons were females, and they appeared to be servants from 10 the neighbouring mansion. They brought more flowers and festoons, and were talking of the event of the morrow. Coming into the chancel they threw down their burdens with a remark that it was too dark to arrange more flowers that night.

"This is where she is to kneel," said one, standing with her arms 15 akimbo before the altar-railing. "And I wish 'twas I instead, Lord send if I don't."

The two girls went on gossiping till other footsteps caused them to turn.

"I won't say 'tisn't she. She has been here two or three times to day. 20 Let's go round this way."

And the servants went towards the door by a circuitous path round the aisle, to avoid meeting with the new-comer.

Egbert, too, thought he would leave the place now that he had heard and seen thus much; but from carelessness or design he went 25 straight down the nave. An instant afterwards he was standing face to face with Geraldine. The servants had vanished.

"Good evening," she said serenely, not knowing him, and supposing him to be a parishioner.

Egbert returned the words hastily, and, in standing aside to let her 30 pass, looked clearly into her eyes and pale face, as if there never had been a time at which he would have done anything on earth for her sake.

She knew him, and started, uttering a weak exclamation. When he reached the door he turned his head, and saw that she was irresolutely 35 holding up her hand, as if to beckon to him to come back.

10 festoons] wreaths   12 burdens] bundles   23–4 now... much;] before other stragglers came,   28 parishioner.] parishioner: many had visited the church that day.   33 him] him then   35 to him] him

"One word, since I have met you," she said in unequal half-whispered tones. "I have felt that I was one-sided in my haste on the day you called to see me in London. I misunderstood you."

Egbert could at least out-do her in self-control, and, astonished that she should have spoken, he answered in a yet colder tone,　5

"I am sorry for that; very sorry, madam."

"And you excuse it?"

"Of course I do, readily. And I hope you, too, will pardon my intrusion on that day, and understand the—circumstances."

"Yes, yes. Especially as I am most to blame for those indiscreet　10 proceedings in our early lives which led to it."

"Certainly you were not most to blame."

"How can you say that?" she answered with a slight laugh, "when you know nothing of what my motives and feelings were?"

"I know well enough to judge, for I was the elder. Let me just recall　15 some points in your own history at that time."

"No."

"Will you not hear a word?"

"I cannot. . . . Are you writing another book?"

"I am doing nothing. I am idling at Monk's Hut."　20

"Indeed!" she said, slightly surprised. "Well, you will always have my good wishes, whatever you may do. If any of my relatives can ever help you—"

"Thank you, madam, very much. I think, however, that I can help myself."　25

She was silent, looking upon the floor; and Egbert spoke again, successfully hiding the feelings of his heart under a light and untrue tone. "Miss Allenville, you know that I loved you devotedly for many years, and that that love was the starting point of all my ambition. My sense of it makes this meeting rather awkward. But men survive　30 almost anything. I have proved it. Their love is strong while it lasts, but it soon withers at sight of a new face. I congratulate you on your coming marriage. Perhaps I may marry some day, too."

"I hope you will find some one worth your love. I am sorry I ever—inconvenienced you as I did. But one hardly knows at that　35 age—"

"Don't think of it for a moment—I really entreat you not to think of

12 not [*not in HW*]　　　13 How can] Can　　　29 starting point]
mainspring

that.'' What prompted the cruelty of his succeeding words he never could afterwards understand. ''It was a hard matter at first for me to forget you, certainly; but perhaps I was helped in my wish by the strong prejudice I originally had against your class and family. I have
5 fixed my mind firmly upon the differences between us, and my youthful fancy is pretty fairly overcome. Those old silly days of devotion were pretty enough, but the devotion was entirely unpractical, as you have seen, of course.''

''Yes, I have seen it,'' she faltered.
10 ''It was scarcely of a sort which survives accident and division, and is strengthened by disaster.''

''Well, perhaps not, perhaps not. You can scarcely care much now whether it was or not; or, indeed, care anything about me or my happiness.''
15 ''I do care.''

''How much? As you do for that of any other wretched human being?''

''Wretched? No!''

''I will tell you—I must tell you!'' she said with rapid utterance.
20 ''This is my secret, this. I don't love the man I am going to marry; but I have agreed to be his wife to satisfy my friends. Say you don't hate me for what I have told. I could not bear that you should not know!''

''Hate you? Oh, Geraldine!''

A hair's-breadth further, and they would both have broken down.
25 ''Not a word more. Now you know my unhappy state, and I shall die content.''

''But, darling—my Geraldine!''

''It is too late. Good-night—good-bye!'' She spoke in a hurried voice, almost like a low cry, and rushed away.
30 Here was a revelation. Egbert moved along to the door, and up the path, in a condition in which his mind caused his very body to ache. He gazed vacantly through the railings of the lawn, which came close to the churchyard; but she was gone. He still moved mechanically on. A little further and he was overtaken by the parish clerk, who,
35 addressing a few words to him, soon recognised his voice.

The clerk's talk, too, was about the wedding. ''Is the marriage

9 it,'' she faltered.] it.''   12 now [*not in HW*]   19–20 you!'' she said
. . . secret, this. I] you! This is my secret, Egbert,'' she burst out. ''I   22 told.
. . . know!''] told!''   24 both [*not in HW*]

likely to be a happy one?" asked Egbert, aroused by the subject.

"Well, between you and me, Mr Mayne, 'tis a made up affair. Some says she can't bear the man."

"Lord Bretton?"

"Yes. I could say more if I dared; but what's the good of it now!" 5

"I suppose none," said Egbert wearily.

He was glad to be again alone, and went on towards Fairland slowly and heavily. Had Geraldine forgotten him, and loved elsewhere with a light heart, he could have borne it; but this sacrifice at a time when, left to herself, she might have listened to him, was an 10 intolerable misery. Her inconsistent manner, her appearance of being swayed by two feelings, her half-reservations, were all explained. "Against her wishes," he said; "at heart she may still be mine. Oh, Geraldine, my poor Geraldine, is it come to this!"

He bitterly regretted his first manner towards her, and turned 15 round to consider whether he could not go back, endeavour to find her, and ask if he could be of any possible use. But all this was plainly absurd. He again proceeded homeward as before.

Reaching Fairland he sat awhile in his empty house without a light, and then went to bed. Owing to the distraction of his mind he lay for 20 three or four hours meditating, and listening to the autumn wind, turning restlessly from side to side, the blood throbbing in his temples and singing in his ears, and the ticking of his watch waxing apparently loud enough to stun him. He conjured up the image of Geraldine in her various stages of preparation on the following day. 25 He saw her coming in at the well-known door, walking down the aisle in a floating cloud of white, and receiving the eyes of the assembled crowd without a flush, or a sign of consciousness; uttering the words, "I take thee to my wedded husband," as quietly as if she were dreaming them. And the husband? Egbert shuddered. How could she 30 have consented, even if her memories stood their ground only half so obstinately as his own? As for himself, he perceived more clearly than ever how intricately she had mingled with every motive in his past career. Some portion of the thought, "marriage with Geraldine," had been marked on every day of his manhood. 35

Ultimately he fell into a fitful sleep, when he dreamed of fighting, wading, diving, boring, through innumerable multitudes, in the

10 listened] again listened   31 stood their ground only] only stood their ground

midst of which Geraldine's form appeared flitting about, in the usual confused manner of dreams—sometimes coming towards him, sometimes receding, and getting thinner and thinner till she was a mere film tossed about upon a seething mass.

5   He jumped up in the bed, damp with a cold perspiration, and in an agony of disquiet. It was a minute or two before he could collect his senses. He went to the window and looked out. It was quite dark, and the wind moaned and whistled round the corners of the house in the heavy intonations which seem to express that ruthlessness has all the
10   world to itself.

"Egbert, do, do come to me!" reached his ears in a faint voice from the darkness.

There was no mistaking it: it was assuredly the tongue of Geraldine.

15   He half dressed himself, ran down stairs, and opened the front door, holding the candle above his head. Nobody was visible.

He set down the light, hastened round the back of the house, and saw a dusky figure turning the corner to get to the gate. He then ran diagonally across the plot, and intercepted the form in the path.
20   "Geraldine!" he said, "can it indeed be you?"

"Yes, it is, it is!" she cried wildly, and fell upon his shoulder.

The hot turmoil of excitement pervading her hindered her from fainting, and Egbert placed his arm round her, and led her into the house, without asking a question, or meeting with any resistance. He
25   assisted her into a chair as soon as they reached the front room.

"I have run away from home, Egbert, and to you!" she sobbed. "I am not insane: they and you may think so, but I am not. I came to find you. Such shocking things have happened since I met you just now. Can Lord Bretton come and claim me?"

30   "Nobody on earth can claim you, darling, against your will. Now tell it all to me."

She spoke on between her tears. "I have loved you ever since, Egbert; but such influences have been brought to bear upon me that at last I have hardly known what I was doing. At last, I thought that
35   perhaps, after all, it would be better to become a lady of title, with a large park and houses of my own, than the wife of any man of genius

17 round] round to   20 said, "can] cried. "Can   21 fell] leaned
22 turmoil] tumult   26 sobbed. "I] sobbed. "There has been a great quarrel. I
28 since I met you just now [*not in HW*]   34 thought that] thought,

who was poor. I loved you all the time, but I was half ashamed that I loved you. I went out continually, that gaiety might obscure the past. And then dark circles came round my eyes—I grew worn and tired. I am not nearly so nice to look at as at that time when we used to meet in the school, nor so healthy either . . . I think I was handsome then." At this she smiled faintly, and raised her eyes to his, with a sparkle of their old mischief in them.

"And now and ever," he whispered.

"How innocent we were then! Fancy, Egbert, our unreserve would have been almost wrong if we had known the canons of behaviour we learnt afterwards. Ah! who at that time would have thought I was to yield to what I did? I wish now that I had met you at the door in Chevron Square, as I promised. But I feared to—I had promised Lord Bretton—and I that evening received a lecturing from my father, who saw you at the concert—he was in a seat further behind. And then, when I heard of your great success, how I wished I had held out a little longer! for I knew your hard labour had been on my account. When we met again last night it seemed awful, horrible— what I had done. Yet how could I tell you plainly? When I got indoors I felt I should die of misery, and I went to my father, and said I could not be married to-morrow. Oh, how angry he was, and what a dreadful scene occurred!" She covered her face with her hands.

"My poor Geraldine!" said Egbert, supporting her with his arm.

"When I was in my room this came into my mind, 'Better is it that thou shouldest not vow, than that thou shouldest vow and not pay.' I could bear it no longer. I was determined not to marry him, and to see you again, whatever came of it. I dressed, and came down stairs noiselessly, and slipped out. I knew where your house was, and I hastened here."

"You will never marry him now?"

"Never. Yet what can I do? Oh! what can I do? If I go back to my father—no, I cannot go back now—it is too late. But if they should find me, and drag me back, and compel me to perform my promise!"

"There is one simple way to prevent that, if, beloved Geraldine, you will agree to adopt it."

"Yes."

---

2 continually] constantly   15 in a seat [*not in HW*]   20 father, and said] father; I said

"By becoming *my* wife, at once. We would return to London as soon as the ceremony was over; and there you may defy them all."

"Oh, Egbert! I have thought of this—"

"You will have no reason to regret it. Perhaps I can introduce you to as intellectual, if odd-mannered and less aristocratic, society than that you have been accustomed to."

"Yes, I know it—I reflected on it before I came ... I will be your wife," she replied tenderly. "I have come to you, and to you I will cling."

Egbert kissed her lips then for the first time in his life. He reflected for some time, if that process could be called reflection which was accompanied with so much excitement.

"The parson of your parish would perhaps refuse to marry us, even if we could get to the church secretly," he said, with a cloud on his brow. "That's a difficulty."

"Oh, don't take me there! I cannot go to Tollamore. I shall be seen, or we shall be parted. Don't take me there."

"No, no; I will not, love. I was only thinking. Are you known in this parish?"

"Well, yes; not, however, to the clergyman. He is a young man—old Mr Keene is dead, you know."

"Then I can manage it." Egbert clasped her in his arms in the delight of his heart. "Now this is our course. I am first going to the surrogate's, and then further; and while I am gone you must stay in this house absolutely alone, and lock yourself in for safety. There is food in the house, and wine in that cupboard; you must stay here in hiding till I come back. It is now five o'clock. I will be here again at latest by eleven. If anybody knocks, remain silent, and the house will be supposed empty, as it lately has been so for a long time. My old servant and waitress must not come here to-day—I will manage that. I will light a fire, which will have burnt down by daylight, so that the room will be warmed for you. Sit there while I set about it."

He lit the fire, placed on the table all the food the house afforded, and went away.

4 Perhaps [*not in HW*]
intellectual if less aristocratic
10 then ... life.] then, and again.
on,

5 as intellectual ... aristocratic,] a more
8–9 "I have ... cling." [*not in HW*]
17 or] and   24 further;] further

CHAPTER VI

Hence will I to my ghostly father's cell;
His help to crave, and my dear hap to tell.

In half an hour Egbert returned, leading a horse.

"I have borrowed this from an old neighbour," he said, "and I   5
have told the woman who waits upon me that I am going on a
journey, and shall lock up the house to-day, so that she will not be
wanted. And now, dearest, I want you to lend me something."

"Whatever it may be, you know it is yours."

"It is that," he answered, lightly touching with the tip of his finger   10
a sparkling ring she wore on hers—the same she had used to wear at
their youthful meetings in past years. "I want it as a pattern for the
size."

She drew it off and handed it to him, at the same time raising her
eyelids and glancing under his with a little laugh of confusion. His   15
heart responded, and he kissed her; but he could not help feeling that
she was by far too fair a prize for him.

She accompanied him to the door, and Mayne mounted the horse.
They parted, and, waiting to hear her lock herself in, he cantered off
by a bridle-path towards a town about five miles off.   20

It was so early that the surrogate on whom he called had not yet
breakfasted, but he was very willing to see Mayne, and took him at
once to the study. Egbert briefly told him what he wanted; that the
lady he wished to marry was at that very moment in his house, and
could go nowhere else for shelter—hence the earliness and urgency of   25
his errand.

The surrogate seemed to see rather less interest in the
circumstances than Mayne did himself; but he at once prepared the
application for a license. When it was done, he made it up into a
letter, directed it, and placed it on the mantelpiece. "It shall go by   30
this evening's post," he said.

"But," said Egbert, "considering the awkward position this lady is
in, cannot a special messenger be sent for the license? It is only seven
or eight miles to ——, and yet otherwise I must wait for two days'
posts."   35

"Undoubtedly; if anybody likes to pay for it, a special messenger
may be sent."

      5 "and] out of breath. "And   12 a pattern] pattern

"There will be no paying; I am willing to go myself. Do you object?"

"No; if the case is really serious, and the lady is dangerously compromised by every delay."

5 Mayne left the vicarage of the surrogate and again rode off; this time it was towards a well-known cathedral town. He felt bewildering sensations during this stroke for happiness, and went on his journey in that state of mind which takes cognisance of little things, without at the time being conscious of them, though they return vividly upon the 10 memory long after.

He reached the city after a ride of seven additional miles, and soon obtained the precious document, and all else that he required. Returning to the inn where the horse had been rested, rubbed down, and fed, he again crossed the saddle, and at ten minutes past eleven he 15 was back at Fairland. Before going to Monk's Hut, where Geraldine was immured, he hastened straight to the parsonage.

The young clergyman looked curiously at him, and at the bespattered and jaded horse outside. "Surely you are too rash in the matter," he said.

20 "No," said Egbert; "there are weighty reasons why I should be in such haste. The lady has at present no home to go to. She has taken shelter with me. I am doing what I consider best in so awkward a case."

The parson took down his hat, and said, "Very well; I will go to the 25 church at once. You must be quick if it is to be done to-day."

Mayne left the horse for the present in the parson's yard, ran round to the clerk, thence to Monk's Hut, and called Geraldine.

It was, indeed, a hasty preparation for a wedding ceremony that these two made that morning. She was standing at the window, quite 30 ready, and feverish with waiting. Kissing her gaily and breathlessly he directed her by a slightly circuitous path to the church; and, when she had been gone about two minutes, proceeded thither himself by the direct road, so that they met in the porch. Within, the clergyman, clerk, and clerk's wife had already gathered; and Geraldine and 35 Egbert advanced to the communion railing.

Thus they became man and wife.

4 every [*not in HW*]   7 happiness] the happiness of two   15 back] again   18–19 the matter] this matter   20 Egbert] Mayne   22 so awkward] such   30 waiting] fear and waiting

"Now he cannot claim me anyhow," she murmured when the service was ended, as she sank almost fainting upon the arm of Mayne.

"Mr Mayne," said the clergyman, aside to him in the vestry, "what is the name of the family at Tollamore House?"

"Strangely enough, Allenville—the same as hers," said he, coolly.

The parson looked keenly and dubiously at Mayne, and Egbert returned the look, whereupon the other turned aside and said nothing.

Egbert and Geraldine returned to their hermitage on foot, as they had left it; and, by rigorously excluding all thoughts of the future, they felt happy with the same old unreasoning happiness as of six years before, now resumed for the first time since that date.

But it was quite impossible that the hastily-married pair should remain at Monk's Hut unseen and unknown, as they fain would have done. Almost as soon as they had sat down in the house they came to the conclusion that there was no alternative for them but to start at once for Melport, if not for London. The difficulty was to get a conveyance. The only horse obtainable here, though a strong one, had already been tired down by Egbert in the morning, and the nearest village at which another could be had was about two miles off.

"I can walk as far as that," said Geraldine.

"Then walk we will," said Egbert. "It will remove all our difficulty." And, first packing up a small valise, he locked the door and went off with her upon his arm, just as the church clock struck one.

That walk through the woods was as romantic an experience as any they had ever known in their lives, though Geraldine was far from being quite happy. On reaching the village, which was larger than Fairland, they were fortunate enough to secure a carriage without any trouble. The village stood on the turnpike road, and a fly, about to return to Melport, where it had come from, was halting before the inn. Egbert hired it at once, and in little less than an hour and a half bridegroom and bride were comfortably housed in a quiet hotel of the seaport town above mentioned.

21 had] hired

CHAPTER VII

How small a part of time they share
That are so wondrous sweet and fair!

They remained three days at Melport without having come to any
decision on their future movements.

On the third day, at breakfast, Egbert took up the local newspaper
which had been published that morning, and his eye presently
glanced upon a paragraph headed "The Tollamore Elopement."

Before reading it he considered for a moment whether he should lay
the journal aside, and for the present hide its contents from the
tremulous creature opposite. But deeming this unadvisable, he gently
prepared her for the news, and read the paragraph aloud.

It was to the effect that the village of Tollamore and its
neighbourhood had been thrown into an unwonted state of
excitement by the disappearance of Miss Allenville on the eve of the
preparations for her marriage with Lord Bretton, which had been
alluded to in their last number. Simultaneously there had
disappeared from a neighbouring village, whither he had come for a
few months' retirement, a gentleman named Mayne, of considerable
literary reputation in the metropolis, and apparently an old
acquaintance of Miss Allenville's. Efforts had been made to trace the
fugitives by the young lady's father and the distracted bridegroom,
Lord Bretton, but hitherto all their exertions had been unavailing.

Subjoined was another paragraph, entitled "Latest particulars."

"It has just been discovered that Mr Mayne and Miss Allenville are already
man and wife. They were boldly married at the parish church of Fairland,
before any person in the village had the least suspicion who or what they
were. It appears that the lady joined her intended husband early that
morning at the cottage he had taken for the season, that they went to the
church by different paths, and after the ceremony walked out of the parish by
a route as yet unknown. In consequence of this intelligence Lord Bretton has
returned to London, and her father is left alone to mourn the young lady's
rashness."

Egbert lifted his eyes and watched Geraldine as he finished reading.
On perceiving his look she tried to smile. The smile thinned away, for

---

2–3 How . . . fair!] "These violent delights have violent ends, | And in their triumph
die."   24 Latest] Very latest   32–3 the young lady's rashness] her loss

there was not cheerfulness enough to support it long, and she said faintly, "Egbert, what must be done?"

"We must, I suppose, leave this place, darling; charming as our life is here."

"Yes; I fear we must."   5

"London seems to be the spot for us at once, before we attract the attention of the people here."

"How well everything might end," she said, "if my father were induced to welcome you, and make the most of your reputation! I wonder, wonder if he would! In that case there would be little amiss."   10

Mayne, after some reflection, said, "I think that I will go to your father before we leave for town. We are certain to be discovered by somebody or other, either here or in London, and that would bring your father, and there would possibly result a public meeting between him and myself at which words might be uttered which could not be   15 forgotten on either side; so that a private meeting and explanation is safest, before anything of that sort can happen."

"I think," she said, looking to see if he approved of her words as they fell, "I think that a still better course would be for me to go to him—alone."   20

Mayne did not care much about this plan at first; but further discussion gave it a more feasible aspect, since Allenville, though stern and proud, was fond of his daughter, and had never crossed her, except when her whims interfered, as he considered, with her interests. Nothing could unmarry them; and Geraldine's mind would   25 be much more at ease after begging her father's forgiveness. The journey was therefore decided on. They waited till nearly evening, and then, ordering round a brougham, Egbert told the man to drive to Tollamore.

The journey to Geraldine was tedious and oppressive to a degree.   30 When, after two hours' driving, they drew near the park precincts, she said shivering,

"I don't like to drive up to the house, Egbert."

"I will do just as you like. What do you propose?"

"To let him wait in the road, under the three oak trees, while you   35 and I walk to the house."

Egbert humoured her in everything; and when they reached the

14 possibly] probably   16–17 is safest] are safest   27 decided on] decided upon   30 to Geraldine was] was to Geraldine

designated spot the driver was stopped, and they alighted. Carefully wrapping her up he gave her his arm, and they started for Tollamore House at an easy pace through the moonlit park, avoiding the direct road as much as possible.

5   Geraldine spoke but little during the walk, especially when they neared the house, and passed across the smooth broad glade which surrounded it. At sight of the door she seemed to droop, and leant heavily upon him. Egbert more than ever wished to confront Mr Allenville himself; morally and socially it appeared to him the right
10 thing to do. But Geraldine trembled when he again proposed it; and he yielded to her entreaty thus far, that he would wait a few minutes till she had entered and seen her father privately, and prepared the way for Egbert to follow, which he would then do in due course.

The spot in which she desired him to wait was a summer-house
15 under a tree about fifty yards from the lawn front of the house, and commanding a view of the door on this side. She was to enter unobserved by the servants, and go straight to her father, when, should he listen to her with the least show of mildness, she would send out for Egbert to follow. If the worst were to happen, and he were to be
20 enraged with her, refusing to listen to entreaties or explanations, she would hasten out, rejoin Egbert, and depart.

In this little summer-house he embraced her, and bade her adieu, after their honeymoon of three short days. She trembled so much that she could scarcely walk when he let go her hand.

25 "Don't go alone—you are not well," said Egbert.

"Yes, yes, dearest, I am—and I will soon return, so soon!" she answered; and he watched her crossing the grass and advancing, a mere dot, towards the mansion. In a short time the appearance of an oblong of light in the shadowy expanse of wall denoted to him that the
30 door was open: her outline appeared on it; then the door shut her in, and all was shadow as before. Even though they were husband and wife the line of demarcation seemed to be drawn again as rigidly as when he lived at the school.

Egbert waited in the solitude of this place minute by minute,
35 restlessly swinging his foot when seated, at other times walking up and down, and anxiously watching for the arrival of some messenger. Nearly half an hour passed, but no messenger came.

The first sign of life in the neighbourhood of the house was in the

30 appeared on] appeared in

shape of a man on horseback, galloping from the stable entrance. Egbert saw this by looking over the wall at the back of the summer-house; and the man passed along the open drive, vanishing in the direction of the lodge. Mayne, not without some presentiment of ill, wondered what it could mean, but thought it just possible that the horseman was a special messenger sent to catch the late post at the nearest town, as was sometimes done by Squire Allenville. So he curbed his impatience for Geraldine's sake.

Next he observed lights moving in the upper windows of the building. "It has been made known to them all that she is come, and they are preparing a room," he thought hopefully.

But nobody came from the door to welcome him; his existence was apparently forgotten by the whole world. In another ten minutes he saw the Melport brougham that had brought them, creeping slowly up to the house. Egbert went round to the man, and told him to drive to the stables and wait for orders.

From the length of Geraldine's absence, Mayne could not help concluding that the impression produced on her father was of a doubtful kind, not quite favourable enough to warrant her in telling him at once that her husband was in waiting. Still, a sense of his dignity as her husband might have constrained her to introduce him as soon as possible, and he had only agreed to wait a few minutes. Something unexpected must, after all, have occurred. And this supposition was confirmed a moment later by the noise of a horse and carriage coming up the drive. Egbert again looked over into the open park, and saw the vehicle reach the carriage entrance, where somebody alighted and went in.

"Her father away from home perhaps, and now just returned," he said.

He lingered yet another ten minutes, and then could endure no longer. Before he could reach the lawn door through which Geraldine had disappeared it opened. A person came out and, without shutting the door, hastened across to where Egbert stood. The man was a servant, without a hat on, and the moment that he saw Mayne he ran up to him.

"Mr Mayne?" he said.

"It is," said Egbert.

5

10

15

20

25

30

35

---

10 she is] we are   24–5 horse and carriage] carriage and pair   29 said] said to himself

"Mr Allenville desires that you will come with me. There is something serious the matter. Miss Allenville is taken dangerously ill, and she wishes to see you."

"What has happened to her?" gasped Egbert breathlessly.

5 "Miss Allenville came unexpectedly home just now, and directly she saw her father it gave her such a turn that she fainted, and ruptured a blood-vessel internally, and fell upon the floor. They have put her to bed, and the doctor has come, but we are afraid she won't live over it. She has suffered from it before."

10 Egbert did not speak, but walked hastily beside the man-servant. The only recollection that he ever had in after years of entering that house was a vague idea of stags' antlers in a long row on the wall, and a sense of great breadth in the stone staircase as he ascended it. Everything else was in a mist.

15 Mr Allenville, on being informed of his arrival, came out and met him in the corridor.

Egbert's mind was so entirely given up to the one thought that the life of Geraldine was in danger, that he quite forgot the peculiar circumstances under which he met Allenville, and the peculiar 20 behaviour necessary on that account. He seized her father's hand, and said abruptly,

"Where is she? Is the danger great?"

Allenville withdrew his hand, turned, and led the way into his daughter's room, merely saying in a low hard tone, "Your wife is in 25 great danger, sir."

Egbert rushed to the bedside and bent over her in agony not to be described. Allenville sent the attendants from the room, and closed the door.

"Father," she whispered feebly, "I cannot help loving him. Would 30 you leave us alone? We are very dear to each other, and perhaps I shall soon die."

"Anything you wish, child," he said with stern anguish; "and anything can hardly include more." Seeing that she looked hurt at this, he spoke more pleasantly. "I am glad to please you—you know I 35 am, Geraldine—to the utmost." He then went out.

"They would not have let you know if Dr Williams had not

4 gasped] said   7 ruptured . . . internally,] burst a blood-vessel,
14 Everything . . . mist. [*not in HW*]   22 great] past   23 withdrew his
hand, [*not in HW*]

insisted," she said. "I could not speak to explain at first—that's how it is you have been left there so long."

"Geraldine, dear, dear Geraldine, why should all this have come upon us?" he said in broken accents.

"Perhaps it is best," she murmured. "I hardly knew what I was doing when I entered the door, or how I could explain to my father, or what could be done to reconcile him to us. He kept me waiting a little time before he would see me, but at last he came into the room. I felt a fulness on my chest, I could not speak, and then this happened to me. Papa has asked no questions."

A silence followed, interrupted only by her fitful breathing:

> A silence which doth follow talk, that causes
> The baffled heart to speak with sighs and tears.

"Do you love me very much now, Egbert?" she said. "After all my vacillation, do you?"

"Yes—how can you doubt?"

"I do not doubt. I know you love me. But will you stay here till I get better? You must stay. Papa is sure to be friendly with you now."

"Don't agitate yourself, dearest, about me. All is right with me here. Your health is the one thing to be anxious about now."

"I have only been taken ill like this once before in my life, and I thought it would never be again."

As she was not allowed to speak much, he remained holding her hand; and after some time she sank into a light sleep. Egbert then went from the chamber for a moment, and asked the physician, who was in the next room, if there was good hope for her life.

"It is a dangerous attack, and she is very weak," he replied, concealing, though scarcely able to conceal, the curiosity with which he regarded Egbert; for the marriage had now become generally known.

The evening and night wore on. Great events in which he could not participate seemed to be passing over Egbert's head; a stir was in progress, of whose results he grasped but small and fragmentary notions. And, on the other hand, it was mournfully strange to notice her father's behaviour during these hours of doubt. It was only when

11 by her fitful breathing:] now and then by her light breathing—   21–2 "I have...again." [*not in HW*]   27 attack] hemorrhage   32 Egbert's] Mayne's   32–3 stir...results] stir, of whose meaning

he despaired that he looked upon Egbert with tolerance. When he hoped, the young man's presence was hateful to him.

Not knowing what to do when out of her chamber, having nobody near him to whom he could speak on intimate terms, Egbert passed a wretched time of three long days. After watching by her for several hours on the third day, he went downstairs, and into the open air. There intelligence was brought him that another effusion, more violent than any which preceded it, had taken place. Egbert rushed back to her room. Powerful remedies were applied, but none availed. A fainting-fit followed, and in two or three hours it became plain to those who understood that there was no Geraldine for the morrow.

Sometimes she was lethargic, and as if her spirit had already flown; then her mind wandered; but towards the end she was sensible of all that was going on, though unable to speak, her strength being barely enough to enable her to receive an idea.

It was a gentle death. She was as acquiescent as if she had been a saint, which was not the least striking and uncommon feature in the life of this fair and unfortunate lady. Her husband held one tiny hand, remaining all the time on the right side of the bed in a nook beside the curtains, while her father and the rest remained on the left side, never raising their eyes to him, and scarcely ever addressing him.

Everything was so still that her weak act of trying to live seemed a silent wrestling with all the powers of the universe. Pale and hopelessly anxious they all waited and watched the heavy shadows close over her. It might have been thought that death felt for her and took her tenderly. She sighed twice or three times; then her heart stood still; and this strange family alliance was at an end for ever.

---

5 of three long days [*not in HW*]   6 on the third day, [*not in HW*]
8 preceded] had preceded   9 her room] the room   11 Geraldine] fair
Geraldine   17–18 the life of [*not in HW*]   26–7 times . . . ever.] times, and
then her heart lay still.

Our Exploits at West Poley

INTRODUCTION

Hardy's second children's story, 'Our Exploits at West Poley', in content so much more realistic than 'Thieves', has a mystery all its own. Sold in 1883 to the popular children's magazine, the *Youth's Companion*, it was published nine years later—apparently without Hardy's knowledge—by another Boston periodical, the *Household*, an obscure monthly 'DEVOTED TO THE INTERESTS OF THE AMERICAN HOUSEWIFE'. Writing to Howard Bliss on 10 December 1928, Florence Hardy said: 'I have never heard of that story: "Our Exploits at West-Poley" though I remember my husband telling me that he had written a story once, for boys, & it was never published. That may be the one.'[1] The story remained buried in the pages of the *Household* until discovered by Purdy almost sixty years after its first publication in six monthly instalments, November 1892–April 1893.[2]

The story's original purchaser, the *Youth's Companion*, began in 1827 as a Sunday School weekly, but by the 1880s it had become the most popular family magazine in the United States and by the end of the century it was to have a circulation of more than half a million.[3] This enormous success can be attributed almost entirely to Daniel S. Ford, co-owner of the *Companion* as of 1857, sole owner—and editor-publisher—from 1867 until his death in 1899. Ford was an exceptionally talented businessman and astute editor: his famous *Companion* premiums scheme, offering mail-order gifts to readers signing up new subscribers, vastly increased circulation, as did his inclusion of material which would appeal to adults as well as children. The blatantly didactic and Christian fiction originally published by the

[1] Beinecke.
[2] Purdy's account of the publication history—much less detailed but not substantially different in outline from mine—first appeared in his introduction to *Our Exploits at West Poley* [limited edn.] (London: Geoffrey Cumberlege, Oxford University Press, 1952), pp. vii–xii.
[3] Richard Cutts, Introduction to *Index to The Youth's Companion 1871–1929*, i (Metuchen, NJ: Scarecrow Press, 1972), pp. viii ff.; entry for Daniel Sharp Ford in *Dictionary of American Biography*.

Companion gradually gave way to stories which were entertaining as well as educational and even—within the obvious limits imposed by the necessity of supplying several stories each week—of some literary merit.

Recognizing that, if children were reading 'adult' novels by Cooper and Scott, there seemed no reason why good 'children's literature' should not have an equally wide appeal, the *Companion* developed a reputation for high literary standards and its contributions were increasingly written by celebrated authors. In the 1880s, for example, stories by Wilkie Collins, Charles Reade, and Harriet Beecher Stowe appeared, even though most of the *Companion* authors remained undistinguished, many being staff members writing under numerous pseudonyms.[4] It was presumably Hardy's established reputation as a novelist that made Ford, in 1883, seek to include him in the *Companion* list of authors. Although it is conceivable that Ford had by some chance read and liked 'Thieves' in *Father Christmas*, there is certainly no reference to it in the surviving *Companion* correspondence, nor, for that matter, any indication that a specific type of children's story was requested—beyond, of course, the expectation that it would have, as Hardy himself put it, 'a healthy tone'.[5]

On 5 April 1883 Hardy accepted the *Companion* offer:

In answer to your letter of the 20th ult. I am happy to be able to state definitely that I will undertake to write the story on the terms detailed in your previous communication. It is, of course, understood that the tale will appear as a serial solely in the Youth's Companion. Your offer to allow publication in book form in the United States only on condition that I receive the usual royalty I gladly accept. My publishers are Messrs Holt & Co. of New York. I propose to deliver the manuscript not later than the end of the present year.

With regard to the title and subject: since writing my former letter I have roughly thought out a plot which at present seems promising. But I should prefer not to commit myself to a title till later on in the year. The general scope, or subtitle, however, might be announced as "A rural tale of adventure in the West of England."

You may depend upon my using my best efforts to please your numerous readers; & that the story shall have a healthy tone, suitable to intelligent youth of both sexes.[6]

[4] See Cutts, Introduction to *Index*, pp. ix–xiii.   [5] *CL* i. 116.   [6] Ibid.

Beginning 'Dear Sirs', the letter was presumably addressed to Perry Mason & Co.,[7] though effectively written to Ford, the company name being an invention designed to preserve his anonymity. At least three earlier letters had been exchanged: the publisher's 'previous communication' presumably soliciting a contribution; Hardy's 'former letter' tentatively[8] accepting—or at least expressing interest in—the offer; and the *Companion* letter of 20 March 1883 ('the 20th ult.'). It is of course possible that there was a still earlier letter in which Hardy approached the firm, their 'previous communication' being a response to his, but the fact that at the time of writing his 'former letter' he appears to have had little or no idea of his subject suggests otherwise. For Hardy to have accepted an offer from a children's magazine is not especially surprising, given that the remuneration was probably generous (in subsequent correspondence he wrote of having been dealt with 'very fairly')[9] and that he had recently been experimenting with different forms and modes of fiction in attempting to establish his literary career. During the preceding five years he had published more short fiction than ever before—nine stories as varied in kind and quality as 'Fellow-Townsmen', 'A Legend of the Year Eighteen Hundred and Four', 'The Three Strangers', and 'The Romantic Adventures of a Milkmaid'—and had also produced a sociological essay, a dramatization, three novels, and at least one poem.[10] Nor would the composition of a children's story have distracted him from more 'serious' pursuits, since 'Exploits' marks the end of the period of mixed—and, in terms of literary value, relatively minor—production that preceded the beginning of work on *The Mayor of Casterbridge* in 1884.

In spite of his assuring the publishers that he would use his 'best efforts to please your numerous readers', it is doubtful that Hardy expended much time or energy on the tale: its numerous internal inconsistencies[11] were perhaps caused by editorial excisions but could

---

[7] As Purdy and Millgate have assumed.

[8] Note TH's use of 'definitely' in the first sentence of the 5 Apr. letter.

[9] To W. P. Frith [late 1884?] (*CL* i. 129).

[10] 'The Dorchester Labourer', *The Mistress of the Farm*, *The Trumpet-Major*, *A Laodicean*, *Two on a Tower*, and 'The Levelled Churchyard'. The other five stories published were 'The Impulsive Lady of Croome Castle' (collected as 'The Duchess of Hamptonshire'), 'Indiscretion', 'The Distracted Young Preacher', 'What the Shepherd Saw', and 'Benighted Travellers' (collected as 'The Honourable Laura').

[11] E.g., the boys visit East Poley on the third day after diverting the river but are told there that the water first appeared 'Yesterday afternoon'; see also the explanatory notes to pp. 191. 6, 202. 30–1, 205. 31, 206. 9, 211. 24.

equally have been the result of authorial carelessness. That Hardy may himself have recognized the inferiority of the story—at least in comparison with his best work—is suggested by the distinctly defensive tone of the letter he sent with the manuscript on 5 November 1883:

In constructing the story I have been careful to avoid making it a mere precept in narrative—a fatal defect, to my thinking, in tales for the young, or for the old. That it carries with it, nevertheless, a sufficiently apparent moral, will I think be admitted.

The important features of plot & incident have received my best attention. The end of each chapter will probably form a sufficiently striking point for breaking off the weekly instalment; but equally good places may be discovered elsewhere, if your editor should desire a different division.[12]

Although 'A Story of English Rustic Life, by Thomas Hardy' headed the list of 'Illustrated Serial Stories' promised for 1884 in the 22 November 1883 *Youth's Companion*, the absence of a specific title suggests that the magazine had gone to press before the arrival of Hardy's manuscript: the description used echoes Hardy's 5 April suggestion that the story could be advertised as 'A rural tale of adventure in the West of England'. When the manuscript did arrive it was apparently not read with entire enthusiasm, for on 14 March 1884 Hardy wrote: 'I return to you, by registered book post, the copy you were good enough to send for correction. The story seems to me to go naturally enough now, & I hope you will think the same—still more that your numerous young readers will think so.'[13] The precise nature of what Hardy was returning remains unknown: it may have been corrected proofs or, more probably—given his reference in the same letter to having 'no correct copy from which [the story] could be printed in England'—a revised manuscript. What is clear is that Hardy complied with a request that he should make substantial alterations to his original text.

Almost three years later, however, the story had not appeared, and on 13 December 1886 Hardy replied to an evidently apologetic (though no longer extant) communication from the associate editor, William Rideing:

please do not pay any attention to the fact that I cannot avail myself of it here as long as you keep it unpublished. The proprietors of the Companion treated me very courteously in the matter, & I should much prefer that you hold it

[12] *CL* i. 123.   [13] Ibid. 126–7.

back as long as there is any chance of your having room for it, to your publishing it elsewhere to oblige me. Possibly if you have no space for it at length you may some day think fit to produce it in a somewhat abridged form—it being a story of an imaginative kind suitable for a Christmas number, or such like.[14]

Hardy's willingness to allow abridgement again seems expressive of his low opinion of the story,[15] as does his apparent indifference to its subsequent fate. Unmentioned in later surviving correspondence or in *Life*, 'Exploits' was not necessarily forgotten—'Indiscretion' does not figure in the autobiography either but was in fact being discussed as late as 1913.[16] 'Memory lapses' at times quite suited Hardy's purposes. And certainly in his later years he tended to disparage his minor fiction in, for example, his 'hunting very small deer' remark about *Poor Man* (see p. 85) and his comment about his 'stray short stories' not being 'worth reprinting'.[17] Perhaps he had little confidence in his ability to write children's fiction and was thus blinded to the merits 'Exploits' did possess, thinking it must be poor indeed—and therefore just as well consigned to oblivion—if the publishers had seen fit to hold it back for so long.

That they should have kept a manuscript for several years was not in itself unusual. W. P. Frith's 'Youthful Models', published in June 1890, must have undergone similar treatment if it was sent shortly after Hardy wrote to the painter about the magazine's credibility—presumably in late 1884, but at least before the June 1885 move to Max Gate.[18] As one *Companion* editor later recalled, 'Manuscripts that might conceivably be used at some future time, possibly years ahead ... were bought in appalling numbers, and filed away in great cabinets, under the classifications—Boys', Girls', Family, Adventure, Humorous—to which they might be assigned some day in the standardized make-up of the paper.'[19]

What was unprecedented—sufficiently so as to become an office legend, according to Charles Miner Thompson (associate editor of

[14] Ibid. 158; note that 'Thieves' was published in a Christmas annual.
[15] He did, however, offer to condense *The Woodlanders* if the *Independent* editors would agree to publish it (*CL* i. 141).
[16] *CL* iv. 306.
[17] To FH, 22 July 1898 (ibid. ii. 197); he did, however, subsequently publish the *Changed Man* collection.
[18] *CL* i. 129; Purdy and Millgate date the letter '[Late 1884?]'.
[19] Quoted by Purdy (Introduction to *Exploits*, p. x).

the *Companion*, 1890–1911; editor-in-chief, 1911–25)—was Ford's giving a story by so distinguished an author to his son-in-law, Hartshorn, for whom he had purchased the small and not particularly prosperous *Household*.[20] Although 'DEVOTED TO THE INTERESTS OF THE AMERICAN HOUSEWIFE', the *Household* resembled the *Companion* quite closely in content and especially in format. Both were primarily short-story papers which also included 'educational' essays, poems, anecdotal pieces, a children's page, a health column, and so forth. More striking are the similarities in layout: the four-column structure, the headline design, the decorative rule between items, the spacing and type-face of the titles—to say nothing of the fine-print 'For The Household' (adapted from the familiar 'For the Companion') preceding the titles of original contributions. (In the case of 'Exploits' the statement is of course false, though it does serve to distinguish the story from previously published material.) Even the firm of Russell & Richardson, the source of the illustrations for 'Exploits' and numerous other *Household* stories, was regularly (though not exclusively) employed by the *Companion*.

Hartshorn may simply have been attempting to follow Ford's recipe for success as exemplified by the *Companion*, but he could equally well have been a figure-head, owner but only nominally editor of the *Household*, allowing his father-in-law to make the major decisions. This would help to explain not only the transference of manuscripts from the *Companion* files to the *Household*—for 'Exploits' was apparently one of several[21]—but also the sharing of staff. Hezekiah Butterworth, for example, was employed by the *Companion* from 1870 to 1894, yet frequently contributed to the *Household*, often writing as a staff-member; his article entitled 'Sordello's Story', for instance, concludes: 'A good subject for a literary society might be—"Which is the greater poem, Sordello or Paracelsus?" Kindly send us your decision.'[22]

---

[20] Ibid., pp. x–xi; TH presumably never knew of his story's publication, but he had heard of the *Household*, for on 25 Jan. 1886 he wrote to Henry Holt:

> Could you inform me whether the American periodicals called "The Household Magazine", "Fireside Companion", "Fireside at Home" (or some such title), & "Ballou's Monthly(?)" (Boston) are of fairly good literary standing & monthly, or weekly? My inquiry is made in reference to advance sheets, &c, for which I sometimes have offers, or have to find a place. (*CL* i. 140)

[21] According to Thompson (Purdy, Introduction to *Exploits*, p. xi).

[22] *Household*, Feb. 1893, 41.

It was in fact Butterworth's 'Hannah, who Sang Countre' [*sic*] which was chosen as the feature-story for the issue of the *Household* containing the first instalment of 'Exploits'. If Hartshorn was making the editorial decisions, he must have shared his father-in-law's not particularly high opinion of Hardy's fiction—or at least of 'Exploits'—for he, too, had held back the manuscript. Apparently given to him some time after 1886[23] but before Thompson joined the *Companion* in 1890,[24] the story was finally published in six monthly instalments from November 1892 to April 1893. On the cover of the November *Household* it is merely listed without reference to an author as ' "Our Exploits at West Poley." A Story for Boys' and placed below ' "Hannah, who Sang Countre" By HEZEKIAH BUTTERWORTH'. (The cover illustration is also taken from 'Hannah'.) Hardy's name does not in fact appear until the conclusion of the first instalment and is omitted altogether from the fourth, though it replaces the subtitle in the fifth and sixth. These absences to some extent account for the story remaining unnoticed. Perhaps, as Purdy suggested, the readers of the *Household* were not the readers of *Tess*,[25] but even if they had been they could have failed to recognize the connection between the Hardy of 'Exploits' and the author of *Tess*, not only because Hardy was unknown as a children's writer but also because even 'THE AMERICAN HOUSEWIFE' might have expected the magazine to play up such a celebrated contributor. It is in fact unlikely that many adults read the story, let alone registered the author's name, since the *Household* circulation was not extensive and those who did subscribe could easily have passed on to their children, unread, 'A Story for Boys' along with the regular 'Children's Page'.

That a boys' adventure story—even one written by Hardy—was not a high publication priority in a women's magazine is altogether less surprising than the *Companion* editors' original decision not to use it themselves. Since copy of some kind was sent to Hardy for correction in early 1884, the story was evidently being considered for publication in the near future: this was not a case of a manuscript being purchased and immediately shelved—the filing away came later.[26]

---

[23] It was evidently still being considered (if not very enthusiastically) for publication by the *Companion* when TH wrote to Rideing on 13 Dec. 1886 (*CL* i. 158–9).

[24] Purdy, Introduction to *Exploits*, x. [25] Ibid. p. xii.

[26] That what was eventually given to Hartshorn was in fact manuscript rather than corrected proof is suggested by the nature of the compositorial errors, many of them evident misreadings of Hardy's hand: 'Mondip' for 'Mendip', 'Chuddar' for 'Cheddar', 'pills' for 'frills', 'leach' for 'loach', and so forth. Alternatively, the *Household*

Why 'Exploits' was held back is not known. Although not Hardy's best work, it is certainly superior to the typical *Companion* story of the 1880s. Perhaps the moral—though, as Hardy claimed, 'sufficiently apparent'—was not sufficiently conventional or, more probably, not formulaically embodied in the plot, the unmitigated success of Steve's 'Exceptionally smart actions' in fact tending to contradict rather than to prove that 'Quiet perseverance in clearly defined courses is, as a rule, better than the erratic exploits that may do much harm'. In spite of Steve's sententious remorsefulness when faced with the rising waters (an unsubtle attempt to make the moral apparent), he again acts out of what he himself has called 'the foolishness of presumption' in blowing up the cave: even a youthful reader would realize that, if prior approval had been sought, it would not have been granted, thus leaving the village water supply unsecured for future generations. Unlike most of the *Companion* fiction of this period, the story was indeed no 'mere precept in narrative'[27] and would in fact have been more apt to incite reckless heroics than to curb them. Perhaps, too, Hardy's inability to simplify moral issues even in a children's story met with editorial disfavour, for the boys discover that there is no unambiguous formula for right behaviour, 'good brains' being as necessary as 'a good heart' in a world where 'it is next to impossible ... to do good to one set of folks without doing harm to another'.

But in the end the most logical explanation for the postponement of publication is that the story was not thought likely to prove interesting enough to the *Companion* readers, as is implied by Hardy's 13 December 1886 letter to Rideing: 'Our children here are younger for their age than yours; & possibly the story is too juvenile for your side of the sea. I fancy you may be mistaken in that; but of course I do not know as well as yourselves.'[28] At times slow-moving, it was presumably still more so as Hardy first wrote it, and perhaps even as he revised it: the *Household* text appears to have been abridged, the first two instalments referring to eight chapters rather than to the six

setting-copy could have been *uncorrected Companion* proof, though once the type was broken up there would have been little reason for keeping it, beyond, of course, its superior cleanliness to the corrected copy, whether manuscript or proof, returned by Hardy in Mar. 1884.

[27] *CL* i. 123; it has, however, been read as one: e.g. Pinion (*Old Mrs Chundle and Other Stories* (London: Macmillan, 1977), 235) maintains that 'All is carefully calculated to discourage rashness.'

[28] *CL* i. 158–9.

actually published, and chapters IV and V being considerably shorter than the others.[29] Similarly suggestive of editorial excisions are the numerous redundant or missing quotation marks, and even the various narrative inconsistencies.[30] It is impossible to know how extensive such revisions would have been—perhaps, as the *Household* subtitles suggest, the material for as much as two chapters was cut. Sharing some of the *Companion* staff, the *Household* may also have shared its policy with regard to contributors' texts. Certainly the *Companion* editors were accustomed to taking considerable liberties, especially with the work of non-professional writers. For example, a manuscript by 'Charles Ellis, East Saginaw, Michigan' elicited the following comment from C. A. Stephens, author and *Companion* staff-member:

Contains some information relative to the migration of wild geese[,] brant and ducks and their arrival in northern Iowa, Minnesota and Dakota; the story of the hunt is rather tame; but the incident of the upset of the tin boat could be made considerably more of. With a day's work, a fairly readable sketch can be made of this.[31]

The manuscript was 'Paid for simply as material' and eventually reworked—and signed—by Frank W. Calkins, a frequent *Companion* contributor.[32] Hardy's reputation had perhaps deterred the *Companion* editors from freely rewriting 'Exploits' until it, too, would fit the mould, and if, as appears, they remained dissatisfied with the revisions he made at their request they perhaps preferred to shelve the story than to send it back a second time. That Hardy had certainly not shortened his material to the extent required is implicit in his 13 December 1886 suggestion that Rideing 'produce it in a somewhat abridged form' if there was 'no space for it at length'.[33]

In attempting to write for those whom he described as 'intelligent youth of both sexes', 'young people who are more than children, yet not quite mature',[34] Hardy perhaps judged them by memories of himself at their age, over-estimating their intellectual interests. It is unlikely that many young teenagers, especially in the United States, would have appreciated the references to Carlyle and Bentham, still

---

[29] First remarked by Purdy (Introduction to *Exploits*, p. xi).

[30] See, e.g., emendations to pp. 178. 36, 191. 32, 195. 8, 203. 31, and n. 11.

[31] Quoted by Cutts (Introduction to *Index*, p. x); original in Bowdoin College, Brunswick, Maine.

[32] Cutts, Introduction to *Index*, p. x.   [33] *CL* i. 158.   [34] Ibid. 116, 129.

less the classical allusions and playful use of schoolboy Latin. More excitement and less literariness would doubtless have met with greater acceptance. Not that 'Exploits' is without incident: rising waters and exploding caves are certainly the stuff of successful adventure stories, but these dramatic episodes are only a small part of a much more leisurely paced overall narrative. The exploration of the cave, the gulling of the East Poley boys, and even the confrontation with the would-be water-thieves are certainly of a different order from the sensational *Companion* tales of Sioux raids, train crashes, naval battles, and so forth. Yet the gentle charm of 'Exploits', what Henry Reed described as 'some small sort of eternal summer',[35] lies precisely in its unhurried evocation of place and character, and especially in its relatively low-key dramas of rural life.

Purdy suggested that the presentation of Leonard, the younger of the two boys, embodied 'a reminiscence of Hardy himself and his boyhood',[36] and it does indeed seem possible that 'Exploits', with its moralizing about thoughtful prudence, may represent an attempt to justify Hardy's own youthful passivity. There can be no doubt, however, that the doughty and 'truly courageous' Steve emerges more sympathetically than his cautious cousin, and it seems in fact unlikely that Hardy had in mind 'originals'—either himself or anyone else— for the two boys, any more than he appears to have modelled West Poley on a specific geographical location. There certainly appears to be no factual basis for Robert Gittings's association of the story with the family of Hardy's cousin Emma Cary,[37] who lived in Faulkland, a small village in the Somerset parish of Hemington. Gittings claims that the ages of the Cary boys corresponded to those of Leonard (thirteen) and Steve (fifteen or sixteen), but the 1881 census returns for Faulkland[38] show that at that date—two years before 'Exploits' was written—the eldest Cary son was nineteen, the second twelve, and the third eight.

As for Faulkland itself as a possible setting for this 'tale of the Mendips' (Hardy's suggested subtitle),[39] the identification is tempting only because it is not an obvious one. That Hardy was not thinking of a place famous for its caves—such as Wookey, where the

[35] Henry Reed, rev. of *Our Exploits at West Poley*, *Listener*, 9 Oct. 1952, 600.
[36] Purdy, Introduction to *Exploits*, p. xii.
[37] Robert Gittings, *The Older Hardy* (London: Heinemann, 1978), 39.
[38] RG11/2404.
[39] *CL* i. 123.

1985 film version of the story (see p. 167) was apparently shot—is made clear by Leonard's initial scepticism about the West Poley hills containing anything more than 'stone and earth', the Mendip Caves, as he points out, being 'nearer Cheddar'. But Faulkland seems *too* improbable a location: though within the Mendip region, it is in an area geographically quite distinct from that around Wookey and Cheddar—by the 1880s, when the Carys emigrated to Australia, it had become predominantly a coal-mining village[40]—and the neighbourhood offers little in the way of limestone caves or any of the other topographical features exploited in Hardy's narrative.

That Hardy knew the Mendips there can be no doubt: they fell within his matured conception of Wessex and lay in or near the routes from Dorchester to such places as Bristol, Bath, Glastonbury, and Wells, with all of which he was familiar from a relatively early date. Even if he did visit his cousin during the more than twenty years she lived in Faulkland,[41] therefore—a circumstance by no means established—it cannot be assumed that he chose that neighbourhood or any other specific part of the Mendip region as his setting. Nick's Pocket, Grim Billy, Giant's Ear, and Goblin's Cellar do not appear to be actual cave names, and the use of 'twin' village names in Somerset—for example, West and East Pennard or, indeed, West and East Coker—is too common to suggest any specific identification. Ultimately, it seems impossible to be more precise than Denys Kay-Robinson who, in *The Landscape of Thomas Hardy*, can only point to 'certain Mendip caves' as the scene of the boys' adventures.[42]

The significance of 'Exploits', then—unlike that of 'Old Mrs Chundle' and 'The Doctor's Legend'—lies not in Hardy's fictionalization of the actual, but in his experimentation with form, and especially with point of view, as he attempted to write for a younger audience. More adventurous than 'Thieves' in its combination of elements from seemingly antithetical genres—allegory and realism, pastoral romance and adventure story—it is in some ways less

---

[40] As shown by the 1881 census. See also *Mendip: A New Study*, ed. Robert Atthill (Newton Abbot: David & Charles, 1976), fig. 3; and C. G. Down and A. J. Warrington, *The History of the Somerset Coalfield* (Newton Abbot: David & Charles, n.d.), 204–5.

[41] It appears from the 1861 (RG9/1657) and 1871 (RG10/2437) census returns that she moved to Faulkland immediately upon her marriage to Thomas Cary in August 1860 and remained there until the family's departure for Australia in 1884.

[42] Denys Kay-Robinson, *The Landscape of Thomas Hardy* (Exeter: Webb & Bower, 1984), 194.

successful as children's literature, its greater length increasing the difficulty of sustaining the kind of narrative interest required by most juvenile readers. (That Hardy felt somewhat at a loss when it came to inventing appropriate new material can perhaps be inferred by his inclusion in both stories of scenes in which children impersonate magicians.) In truth the children's story about boys' exploits seems of less interest than the adult's story about a man's presentation of those adventures, especially since Leonard, as a retrospective narrator reviewing the past with the advantages of hindsight and maturity, is clearly engaged, consciously or otherwise, in attempts to manipulate the reader's response in ways favourable to himself.[43]

'Exploits' as children's literature is not, however, without its admirers. Purdy's edition, published by Oxford University Press in 1952 in both a limited edition of 1,050 copies and in a (reset) trade edition, was sufficiently popular to justify the production in 1978 of a new edition, promoted specifically—and successfully—as a children's book. The 1978 edition was also brought out in paperback in 1981 and is still in print, as is the Puffin Classics edition, published in 1983. 'Exploits' has also been collected several times, not only in Pinion's *Old Mrs Chundle and Other Stories* but also in volumes intended for a juvenile audience. It is, for example, one of the ten stories in Roger Lancelyn Green's *Tales of Make-Believe* (London: Dent, 1960), a collection which also includes Dickens's 'The Adventures of Captain Boldheart' and Kipling's 'The Tabu Table', and it is the leading story—taking precedence over selections from Twain's *The Adventures of Tom Sawyer* and Dennis McEldowney's 'By the Lake'—in James Stark's *Our Exploits at West Poley and Other Cave Stories* (Agincourt: Book Society of Canada, 1972), a school reader complete with 'Notes, Work and Study Programme, and Suggested Projects'. An adaptation by E. C. Parnwell, *Our Cave at West Poley*, was also published in 1953 as one of the Oxford University Press's Tales Retold for Easy Reading—other titles include *Tales from Gulliver's Travels*, *A Christmas Carol*, *Great Expectations*, *Jane Eyre*, *Wives and Daughters*, and *Adam Bede*—a series apparently designed for Third-World children learning English.[44] Further proof of the story's popularity can be found in its translation into Russian by S. Maizels and J. Polykova

---

[43] See Pamela Dalziel, 'A Critical Edition of Thomas Hardy's Uncollected Stories', D.Phil. thesis (University of Oxford, 1989), 363 ff.

[44] Words such as 'cheese', 'apples', 'inn', 'beard', 'pool', and 'drown' are footnoted.

(Moscow: Detgiz, 1959) and in its two adaptations as a film by the Children's Film (and Television) Foundation ('The Secret Cave', 1953; 'Exploits at West Poley', 1985).

BIBLIOGRAPHICAL DESCRIPTION

Periodical Publication

The Household, 25 (Nov.–Dec. 1892); 26 (Jan.–Apr. 1893) (6 instalments)

November, 343, col. 1; 344, cols. 1–4: chapter I. The title reads:
For The Household. | OUR EXPLOITS AT WEST POLEY. [*swash* A] | A Story for Boys. | EIGHT CHAPTERS.—CHAPTER I. There is one illustration with the caption, 'Our Exploits at West Poley.' Hardy's name appears at the conclusion of the instalment.

December, 384, cols. 3–4; 385, cols. 1–4; 386, col. 1: chapter II. The title appears in the same form as in the November issue, except that the chapter number has been changed and the following line added:
How We Shone in the Eyes of the Public.
There is one illustration by 'RUSSELL & RICHARDSON SC.' with the caption, ' "There we stood, waving our white sticks, hoping we should succeed." ' Hardy's name appears at the conclusion of the instalment.

January, 5, cols. 2–4; 6, cols. 1–2: chapter III. The first three lines of the title appear in the same form as in the November and December issues; the lines following read:
SIX CHAPTERS.   CHAPTER III. | How We Were Caught in Our Own | Trap.
Hardy's name appears at the conclusion of the instalment.

February, 41, col. 4; 42, cols. 1–4: chapter IV. The first and second lines of the title appear in the same form as the second and third lines in the earlier issues; the lines following read:
CHAPTER IV. | How Older Heads than Ours Became | Concerned.
There is one illustration by 'RUSSELL & RICHARDSON SC.' with the caption, ' "Hu, hu, hu, hu! O, ho—I am drownded!" ' Hardy's name does not appear in this instalment.

March, 78, cols. 1–4; 79, col. 1: chapter V. The title reads:
For the Household. | OUR EXPLOITS AT WEST POLEY.

[*swash* A] | THOMAS HARDY. | CHAPTER V. | How We Became Close Allies with the | Villagers.

There are two illustrations with the captions, ' "Upheld by the rope I floated across to the spot under the opening." ' and ' "Now, my boy, we are all here. What have you to tell?" '

April, 114, cols. 1–4; 115, cols. 1–3: chapter VI. The first four lines of the title appear in the same form as in the March issue, except that the definite article preceding 'Household' has been capitalized and the chapter number changed; the line following reads:

How all Our Difficulties Came to an End.

There is one illustration with the caption, ' "It was Steve— apparently dead, or unconscious." '

NOTE ON THE TEXT

The copy-text is the sole surviving authoritative text, the November 1892–April 1893 *Household* printing (*H*). Since the only variants are editorial emendations of the copy-text, lemmata and recorded variants are not followed by sigla.

OUR EXPLOITS AT WEST POLEY

A Story For Boys

CHAPTER I

On a certain fine evening of early autumn—I will not say how many years ago—I alighted from a green gig, before the door of a farmhouse at West Poley, a village in Somersetshire. I had reached the age of thirteen, and though rather small for my age, I was robust and active. My father was a schoolmaster, living about twenty miles off. I had arrived on a visit to my Aunt Draycot, a farmer's widow, who, with her son Stephen, or Steve, as he was invariably called by his friends, still managed the farm, which had been left on her hands by her deceased husband.

Steve promptly came out to welcome me. He was two or three years my senior, tall, lithe, ruddy, and somewhat masterful withal. There was that force about him which was less suggestive of intellectual power than (as Carlyle said of Cromwell) "Doughtiness—the courage and faculty to do."

When the first greetings were over, he informed me that his mother was not indoors just then, but that she would soon be home. "And, do you know, Leonard," he continued, rather mournfully, "she wants me to be a farmer all my life, like my father."

"And why not be a farmer all your life, like your father?" said a voice behind us.

We turned our heads, and a thoughtful man in a threadbare, yet well-fitting suit of clothes, stood near, as he paused for a moment on his way down to the village.

"The straight course is generally the best for boys," the speaker continued, with a smile. "Be sure that professions you know little of have as many drudgeries attaching to them as those you know well—it is only their remoteness that lends them their charm." Saying this he nodded and went on.

"Who is he?" I asked.

"Oh—he's nobody," said Steve. "He's a man who has been all over the world, and tried all sorts of lives, but he has never got rich, and now he has retired to this place for quietness. He calls himself the Man who has Failed."

After this explanation I thought no more of the Man who had
5 Failed than Steve himself did; neither of us was at that time old enough to know that the losers in the world's battle are often the very men who, too late for themselves, have the clearest perception of what constitutes success; while the successful men are frequently blinded to the same by the tumult of their own progress.

10 To change the subject, I said something about the village and Steve's farm-house—that I was glad to see the latter was close under the hills, which I hoped we might climb before I returned home. I had expected to find these hills much higher, and I told Steve so without disguise.

15 "They may not be very high, but there's a good deal inside 'em," said my cousin, as we entered the house, as if he thought me hypercritical, "a good deal more than you think."

"Inside 'em?" said I, "stone and earth, I suppose."

"More than that," said he. "You have heard of the Mendip Caves,
20 haven't you?"

"But they are nearer Cheddar," I said.

"There are one or two in this place, likewise," Steve answered me. "I can show them to you to-morrow. People say there are many more, only there is no way of getting into them."

25 Being disappointed in the height of the hills, I was rather incredulous about the number of the caves; but on my saying so, Steve rejoined, "Whatever you may think, I went the other day into one of 'em—Nick's Pocket—that's the cavern nearest here, and found that what was called the end was not really the end at all. Ever since then
30 I've wanted to be an explorer, and not a farmer; and in spite of that old man, I think I am right."

At this moment my aunt came in, and soon after we were summoned to supper; and during the remainder of the evening nothing more was said about the Mendip Caves. It would have been
35 just as well for us two boys if nothing more had been said about them at all; but it was fated to be otherwise, as I have reason to remember.

Steve did not forget my remarks, which, to him, no doubt, seemed to show a want of appreciation for the features of his native district.

19† Mendip] Mondip   21† Cheddar] Chuddar

The next morning he returned to the subject, saying, as he came indoors to me suddenly, "I mean to show ye a little of what the Mendips contain, Leonard, if you'll come with me. But we must go quietly, for my mother does not like me to prowl about such places, because I get muddy. Come here, and see the preparations I have made."

He took me into the stable, and showed me a goodly supply of loose candle ends; also a bit of board perforated with holes, into which the candles would fit, and shaped to a handle at one extremity. He had provided, too, some slices of bread and cheese, and several apples. I was at once convinced that caverns which demanded such preparations must be something larger than the mere gravel-pits I had imagined; but I said nothing beyond assenting to the excursion.

It being the time after harvest, while there was not much to be attended to on the farm, Steve's mother could easily spare him, "to show me the neighbourhood," as he expressed it, and off we went, with our provisions and candles.

A quarter of a mile, or possibly a little more—for my recollections on matters of distance are not precise—brought us to the mouth of the cave called Nick's Pocket, the way thither being past the village houses, and the mill, and across the mill-stream, which came from a copious spring in the hillside some distance further up. I seem to hear the pattering of that mill-wheel when we walked by it, as well as if it were going now; and yet how many years have passed since the sound beat last upon my ears.

The mouth of the cave was screened by bushes, the face of the hill behind being, to the best of my remembrance, almost vertical. The spot was obviously well known to the inhabitants, and was the haunt of many boys, as I could see by footprints; though the cave, at this time, with others thereabout, had been but little examined by tourists and men of science.

We entered unobserved, and no sooner were we inside, than Steve lit a couple of candles and stuck them into the board. With these he showed the way. We walked on over a somewhat uneven floor, the novelty of the proceeding impressing me, at first, very agreeably; the light of the candles was sufficient, at first, to reveal only the nearer stalactites, remote nooks of the cavern being left in well-nigh their original mystic shadows. Steve would occasionally turn, and accuse me, in arch tones, of being afraid, which accusation I (as a boy would naturally do) steadfastly denied; though even now I can recollect that I experienced more than once some sort of misgiving.

"As for me—I have been there hundreds of times," Steve said proudly. "We West Poley boys come here continually to play 'I spy,'
5 and think nothing of running in with no light of any sort. Come along, it is home to me. I said I would show you the inside of the Mendips, and so I will."

Thus we went onward. We were now in the bowels of the Mendip hills—a range of limestone rocks stretching from the shores of the
10 Bristol Channel into the middle of Somersetshire. Skeletons of great extinct beasts, and the remains of prehistoric men have been found thereabouts since that time; but at the date of which I write science was not so ardent as she is now, in the pursuit of the unknown; and we boys could only conjecture on subjects in which the boys of the
15 present generation are well-informed.

The dim sparkle of stalactite, which had continually appeared above us, now ranged lower and lower over our heads, till at last the walls of the cave seemed to bar further progress.

"There, this spot is what everybody calls the end of Nick's Pocket,"
20 observed Steve, halting upon a mount of stalagmite, and throwing the beams of the candles around. "But let me tell you," he added, "that here is a little arch, which I and some more boys found the other day. We did not go under it, but if you are agreed we will go in now and see how far we can get, for the fun of the thing. I brought these pieces of
25 candle on purpose." Steve looked what he felt—that there was a certain grandeur in a person like himself, to whom such mysteries as caves were mere playthings, because he had been born close alongside them. To do him justice, he was not altogether wrong, for he was a truly courageous fellow, and could look dangers in the face
30 without flinching.

"I think we may as well leave fun out of the question," I said, laughing; "but we will go in."

Accordingly he went forward, stooped, and entered the low archway, which, at first sight, appeared to be no more than a slight
35 recess. I kept close at his heels. The arch gave access to a narrow tunnel or gallery, sloping downwards, and presently terminating in another cave, the floor of which spread out into a beautiful level of sand and shingle, interspersed with pieces of rock. Across the middle

10† middle of] middle of the

of this subterranean shore, as it might have been called, flowed a pellucid stream. Had my thoughts been in my books, I might have supposed we had descended to the nether regions, and had reached the Stygian shore; but it was out of sight, out of mind, with my classical studies then.

Beyond the stream, at some elevation, we could see a delightful recess in the crystallized stone work, like the apse of a Gothic church.

"How tantalizing!" exclaimed Steve, as he held the candles above his head, and peered across. "If it were not for this trickling riband of water, we could get over and climb up into that arched nook, and sit there like kings on a crystal throne!"

"Perhaps it would not look so wonderful if we got close to it," I suggested. "But, for that matter, if you had a spade, you could soon turn the water out of the way, and into that hole." The fact was, that just at that moment I had discovered a low opening on the left hand, like a human mouth, into which the stream would naturally flow, if a slight barrier of sand and pebbles were removed.

On looking there also, Steve complimented me on the sharpness of my eyes. "Yes," he said, "we could scrape away that bank, and the water would go straight into the hole surely enough. And we will. Let us go for a spade!"

I had not expected him to put the idea into practice; but it was no sooner said than done. We retraced our steps, and in a few minutes found ourselves again in the open air, where the sudden light overpowered our eyes for awhile.

"Stay here, while I run home," he said. "I'll not be long."

I agreed, and he disappeared. In a very short space he came back with a spade in his hand, and we again plunged in. This time the candles had been committed to my charge. When we had passed down the gallery into the second cave, Steve directed me to light a couple more of the candles, and stick them against a piece of rock, that he might have plenty of light to work by. This I did, and my stalwart cousin began to use the spade with a will, upon the breakwater of sand and stones.

The obstacle, which had been sufficient to turn the stream at a right angle, possibly for centuries, was of the most fragile description. Such instances of a slight obstruction diverting a sustained onset often occur in nature on a much larger scale. The Chesil Bank, for example, connecting the peninsula of Portland, in Dorsetshire, with the mainland, is a mere string of loose pebbles; yet it resists, by its shelving surface and easy curve, the mighty roll of the Channel seas, when urged upon the bank by the most furious southwest gales.

In a minute or two a portion of the purling stream discovered the
5   opening Steve's spade was making in the sand, and began to flow through. The water assisted him in his remaining labours, supplementing every spadeful that he threw back, by washing aside ten. I remember that I was child enough, at that time, to clap my hands at the sight of larger and larger quantities of the brook
10   tumbling in the form of a cascade down the dark chasm, where it had possibly never flowed before, or at any rate, never within the human period of the earth's history. In less than twenty minutes the whole stream trended off in this new direction, as calmly as if it had coursed there always. What had before been its bed now gradually drained
15   dry, and we saw that we could walk across dryshod, with ease.

We speedily put the possibility into practice, and so reached the beautiful, glistening niche, that had tempted us to our engineering. We brought up into it the candles we had stuck against the rockwork further down, placed them with the others around the niche, and
20   prepared to rest awhile, the spot being quite dry.

"That's the way to overcome obstructions!" said Steve, triumphantly. "I warrant nobody ever got so far as this before—at least, without wading up to his knees, in crossing that watercourse."

My attention was so much attracted by the beautiful natural
25   ornaments of the niche, that I hardly heeded his remark. These covered the greater part of the sides and roof; they were flesh-coloured, and assumed the form of frills, lace, coats of mail; in many places they quaintly resembled the skin of geese after plucking, and in others the wattles of turkeys. All were decorated with water crystals.
30   "Well," exclaimed I, "I could stay here always!"

"So could I," said Steve, "if I had victuals enough. And some we'll have at once."

Our bread and cheese and apples were unfolded, and we speedily devoured the whole. We then tried to chip pieces from the rock, and
35   but indifferently succeeded, though while doing this we discovered some curious stones, like axe and arrow heads, at the bottom of the niche; but they had become partially attached to the floor by the limestone deposit, and could not be extracted.

27† frills] pills

"This is a long enough visit for to-day," said my cousin, jumping up as one of the candles went out. "We shall be left in the dark if we don't mind, and it would be no easy matter to find our way out without a light."

Accordingly we gathered up the candles that remained, descended from the niche, recrossed the deserted bed of the stream, and found our way to the open air, well pleased enough with the adventure, and promising each other to repeat it at an early day. On which account, instead of bringing away the unburnt candles, and the wood candlestick, and the spade, we laid these articles on a hidden shelf near the entrance, to be ready at hand at any time.

Having cleaned the tell-tale mud from our boots, we were on the point of entering the village, when our ears were attracted by a great commotion in the road below.

"What is it?" said I, standing still.

"Voices, I think," replied Steve. "Listen!"

It seemed to be a man in a violent frenzy. "I think it is somebody out of his mind," continued my cousin. "I never heard a man rave so in my life."

"Let us draw nearer," said I.

We moved on, and soon came in sight of an individual, who, standing in the midst of the street, was gesticulating distractedly, and uttering invectives against something or other, to several villagers that had gathered around.

"Why, 'tis the miller!" said Steve. "What can be the matter with him?"

We were not kept long in suspense, for we could soon hear his words distinctly. "The money I've sunk here!" he was saying; "the time—the honest labour—all for nothing! Only beggary afore me now! One month it was a new pair of mill-stones; then the back wall was cracked with the shaking, and had to be repaired; then I made a bad speculation in corn and dropped money that way! But 'tis nothing to this! My own freehold—the only staff and dependence o' my family—all useless now—all of us ruined!"

"Don't you take on so, Miller Griffin," soothingly said one who proved to be the Man who had Failed. "Take the ups with the downs, and maybe 'twill come right again."

"Right again!" raved the miller; "how can what's gone forever come back again as 'twere afore—that's what I ask my wretched self—how can it?"

"We'll get up a subscription for ye," said a local dairyman.

"I don't drink hard; I don't stay away from church, and I only grind
5   into Sabbath hours when there's no getting through the work otherwise, and I pay my way like a man!"

"Yes—you do that," corroborated the others.

"And yet, I be brought to ruinous despair, on this sixth day of September, Hannah Dominy; as if I were a villain! Oh, my mill, my
10   mill wheel—you'll never go round any more—never more!" The miller flung his arms upon the rail of the bridge, and buried his face in his hands.

"This raving is but making a bad job worse," said the Man who had Failed. "But who will listen to counsel on such matters."

15   By this time we had drawn near, and Steve said, "What's the cause of all this?"

"The river has dried up—all on a sudden," said the dairyman, "and so his mill won't go any more."

I gazed instantly towards the stream, or rather what had been the
20   stream. It was gone; and the mill wheel, which had pattered so persistently when we entered the cavern, was silent. Steve and I instinctively stepped aside.

"The river gone dry!" Steve whispered.

"Yes," said I. "Why, Steve, don't you know why?"

25   My thoughts had instantly flown to our performance of turning the stream out of its channel in the cave, and I knew in a moment that this was the cause. Steve's silence showed me that he divined the same thing, and we stood gazing at each other in consternation.

CHAPTER II

30   How We Shone in the Eyes of the Public.

As soon as we had recovered ourselves we walked away, unconsciously approaching the river-bed, in whose hollows lay the dead and dying bodies of loach, sticklebacks, dace, and other small fry, which before our entrance into Nick's Pocket had raced merrily up

---

33† loach, sticklebacks] leach, stickbacks

and down the waterway. Further on we perceived numbers of people ascending to the upper part of the village, with pitchers on their heads, and buckets yoked to their shoulders.

"Where are you going?" said Steve to one of these.

"To your mother's well for water," was the answer. "The river we have always been used to dip from is dried up. Oh, mercy me, what with the washing and cooking and brewing I don't know what we shall do to live, for 'tis killing work to bring water on your back so far!"

As may be supposed, all this gave me still greater concern than before, and I hurriedly said to Steve that I was strongly of opinion that we ought to go back to the cave immediately, and turn the water into the old channel, seeing what harm we had unintentionally done by our manœuvre.

"Of course we'll go back—that's just what I was going to say," returned Steve. "We can set it all right again in half an hour, and the river will run the same as ever. Hullo—now you are frightened at what has happened! I can see you are."

I told him that I was not exactly frightened, but that it seemed to me we had caused a very serious catastrophe in the village, in driving the miller almost crazy, and killing the fish, and worrying the poor people into supposing they would never have enough water again for their daily use without fetching it from afar. "Let us tell them how it came to pass," I suggested, "and then go and set it right."

"Tell 'em—not I!" said Steve. "We'll go back and put it right, and say nothing about it to any one, and they will simply think it was caused by a temporary earthquake, or something of that sort." He then broke into a vigorous whistle, and we retraced our steps together.

It occupied us but a few minutes to rekindle a light inside the cave, take out the spade from its nook, and penetrate to the scene of our morning exploit. Steve then fell to, and first rolling down a few large pieces of stone into the current, dexterously banked them up with clay from the other side of the cave, which caused the brook to swerve back into its original bed almost immediately. "There," said he, "it is all just as it was when we first saw it—now let's be off."

We did not dally long in the cavern; but when we gained the exterior we decided to wait there a little time till the villagers should have discovered the restoration of their stream, to watch the effect.

Our waiting was but temporary; for in quick succession there burst upon our ears a shout, and then the starting of the mill-wheel patter.

At once we walked into the village street with an air of unconcern. The miller's face was creased with wrinkles of satisfaction; the countenances of the blacksmith, shoemaker, grocer and dairyman were perceptibly brighter. These, and many others of West Poley, were gathered on the bridge over the mill-tail, and they were all holding a conversation with the parson of the parish, as to the strange occurrence.

Matters remained in a quiet state during the next two days. Then there was a remarkably fine and warm morning, and we proposed to cross the hills and descend into East Poley, the next village, which I had never seen. My aunt made no objection to the excursion, and we departed, ascending the hill in a straight line, without much regard to paths. When we had reached the summit, and were about half way between the two villages, we sat down to recover breath. While we sat a man overtook us, and Steve recognized him as a neighbour.

"A bad job again for West Poley folks!" cried the man, without halting.

"What's the matter now?" said Steve, and I started with curiosity.

"Oh, the river is dry again. It happened at a quarter past ten this morning, and it is thought it will never flow any more. The miller he's gone crazy, or all but so. And the washerwoman, she will have to be kept by the parish, because she can't get water to wash with; aye, 'tis a terrible time that's come. I'm off to try to hire a water-cart, but I fear I shan't hear of one."

The speaker passed by, and on turning to Steve I found he was looking on the ground. "I know how that's happened," he presently said. "We didn't make our embankment so strong as it was before, and so the water has washed it away."

"Let's go back and mend it," said I; and I proposed that we should reveal where the mischief lay, and get some of the labourers to build the bank up strong, that this might not happen again.

"No," said Steve, "since we are half way we will have our day's pleasure. It won't hurt the West Poley people to be out of water for one day. We'll return home a little earlier than we intended, and put it all in order again, either ourselves, or by the help of some men."

Having gone about a mile and a half further we reached the brow of the descent into East Poley, the place we had come to visit. Here we beheld advancing towards us a stranger whose actions we could not at first interpret. But as the distance between us and him lessened we discerned, to our surprise, that he was in convulsions of laughter. He would laugh until he was tired, then he would stand still gazing on the ground, as if quite preoccupied, then he would burst out laughing again and walk on. No sooner did he see us two boys than he placed his hat upon his walking-stick, twirled it and cried "Hurrah!"

I was so amused that I could not help laughing with him; and when he came abreast of us Steve said, "Good morning; may I ask what it is that makes you laugh so?"

But the man was either too self-absorbed or too supercilious to vouchsafe to us any lucid explanation. "What makes me laugh?" he said. "Why, good luck, my boys! Perhaps when you are as lucky, you will laugh too." Saying which he walked on and left us; and we could hear him exclaiming to himself, "Well done—hurrah!" as he sank behind the ridge.

Without pausing longer we descended towards the village, and soon reached its outlying homesteads. Our path intersected a green field dotted with trees, on the other side of which was an inn. As we drew near we heard the strains of a fiddle, and presently perceived a fiddler standing on a chair outside the inn door; whilst on the green in front were several people seated at a table eating and drinking, and some younger members of the assembly dancing a reel in the background.

We naturally felt much curiosity as to the cause of the merriment, which we mentally connected with that of the man we had met just before. Turning to one of the old men feasting at the table, I said to him as civilly as I could, "Why are you all so lively in this parish, sir?"

"Because we are in luck's way just now, for we don't get a new river every day. Hurrah!"

"A new river?" said Steve and I in one breath.

"Yes," said one of our interlocutors, waving over the table a ham-bone he had been polishing. "Yesterday afternoon a river of beautiful water burst out of the quarry at the higher end of this bottom; in an hour or so it stopped again. This morning, about a quarter past ten, it burst out again, and it is running now as if it would run always."

"It will make all land and houses in this parish worth double as

much as afore," said another; "for want of water is the one thing that
has always troubled us, forcing us to sink deep wells, and even then
being hard put to, to get enough for our cattle. Now we have got a
river, and the place will grow to a town."

5   "It is as good as two hundred pounds to me!" said one who looked
like a grazier.

"And two hundred and fifty to me!" cried another, who seemed to
be a brewer.

"And sixty pound a year to me, and to every man here in the
10   building trade!" said a third.

As soon as we could withdraw from the company, our thoughts
found vent in words.

"I ought to have seen it!" said Steve. "Of course if you stop a
stream from flowing in one direction, it must force its way out in
15   another."

"I wonder where their new stream is," said I.

We looked round. After some examination we saw a depression in
the centre of a pasture, and, approaching it, beheld the stream
meandering along over the grass, the current not having had as yet
20   sufficient time to scour a bed. Walking down to the brink, we were lost
in wonder at what we had unwittingly done, and quite bewildered at
the strange events we had caused. Feeling, now, that we had walked
far enough from home for one day, we turned, and, in a brief time,
entered a road pointed out by Steve, as one that would take us to West
25   Poley by a shorter cut than our outward route.

As we ascended the hill, Steve looked round at me. I suppose my
face revealed my thoughts, for he said, "You are amazed, Leonard, at
the wonders we have accomplished without knowing it. To tell the
truth, so am I."

30   I said that what staggered me was this—that we could not turn
back the water into its old bed now, without doing as much harm to
the people of East Poley by taking it away, as we should do good to the
people of West Poley by restoring it.

"True," said Steve, "that's what bothers me. Though I think we
35   have done more good to these people than we have done harm to the
others; and I think these are rather nicer people than those in our
village, don't you?"

I objected that even if this were so, we could have no right to take

21† done, and] done, and being

water away from one set of villagers and give it to another set without consulting them.

Steve seemed to feel the force of the argument; but as his mother had a well of her own he was less inclined to side with his native place than he might have been if his own household had been deprived of water, for the benefit of the East Poleyites. The matter was still in suspense, when, weary with our day's pilgrimage, we reached the mill.

The mill-pond was drained to its bed; the wheel stood motionless; yet a noise came from the interior. It was not the noise of machinery, but of the nature of blows, followed by bitter expostulations. On looking in, we were grieved to see that the miller, in a great rage, was holding his apprentice by the collar, and beating him with a strap.

The miller was a heavy, powerful man, and more than a match for his apprentice and us two boys besides; but Steve reddened with indignation, and asked the miller, with some spirit, why he served the poor fellow so badly.

"He says he'll leave," stormed the frantic miller. "What right hev he to say he'll leave, I should like to know!"

"There is no work for me to do, now the mill won't go," said the apprentice, meekly; "and the agreement was that I should be at liberty to leave if work failed in the mill. He keeps me here and don't pay me; and I be at my wits' end how to live."

"Just shut up!" said the miller. "Go and work in the garden! Mill-work or no mill-work, you'll stay on."

Job, as the miller's boy was called, had won the good-will of Steve, and Steve was now ardent to do him a good turn. Looking over the bridge, we saw, passing by, the Man who had Failed. He was considered an authority on such matters as these, and we begged him to come in. In a few minutes the miller was set down, and it was proved to him that, by the terms of Job's indentures, he was no longer bound to remain.

"I have to thank you for this," said the miller, savagely, to Steve. "Ruined in every way! I may as well die!"

But my cousin cared little for the miller's opinion, and we came away, thanking the Man who had Failed for his interference, and receiving the warmest expressions of gratitude from poor Job; who, it

28† who had] who

appeared, had suffered much ill-treatment from his irascible master, and was overjoyed to escape to some other employment.

We went to bed early that night, on account of our long walk; but we were far too excited to sleep at once. It was scarcely dark as yet, 5 and the nights being still warm the window was left open as it had been left during the summer. Thus we could hear everything that passed without. People were continually coming to dip water from my aunt's well; they gathered round it in groups, and discussed the remarkable event which had latterly occurred for the first time in 10 parish history.

"My belief is that witchcraft have done it," said the shoemaker, "and the only remedy that I can think o', is for one of us to cut across to Bartholomew Gann, the white wizard, and get him to tell us how to counteract it. 'Tis a long pull to his house for a little man, such as I be, 15 but I'll walk it if nobody else will."

"Well, there's no harm in your going," said another. "We can manage by drawing from Mrs Draycot's well for a few days; but something must be done, or the miller'll be ruined, and the washerwoman can't hold out long."

20 When these personages had drawn water and retired, Steve spoke across from his bed to me in mine. "We've done more good than harm, that I'll maintain. The miller is the only man seriously upset, and he's not a man to deserve consideration. It has been the means of freeing poor Job, which is another good thing. Then, the people in 25 East Poley that we've made happy are two hundred and fifty, and there are only a hundred in this parish, even if all of 'em are made miserable."

I returned some reply, though the state of affairs was, in truth, one rather suited to the genius of Jeremy Bentham than to me. But the 30 problem in utilitarian philosophy was shelved by Steve exclaiming, "I have it! I see how to get some real glory out of this!"

I demanded how, with much curiosity.

"You'll swear not to tell anybody, or let it be known anyhow that we are at the bottom of it all?"

35 I am sorry to say that my weak compunctions gave way under stress of this temptation; and I solemnly declared that I would reveal nothing, unless he agreed with me that it would be best to do so. Steve made me swear, in the tone of Hamlet to the Ghost, and when I had done this, he sat up in his bed to announce his scheme.

"First, we'll go to Job," said Steve. "Take him into the secret; show him the cave; give him a spade and pickaxe; and tell him to turn off the water from East Poley at, say, twelve o'clock, for a little while. Then we'll go to the East Poley boys and declare ourselves to be magicians."

"Magicians?" I said.

"Magicians, able to dry up rivers, or to make 'em run at will," he repeated.

"I see it!" I almost screamed, in my delight.

"To show our power, we'll name an hour for drying up theirs, and making it run again after a short time. Of course we'll say the hour we've told Job to turn the water in the cave. Won't they think something of us then?"

I was enchanted. The question of mischief or not mischief was as indifferent to me now as it was to Steve—for which indifference we got rich deserts, as will be seen in the sequel.

"And to look grand and magical," continued he, "we'll get some gold lace that I know of in the garret, on an old coat my grandfather wore in the Yeomanry Cavalry, and put it round our caps, and make ourselves great beards with horse-hair. They will look just like real ones at a little distance off."

"And we must each have a wand!" said I, explaining that I knew how to make excellent wands, white as snow, by peeling a couple of straight willows; and that I could do all that in the morning while he was preparing the beards.

Thus we discussed and settled the matter, and at length fell asleep—to dream of to-morrow's triumphs among the boys of East Poley, till the sun of that morrow shone in upon our faces and woke us. We arose promptly and made our preparations, having carte blanche from my Aunt Draycot to spend the days of my visit as we chose.

Our first object on leaving the farmhouse was to find Job Tray, apprise him of what it was necessary that he should know, and induce him to act as confederate. We found him outside the garden of his lodging; he told us he had nothing to do till the following Monday, when a farmer had agreed to hire him. On learning the secret of the river-head, and what we proposed to do, he expressed his glee by a low laugh of amazed delight, and readily promised to assist as bidden. It took us some little time to show him the inner cave, the

tools, and to arrange candles for him, so that he might enter without difficulty just after eleven and do the trick. When this was all settled we put Steve's watch on a ledge in the cave, that Job might know the exact time, and came out to ascend the hills that divided the eastern
5   from the western village.

For obvious reasons we did not appear in magician's guise till we had left the western vale some way behind us. Seated on the limestone ridge, removed from all observation, we set to work at preparing ourselves. I peeled the two willows we had brought with us to be used
10   as magic wands, and Steve pinned the pieces of old lace round our caps, congratulating himself on the fact of the lace not being new, which would thus convey the impression that we had exercised the wizard's calling for some years. Our last adornments were the beards; and, finally equipped, we descended on the other side.

15   Our plan was now to avoid the upper part of East Poley, which we had traversed on the preceding day, and to strike into the parish at a point further down, where the humble cottages stood, and where we were both absolutely unknown. An hour's additional walking brought us to this spot, which, as the crow flies, was not more than
20   half so far from West Poley as the road made it.

The first boys we saw were some playing in an orchard near the new stream, which novelty had evidently been the attraction that had brought them there. It was an opportunity for opening the campaign, especially as the hour was long after eleven, and the cessation of water
25   consequent on Job's performance at a quarter past might be expected to take place as near as possible to twelve, allowing the five and forty minutes from eleven-fifteen as the probable time that would be occupied by the stream in travelling to the point we had reached.

I forget at this long distance of years the exact words used by Steve
30   in addressing the strangers; but to the best of my recollection they were, "How d'ye do, gentlemen, and how does the world use ye?" I distinctly remember the sublimity he threw into his gait, and how slavishly I imitated him in the same.

The boys made some indifferent answer, and Steve continued,
35   "You will kindly present us with some of those apples, I presume, considering what we are?"

They regarded us dubiously, and at last one of them said, "What are you, that you should expect apples from us?"

"We are travelling magicians," replied Steve. "You may have

heard of us, for by our power this new river has begun to flow. Rhombustas is my name, and this is my familiar Balcazar."

"I don't believe it," said an incredulous one from behind.

"Very well, gentlemen; we can't help that. But if you give us some apples we'll prove our right to the title." 5

"Be hanged if we will give you any apples," said the boy who held the basket; "since it is already proved that magicians are impossible."

"In that case," said Steve, "we—we—"

"Will perform just the same," interrupted I, for I feared Steve had forgotten that the time was at hand when the stream would be 10 interrupted by Job, whether we willed it or not.

"We will stop the water of your new river at twelve o'clock this day, when the sun crosses the meridian," said Rhombustas, "as a punishment for your want of generosity."

"Do it!" said the boys incredulously. 15

"Come here, Balcazar," said Steve. We walked together to the edge of the stream; then we muttered, *Hi, hae, haec, horum, harum, horum*, and stood waving our wands.

"The river do run just the same," said the strangers derisively.

"The spell takes time to work," said Rhombustas, adding in an 20 aside to me, "I hope that fellow Job has not forgotten, or we shall be hooted out of the place."

There we stood, waving and waving our white sticks, hoping and hoping we should succeed; while still the river flowed. Seven or ten minutes passed thus; and then, when we were nearly broken down by 25 ridicule, the stream diminished its volume. All eyes were instantly bent on the water, which sank so low as to be in a short time but a narrow rivulet. The faithful Job had performed his task. By the time that the clock of the church tower struck twelve the river was almost dry. 30

The boys looked at each other in amazement, and at us with awe. They were too greatly concerned to speak except in murmurs to each other.

"You see the result of your conduct, unbelieving strangers," said Steve, drawing boldly up to them. "And I seriously ask that you hand 35 over those apples before we bring further troubles upon you and your village. We give you five minutes to consider."

"We decide at once!" cried the boys. "The apples be yours and welcome."

"Thank you, gentlemen," said Steve, while I added, "For your readiness the river shall run again in two or three minutes' time."

"Oh—ah, yes," said Steve, adding heartily in undertones, "I had forgotten that!"

5   Almost as soon as the words were spoken we perceived a little increase in the mere dribble of water which now flowed, whereupon he waved his wand and murmured more words. The liquid thread swelled and rose; and in a few minutes was the same as before. Our triumph was complete; and the suspension had been so temporary

10 that probably nobody in the village had noticed it but ourselves and the boys.

CHAPTER III

How We Were Caught in Our Own Trap.

At this acme of our glory who should come past but a hedger whom

15 Steve recognized as an inhabitant of West Poley; unluckily for our greatness the hedger also recognized Steve.

"Well, Maister Stevey, what be you doing over in these parts then? And yer little cousin, too, upon my word! And beards—why ye've made yerselves ornamental! haw, haw!"

20   In great trepidation Steve moved on with the man, endeavouring thus to get him out of hearing of the boys.

"Look here," said Steve to me on leaving that outspoken rustic; "I think this is enough for one day. We'd better go further before they guess all."

25   "With all my heart," said I. And we walked on.

"But what's going on here?" said Steve, when, turning a corner of the hedge, we perceived an altercation in progress hard by. The parties proved to be a poor widow and a corn-factor, who had been planning a water-wheel lower down the stream. The latter had

30 dammed the water for his purpose to such an extent as to submerge the poor woman's garden, turning it into a lake.

"Indeed, sir, you need not ruin my premises so!" she said with tears in her eyes. "The mill-pond can be kept from overflowing my garden by a little banking and digging; it will be just as well for your purpose

27† altercation] alteration

to keep it lower down, as to let it spread out into a great pool here. The house and garden are yours by law, sir; that's true. But my father built the house, and, oh, sir, I was born here, and I should like to end my days under its roof!"

"Can't help it, mis'ess," said the corn-factor. "Your garden is a mill-pond already made, and to get a hollow further down I should have to dig at great expense. There is a very nice cottage up the hill, where you can live as well as here. When your father died the house came into my hands; and I can do what I like with my own."

The woman went sadly away indoors. As for Steve and myself, we were deeply moved as we looked at the pitiable sight of the poor woman's garden, the tops of the gooseberry bushes forming small islands in the water, and her few apple trees standing immersed half-way up their stems.

"The man is a rascal," said Steve. "I perceive that it is next to impossible, in this world, to do good to one set of folks without doing harm to another."

"Since we have not done all good to these people of East Poley," said I, "there is a reason for restoring the river to its old course through West Poley."

"But then," said Steve, "if we turn back the stream, we shall be starting Miller Griffin's mill; and then, by the terms of his 'prenticeship, poor Job will have to go back to him and be beaten again! It takes good brains no less than a good heart to do what's right towards all."

Quite unable to solve the problem into which we had drifted, we retraced our steps, till, at a stile, within half a mile of West Poley, we beheld Job awaiting us.

"Well, how did it act?" he asked with great eagerness. "Just as the hands of your watch got to a quarter past eleven, I began to shovel away, and turned the water in no time. But I didn't turn it where you expected—not I—'twould have started the mill for a few minutes, and I wasn't going to do that."

"Then where did you turn it?" cried Steve.

"I found another hole," said Job.

"A third one?"

"Ay, hee, hee! a third one! So I pulled the stones aside from this new hole, and shovelled the clay, and down the water went with a gush. When it had run down there a few minutes, I turned it back to

the East Poley hole, as you ordered me to do. But as to getting it back
to the old West Poley hole, that I'd never do."

Steve then explained that we no more wished the East village to
have the river than the West village, on account of our discovery that
5 equal persecution was going on in the one place as in the other. Job's
news of a third channel solved our difficulty. "So we'll go at once and
send it down this third channel," concluded he.

We walked back to the village, and, as it was getting late, and we
were tired, we decided to do nothing that night, but told Job to meet
10 us in the cave on the following evening, to complete our work there.

All next day my cousin was away from home, at market for his
mother, and he had arranged with me that if he did not return soon
enough to join me before going to Nick's Pocket, I should proceed
thither, where he would meet me on his way back from the market-
15 town. The day passed anxiously enough with me, for I had some
doubts of a very grave kind as to our right to deprive two parishes of
water on our own judgment, even though that should be, as it was,
honestly based on our aversion to tyranny. However, dusk came on at
last, and Steve not appearing from market, I concluded that I was to
20 meet him at the cave's mouth.

To this end I strolled out in that direction, and there being as yet no
hurry, I allowed myself to be tempted out of my path by a young
rabbit, which, however, I failed to capture. This divergence had
brought me inside a field, behind a hedge, and before I could resume
25 my walk along the main road, I heard some persons passing along the
other side. The words of their conversation arrested me in a moment.

" 'Tis a strange story if it's true," came through the hedge in the
tones of Miller Griffin. "We know that East Poley folk will say queer
things; but the boys wouldn't say that it was the work of magicians if
30 they hadn't some ground for it."

"And how do they explain it?" asked the shoemaker.

"They say that these two young fellows passed down their lane
about twelve o'clock, dressed like magicians, and offered to show their
power by stopping the river. The East Poley boys challenged 'em;
35 when, by George, they did stop the river! They said a few words, and it
dried up like magic. Now mark my words, my suspicion is this: these
two gamesters have somehow got at the river head, and been tampering
with it in some way. The water that runs down East Poley bottom is the
water that ought, by rights, to be running through my mill."

"A very pretty piece of mischief, if that's the case!" said the shoemaker. "I've never liked them lads, particularly that Steve—for not a boot or shoe hev he had o' me since he's been old enough to choose for himself—not a pair, or even a mending. But I don't see how they could do all this, even if they had got at the river head. 'Tis a spring out of the hill, isn't it? And how could they stop the spring?"

It seemed that the miller could offer no explanation, for no answer was returned. My course was clear: to join Job and Steve at Nick's Pocket immediately; tell them that we were suspected, and to get them to give over further proceedings, till we had stated our difficulties to some person of experience—say the Man who had Failed.

I accordingly ran like a hare over the clover inside the hedge, and soon was far away from the interlocutors. Drawing near the cave, I was relieved to see Steve's head against the sky. I joined him at once, and recounted to him, in haste, what had passed.

He meditated. "They don't even now suspect that the secret lies in the cavern," said he.

"But they will soon," said I.

"Well, perhaps they may," he answered. "But there will be time for us to finish our undertaking, and turn the stream down the third hole. When we've done that we can consider which of the villages is most worthy to have the river, and act accordingly."

"Do let us take a good wise man into our confidence," I said.

After a little demurring, he agreed that as soon as we had completed the scheme we would state the case to a competent adviser, and let it be settled fairly. "And now," he said, "where's Job; inside the cave, no doubt, as it is past the time I promised to be here."

Stepping inside the cave's mouth, we found that the candles and other things which had been deposited there were removed. The probability being that Job had arrived and taken them in with him, we groped our way along in the dark, helped by an occasional match which Steve struck from a box he carried. Descending the gallery at the further end of the outer cavern, we discerned a glimmer at the remote extremity, and soon beheld Job working with all his might by the light of one of the candles.

"I've almost got it into the hole that leads to neither of the Poleys, but I wouldn't actually turn it till you came," he said, wiping his face.

We told him that the neighbours were on our track, and might soon guess that we performed our tricks in Nick's Pocket, and come there, and find that the stream flowed through the cave before rising in the spring at the top of the village; and asked him to turn the water at once, and be off with us.

5 "Ah!" said Job, mournfully, "then 'tis over with me! They will be here to-morrow, and will turn back the stream, and the mill will go again, and I shall have to finish my time as 'prentice to the man who did this!" He pulled up his shirt sleeve, and showed us on his arm several stripes and bruises—black and blue and green—the tell-tale
10 relics of old blows from the miller.

Steve reddened with indignation. "I would give anything to stop up the channels to the two Poleys so close that they couldn't be found again!" he said. "Couldn't we do it with stones and clay? Then if they came here 'twould make no difference, and the water would flow
15 down the third hole forever, and we should save Job and the widow after all."

"We can but try it," said Job, willing to fall in with anything that would hinder his recall to the mill. "Let's set to work."

Steve took the spade, and Job the pickaxe. First they finished what
20 Job had begun—the turning of the stream into the third tunnel or crevice, which led to neither of the Poleys. This done, they set to work jamming stones into the other two openings, treading earth and clay around them, and smoothing over the whole in such a manner that nobody should notice they had ever existed. So intent were we on
25 completing it that—to our utter disaster—we did not notice what was going on behind us.

I was the first to look round, and I well remember why: my ears had been attracted by a slight change of tone in the purl of the water down the new crevice discovered by Job, and I was curious to learn
30 the reason of it. The sight that met my gaze might well have appalled a stouter and older heart than mine. Instead of pouring down out of sight, as it had been doing when we last looked, the stream was choked by a rising pool into which it boiled, showing at a glance that what we had innocently believed to be another outlet for the stream
35 was only a blind passage or *cul de sac*, which the water, when first turned that way by Job, had not been left long enough to fill before it was turned back again.

"Oh, Steve—Job!" I cried, and could say no more.

14† came] come

They gazed round at once, and saw the situation. Nick's Pocket had become a cauldron. The surface of the rising pool stood, already, far above the mouth of the gallery by which we had entered, and which was our only way out—stood far above the old exit of the stream to West Poley, now sealed up; far above the second outlet to East Poley, discovered by Steve, and also sealed up by our fatal ingenuity. We had been spending the evening in making a closed bottle of the cave, in which the water was now rising to drown us.

"There is one chance for us—only one," said Steve in a dry voice.

"What one?" we asked in a breath.

"To open the old channel leading to the mill," said Steve.

"I would almost as soon be drowned as do that," murmured Job gloomily. "But there's more lives than my own, so I'll work with a will. Yet how be we to open any channel at all?"

The question was, indeed, of awful aptness. It was extremely improbable that we should have power to reopen either conduit now. Both those exits had been funnel-shaped cavities, narrowing down to mere fissures at the bottom; and the stones and earth we had hurled into these cavities had wedged themselves together by their own weight. Moreover—and here was the rub—had it been possible to pull the stones out while they remained unsubmerged, the whole mass was now under water, which enlarged the task of reopening the channel to Herculean dimensions.

But we did not know my cousin Steve as yet. "You will help me here," he said authoritatively to Job, pointing to the West Poley conduit. "Lenny, my poor cousin," he went on, turning to me, "we are in a bad way. All you can do is to stand in the niche, and make the most of the candles by keeping them from the draught with your hat, and burning only one at a time. How many have we, Job?"

"Ten ends, some long, some short," said Job.

"They will burn many hours," said Steve. "And now we must dive, and begin to get out the stones."

They had soon stripped off all but their drawers, and, laying their clothes on the dry floor of the niche behind me, stepped down into the middle of the cave. The water here was already above their waists, and at the original gulley-hole leading to West Poley spring was proportionately deeper. Into this part, nevertheless, Steve dived. I have recalled his appearance a hundred—aye, a thousand—times

7† closed] close

since that day, as he came up—his crown bobbing into the dim candle-light like a floating apple. He stood upright, bearing in his arms a stone as big as his head.

"That's one of 'em!" he said as soon as he could speak. "But there
5 are many, many more!"

He threw the stone behind; while Job, wasting no time, had already dived in at the same point. Job was not such a good diver as Steve, in the sense of getting easily at the bottom; but he could hold his breath longer, and it was an extraordinary length of time before
10 his head emerged above the surface, though his feet were kicking in the air more than once. Clutched to his chest, when he rose, was a second large stone, and a couple of small ones with it. He threw the whole to a distance; and Steve, having now recovered breath, plunged again into the hole.

15 But I can hardly bear to recall this terrible hour even now, at a distance of many years. My suspense was, perhaps, more trying than that of the others, for, unlike them, I could not escape reflection by superhuman physical efforts. My task of economizing the candles, by shading them with my hat, was not to be compared, in difficulty, to
20 theirs; but I would gladly have changed places, if it had been possible to such a small boy, with Steve and Job, so intolerable was it to remain motionless in the desperate circumstances.

Thus I watched the rising of the waters, inch by inch, and on that account was in a better position than they to draw an inference as to
25 the probable end of the adventure.

There were a dozen, or perhaps twenty, stones to extract before we could hope for an escape of the pent mass of water; and the difficulty of extracting them increased with each successive attempt in two ways: by the greater actual remoteness of stone after stone, and by its
30 greater relative remoteness through the rising of the pool. However, the sustained, gallant struggles of my two comrades succeeded, at last, in raising the number of stones extracted to seven. Then we fancied that some slight passage had been obtained for the stream; for, though the terrible pool still rose higher, it seemed to rise less
35 rapidly.

After several attempts, in which Steve and Job brought up nothing, there came a declaration from them that they could do no more. The lower stones were so tightly jammed between the sides of the fissure that no human strength seemed able to pull them out.

Job and Steve both came up from the water. They were exhausted and shivering, and well they might be. "We must try some other way," said Steve.

"What way?" asked I.

Steve looked at me. "You are a very good little fellow to stand this so well!" he said, with something like tears in his eyes.

They soon got on their clothes; and, having given up all hope of escape downward, we turned our eyes to the roof of the cave, on the chance of discovering some outlet there.

There was not enough light from our solitary candle to show us all the features of the vault in detail; but we could see enough to gather that it formed anything but a perfect dome. The roof was rather a series of rifts and projections, and high on one side, almost lost in the shades, there was a larger and deeper rift than elsewhere, forming a sort of loft, the back parts of which were invisible, extending we knew not how far. It was through this overhanging rift that the draught seemed to come which had caused our candle to gutter and flare.

To think of reaching an opening so far above our heads, so advanced into the ceiling of the cave as to require a fly's power of walking upside down to approach it, was mere waste of time. We bent our gaze elsewhere. On the same side with the niche in which we stood there was a small narrow ledge quite near at hand, and to gain it my two stalwart companions now exerted all their strength.

By cutting a sort of step with the pickaxe, Job was enabled to obtain a footing about three feet above the level of our present floor, and then he called to me.

"Now, Leonard, you be the lightest. Do you hop up here, and climb upon my shoulder, and then I think you will be tall enough to scramble to the ledge, so as to help us up after you."

I leapt up beside him, clambered upon his stout back as he bade me, and, springing from his shoulder, reached the ledge. He then handed up the pickaxe, directed me how to make its point firm into one of the crevices on the top of the ledge; next, to lie down, hold on to the handle of the pickaxe and give him my other hand. I obediently acted, when he sprang up, and turning, assisted Steve to do likewise.

We had now reached the highest possible coign of vantage left to us, and there remained nothing more to do but wait and hope that the encroaching water would find some unseen outlet before reaching our level.

Job and Steve were so weary from their exertions that they seemed almost indifferent as to what happened, provided they might only be allowed to rest. However, they tried to devise new schemes, and looked wistfully over the surface of the pool.

5   "I wonder if it rises still?" I said. "Perhaps not, after all."

"Then we shall only exchange drowning for starving," said Steve.

Job, instead of speaking, had endeavoured to answer my query by stooping down and stretching over the ledge with his arm. His face was very calm as he rose again. "It will be drowning," he said almost

10   inaudibly, and held up his hand, which was wet.

CHAPTER IV

How Older Heads than Ours Became Concerned.

The water had risen so high that Job could touch its surface from our retreat.

15   We now, in spite of Job's remark, indulged in the dream that, provided the water would stop rising, we might, in the course of time, find a way out somehow, and Job by-and-by said, "Perhaps round there in the dark may be places where we could crawl out, if we could only see them well enough to swim across to them. Couldn't we send a

20   candle round that way?"

"How?" said I and Steve.

"By a plan I have thought of," said he. Taking off his hat, which was of straw, he cut with his pocket-knife a little hole in the middle of the crown. Into this he stuck a piece of candle, lighted it, and lying

25   down to reach the surface of the water as before, lowered the hat till it rested afloat.

There was, as Job had suspected, a slight circular current in the apparently still water, and the hat moved on slowly. Our six eyes became riveted on the voyaging candle as if it were a thing of

30   fascination. It travelled away from us, lighting up in its progress unsuspected protuberances and hollows, but revealing to our eager stare no spot of safety or of egress. It went further and yet further into darkness, till it became like a star alone in a sky. Then it crossed from left to right. Then it gradually turned and enlarged, was lost behind

35   jutting crags, reappeared, and journeyed back towards us, till it again floated under the ledge on which we stood, and we gathered it in. It

had made a complete circuit of the cavern, the circular motion of the water being caused by the inpour of the spring, and it had showed us no means of escape at all.

Steve spoke, saying solemnly, "This is all my fault!"

"No," said Job. "For you would not have tried to stop the millstream if it had not been to save me."

"But I began it all," said Steve, bitterly. "I see now the foolishness of presumption. What right had I to take upon myself the ordering of a stream of water that scores of men three times my age get their living by?"

"I thought overmuch of myself, too," said Job. "It was hardly right to stop the grinding of flour that made bread for a whole parish, for my poor sake. We ought to ha' got the advice of some one wi' more experience than ourselves."

We then stood silent. The impossibility of doing more pressed in upon our senses like a chill, and I suggested that we should say our prayers.

"I think we ought," said Steve, and Job assenting, we all three knelt down. After this a sad sense of resignation fell on us all, and there being now no hopeful attempt which they could make for deliverance, the sleep that excitement had hitherto withstood overcame both Steve and Job. They leant back and were soon unconscious.

Not having exerted myself to the extent they had done I felt no sleepiness whatever. So I sat beside them with my eyes wide open, holding and protecting the candle mechanically, and wondering if it could really be possible that we were doomed to die.

I do not know how or why, but there came into my mind during this suspense the words I had read somewhere at school, as being those of Flaminius, the consul, when he was penned up at Thrasymene: "Friends, we must not hope to get out of this by vows and prayers alone. 'Tis by fortitude and strength we must escape." The futility of any such resolve in my case was apparent enough, and yet the words were sufficient to lead me to scan the roof of the cave once more.

When the opening up there met my eye I said to myself, "I wonder where that hole leads to?" Picking up a stone about the size of my fist I threw it with indifference, though with a good aim, towards the spot. The stone passed through the gaping orifice, and I heard it alight within like a tennis ball.

But its noise did not cease with its impact. The fall was succeeded by a helter-skelter kind of rattle which, though it receded in the distance, I could hear for a long time with distinctness, owing, I suppose, to the reflection or echo from the top and sides of the cave. It denoted that on the other side of that dark mouth yawning above me there was a slope downward—possibly into another cave, and that the stone had ricocheted down the incline. "I wonder where it leads?" I murmured again aloud.

Something greeted my ears at that moment of my pronouncing the words "where it leads" that caused me well nigh to leap out of my shoes. Even now I cannot think of it without experiencing a thrill. It came from the gaping hole.

If my readers can imagine for themselves the sensations of a timid bird, who, while watching the approach of his captors to strangle him, feels his wings loosening from the tenacious snare, and flight again possible, they may conceive my emotions when I realized that what greeted my ears from above were the words of a human tongue, direct from the cavity.

"Where, in the name of fortune, did that stone come from?" The voice was the voice of the miller.

"Be dazed if I know—but 'a nearly broke my head!" The reply was that of the shoemaker.

"Steve—Job!" said I. They awoke with a start and exclamation. I tried to shout, but could not. "They have found us—up there—the miller—shoemaker!" I whispered, pointing to the hole aloft.

Steve and Job understood. Perhaps the sole ingredient, in this sudden revival of our hopes, which could save us from fainting with joy, was the one actually present—that our discoverer was the adversary whom we had been working to circumvent. But such antagonism as his weighed little in the scale with our present despairing circumstances.

We all three combined our voices in one shout—a shout which roused echoes in the cavern that probably had never been awakened since the upheaval of the Mendips, in whose heart we stood. When the shout died away we listened with parted lips.

Then we heard the miller speak again. "Faith, and believe me—'tis the rascals themselves! A-throwing stones—a-trying to terrify us off the premises! Did man ever know the like impudence? We have found the clue to the water mystery at last—may be at their pranks at this very moment! Clamber up here; and if I don't put about their backs the greenest stick that ever growed, I'm no grinder o' corn!''

Then we heard a creeping movement from the orifice over our heads, as of persons on their hands and knees; a puffing, as of fat men out of breath; sudden interjections, such as can be found in a list in any boys' grammar-book, and, therefore, need not be repeated here. All this was followed by a faint glimmer, about equal to that from our own candle, bursting from the gap on high, and the cautious appearance of a head over the ledge.

It was the visage of the shoemaker. Beside it rose another in haste, exclaiming, "Urrr—r! The rascals!" and waving a stick. Almost before we had recognized this as the miller, he, climbing forward with too great impetuosity, and not perceiving that the edge of the orifice was so near, was unable to check himself. He fell over headlong, and was precipitated a distance of some thirty feet into the whirling pool beneath.

Job's face, which, until this catastrophe, had been quite white and rigid at sight of his old enemy, instantly put on a more humane expression. "We mustn't let him drown," he said.

"No," said Steve, "but how can we save him in such an awkward place?"

There was, for the moment, however, no great cause for anxiety. The miller was a stout man, and could swim, though but badly—his power to keep afloat being due rather to the adipose tissues which composed his person, than to skill. But his immersion had been deep, and when he rose to the surface he was bubbling and sputtering wildly.

"Hu, hu, hu, hu! O, ho—I am drownded!" he gasped. "I am a dead man and miller—all on account of those villainous—I mean good boys!—If Job would only help me out I would give him such a dressing—blessing I would say—as he never felt the force of before. Oh, bub, bub, hu, hu, hu!"

Job had listened to this with attention. "Now, will you let me rule in this matter?" he said to Steve.

"With all my heart," said Steve.

"Look here, Miller Griffin," then said Job, speaking over the pool, "you can't expect me or my comrades to help ye until you treat us civilly. No mixed words o' that sort will we stand. Fair and square, or not at all. You must give us straightforward assurance that you will do us no harm; and that if the water runs in your stream again, and the mill goes, and I finish out my 'prenticeship, you treat me well. If you won't promise this, you are a dead man in that water to-night."

5 "A master has a right over his 'prentice, body and soul!" cried the miller, desperately, as he swam round, "and I have a right over you—and I won't be drownded!"

"I fancy you will," said Job, quietly. "Your friends be too high above to get at ye."

10 "What must I promise ye, then, Job—hu—hu—hu—bub, bub, bub!"

"Say, If I ever strike Job Tray again, he shall be at liberty to leave my service forthwith, and go to some other employ, and this is the solemn oath of me, Miller Griffin. Say that in the presence of these 15 witnesses."

"Very well—I say it—bub, bub—I say it." And the miller repeated the words.

"Now I'll help ye out," said Job. Lying down on his stomach he held out the handle of the shovel to the floating miller, and hauled him 20 towards the ledge on which we stood. Then Steve took one of the miller's hands, and Job the other, and he mounted up beside us.

"Saved,—saved!" cried Miller Griffin.

"You must stand close in," said Steve, "for there isn't much room on this narrow shelf."

25 "Ay, yes I will," replied the saved man gladly. "And now, let's get out of this dark place as soon as we can—Ho!—Cobbler Jones!—here we be coming up to ye—but I don't see him!"

"Nor I," said Steve. "Where is he?"

The whole four of us stared with all our vision at the opening the 30 miller had fallen from. But his companion had vanished.

"Well—never mind," said Miller Griffin, genially; "we'll follow. Which is the way?"

"There's no way—we can't follow," answered Steve.

"*Can't follow!*" echoed the miller, staring round, and perceiving for 35 the first time that the ledge was a prison. "What—*not saved!*" he shrieked. "Not able to get out from here?"

"We be not saved unless your friend comes back to save us," said Job. "We've been calculating upon his help—otherwise things be as bad as they were before. We three have clung here waiting for death these two hours, and now there's one more to wait for death—unless the shoemaker comes back."

Job spoke stoically in the face of the cobbler's disappearance, and Steve tried to look cool also; but I think they felt as much discouraged as I, and almost as much as the miller, at the unaccountable vanishing of Cobbler Jones.

On reflection, however, there was no reason to suppose that he had basely deserted us. Probably he had only gone to bring further assistance. But the bare possibility of disappointment at such times is enough to take the nerve from any man or boy.

"He *must* mean to come back!" the miller murmured lugubriously, as we all stood in a row on the ledge, like sparrows on the moulding of a chimney.

"I should think so," said Steve, "if he's a man."

"Yes—he must!" the miller anxiously repeated. "I once said he was a two-penny sort of workman to his face—I wish I hadn't said it, oh—how I wish I hadn't; but 'twas years and years ago, and pray heaven he's forgot it! I once called him a stingy varmint—that I did! But we've made that up, and been friends ever since. And yet there's men who'll carry a snub in their buzzoms; and perhaps he's going to punish me now!"

"'Twould be very wrong of him," said I, "to leave us three to die because you've been a wicked man in your time, miller."

"Quite true," said Job.

"Zounds take your saucy tongues!" said Griffin. "If I had elbow room on this miserable perch I'd—I'd—"

"Just do nothing," said Job at his elbow. "Have you no more sense of decency, Mr Griffin, than to go on like that, and the waters rising to drown us minute by minute?"

"Rising to drown us—hey?" said the miller.

"Yes, indeed," broke in Steve. "It has reached my feet."

CHAPTER V

How We Became Close Allies with the Villagers.

Sure enough, the water—to which we had given less attention since the miller's arrival—had kept on rising with silent and pitiless regularity. To feel it actually lapping over the ledge was enough to paralyze us all. We listened and looked, but no shoemaker appeared. In no very long time it ran into our boots, and coldly encircled our ankles.

Miller Griffin trembled so much that he could scarcely keep his standing. "If I do get out of this," he said, "I'll do good—lots of good—to everybody! Oh, oh—the water!"

"Surely you can hold your tongue if this little boy can bear it without crying out!" said Job, alluding to me.

Thus rebuked, the miller was silent; and nothing more happened till we heard a slight sound from the opening which was our only hope, and saw a slight light. We watched, and the light grew stronger, flickering about the orifice like a smile on parted lips. Then hats and heads broke above the edge of the same—one, two, three, four—then candles, arms and shoulders; and it could be seen then that our deliverers were provided with ropes.

"Ahoy—all right!" they shouted, and you may be sure we shouted back a reply.

"Quick, in the name o' goodness!" cried the miller.

A consultation took place among those above, and one of them shouted, "We'll throw you a rope's end and you must catch it. If you can make it fast, and so climb up one at a time, do it.

"If not, tie it round the first one, let him jump into the water; we'll tow him across by the rope till he's underneath us, and then haul him up."

"Yes, yes, that's the way!" said the miller. "But do be quick—I'm dead drowned up to my thighs. Let me have the rope."

"Now, miller, that's not fair!" said one of the group above—the Man who had Failed, for he was with them. "Of course you'll send up the boys first—the little boy first of all."

"I will—I will—'twas a mistake," Griffin replied with contrition.

The rope was then thrown; Job caught it, and tied it round me. It was with some misgiving that I flung myself on the water; but I did it, and, upheld by the rope, I floated across to the spot in the pool that was perpendicularly under the opening, when the men all heaved, and I felt myself swinging in the air, till I was received into the arms of half the parish. For the alarm having been given, the attempt at rescue was known all over the lower part of West Poley.

My cousin Steve was now hauled up. When he had gone the miller burst into a sudden terror at the thought of being left till the last, fearing he might not be able to catch the rope. He implored Job to let him go up first.

"Well," said Job; "so you shall—on one condition."

"Tell it, and I agree."

Job searched his pockets, and drew out a little floury pocket-book, in which he had been accustomed to enter sales of meal and bran. Without replying to the miller, he stooped to the candle and wrote. This done he said, "Sign this, and I'll let ye go."

The miller read: I hereby certify that I release from this time forth Job Tray, my apprentice, by his wish, and demand no further service from him whatever. "Very well—have your way," he said; and taking the pencil subscribed his name. By this time they had untied Steve and were flinging the rope a third time; Job caught it as before, attached it to the miller's portly person, shoved him off, and saw him hoisted. The dragging up on this occasion was a test to the muscles of those above; but it was accomplished. Then the rope was flung back for the last time, and fortunate it was that the delay was no longer. Job could only manage to secure himself with great difficulty, owing to the numbness which was creeping over him from his heavy labours and immersions. More dead than alive he was pulled to the top with the rest.

The people assembled above began questioning us, as well they might, upon how we had managed to get into our perilous position. Before we had explained, a gurgling sound was heard from the pool. Several looked over. The water whose rising had nearly caused our death was sinking suddenly; and the light of the candle, which had been left to burn itself out on the ledge, revealed a whirlpool on the surface. Steve, the only one of our trio who was in a condition to observe anything, knew in a moment what the phenomenon meant.

The weight of accumulated water had completed the task of reopening the closed tunnel or fissure which Job's and Steve's diving had begun; and the stream was rushing rapidly down the old West Poley outlet, through which it had run from geological times. In a few minutes—as I was told, for I was not an eye-witness of further events this night—the water had drained itself out, and the stream could be heard trickling across the floor of the lower cave as before the check.

In the explanations which followed our adventure, the following facts were disclosed as to our discovery by the neighbours.

The miller and the shoemaker, after a little further discussion in the road where I overheard them, decided to investigate the caves one by one. With this object in view they got a lantern, and proceeded, not to Nick's Pocket, but to a well-known cave nearer at hand called Grim Billy, which to them seemed a likely source for the river.

5   This cave was very well known up to a certain point. The floor sloped upwards, and eventually led to the margin of the hole in the dome of Nick's Pocket; but nobody was aware that it was the inner part of Nick's Pocket which the treacherous opening revealed. Rather was the unplumbed depth beneath supposed to be the mouth of an

10 abyss into which no human being could venture. Thus when a stone ascended from this abyss (the stone I threw) the searchers were amazed, till the miller's intuition suggested to him that we were there. And, what was most curious, when we were all delivered, and had gone home, and had been put into warm beds, neither the miller nor

15 the shoemaker knew for certain that they had lighted upon the source of the mill stream. Much less did they suspect the contrivance we had discovered for turning the water to East or West Poley, at pleasure.

   By a piece of good fortune, Steve's mother heard nothing of what had happened to us till we appeared dripping at the door, and could

20 testify to our deliverance before explaining our perils.

   The result which might have been expected to all of us, followed in the case of Steve. He caught cold from his prolonged duckings, and the cold was followed by a serious illness.

   The illness of Steve was attended with slight fever, which left him

25 very weak, though neither Job nor I suffered any evil effects from our immersion.

   The mill-stream having flowed back to its course, the mill was again started, and the miller troubled himself no further about the river-head; but Job, thanks to his ingenuity, was no longer the

30 miller's apprentice. He had been lucky enough to get a place in another mill many miles off, the very next day after our escape.

   I frequently visited Steve in his bed-room, and, on one of these occasions, he said to me, "Suppose I were to die, and you were to go away home, and Job were always to stay away in another part of

35 England, the secret of that mill-stream head would be lost to our village; so that if by chance the vent this way were to choke, and the water run into the East Poley channel, our people would not know how to recover it. They saved our lives, and we ought to make them the handsome return of telling them the whole manœuvre."

This was quite my way of thinking, and it was decided that Steve should tell all as soon as he was well enough. But I soon found that his anxiety on the matter seriously affected his recovery. He had a scheme, he said, for preventing such a loss of the stream again.

Discovering that Steve was uneasy in his mind, the doctor—to whom I explained that Steve desired to make personal reparation—insisted that his wish be gratified at once—namely, that some of the leading inhabitants of West Poley should be brought up to his bedroom, and learn what he had to say. His mother assented, and messages were sent to them at once.

The villagers were ready enough to come, for they guessed the object of the summons, and they were anxious, too, to know more particulars of our adventures than we had as yet had opportunity to tell them. Accordingly, at a little past six that evening, when the sun was going down, we heard their footsteps ascending the stairs, and they entered. Among them there were the blacksmith, the shoemaker, the dairyman, the Man who had Failed, a couple of farmers; and some men who worked on the farms were also admitted.

Some chairs were brought up from below, and, when our visitors had settled down, Steve's mother, who was very anxious about him, said, "Now, my boy, we are all here. What have you to tell?"

Steve began at once, explaining first how we had originally discovered the inner cave, and how we walked on till we came to a stream.

"What we want to know is this," said the shoemaker, "is that great pool we fetched you out of, the head of the mill-stream?"

Steve explained that it was not a natural pool, and other things which the reader already knows. He then came to the description of the grand manœuvre by which the stream could be turned into either the east or the west valley.

"But how did you get down there?" asked one. "Did you walk in through Giant's Ear, or Goblin's Cellar, or Grim Billy?"

"We did not enter by either of these," said Steve. "We entered by Nick's Pocket."

"Ha!" said the company, "that explains all the mystery."

" 'Tis amazing," said the miller, who had entered, "that folks should have lived and died here for generations, and never ha' found out that Nick's Pocket led to the river spring!"

"Well, that isn't all I want to say," resumed Steve. "Suppose any people belonging to East Poley should find out the secret, they would go there and turn the water into their own vale; and, perhaps, close up the other channel in such a way that we could scarcely open it again. But didn't somebody leave the room a minute ago?—who is it that's going away?"

"I fancy a man went out," said the dairyman looking round. One or two others said the same, but dusk having closed in it was not apparent which of the company had gone away.

Steve continued: "Therefore before the secret is known, let somebody of our village go and close up the little gallery we entered by, and the upper mouth you look in from. Then there'll be no danger of our losing the water again."

The proposal was received with unanimous commendation, and after a little more consultation, and the best wishes of the neighbours for Steve's complete recovery, they took their leave, arranging to go and stop the cave entrances the next evening.

As the doctor had thought, so it happened. No sooner was his sense of responsibility gone, than Steve began to mend with miraculous rapidity. Four and twenty hours made such a difference in him that he said to me, with animation, the next evening: "Do, Leonard, go and bring me word what they are doing at Nick's Pocket. They ought to be going up there about this time to close up the gallery. But 'tis quite dark—you'll be afraid."

"No—not I," I replied, and off I went, having told my aunt my mission.

It was, indeed, quite dark, and it was not till I got quite close to the mill that I found several West Poley men had gathered in the road opposite thereto. The miller was not among them, being too much shaken by his fright for any active enterprise. They had spades, pickaxes, and other tools, and were just preparing for the start to the caves.

I followed behind, and as soon as we reached the outskirts of West Poley, I found they all made straight for Nick's Pocket as planned. Arrived there they lit their candles and we went into the interior. Though they had been most precisely informed by Steve how to find the connecting gallery with the inner cavern, so cunningly was it hidden by Nature's hand that they probably would have occupied no small time in lighting on it, if I had not gone forward and pointed out the nook.

They thanked me, and the dairyman, as one of the most active of the group, taking a spade in one hand, and a light in the other, prepared to creep in first and foremost. He had not advanced many steps before he reappeared in the outer cave, looking as pale as death.

CHAPTER VI

How all Our Difficulties Came to an End.

"What's the matter!" said the shoemaker.

"Somebody's there!" he gasped.

"It can't be," said a farmer. "Till those boys found the hole, not a being in the world knew of such a way in."

"Well, come and harken for yourselves," said the dairyman.

We crept close to the gallery mouth and listened. Peck, peck, peck; scrape, scrape, scrape, could be heard distinctly inside.

"Whoever they call themselves, they are at work like the busy bee!" said the farmer.

It was ultimately agreed that some of the party should go softly round into Grim Billy, creep up the ascent within the cave, and peer through the opening that looked down through the roof of the cave before us. By this means they might learn, unobserved, what was going on.

It was no sooner proposed than carried out. The baker and shoemaker were the ones that went round, and, as there was nothing to be seen where the others waited, I thought I would bear them company. To get to Grim Billy, a circuit of considerable extent was necessary; moreover, we had to cross the mill-stream. The mill had been stopped for the night, some time before, and, hence, it was by a pure chance we noticed that the river was gradually draining itself out. The misfortune initiated by Steve was again upon the village.

"I wonder if the miller knows it?" murmured the shoemaker. "If not, we won't tell him, or he may lose his senses outright."

"Then the folks in the cave are enemies!" said the farmer.

"True," said the baker, "for nobody else can have done this—let's push on."

Grim Billy being entered, we crawled on our hands and knees up the slope, which eventually terminated at the hole above Nick's Pocket—a hole that probably no human being had passed through before we were hoisted up through it on the evening of our marvellous escape. We were careful to make no noise in ascending, and, at the edge, we gazed cautiously over.

A striking sight met our view. A number of East Poley men were assembled below on the floor, which had been for awhile submerged by our exploit; and they were working with all their might to build and close up the old outlet of the stream towards West Poley, having already, as it appeared, opened the new opening towards their own village, discovered by Steve. We understood it in a moment, and, descending with the same softness as before, we returned to where our comrades were waiting for us in the other cave, where we told them the strange sight we had seen.

"How did they find out the secret?" the shoemaker inquired under his breath. "We have guarded it as we would ha' guarded our lives."

"I can guess!" replied the baker. "Have you forgot how somebody went away from Master Steve Draycot's bedroom in the dusk last night, and we didn't know who it was? Half an hour after, such a man was seen crossing the hill to East Poley; I was told so to-day. We've been surprised, and must hold our own by main force, since we can no longer do it by stealth."

"How, main force?" asked the blacksmith and a farmer simultaneously.

"By closing the gallery they went in by," said the baker. "Then we shall have them in prison, and can bring them to book rarely."

The rest being all irritated at having been circumvented so slily and selfishly by the East Poley men, the baker's plan met with ready acceptance. Five of our body at once chose hard boulders from the outer cave, of such a bulk that they would roll about half-way into the passage or gallery—where there was a slight enlargement—but which would pass no further. These being put in position, they were easily wedged there, and it was impossible to remove them from within, owing to the diminishing size of the passage, except by more powerful tools than they had, which were only spades. We now felt sure of our antagonists, and in a far better position to argue with them than if they had been free. No longer taking the trouble to preserve silence, we, of West Poley, walked in a body round to the other cave—Grim Billy—ascended the inclined floor like a flock of goats, and arranged ourselves in a group at the opening that impended over Nick's Pocket.

The East Poley men were still working on, absorbed in their labour, and were unconscious that twenty eyes regarded them from above like stars.

"Let's halloo!" said the baker.

Halloo we did with such vigour that the East Poley men, taken absolutely unawares, well nigh sprang into the air at the shock it produced on their nerves. Their spades flew from their hands, and they stared around in dire alarm, for the echoes confused them as to the direction whence their hallooing came. They finally turned their eyes upwards, and saw us individuals of the rival village far above them, illuminated with candles; and with countenances grave and stern as a bench of unmerciful judges.

"Men of East Poley," said the baker, "we have caught ye in the execution of a most unfair piece of work. Because of a temporary turning of our water into your vale by a couple of meddlesome boys—a piece of mischief that was speedily repaired—you have thought fit to covet our stream. You have sent a spy to find out its secret, and have meanfully come here to steal the stream for yourselves forever. This cavern is in our parish, and you have no right here at all."

"The waters of the earth be as much ours as yours," said one from beneath. But the remainder were thunderstruck, for they knew that their chance had lain entirely in strategy and not in argument.

The shoemaker then spoke: "Ye have entered upon our property, and diverted the water, and made our parish mill useless, and caused us other losses. Do ye agree to restore it to its old course, close up the new course ye have been at such labour to widen—in short, to leave things as they have been from time immemorial?"

"No-o-o-o!" was shouted from below in a yell of defiance.

"Very well, then," said the baker, "we must make you. Gentlemen, ye are prisoners. Until you restore that water to us, you will bide where you be."

The East Poley men rushed to escape by the way they had entered. But half way up the tunnel a barricade of adamantine blocks barred their footsteps. "Bring spades!" shouted the foremost. But the stones were so well wedged, and the passage so small, that, as we had anticipated, no engineering force at their disposal could make the least impression upon the blocks. They returned to the inner cave disconsolately.

"D'ye give in?" we asked them.

"Never!" said they doggedly.

"Let 'em sweat—let 'em sweat," said the shoemaker, placidly. "They'll tell a different tale by to-morrow morning. Let 'em bide for
5 the night, and say no more."

In pursuance of this idea we withdrew from our position, and, passing out of Grim Billy, went straight home. Steve was excited by the length of my stay, and still more when I told him the cause of it. "What—got them prisoners in the cave?" he said. "I must go myself
10 to-morrow and see the end of this!"

Whether it was partly due to the excitement of the occasion, or solely to the recuperative powers of a strong constitution, cannot be said; but certain it is that next morning, on hearing the villagers shouting and gathering together, Steve sprang out of bed, declaring
15 that he must go with me to see what was happening to the prisoners. The doctor was hastily called in, and gave it as his opinion that the outing would do Steve no harm, if he were warmly wrapped up; and soon away we went, just in time to overtake the men who had started on their way.

20 With breathless curiosity we entered Grim Billy, lit our candles and clambered up the incline. Almost before we reached the top, exclamations ascended through the chasm to Nick's Pocket, there being such words as, "We give in!" "Let us out!" "We give up the water forever!"

25 Looking in upon them, we found their aspect to be very different from what it had been the night before. Some had extemporized a couch with smock-frocks and gaiters, and jumped up from a sound sleep thereon; while others had their spades in their hands, as if undoing what they had been at such pains to build up, as was proved
30 in a moment by their saying eagerly, "We have begun to put it right, and shall finish soon—we are restoring the river to his old bed—give us your word, good gentlemen, that when it is done we shall be free!"

"Certainly," replied our side with great dignity. "We have said so already."

35 Our arrival stimulated them in the work of repair, which had hitherto been somewhat desultory. Then shovels entered the clay and rubble like giants' tongues; they lit up more candles, and in half an hour had completely demolished the structure raised the night before with such labour and amazing solidity that it might have been

expected to last forever. The final stone rolled away, the much tantalized river withdrew its last drop from the new channel, and resumed its original course once more.

While the East Poley men had been completing this task, some of our party had gone back to Nick's Pocket, and there, after much exertion, succeeded in unpacking the boulders from the horizontal passage admitting to the inner cave. By the time this was done, the prisoners within had finished their work of penance, and we West Poley men, who had remained to watch them, rejoined our companions. Then we all stood back, while those of East Poley came out, walking between their vanquishers, like the Romans under the Caudine Forks, when they surrendered to the Samnites. They glared at us with suppressed rage, and passed without saying a word.

"I see from their manner that we have not heard the last of this," said the Man who had Failed, thoughtfully. He had just joined us, and learnt the state of the case.

"I was thinking as much," said the shoemaker. "As long as that cave is known in Poley, so long will they bother us about the stream."

"I wish it had never been found out," said the baker bitterly. "If not now upon us, they will be playing that trick upon our children when we are dead and gone."

Steve glanced at me, and there was sadness in his look.

We walked home considerably in the rear of the rest, by no means at ease. It was impossible to disguise from ourselves that Steve had lost the good feeling of his fellow parishioners by his explorations and their results.

As the West Poley men had predicted, so it turned out. Some months afterwards, when I had gone back to my home and school, and Steve was learning to superintend his mother's farm, I heard that another midnight entry had been made into the cave by the rougher characters of East Poley. They diverted the stream as before, and when the miller and other inhabitants of the west village rose in the morning, behold, their stream was dry! The West Poley folk were furious, and rushed to Nick's Pocket. The mischief-makers were gone, and there was no legal proof as to their identity, though it was indirectly clear enough where they had come from. With some difficulty the water was again restored, but not till Steve had again been spoken of as the original cause of the misfortunes.

About this time I paid another visit to my cousin and aunt. Steve seemed to have grown a good deal older than when I had last seen him, and, almost as soon as we were alone, he began to speak on the subject of the mill-stream.

"I am glad you have come, Leonard," he said, "for I want to talk
5 to you. I have never been happy, you know, since the adventure; I don't like the idea that by a freak of mine our village should be placed at the mercy of the East Poleyites; I shall never be liked again unless I make that river as secure from interruption as it was before."

10   "But that can't be," said I.

"Well, I have a scheme," said Steve musingly. "I am not so sure that the river may not be made as secure as it was before."

"But how? What is the scheme based on?" I asked, incredulously.

"I cannot reveal to you at present," said he. "All I can say is, that I
15 have injured my native village, that I owe it amends, and that I'll pay the debt if it's a possibility."

I soon perceived from my cousin's manner at meals and elsewhere that the scheme, whatever it might be, occupied him to the exclusion of all other thoughts. But he would not speak to me about it. I
20 frequently missed him for spaces of an hour or two, and soon conjectured that these hours of absence were spent in furtherance of his plan.

The last day of my visit came round, and to tell the truth I was not sorry, for Steve was so preoccupied as to be anything but a pleasant
25 companion. I walked up to the village alone, and soon became aware that something had happened.

During the night another raid had been made upon the river head—with but partial success, it is true; but the stream was so much reduced that the mill-wheel would not turn, and the dipping pools
30 were nearly empty. It was resolved to repair the mischief in the evening, but the disturbance in the village was very great, for the attempt proved that the more unscrupulous characters of East Poley were not inclined to desist.

Before I had gone much further, I was surprised to discern in the
35 distance a figure which seemed to be Steve's, though I thought I had left him at the rear of his mother's premises.

He was making for Nick's Pocket, and following thither I reached the mouth of the cave just in time to see him enter.

"Steve!" I called out. He heard me and came back. He was pale, and there seemed to be something in his face which I had never seen there before.

"Ah—Leonard," he said, "you have traced me. Well, you are just in time. The folks think of coming to mend this mischief as soon as their day's work is over, but perhaps it won't be necessary. My scheme may do instead."

"How—do instead?" asked I.

"Well, save them the trouble," he said with assumed carelessness. "I had almost decided not to carry it out, though I have got the materials in readiness, but the doings of the night have stung me; I carry out my plan."

"When?"

"Now—this hour—this moment. The stream must flow into its right channel, and stay there, and no man's hands must be able to turn it elsewhere. Now good-bye, in case of accidents."

To my surprise, Steve shook hands with me solemnly, and wringing from me a promise not to follow, disappeared into the blackness of the cave.

For some moments I stood motionless where Steve had left me, not quite knowing what to do. Hearing footsteps behind my back, I looked round. To my great pleasure I saw Job approaching, dressed up in his best clothes, and with him the Man who had Failed.

Job was glad to see me. He had come to West Poley for a holiday, from the situation with the farmer which, as I now learned for the first time, the Man who had Failed had been the means of his obtaining. Observing, I suppose, the perplexity upon my face, they asked me what was the matter, and I, after some hesitation, told them of Steve. The Man who had Failed looked grave.

"Is it serious?" I asked him.

"It may be," said he, in that poetico-philosophic strain which, under more favouring circumstances, might have led him on to the intellectual eminence of a Coleridge or an Emerson. "Your cousin, like all such natures, is rushing into another extreme, that may be worse than the first. The opposite of error is error still; from careless adventuring at other people's expense he may have flown to rash self-sacrifice. He contemplates some violent remedy, I make no doubt. How long has he been in the cave? We had better follow him."

Before I could reply, we were startled by a jet of smoke, like that from the muzzle of a gun, bursting from the mouth of Nick's Pocket;

and this was immediately followed by a deadened rumble like thunder underground. In another moment a duplicate of the noise reached our ears from over the hill, in the precise direction of Grim Billy.

5 "Oh—what can it be?" said I.

"Gunpowder," said the Man who had Failed, slowly.

"Ah—yes—I know what he's done—he has blasted the rocks inside!" cried Job. "Depend upon it, that's his plan for closing up the way to the river head."

10 "And for losing his life into the bargain," said our companion. "But no—he may be alive. We must go in at once—or as soon as we can breathe there."

Job ran for lights, and before he had returned we heard a familiar sound from the direction of the village. It was the patter of the mill-
15 wheel. Job came up almost at the moment, and with him a crowd of the village people.

"The river is right again," they shouted. "Water runs better than ever—a full, steady stream, all on a sudden—just when we heard the rumble underground."

20 "Steve has done it!" I said.

"A brave fellow," said the Man who had Failed. "Pray that he is not hurt."

Job had lighted the candles, and, when we were entering, some more villagers, who at the noise of the explosion had run to Grim
25 Billy, joined us. "Grim Billy is partly closed up inside!" they told us. "Where you used to climb up the slope to look over into Nick's Pocket, 'tis all altered. There's no longer any opening there; the whole rock has crumbled down as if the mountain had sunk bodily."

Without waiting to answer, we, who were about to enter Nick's
30 Pocket, proceeded on our way. We soon had penetrated to the outer approaches, though nearly suffocated by the sulphurous atmosphere; but we could get no further than the first cavern. At a point somewhat in advance of the little gallery to the inner cave, Nick's Pocket ceased to exist. Its roof had sunk. The whole superimposed mountain, as it
35 seemed, had quietly settled down upon the hollow places beneath it, closing like a pair of bellows, and barring all human entrance.

But alas, where was Steve? "I would liever have had no water in West Poley forevermore than have lost Steve!" said Job.

37† liever] never

"And so would I!" said many of us.

To add to our terror, news was brought into the cave at that moment that Steve's mother was approaching; and how to meet my poor aunt was more than we could think.

But suddenly a shout was heard. A few of the party, who had not penetrated so far into the cave as we had done, were exclaiming, "Here he is!" We hastened back, and found they were in a small side hollow, close to the entrance, which we had passed by unheeded. The Man who had Failed was there, and he and the baker were carrying something into the light. It was Steve—apparently dead, or unconscious.

"Don't be frightened," said the baker to me. "He's not dead; perhaps not much hurt."

As he had declared, so it turned out. No sooner was Steve in the open air, than he unclosed his eyes, looked round with a stupefied expression, and sat up.

"Steve—Steve!" said Job and I, simultaneously.

"All right," said Steve, recovering his senses by degrees. "I'll tell— how it happened—in a minute or two."

Then his mother came up, and was at first terrified enough, but on seeing Steve gradually get upon his legs, she recovered her equanimity. He soon was able to explain all. He said that the damage to the village by his tampering with the stream had weighed upon his mind, and led him to revolve many schemes for its cure. With this in view he had privately made examination of the cave; when he discovered that the whole superincumbent mass, forming the roof of the inner cave, was divided from the walls of the same by a vein of sand, and, that it was only kept in its place by a slim support at one corner. It seemed to him if this support could be removed, the upper mass would descend by its own weight, like the brick of a brick-trap when the peg is withdrawn.

He laid his plans accordingly; procuring gunpowder, and scooping out holes for the same, at central points in the rock. When all this was done, he waited a while, in doubt as to the effect; and might possibly never have completed his labours, but for the renewed attempt upon the river. He then made up his mind, and attached the fuse. After lighting it, he would have reached the outside safely enough but for the accident of stumbling as he ran, which threw him so heavily on the ground, that, before he could recover himself and go forward, the explosion had occurred.

All of us congratulated him, and the whole village was joyful, for no less than three thousand, four hundred and fifty tons of rock and earth—according to calculations made by an experienced engineer a short time afterwards—had descended between the river's head and
5 all human interference, so that there was not much fear of any more East Poley manœuvres for turning the stream into their valley.

The inhabitants of the parish, gentle and simple, said that Steve had made ample amends for the harm he had done; and their good-will was further evidenced by his being invited to no less than
10 nineteen Christmas and New Year's parties during the following holidays.

As we left the cave, Steve, Job, Mrs Draycot and I walked behind the Man who had Failed.

"Though this has worked well," he said to Steve, "it is by the
15 merest chance in the world. Your courage is praiseworthy, but you see the risks that are incurred when people go out of their way to meddle with what they don't understand. Exceptionally smart actions, such as you delight in, should be carefully weighed with a view to their utility before they are begun. Quiet perseverance in
20 clearly defined courses is, as a rule, better than the erratic exploits that may do much harm."

Steve listened respectfully enough to this, but he said to his mother afterwards: "He has failed in life, and how can his opinions be worth anything?"
25 "For this reason," said she. "He is one who has failed, not from want of sense, but from want of energy; and people of that sort, when kindly, are better worth attending to than those successful ones, who have never seen the seamy side of things. I would advise you to listen to him."
30 Steve probably did; for he is now the largest gentleman-farmer of those parts, remarkable for his avoidance of anything like speculative exploits.

THE END.

Old Mrs Chundle

INTRODUCTION

Unpublished during Hardy's lifetime, unmentioned in his autobiography or surviving correspondence, 'Old Mrs Chundle' might have disappeared altogether if it had not been for the persistence of Crosby Gaige. A successful Broadway producer, Gaige's interests were wideranging and included publishing and book-collecting—specifically the works of his contemporaries, beginning with Hardy and ending with Virginia Woolf. According to Gaige's autobiography, *Footlights and Highlights*, his collection was 'rich in personalized items'—'manuscripts, correspondence, corrected proof sheets, autographed copies'[1]—and it was presumably on Gaige's behalf[2] that the London literary agent Curtis Brown attempted (without success) to purchase a Hardy manuscript in September 1927.[3] Undissuaded, Gaige tried to obtain something of Hardy's to publish in what he described as his 'series of books by well-known contemporaries, each limited in number, planned by a top-notch designer, and printed in shops equipped to do especially fine work'.[4] But on 8 December 1927 Florence Hardy was obliged to tell Curtis Brown, who was acting as intermediary, that 'The Duke's Reappearance' had already been published in a volume in both England and the United States,[5] and on 5 June 1928 that Macmillan would doubtless strongly object to

---

[1] Crosby Gaige, *Footlights and Highlights* (New York: E. P. Dutton, 1948), 200.

[2] In her 8 Dec. 1927 letter to Curtis Brown (typed transcript; Beinecke) FEH referred to Gaige as 'your friend'.

[3] FEH's 25 Sept. 1927 letter to Curtis Brown (Robert H. Taylor Collection, Princeton University) states that no manuscripts were available, or likely to be, most having been distributed 'among the different museums etc. that wished to have them'.

[4] Gaige, *Footlights and Highlights*, 201.

[5] Typed transcript (Beinecke). The 1927 New York private printing of eighty-nine copies of 'The Duke's Reappearance' (see Carroll A. Wilson, *Thirteen Author Collections of the Nineteenth Century and Five Centuries of Familiar Quotations*, i (privately printed for Charles Scribner's Sons, New York, 1950), 109) may have been Gaige's; if so, it was perhaps already printed before FEH's letter arrived and, as an unauthorized edition, would not have been subsequently mentioned to her.

the publication of a special edition of the *Winter Words* poems.[6] In this later letter she did, however, offer 'Old Mrs Chundle':

I have in my possession the MS. of an unpublished story by my husband, which he wrote many years ago but never published. It was intended to form one of the collection known as "Life's Little Ironies" but for certain personal reasons my husband held it back. He intended to publish it at some time I think as he copied it out carefully some years ago. It has not even been typed and no-one but myself has read it. Would this be suitable do you think?

Florence Hardy was willing to let Gaige not only publish the story but also purchase the manuscript,[7] though she withdrew the latter offer upon learning from legal counsel that all unpublished manuscripts were the joint property of her husband's literary executors, namely Sydney Cockerell and herself.[8] Gaige was evidently eager to publish the story, and on 22 June Florence Hardy, apparently not expecting any objections, sent the agreement to her co-executor for signature. That she and Cockerell had previously discussed the story's appearing in a private printing by herself can be inferred from the covering letter: 'On consideration I felt that it would be better to let Crosby Gaige do the publishing. He does it perfectly I am told, & I don't want to go into the business. Perhaps I've done too many 1st editions already.'[9] Cockerell, however, had evidently not seen the story at this point—Florence Hardy wrote that she would have a typewritten copy made almost immediately[10]—and after reading it he objected to the proposed publication, ostensibly (according to her) 'on the ground that the story is a poor one'.[11] For her own part Florence Hardy claimed that he was refusing to sign the agreement 'merely because he was not consulted in the first instance'.[12] Probably both motivations figured in his initial response, which appears to have emphasized the inappropriate independence of her action as well as the desirability of obtaining another opinion, for on 26 June she wrote:

I am sorry if I have given you trouble about "Mrs Chundle". I thought I would save you letter-writing etc, by doing it 'off my own bat'. I did not say anything about it to Barrie, as I thought he was worried sufficiently about T.H.'s affairs,

---

[6] Adams.   [7] FEH to Curtis Brown, 12 June 1928 (UCLA).
[8] To Curtis Brown, 16 June 1928 (Adams).
[9] Beinecke.   [10] 22 June 1928 (Beinecke).
[11] To Michael Joseph (general manager at Curtis Brown), 3 July 1928 (Adams).
[12] To Joseph, 3 July 1928 (Adams).

& have no wish to become a nuisance to him. I'll show it to him if you think fit.[13]

Whether it was Florence Hardy or Cockerell who in fact gave James Barrie a typescript is not clear, though it was probably the latter; in any case—according to Cockerell's diary—by 29 June Barrie had read the story and sided with him on the question of publication.[14] Florence Hardy seems to have felt that the two men were ganging up on her, as they had immediately after her husband's death when she was too tired and distressed to prevent the interment of his ashes at Westminster Abbey, only his heart being buried in his chosen resting-place of Stinsford.[15] There had also been disagreement over a Hardy memorial, Cockerell proposing to erect on Rainbarrow a column like the one raised to Sir Thomas Masterman Hardy of Trafalgar fame, and Florence Hardy utterly rejecting the idea that her husband would have wanted—as Cockerell claimed he did—such a prominent monument.[16] She eventually won that battle, but in the meantime had to fight another over *Early Life* and *Later Years*, the two ostensibly biographical volumes published over her name. Granted by Hardy's 'Private Memorandum' the freedom to remove from the materials he had left behind him anything which 'should seem to be indiscreet, belittling, monotonous, trivial, provocative, or in other ways unadvisable' and to include 'other details that may be deemed necessary',[17] she was obliged to decide what changes would best fulfil her husband's intentions as she understood them[18]—a position rendered particularly difficult by her knowledge (at this point still exclusive) of his authorship. Although she did incorporate suggestions—including substantial additions and deletions—from various readers (notably Barrie), she also rejected a number of proposed alterations from those same sources.

Cockerell's admission on 29 June 1928 that he had discussed with Barrie both the *Early Life* proofs and 'Old Mrs Chundle' led to a violent quarrel, as he noted in his diary entry for that date:

[13] Beinecke.   [14] Cockerell 1928 diary (BL Add. MS 52666), fo. 35ʳ.
[15] See *Biography*, 574–7, and 'Thomas Hardy's Will', in *Thomas Hardy's Will and Other Wills of his Family*, ed. J. Stevens Cox (Mount Durand, Guernsey: Toucan Press, 1967), clause 1, 1.
[16] Cockerell, 'Memorials to Thomas Hardy', letter to *The Times*, 17 Jan. 1928, 15; Wilfrid Blunt, *Cockerell* (London: Hamish Hamilton, 1964), 218–20.   [17] DCM.
[18] See Millgate, *Life*, pp. xix–xxvi; FEH's motives were not always disinterested, especially with regard to the removal of references to EH.

Spent all the morning going over proofs of the Hardy memoir with Barrie. . . . I met Mrs Hardy & went with her to Dorchester by the 4.30 train. . . . She was very tired. After dinner we started on the proofs. She was greatly displeased at my having gone over the proofs with Barrie & consulted him about a story of Hardy's called Old Mrs Chundle, which he and I think should not be printed. I had done this in all innocence, knowing that she had sent him a set of the proofs & thinking that she would approve.[19]

The following evening apparently saw more proof-correction and 'more severe reproaches' which 'Went on till midnight'.[20] Nor did the next day bring peace: 'Another stormy outburst from F.H. who had not slept. All this fuss, as it seemed to me, quite uncalled for, as I had only been doing my best to help her to improve her book in little ways.'[21] The violence of Florence Hardy's reaction was doubtless attributable in part to what Barrie described as 'her extreme fatigue and nervous exhaustion',[22] in part to her fear and resentment[23] of the two men who seemed again to be uniting to pressure her into actions—specifically 'improving' the 'biography'—which she would ultimately regret.

It is difficult to know whether Florence Hardy genuinely believed that she was fulfilling her husband's intentions in arranging for the publication of 'Old Mrs Chundle'. Her initial statement to Curtis Brown is not without qualification: 'He intended to publish it at some time *I think* as he copied it out carefully some years ago' (emphasis added).[24] It was only after Cockerell had objected that she wrote to Michael Joseph (then general manager for Curtis Brown) of Hardy's having 'expressly [given her] permission to have the story printed',[25] and similarly told Cockerell himself:

I can positively affirm that my husband gave me that MS. with instructions that it might be printed. He copied it out carefully himself, & fastened the pages together, thus showing that he did *not* consider it valueless—though he certainly did not wish it published during his lifetime.[26]

---

[19] Cockerell 1928 diary, fo. 35^r.   [20] Ibid., fo. 35^r.   [21] Ibid., fo. 35^v.

[22] As recorded by Cockerell in his diary entry for 2 July 1928 (ibid., fo. 35^v).

[23] FEH had some justification for expecting Barrie to support her, since on 14 June she had apparently told Cockerell that it was 'as good as settled' that she and Barrie were to marry the following year; by January it was clear, however, that the marriage was not to take place (Cockerell 1928 diary, fo. 33^r; 1929 diary (BL Add. MS 52667), fo. 6^r; Blunt, *Cockerell*, 223).

[24] 5 June 1928 (Adams).   [25] 3 July 1928 (Adams).

[26] 24 July 1928 (Beinecke).

Cockerell was not convinced. He had promised to sign the agreement 'if a competent judge—Mr. F. M[.] Forster, for example, approve[d] of the publication',[27] but Forster, perhaps reluctant to offend either Florence Hardy or Cockerell,[28] refused to commit himself. Having promised to 'do [his] best to send an impartial criticism',[29] he sent in fact an evasive one:

I like the story. The humour made me laugh a great deal. If it was the work of any writer of ordinary reputation I should urge you to publish it. As it is I can't quite make up my mind—I think you should get another opinion. One doesn't want the reviewers to say 'this is a rejected scrap', & nothing else, & in view of Mr Hardy's high position there is a danger of this.[30]

Florence Hardy chose to read the judgement favourably ('E.M. Forster thinks the story good, in a way'),[31] Cockerell evidently did not, and the impasse continued.

The deterioration of her relationship with Cockerell is reflected in the increasing formality of her letters: the pre-disagreement 'Yours ever— F.E.H.'[32] becomes on 11 July 1928 'Yours very sincerely, Florence Hardy'; on 24 July the 'very' is omitted and the opening 'Dear Sydney' has even given place to 'Dear Mr Cockerell'.[33] On 8 August Cockerell noted in his diary that their 'differences of the weekend of June 29–July 2 [were] composed',[34] though apparently not resolved, for three days later she replied to a telegram from Curtis Brown regarding the proposed publication: 'I can only repeat that my co-executor Mr Sydney Cockerell still withholds his consent.'[35]

But, in spite of Cockerell's objections, 'Old Mrs Chundle' was published a few months later. How Florence Hardy eventually

[27] As recorded in FEH to Joseph, 3 July 1928 (Adams).
[28] Forster, described by FEH as 'a close personal friend' (to Joseph, 5 July; Adams), apparently also found Cockerell difficult, for on 3 July he wrote:
I am not surprised you find Cockerell a trial. I could not work with him for five minutes, and if he has been as insensitive with you as he has with me [over another and unconnected matter] I cannot believe that M' Hardy would wish you to undergo the trials of the coexecutorship. (Adams; Forster's square brackets)
[29] To FEH, 3 July 1928 (Adams).
[30] As quoted in FEH to Cockerell, 11 July 1928 (Beinecke).
[31] To Cockerell, 11 July 1928 (Beinecke).
[32] E.g. 6 May, 22 June, and 26 June 1928 (Beinecke).
[33] Beinecke.   [34] Cockerell 1928 diary, fo. 40ᵛ.
[35] 11 Aug. 1928 (typed transcript; Harry Ransom Humanities Research Center, University of Texas at Austin).

managed to act without his approval can perhaps be explained by the twelfth clause of her husband's will:

I bequeath all my unpublished Manuscripts papers letters and documents of a literary character to my Literary Executors hereinafter named and I leave it to their absolute discretion (after considering the instructions I may leave with my wife or in writing) to decide which (if any) of my Manuscripts papers letters and documents may be published after my death ...[36]

Since Florence Hardy insisted that she had permission to print the story, she would have been able to point to her husband's stipulation that instructions left with her should be given first consideration.

In any case, the eventual publication was certainly not the result of a change of opinion on Cockerell's part: Florence Hardy must simply have decided to act alone as literary executor, at least in this instance. Cockerell's letter to the *Times Literary Supplement*, published 14 March 1935, while acknowledging his literary executorship, disclaimed all responsibility for the recent private printing of 'Indiscretion' and emphasized that 'Old Mrs Chundle' had been published in spite of his 'very strong objection'.[37] Writing to Purdy in 1948 he reiterated: 'I very strongly disapproved of the printing of "Old Mrs Chundle["], and so did Barrie. But FEH was obdurate about it.'[38]

Even before the story was published, however, she tried to draw back from what she had done: 'Old Mrs Chundle' appeared in the February 1929 issue of the Philadelphia *Ladies' Home Journal* (published 'ON THE FIRST DAY OF EACH MONTH') and as early as 12 January that year she had written to Cockerell about preventing the publication of Gaige's limited edition.[39] By that date it would clearly have been too late to do anything about the *Ladies' Home Journal*, and in writing to Bliss on 15 January she referred to the publication as a *fait accompli*: 'I am much relieved by your opinion concerning "Old Mrs Chundle". At the same time I much regret that it was ever printed.'[40] The following day she 'surrendered' to Cockerell:

I have got Mr Curtis Brown to stop, at any rate until we have talked over the matter—the publication in the limited edition of 'Old Mrs Chundle" [*sic*]. I have taken back his cheque, & please do not sign any agreement if any is sent

[36] *Thomas Hardy's Will*, 3.

[37] Sydney Cockerell, 'Early Hardy Stories', letter to the *Times Literary Supplement*, 14 Mar. 1935.

[38] 2 Nov. 1948 (Millgate collection).   [39] Beinecke.

[40] Morris Parrish Collection, Princeton University.

to you. I find I was misled—& I also very deeply regret the publication in 'The Ladies [*sic*] Home Journal'. It will not be published in England in any case. About the publication of letters etc, & the few unpublished poems I intend to leave everything in your hands as I fear I am liable to make very serious mistakes ...[41]

But in a letter of the same date which evidently crossed with hers, Cockerell executed a retreat of his own in response to her earlier suggestion that he should discuss the Gaige edition with Curtis Brown: 'I would rather leave any decisions about M[rs] Chundle entirely in your hands, as I think was arranged between us.'[42] Cockerell may have changed his mind after seeing her on 18 January, when he described her as 'on the verge of a nervous breakdown', since he did see Curtis Brown 'about Hardy matters' the following week.[43] Perhaps it was already too late—copies of *Old Mrs. Chundle* were delivered to Random House and the Fountain Press by the printers, Merrymount Press, in the latter part of January 1929[44] and some may already have been in circulation—or perhaps Florence Hardy simply reverted to her original position. The story was in any case published by Gaige in a limited edition of 755 copies,[45] and Cockerell was later to claim that upon reading 'some condemnation' of it Florence Hardy told him 'in a flood of tears that she would never again go against [his] judgment'.[46]

Whether or not Hardy would have approved of the story's volume publication—or indeed of its collection here or in the New Wessex

[41] Beinecke; the *Ladies' Home Journal* could, however, be sent for 'a shilling *anywhere in England*' (Feb. 1929 issue, 3). FEH's 11 July 1928 letter to Daniel Macmillan suggests that an English edition of 'Old Mrs Chundle' had been discussed, but on 11 Jan. 1929 she wrote: 'I have decided that on no account would I like that story to be published in England, & much regret its having been published in America[.] So would you please burn the typewritten copy' (BL Add. MS 54926).

[42] Draft (Beinecke).   [43] Cockerell 1929 diary, fo. 6[v].

[44] John Bianchi (of the Merrymount Press) to Purdy, 8 Oct. 1942 (Millgate collection).

[45] Both the Gaige edition and the *Ladies' Home Journal* printing were evidently set from one of the three typescripts—or copy derived from it—FEH sent to Curtis Brown (FEH to Curtis Brown, 9 June 1928, UCLA), since many of the texts' variant readings can be found in a surviving typescript bearing a Curtis Brown address label and accompanied by a note from FEH (David Holmes collection). The typescript itself, however, contains no markings of any kind and was presumably not used as setting-copy.

[46] To Purdy, 2 Nov. 1948 (Millgate collection); Cockerell may have been referring to his meeting with FEH of 18 Jan. 1929, during which she apparently could not 'reproach herself enough' (Cockerell 1929 diary, fo. 6[r]).

Edition[47]—is difficult to establish. The fact that he kept the manu-script does suggest that he thought it might ultimately be printed, and he apparently did copy it out—though by no means 'carefully', as his widow claimed[48]—some time after 1900. The manuscript concludes with two notes in his hand: '(Written about 1888–1890. Probably intended to be included in the volume entitled "Life's Little Ironies", or "Wessex Tales.")' and '[Copied from the original rough draft]'. Sufficiently imprecise as it is, the stated date of composition is further called into question by the fact that it is a revision: Hardy first wrote '1900', then altered it to '1890' and added '1888–' above the line. Perhaps he simply realized that his initial statement was contradic-tory—*Wessex Tales* having been published in 1888 and *Life's Little Ironies* in 1894—and changed it accordingly. Although it is unlikely that 'Old Mrs Chundle' was in fact intended for either of these collec-tions—it seems too slight, in terms of both content and length,[49] to have been included—it probably does belong to the 1888–90 period rather than to 1900. Hardy's statement in 1914 to the literary agent W. M. Colles that he had 'not written a prose story, long or short, since the last century',[50] seems to be true—at least in respect of non-collaborative works. Between November 1899 and January 1900 he completed 'Enter a Dragoon' and 'A Changed Man', the last two short stories published under his name, but only with apparent diffi-culty and under some pressure from editors.[51] Between 1888 and 1890, on the other hand, he wrote more short fiction than ever before or again, including most of the *Noble Dames* stories, 'The Waiting Supper', 'A Tragedy of Two Ambitions', and 'The Melancholy Hussar'.[52] Although there is some justification for associating 'Old Mrs Chundle' with 'A Changed Man' (see p. 226), printed in 1900—which is perhaps why Hardy initially assigned the un-published story to that year—it seems unlikely that he would have

[47] The story appears in both *Old Mrs Chundle and Other Stories* (London: Macmillan, 1977) and *Collected Short Stories* (London: Macmillan, 1988).

[48] See p. 218; the missing quotation marks, elongated periods, malformed letters, and so forth indicate that the MS was in fact written with considerable haste.

[49] Although longer than some of the 'Crusted Characters' stories, its Purbeck setting suggests that it was not intended to form part of this group, which is associated exclusively with Longpuddle.

[50] *CL* v. 22.   [51] Ibid. ii. 238, 240, 245–6.

[52] *Biography*, 290, 292, 300; Purdy, 65. Purdy (85) also assigns 'The Son's Veto', 'For Conscience' Sake', 'On the Western Circuit', 'To Please His Wife', and 'A Few Crusted Characters' to 'the latter half of 1890 and the early months of 1891'.

written a story known to be unpublishable in the foreseeable future at a time when he so much preferred to work on his poetry.

That Hardy, as his widow admitted, did not wish 'Old Mrs Chundle' to be published during his lifetime is self-evident. His reasons were almost certainly personal rather than literary: having incurred in 1889 (the year, as falling within the specified 1888–90 period, is perhaps significant) the current Earl of Ilchester's displeasure at the appearance of 'The First Countess of Wessex' (see p. 244), a fictionalized account of the first Earl's marriage, Hardy was presumably reluctant to print another story so closely based on actual people and events. In her 2 July 1928 letter to Forster, Florence Hardy said that 'Old Mrs Chundle' was 'founded on fact'[53] and, in conversation with Purdy the following year, she added that Hardy often repeated the story, which had been told to him by Henry Moule, himself the 'original' of the curate–protagonist.[54] The hitherto unchallenged assumption has been that the Moule in question was Henry Joseph Moule, eldest son of the famous Henry Moule, vicar of Fordington. Henry Joseph was one of Hardy's closest friends, especially from 1883 onwards when both had settled in Dorchester, and their mutual—if not identical—interest in local history, folklore, and tale-telling generally would have provided ample opportunity for the sharing of such a story as the one which eventually developed into 'Old Mrs Chundle'.[55] His local reputation as a painter in water-colours has also tended to encourage the identification of him with the fictional curate.

Such an identification, however, is substantially undercut by the fact that Henry Joseph was never ordained or even trained for the ministry, and what seems most likely is that he told the story about his father, who as a young man was indeed, like the story's protagonist, curate-in-charge of a small Dorset parish. Famous for his social activism and invention of the earth-closet, the Revd Henry Moule also wrote on subjects as diverse as the warming of churches and the extraction of gas from shale,[56] and the installation of a sound-tube for a deaf parishioner would have been quite in keeping with his in-

---

[53] King's College, Cambridge.   [54] Purdy, 268.

[55] *CL* iii. 114–15; Hardy, 'H. J. M.—Some Memories and Letters', in *Dorchester Antiquities*, by H. J. Moule (Dorchester: Henry Ling, 1906); 'Death of Mr. H. J. Moule', *Dorset County Chronicle*, 17 Mar. 1904, 5; *Biography*, 224.

[56] See the list of works appended to his *Paupers, Criminals and Cholera at Dorchester in 1854* (Mount Durand, Guernsey: Toucan Press, 1968).

defatigable desire to solve practical difficulties. He is not remembered as a water-colourist—though he was certainly interested in the arts[57] and may have done some sketching in his youth—but the sketching expedition seems in any case to have little significance other than as a plot device for contriving an encounter unconnected with the curate's pastoral duties. Although Hardy's starting-point was apparently factual—as in 'The First Countess of Wessex' or, indeed, the other Henry Moule story, 'A Changed Man'—he was, after all, writing fiction, not biography.

Liberties were also taken with the setting, clearly identifiable though it is as the south-east corner of Dorset, the location of such familiar Wessex places as Corvsgate (from 'Corfgetes', the Saxon name for Corfe Castle), Enckworth (Encombe), and Anglebury (Wareham).[58] Two miles from 'Corvsgate' and three from 'Enckworth', the cottage was probably located, or imagined, west of the castle ruins and east of Creech Barrow—mentioned with casual familiarity by Mrs Chundle and presumably, given her limited travels, not too far distant. The name 'Kingscreech' was no doubt a merging of Creech—be it Barrow, Bottom, Heath, Hamlet, or Grange—with Kingston, thought by Pinion to be the 'original'[59] (and perhaps indeed the approximate) location Hardy had in mind. Kay-Robinson, pointing out that Kingston was not in the charge of a curate and that neither of its churches had the interior features of Kingscreech, suggests Steeple instead, but is forced to acknowledge that the pulpit is without the eight steps described in the story.[60] None of the Purbeck identifications seems quite right, however, for the simple reason that the church of the story is almost certainly based on St Mary the Virgin, Gillingham, where Henry Moule was curate-in-charge from 1825 to 1829. A sketch of the chancel by Moule's son Henry Joseph, made during a return visit to his birthplace

---

[57] See Handley C. G. Moule, *Memories of a Vicarage* (London: Religious Tract Society, 1913), 82.

[58] All three figure in *The Hand of Ethelberta* (see Hermann Lea, *Thomas Hardy's Wessex* (London: Macmillan, 1913), 240 ff.); Corvsgate is also mentioned in *Desperate Remedies*, Anglebury in *Far from the Madding Crowd*, *The Mayor of Casterbridge*, *Tess of the d'Urbervilles*, and 'The Withered Arm'.

[59] F. B. Pinion, *A Hardy Companion: A Guide to the Works of Thomas Hardy and their Background* (London: Macmillan, 1968; rev. edn. 1976), 382.

[60] Denys Kay-Robinson, *The Landscape of Thomas Hardy* (Exeter: Webb & Bower, 1984), 144.

(presumably between 1840 and 1844),[61] is dominated by an octagonal wooden pulpit raised high above the floor.[62] Hardy may have seen the water-colour and, in any case, he would have seen the pulpit itself on any visit to the church before 1883.[63] Like Kingscreech, St Mary's also had a gallery—more than one, in fact[64]—in which irreverent conduct reminiscent of the boys' laughter in the story seems to have continued into the twentieth century: in 1911 'the Vicar had to remind the sidesmen of the necessity of keeping a watch on the occupants of the galleries, where now and again there had been disorderly behaviour during Divine Service'.[65]

That Hardy should have located Kingscreech some forty-odd kilometres south-east of Gillingham is not surprising in view of the story's Moule association. Though never as close to Henry Moule's other sons—or, indeed, to any other male friend—as he had been to Horace Moule, who committed suicide in 1873,[66] Hardy remained on friendly terms with all 'the seven brethren'[67] throughout their lives, and would not have wished to give offence by seeming to disparage their father, for whom he in fact had considerable respect.[68] By changing the setting

[61] The sketch is one of fifteen water-colours of Gillingham photographed by H. C. Flashman and presented to the Gillingham Local History Society (their current location) after the exhibition of the originals, lent by E. C. H. Moule (Henry Joseph's nephew), in 1956. E. C. H. Moule (to C. R. A. Wallis, then secretary of the Society, 17 July 1956) said that the 'drawings were certainly made before [1844]', when his uncle went up to Cambridge. The two views of Gillingham show the church in its 'restored' (post-1839) state and the sketch of the chancel includes the Gothic altar chairs, placed in the sanctuary 'Between the reopening of the church and 1842' (A. F. H. V. Wagner, *The Church of St. Mary the Virgin Gillingham: An Historical Account* ([Gillingham], 1956), 23).

[62] '[T]he curate mounted the eight steps into the wooden octagon' ('Old Mrs Chundle').

[63] The pulpit in the sketch may not have been the actual one Henry Moule used as a curate, since on 16 July 1839 it was decided that 'a new pulpit at a price not exceeding £5 should be set up', rather than, as the contract specified, fixing the 'present pulpit [also octagonal] ... as shown upon ground plan [i.e. in the centre of the nave]'. The pulpit now in the church was installed in 1883 (Wagner, *Church of St. Mary the Virgin*, 20, 25, and illustration facing 19).

[64] The two small galleries in each aisle mentioned in the Revd Henry Deane's 1837–8 description of the church were replaced in 1839 by galleries 'along the whole length of both aisles' and a west gallery. The latter was removed between 1908 and 1910, followed by the north and south galleries in 1918 (Wagner, *Church of St. Mary the Virgin*, 18, 19, 26–7).

[65] Quoted by Wagner, *Church of St. Mary the Virgin*, 26.

[66] *Biography*, 66–71, 153–6.   [67] *CL* vi. 87.

[68] See ibid. i. 70; TH also claimed that he had partially modelled Angel Clare's father in *Tess* on Henry Moule (ibid. ii. 248, vii. 40).

he had presumably hoped to prevent recognition of his 'original', but must have decided that the parallels were still too obvious to risk publication: the anecdote may have been well known in Dorset, and in any case the Moules would have recognized it and perhaps been pained by this immortalization of their father's youthful shortcomings. There had been no need to hesitate over the publication of the other Moule story, 'A Changed Man', since it unambiguously celebrated the vicar's courageous labours during the 1854 cholera epidemic, while such fictional embellishments as the protagonist's military career or his wife's desertion bore too little resemblance to Moule's life to be mistaken for fact. The portrait of the curate in 'Old Mrs Chundle', on the other hand, is hardly so laudatory and could equally well have been founded on fact as on fiction, though—like Hardy's other 'true' stories—it probably combined the two.

BIBLIOGRAPHICAL DESCRIPTION

Manuscript

The MS was among the Max Gate papers at FEH's death and is now in the Dorset County Museum. Entirely in TH's hand, it was—according to the note he added on the final leaf—'[Copied from the original rough draft]', presumably sometime after 1900. Revisions were introduced in at least two stages: as TH was writing it out and after completion.

The MS is comprised of thirteen regularly foliated leaves, measuring on average 25.45 by 20.45 cm. Ragged at the left edge, they appear to have been torn from a notebook of ruled paper with twenty-six lines 8.7 mm. apart per leaf, a top margin of 21–2 mm., and a bottom margin of 15 mm. Cream in colour with light blue lines, the paper has no watermarks or chain lines and is 0.13 mm. thick. The leaves have been pierced twice through and fastened at the top left corner—presumably by TH (see p. 218)—with a pink lace. Fos. 1^v and 13^v are stamped with the Dorset County Museum stamp.

NOTE ON THE TEXT

The copy-text is the sole surviving authoritative text, the holograph MS. In the variants lists the source of the lemma is the corrected MS and that of the recorded variant is the unrevised MS unless otherwise specified.

OLD MRS CHUNDLE

The curate had not been a week in the parish, but the autumn
morning proving fine he thought he would make a little water-colour
sketch, showing a distant view of the Corvsgate ruin two miles off,
which he had passed on his way hither. The sketch occupied him a
5 longer time than he had anticipated. The luncheon hour drew on, and
he felt hungry.

Quite near him was a stone-built old cottage of respectable and
substantial build. He entered it, and was received by an old woman.

"Can you give me something to eat, my good woman?" he said.
10 She held her hand to her ear.

"Can you give me something for lunch?" he shouted. "Bread-and-
cheese—anything will do."

A sour look crossed her face, and she shook her head. "That's
unlucky," murmured he.

15 She reflected and said more urbanely: "Well, I'm going to have my
own bit o' dinner in no such long time hence. 'Tis taters and cabbage,
boiled with a scantling o' bacon. Would ye like it? But I suppose 'tis
the wrong sort, and that ye would sooner have bread-and-cheese?"

"No, I'll join you. Call me when it is ready. I'm just out here."
20 "Ay, I've seen ye. Drawing the old stones, baint ye? Sure 'tis well
some folk have nothing better to do with their time. Very well. I'll call
ye, when I've dished up."

He went out and resumed his painting; till in about seven or ten
minutes the old woman appeared at her door and held up her hand.
25 The curate washed his brush, went to the brook, rinsed his hands and
proceeded to the house.

"There's yours" she said, pointing to the table. "I'll have my bit
here." And she denoted the settle.

11–12 lunch?" . . . "Bread-and-cheese] lunch? Bread-&-cheese [Bread-&-cheese
undeleted]   13–15 and she shook . . . She] but she [he *of* she *undeleted*]
15 said more urbanely:] said: 17–18 But . . . would] or would ye [would
undeleted]

"Why not join me?"

"Oh, faith, I don't want to eat with my betters—not I." And she continued firm in her resolution, and eat apart.

The vegetables had been well cooked over a wood fire—the only way to cook a vegetable properly—and the bacon was well-boiled. The curate ate heartily: he thought he had never tasted such potatoes and cabbage in his life, which he probably had not, for they had been just brought in from the garden, so that the very freshness of the morning was still in them. When he had finished he asked her how much he owed for the repast, which he had much enjoyed.

"Oh, I don't want to be paid for that bit of snack 'a b'lieve!"

"But really you must take something. It was an excellent meal."

" 'Tis all my own growing, that's true. But I don't take money for a bit o' victuals. I've never done such a thing in my life."

"I should feel much happier if you would."

She seemed unsettled by his feeling, and added as by compulsion, "Well, then; I suppose twopence won't hurt ye?"

"Twopence?"

"Yes. Twopence."

"Why, my good woman, that's no charge at all. I am sure it is worth this, at least." And he laid down a shilling.

"I tell 'ee 'tis *twopence*, and no more!" she said firmly. "Why, bless the man, it didn't cost me more than three halfpence, and that leaves me a fair quarter profit. The bacon is the heaviest item; that may perhaps be a penny. The taters I've got plenty of, and the cabbage is going to waste."

He thereupon argued no further, paid the limited sum demanded, and went to the door. "And where does that road lead?" he asked, by way of engaging her in a little friendly conversation before parting, and pointing to a white lane which branched from the direct highway near her door.

"They tell me that it leads to Enckworth."

"And how far is Enckworth?"

"Three mile, they say. But God knows if 'tis true."

"You haven't lived here long, then?"

"Five-and-thirty year come Martinmas."

"And yet you have never been to Enckworth?"

"Not I. Why should I ever have been to Enckworth? I never had

4 had been] were   13 'Tis] Yes: 'tis

any business there—a great mansion of a place, holding people that I've no more doings with than with the people of the moon. No: there's on'y two places I ever go to from year's end to year's end: that's once a fortnight to Anglebury, to do my bit o' marketing; and once a week to my parish church."

"Which is that?"

"Why, Kingscreech."

"Oh—then you are in my parish?"

"Maybe. Just on the outskirts."

"I didn't know the parish extended so far. I'm a new comer. Well, I hope we may meet again. Good afternoon to you."

When the curate was next talking to his rector he casually observed: "By the way, that's a curious old soul who lives out towards Corvsgate—old Mrs—I don't know her name—a deaf old woman."

"You mean old Mrs Chundle, I suppose."

"She tells me she's lived there five-and-thirty years, and has never been to Enckworth, three miles off. She goes to two places only, from year's end to year's end—to the market town, and to church on Sundays."

"To church on Sundays. H'm. She rather exaggerates her travels, to my thinking. I've been rector here thirteen years, and I have certainly never seen her at church in my time."

"A wicked old woman. What can she think of herself for such deception!"

"She didn't know you belonged here when she said it, and could find out the untruth of her story. I warrant she wouldn't have said it to me!" And the rector chuckled.

On reflection the curate felt that this was decidedly a case for his ministrations, and on the first spare morning he strode across to the cottage beyond the ruin. He found its occupant of course at home.

"Drawing picters again?" she asked, looking up from the hearth, where she was scouring the fire-dogs.

"No. I come on more important matters, Mrs Chundle. I am the new curate of this parish."

"You said you was last time. And after you had told me and went

7† Kingscreech *Ed.*] Kingcreech *MS*   10 I'm a new comer. [*added*]
25 here when she said it,] here,   35 after you had] even before you
35 me] me I tho [*not continued*]

away I said to myself, he'll be here again sure enough, hang me if I
didn't. And here you be."

"Yes. I hope you don't mind?"

"Oh, no. You find us a roughish lot, I make no doubt?"

"Well, I won't go into that. But I think it was a very culpable—   5
unkind thing of you to tell me you came to church every Sunday,
when I find you've not been seen there for years."

"Oh—did I tell 'ee that?"

"You certainly did."

"Now I wonder what I did that for?"   10

"I wonder too."

"Well, you could ha' guessed, after all, that I didn't come to any
service. Lord, what's the good o' my lumpering all the way to church
and back again, when I'm as deaf as a plock? Your own commonsense
ought to have told 'ee that 'twas but a figure o' speech, seeing you was   15
a pa'son."

"Don't you think you could hear the service if you were to sit close
to the reading-desk and pulpit?"

"I'm sure I couldn't. O no—not a word. Why I couldn't hear
anything even at that time when Isaac Coggs used to cry the Amens   20
out loud beyond anything that's done nowadays, and they had the
barrel-organ for the tunes—years and years agone, when I was
stronger in my narves than now."

"H'm—I'm sorry. There's one thing I could do, which I would
with pleasure, if you'll use it. I could get you an ear-trumpet. Will you   25
use it?"

"Ay, sure. That I woll. I don't care what I use—'tis all the same to
me."

"And you'll come?"

"Yes. I may as well go there as bide here, I suppose."   30

The ear-trumpet was purchased by the zealous young man, and the
next Sunday, to the great surprise of the parishioners when they
arrived, Mrs Chundle was discovered in the front seat of the nave of
Kingscreech Church, facing the rest of the congregation with an
unmoved countenance.   35

She was the centre of observation through the whole morning

20–1 Amens . . . nowadays,] Amens,   22 agone,] agone now
23 now] nowadays [now *undeleted*]   32–3 parishioners when they arrived,]
parishioners,

service. The trumpet, elevated at a high angle, shone and flashed in
the sitters' eyes as the chief object in the sacred edifice.

The curate could not speak to her that morning, and called the next
day to inquire the result of the experiment. As soon as she saw him in
5 the distance she began shaking her head.

"No; no;" she said decisively as he approached. "I knowed 'twas
all nonsense."

"What?"

" 'Twasn't a mossel o' good, and so I could have told 'ee before. A
10 wasting your money in jimcracks upon a' old 'ooman like me."

"You couldn't hear? Dear me—how disappointing."

"You might as well have been mouthing at me from the top o'
Creech Barrow."

"That's unfortunate."

15 "I shall never come no more—never—to be made such a fool of as
that again."

The curate mused. "I'll tell you what, Mrs Chundle. There's one
thing more to try, and only one. If that fails I suppose we shall have to
give it up. It is a plan I have heard of, though I have never myself tried
20 it; it's having a sound-tube fixed, with its lower mouth in the seat
immediately below the pulpit, where you would sit, the tube running
up inside the pulpit with its upper end opening in a bell-mouth just
beside the book-board. The voice of the preacher enters the bell-
mouth, and is carried down directly to the listener's ear. Do you
25 understand?"

"Exactly."

"And you'll come, if I put it up at my own expense?"

"Ay, I suppose. I'll try it, e'en though I said I wouldn't. I may as
well do that as do nothing, I reckon."

30 The kind-hearted curate, at great trouble to himself, obtained the
tube and had it fixed vertically as described, the upper mouth being
immediately under the face of whoever should preach, and on the
following Sunday morning it was to be tried. As soon as he came from
the vestry the curate perceived to his satisfaction Mrs Chundle in the
35 seat beneath, erect and at attention, her head close to the lower orifice
of the sound-pipe, and a look of great complacency that her soul

---

24 directly] direct [*undeleted*]   29 nothing, I reckon."] nothing." [*altered in same
line*]   32 should preach] preached [preach *undeleted*]   36–233. 2 sound-pipe
... way.] sound-pipe.

required a special machinery to save it, while other people's could be saved in a commonplace way. The rector read the prayers from the desk on the opposite side, which part of the service Mrs Chundle could follow easily enough by the help of the prayer-book; and in due course the curate mounted the eight steps into the wooden octagon,   5
gave out his text, and began to deliver his discourse.

It was a fine frosty morning in early winter, and he had not got far with his sermon when he became conscious of a steam rising from the bell-mouth of the tube, obviously caused by Mrs Chundle's breathing at the lower end, and it was accompanied by a suggestion of onion-   10
stew. However he preached on awhile, hoping it would cease, holding in his left hand his finest cambric handkerchief kept especially for Sunday morning services. At length, no longer able to endure the odour, he lightly dropped the handkerchief into the bell of the tube, without stopping for a moment the eloquent flow of his words; and he   15
had the satisfaction of feeling himself in comparatively pure air.

He heard a fidgeting below; and presently there arose to him over the pulpit-edge a hoarse whisper: "The pipe's chokt!"

"Now, as you will perceive, my brethren," continued the curate, unheeding the interruption; "by applying this test to ourselves, our   20
discernment of—"

"The pipe's chokt!" came up in a whisper yet louder and hoarser.

"Our discernment of actions as morally good, or indifferent, will be much quickened, and we shall be materially helped in our—"

Suddenly came a violent puff of warm wind, and he beheld his   25
handkerchief rising from the bell of the tube and floating to the pulpit-floor. The little boys in the gallery laughed, thinking it a miracle. Mrs Chundle had, in fact, applied her mouth to the bottom end, blown with all her might, and cleared the tube. In a few seconds the atmosphere of the pulpit became as before, to the curate's great   30
discomfiture. Yet stop the orifice again he dared not, lest the old woman should make a still greater disturbance and draw the attention of the congregation to this unseemly situation.

"If you carefully analyze the passage I have quoted," he continued in somewhat uncomfortable accents, "you will perceive that it   35
naturally suggests three points for consideration—"

("It's not onions: it's peppermint," he said to himself.)

3 part of the service [*added*]   27 The ... miracle. [*added*]   31 orifice]
pipe [*altered in same line*]

"Namely, mankind in its unregenerate state—"

("And cider.")

"The incidence of the law, and lovingkindness or grace, which we will now severally consider—"

5 ("And pickled cabbage. What a terrible supper she must have made!")

"Under the twofold aspect of external and internal consciousness."

Thus the reverend gentleman continued strenuously for perhaps five minutes longer: then he could stand it no more. Desperately 10 thrusting his thumb into the hole he drew the threads of his distracted discourse together, the while hearing her blow vigorously to dislodge the plug. But he stuck to the hole, and brought his sermon to a premature close.

He did not call on Mrs Chundle the next week, a slight cooling of 15 his zeal for her spiritual welfare being manifest; but he encountered her at the house of another cottager whom he was visiting; and she immediately addressed him as a partner in the same enterprize.

"I could hear beautiful!" she said. "Yes; every word! Never did I know such a wonderful machine as that there pipe. But you forgot 20 what you was doing once or twice, and put your handkercher on the top o' en, and stopped the sound a bit. Please not to do that again, for it makes me lose a lot. Howsomever, I shall come every Sunday morning reg'lar now, please God."

The curate quivered internally.

25 "And will ye come to my house once in a while and read to me?"

"Of course."

Surely enough the next Sunday the ordeal was repeated for him. In the evening he told his trouble to the rector. The rector chuckled.

"You've brought it upon yourself" he said. "You don't know this 30 parish so well as I. You should have left the old woman alone."

"I suppose I should!"

"Thank Heaven, she thinks nothing of my sermons, and doesn't come when I preach. Ha, ha!"

"Well," said the curate somewhat ruffled, "I must do something. I 35 cannot stand this. I shall tell her not to come."

"You can hardly do that."

"And I've half-promised to go and read to her. But—I shan't go."

---

8 reverend gentleman continued] curate co [*not continued*]   11 vigorously] desperately [*altered in same line*]

"She's probably forgotten by this time that you promised."

A vision of his next Sunday in the pulpit loomed horridly before the young man, and at length he determined to escape the experience. The pipe should be taken down. The next morning he gave directions, and the removal was carried out.

A day or two later a message arrived from her, saying that she wished to see him. Anticipating a terrific attack from the irate old woman he put off going to her for a day, and when he trudged out towards her house on the following afternoon it was in a vexed mood. Delicately nurtured man as he was he had determined not to re-erect the tube, and hoped he might hit on some new *modus vivendi*, even if at any inconvenience to Mrs Chundle, in a situation that had become intolerable as it was last week.

"Thank Heaven, the tube is gone," he said to himself as he walked; "and nothing will make me put it up again!"

On coming near he saw to his surprise that the calico curtains of the cottage windows were all drawn. He went up to the door, which was ajar; and a little girl peeped through the opening.

"How is Mrs Chundle?" he asked blandly.

"She's dead, sir" said the girl in a whisper.

"Dead? . . . Mrs Chundle dead?"

"Yes, sir."

A woman now came. "Yes, 'tis so, sir. She went off quite sudden-like about two hours ago. Well, you see, sir, she was over seventy years of age, and last Sunday she was rather late in starting for church, having to put her bit o' dinner ready before going out; and was very anxious to be in time. So she hurried overmuch, and runned up the hill, which at her time of life she ought not to have done. It upset her heart, and she's been poorly all the week since, and that made her send for 'ee. Two or three times she said she hoped you would come soon, as you'd promised to, and you were so staunch and faithful in wishing to do her good, that she knew 'twas not by your own wish you didn't arrive. But she would not let us send again, as it might trouble 'ee too much, and there might be other poor folks needing you. She worried to think she might not be able to listen to 'ee

2–3 the young man] him [*altered in same line*]   5 and [*added*]   5 carried out] done [*altered in same line*]   10 determined] determined to carry out his duty [*not continued*]   26 going] start [*not continued*]   29–30 since . . . 'ee. *MS(3)*] since, & it made . . . *MS(2)* [& it *deleted*]] since. *MS(1)*

next Sunday, and feared you'd be hurt at it, and think her remiss. But she was eager to hear you again later on. However, 'twas ordained otherwise for the poor soul, and she was soon gone. 'I've found a real friend at last,' she said. 'He's a man in a thousand. He's not
5 ashamed of a' old woman, and he holds that her soul is worth saving as well as richer people's.' She said I was to give you this.''

It was a small folded piece of paper, directed to him and sealed with a thimble. On opening it he found it to be what she called her will, in which she had left him her bureau, case-clock, settle, four-post
10 bedstead, and framed sampler—in fact all the furniture of any account that she possessed.

The curate went out, like Peter at the cock-crow. He was a meek young man, and as he went his eyes were wet. When he reached a lonely place in the lane he stood still thinking, and kneeling down in
15 the dust of the road rested his elbow in one hand and covered his face with the other. Thus he remained some minute or so, a black shape on the hot white of the sunned trackway; till he rose, brushed the knees of his trousers, and walked on.

The end.

2 was eager] hoped   2 hear you again] come   6 people's ... this.'']
people's.' '' ¶ The curate went out, like Peter at the cock-crow. He was a meek young
man, & as he went his eyes were [*see TN*]   9–10 four-post bedstead, [*added*]
17 hot [*added*]   17 sunned trackway] road

The Doctor's Legend

INTRODUCTION

The 26 March 1891 Easter Number of the New York *Independent* included the following announcement: 'We offer unusual attractions in the opening half of a story by Elizabeth Stuart Phelps, and another story, written especially for THE INDEPENDENT, by the famous English novelist, Thomas Hardy.'[1] The Hardy story was 'The Doctor's Legend' and it appeared as the final item—following a short poem and part one of Phelps's 'The Law and the Gospel. An Easter Story'—in the 'Old and Young' department. It was not the first time that the readers of the *Independent* had been offered one of Hardy's stories: the solicited contribution 'Emmeline; or Passion versus Principle' (previously published as 'The Impulsive Lady of Croome Castle' and subsequently collected in *A Group of Noble Dames* as 'The Duchess of Hamptonshire') had appeared seven years earlier, in the issue of 7 February 1884.[2] 'Emmeline' had obviously met with favour, for on 3 March 1885 John Bowen, son of the paper's proprietor Henry Bowen, attempted to acquire a second Hardy story.[3] Pleading 'previous engagements'—he was in the midst of writing *The Mayor of Casterbridge*—Hardy asked that the matter be allowed 'to stand over for the present'.[4] When pressed again eight months later, he offered the US serialization of *The Woodlanders*, but John Bowen had reservations both about its length and about simultaneous transatlantic publication, and arrangements were not concluded.[5] A further request evidently came from the *Independent* in the autumn of 1890 and on 14 November Hardy, now corresponding with Henry Bowen, agreed to supply a story:

I should have much pleasure in writing a short story for The Independent. As you probably are aware, when exclusive publication is asked for in any periodical—as it usually is by the more prominent in America—I am obliged to fix a higher price than in cases where I publish the same matter simultaneously on this side also. The price I now receive for the exclusive newspaper

---

[1] *Independent*, 26 Mar. 1891, 16.   [2] *CL* vii. 98–9.   [3] Ibid. i. 132.
[4] Ibid.   [5] Ibid. 137–8, 141.

right is ten pounds per thousand words; & if this should be satisfactory to you I will prepare a story of from 5,000 to 8,000 words. As it would be specially written I would do my best to keep it in harmony with the general tone of The Independent (with which I am familiar.)[6]

Whether or not Hardy really meant to write something specifically with the *Independent* in mind is unknowable: at this time he was planning several stories (most of those collected in *Life's Little Ironies* were written in late 1890 or early 1891)[7] and one of these could perhaps have been intended for the *Independent* before its finished form rendered it inappropriate for a leading Congregationalist paper. In any case, 'The Doctor's Legend' was almost certainly not written expressly for the *Independent*, despite the claims to that effect made both in the paper's announcement and in Hardy's note on the manuscript (see p. 245). At 3,800 words it is considerably shorter than the 5,000–8,000-word story initially proposed; it is also very clearly linked with the *Group of Noble Dames* stories completed in April 1890,[8] more than six months before Hardy accepted Henry Bowen's invitation.

On 7 March 1890 Hardy had offered Harper & Brothers the US serial rights to the original *Group of Noble Dames* collection, describing it as:

a Tale of Tales—a series of linked stories ... The scenes, which are numerous, will be laid in the old mansions and castles hereabouts: the characters are to be proportionately numerous, & to be exclusively persons of title of the last century (names disguised, but incidents approximating to fact).[9]

Significantly, Hardy did not mention either the number or the titles of the tales, so that at this point 'The Doctor's Legend' could have been one of those being considered for inclusion. That it should indeed be associated with the six *Noble Dames* stories serialized in *Harper's Weekly* and the *Graphic* in late 1890 is suggested primarily by its subject-matter, its story-telling frame, and its use of a narrator identified only by his profession. The *Noble Dames* collection was expanded in January 1891 to incorporate four stories published earlier than the *Harper's* and *Graphic* serializations, but these, though similar in subject-matter, were not framed in their original versions. It is true that the frame of 'The Doctor's Legend' is not extensively developed, but neither, it would seem, were those of the early versions of the stories

[6] Ibid. 219–20.   [7] Purdy, 85.   [8] Ibid. 64.   [9] *CL* vii. 113.

which made up the original *Group of Noble Dames*. Foliated individually, the manuscripts of these six suggest that they were written
independently and that much of the linking narrative frame was
added later.[10]

'The Doctor's Legend', then, was probably written or at least conceived during the same period as the original *Noble Dames* collection,
late 1889 or early 1890. The use of the doctor as narrator, however,
suggests that the decision to exclude it from the group had been made
before 'Barbara (Daughter of Sir John Grebe)'—subsequently entitled 'Barbara of the House of Grebe'—was written, or at least before
it was attributed to the Old Surgeon, since Hardy presumably would
not have used two medical men as narrators in the same collection.
'Barbara' can, in fact, be plausibly seen as a replacement for 'The
Doctor's Legend'. The two stories are, after all, quite similar[11]—in
their general gruesomeness and sardonic tone and, more specifically,
in their emphasis on the response of a sensitive temperament to a
horrifying object[12] and their inclusion of such details as the nobleman
dying without issue and the family becoming the subject of a sermon.

From a literary point of view 'The Doctor's Legend' is certainly
inferior to 'Barbara', and its slightness—in terms of length as well as
content—may have influenced Hardy's decision to omit it from the
Noble Dames group. The story's focus, too, perhaps seemed inappropriate: although its scenes are laid in one of 'the old mansions' of
Dorset and most of its characters are 'persons of title of the last
century (names disguised, but incidents approximating to fact)',
neither of its noble dames is actually the central figure.[13] But what
probably most deterred Hardy from publishing the story in *A Group of
Noble Dames* was its too close correspondence to the history of the
family he described in *Life* as 'the tragic Damers'.[14] Joseph Damer
(created Lord Milton 1753, Earl of Dorchester 1792; died 1798) purchased Milton Abbey in 1752 and proceeded to rebuild the house and
reshape the surrounding valley, eventually transplanting the entire

[10] MS (Library of Congress); Purdy, 64–5.

[11] Purdy (299) remarked that 'In some details ["The Doctor's Legend"] is slightly
reminiscent of the Old Surgeon's story, "Barbara of the House of Grebe".'

[12] Both the skull in 'The Doctor's Legend' and the mutilated statue in 'Barbara' are
also associated with allegorical figures of Death.

[13] First remarked by Pinion (*A Hardy Companion: A Guide to the Works of Thomas Hardy
and their Background* (London: Macmillan, 1968; rev. edn., 1976), 81).

[14] *Life*, 249; first suggested by Weber (*Revenge is Sweet* (Waterville, Me.: Colby
College Library, 1940), 14).

village of Milton Abbas to a new site half a mile away. Because the bones of former parishioners were treated irreverently during the conversion of the old churchyard into lawns, he was said to have been cursed and to have died of a 'gruesome disease'.[15] Hardy, well acquainted with the legend, wrote on 23 February 1905 to Herbert Pentin, a local historian and the current vicar of Milton Abbas:

What a sinister figure arises from the past in the person of Ld Dorchester! "The evil that men do lives after them". You probably know the traditionary story about him & the Monks' bones, &c? It is extraordinary how firmly it was believed in by the old men who used to repeat it to me when I was young.[16]

Although 'The Doctor's Legend' makes use of this local tradition, its narrative development depends upon the wholly imaginary Death's Head plot, thereby demonstrating that 'whimsical use of history' which has been said to characterize the stories in *A Group of Noble Dames*.[17] Hardy took the basic ingredients of the existing accounts and, where necessary, altered them to suit his creative purposes: Joseph Damer, like the fictional squire, did marry 'the daughter of an ancient and noble [Dorset] house' and his 'immense fortune' did descend to him from a relative who had been a money-lender (actually his great-uncle in Ireland,[18] not an uncle in 'some northern city'); on the other hand, he had four children, not one, three of whom survived him, and, although the title did become extinct within a few years of his death, the family name was revived by three of his sister's grandchildren.[19] Other historical details are similarly distorted, though often in the letter rather than in the spirit: Joseph Damer may not have been enraged by a child in search of flowers, but he is said to have been irritated by the local Grammar School boys who tres-

---

[15] Herbert Pentin, 'The Old Town of Milton Abbey', *Proceedings of the Dorset Natural History and Antiquarian Field Club*, 25 (1904), 5; J. P. Traskey, *Milton Abbey: A Dorset Monastery in the Middle Ages* (Tisbury: Compton Press, 1978), 197.

[16] *CL* iii. 156; see also iv. 58.

[17] Kristin Brady, *The Short Stories of Thomas Hardy: Tales of Past and Present* (London: Macmillan, 1982), 51.

[18] Referred to by Walpole, one of TH's sources, as 'an old uncle in Ireland' (*The Letters of Horace Walpole, Earl of Orford*, ed. Peter Cunningham (9 vols.; London: Richard Bentley, 1857–9), v. 43–4); all quotations from Walpole are from this edn.; see also n. 27.

[19] John Hutchins, *The History and Antiquities of the County of Dorset*, 3rd. edn., rev. by William Shipp and James Whitworth Hodson (Westminster: John Bowyer Nichols and Sons, 1873), iv. 387–8; Traskey, *Milton Abbey*, 190.

passed on his ground, stealing his fruit and disturbing his game; John Damer, his eldest son, may not have been driven insane by the sight of a death's head, but he did commit suicide when he had run up debts his father (like the fictitious lord) refused to pay.[20] Using as a starting-point such recorded facts as the younger Damer's suicide and his wife's sculptural talents,[21] Hardy imaginatively reconstructed history, a process described in his 1896 Preface to *A Group of Noble Dames*:

The pedigrees of our county families, arranged in diagrams on the pages of county histories, mostly appear at first sight to be as barren of any touch of nature as a table of logarithms. But given a clue—the faintest tradition of what went on behind the scenes, and this dryness as of dust may be transformed into a palpitating drama.... [A]nybody practised in raising images from such genealogies finds himself unconsciously filling into the framework the motives, passions, and personal qualities which would appear to be the single explanation possible of some extraordinary conjunction in times, events, and personages that occasionally marks these reticent family records.[22]

Hardy's primary source for the 'dry as dust' information metamorphosed in several of the *Noble Dames* stories[23] was John Hutchins's *The History and Antiquities of the County of Dorset*, one of his favourite books. His personal copy of the third edition is well worn and contains extensive markings and annotations, several of them in the Milton Abbas chapter.[24] *History and Antiquities* contains not only family pedigrees but also architectural descriptions and histories, probably the source for numerous details in 'The Doctor's Legend' relating to the abbey and its estates, from the preserved Abbots' Hall to the new, barn-like village church.[25] At times the borrowings are extensive, though never slavish; compare, for example, Hutchins's account of the removal of the church-bells with Hardy's:

It being represented to his Lordship that bell-ringing tended to drunkenness, he sold all the bells in the abbey-tower, two only excepted, which were transferred to the new church ... A tradition still lingers in the parish, that when the inhabitants saw the bells, after the sale, drawn through the village on their way to their respective destinations, they stood at their house-doors

---

[20] Pentin, 'Milton Abbey', 6; Walpole, *Letters*, vi. 368.
[21] Hutchins, *History and Antiquities*, iv. 388.
[22] *A Group of Noble Dames*, p. vii; the wording is identical in the 1896 and 1912 edns.
[23] See Brady, *Short Stories*, 85 ff.   [24] DCM.
[25] Hutchins, *History and Antiquities*, iv. 395, 406.

shedding tears for the loss of that peculiarly English music, endeared to them by so many hallowed associations.[26]

As the natives persistently came and got drunk in the ringing-loft, the peer determined to put a stop to it. He sold the ring of bells to a founder in a distant city, and to him one day the whole beautiful set of them was conveyed on waggons away from the spot on which they had hung and resounded for so many centuries, and called so many devout souls to prayer. When the villagers saw their dear bells going off in procession, never to return, they stood at their doors and shed tears. ('The Doctor's Legend')

Scarcely less significant is Hardy's indebtedness to Horace Walpole. According to *Life*, in 1868 he read 'Walpole's *Letters to Sir Horace Mann* in six volumes',[27] and certainly a wide familiarity with these and other Walpole letters is indicated by numerous references in his own correspondence, notebooks, autobiography, and fiction[28]—including 'The Doctor's Legend'. Walpole is the 'writer of that time who knew [the lord] well', and his 20 August 1776 letter to Mann is the source for the quotation 'one whom anything would petrify but nothing would soften'.[29] Hardy presumably had this letter in mind when in his copy of Hutchins he annotated the reference to John Damer's death 'suicide: see Walpole's Letters',[30] and it is certainly echoed within 'The Doctor's Legend' in the references to the son's unpaid debts ('I've been telling the old man of my debts, too, and he says he won't pay them') and his unpresentable companions ('he had many friends of both sexes with whom his refined and accomplished wife was unacquainted'), and especially in the account of the suicide itself:

"At four o'clock the next morning news was brought to the house that my lord's heir had shot himself dead with a pistol at a tavern not far off.

"His reason for the act was absolutely inexplicable to the outer world. The heir to an enormous property and a high title, the husband of a wife as gifted

---

[26] Ibid. 406.

[27] *Life*, 61; in spite of his mistake about the number of volumes (there are only four), TH probably did read the 1843–4 edn. (London: Bentley) of letters to Mann. It is in any case certain that he was familiar with Peter Cunningham's edn. of Walpole's letters; see *CL* i. 64 and *The Literary Notebooks of Thomas Hardy*, ed. Lennart A. Björk (2 vols.; London: Macmillan, 1985), i. 355.

[28] E.g. *CL* i. 64, ii. 43, iv. 229; *Literary Notebooks*, ed. Björk, i. 118; *Life*, 13, 389, 406; *The Hand of Ethelberta*, 457–8.

[29] Walpole (*Letters*, vi. 368) actually wrote 'Lord Milton, whom anything can petrify and nothing soften'. [30] Hutchins, *History and Antiquities*, iv. 387 (DCM).

as she was charming; of all the men in English society he seemed to be the last likely to undertake such a desperate deed.

Compare Walpole:

[John Damer] and his two brothers most unexpectedly notified to their father that they owed above seventy thousand pounds. The proud lord, for once in the right, refused to pay the debt, or see them.... On Thursday, Mr. Damer supped at the Bedford Arms in Covent Garden, with four common women, a blind fiddler, and no other man. At three in the morning he dismissed his seraglio, bidding each receive her guinea at the bar, and ordering Orpheus to come up again in half-an-hour. When he returned, he found a dead silence, and smelt gunpowder. He called, the master of the house came up, and found Mr. Damer sitting in his chair, dead, with a pistol by him, and another in his pocket! ...

What a catastrophe for a man at thirty two, heir to two and twenty thousand a year! We are persuaded lunacy, not distress, was the sole cause of his fate.[31]

John Damer's 'lunacy' (the verdict in fact brought in by the Coroner's jury)[32] may have been one of those behind-the-scenes clues which led to Hardy's fabrication of the Death's Head narrative, prompting the characterization of the son in the story as 'exceedingly timid', 'impressionable', and suffering from 'nervous debility', rather than as described by Walpole: 'grave, cool, reasonable, and reserved'.[33] In contrast, the portrait of the 'bright', 'refined', and 'accomplished' daughter-in-law with her knowledge of Latin and Greek and 'great skill as a sculptress in marble and other materials' closely accords with Walpole's account of Anne Seymour Conway Damer in a later letter to Mann:

She has one of the most solid understandings I ever knew, astonishingly improved, but with so much reserve and modesty, that I have often told Mr. Conway he does not know the extent of her capacity and the solidity of her reason. We have by accident discovered, that she writes Latin like Pliny, and is learning Greek. In Italy she will be a prodigy. She models like Bernini, has excelled the moderns in the similitudes of her busts, and has lately begun one in marble.[34]

Hardy's reference to the lord's constructing 'an ingenious and creditable genealogical tree', after discovering in the County history that 'one of the knights who came over with William the Conqueror bore a

---

[31] Walpole, *Letters*, vi. 368.
[32] *The London Chronicle for the Year 1776*, 15–17 Aug., 167.
[33] Walpole, *Letters*, vi. 368.   [34] 7 Sept. 1781 (Walpole, *Letters*, viii. 76).

name which somewhat resembled his own',[35] perhaps owes something to Walpole's 22 October 1766 letter to George Montagu:

You know my Lord Milton, from nephew of the old usurer Damer, of Dublin, has endeavoured to erect himself into the representative of the ancient Barons Damory—

> "— Momento turbinis exit
> Marcus Dama."[36]

Damer's supposed descent from Sir Richard Damory was in fact sufficiently credible to be recorded in Collins's *Peerage* and repeated by Hutchins,[37] but it of course better suited Hardy's fictional purposes for the pedigree to have been spuriously constructed, thereby providing yet another instance of the lord's dishonesty and ambition and emphasizing still further the rapidity of his rise and fall.

That Hardy did not publish 'The Doctor's Legend' in England is not, then, surprising: he had not forgotten the Earl of Ilchester's anger at the publication in 1889 of 'The First Countess of Wessex'[38] (largely based on Hutchins's account of the first Earl's marriage),[39] and doubtless had no wish for a repetition of such unpleasantness with his near neighbours the Dawson Damers of Came House.[40] Although the story's only named character is Lady Cicely (in manuscript originally Lady Cicely Douce, Hardy presumably deciding not to repeat both of Lady Caroline Damer's initials), its plot details, especially the notorious removal of the village, would have left little doubt as to the 'originals'. To send the story to the New York *Independent*—whose English readership was negligible and whose editors wanted exclusive first publication rights—was therefore a convenient way to publish without giving offence. In a letter to the *Independent* of 17 February 1891—not included in *Collected Letters* but offered for sale by a US bookseller in 1956—Hardy apologized for his late submission of copy (a factor which perhaps explains the manuscript's having

---

[35] In a paragraph annotated by TH, Hutchins (*History and Antiquities*, iv. 386) wrote: 'William Damery ... came to England with William the Conqueror'.

[36] Walpole, *Letters*, v. 20.

[37] Arthur Collins, *The Peerage of England* (4th edn.; London: H. Woodfall, &c., 1768), vii. 608; Hutchins, *History and Antiquities*, iv. 387.

[38] TH was still referring to the incident in letters of 1905 and 1915 (*CL* iii. 190, v. 134).

[39] Hutchins, *History and Antiquities*, ii. 663, 667, 679.

[40] At the death of Joseph Damer's daughter Caroline, Came passed to George Lionel Dawson and Milton Abbey to William Henry Dawson, both grandsons of Damer's sister Mary (ibid. iv. 387–8).

been written out by his wife), named a lower price (seven pounds ten shillings per thousand words) than that proposed the previous November, repeated his assurance that the story was 'written expressly for *The Independent*', and expressed his confidence that its 'general tone' would 'be found in harmony with the spirit of that paper'.[41] Whether or not Henry Bowen considered 'The Doctor's Legend' good value even at the reduced rate is not known, but it is perhaps significant that no correspondence relating to a request for a third contribution appears to survive.

Like 'Destiny and a Blue Cloak', 'The Doctor's Legend' remained obscure until 1940, when it was collected in Weber's *Revenge is Sweet*. More recently the story has appeared in Pinion's *Old Mrs Chundle and Other Stories* and *Collected Short Stories*, and also in Peter Haining's *The Supernatural Tales of Thomas Hardy* (London: W. Foulsham & Co., 1988).

BIBLIOGRAPHICAL DESCRIPTIONS

Manuscript

The MS was for many years in the possession of Bliss Carman, one of the *Independent* editors in 1891, and was eventually advertised as item 663 in Part I of the 7–10 January 1929 Jerome Kern sale catalogue (New York: Anderson Galleries). The catalogue description ('Original Autograph') and facsimile of the first page prompted Howard Bliss, as a prospective purchaser, to ask Cockerell to point out that most of the MS is written in EH's hand.[1] Cockerell complied (his telegram still accompanies the MS), the price fell, and Bliss purchased the MS for $1,000. Subsequently purchased and resold by the dealer L. D. Feldman, the MS is now in the Berg Collection of the New York Public Library.

The MS is evidently a copy of an earlier draft and is written predominantly in EH's hand, though virtually all the corrections and revisions are TH's. TH wrote the first three lines of heading ('[Written expressly for *The Independent*.] | The Doctor's Legend | By Thomas Hardy.'), and probably the fourth line ('I'). The first two words of text ('‘Not more') and 'The End.' are also in his hand.

---

[41] *News of Autographs at Goodspeed's*, Nov.–Dec. 1956, item 47.

[1] 29 Dec. 1928 letter (Beinecke).

The MS is comprised of sixteen regularly foliated leaves, measuring on average 25.75 by 20.9 cm. The dark cream paper has artificially imposed chain lines but no watermarks and is 0.11 mm. thick. Fo. 1 has been torn vertically in half and repaired with tape; fo. 5 has been torn horizontally between the ninth and tenth lines and similarly repaired. Used as setting-copy for the *Independent* printing, the MS contains numerous blue-pencil markings, including the double underlining of 'Not' (the first word of text), the deletion of '[Written expressly for *The Independent*.]' and 'The End.', as well as what seem to be stint marks. The latter appear in the left margin at irregular intervals: 1B begins at the title; 2B at fo. 2. 13 (p. 248. 26); 3B at fo. 4. 3 (p. 250. 3); 4B at fo. 5. 3 (p. 250. 23); 5B at fo. 6. 17[2] (p. 251. 28); 6B at fo. 8. 11 (p. 253. 10); 7B at fo. 9. 22 (p. 254. 12); 8B at fo. 11. 5 (p. 255. 7); 9B at fo. 12. 2 (p. 255. 27); 10B at fo. 13. 3 (p. 256. 16); 11B at fo. 14. 2 (p. 258. 4); 12B at fo. 15. 3 (p. 257. 27); 13B at fo. 16. 3 (p. 258. 17). Disregarding the first and last, six of the sections (3B and 8B–12B) are of approximately the same length (twenty-three lines), while the other five are bafflingly irregular (ranging from thirty-four to forty-one lines). The divisions do not correspond to the *Independent* columns; they may, however, represent compositorial stints (for equally short—though regular—takes see the description of the second 'Spectre' typescript) or perhaps some form of casting off. Significantly, the MS of TH's story 'Emmeline; or Passion versus Principle',[3] published by the *Independent* seven years previously, contains markings which also appear to have no relation to the divisions of the printed text and occur at similarly irregular intervals, ranging from twenty-nine to forty-two lines.

Each leaf carries the identifying device formerly used by the Berg Collection (an ink dot below the last word of the penultimate line) and is also stamped 'NYPL' (1 by 6 mm.) on the verso. Erased at the top left corner of fo. 1 is what appears to be a pencil record of the dealer's price: an illegible word (or set of initials) written above '$950.⁰⁰'. 'Feldman 5.29.63' and '1000—' are written in pencil on fo. 16ᵛ, and 'Feldman 5.29.64' [*sic*] appears on the verso of Cockerell's telegram. The folder has a Jerome Kern bookplate.

---

[2] TH's interlineations are not included in the line-count.   [3] Pierpont Morgan.

Periodical Publication

New York *Independent*, 26 Mar. 1891

The text begins in col. 3 of p. 35 (there are four columns per page) and concludes in col. 1 of p. 37. The title reads:

THE DOCTOR'S LEGEND. | [*rule 31 mm.*] | BY THOMAS HARDY. | [*rule 8 mm.*]

NOTE ON THE TEXT

The copy-text is the MS, as written out by EH and revised by TH. The earliest version of the text (MS(1)) is therefore always in EH's hand. The only other surviving textual witness, the 26 March 1891 *Independent* printing (*IN*), was authorized, but the shortness of the interval between submission and publication and the restriction of the variants almost entirely to details of pointing and styling constitute strong indications that TH did not read proof. The *IN* variants, therefore, have not been incorporated into the edited text, though they are recorded.

In the variants lists the source of lemmata not followed by sigla is the MS.

The Doctor's Legend

I

"Not more than half-a-dozen miles from the Wessex coast" (said the doctor) "is a mansion which appeared newer in the last century than it appears at the present day after years of neglect and occupation by
5 inferior tenants. It was owned by a man of five-and-twenty, than whom a more ambitious personage never surveyed his face in a glass. His name I will not mention out of respect to those of his blood and connections who may remain on earth, if any such there be. In the words of a writer of that time who knew him well, he was 'one whom
10 anything would petrify but nothing would soften'.

"This worthy gentleman was of so elevated and refined a nature that he never gave a penny to women who uttered bad words in their trouble and rage, or who wore dirty aprons in view of his front door. On those misguided ones who did not pull the fore-lock to him in
15 passing, and call him 'your Honour' and 'Squire', he turned the shoulder of scorn, especially when he wore his finer ruffles and gold seals.

"Neither his personal nor real estate at this time was large; but the latter he made the most of by jealously guarding it, as of the former by
20 his economies. Yet though his fields and woods were well-watched by his gamekeepers and other dependants, such was his dislike to intrusion that he never ceased to watch the watchers. He stopped footpaths and enclosed lands. He made no exception to these sentiments in the case of his own villagers, whose faces were never to
25 be seen in his private grounds except on pressing errands.

"Outside his garden-wall, near the entrance to the park, there lived a poor woman with an only child. This child had been so unfortunate as to trespass upon the Squire's lawn on more than one occasion, in

8 connections *MS(2)TH*] name *MS(1)*   12 uttered *MS(2)TH*] said *MS(1)*
14 fore- *MS(2)TH* [*added*]   26 near *MS(2)EH*] near to *MS(1)*   27 child.
This *MS(2)TH*] child and this *MS(1)* [his *of* this *undeleted*]

search of flowers; and on this incident, trivial as it was, hung much that was afterwards of concern to the house and lineage of the Squire. It seems that the Squire had sent a message to the little girl's mother concerning the nuisance; nevertheless, only a few days afterwards, he saw the child there again. This unwarrantable impertinence, as the owner and landlord deemed it to be, irritated him exceedingly; and, with his walking cane elevated, he began to pursue the child to teach her by chastisement what she would not learn by exhortation.

"Naturally enough, as soon as the girl saw the Squire in pursuit of her she gave a loud scream, and started off like a hare; but the only entrance to the grounds being on the side which the Squire's position commanded, she could not escape, and endeavoured to elude him by winding, and doubling in her terrified course. Finding her, by reason of her fleetness, not so easy to chastise as he had imagined, her assailant lost his temper—never a very difficult matter—and the more loudly she screamed the more angrily did he pursue. A more untoward interruption to the peace of a beautiful and secluded spot was never seen.

"The race continued, and the Squire, now panting with rage and exertion, drew closer to his victim. To the horrified eyes of the child, when she gazed over her shoulder, his face appeared like a crimson mask set with eyes of fire. The glance sealed her fate in the race. By a sudden start forward he caught hold of her by the skirt of her short frock flying behind. The clutch so terrified the child that, with a louder shriek than ever, she leapt from his grasp, leaving the skirt in his hand. But she did not go far; in a few more moments she fell on the ground in an epileptic fit.

"This strange, and, but for its painfulness, even ludicrous scene, was witnessed by one of the gardeners who had been working near, and the squire haughtily directed him to take the prostrate and quivering child home; after which he walked off, by no means pleased

1–3 flowers ... seems that *MS(3)TH*] ... much afterwards ... *MS(2)TH*] flowers. *MS(1)* [*see TN*]   6 owner *MS(2)TH*] Squire *MS(1)*   9 Naturally enough, *MS(2)TH* [*added*]   16 loudly *MS(2)TH* [*added*]   16–18 A more ... seen. *MS(2)TH* [*added*]   19–20 now panting ... victim. *MS(4)TH*] drew closer to his victim, now panting with rage & exertion. *MS(3)TH*] drew closer, panting ... *MS(2)TH*] drew closer, now panting ... *MS(1)* [panting ... exertion *undeleted*] 22 The glance ... race. *MS(2)TH* [*added*]   23 short *MS(2)TH* [*added*] 24 frock flying behind. *MS(2)TH*] frock. *MS(1)*   24 the child *MS(2)TH*] her, *MS(1)*   26 few more moments *MS(2)TH*] moment *MS(1)* [*undeleted*] 30–1 prostrate and quivering *MS(2)TH* [*added*]

with himself at the unmanly and undignified part which a violent temper had led him to play.

"The mother of the girl was in great distress when she saw her only child brought home in such a condition: she was still more distressed,
5 when in the course of a day or two, it became doubtful if fright had not deprived the girl entirely of her reason, as well as of her health. In the singular, nervous malady which supervened the child's hair came off, and her teeth fell from her gums; till no one could have recognised in the mere scare-crow that she appeared, the happy and laughing
10 youngster of a few weeks before.

"The mother was a woman of very different mettle from her poor child. Impassioned and determined in character, she was not one to provoke with impunity. And her moods were as enduring as they were deep. Seeing what a wreck her darling had become she went on foot to
15 the manor-house, and, contrary to the custom of the villagers, rang at the front door, where she asked to see that ruffian the master of the mansion who had ruined her only child. The Squire sent out a reply that he was very sorry for the girl, but that he could not see her mother, accompanying his message by a *solatium* of five shillings.
20 "In the bitterness of her hate, the woman threw the five-shilling-piece through the panes of the dining-room window, and went home to brood again over her idiotized child.

"One day a little later, when the girl was well enough to play in the lane, she came in with a bigger girl who took care of her.
25 "'Death's Head—I be Death's Head—hee, hee!' said the child.

"'What?' said her mother, turning pale.

"The girl in charge explained that the other children had nick-named her daughter 'Death's Head' since she had lost her hair, from her resemblance to a skull.
30 "When the elder girl was gone the mother carefully regarded the child from a distance. In a moment she saw how cruelly apt the *sobriquet* was. The bald scalp, the hollow cheeks—by reason of the

1 unmanly and *MS(2)TH* [*added*]   9 that *MS(2)TH* [*added*]   12 and determined *MS(2)TH* [*added*]   13–14 provoke...deep. *MS(3)TH* [*altered in same line*]] provoke with impunity. *MS(2)TH*] thoughtlessly provoke. *MS(1)* [provoke *undeleted*]   20–1 five-shilling-piece *MS(2)EH* [*altered in same line*]] five shillings *MS(1)* [*only final* s *deleted*]   21 dining-room *MS(2)TH*] drawing-room *MS(1)* [-room *undeleted*]   22 idiotized *MS(2)TH*] idolized *IN*   24 bigger *MS(2)TH* [*added*]   28 Head' since she...hair, *MS(2)TH*] head', *MS(1)* [*see TN*]

absence of teeth—and the saucer eyes, the cadaverous hue, had, indeed, a startling likeness to that bony relic of mortality.

"At this time the Squire was successfully soliciting in marriage a certain Lady Cicely, the daughter of an ancient and noble house in that county. During the ensuing summer their nuptials were 5 celebrated, and the young wife brought home amid great rejoicing, and ringing of bells, and dancing on the green, followed by a bonfire after dark on the hill. The woman whose disfigured child was as the apple of her eye to her, saw all this, and the greater the good fortune that fell to the Squire, the more envenomed did she become. 10

"The newly-wedded lady was much liked by the villagers in general, to whom she was very charitable, intelligently entering into their lives and histories, and endeavouring to relieve their cares. On a particular evening of the ensuing Autumn when she had been a wife but a few months, after some parish-visiting, she was returning 15 homeward to dinner on foot, her way to the mansion lying by the churchyard-wall. It was barely dusk, but a full harvest moon was shining from the east. At this moment of the Lady Cicely's return, it chanced that the widow with her afflicted girl was crossing the churchyard by the footpath from gate to gate. The churchyard was in 20 obscurity, being shaded by the yews. Seeing the lady in the adjoining highway, the woman hastily left the footpath with the child, crossed the graves to the shadow of the wall outside which the lady was passing, and pulled off the child's hood so that the baldness was revealed. Whispering to the child, 'Grin at her my deary!' she held up 25 the little girl as high as she could, which was just sufficient to disclose her face over the coping of the wall to a person on the other side.

"The moonlight fell upon the sepulchral face and head,

1 the cadaverous hue, *MS(2)TH* [*added*]   4 Cicely *MS(2)TH*] Cicely Douce *MS(1)*   5 their *MS(2)TH*] the *MS(1)* [*undeleted*]   6 amid *MS(2)TH*] with *MS(1)*   7–8 green . . . hill. *MS(2)TH*] green. *MS(1)*   13 and histories, *MS(2)TH* [*added*]   13–14 On a particular *MS(2)TH*] One *MS(1)*   14–15 when she . . . months, *MS(2)TH* [*added*]   20–1 The churchyard was . . . yews. *MS(2)TH* [*added*]   21–2 adjoining highway *MS(2)TH*] highway without the wall *MS(1)* [*highway undeleted*]   23 shadow of the *MS(3)TH*] inner face of the w *MS(2)TH* [*not continued; added*]   25 revealed. Whispering *MS(2)* [*period and* W *TH*]] revealed at the same time whispering *MS(1)*   26–7 as high . . . side. *MS(4)TH*] . . . the wall. *MS(3)TH* [*altered in same line*]] . . . sufficient to reveal *MS(2)TH*] so that her face came just over the coping of the wall. *MS(1)*   28 sepulchral *MS(2)TH*] disfigured *MS(1)*

intensifying the child's daytime aspect till it was only too much like that which had suggested the nickname. The unsuspecting and timid lady—a perfect necrophobist by reason of the care with which everything unpleasant had been kept out of her dainty life—saw the
5 death-like shape, and, shrieking with sudden terror, fell to the ground. The lurking woman with her child disappeared in another direction, and passed through the churchyard gate homeward.

"The Lady Cicely's shriek brought some villagers to the spot. They found her quivering, but not senseless; and she was taken home.
10 There she lay prostrate for some time under the doctor's hands.

I I

"It was the following spring, and the time drew near when an infant was to be born to the Squire. Great was the anxiety of all concerned, by reason of the fright and fall from which the Lady Cicely had
15 suffered in the latter part of the preceding year. However the event which they were all expecting took place, and, to the joy of her friends, no evil consequences seemed to have ensued from the terrifying incident before-mentioned. The child of Lady Cicely was a son and heir.

20 "Meanwhile the mother of the afflicted child watched these things in silence. Nothing—not even malevolent tricks upon those dear to him—seemed to interrupt the prosperity of the Squire. An Uncle of his, a money-lender in some northern city, died childless at this time, and left an immense fortune to his nephew the Lady Cicely's
25 husband; who, fortified by this acquisition, now bethought himself of a pedigree as a necessity, so as to be no longer beholden to his wife for all the ancestral credit that his children would possess. By searching in the County history he happily discovered that one of the knights who came over with William the Conqueror bore a name which somewhat

---

1 daytime *MS(2)TH*] natural *MS(1)*   2 which had suggested the *MS(2)TH*]
of its *MS(1)*   3–4 —a perfect . . . life— *MS(4)TH* [*altered in same line*]] . . . kept
from her *MS(3)TH*] . . . kept <out> *MS(2)TH* [*not continued; added*]   4 saw the
MS(2)TH] saw its *MS(1)* [*its altered rather than deleted*]   5 shape, *MS(2)TH*] form
MS(1)   6 lurking *MS(2)TH* [*added*]   8 Lady Cicely's *MS(2)TH*] lady's
MS(1) [*only* l *and* s *deleted*]   10 hands] hand *IN*   14 and fall *MS(2)TH*
[*added*]   14 Lady Cicely *MS(2)TH*] lady *MS(1)* [*only* l *deleted*]   23 his
MS(2)TH] hers *MS(1)*

resembled his own, and from this he constructed an ingenious and creditable genealogical tree; the only rickety point in which occurred at a certain date in the previous century. It was the date whereat it became necessary to show that his great-grandfather (in reality a respectable village tanner) was the indubitable son of a scion of the ⁵ knightly family before alluded to, despite the fact that this scion had lived in quite another part of the county. This little artistic junction, however, was satisfactorily manipulated, and the grafting was only to be perceived by the curious.

"His upward progress was uninterrupted. His only son grew to be ¹⁰ an interesting lad, though, like his mother, exceedingly timid and impressionable. With his now great wealth, the Squire began to feel that his present modest country-seat was insufficient, and there being at this time an Abbey and its estates in the market, by reason of some dispute in the family hitherto its owners, the wealthy gentleman ¹⁵ purchased it. The Abbey was of large proportions, and stood in a lovely and fertile valley surrounded by many attached estates. It had a situation fit for the home of a prince, still more for that of an Archbishop. This historic spot, with its monkish associations, its fish-ponds, woods, village, abbey-church, and Abbots' bones beneath ²⁰ their incised slabs, all passed into the possession of our illustrious self-seeker.

"Meeting his son when the purchase was completed, he smacked the youth on the shoulder.

"'We've estates, and rivers, and hills, and woods, and a beautiful ²⁵ Abbey unrivalled in the whole of Wessex—Ha, ha!' he cried.

"'I don't care about Abbeys,' said the gentle son. 'They are gloomy; this one particularly.'

"'Nonsense!' said his father. 'And we've a village, and the Abbey church into the bargain.' ³⁰

"'Yes.'

"'And dozens of mitred Abbots in their stone coffins underground,

---

3 century. It ... whereat it *MS(3)TH*] ... date at which it *MS(2)TH*] century, where it *MS(1)*   7 in quite *MS(3)TH* [*altered in same line*]] in *MS(2)EH* [*added; see TN*]   7 county] country *IN*   7 This little artistic junction, *MS(3)TH*] This little artistic touc *MS(2)TH* [*not continued*]] This, *MS(1)*   8 manipulated *MS(2)TH*] arranged *MS(1)*   11 though, like his mother, *MS(2)TH*] though *MS(1)*   15 wealthy *MS(2)TH* [*added*]   17 attached *MS(2)TH*] large *MS(1)*   24 the youth *MS(2)TH*] him *MS(1)*

and tons of monks—all for the same money. . . . Yes the very dust of those old rascals is mine! Ho-ho!'

"The son turned pale. 'Many were holy men,' he murmured, 'despite the errors in their creed.'

5　　"'D— ye, grow up, and get married, and have a wife who'll disabuse you of that ghostly nonsense!' cried the Squire.

"Not more than a year after this, several new peers were created for political reasons with which we have no concern. Among them was the subject of this legend; much to the chagrin of some of his
10　neighbours, who considered that such rapid advancement was too great for his deserts. On this point I express no opinion.

"He now resided at the Abbey, outwardly honoured by all in his vicinity, though perhaps less honoured in their hearts; and many were the visitors from far and near. In due course his son grew to
15　manhood and married a beautiful woman, whose beauty nevertheless was no greater than her taste and accomplishments. She could read Latin and Greek, as well as one or two modern languages; above all she had great skill as a sculptress in marble and other materials.

"The poor widow in the other village seemed to have been blasted
20　out of existence by the success of her long-time enemy. The two could not thrive side by side. She declined and died; her death having, happily, been preceded by that of her child.

"Though the Abbey, with its little cells, and quaint turnings, satisfied the curiosity of visitors, it did not satisfy the noble lord (as
25　the Squire had now become). Except the Abbot's Hall, the rooms were miserably small for a baron of his wealth, who expected soon to be an Earl, and the parent of a line of Earls.

"Moreover the village was close to his very doors—on his very lawn, and he disliked the proximity of its inhabitants, his old craze for
30　seclusion remaining with him still. On Sundays they sat at service in the very Abbey Church which was part of his own residence. Besides, as his son had said, the conventual buildings formed a gloomy dwelling, with its dark corridors, monkish associations, and charnel-like smell.

35　　"So he set to work, and did not spare his thousands. First, he carted

5 D—ye,] Oh *IN*　　　　　　　13 vicinity . . . hearts; *MS(2)TH*] vicinity; *MS(1)*
17 as well as *MS(2)TH*] no less than *MS(1)*　　　　19 other *MS(2)TH* [*added*]
19 have been *MS(2)TH*] be *MS(1)*　　　　　　20 long-time *MS(2)TH* [*added*]
29–30 inhabitants . . . still. *MS(2)TH*] inhabitants. *MS(1)*

the village bodily away to a distance of a mile or more, where he built new, and, it must be added, convenient cottages, and a little barn-like church. The spot on which the old village had stood was now included in his lawn. But the villagers still intruded there, for they came to ring the Abbey-Church bells—a fine peal, which they 5 professed (it is believed truly) to have an immemorial right to chime.

"As the natives persistently came and got drunk in the ringing-loft, the peer determined to put a stop to it. He sold the ring of bells to a founder in a distant city, and to him one day the whole beautiful set of them was conveyed on waggons away from the spot on which they 10 had hung and resounded for so many centuries, and called so many devout souls to prayer. When the villagers saw their dear bells going off in procession, never to return, they stood at their doors and shed tears.

"It was just after this time that the first shadow fell upon the new 15 lord's life. His wife died. Yet the renovation of the residence went on apace. The Abbey was pulled down wing by wing, and a fair mansion built on its site. An additional lawn was planned to extend over the spot where the cloisters had been, and for that purpose the ground was to be lowered and levelled. The flat tombs covering the Abbots 20 were removed one by one, as a necessity of the embellishment, and the bones dug up.

"Of these bones it seemed as if the excavators would never reach the end. It was necessary to dig ditches and pits for them in the plantations, and from their quantity there was not much respect 25 shown to them in wheeling them away.

III

"One morning, when the family were rising from breakfast, a message was brought to my lord that more bones than ever had been found in clearing away the ground for the ball-room, and for the 30 foundations of the new card-parlour. One of the skeletons was that of a mitred abbot—evidently a very holy person. What were they to do with it?

6 (it is believed truly) *MS(2)TH* [*added*]   9 city, and to him *MS(2)TH*] city to whom *MS(1)*   16 of the residence *MS(2)TH* [*added*]   17 mansion *MS(2)TH*] residence *MS(1)*   25–6 plantations … away. *MS(2)TH*] plantations. *MS(1)*   31 card-parlour *MS(2)TH*] card-room *MS(1)* [card- *undeleted*]

" 'Put him into any hole,' says my lord.

"The foreman came a second time, 'There is something strange in those bones, my lord,' he said; 'we remove them by barrowfuls, and still they seem never to lessen. The more we carry away, the more
5 there are left behind.'

"The son looked disturbed, rose from his seat and went out of the room. Since his mother's death he had been much depressed, and seemed to suffer from nervous debility.

" 'Curse the bones!' said the peer, angry at the extreme sensitiveness
10 of his son, whose distress and departure he had observed. 'More, do ye say? Throw the wormy rubbish into any ditch you can find!'

"The servants looked uneasily at each-other, for the old Catholicism had not at that time ceased to be the religion of these islands so long as it has now, and much of its superstition and weird
15 fancy still lingered in the minds of the simple folk of this remote nook.

"The son's wife, the bright and accomplished woman aforesaid, to enliven the subject told her father-in-law that she was designing a marble tomb for one of the London churches, and the design was to be a very artistic allegory of Death and the Resurrection; the figure of an
20 Angel on one side, and that of Death on the other (according to the extravagant symbolism of that date, when such designs as this were much in vogue). Might she, the lady asked, have a skull to copy in marble for the head of Death?

"She might have them all, and welcome, her father-in-law said. He
25 would only be too glad.

"She went out to the spot where the new foundations were being dug, and from the heap of bones chose the one of those sad relics which seemed to offer the most perfect model for her chisel.

" 'It is the last Abbot's, my lady,' said the clerk of the works.
30 " 'It will do,' said she; and directed it to be put into a box and sent to the house in London where she and her husband at present resided.

"When she met her husband that day he proposed that they should return to town almost immediately. 'This is a gloomy place,' said he. 'And if ever it comes into my hands I shan't live here much. I've been

---

6 looked disturbed, *MS(2)TH*] turned pale, *MS(1)*   6 went *MS(2)TH?*] went away *MS(1)*   10 distress *MS(2)TH*] pallor *MS(1)*   19 a very artistic *MS(2)TH*] an *MS(1)*   21–2 date . . . vogue). *MS(2)TH*] date. *MS(1)* 26–7 out to the spot . . . dug, *MS(2)TH*] out, *MS(1)*   27 chose the *MS(2)TH*] chose *MS(1)*   28 the most perfect *MS(2)TH*] a good *MS(1)*   33 This *MS(2)TH*] It *MS(1)*

telling the old man of my debts, too, and he says he won't pay them
... be hanged if he will, until he has a grandson at least. ... So let's be
off.'

"They returned to town. This young man the son and heir, though
quiet and nervous, was not a very domestic character; he had many 5
friends of both sexes with whom his refined and accomplished wife
was unacquainted. Therefore she was thrown much upon her own
resources; and her gifts in carving were a real solace to her. She
proceeded with her design for the tomb of her acquaintance; and the
Abbot's skull having duly arrived, she made use of it as her model as 10
she had planned.

"Her husband being as usual away from home, she worked at her
self-imposed task till bed-time—and then retired. When the house
had been wrapped in sleep for some hours the front door was opened,
and the absent one entered, a little the worse for liquor—for drinking 15
in those days was one of a nobleman's accomplishments. He ascended
the stairs, candle in hand, and feeling uncertain whether his wife had
gone to bed or no, entered her studio to look for her. Holding the
candle unsteadily above his head, he perceived a heap of modelling
clay; behind it a sheeted figure with a death's-head above it—this 20
being in fact the draped dummy arrangement that his wife had built
up to be ultimately copied in marble for the allegory she had designed
to support the mural tablet.

"The sight seemed to overpower the gazer with horror; the candle
fell from his hand; and in the darkness he rushed downstairs and out 25
of the house.

" 'I've seen it before!' he cried in mad and maudlin accents. 'Where?
when?'

"At four o'clock the next morning news was brought to the house
that my lord's heir had shot himself dead with a pistol at a tavern not 30
far off.

"His reason for the act was absolutely inexplicable to the outer
world. The heir to an enormous property and a high title, the

2 at least *MS(2)TH* [*added*]   4 This young man *MS(2)TH* [*added*]
5 character; he *MS(2)TH*] character: & *MS(1)*   6 refined and accomplished
MS(2)TH] gentle & gifted *MS(1)*   14 had been *MS(2)TH*] was *MS(1)*
14 sleep for some hours *MS(2)TH*] sleep, *MS(1)*   15–16 —for drinking ...
accomplishments. *MS(2)TH* [*added*]   19 modelling *MS(2)TH* [*added*]
22 ultimately *MS(2)TH* [*added*]   33 property *MS(2)EH* [*altered in same line*]]
fortune *MS(1)*   33 a high *MS(2)TH* [*added*]

husband of a wife as gifted as she was charming; of all the men in English society he seemed to be the last likely to undertake such a desperate deed.

"Only a few persons—his wife not being one of them, though his
5 father was—knew of the sad circumstance in the life of the suicide's mother the late Lady Cicely, a few months before his birth—in which she was terrified nearly to death by the woman who held up poor little 'Death's-Head', over the churchyard wall.

"Then people said that in this there was retribution upon the
10 ambitious lord for his wickedness, particularly that of cursing the bones of the holy men of God. I give the superstition for what it is worth. It is enough to add, in this connection, that the old lord died, some say like Herod, of the characteristics he had imputed to the inoffensive human remains. However that may be in a few years the
15 title was extinct, and now not a relative or scion remains of the family that bore his name.

"A venerable dissenter, a fearless ascetic of the neighbourhood, who had been deprived of his opportunities through some objections taken by the peer, preached a sermon the Sunday after his funeral,
20 and mentioning no names, significantly took as his text, Isaiah XIV. 10–23:—

"'Art thou also become weak as we? Art thou become like unto us? Thy pomp is brought down to the grave, and the noise of thy viols: the worm is spread under thee, and the worms cover thee. How art thou
25 fallen from Heaven, O Lucifer, son of the morning! How art thou cut down to the ground, which didst weaken the nations. . . . I will rise up against him, saith the Lord of hosts, and cut off from Babylon the name, and remnant, and son, and nephew, saith the Lord.'

"Whether as a Christian moralist he was justified in doing this I
30 leave others to judge."

2 he *MS(2)TH?*] she *MS(1)* [he *undeleted*]   5 the suicide's *MS(2)TH*] his *MS(1)*   6 mother the late Lady Cicely, *MS(2)TH*] mother, *MS(1)*   11–12 I give . . . worth. *MS(3)TH*] The superstition is given for . . . worth. *MS(2)TH* [*added; only* is given *deleted*]   12 add, *MS(3)TH*] state *MS(2)TH*] say, *MS(1)*   14 human *MS(2)TH* [*added*]   14 remains. However that may be *MS(2)TH*] remains, and that *MS(1)*   15 and *MS(2)TH*] & that *MS(1)*   15 remains *MS(2) EH* [*altered in same line*]] remained *MS(1)*   17 dissenter *MS(2)TH*] clergyman *MS(1)*   17 ascetic *MS(2)TH*] moralist *MS(1)*   18 opportunities *MS(2)TH*] advancement *MS(1)*   25 cut *MS(2)TH*] cast *MS(1)*

Here the doctor concluded his story, and the thoughtfulness which it had engendered upon his own features spread over those of his hearers, as they sat with their eyes fixed upon the fire.

The End.

1 Here *MS(3)TH*] Herewith *MS(2)TH* [*added;* Here *undeleted*]   1 doctor
MS(2)EH?] doctors *MS(1)* [doctor *undeleted*]

The Spectre of the Real

INTRODUCTION

Occupying a unique place in the Hardy canon as his only acknowledged collaborative work, 'The Spectre of the Real' had its origins in the special nature of Hardy's relationship with his co-author, the novelist Florence Henniker, daughter of Richard Monckton Milnes, Lord Houghton, and wife of Arthur Henry Henniker–Major, a distinguished professional soldier. Hardy met Florence Henniker in Dublin on 19 May 1893 and was immediately attracted to her, describing her in his notebook entry for that date as 'A charming, *intuitive* woman apparently'.[1] The intensity of his subsequent feelings, glimpsed in the surviving letters and openly celebrated in some of his most moving poems,[2] led him to adopt any stratagems—from architectural lessons to literary discussions—which might help to establish an intimate friendship. For her part, as a successful but not particularly celebrated novelist, she was not reluctant to be on familiar terms with the author of *Tess of the d'Urbervilles*. It was, however, Hardy who was the suitor and he behaved as such, not scrupling to stoop to flattery. He read and praised her work, wrote a promotional paragraph about her,[3] described her as 'a real woman of letters', and declared in his letter of 29 June: 'If ever I were to consult any woman on a point in my own novels I should let that woman be yourself—my belief in your insight and your sympathies being strong, and increasing'.[4]

Although it quickly became clear that Henniker had no intention of entering into a romantic liaison with Hardy, at the time when the possibility of their literary collaboration was first raised he had not yet given up hope. It seems significant that in a letter of 20 July his

---

[1] *Life*, 270.

[2] E.g. 'At an Inn', 'A Broken Appointment', 'The Division', 'In Death Divided', 'The Month's Calendar', 'A Thunderstorm in Town'.

[3] TH's 'The Hon. Mrs. Henniker' was published anonymously in the *Illustrated London News*, 18 Aug. 1894.

[4] *CL* ii. 20, 18.

promise to 'think over the scheme of our collaborating in the talked of story' is immediately preceded by a reference to her conventional Christian views (and moral standards): 'I cannot help wishing you were free from certain retrograde superstitions: and I believe you will be some day, and none the less happy for the emancipation.'[5] Since Hardy said that he would 'think over' the scheme, it was probably Henniker who had suggested it during his visit to her the previous day, perhaps desiring to direct his attentions into safe literary channels as much as to benefit professionally from an association with such a celebrated author. For him there was, of course, no possibility of gain except in personal terms, and there is some indication that he seriously took up the idea of their collaboration only as a kind of last resort following their trip to Winchester on 8 August, the occasion when Henniker made it clear that the relationship could not be as he wished.[6] A literary partnership would at least provide an excuse for meetings and correspondence, and Hardy may still have hoped that friendship might eventually lead to something more.

But collaborating with Henniker did not prove to be easy. Although she doubtless spoke truly when in subsequent years she insisted that Hardy's kindness in offering 'hints & suggestions' for her work was both 'an advantage' and 'a great compliment',[7] she was in fact quite sensitive to his criticisms. Unlike the novice author Evangeline Smith, who in 1876 had sent Hardy a rejected story for comment—unlike, indeed, Agnes Grove and Florence Dugdale, who succeeded Henniker as his literary protégées (see pp. 332 ff.)—Henniker had already published three quite successful novels,[8] and she to some extent approached Hardy more as a fellow author than as a pupil. That Hardy was aware of this is suggested by the conciliatory tone of his 6 September 1893 letter concerning the stories she had sent him:

I was very glad to receive your letter, dear Mrs Henniker, & to hear about the stories, & that you received my scribblings for amendments on their pages without any of the umbrage you might have felt at the liberty I took in making them.

[5] Ibid. 26.　　[6] See *Biography*, 339–40.
[7] To Coulson Kernahan, 23 July 1896 (Berg Collection, New York Public Library); Raymond Blathwayt, 'The Hon. Mrs. Arthur Henniker', *Woman at Home*, July 1895, 55.
[8] *Sir George* (London: Richard Bentley and Son, 1891), *Bid Me Good-bye* (London: Richard Bentley and Son, 1892; hereafter *BMG*), and *Foiled* (London: Hurst and Blackett, 1893). References to these and FH's other books—*Outlines* (London: Hutchinson, 1894), *In Scarlet and Grey* (London: John Lane, 1896; hereafter *SG*),

If I may venture to say it, I think you have made a serious mistake in leaving "His Excellency" out of the collection. . . . The simple & sole fault of the tale was its conventional ending, as I said, which might easily have been remedied by rewriting a conclusion. I enclose for what it is worth a third suggestion on that point, which occurred to me just after dispatching my last letter.

I should call the book "The Statesman's Love-Lapse, & other stories namely . ." . . .

[P.S.] (On second thoughts it is not worth while to enclose the note on the story.)[9]

Several weeks later, after recommending the collection to the literary agent A. P. Watt, Hardy expressed his hope that Henniker had carried out his suggestions, especially those concerning a story called 'A Lost Illusion': and so made the volume more attractive to a potential publisher.[10] It is difficult to know just what her response was. She neither adopted his title (the volume was published as *Outlines*) nor included 'His Excellency', but she perhaps did alter 'A Lost Illusion': in the final scene of the story as published (it was retitled 'A Sustained Illusion') the central figure, Purcell, after being given cause to question his granddaughter's respectability, believes her cover-up lie and dies before she breaks down and admits the truth. Since Henniker's conclusions were often weak—prompting Hardy to suggest alternatives—the original version probably ended with the first revelation scene.

With 'The Spectre of the Real' Hardy was of course much more actively involved in the compositional process—though not to the extent that has hitherto been assumed. Purdy's theory—expanded by Millgate and repeated by Simon Gatrell and Jeffrey S. Cramer—proposes that 'the collaboration consisted in Hardy's discussing the outlines of his story with Mrs. Henniker and incorporating in the finished work some brief paragraphs she had written'.[11] But, as will be demonstrated, the surviving correspondence, Henniker's fiction, and

Sowing the Sand (London: Harper & Brothers, 1898; hereafter *SS*), *Contrasts* (London: John Lane, 1903), *Our Fatal Shadows* (London: Hurst and Blackett, 1907; hereafter *FS*), and *Second Fiddle* (London: Eveleigh Nash, 1912; hereafter *SF*)—are incorporated in the text.

[9] *CL* ii. 29.   [10] 22 Oct. 1893 (*CL* ii. 37).

[11] Purdy, 347; *Biography*, 343–4; Simon Gatrell, 'The Early Stages of Hardy's Fiction', in *Thomas Hardy Annual No. 2*, ed. Norman Page (London: Macmillan, 1984), 19–20; Jeffrey S. Cramer, Introduction to 'The Spectre of the Real', *The Thomas Hardy Year Book*, 13 (1986), 8.

especially the two typescripts and the proofs of 'Spectre'—the first typescript revised by Henniker and then by Hardy, the second typescript (based on the corrected first typescript) and proofs revised by Hardy alone—suggest a considerably more complicated history. It can be summarized thus: after discussing the project, including potential plots, with Henniker, Hardy sent her two outlines; she selected one and wrote it up as a scenario which he altered slightly; she then wrote out the story in full and sent the manuscript to Hardy, who extensively revised it and completely rewrote the conclusion before dispatching it to be typed; after she had lightly corrected that first typescript he altered it substantially, had a second typescript made, revised it, sent it to *To-Day*, and finally corrected the proofs when they arrived.

Work on the story—originally entitled 'Desire'—must have begun by early September 1893, for on the 10th Hardy wrote to Henniker: 'I send the "Desire" sketch, with the trifling modification. I think the insertion in red at the end improves it.'[12] Evidently she did not immediately reply, for three days later he wrote again to say: 'I hope you received the skeleton MS. If you don't like either of the two stories will you be frank, & tell me? I can send others, as I have several partly thought out: & it *must* be a good one.'[13] Since Hardy asked for Henniker's frank opinion, the original idea for 'Desire' had presumably been his, possibly influenced by earlier discussions they had had together, while the reference to 'two stories' points to Hardy's having previously sent her outlines of some kind,[14] perhaps the 'sketch-plots' she returned the following month.[15] As for 'the skeleton MS' sent to Henniker, it has hitherto been assumed that this was Hardy's outline,[16] but his classification of it as a 'sketch' suggests something more developed (such as a scenario), while his use of the placatory 'trifling' clearly implies that it was her work he was modifying. Significantly, too, when he later suggested that they 'put back the Desire for the present', he asked if she would 'mind the trouble of writing . . . out' a 'still better story' if he could think of one.[17]

Hardy's attempt to downplay his revision of the 'skeleton MS' was

---

[12] *CL* ii. 30.   [13] Ibid. 31.

[14] They were probably similar to the unused story plots now in DCM and transcribed (inaccurately) in Evelyn Hardy, 'Plots for Five Unpublished Short Stories', *London Magazine*, 5 (Nov. 1958), 33–45, and in *Old Mrs Chundle and Other Stories* (London: Macmillan, 1977), 115–28.

[15] *CL* ii. 38.   [16] Gatrell, 'Early Stages', 19.   [17] 6 Oct. 1893 (*CL* ii. 36).

apparently unsuccessful, since on 16 September he was obliged to reassure her: 'As to my having "contempt" as you suggest, for your rendering of the "Desire", you know I *never* can have that for *anything* you do.'[18] His protestations were, however, somewhat disingenuous: if he did not have 'contempt' for her work, he would at least have preferred it to have been different. Earlier in the same letter he had written:

Yes: I *do* sigh a little; over your position less than over your conventional views. I do not mind its results upon the present little story (which please alter as you like)—but upon your future literary career. If you mean to make the world listen to you, you must say now what they will all be thinking & saying five & twenty years hence: & if you do that you must offend your conventional friends.

It is true that Henniker's fiction suffers from her adherence to convention—the wicked and even the erring virtuous are killed off at an alarming rate—and doubtless Hardy did wish her to be successful, but his advice was scarcely disinterested. Having failed to convince her of the personal desirability of becoming the 'enfranchised woman' he sought,[19] hence potentially more sympathetic to his romantic overtures, he somewhat unfairly invoked the possible literary consequences of her 'conventional views'. What becomes increasingly clear is that he remained more concerned with the possibilities of their relationship than with the quality of their story.

As a professional writer with an established reputation, he could hardly be indifferent to the latter, however, and, after receiving the completed manuscript from her on 22 September,[20] he was apparently unable to refrain from suggesting alterations, although the letter in question has not survived. On 6 October, in any case, he again felt compelled to apologize: 'I did not at all *mean* my last note to be unkind, & am sorry that it seemed so, & hurt you about the MS. ... Never would I give *you* pain!'[21] A sense of frustration is apparent throughout this letter—in his reproach because she had not sent a specific address in Scotland, in his jealous comparison of himself, 'a mere scribbler who would not kill a fly', to her 'millionaire sportsmen' companions, and above all in his complaint about her absence:

[18] *CL* ii. 33.   [19] To FH, 16 July 1893 (*CL* ii. 24).   [20] *CL* ii. 34.
[21] Ibid. 35.

I have several things to ask you on our literary partnership, but I cannot enter into them till a distinct postal communication is re-established between us—or, still better, a meeting is feasible. . . . It is unfortunate that just when this scheme rendered it necessary for us to communicate freely & easily you shd have rushed off to such outlandish latitudes: otherwise we should almost have been in print by this time.

Their collaboration had failed not only as a means of increasing intimacy but also, so it seemed, as a literary venture, for, in spite of his assurances that he wished 'as much as ever to carry out the joint story', Hardy was beginning to wonder whether their conflicting views could in fact be reconciled. He accordingly suggested putting back 'Desire' for 'the present' in favour of 'a still better story'.

This tactful attempt to withdraw from what was becoming an impossible situation was evidently not supported by Henniker, however, for on 22 October, after dispatching the stories for the *Life's Little Ironies* volume to Osgood, McIlvaine, Hardy again 'turn[ed] to the "Desire"'.[22] Discussion in the interim must have focused largely upon the question of alternative endings, for in explanation of the need for a new title he wrote: 'I have planned to carry out Ending II—since you like it so much better: I feel I ought not to force the other upon you—wh. is too uncompromising for one of the pretty sex to have a hand in. The question now is, what shall we call it?—"The ressurection [*sic*] of a Love"?' Hardy was obviously doing his utmost not to offend his collaborator, consulting her not only about the title of their joint project but also about the name for the heroine of his next novel (significantly, Sue Bridehead's second name is Florence). Moreover, he insisted that Henniker's 'remarks on the various possibilities of the "Desire" [were] very thoughtful & good', and that he did not object to her criticisms ('please do any amount of them, dear fellow-scribbler').

But Hardy's artistic conscience again refused to be stifled altogether, and three days later he tentatively withdrew his previous concession: 'A word as to our story: in working it out I find it may possibly be necessary to effect a compromise between the two endings: for on no account must it end weakly.'[23] By 28 October he was able to report that the story was 'finished virtually' and that the manuscript had been sent 'early this morning' to a professional typist with instructions to send the resulting typescript directly to

[22] Ibid. 38.   [23] Ibid. 39.

Henniker.[24] Hardy had come up with a new ending, one which, whether 'good or bad', he saw as having 'the merit of being in exact keeping with Lord P.'s character',[25] and he broached the subject of this and other revisions cautiously, promising to defer to her wishes:

> Will you please read it from the beginning (*without* glancing first at the end!) so as to get the intended effect, & judge of its strength or weakness. It is, as you wished, very tragic; a modified form of Ending II—which I think better than any we have thought of before. If anything in it is what you don't like please tell me quite freely,—& it shall be modified. As I said last time, all the wickedness (if it has any) will be laid on my unfortunate head, while all the tender & proper parts will be attributed to you. Without wishing to make you promise, I suggest that we keep it a secret to our two selves which is my work & which yours. We may be amusingly bothered by friends & others to confess.

To reconstruct the original version of Ending II preferred by Henniker is impossible, but what seems clear is that it, too, was 'very tragic'—her own fiction, although conventional, very rarely ends happily—though without involving Parkhurst's suicide. More typical of Henniker would have been the accidental deaths of both Jim and Parkhurst, and perhaps of Rosalys as well. As for the 'uncompromising' Ending I referred to in the 22 October letter, it is tempting to think that it might have involved yet another reworking of the Elfride–Knight, Tess–Angel situation: confession followed by rejection. As it stands the conclusion is of course a variation on that theme, even though the 'real' may on this occasion not have been voluntarily revealed, and it is therefore not surprising that Hardy thought it the best.

Having substantially—and independently—altered the plot of their story, Hardy attempted to reinstate Henniker as co-author by inviting her to revise the account of the wedding morning and to make the final choice of title:

> In reading it over, particularly the bride's doings in the morning from dawn till the wedding-hour, please insert in pencil any details that I have omitted, & that would only be known to a woman. I may not be quite correct in what I

---

[24] Ibid. 39; all quotations in the following paragraphs are from this letter unless otherwise identified.

[25] Parkhurst commits suicide after marrying Rosalys in ignorance of the fact that she has been a widow for only a few hours, the accidental death of her long estranged husband having occurred shortly after the latter's unexpected return and resumption of sexual relations the previous night.

have hastily written, never having had the pleasure of being a bride-elect myself. . . .

Our old title was in itself rather good, but as it does not quite apply, I have provisionally substituted "The Spectre of the Real".—"The Looming of the Real" is perhaps almost better. I have also thought of "A passion & after"; "To-day's kiss & yesterday's."—"Husband's corpse & husband's kiss" "A shattering of Ideals". When you have read the modifications you will be able to choose; or suggest.

Henniker perhaps chose the title and she did make a few pencil alterations still visible on the typescript, but these were of a relatively minor kind, neither adding details to the wedding-morning passages nor modifying the ending. What she evidently did insist upon, however, was the reinstatement of some descriptive passages of hers that Hardy had excised during his revision of the manuscript. He was clearly sensitive on this point and in the 28 October letter had attempted to forestall objections:

I will send you back the pages of detail omitted, if you wd like to have them, as they may be useful. You will *quite* understand that they were not omitted because they weren't good; but because the scale of the story was too small to admit them without injury to the proportion of the whole. I refer particularly to the description of the pool, & the bird tracks; which I *much* wished to retain.

Hardy also mentioned that he had asked the typist to return the manuscript 'in case [he] should want to insert a little more detail from it', but he probably did not expect to have to restore quite as much as he did—not only the pool and bird-tracks passage but also shorter descriptions of butterflies playing hide-and-seek, Rosalys whistling to a robin, and birds sleeping in the park (pp. 318, 313, 314, 324). All these passages were added to the typescript in Hardy's hand but are clearly restorations of Henniker's work. They were, however, rewritten—as Hardy's false starts and alterations demonstrate—and apparently moved on occasion from their original manuscript positions, for the typescript shows traces of two abandoned attempts to incorporate them: in the margin of fo. 17, alongside the paragraph about the (lack of) view from the summer-house (p. 312), a largely illegible erasure includes the words 'copper-coloured butterfly' and 'in the hedge with a little blue companion'; on the verso of fo. 35, keyed for insertion after the sentence beginning 'When the doctor had left', is the undeleted fragment of a version of the pool and bird-tracks passage, 'The lake was before her, & from the mud at the edge' (p. 329).

That the descriptive passages were finally included is evidence not only of Henniker's strength of will but also of Hardy's willingness to accommodate her—and by extension the depth of his feelings—even at some cost to his professional integrity, for the details are essentially superfluous, contributing little or nothing to the story in terms of imagery, theme, mood, or even local colour. As such they are typical of Henniker's work: all her stories contain obtrusive description for its own sake,[26] usually involving birds, occasionally butterflies and small animals. The style, too, is essentially Henniker's, prosaic and thick with clichés. Compare, for example, the following lines from 'Spectre'—even as improved by Hardy—with a passage from Henniker's *Bid Me Good-bye*:

not a creature was conscious of the presence of these two but a little squirrel they had disturbed in a beech ...

Suddenly the plovers rose into the air, uttering their customary wails, and dispersing like a group of stars from a rocket; and the herons drew up their flail-like legs, and flapped themselves away.

She was conscious that St. Aubyn was knocking off the head of a large-leaved plant at their feet; that a squirrel looked at them with his shy bright eyes, and sprang into a hollow tree above their heads; that a pheasant, with a frightened whirr of wings, started up from the thicket and soared away into the sky. (*BMG* 126)

Henniker's written contributions to 'Spectre' were not, however, limited to such descriptive passages, as has hitherto been believed. Millgate, developing Purdy's conclusions, assumes that 'the pages of detail' to be returned to Henniker were all she wrote and that they were separate from the manuscript sent to the typist.[27] But since

---

[26] On rare occasions the passages have a foreshadowing or mood-establishing function, as in the description in *Foiled* (iii. 25) of Léo watching a sparrow-hawk seize 'in his cruel talons' a 'helpless small creature' (compare the much more powerful and better integrated account of the hawk and wild duck in *The Hand of Ethelberta*) shortly before she is herself victimized, or the final lines of 'An Hour in October' reflecting the death of Hilary Chesney's happiness (note also the similarity to descriptions in 'Spectre'): 'The sky was red with the glow of an expiring fire, and would soon be uniform and sombre. The wailing cry of the water-fowl came towards her from a long distance. And all around her the leaves were falling....' (*Contrasts*, 269; FH's ellipsis).

[27] *Biography*, 343.

Hardy had asked for the manuscript back as a potential source of additional detail, it seems clear that the manuscript as returned to him contained both narrative and detail mixed together—otherwise the omitted descriptive passages could simply have been kept back in the first place. That Hardy should have mentioned 'pages' of detail is not in itself problematic in light of Henniker's large hand and the length—up to three hundred words—of some of her descriptive passages in other works; nor, of course, were all her descriptions necessarily reinstated. The phrase, too, could merely have been a concise designation for pages 'predominantly of detail', 'containing detail', and so forth. It is in any case improbable that Hardy, after reading page after page of stock description in Henniker's first three novels, would have asked her to supply similar passages for their story.

The manuscript sent to the typist on 28 October, then, was presumably the one Hardy had received from Henniker on 22 September. It had, of course, been extensively revised since then—as is suggested by Hardy's references to 'tak[ing] the "Desire" in hand' on 22 October, 'working it out' on 25 October, and having 'finished [it] virtually' on 28 October[28]—but not to the extent of necessitating the production of a new manuscript, except perhaps of the rewritten ending. If it had been completely recopied, after all, it would not have contained the omitted detail that Hardy wanted to have available for possible reinsertion. Hardy's reworking of Henniker's material—and, indeed, of his own—was not, however, limited to the pre-typescript stage. Having asked her to forward the typewritten copy to him so that he could 'go through it for final corrections, & send it off',[29] Hardy found when he received it that his 'corrections' in fact amounted to substantial revisions sufficient to justify a fresh typescript. Since he further revised that second typescript before sending it to *To-Day*—using the carbon copy, having presumably arranged for the ribbon copy to be sent to his collaborator—and in due course corrected the proofs, it is not surprising that Purdy, misled by the numerous Hardyan phrases and the characteristic plot, should have claimed that 'The work was largely Hardy's'.[30] But to a reader familiar with Henniker's fiction the style is for the most part unquestionably hers, as, indeed, a perceptive contemporary reviewer suggested: 'The style seems Mrs. Henniker's, so possibly Mr. Hardy furnished the plot.'[31]

[28] *CL* ii. 38, 39.   [29] 28 Oct. 1893 (*CL* ii. 40).   [30] Purdy, 346.
[31] Rev. of *In Scarlet and Grey, Literary World*, 14 Nov. 1896, 375.

Because Henniker's prose is distinctive primarily in its very banality, this claim is (given the absence of her manuscript) somewhat difficult to substantiate in detail: Hardy, too, was quite capable of succumbing to pedestrianism on occasion. Moreover, the very nature of the collaboration makes it difficult to identify with any confidence work that was *exclusively* hers: seemingly typical Henniker sentences were no doubt written by her but could well contain minor Hardy revisions. This degree of interaction renders useless any attempt to carry out a computerized stylistic analysis to determine their respective contributions, since a Hardyan prepositional sequence could easily turn up in a sentence otherwise wholly Henniker's. For the same reason it is impossible to distinguish examples of 'masculine' and 'feminine' prose in the story, and in any case Henniker firmly belongs, both ideologically and stylistically, to the group of female writers who imitated the prevailing modes of the dominant (patriarchal) tradition.[32]

In seeking internal evidence of Henniker's contribution to 'Spectre' one must in fact turn to the content—not to the plot, since that is essentially Hardy's, but to the detailed working out of the events. For example, Henniker's characters tend, like Parkhurst, to answer questions with physical gestures[33] and to smile with their eyes;[34] during times of intense emotion they become oblivious, like Rosalys, of their surroundings[35] or feel as if they are living through a dream (a sensation experienced by at least thirteen other Henniker characters).[36] Significantly, Hardy attempted to improve upon that last trite idea by adding a reference to Jim's voice being heard 'as the phantom of a dead sound'. A few passages warrant comparison:

He bade them a cool good-bye and left. She watched his retreating figure . . . He never turned his head.[37]

[32] See Toril Moi, 'Feminist Literary Criticism', in Ann Jefferson and David Robey (eds.), *Modern Literary Theory: A Comparative Introduction* (2nd edn.; London: B. T. Batsford, 1986), 220, and Elaine Showalter, *A Literature of their Own: British Women Novelists from Brontë to Lessing* (Princeton: Princeton University Press, 1977), 13.

[33] P. 319, as does Jim, p. 302; the signalling phrase is always 'For all answer' (*BMG* 149; *Foiled*, iii. 259; *Outlines*, 137–8; *SF* 196).

[34] P. 319; *BMG* 149, 159; *Foiled*, ii. 36; *Outlines*, 153; *Contrasts*, 273; *SF* 144.

[35] Pp. 303, 306; *BMG* 226; *Foiled*, i. 194; *SS* 33.

[36] P. 321; *BMG* 126, 218, 239, 243; *Outlines*, 58, 133; *SG* 27, 74, 157; *SS* 217; *Contrasts*, 168, 188, 264, 290; *FS* 268.

[37] In this paragraph and the following one quotations are from the first typescript (before it was revised), the surviving witness closest to FH's MS.

Then with rather a cold shake of the hand to Mary ... he started to walk home. And he never turned his head to look back, though Mary watched him until a bend in the avenue concealed him from sight. (*BMG 131*)

One last long kiss; and then from the shadow in which he stood he watched her skirting the lake and hurrying along in the shelter of the yew hedges ...

One last pressure of the little hand, and she was through the gate, running down the lime avenue ... with her child-like smile shining on her lips and eyes. (*BMG 158–9*)

the whole impression left by the church being one of singular harmony, loveliness, and above all, repose—which contrasted greatly with her experiences just then.

To both of them the contrast between its smiling tranquility and the restless ache of human life was so profound ... (*SS* 186)

If her mother had not been beside her she would have screamed out aloud in her pain.

She could almost have screamed for the very pain of keeping back her tears. (*Outlines*, 75)[38]

Other passages characteristic of Henniker include the evening at Colonel Lacy's with its banal dinner conversation and, especially, Rosalys's concern for the cab-horse and her comment about butchers not having hearts like other men.[39]

Henniker's prose is also marked by the repeated use of stock descriptive phrases: skies are velvet-like, cheeks pink and eyes shining, faces white and tired.[40] Images likewise recur, particularly allusions to the world of romance and fairy-tale or to favourite biblical passages:

---

[38] Cf. *Contrasts*, 209, 224. A similar phrase appears in *Jude* (148)—'If he had been a woman he must have screamed under the nervous tension'—but the idea is certainly more characteristic of FH than TH and may in fact have been suggested by 'Spectre'.

[39] Cf. *BMG* 88–9, 50. Virtually all FH's stories contain some reference to animals, the treatment of them serving as a touchstone for character. TH's fiction—notably *Tess* and *Jude*—also expresses his concern for animals, but much less obtrusively. Unlike TH, FH was unconsciously inconsistent (presumably because of her social position and military connections): her male animal-lovers are often keen, though 'humane', sportsmen and/or soldiers. The irony of Rosalys's remarking how revolting it must be to marry a butcher just as she is about to enter the church with a potential butcher of men is no doubt unintentional.

[40] Pp. 303, 311 (both phrases were revised by TH): *SG* 11, *Contrasts*, 130; p. 303: *Outlines*, 57, *SG* 16–17; p.321: *BMG* 178.

the grand walk whose pebbles shone like precious stones ...
[a] princess emerging from her palace into a garden of roses and fountains to meet her lover-prince ...

as she walked down the gravel paths where every pebble shone like a jewel in the strange light, it seemed to her that she was the heroine of a fairy story; a princess in an enchanted castle ... (*BMG* 6)[41]

he might have been the direct descendant of a line of picked crusaders ... one who might have been a Viking, or knightly hero of romance ... (*Contrasts*, 74)

From the crown of his head even to the sole of his foot there was no blemish in him.

From the crown of that exquisite *blonde cendré* head ... down to her little *suède* shoe, there is no fault to be found ... (*FS* 60)[42]

Significantly, three of these four passages from 'Spectre'—the exception being the biblical allusion—were substantially revised by Hardy.

Such evidence helps to confirm that the first six sections were predominantly Henniker's work—as, indeed, does the choice of setting. By 1893 the concept of Wessex had become one of the most dominant elements in Hardy's fiction,[43] and it seems unlikely that, even in a story which as a collaboration would in some sense be distinct from his other work, he would have created a location so topographically undefined and unsituated as Ambrose Towers. With its sixteenth-century 'red tower', 'shrouded mullions', and 'old brick walls' surrounded by 'broad paths and garden-lands', Ambrose Towers could be any number of English country estates. As such it is typical of Henniker's fiction, as is the use of actual London addresses: Eaton Place (later changed to Belgrave Road) and Porchester Terrace. If the inclusion of recognizable London locations—Kensington Gardens, the 'great meat-market' (Smithfield), the 'fashionable hotel on the Embankment' (the Savoy)—is typical of both Henniker and Hardy, the choice and description of the 'East-London church', unmistakably Saint Bartholomew the Great, does

[41] See also *BMG* 80; *SS* 81, 229; *Contrasts*, 287; *SF* 123.

[42] That these two passages were written by the same author is suggested by the reversal of the 2 Sam. 14: 25 sequence ('from the sole of his foot even to the crown of his head ...').

[43] See Simon Gatrell, *Hardy the Creator: A Textual Biography* (Oxford: Clarendon Press, 1988), 118 ff.

suggest Henniker's authorship.[44] Writing to her in June 1893 about their arranged architectural lesson, Hardy had said: 'Westminster Abbey, St. Saviour's Southwark, and St. Bartholemew's [*sic*] Smithfield, contain excellent features for study.'[45] The inclusion of architectural details in 'Spectre' can be seen as part of the dialogue between Hardy and Henniker, her attempt to demonstrate that she was, indeed, as Hardy had predicted, 'an apt scholar'. The Smithfield church is today still a 'beautiful building, with its Norman apse and transverse arches of horse-shoe form, and the massive curves and cushion-capitals that [support] the tower-end; the whole impression left by the church being one of singular harmony, loveliness, and above all, repose ...' And the sunlight continues to illuminate 'the quaint tomb where the founder of the building [lies] in his dreamless sleep'. There is, however, no 'fine old Norman porch': the original porch was destroyed when Henry VIII dissolved the monasteries and the present ones (West and North) were in fact built in 1893,[46] the year 'Spectre' was written. Perhaps Henniker was confused by the building work and assumed that in the late 1870s, the approximate date of these opening chapters,[47] the church entrance was indeed still Norman.

But even if Henniker is accepted as the primary author of the bulk of the story, it remains certain that Hardy introduced revisions and additions which are now difficult to identify with confidence, especially since Henniker's conventionality did not inhibit her from writing of life's little ironies and disillusionments. Even the authorship of a line as Hardyan as Rosalys's comment about the vicar being 'too stupid to give anyone a pang' is doubtful, for Henniker, devout Christian though she was, could allow a character to refer to a parson as 'a well-meaning ass' (*SG* 156). Similarly, the remark about Parkhurst's chivalrous feelings towards women 'originating perhaps in the fact that he knew very little about them' could as easily have been written by the author of *Foiled*—in which the victimized hero exclaims, 'It was

[44] One wonders if FH was aware that St Bartholomew's was (as it still is) the church of the Worshipful Company of Butchers: as such—at least for her—it would have been an appropriately morbid place for a marriage which would end in unhappiness and disillusion.   [45] *CL* ii. 11.

[46] E. A. Webb, *The Records of St. Bartholomew's Priory and of the Church and Parish of St. Bartholomew the Great West Smithfield*, ii (Oxford: Oxford University Press, 1921), 109, 115.

[47] Assuming that the discussion of the Home-Rule question seven years after Jim's departure is not anachronistic.

the sort of infernal ingenuity of which no one but a woman could have been capable!' (iii. 255)—as by the author of *Jude*, although the reviewer Coulson Kernahan, pretending to know but not to reveal who had written what, was probably correct in attributing it to Hardy.[48] That it was a manuscript addition is suggested by its pointing in the first typescript, where a dash marks its conclusion but no punctuation separates it from the preceding clause—an oversight more likely to occur in revision than in composition. Although Henniker made very few alterations when reading over the typescript, this particular error was sufficiently glaring even for her to notice and correct.

Textual evidence interpreted in the context of external evidence must primarily be relied upon in attempting to determine which passages are Hardy's. Henniker's bowdlerization of the story before collecting it in *In Scarlet and Grey* provides some clues: in the revised text Jim and Rosalys meet 'at hotels or restaurants' instead of 'in the private rooms of hotels'; Rosalys's desire wanes because 'the novelty of wifedom was past' not because 'the sensuous part of her character was satisfied'; their passion is 'resistless' instead of 'almost unholy'; and Rosalys has supposedly 'rejected all other men' rather than kept herself from them. But it is difficult to know whether Hardy in fact wrote the entire passage in which the offending phrases occurred or merely the phrases themselves. It was apparently only Hardy's addition in the first typescript of '& sinful' to Henniker's own prose which necessitated her alteration in *In Scarlet and Grey* of 'Somehow I feel so dreadfully sad and sinful' to 'Somehow I feel so depressed, so dreadfully sad'. On the other hand, her most extensive bowdlerizations—deletions of Jim's unwanted embrace at the end of VI and the (not very) veiled allusions to his renewed sexual relations with Rosalys at the beginning of VII—suggest a much greater involvement on Hardy's part, and it was probably at this point that he departed radically from Henniker's manuscript in order to rewrite the ending. For one of the sentences in this section ('When—did you part from her?') there is also textual evidence of Hardy's authorship, since in the first typescript Henniker, presumably not understanding his rhetorical punctuation, deleted the dash, which Hardy subsequently restored. There are clear similarities, too, between this passage and the scene in *Jude* in which Arabella confesses her bigamy after spend-

---

[48] Coulson Kernahan, 'A Woman Who Expected the Impossible', rev. of *Second Fiddle*, *Bookman*, Mar. 1912, 299.

ing the night with Jude, notably his shock as he stands 'pale and fixed', his 'sense of degradation at his revived experiences with her', and her self-justification: 'They don't think much of such as that over there! Lots of 'em do it.'[49] Although such Hardyan echoes are of course frequent throughout 'Spectre' and do not necessarily indicate the authorship of the passage in which they occur, in this instance the 'objectionable' nature of the content provides a reasonably reliable indicator.

That Hardy also wrote the subsequent narration of the wedding-day events is implied by his invitation to Henniker to supply details of the 'bride's doings'. If she appears not to have offered any suggestions about such essentially feminine preparations, she did delete the reference to Rosalys feeling that Parkhurst's title would be 'a handy thing, a very handy thing, for a woman with a big house and park like hers'. The deletion is Henniker's only extensive revision to the typescript and it is perhaps worth remarking that almost half of her alterations of wording (ten out of twenty-four) were made in the last three typescript pages of section VI and in section VII, as would be appropriate if these were predominantly Hardy's. Moreover, VII contains none of the characteristic Henniker phrases and incidents mentioned above.

The familiar features of the story first pointed out by Purdy—'the clandestine romance and marriage of a "noble lady" and a poor officer, the return of the vanished husband on the eve of his wife's remarriage, the removal of a troublesome character by drowning in a water-meadow'[50]—as well as the post-nuptial disillusionment, the agreement to separate, and so forth, indicate little more than that the plot was Hardy's. Some similarities in detail and phrasing between 'Spectre' and Hardy's earlier fiction are, however, sufficiently striking to suggest his authorship of specific passages. 'An Imaginative Woman', clearly inspired by his feelings for Henniker and written during the late summer of 1893[51] when they were beginning their collaborative work, parallels 'Spectre' in its use of a newspaper paragraph to report the suicide of Trewe who, like Parkhurst, shoots himself through the head with a revolver. 'Spectre' also offers an echo of 'A Tragedy of Two Ambitions' when Rosalys regards the lake very much as the two brothers contemplate the meads where their father drowned:

---

[49] *Jude*, 222, 223.   [50] Purdy, 346.   [51] *CL* ii. 22, 32; *Biography*, 342.

There was the lake from which the water had flowed down the river that had drowned Jim ...

There were the hatches, there was the culvert; they could see the pebbly bed of the stream through the pellucid water.[52]

That there should be some resemblance between these stories is not surprising, since, as Hardy wrote to Henniker, it was the preparation of the *Life's Little Ironies* volume—involving not only collection but also revision,[53] hence rereading—which delayed his work on their project: 'I could not take the "Desire" in hand till to-day, having been hunting up the tales I told you of ("Two Ambitions" being one of them). They are now fastened together to be dispatched to the publisher ...'[54] 'A Mere Interlude' was perhaps also reread at this time—in terms of content if not of quality it can be grouped with the *Life's Little Ironies* stories—for, as Baptista allows 'circumstances to pilot her along' and 'things to drift',[55] so Rosalys allows 'things to take their course', each remarrying within hours of the drowning of her first husband.

Still more striking similarities are to be found in 'The Waiting Supper', which could equally well have been considered for inclusion in *Life's Little Ironies*. In addition to the familiar 'poor man and the lady' situation (complete with nocturnal meetings and the discussion of a secret marriage), the unexpected return of the husband owing to the newspaper announcement of his wife's remarriage, and the death by drowning, there are several verbal parallels: when Christine arrives for the wedding ceremony, Nicholas kisses her 'with a sort of surprise, as if he had expected that at the last moment her heart would fail her' (*CM* 37), while Jim greets Rosalys with 'I was half afraid you might have failed me at the last moment'; Bellston defines his profession as 'Travel and exploration' (*CM* 41), while Jim describes himself as a 'traveller and explorer'; Christine sends Nicholas away saying, 'I will tell you everything of my history then' (*CM* 64), while Jim leaves Rosalys promising, 'and

---

[52] *Life's Little Ironies*, 105; the wording is identical in the 1888 serialization.
[53] See Purdy, 81–3.
[54] 22 Oct. 1893 (*CL* ii. 38).
[55] *A Changed Man*, 276, 288; subsequent references appear in the text preceded by *CM*. Unless otherwise stated, all quotations from this volume are identical in the serial texts.

then I'll tell you all my history'. The accounts of the drownings are also similar:[56]

> It was supposed that ... he had taken a short cut through the grounds ... and coming to the fall under the trees had expected to find there the plank which, during his occupancy of the premises with Christine and her father, he had placed there for crossing into the meads on the other side ... (*CM* 81)

> it is supposed he took the old short cut across the moor where there used to be a path when he was a lad at home, crossing the big river by a plank.

Equally remarkable are the resemblances between 'Spectre' and *The Pursuit of the Well-Beloved*, serialized October–December 1892, less than a year before work began on the collaborative story. The novel— at least in the serial version, which differs substantially from the volume-edition text—contains several of the familiar Hardyan plot devices, including a clandestine marriage, the return of a long-estranged spouse in response to a newspaper paragraph, and the convenient disposal of a character through drowning or, in this case, attempted drowning. The development of Jim's and Rosalys's post-marital disillusionment, too, is reminiscent of Pearston's and Marcia's in *Pursuit*: violent quarrels are interspersed with periods of dreary indifference, culminating in an agreement to separate. More-over, Jim's 'emancipated' views—his insistence on the 'practical nul-lity of their marriage-contract if they simply kept in different hemis-pheres without a word'—echo Marcia's 'advanced' and 'novel' social principles, articulated in her letter to Pearston: 'If I strictly confine myself to one hemisphere, and you ... to the other, any new tie we may form can affect nobody but ourselves.'[57] So, too, Jim's response when Rosalys acknowledges her desire to eradicate the evidence of their marriage closely parallels Isaac Pearston's when confronted by Avice the Second's discontent:

> That's a pleasant remark to make to a husband!
> That's a pretty thing for a wife to say! (*Pursuit*, 577)

Rosalys's agonized expression of her love for Parkhurst is similarly reminiscent of Avice the Third's confession about Mons Leverre:

[56] First remarked in Jeffrey S. Cramer, 'Hardy, Henniker, and "The Spectre of the Real"', *Thomas Hardy Society Review* (1977), 90–1. The *A Changed Man* text resembles 'Spectre' somewhat more closely than does the 1888 serial text: if TH did reread the story in 1893 with a view to its possible collection he could have reworked it then.

[57] *The Pursuit of the Well-Beloved*, *Illustrated London News*, 101 (1892), 481, 514. Subse-quent references to the serial version of the novel appear in the text.

I ought not to have done it . . . I tried not to. But I was so fearfully lonely! . . . I
didn't know you were coming back any more . . .

I can't—help crying—I know I ought not to—but I loved him very much . . .
And I didn't know he would come again! . . . I'll try—not to mind . . .
(*Pursuit*, 742)

Significantly, almost all of these parallels with both the novel and the
stories either occur in VII or were added by Hardy to the first typescript of 'Spectre', leaving little doubt of his authorship or of the
extent to which he self-plagiarized, no doubt unconsciously, when his
creative energies were not fully engaged.

The authorship of many phrases and sentences can of course be
determined by the holograph revisions to the two typescripts and
proofs, bearing in mind that apparent Hardy additions are not necessarily his, as the restoration of some of Henniker's descriptive passages has clearly shown. Whether Henniker saw the revised first
typescript or took any action in respect of either the second typescript
(assuming she did receive the ribbon copy) or the proofs is not clear.
Her hand, in any case, appears only in the first typescript and not
frequently there, her changes in wording being almost all stylistic: the
addition of 'that', the substitution of 'lovely' for 'handsome', 'drive'
for 'trot', 'Jove' for 'Gad', and so forth. Hardy accepted all but two of
her corrections: he was doubtless willing to make some concessions
after so radically altering her manuscript, and he had in any case
promised to modify what she did not like. Her revision of 'write' for
'pen', however, he changed to 'begin somehow', presumably because
he was using 'write' in the following sentence, and, although he
initially incorporated her alteration of 'an officer' to 'a soldier', he later
restored the original reading.

The latter instance is one of the few where Henniker's revision is
not essentially stylistic. The context is Mrs Ambrose's not wanting
her daughter to marry someone 'who has nothing but the pay of an
officer in the Line to live upon', and presumably Henniker, herself
married to an officer, felt she should not belittle their salaries or status.
It was, however, her persistent tendency to downgrade the social
positions of both Jim and Rosalys: she changed Jim's London residence from an 'hotel' to 'rooms', and when reprinting the story in her
own collective volume she moved Rosalys's house from Eaton Place
to Belgrave Road, a 'respectable' rather than 'highly respect-

able'—itself a Hardy addition—'place of residences'. The reason for these alterations is obscure; although the reference to Jim's hotel occurs in a passage almost certainly written by Hardy, it was presumably Henniker who originally named Eaton Place. Perhaps she simply wanted to distance these fictitious characters, whom Hardy's alterations were rendering increasingly unpleasant, from her own social circle. What is clear is that in Hardy's conception of the story Jim was somewhat more socially acceptable: Hardy altered the reference to Jim's father's 'house and property' to 'house and properties' and added the description of Jim as a ' "traveller and explorer" of the little known interiors of Asiatic countries', an occupation which would have made him an interesting dinner guest, though not sufficiently so to prevent him from being the last to enter the Lacys' dining-room. In light of Hardy's various 'poor man' suitors, all of whom are to some extent 'superior' to others of their class, it is not surprising that Hardy should have insisted on Jim's being an officer rather than a soldier in the ranks, and it is of course more credible that Rosalys should be dazzled by an officer.

Hardy tended to emphasize Rosalys's sexual attraction to Jim, adding to the first typescript the details of her 'ready mouth' and 'quick breath' and perhaps to the manuscript the reference to her 'full under-lip' trembling: the typing of 'full' over 'face' suggests that the typist was working from heavily revised copy. Possibly also a Hardy addition to the manuscript is the sentence fragment in the first typescript, 'No premonitions that the entirely physical character of his affection for her, and perhaps of hers for him, was an almost certain proof of its transitoriness.'[58] Hardy certainly wrote 'She had thoroughly abandoned herself to his good looks, his recklessness, his eagerness', added to the first typescript, and probably also the rest of the sentence, 'and, now that the sensuous part of her character was satisfied, her fervour also began to burn itself down'—most of which was subsequently bowdlerized by Henniker. In the final scenes Hardy not only reinvoked this sexual desire by inserting 'Come—damn you, dear—put up your mouth as you used to!' but also confirmed Rosalys's continuing inability to resist Jim's advances in those self-condemnatory lines later so carefully excised from Henniker's *In Scarlet and Grey*: 'O—O—what have I done! What a fool—what a weak fool!'; 'O, how weak, how weak was I!' Henniker's deletion of the

---

[58] Cf. the consequences of his revision at p. 320. 21–4.

reference to Rosalys coveting Parkhurst's title (her only major alteration to the first typescript) no doubt reflects a reluctant acceptance
of the accentuation of Rosalys's sexuality but at the same time a
refusal to allow love of social position to be numbered among her
heroine's failings. It does in fact seem out of character for a woman
who, although 'mentally matured under the touch of the gliding
seasons', originally wished to marry an army officer in the customary
way and 'get on as other people do'.

That after their marriage Jim and Rosalys did 'get on as other
people do'—though not in the sense Rosalys meant—is a common
Hardy theme, and one which he brought out strongly in his revisions.
In his addition to the opening paragraph of the story he wrote of 'that
poetical drama of two which the world has often beheld; which leads
up to a contract that causes a slight sinking in the poetry, and a
perceptible lack of interest in the play'. Similarly, in the first typescript 'this little romance' is altered to 'this little excursion to purchase disillusion'. The length, pointing, style, and especially content
of the following sentence—its central idea anticipatory of the Regis-
trar's office scene in *Jude*—suggest that it, too, was originally a Hardy
addition:

> Two or three other couples were also in the church on the same errand: a
> haggard woman in a tawdry white bonnet, hanging on to the arm of a short
> crimson-faced man, who had evidently been replenishing his inside with gin
> to nerve himself to the required pitch for the ordeal: a girl with a coarse, hard
> face, accompanied by a slender youth in shabby black: a tall man, of refined
> aspect, in very poor clothes, whose hollow cough shook his thin shoulders and
> chest, and told his bride that her happiness, such as it was, would probably
> last but the briefest space.

Many of Hardy's other revisions to the first typescript are attempts
to flesh out Henniker's prose. His most frequent criticism of her stories
over the years was that they were 'too little': of 'Lady Gillian' he
wrote, 'Like nearly all your stories, it makes one wish there were more
of it.'[59] It is true that, while Henniker always included long descriptive passages, her narratives, especially in the stories, were often
presented in little more than scenario form, invariably creating an
impression of haste. 'I fancy you write your MSS. a little too rapidly',
wrote Hardy in one of his earliest letters to her, and in an interview

[59] *CL* ii. 252, 245; see also ii. 215, 264, iii. 190, 214.

with Raymond Blathwayt she herself admitted, 'I write very quickly, and some of my short stories I have done in two or three days.'[60] Some of Hardy's attempts to compensate for the frequently skeletal character of her prose involved only the addition of single adjectives: 'harsh' stable-clock, 'alert' birds, 'gigantic' vans, 'covered' carts, 'quaint' tomb, 'fashionable' hotel. Sometimes the revisions were more extensive, when, for example, he added descriptive phrases like 'a fat and genial lady' or expanded 'the walls' to 'the old brick walls—red in the daytime, sable now'. Hardy also attempted to make her descriptions more evocative: the 'huge' shadow becomes 'funereal', the 'velvet-like sky' gives way to 'reaching deeps of sky', and so forth.

A similar process of revision can be traced in the second typescript. Another instance of Henniker's characteristic 'velvet-like' sky is altered, this time to 'a bottomless deep of blue'; so, too, the 'last long' kiss becomes 'clinging', the 'handsome, boyish' face 'healthy, virile', the 'hot' country 'enervating'. Some of Hardy's familiar preoccupations also emerge from the revisions, as when, for example, Jim's comment, 'Further back than my grandfather I am a little hazy as to my ancestors', is replaced by the description of his surname in relation to Rosalys's as 'merely the older one of the little freeholder turned out of this spot by your ancestor when he came'. And, unsurprisingly, Hardy still further emphasized the sexual suggestiveness of the story: Rosalys and Jim have luncheon 'in a room all to themselves'; Parkhurst almost wishes that she were not so good and perfect 'and innocent'; and Jim remarks of his relationship with Mélanie, 'People do these things'.

Relatively few changes were made in proof. Most are stylistic, renewed attempts to rework Henniker's banal prose: 'many yards' of turf becomes 'a smooth plush', Jim's 'handsome' countenance 'now familiar', the 'sad' arbour 'queer'. Not that characterization or thematic concerns were ignored: by merely adding 'to pay his debts' to the account of the disposal of Jim's father's property, for example, Hardy accentuated Jim's irresponsibility and extended his profligacy into areas beyond the sexual.

The proofs on which Hardy made. these—his final—corrections were for Jerome K. Jerome's *To-Day*, a weekly periodical devoted primarily to short fiction, Jerome having purchased the story through the literary agent A. P. Watt. On 30 October 1893, two days

[60] 10 June 1893 (*CL* ii. 13); Blathwayt, 'The Hon. Mrs. Arthur Henniker', 55.

after Hardy had dispatched the manuscript for typing, he informed Henniker that he would be 'writing to Watt this evening about our story'.[61] A copy of 'Spectre' would not have been sent with that letter to Watt, but one must have followed soon after, since on 1 December Hardy was able to tell Henniker:

I am glad to know that Watt sent you your dues—well-earned—on "The Spectre". (£71:15:6 the sum shd be—i.e. half the total paid for the story, £159:10:0, less half his commission.) Considering the shortness of the tale—8000 to 9000 words—the price is a very fair one for serial use only—£18 per thousand words. As to your paying a share of the type-writing, certainly not; the charge was quite small.[62]

Hardy's revision of the first typescript, then, the typing and revision of the second typescript, and the actual sale of the story, must all have taken place in November 1893.

'Spectre' did not, however, appear in *To-Day* until November 1894. That Hardy had seen and corrected the proofs some months earlier is indicated by his 26 August 1894 letter to Jerome: 'By the way, is F.H.'s & my story to be illustrated? & when? I rather liked it when I read over the proofs.'[63] This somewhat unusual delay—it was not common for a periodical story to be left standing in type for such an extended period[64]—can be explained by Jerome's decision to hold back 'Spectre' for the special Christmas or Winter Number, published at sixpence (rather than the usual twopence) on 17 November 1894. Taking full advantage of Hardy's celebrity, the *To-Day* 3 November advertisement for the Winter Number promised 'a COMPLETE STORY by THOMAS HARDY', and an announcement the following week included his name at the head of the list of contributors—in which Henniker's did not figure at all, though in the list of contents she is named as the story's co-author.[65]

The *To-Day* printing was not in fact the first. Sold to the US newspaperman and novelist Irving Bacheller, 'Spectre' was distributed through his syndicate and appeared in the *Philadelphia Press*, 15–21 November 1894; the *Kansas City Star*, 17–22 November; the *Min-*

---

[61] *CL* ii. 41　　　[62] Ibid. 43.　　　[63] Ibid. 62.

[64] This does appear to be what happened: the nature of the variants between the corrected proofs and the printed text—the addition or removal of quotation marks and hyphens, the alteration of colons to dashes when introducing speech, and so forth—suggests corrections (presumably editorial) to revises rather than a new type-setting.

[65] *To-Day*, 3 Nov. 1894, 393; 10 Nov. 1894, 9.

neapolis Tribune, 19–23 November; the New York *Press*, 19–23 November; the *Nebraska State Journal*, 20–24 November; and the San Francisco *Examiner*, 2 and 9 December.[66] The first two instalments of the *Philadelphia Press* serialization, then, anticipated the *To-Day* publication. These syndicated newspaper printings have no textual authority, however, and Hardy and Henniker were perhaps not even aware of their existence. Writing to Henniker on 28 October of the previous year, Hardy had asked: 'This question also arises: shall we print the story in America &c. simultaneously. It will cause a delay of a few weeks perhaps (not so long *possibly*). On the other hand if we sacrifice America for the sake of being sooner out here, we may lose, say, £20 or £25.'[67] They apparently decided to have the story published simultaneously, and Watt presumably sold the US as well as the English serial rights—Hardy refers broadly to the price being a fair one 'for serial use'.[68] Jerome, himself one of the Bacheller syndicate authors, may in fact have bought the rights for both countries and arranged the US sale, though Bacheller did purchase fiction through at least one London agent.[69] What is in any case clear from the wording and pointing of the six syndicate settings is that they all derive from the uncorrected *To-Day* proofs. The large number of shared variants among the newspaper printings further reveals that there was an intervening text, probably proof sheets from Bacheller's type-setting of the story.[70] It can, however, be demonstrated on similar grounds that the *Nebraska State Journal* text was in fact set from that in the *Kansas City Star*.

To trace the nature and extent of editorial or compositorial interference in these syndicated printings is a fascinating exercise and one which is significant in terms of the story's publication history,[71] but since none of the changes was in any sense authorial it seems

[66] The *Minneapolis Tribune* and *Nebraska State Journal* printings have not hitherto been identified; David Bonnell Green found the *Philadelphia Press* printing ('The First Publication of "The Spectre of the Real"', *Library*, 15 (1960), 60–1); Cramer the other three ('Hardy, Henniker', 89–91).

[67] *CL* ii. 40.   [68] 1 Dec. 1893 (*CL* ii. 43).

[69] Irving Bacheller, *Coming Up the Road: Memories of a North Country Boyhood* (Indianapolis: Bobbs-Merrill, 1928), 273.

[70] According to Elmo Scott Watson, Bacheller's material was 'supplied to newspapers in proof sheets or copy form' (*A History of the Newspaper Syndicates in the United States 1865–1935* (Chicago: n.p., 1936), 43).

[71] For complete collations of the syndicated texts, see Pamela Dalziel, 'A Critical Edition of Thomas Hardy's Uncollected Stories', D. Phil. thesis (University of Oxford, 1989), 594 ff.

inappropriate, and would certainly be disproportionate, to offer a detailed analysis of them here. It is perhaps worth noting, however, that three of the syndicated printings were abridged. In the *Minneapolis Tribune* and the *Philadelphia Press* the cuts are relatively minor, amounting in the former to two short paragraphs relating to Mélanie, probably omitted in error, and in the latter to two descriptive passages and the account of Rosalys's bitterness when Jim leaves for Burma, evidently deleted in order to limit the length of the instalment to two columns. Space restrictions also appear to have dictated most of the New York *Press* excisions, almost all of which occur in the third instalment, again abridged to fit into two columns. Omissions in the fourth instalment involve only a couple of minor descriptive passages and the bowdlerization of 'damn you', but in the fifth they are sufficiently radical to create a distinct story: all reference to Parkhurst's suicide has been removed, the narrative ending 'happily ever after' with Rosalys and Parkhurst at the altar railings. Presumably editorial, this revision was prepared for in advance by removing from the third instalment the comments about Parkhurst's rigid notions of honour. The resulting narrative is remarkably coherent, but it throws more strongly into relief the contrivance of Jim's convenient death and of course creates quite a different effect, the happy ending negating much of the preceding irony and cynicism. What one Bacheller syndicate advertisement described as 'A pathetic love story'[72] becomes in the New York *Press* altogether more conventional and sentimental, as is, indeed, heralded by the tone of the summaries of the preceding action supplied at the beginning of the second and subsequent instalments: Jim, for instance, is described as 'Impetuous Jim, an ambitious young soldier without fortune', while to the statement 'Of course Rosalys agrees [to be married secretly]' is appended 'What girl wouldn't?'[73]

No mention of Henniker as co-author is made in any of the Bacheller printings, and in the *Minneapolis Tribune* no author at all is named. It was with its 1896 collection in Henniker's *In Scarlet and Grey*, published simultaneously by John Lane, London, and Roberts Brothers, Boston, that 'Spectre' first appeared in the United States as a collaborative work. Both title-pages prominently display Hardy's name (though on the cover of the English edition only Henniker's appears), and if, as her bowdlerizations and comments suggest,

[72] *Nebraska State Journal*, 19 Nov. 1894, 3.   [73] New York *Press*, 20 Nov. 1894, 7.

Henniker was less than pleased with Hardy's final version of the story, she was clearly prepared to exploit his reputation. The inclusion of a Hardy collaboration must have enhanced the potential interest in her volume, as was in fact acknowledged by a contemporary reviewer:

One has learnt to look forward with very pleasant anticipations to each fresh work from the pen of Mrs. Henniker; and, in the case of her latest production, curiosity had been further stimulated by the announcement that the book would contain a contribution from Mr. Thomas Hardy.[74]

Writing to Henniker on 12 October 1896, Hardy congratulated her: '1000 copies' sale makes, I believe, what publishers consider a success; so you have achieved it.'[75] The sales of *In Scarlet and Grey* were sufficient for it to be reprinted in three so-called 'editions', as well as in John Lane's 'Canvas-Back Library', but its success was perhaps attributable less to its own merits or to Hardy's reputation than to the fact that it was published in the popular Keynotes series, which included not only George Egerton's notorious *Keynotes* and *Discords* but also other best-sellers such as Grant Allen's *The Woman Who Did* and Arthur Machen's *The Great God Pan*.

Although the reviews of *In Scarlet and Grey* were on the whole positive, the assessments of 'Spectre' radically differed. One of the earliest, in the 1 August 1896 *Speaker*, stated: 'We are paying no small compliment to Mrs. Henniker when we say that her unassisted work in this volume seems to us fully as effective, as artistic, and as pungent in its irony as that portion wherein the great master of modern English fiction has lent his aid.'[76] The 26 September *New Saturday* notice was also favourable, praising 'Spectre' as a 'powerful story',[77] but on the same day the *Athenaeum* review insisted that the characteristic morbidity of the Keynotes series was 'unpleasantly emphasized' in 'Spectre', which 'might well have been omitted', and advised Henniker not to allow 'her humour and pathos to be overlaid by the advancing pessimism of a collaborator, however illustrious'.[78] The 24 October *Academy* similarly described the story as 'the most inferior in the book', regrettably 'marred by those deflections from good taste which seem to have become characteristic of Mr. Hardy's later art', and the 31 October *Spectator* was only marginally less condemnatory: '[The

[74] *Speaker*, 1 Aug. 1896, 128.   [75] *CL* ii. 134.   [76] *Speaker*, 128.
[77] *New Saturday*, 99.   [78] *Athenaeum*, 417.

story] is undoubtedly very effective and indeed gruesome, but also superfluously repulsive. . . . Mr. Thomas Hardy, in his later phases, is hardly a judicious literary counsellor.'[79]

It was perhaps to these last two reviews that Hardy was alluding in his letter to Henniker of 8 November 1896:

The Jeunes are surprised at the unfounded attacks on me that the volume [*In Scarlet and Grey*] is made the vehicle of. She read "The Spectre" & Sir F. read it, & neither could discover the impropriety reiterated by the pure-minded reviewers—bless their prurient hearts! But you must keep better literary company in future than is

Your sincere friend

T.H.[80]

To some extent Henniker must have identified with the 'pure-minded reviewers'. Shortly after the volume was published she expressed her reservations about 'Spectre' in a letter to Coulson Kernahan: 'Though of course Mr H's share has great cleverness, it is not really a *sympathetic*, or pleasant story. For, before the tragedy of the close, *some* of it might have been more agreeable.'[81] Her less than enthusiastic response—a not surprising one in view of the extent and nature of Hardy's revisions—reflects what appears to have been a mutual unwillingness to enter into further collaboration. Because of Henniker's sensitivity to criticism and Hardy's virtual inability to refrain from revision once a manuscript—his own or someone else's—was in front of him, their literary partnership, far from intensifying their intimacy as Hardy had hoped, had occasionally threatened to estrange them altogether. That the situation remained delicate even after the story's completion is evident from Hardy's 18 December 1893 letter concerning the placing of Henniker's 'Bad and Worthless': 'I packed up the type-written story, & sent it on to Mr Shorter, *without altering a line*. One *letter* I had altered, & did not remember till it was sealed up: in the spelling of "Gawd"—which is Kipling's, & should decidedly be avoided. But you can restore it in proof if you care to.'[82] In a postscript Hardy was still more conciliatory: 'You must overlook the liberty I took in suggesting alteration of the tale. I am vexed with myself for it.'

But if Henniker did not want Hardy's criticism, she was perfectly willing—at least during these early years of their friendship—to

[79] *Academy*, 305; *Spectator*, 593.   [80] *CL* ii. 137.
[81] 23 July 1896 (Berg Collection, New York Public Library).   [82] *CL* ii. 44.

accept his assistance in placing her stories or, indeed, to have his name linked publicly with hers. When in March 1895 Shorter accepted her 'A Page from a Vicar's History'—originally recommended to him by Hardy[83]—Henniker suggested that Hardy be named as co-author. Hardy, however, adamantly refused. 'I should be manifestly wrong to put my name as joint-author,' he wrote to Shorter,

when it bears such clear internal evidence of the sex of the writer ... that I could not possibly have had much to do with it—as was the case, my share having been editorial, my actual writing being limited to the rather commonplace incident of the last page or so. Possibly Mrs Henniker might be induced to reconsider her decision, or to write a new ending: otherwise I see no course left but to withdraw the story from publication.[84]

Hardy's contribution to the story may indeed have been minor, but it seems more likely that he now had no illusions about the nature of his friendship with Henniker and was not prepared to compromise his reputation for her sake. The incident evidently marked a turning-point in their literary relationship. In August of the same year he reproached her for not continuing as his pupil, and in September he wrote: 'I fear that after the Vicar I cannot be of much service in saying anything that would commend your stories to an editor or publisher.'[85] Nearly three years later he did offer to recommend one of her stories to the New York *Independent*, but she, correctly anticipating that his response would be unfavourable, was reluctant to let him read it,[86] and seems thereafter to have sent him only published work.

To many contemporaries Hardy's motivation in collaborating with Henniker must have seemed inexplicable. The New York *Critic* reviewer of *In Scarlet and Grey* commented: ' "No reason can be assigned for the rash act" is the concluding sentence of the book; and, if it may be taken to refer to Mr. Hardy's partnership in it, it will do very well for our own verdict.'[87] The fundamental reason was, of course, the one that has for centuries been associated with irrational behaviour, and it is no doubt as a reflection of Hardy's relationship with Henniker that the story remains of greatest interest. It is, however, by no means lacking in interest purely as a literary work, especially as a product of its historical moment and as a contribution—if primarily

---

[83] Ibid. vii. 127.   [84] Ibid. ii. 71–2.   [85] Ibid. 84, 87.
[86] Ibid. 197, 201, 205.   [87] *Critic*, 23 Jan. 1897, 57.

Henniker's and ultimately negative—to the current 'New Fiction' debate.[88]

Typescripts and Proofs

The two typescripts and *To-Day* proofs were for many years in the possession of Ernest Bramah Smith (better known as 'Ernest Bramah', the author of the once popular Carrados and Kai Lung stories), who was an editorial assistant to Jerome K. Jerome, the editor of *To-Day*, when 'Spectre' was published in 1894. On 24 February 1959 they were sold at Sotheby's (lot 481) to the dealer John Fleming, who in turn sold them on 18 May 1961 to Frederick B. Adams, their present owner.

Typescript 1 (1TS)

1TS consists of a title-leaf and thirty-seven leaves of text regularly numbered 1 to 37. The title-leaf reads:
THE SPECTRE OF THE REAL. | [*rule 91.7mm.*] | [century *in TH's hand, written above deleted typed* age] | An end - of - the - century Narrative. | [*rule 74mm.*] | by | T h o m a s   H a r d y and   F l o r e n c e   H e n n i k e r. | [*rule 109.3mm.*]
The leaves measure 27 by 20.5 cm. and are 0.14 mm. thick. The cream paper has artificially imposed chain lines and a watermark of a crown above 'Abbey Mills | Greenfield'.

The second leaf (1 in TH's foliation) was cut in two and approximately a third of a typed line and half of the left margin were then cut away. The two resulting pieces of the leaf were pasted on to an irregularly shaped piece of paper measuring 6.55 cm. at the left edge and 12.1 cm. at the right by 20.5 cm. As this patch shows through on the recto of the leaf it measures 11(left)/4.7(right) by 20.5 cm. A smaller patch measuring 2.2 by 3.6 cm. was also pasted on to the verso of the leaf at the top right of the first patch, which was apparently not quite large enough. This second patch shows through on the recto in the left margin, where it measures 0.95(left)/0.85(right) by 3.15 cm. The patches are of different paper from the rest of 1TS:

---

[88] See Dalziel, 'Thomas Hardy's Uncollected Stories', 575 ff.

the large one is of a slightly lighter cream shade and is 0.105 mm. thick; the small one is light beige in colour and 0.14 mm. thick. The original leaf was cropped at the top and bottom so that it would not differ in length from the other leaves. The explanation for this somewhat complicated patching is in fact very simple. TH wrote in the margin a passage to be incorporated in the text (part of the line encircling the addition can still be seen) and must have subsequently decided that it was not sufficiently legible. The patching enabled him to cut away the passage as originally added and write it out again more clearly in the space opened up in the body of the text by the inserted piece of paper.

The TH holograph corrections of 1TS are numerous, including an extensive addition on fo. 24^v and the beginning of an earlier version of this addition on fo.35^v. A few alterations by FH, usually erased and then rewritten in ink by TH, are also present. Some of the corrections of typographical errors appear to have been made by the typist.

There are two distinct sets of what seem to be editorial or compositorial markings on the leaves. One, consisting of short pencil lines in the right margins at intervals of approximately one hundred words (including holograph interlineations), is apparently an attempt to come up with a fairly accurate word-count. The other divides the story into four parts (corresponding to I–II, III–IV, V–VI, VII) and each of these into three or four sub-sections. The four-part division is indicated by blue-crayon markings: a swirled line after II, 'End of 2nd part' after IV, and 'End of 3 Part.' after VI. The sub-sections are signalled by the pencil underlining of a sentence (except at the beginning of a part) and a large numeral written in blue crayon (except for the numerals in part 3 and the 3 of part 4, all of which are in pencil). Although they occur at bewilderingly irregular intervals, these subsection markings presumably represent some kind of casting off. 1 of part 1 begins at the opening paragraph; 2 at fo. 3. 2 (p. 301. 10); 3 at fo. 7. 3 (p. 304. 12); 4 at fo. 9. 16^1 (p. 306. 17); 1 of part 2 at the beginning of III (fo. 12; p. 308. 2); 2 at fo. 13. 4^2 (p. 309. 10); 3 at fo. 18. 10^3 (p. 313. 6); 1 of part 3 at the beginning of V (fo. 21; p. 315. 21); 2 at

---

[1] The traces of an erased line beneath the preceding sentence suggest that this is a revised marking.

[2] Holograph interlineations are not included in the line-count.

[3] There was evidently some indecision about where to begin this section: the fourth sentence following the indicated starting-point was once underlined, and the second sentence preceding it still is.

fo. 24. 17 (p. 319. 3); 3 at fo. 31. 12 (p. 325. 4); 1^4 of part 4 at the beginning of VII (fo. 32; p. 325. 22); 3 (there is no 2) at fo. 37. 8 (p. 331. 16), though no sentence is in fact underlined. Finally, on fo. 37^v there are some (presumably compositorial) pencil calculations:

$$10 \text{ small} \qquad 5 \text{ \$mall}$$
$$\frac{27}{3} - \frac{1}{3} \text{ rw}$$

Since 1TS represents an earlier version of the story than does the second typescript, which was prepared from 1TS and then revised before being used as setting-copy for the *To-Day* printing, it is particularly difficult to account for these markings and, indeed, for 1TS's being sent—or more probably forwarded by the agent, Watt—to the magazine at all. While TH was revising the second typescript, 1TS could have been submitted simply to give Watt and any potential purchasers some idea of its content and quality, but such a sequence of events still does not explain the markings. There is some correspondence between the various lengths of the marked sub-sections and those of single pages (or, in a few instances, of two facing pages) of a typical illustrated story in *To-Day* and it is conceivable that the superfluous 1TS was passed on to the illustrator—or, indeed, that TH originally sent it to the magazine in response to a request for an extra copy. Although the markings do not bear any relation to the pagination of 'Spectre' as eventually printed, different pagination was presumably necessitated by the decision to hold back the story for the special Winter Number rather than to serialize it in four instalments, as the markings on both typescripts show to have been originally intended.

Typescript 2 (2TS)

2TS is comprised of thirty-three leaves, all carbon copies except for the ribbon-copy title-leaf. The first leaf and the following one are numbered in pencil '(1)' and '(1^4)', respectively, in an unidentified hand; the remaining leaves are regularly foliated 2 to 32, though 8 is numbered in pencil in an unidentified hand. The title-leaf reads:

T H E   S P E C T R E   O F   T H E   R E A L | [T *and* V *of* NARRATIVE *written above deleted typed* V *and* T, *respectively*] AN

---

[4] In fact just a circular marking without a numeral.

END - OF - THE - CENTURY NARRATIVE | By | THOMAS HARDY and FLORENCE HENNIKER. | *CARBON COPY*

In the top-right corner TH wrote in pencil:

To the printer: | Insert all *accents* & hyphens, | & punctuate precisely as | in copy. | T. H.

Pinned (originally glued) to the leaf is a pencil note in an unidentified hand:[5]

From | T. Hardy | Max Gate, | Dorchester, | Dorset.

The leaves measure 32.2 by 20.3 cm. and are 0.075 mm. thick. The cream paper (somewhat darker in shade than that of 1TS) has artificially imposed chain lines and no watermarks.

The typescript, containing numerous TH revisions, was used as setting-copy for the *To-Day* printing. A compositor's name or initials is written in pencil on most leaves, usually at the head of the page, but occasionally by or before the beginning of the first complete paragraph of text (signified in the list below by a double dagger):

Folio number	Page and line number		Compositorial signature
(1^4)	299		Mountain
2	300	14	BY
3	301	23‡	Lewis
4	302	22	Wiles
5	303	13	WA
6	304	20	Baldwin
7	305	24	Cave
8	306	28‡	Wilkins
9	308	1	Post [this mood was unduly prominent *(the first words on the next page) written in the bottom margin in an unidentified hand*]
10	309	10‡	DQ
11	310	7	AH
12	311	3	Faunch
13	312	8	Heil
14	313	11‡	Wiles
15	314	13	Lewis
16	315	12	[*no signature*]

---

[5] The fact that the paper is the same as for 2TS suggests that the hand is probably the typist's.

17	315 20	WA
18	316 18	DQ [she was (*the final words on the preceding page) written in 'DQ''s hand in top margin*]
19	317 26‡	Faunch
20	318 21	Post
21	319 28	[*no signature*]
22	320 4	Baldwin
23	321 8	BY
24	322 8	Heil
25	323 13	AH
26	324 13^6	Mountain
27	325 19	Cave
28	326 23	Lewis
29	328 1	BY
30	329 3	WA
31	330 9	Wilkins
32	331 11	Faunch

In addition, 'Chapter' has been added in pencil before each of the section numbers (except for II) and, in this same hand, 'End of Part I', 'End of II', and 'End of III', at the conclusion of II,[7] IV, and VI, respectively. On fo. 32^v 'Revise' is written in blue crayon and 'Divide into 4' in pencil; there are also some pencil calculations:

$$
\begin{array}{cc}
35 & 400 \\
12 & \\
\hline
0 &
\end{array}
$$

Proofs

The eight slips of the *To-Day* galley proofs are of irregular length and width, the longest measuring 69.1(left)/68.9(right) by 14.05(top)/12.8(bottom) cm., the shortest 61 (left)/60.9(right) by 13(top)/13.9(bottom) cm. The slips are light beige in colour and are 0.11 mm. thick.

Only TH's hand appears on the proofs. At the top of the first slip he wrote '*Press.*' and beneath it, marked for insertion after the title

---

[6] The name is actually written in the left margin, but the stint appears to begin at the first line of the page.

[7] This was evidently a correction, as 'End of Part I' was also added and subsequently deleted at the conclusion of III.

('THE SPECTRE OF THE REAL'), 'By Thomas Hardy and Florence Henniker.' All other markings are corrections and revisions.

Periodical Publication

To-Day, Winter Number (17 Nov. 1894)
The double-columned text begins on p. [5] (the first page of text in the magazine) and concludes on p. 15. The title reads: THE SPECTRE OF THE REAL. | By THOMAS HARDY AND FLORENCE HENNIKER. | *Illustrated by H. R. MILLAR.* | [*double rule 52.5 mm.*] The copyright notice (1894, by Thomas Hardy and Florence Henniker) appears at the bottom of p. [5]. There are five illustrations, the second of which takes up a full page. The captions read: 'THEY SAT DOWN IN AN ARBOUR.', '"I WANT TO HAVE A WORD WITH YOU."', 'HE DISAPPEARED UNDER THE TREES.', 'HIS BODY WAS FOUND IN THE WATER-WEEDS.', and 'ENTERED HIS DRESSING-ROOM AND SHOT HIMSELF.'

Volume Publication as Part of a Collection

In Scarlet and Grey: English edition
Title-page: [*all within a 140.5 by 88 mm. pictorial frame designed by Patten Wilson*] In Scarlet and Grey | STORIES OF SOLDIERS AND OTHERS BY | Florence Henniker | AND | THE SPECTRE OF THE REAL BY | Thomas Hardy and Florence Henniker | LONDON: JOHN LANE, VIGO ST | BOSTON: ROBERTS BROS., 1896
Collation: 8°: π^4A–N^8[O–P]^8. Pp. [viii] + 240. [i] half-title: IN SCARLET AND GREY. [ii] blank. [iii] title-page. [iv] notice of US copyright and printer's imprint (T. and A. Constable, Edinburgh). [v] dedication. [vi] blank. [vii] contents page. [viii] Keynotes key decoration. [1]–208 text. [1]–14 advertisements. [15]–[16] blank. 1–16 advertisements.
Binding: the boards and spine are covered with red cloth. The front cover is blocked in black with the Wilson pictorial frame—slightly larger (152.5 by 95 mm.) than that of the title-page—and lettered: In | Scarlet & Grey | Florence Henniker
Blocked in black on the back cover is a 54 by 28 mm. ornament, consisting of the Keynotes key separating the '8' and '9' of '1896'. The spine is also blocked in black with the key and gold-lettered:

In Scarlet | and | Grey | • | Florence | Henniker | [*key 54 by 17.5 mm.*] | ■ JOHN | LANE ■ | THE BOD- | LEY HEAD
The end-papers are plain.
The text of 'The Spectre of the Real' appears on pp. [164]–208.

In Scarlet and Grey: US edition
Title-page: [*all within a slightly larger version (150.5 by 90.5 mm.) of the Wilson pictorial frame used for the English edition*] In Scarlet and Grey | STORIES OF SOLDIERS AND OTHERS BY | Florence Henniker | AND | THE SPECTRE OF THE REAL BY | Thomas Hardy and Florence Henniker | BOSTON: ROBERTS BROS., 1896 | LONDON: JOHN LANE, VIGO ST
Collation: 8°: $\pi^4 1$–$13^8 14^6$. Pp. [viii] + 220. [i] half-title: IN SCARLET AND GREY. [ii] Keynotes key decoration. [iii] title-page. [iv] copyright notice (1896, by Roberts Brothers) and printer's imprint (University Press, John Wilson and Son, Cambridge, U.S.A.). [v] dedication. [vi] blank. [vii] contents page. [viii] blank. [1]–210 text. [211]–[220] advertisements.
Binding: the boards and spine are covered in medium-blue cloth. The front cover is blocked in dark green with the Wilson pictorial frame—slightly larger (151.5 by 91 mm.) than that of the title-page—and lettered:
IN SCARLET AND GREY | BY | FLORENCE HENNIKER | [*ornament 3 by 11 mm.*] | THE SPECTRE OF THE REAL | BY | THOMAS HARDY AND FLORENCE HENNIKER
The back cover is blocked in dark green with the Keynotes key ornament (54 by 17.5 mm.). The spine is gold-lettered:
IN SCARLET | AND GREY | [*rule 8.5 mm.*] | F. HENNIKER | WITH | THE SPECTRE OF | THE REAL | • | THOMAS HARDY | AND | FLORENCE HENNIKER | ROBERTS | BROTHERS
The end-papers are plain. There are two free end-papers both at the front and at the back of the volume. The 'extra' set is of a different paper stock (the same colour but thinner) from that of the first set.
The text of 'The Spectre of the Real' appears on pp. [165]–210. The advertisements bound in at the back of the volume differ from those in the English edition.

In Scarlet and Grey: second printing of the English edition ('Second Edition')

Collation: 8°: π^4A–N^8[O]^8. Pp. [viii] + 224. [i] half-title: IN SCARLET AND GREY. [ii] notice of US copyright. [iii] title-page. [iv] '*Second Edition*' and printer's imprint (T. and A. Constable, Edinburgh). [v] dedication. [vi] blank. [vii] contents page. [viii] Keynotes key decoration. [1]–208 text. [1]–14 advertisements. [15]–[16] blank.

Binding: as for the first English printing, except that the red cloth is of a lighter shade, on the front cover the pictorial frame is enclosed within a rule frame and the spacing of the lettering is slightly different, the back cover is plain, and the spine is lettered in black and does not include the publisher's name.

The text of 'The Spectre of the Real' appears on pp. [164]–208 and was not reset, but the John Lane advertisements bound in at the back of the volume were changed and in fact include one for *In Scarlet and Grey* itself.

In Scarlet and Grey: third printing of the English edition ('Third Edition')[8]

Title-page: as for the first and second English printings.

Collation: as for the second English printing, except that on [iv] '*Second Edition*' has been replaced by '*Third Edition*'.

Binding: as for the second English printing.

The text of 'The Spectre of the Real' appears on pp. [164]–208 and was not reset; the advertisements are the same as those included in the second English printing.

In Scarlet and Grey: John Lane Canvas-Back Library 'edition'[9]

Title-page: [*all enclosed within a 143 by 81 mm. rule frame within which are four smaller rule frames: one 32 by 77.8 mm., enclosing lines 1–2; one 20.5 by 77.8 mm., enclosing line 3; one 56 by 77.8 mm., enclosing lines 4–7; and one 22 by 77.8 mm., enclosing lines 8–9*] In Scarlet and Grey | STORIES OF SOLDIERS AND OTHERS | By FLORENCE HENNIKER | AND | The Spectre of the Real | By THOMAS HARDY AND | FLORENCE HENNIKER | JOHN LANE: THE BODLEY HEAD | LONDON AND NEW YORK

[8] The only known copy of this volume is in the University of London library.

[9] The only known copy of this volume is in the Miller Library, Colby College, Waterville, Maine. I am grateful to the former curator, Dr J. Fraser Cocks, III, and to Professor Michael Millgate for providing bibliographical information and xeroxes.

Collation: 8°: π⁴A–N⁸. Pp. [viii] + 208. [i] half-title: THE CANVAS-BACK LIBRARY | IN SCARLET AND GREY. [ii] advertisement. [iii] title-page. [iv] copyright notice (by John Lane), publisher's note ('This Work may still be obtained in the Cloth Bound Library Edition. Crown 8vo. Price 3s. 6d. net.'), and printer's imprint (Richard Folkard & Son, London). [v] dedication. [vi] blank. [vii] contents page. [viii] Keynotes key decoration. [1]–208 text.

Binding: the front and back boards are covered in almond-green paper and bordered with red rules. The front cover is lettered in red:

> IN [*swash* N] SCARLET [*swash* A, R, T] AND [*swash* A, N] GREY [*swash* R, Y] | By | FLORENCE [*swash* R, N] HENNIKER [*swash* N, N, K, R] | The Canvas-Back [*swash* k] Library

The spine is covered in light-tan cloth, bordered at the top and bottom with red rules, and lettered in red:

> IN [*swash* N] SCARLET [*swash* A, R, T] | AND [*swash* A, N] | GREY [*swash* R] | By | FLORENCE [*swash* R, N] | HENNIKER [*swash* N, N, K, R] | JOHN LANE

The end-papers are plain.

The text of 'The Spectre of the Real' appears on pp. [164]–208 and was not reset.

NOTE ON THE TEXT

'Spectre' survives in three authoritative pre-publication texts: the ribbon copy of the first typescript (1 TS), showing holograph revisions by both FH and TH; a carbon copy, showing holograph revisions by TH only, of the second typescript (2TS), which was professionally prepared from 1 TS as revised; and a set of the *To-Day* proofs (PR), also showing holograph revisions by TH. As the witness closest to the lost MS (presumably destroyed in accordance with TH's and FH's decision to keep secret their respective shares in the story's composition), 1 TS as revised has been taken as copy-text. Since the variants introduced by the typist in 2TS and by the compositors in PR have been regarded as textual corruption rather than as collaboration, TH's pointing and styling revisions in 2TS and PR have been incorporated only when not made in response to non-authorial alterations. In the following quotation, for example, the comma after 'dredging' has been retained in spite of TH's having changed it to a semi-colon in PR, evidently in response to the compositor's addition of commas after 'mud' and 'water': '... Rosalys gazed absently out of the window at the lake, that some men were dredging, the mud left bare by draining down the water being imprinted with hundreds of little footmarks of plovers feeding there.' Similarly, where the typist or compositor omitted a punctuation mark and TH has added one which differs from that in 1TS, the original pointing has normally been retained. Where TH accepted FH's corrections, as he did on all but two occasions, those changes have been included in the edited text, as have all TH's alterations of wording in 1TS, 2TS, and PR, again excepting those which were influenced by non-authoritative readings. For example, the edited text retains the 1TS reading 'past' in the phrase 'Jim watched her light figure past the lake', since 'passing', TH's emendation in 2TS, was a correction of the typist's 'pass'. Such instances are rare, however, and for the most part the wording of the edited text coincides with that of PR. It has thus seemed appropriate in the lists of wording variants to use daggers to indicate those readings which differ from PR rather than—as in the punctuation and styling variants lists—those which differ from the copy-text, 1TS.

The variants introduced in the six Bacheller syndicate printings have neither been incorporated into the edited text nor recorded in this edition:[1] evidently derived from uncorrected *To-Day* proofs and almost certainly published without the knowledge of either TH or FH, they are entirely lacking in authorial authority. Apparently also non-authoritative are the variants which appear only in the published *To-Day* text (*TD*): although TH and FH were fully aware of this printing, the variants, predominantly in styling (hyphenation, the substitution of dashes for colons when introducing speech, and so forth), were probably introduced by a member of the magazine's staff when checking revises. They have therefore not been incorporated into the edited text, though they are recorded in the list of variant readings. Since the variants introduced by FH when revising—primarily bowdlerizing—'Spectre' for her collective volume, *In Scarlet and Grey* (*SG*), are authoritative only in relation to her intentions, not TH's, they too are recorded without being incorporated into the (Hardy-centric) edited text.

[1] A complete listing of the Bacheller variants can, however, be found in Dalziel, 'Thomas Hardy's Uncollected Stories', 594 ff.

The sequence of texts as recorded in reverse chronological order in the variants lists is: *SG*, *TD*, PR, 2TS, 1TS. The US edition of *In Scarlet and Grey* (*SG*a) was apparently set from uncorrected proofs of the English edition and agrees with *SG* unless otherwise indicated. The three later English 'editions' of *In Scarlet and Grey*—the so-called Second Edition, Third Edition, and Canvas-Back Library Edition— were not in fact reset, nor, of course, was the facsimile of the US edition issued by Garland Publishing of New York in 1977. The two subsequent appearances of the story, the first edited by Jeffrey S. Cramer in *The Thomas Hardy Year Book* (1986) and the second by Peter Haining in *The Supernatural Tales of Thomas Hardy* (1988), were both derived from the *SG* text. The text in this edition, then, is not only the first to recover TH's pointing and wording from the three pre-publication witnesses but also the first since the original 1894 publication to be free of bowdlerization.

THE SPECTRE OF THE REAL

An end-of-the-century Narrative

I

A certain March night of this present "waning age" had settled down upon the woods and the park and the parapets of Ambrose Towers. The harsh stable-clock struck a quarter-to-ten. Thereupon a girl in light evening attire and wraps came through the entrance-hall, opened the front door and the small wrought-iron gate beyond it which led to the terrace, and stepped into the moonlight. Such a person, such a night, and such a place were unexceptionable materials for a scene in that poetical drama of two which the world has often beheld; which leads up to a contract that causes a slight sinking in the poetry, and a perceptible lack of interest in the play.

She moved so quietly that the alert birds resting in the great cedar-tree never stirred. Gliding across its funereal shadow over a smooth plush of turf, as far as to the Grand Walk whose pebbles shone like the floor-stones of the Apocalyptic City, she paused and looked back at the old brick walls—red in the daytime, sable now—at the shrouded

title† *An ... Narrative* [*not in* PR+] +   title *century* *1TS(2)TH*] age *1TS(1)*
2–3 A certain ... Towers. *2TS(2)* [parapets *THp&i*]] ... park and the mansion of ...
1TS(3)TH] ... settled upon ... *1TS(2)THp* [*added*]   4 harsh *1TS(2)TH* [*added*]
4 Thereupon *1TS(2)TH*] Whereupon *1TS(1)* [*only* W *altered*]   4–5 in light ...
wraps *1TS(3)THp* [*only* s *added*]] ... & wrap *1TS(2)TH* [*added*]   6 wrought-
1TS(2)TH [*added*]   7–11 into the ... play. ¶ *2TS(3)*] ... poetry. ¶ *1TS(2)THp*
[*reading uncertain*]] into the moonlight. *1TS(1)* [*see* TN] +   9 materials
1TS(3)TH [*added*]   10 often beheld; *2TS(2)THp&i*] beheld before; *1TS(2)TH*
[beheld *undeleted in* 2TS]   10 causes *1TS(2)TH*, *2TS(2)TH*] carries *2TS(1)*
11 and a perceptible lack ... play. *2TS(3)* [perceptible *TH*]] and a distinct lack ...
2TS(2) [distinct *TH*]] and a certain lack ... *1TS(3)TH* [*added*]   12 alert
1TS(2)TH [*added*]   13 Gliding *PR(2)TH*] Flitting *1TS*   13 funereal *1TS(2)TH*]
huge *1TS(1)*   13–14 a smooth plush *PR(2)TH*] many yards *1TS*   14 as to
1TS(2)TH] as *1TS(1)*   14–15 the floor-stones ... City, *2TS(3)TH* [the floor-
added in same line before deleted the *which begins previous reading*]] the stones of ...
2TS(2)TH] precious-stones, *1TS*   16 the old ... now—at *1TS(3)TH*] the dark
brick ... *1TS(2)TH*] the walls, *1TS(1)*

mullions, the silhouette of the tower; though listening rather than seeing seemed her object in coming to the pause. The clammy wings of a bat brushed past her face, startling her and making her shiver a little. The stamping of one or two horses in their stalls surprised her
5 by its distinctness and isolation. The servants' offices were on the other side of the house, and the lady who, with the exception of the girl on the terrace, was its only occupant, was resting on a sofa behind one of the curtained windows. So Rosalys went on her way unseen, trod the margin of the lake, and plunged into the distant shrubberies.
10   The clock had reached ten. As the last strokes of the hour rang out a young man scrambled down the sunk-fence bordering the pleasure-ground, leapt the iron railing within, and joined the girl who stood awaiting him. In the half-light he could not see how her full under-lip trembled, or the fire of joy that kindled in her eyes. But perhaps he
15 guessed, from daylight experiences, since he passed his arm round her shoulders with assurance, and kissed her ready mouth many times. Her head still resting against his arm they walked towards a bench, the rough outlines of which were touched at one end only by the moon-rays. At the dark end the pair sat down.
20   "I cannot come again" said the girl.
   "Oh?" he vaguely returned. "This is new. What has happened? I thought you said your mother supposed you to be working at your Harmony, and would never imagine our meeting here?" The voice sounded just a trifle hard for a lover's.
25   "No, she would not. And I still detest deceiving her. I would do it for no one but you, Jim. But what I meant was this: I feel that it can all lead to nothing. Mother is not a bit more worldly than most people, but she naturally does not want her only child to marry a man who has nothing but the pay of an officer in the Line to live upon. At

---

1 mullions, *1TS(2)TH*] mullions, and *1TS(1)*   1–2 tower ... pause. *1TS(5)TH*] ... seeing was her ... *1TS(4)TH*] ... object in turning <*illegible*> *1TS(3)TH* [ng *and illegible word erased*]] ... listening was *1TS(2)TH* [*not continued*]] tower. *1TS(1)* [*see TN*]   4 stamping ... horses *2TS(2)TH*] sound of one or two horses stamping *1TS* [*only* sound *and* stamping *deleted in 2TS*]   5 distinctness and isolation. *1TS(2)TH*] distinctness. *1TS(1)*   7† only *1TS*] sole *2TS*   8–9 trod the margin of *1TS(2)TH*] skirted *1TS(1)*   10† strokes *1TS*] stroke *2TS*   14 fire *1TS(2)TH*] spark *1TS(1)*   15 from daylight experiences, *1TS(2)TH* [*added*]   15 since *2TS(2)TH*] as *1TS*   16 with assurance *2TS(2)TH* [*added*]   16 ready mouth *1TS(2)TH* [*added*]   24 just a trifle *1TS(2)TH* [*added*]   24 hard *2TS(2)TH*] hard and angry *1TS*   26 feel that *1TS(2)FHp&TH*] feel *1TS(1)*   29 an officer *1TS(1)*, *1TS(3)TH*] a soldier *1TS(2)FHp&TH*

her death (you know she has only a life-interest here), I should have to go away unless my uncle, who succeeds, chose to take me to stay with him. I have no fortune of my own beyond a mere pittance. Two hundred a year."

Jim's reply was something like a sneer at the absent lady: 5
"You may as well add to the practical objection the sentimental one; that she wouldn't allow you to change your fine old crusted name for mine, which is merely the older one of the little freeholder turned out of this spot by your ancestor when he came."

"Dear, dear Jim, don't say those horrid things! As if *I* had ever even 10
thought of that for a moment!"

He shook her hand off impatiently, and walked out into the moonlight. Certainly as far as physical outline went he might have been the direct product of a line of Paladins or hereditary Crusaders. He was tall, straight of limb, with an aquiline nose, and a mouth 15
fitfully scornful. Rosalys sat almost motionless, watching him. There was no mistaking the ardour of her feelings; her power over him seemed to be lessened by his consciousness of his influence upon the lower and weaker side of her nature. It gratified him as a man to feel it; and though she was beautiful enough to satisfy the senses of the 20
critical, there was perhaps something of contempt inwoven with his love. His victory had been too easy, too complete.

"Dear Jim, you are not going to be vexed? It really isn't my fault that I can't come out here again! Mother will be downstairs to-morrow, and then she might take it into her head to look at any time 25
into the schoolroom and see how the Harmony gets on."

"And you are going off to London soon?" said Jim, still speaking gloomily.

2 chose *PR(2)TH*] chooses *1TS* [cho *undeleted in PR*] 5 sneer...lady: *1TS(2)TH* [*restored*]] ...at either... *1TS(3)TH* [*not continued; see TN*]] sneer: *1TS(1)* 6–7 to the...one; *1TS(4)TH* [*1st the written over initial to of previous reading*]] to practical... sentimental to *1TS(3)TH* [*not continued; final to presumably the beginning of* too]] ... sentimental as well— *1TS(2)TH* [*added*] 7 fine old crusted *2TS(2)TH*] ancient *1TS* 8–9 mine...came." *2TS(3)TH*] ...the quite mouldy one... *2TS(2)TH*] mine. Further back than my grandfather I am a little hazy as to my ancestors." *1TS* 13 outline *1TS(2)TH*] outlines *1TS(1)* 14 product *2TS(2)TH*] descendant *1TS* 14 Paladins or hereditary *1TS(2)TH*] picked *1TS(1)* 16 fitfully *2TS(2)TH*] rather *1TS* 17 feelings; *1TS(2)TH*] feelings and *1TS(1)* 18 seemed to be *2TS(2)TH*] might have been *1TS* 19 as a man *1TS(2)TH* [*added*] 20 it; and *2TS(2)TH*] it; but *1TS* 21† inwoven *1TS*] interwoven *2TS* 22 easy, too *1TS(2)TH*] easy and *1TS(1)* 27 said...speaking *1TS(2)TH*] Jim spoke still *1TS(1)* [*only* spoke *deleted*] 28 gloomily. *2TS(2)TH*] sulkily. *1TS*

"I am afraid so. But couldn't you come there too? I know your leave is not up for a great many weeks?"

He was silent for longer than she had ever known him at these times. Rosalys left her seat on the bench and threw her arms
5 impulsively round him.

"I *can't* go away unless you will come to London when we do, Jim!"

"I will; but on one condition."

"What condition? You frighten me!"

"That you will marry me when I do join you there."

10 The quick breath that heaved in Rosalys ebbed silently; and she leant on the rustic bench with one hand, a trembling being apparent in her garments.

"You really—mean it, Jim darling?"

He swore that he did; that life was quite unendurable to him as he
15 then experienced it. When she was once his wife nothing could come between them; but of course the marriage need not be known for a time—indeed must not. He could not take her abroad. The climate of Burmah would be too trying for her; and, besides, they really would not have enough to live upon.

20 "Couldn't we get on as other people do?" said Rosalys, trying not to cry at these arguments. "I am so tired of concealment, and I don't like to marry privately! It seems to me, much as I love being with you, that there is a sort of—well—vulgarity in our clandestine meetings, as we now enjoy them. Therefore how should I ever have strength
25 enough to hide the fact of my being your wife, to face my mother day after day with the shadow of this secret between us?"

For all answer Jim kissed her, and stroked her silky brown curls.

"I suppose I shall end in agreeing with you—I always do!" she said, her mouth quivering. "Though I *can* be very dogged and
30 obstinate too, Jim! Do you know that all my governesses have said I was the most stubborn child they ever came across? But then, in that case, my temper must be really aroused. You have never seen me as I

10 The quick ... and she *2TS(2)* [silently; *TH*]] ... ebbed; and ... *1TS(2)TH*]
Rosalys *1TS(1)*   11 leant on *PR(2)TH*] held on to *1TS* [on *undeleted in PR*]
11–12 a trembling ... garments. *2TS(2)TH*] trembling from head to foot. *1TS*
[trembling *undeleted in 2TS*]   14 swore *1TS(2)TH*] said *1TS(1)*   14–15 he then
experienced it *1TS(2)TH*] it then was *1TS(1)* [then *undeleted*]   15† could *1TS*]
would *2TS*   20 Rosalys *1TS(2)TH*] the girl *1TS*   22 me *1TS* [*restored in*
2TS]] me that *2TS(2)TH* [that *deleted*]   25 hide *1TS(2)FHp&TH*] conceal
1TS(1)   29 quivering *2TS(2)TH*] trembling *1TS*

am when angry. Perhaps, Jim, you would get to hate me?" She looked at him wistfully with her wet eyes.

"I shall never cease to love you desperately, as I do now!" declared the young man. "How lovely you look, little Rosalys, with that one moonbeam making your forehead like pure white marble. But time is   5
passing. You must go back, my darling, I'm afraid. And you won't fail me in London? I shall make all the plans. Good-bye—good-bye!"

One clinging, intermittent kiss; and then from the shadow in which he stood Jim watched her light figure past the lake, and hurrying along in the shelter of the yew hedges towards the great house, asleep   10
under the reaching deeps of sky, and the vacant gaze of the round white moon.

II

When clouds are iron-grey above the prim drab houses, and a hard east wind blows flakes of dust, stable-straws, scraps of soiled   15
newspaper, and sharp pieces of grit into the eyes of foot-passengers, a less inviting and romantic dwelling-spot than Eaton Place can hardly be experienced.

But the Prince's daughter of the Canticles, emerging from her palace to see the vine flourish and the pomegranates bud forth with   20
her Beloved, could not have looked more unconscious of grime than Rosalys Ambrose as she came down the steps of one of the tall houses in the aforesaid highly respectable place of residences. Her cheeks were hotly pink, her eyes shining, her lips parted. Having once made

2 with her *PR(2)TH*] with *1TS*   2 eyes *1TS(2)TH*] eyelids *1TS(1)* [eye *undeleted*]
8 clinging, *2TS(2)TH*] last long *1TS*   8 intermittent *1TS(2)TH* [*added*]   9 Jim
2TS(2)TH] he *1TS*   9† light figure past *1TS(2)TH*] light figure passing *2TS(2)*
[ing *TH*]] light figure pass *2TS(1)*] skirting *1TS(1)*   11† under the *1TS*] under
2TS   11 reaching deeps of *1TS(2)TH*] velvet-like *1TS(1)*   14 clouds are
1TS(3)TH] sky is *1TS(2)TH?p*] the sky is *1TS(1)* [*only* the deleted *in 1st revision*]
14 drab *2TS(2)TH*] yellow *1TS*   14 houses *1TS, 2TS(2)TH*] house *2TS(1)* [*undeleted*]
15 stable-straws *1TS(2)TH* [*added*]   15 soiled *2TS(2)TH*] dirty *1TS*   17 Eaton
Place *1TS*] Belgrave Road *SG*   18 experienced. *1TS(2)TH*] known. *1TS(1)*
19 the Prince's ... Canticles, *2TS(4)TH*] the P *2TS(3)TH* [*not continued; completely
deleted*]] no p *2TS(2)TH* [*not continued*]] no Princess *1TS* [*only final* s *deleted in 2TS*]
20 to see ... forth with *2TS(2)TH*] into a garden of roses and fountains, to meet *1TS*
21 Beloved, *2TS(2)TH*] lover-prince, *1TS*   21 not *2TS(2)TH* [*added*]   21 grime
1TS, PR(2)TH] crime *PR(1)*   23 highly respectable *2TS(2)TH* [*added*]]
respectable *SG*   23† of residences *1TS(2)TH* [*added*]] of residence *2TS*   24 once
1TS(2)TH [*added*]

up her mind, "Qualms of prudence, pride and pelf" had died within her passionate little heart. After to-day she would belong absolutely to Jim, be his alone, through all the eternities, as it seemed; and of what account was anything else in the world? The entirely physical
5　character of his affection for her, and perhaps of hers for him, was an unconjectured element herein which might not render less transitory the most transitory of sweet things. Thus hopefully she stepped out of the commonplace home that would, in one sense, be hers no more.

　　The raw wind whistled up the street, and deepened the colour in
10　her face. She was plainly dressed in grey, and wore a rather thick veil, natural to the dusty day: it could not however conceal the sparkle of her eyes: veils, even thick ones, happily, never do. Hailing a hansom she told the driver to take her to the corner of the Embankment.

　　In the midst of her pre-occupation she noticed as the cab turned the
15　corner out of Eaton Place that the bony chestnut-horse went lame. Rosalys was superstitious as well as tender-hearted, and she deemed that some stroke of ill-luck might befall her if she drove to be married behind a suffering animal. She alighted and paid off the man, and in her excitement gave him three times his fare. Hurrying forward on
20　foot she heard her name called, and received a cordial greeting from a tall man with grey whiskers, in whom she recognized Mr Durrant, Jim's father. It occurred to her for a second that he might have discovered the plot and have lain in wait to prevent it. However, he spoke in his usual half-respectful, half-friendly tones, not noticing her
25　frightened face. Mr Durrant was a busy man. Besides holding several very important land-agencies in the county where Rosalys lived, he had business in the city to transact at times. He explained to Miss Ambrose that some urgent affairs he was supervising for a client of his, Lord Parkhurst, had now brought him up to London for a few
30　weeks.

　　1 had *2TS(2)TH* [*added*]　　　4 else in the world? The *2TS(2)TH*] else? No premonitions had she that the *1TS(2)* [had she *TH; in 2TS deletion p&i and he of* the *undeleted*]] ... premonitions that the *1TS(1)*　　　6–7 unconjectured ... things. *2TS(3)TH*] ... element which ... of things. *2TS(2)THp*] almost certain proof of its transitoriness. *1TS*　　　9† colour in *1TS*] colour on *2TS*　　　11 natural ... day: it *1TS(2)TH*] which *1TS(1)*　　　12 eyes ... do. *2TS(2)* [even thick ones, *TH*]] eyes: thick veils, happily ... *1TS(2)TH*] eyes. *1TS(1)*　　　13 take her *1TS(2)TH*] drive *1TS(1)*　　　15 corner out *1TS*] corner *SGa*　　　15 Eaton Place *1TS*] Belgrave Road *SG*　　　17† befall her *1TS*] befall *2TS*　　　18 behind *2TS(2)TH*] behind such *1TS*　　　26 county *1TS, 2TS(2)TH*] country *2TS(1)*　　　28 some *1TS(2)TH* [*added*]　　　28–9 he was supervising ... Parkhurst, *1TS(2)TH* [*added*]

"Lord Parkhurst is away?" she asked, to say something. "I hear of him sometimes through his uncle Colonel Lacy."

"Yes. A thorough sailor. Mostly afloat," Mr Durrant replied. "Well—we're rather out of the way in Porchester Terrace; otherwise, my wife would be so pleased if you would come to tea, Miss Ambrose? 5 My son Jim, lazy young beggar, is up here now, too—going to plays and parties. Well, well, it's natural he should like to amuse himself before he leaves for Burmah, poor boy. Are you looking for a hansom? Yes? Hi!" And he waved his stick.

"Thank you so much" said Miss Ambrose. "And I will tell 10 Mamma where you and Mrs Durrant are staying."

She was surprised at her own composure. Her unconscious father-in-law elect helped her into the cab, took off his hat, and walked rapidly away. Rosalys felt her heart stand still when she drew up at the place of meeting. She saw Jim, very blooming and very well- 15 dressed, awaiting her, outwardly calm, at any rate. He jumped into her vehicle and they drove on city-wards.

"You are only ten minutes late, dearest," he said. "Do you know, I was half afraid you might have failed me at the last moment?"

"You don't believe it, Jim!" 20

"Well, I sometimes think I ought not to expect you to keep engagements with me so honestly as you do. Good, brave, little Rosalys!"

They moved on through the press of struggling omnibuses, gigantic vans, covered carts, and foot-passengers who darted at imminent risk 25 of their lives amid the medley of wheels, horses, and shouting drivers. The noise jarred Rosalys' head, and she began to be feverishly anxious.

The church stood in the neighbourhood of a great meat-market, and the pavement was crowded by men in blue linen blouses, their 30 clothes sprinkled with crimson stains. The young girl gave a shiver of disgust.

1–4 "Lord ... Well— *2TS(2)* [A thorough sailor. Mostly *TH*]] ... "Yes. Always afloat," ... *1TS(2)TH* [*added*]   4 Terrace; otherwise *1TS(2)TH*] Terrace," he said. "Otherwise *1TS(1)*   8 leaves for *1TS(2)TH*] goes to *1TS(1)*   10 Miss Ambrose *1TS(3)TH*] the young woman *1TS(2)TH*] the girl *1TS(1)* [the *undeleted in 1st revision*]   12 composure *1TS(2)TH*] calmness *1TS(1)*   15 and very *1TS(2)TH*] and *1TS(1)*   24 gigantic *1TS(2)TH* [*added*]   25 covered *1TS(2)TH* [*added*]   25 foot-passengers who darted *1TS(2)TH*] foot-passengers, darting *1TS(1)* [dart *undeleted*]   31 young *1TS(2)TH* [*added*]

"How revolting it must be to have a butcher for a husband! They can't have hearts like other men. . . . What a gloomy part of London this is to be married in, Jim!"

"Ah—yes! Everything looks gloomy with the east wind blowing.
5 Now, here we are! Jump out, little woman!"

He handed money to the driver, who went off with the most cursory thoughts of the part that he had played in this little excursion of a palpitating pair into the unknown.

"Jimmy darling; oughtn't you, or one of us, to have lived here for
10 fifteen days?" she said as they entered the fine old Norman porch, to which she was quite blind in her pre-occupation.

Durrant laughed. "I have declared that I did," he answered coolly. "I hope, in the circumstances, that it's a forgivable lie. Cheer up, Rosalys; don't all of a sudden look so solemn!"

15 There were tears in her eyes. The gravity of the step she was about to take had begun to frighten her.

They had some time to wait before the clergyman condescended to come out of the vestry and perform the ceremony which was to unite her to Jim. Two or three other couples were also in the church on the
20 same errand: a haggard woman in a tawdry white bonnet, hanging on to the arm of a short crimson-faced man, who had evidently been replenishing his inside with gin to nerve himself to the required pitch for the ordeal: a girl with a coarse, hard face, accompanied by a slender youth in shabby black: a tall man, of refined aspect, in very
25 poor clothes, whose hollow cough shook his thin shoulders and chest, and told his bride that her happiness, such as it was, would probably last but the briefest space.

Rosalys glanced absently at the beautiful building, with its Norman apse and transverse arches of horse-shoe form, and the
30 massive curves and cushion-capitals that supported the tower-end; the whole impression left by the church being one of singular

---

7–8 excursion . . . unknown. *2TS(4)TH*] . . . a pair . . . *2TS(3)TH*] excursion to purchase possible disillusion. *2TS(2)* [possible *TH*]] excursion to purchase disillusion. *1TS(3)TH*] adventure in search <*illegible*> *1TS(2)THp*] romance. *1TS(1)*
12 Durrant *1TS(2)TH*] Jim *1TS(1)*   13 hope, in *1TS(2)TH*] hope, under *1TS(1)*
16 had begun *1TS(2)TH*] was beginning *1TS(1)*   22 replenishing his inside *1TS(2)TH*] regaling himself *1TS(1)*   22 pitch *1TS*, *2TS(3)TH*] strength *2TS(2)TH*   23 the ordeal *1TS*] throwing himself away *2TS(2)TH* [*never adopted; i.e.* the ordeal *undeleted*]   26 happiness, such as it was, *1TS(2)TH*] happiness *1TS(1)*   27 the briefest *2TS(2)TH*] a very short *1TS*

harmony, loveliness, and above all, repose—which struck even her by its great contrast with her experiences just then. As the clergyman emerged from the vestry a shaft of sunlight smote the altar, touched the quaint tomb where the founder of the building lay in his dreamless sleep, and quivered on the darned clothes of the 5 consumptive bridegroom.

Jim and Rosalys moved forward, and then the light shone for a moment, too, upon his yellow hair and handsome face. To the woman who loved him it seemed that "From the crown of his head even to the sole of his foot there was no blemish in him." 10

The curate looked sharply at the four couples; angrily, Rosalys fancied, at her. But it was only because the east-wind had given him an acute tooth-ache that his gaze was severe, and his reading spiritless.

The four couples having duly contracted their inviolable unities, 15 and slowly gone their ways through the porch, Jim and Rosalys adjourned to a fashionable hotel on the Embankment, where in a room all to themselves they had luncheon, over which Rosalys presided with quite a housewifely air.

"When shall I see you again?" he said, as he put her into a cab two 20 or three hours later on in the afternoon.

"*You* must arrange all that, Jim. Somehow I feel so dreadfully sad and sinful now, all of a sudden! Have I been wicked? I don't know!"

Her tone changed as she met his passionate gaze, and she said very low, with a lump in her throat: 25

"O my dear darling! I care for nothing in the whole wide world, now that I belong to you!"

1–2 struck ... contrast *1TS(2)TH*] contrasted greatly *1TS(1)* [contrast *undeleted*]
4 quaint *1TS(2)TH* [*added*]   4–5 in his dreamless sleep *1TS(2)TH*] asleep
1TS(1) [sleep *undeleted*]   6 bridegroom. *1TS(2)TH*] man. *1TS(1)*   7–8 for
a moment, too, *1TS(2)TH*] too for a moment, *1TS(1)* [for a moment, *undeleted*]
8–9 To ... seemed that *1TS(2)TH*] It seemed to the woman that loved him *1TS(1)* [o
the woman *and* loved him *undeleted*]   15–16 having ... porch, *1TS(2)TH*] being
duly contracted, *1TS(1)* [duly contracted *undeleted*]   17 a fashionable *1TS(3)TH*
[*altered in same line*]] a handsome *1TS(2)TH*] an *1TS(1)*   17–18 in a ...
themselves *2TS(3)TH* [*added; originally followed by a comma and marked for insertion after*
luncheon]   18–19 luncheon ... air. *1TS(2)TH*] luncheon. *1TS(1)* [*see TN*]
20–1 two ... later on *1TS(3)TH*] later *1TS(2)TH*] late *1TS(1)* [*undeleted in 1st*
revision]   22–3 dreadfully ... sinful *1TS(2)* [& sinful *TH*]] depressed, so
dreadfully sad *SG*] dreadfully sad *1TS(1)*   24 Her *PR(2)TH*] Suddenly her *1TS*
[her *undeleted in PR; capitalization signified by double underscoring*]   25 low ... throat:
1TS(2)TH] low: *1TS(1)*

III

The London weeks went by with all their commonplaces, all their novelties. Mr Durrant, senior, had finished his urgent business, and returned to his square and uninteresting country-house. But Jim
5 lingered on in town, although conscious of some subtle change in himself and his view of things. He and Rosalys met whenever it was possible, which was pretty frequently. Often they contrived to do so at hastily arranged luncheons and teas in the private rooms of hotels; sometimes, when Mrs Ambrose was suddenly called away, at Jim's
10 own rooms. Sometimes they adventured to queer suburban restaurants.

In the lapse of these weeks the twain began somehow to lose a little of their zest for each other's society. Jim himself was aware of it before he had yet discovered that something of the same disappointment was
15 dulling her heart too. On his own side it was the usual lowering of the fire—the slackening of a man's passion for a woman when she becomes his property. On hers it was a more mixed feeling. No doubt her love for Jim had been of but little higher quality than his for her. She had thoroughly abandoned herself to his good looks, his
20 recklessness, his eagerness; and, now that the sensuous part of her character was satisfied, her fervour also began to burn itself down. But beyond, above, this, the concealment of her marriage was

2 London *1TS(2)TH [added]*   2–3 by with ... novelties. *1TS(2)TH]* by.
1TS(1)   4 country-house *2TS(3)TH]* country home *1TS, 2TS(2)]* country house
2TS(1) [country *undeleted]*   5 town *1TS(2)TH]* London *1TS(1)*   6 view of
things *1TS(2)TH]* surroundings *1TS(1)*   7 they contrived to do so *1TS(2)TH*
[*added]*   8 in the private rooms of hotels *1TS]* at hotels or restaurants *SG*
10 they adventured to queer *1TS(3)TH [altered in same line]*] ... to strange *1TS(2)TH]*
at *1TS(1)*   11 restaurants *1TS]* coffee-houses *SG*   12 these *1TS(2)TH*
[*added]*] these three *SGa*   12 the twain *1TS(2)TH]* they *1TS(1)* [the *undeleted]*
12 somehow *1TS(2)TH]* somehow or other *1TS(1)*   13 himself *1TS(2)TH*
[*added]*   13 aware *PR(2)TH]* conscious *1TS*   14 discovered that
1TS(2)FHp&TH] discovered *1TS(1)*   15 own *1TS(2)TH [added]*
15–16 lowering of the fire— *1TS(2)TH]* case of *1TS(1)*   18 Jim had *2TS]* Jim
has *1TS*   18–20 her. She ... eagerness; *1TS(3)TH]* having become thoroughly
<*illegible erasure*> to his good looks, his recklessness, his <*illegible erasure*> for her;
1TS(2)TH [only having become *and* for her; *deleted]*] her; *1TS(1)*   20 and, now
that *1TS(2)TH]* and when *1TS(1)*   20–1 sensuous ... satisfied, *1TS]* novelty of
wifedom was past, *SG*   21 satisfied ... burn *PR(2)* [fervour *and* began to burn
TH]] satisfied, her passion also had burnt *1TS(2)TH]* satisfied had burnt *1TS(1)*
[burnt *undeleted]*   22 beyond, above, *1TS(3)TH [altered in same line]*] beyond
1TS(2)TH] in addition to *1TS(1)*

repugnant to Rosalys. When the rapture of the early meetings had died away she began to loathe the sordid deceit which these involved: the secretly despatched letters, the unavoidably brazen lies to her mother, who, if she attached overmuch importance to money and birth, yet loved her daughter in all good faith and simplicity. Then 5 once or twice Jim was late at their interviews. He seemed indifferent and pre-occupied. His manner stung Rosalys into impatient utterance at the end of a particular meeting in which this mood was unduly prominent.

"You forget all I have given up for you!" she cried. "You make a 10 fool of me in allowing me to wait here for you. It is humiliating and vulgar! I hate myself for behaving as I do!"

"The renunciations are not all on your side," he answered caustically. "You forget all that the loss of his freedom means to a man!" 15

Her heart swelled, and she had great difficulty in keeping back her tears. But she took refuge in sullenness.

"Unfortunately we can't undo our folly!" she murmured. "You will have to make the best of it as well as I. I suppose the awakening to a sense of our idiocy was bound to come sooner or later. But—I didn't 20 think it would come so soon! Jim, look at me! Are you really angry? Don't for God's sake go and leave me like this!"

He was walking slowly towards the great iron gate leading out of Kensington Gardens; a dogged cast on his now familiar countenance.

"Don't make a scene in public, for Heaven's sake, Rosalys!" 25 Feeling that he had spoken too brutally he suddenly paused, and changed:

"I am sorry, little woman, if I was cross! But things have combined to harass me lately. Of course we won't part from one another in anger." 30

Jim glanced at her straight profile with its full under-lip and firmly curved chin, at the lashes on either lid, and the glossy brown hair twisted in coils under her hat. But the sight of this loveliness, now all

1 Rosalys *1TS(2)TH*] her *1TS₂,1*)   8–9 utterance ... prominent. *1TS(4)TH*]
... a meeting ... *1TS(3)TH*] ... which these *1TS(2)TH* [*not continued*]] utterance.
1TS(1)   13–14 answered caustically. *1TS(2)TH*] answered, with a half sneer
1TS(1)   24 now familiar *PR(2)TH*] handsome *1TS*   26 Feeling *1TS(2)TH*]
But feeling *1TS(1)* [*feeling undeleted; capitalization signified by double underscoring*]
26–7 paused, and changed: *1TS(2)TH*] paused. *1TS(1)*

his own, failed to arouse the old emotions. He simply contemplated her approvingly from an artistic point of view.

They had reached the gateway, and she placed her hand on his arm.

5   "Good-bye. When shall we next meet? To-day is Tuesday. Shall it be Friday?"

"I am afraid I must go out of London on Thursday for a day or two. I'll write, dear. Let me call a hansom."

She thanked him in a cold voice again, and with a last handshake,
10 and a smile that hovered on sorrow, left him and drove away towards Belgravia.

Once or twice later on they met; the next interview being shorter and sadder perhaps than the last. The one that followed it ended in bitterness.

15   "This had better be our long good-bye, I suppose?" said she.

"Perhaps it had.... You seem to be always looking out for causes of reproach, Rosalys. I don't know what has come over you."

"It is *you* who have changed!" she cried, with a little stamp. "And you are by far the most to blame of us two. You forget that I should
20 never have contemplated marriage as a possibility! You have made me lie to my mother, do things of which I am desperately ashamed, and now you don't attempt to disguise your weariness of me!"

It was Jim's turn to lose his temper now. "You forget that *you* gave me considerable encouragement! Most girls would not have come ouι
25 again and again to surreptitious meetings with a man who was in love with them,—girls brought up as you have been!"

She started as in a spasm. A momentary remorse seized him. He realized that he had been betrayed into speaking as no man of kindly good-feeling could speak. He made a tardy, scarcely gracious
30 apology, and they parted. A few days afterwards he wrote a letter full of penitence for having hurt her, and she answered almost

9 cold *2TS(2)TH*] hard cold *1TS* [cold *undeleted*]   10 sorrow *1TS(2)TH*]
tears *1TS(1)*   12 later on *2TS(2)TH*] again *1TS*   15 she. *1TS(2)TH*] the
girl. *1TS(1)*   23 -4 It was ... Most *1TS(2)TH*] "*You* forget ... encouragement!"
It was Jim's turn to lose his temper now. "Most *1TS(1)* [*2nd sentence circled and
marked for inclusion at beginning of paragraph*]   25 surreptitious meetings with
1TS(2)TH] surreptitiously meet *1TS(1)* [surreptitious *undeleted*]   27 She ... spasm.
1TS(4)TH [*altered in same line*]] ... as in pain. *1TS(3)TH* [*see TN*]   27 momentary
1TS(2)TH] momentary feeling of *1TS(1)*   28 had been betrayed into *2TS(2)TH*]
was *1TS*   28 kindly *2TS(2)TH*] gentlemanly *1TS*   29 scarcely gracious
2TS(2)TH] half-ungracious *1TS* [gracious *undeleted in 2TS*]

affectionately. But each knew that their short-lived romance was dead as the wind-flowers that had blossomed at its untimely birth.

IV

In August this pair of disappointed people met once more amid their old surroundings. Perhaps their enforced absence from one another 5 gave at first some zest to their reunion. Jim was at times tender, and like his former self; Rosalys, if sad and subdued, less sullen and reproachful than she had been in London.

Mrs Ambrose had fallen into delicate health, and her daughter was in consequence able to dispose of her time outside the house as she 10 wished. The moonlight meetings with Jim were discontinued, but husband and wife went for long strolls sometimes in the remoter nooks of the park, through winding walks in the distant shrubberies, and down paths hidden by high yew-hedges from intruding eyes that might look with suspicion on their being together. 15

On one especially beautiful August day they paced side by side, talking at moments with something of their old tenderness. The sky above the dark-green barriers on either hand was a bottomless deep of blue. The yew-boughs were covered in curious profusion by the handiwork of energetic spiders, who had woven their glistening webs in 20 every variety of barbaric pattern. In shape some resembled hammocks, others ornamental purses, others deep bags, in the middle of which a large yellow insect remained motionless and watchful.

"Shall we sit for a little while in the summer-house?" said Rosalys at last, in flat accents, for a tête-à-tête with Jim had long ceased to 25

2 wind-flowers *2TS(2)TH*] flowers *1TS* [*undeleted in 2TS*]   13 nooks
1TS(2)TH] parts *1TS(1)*   13 park, *1TS(2)TH*] park and *1TS(1)*   13 winding
2TS(2)TH] dusky *1TS*   13 distant *1TS(2)TH*] more distant *1TS(1)* [distant
undeleted]   13–14 shrubberies, and *1TS(2)TH*] shrubberies *1TS(1)*   14 paths
1TS(1) [*restored*]] paths to the woods *1TS(2)TH* [*deleted*]   14 from *2TS(2)TH*]
from all *1TS*   14–15 eyes ... together. *2TS(3)TH*] eyes who should pry into their
secret. *2TS(2)TH*] eyes. *1TS*   17 at moments *2TS(2)TH* [*added*]   18 dark-green
1TS(2)TH] dark *1TS(1)* [dark *undeleted*]   18 hand *1TS, 2TS(2)TH*] side *2TS(1)*
18 a bottomless deep of *2TS(2)TH*] of a velvet-like *1TS*   20 handiwork *1TS(1)*
[*restored*]] enlaced handiwork *1TS(2)TH* [enlaced *deleted*]   21–3† In shape ...
watchful. *1TS(3)TH*] ... hammocks, others purses ... *2TS*] ... resembled ornamental
purses ... *1TS(2)TH* [*added*]   24–5 Rosalys at last, *2TS(2)TH*] Rosalys,
1TS(2)TH] Rosalys. She spoke *1TS(1)*   25 flat *1TS(2)TH*] spiritless *1TS(1)*
25 for *2TS(2)TH*] for the thought of *1TS*

give her any really strong beats of pleasure. "I want to talk to you
further about plans; how often we had better write, and so on."
They sat down, in an arbour made of rustic logs, which overlooked
the mere. The wood-work had been left rough within, and dusty
5 spider-webs hung in the crevices; here and there the bark had fallen
away in strips; above, on the roof, there were clumps of fungi, looking
like tufts of white fur.

"This is a sunless, queer sort of place you have chosen," he said,
looking round critically.

10 The boughs had grown so thickly in the foreground that the
glittering margin of water was hardly perceptible between their
interlacing twigs, and no visible hint of a human habitation was
given, though the rustic shelter had been originally built with the
view of affording a picturesque glimpse of the handsome old brick
15 house wherein the Ambroses had lived for some three centuries.

"You might have found a more lively scene for what will be,
perhaps, our last interview for years," Jim went on.

"Are you really going so soon?" she asked, passing over the
complaint.

20 "Next week. And my father has made all sorts of arrangements for
me. Besides, he is beginning to suspect that you and I are rather too
intimate. And your mother knows, somehow or other, that I have
been up here several times of late. We must be careful."

"I suppose so," she answered absently, looking out under the log
25 roof at a chaffinch swinging himself backwards and forwards on a
larch bough. A sort of dreary indifference to her surroundings; a sense
of being caged and trapped had begun to take possession of Rosalys.
The present was full of perplexity, the future objectless. Now and
then, when she looked at Jim's lithe figure, and healthy, virile face,

1 really strong *2TS(2)TH* [*added*]   1 beats *1TS(3)TH*] thrills *1TS(2)TH*]
thrill *1TS(1)* [*undeleted in 1st revision*]   2 further *2TS(2)TH* [*added*]
4 wood-work *2TS(2)TH*] wood *1TS* [*undeleted in 2TS*]   8 queer *PR(2)TH*] sad
1TS   12 no *1TS(2)TH*] there was no *1TS(1)* [*no undeleted*]   12 of a
1TS(2)TH] of *1TS(1)*   12–13 habitation was given, though *1TS(3)TH*] ...
was of *1TS(2)TH* [*not continued*]] habitation, although *1TS(1)* [*though undeleted*]
13–14 the view of *1TS(2)TH*] a view to *1TS(1)* [*view undeleted*]   14 old
2TS(2)TH] red *1TS*   15 wherein *2TS(2)TH*] where *1TS* [*where undeleted in
2TS*]   16 scene *1TS(2)TH*] one *1TS(1)*   18–19 she asked ... complaint.
1TS(2)TH [*added*]   22 And your mother *2TS(2)TH*] He *1TS*   23 here *1TS*
[*not in SG*]   23 We *1TS(1)*, *2TS(2)TH*] You *1TS(2)TH*   26† larch *1TS*]
large *2TS*   27 Rosalys. *1TS(2)TH*] her. *1TS(1)*   29 healthy, virile
2TS(2)TH] handsome, boyish *1TS*

she felt that perhaps she might have been able to love him still if only he had cared for her with a remnant of his former passionate devotion. But his indifference was even more palpable than her own. They sat and talked on within the dim arbour for a little while. Then Jim made one of the unfortunate remarks that always galled her to the quick. She rose in anger, answered him with cold sarcasm, and hastened away down the little wood. He followed, a rather ominous light shining in his eyes.

"Your temper is really growing insufferable, Rosalys!" he cried, and clenched his hand roughly on her arm to detain her.

"How dare you!" said the girl. "For God's sake leave me, and don't come back again! I rejoice to think that in a few days it will not be in your power to insult me any more!"

"Damn it—I am going to leave you, am I not! I only want to keep you here for a moment to come to some understanding! ... Indeed you'll be surprised to find how very much I am going to leave you, when you hear what I mean! My ideas have grown considerably emancipated of late, and therefore I tell you that there is no reason on earth why any soul should ever know of that miserable mistake we made in the spring."

She winced a little; it was an unexpected move; and her eyes lingered uneasily on a copper-coloured butterfly playing a game of hide-and-seek with a little blue companion.

"Who," he continued, "is ever going to search the register of that old East-London church? We must philosophically look on the marriage as an awkward fact in our lives, which won't prevent our loving elsewhere when we feel inclined. In my opinion this early error will carry one advantage with it—that we shall be unable to extinguish any love we may each feel for another person by a sordid matrimonial knot—unless, indeed, after seven years of obliviousness to one another's existence."

6 cold sarcasm *1TS(2)TH*] a cold sneer *1TS(1)* [cold *undeleted*]   7† followed
1TS] followed her *2TS*   9–10 he cried, and *1TS(2)TH*] He *1TS(1)*   10 clenched
PR(2)TH] laid *1TS*   10 on *1TS* [*restored in PR*]] round *PR(2)TH* [*deleted*]
11 you *1TS(2)FHp&TH*] you, sir *1TS(1)*   11 said *1TS(2)TH*] cried *1TS(1)*
15 Indeed *1TS(2)TH* [*added*]   17 considerably *2TS(2)TH*] very *1TS*
18† you that *1TS*] you *2TS*   19 soul *1TS(2)TH*] soul on earth *1TS(1)*
19 mistake *1TS(2)TH*] mistake which *1TS(1)*   21–3 move ... companion.
2TS(2) [uneasily *TH*]] ... lingered vacantly on ... *1TS(3)TH*] move; & stood as if
1TS(2)TH [*not continued*]] move. *1TS(1)*   27 elsewhere *1TS*] anybody else *SG*
29† each *1TS* [*not in 2TS+*]   30 knot *2TS(2)TH*] contract *1TS*

"I'll—try to—emancipate myself likewise," she said slowly. "It will be well to forget this tragedy of our lives! And the most tragic part of it is—that we are not even sorry that we don't love each other any more!"

5 "The truest words you ever spoke!"

"And the surest event that was ever to come, given your nature—"

"And yours!"

She hastened on down the grass walk into the broad gravelled path leading to the house. At the corner stood Mrs Ambrose, who was

10 better, and had come out for a stroll—assuming as an invalid the privilege of wearing a singular scarlet gown and a hat in which a number of black quills stood startlingly erect.

"Ah—Rosy!" she cried. "Oh, and Mr Durrant? What a colour you have got, child!"

15 "Yes. Mr Durrant and I have been having a furious political discussion, mamma. I have grown quite hot over it. He is more unreasonable than ever. But when he gets abroad he won't be as he is now. A few years of India will change all that." And to carry on the idea of her unconcern she turned to whistle to a bold robin that had

20 flitted down from a larch tree, perched on the yew hedge, and looked inquiringly at her, answering her whistle with his pathetic little pipe.

Durrant had come up behind. "Yes," he said cynically. "One never knows how an enervating country may soften one's brains."

He bade them a cool good-bye and left. She watched his retreating

25 figure, the figure of the active, the strong, the handsome animal, who had scarcely won the better side of her nature at all. He never turned his head. So this was the end!

The bewildering bitterness of it well-nigh paralysed Rosalys for a few moments. Why had they been allowed—he and she—to love one

30 another with that eager, almost unholy, passion, and then to part with less interest in each other than ordinary friends? She felt

---

6–7 "And the surest ... yours!" *1TS(3)TH* [*altered in same line*]] ... nature & mine!" *1TS(2)TH* [*added*]   10–12 stroll ... erect. *PR(2)* [*transposition of* as an invalid *and* assuming *marked by TH*]] stroll—as an invalid assuming the ... *2TS(3)* [*singular TH; altered in same line*]] ... a surprising scarlet ... *2TS(2)* [*surprising TH*]] ... a scarlet ... *1TS(3)TH*] ... stood erect. *1TS(2)TH*] stroll. *1TS(1)*   18–21 And to carry ... pipe. *1TS(5)TH*] ... a robin ... *1TS(4)TH*] ... perched inquiringly on the yew hedge, *1TS(3)TH* [*not continued; see TN*]] ... unconcern she paus *1TS(2)TH* [*not continued; added*]   23 an enervating *2TS(2)TH*] a hot *1TS*   26 scarcely *2TS(2)TH*] never *1TS*   28 it *1TS(2)TH*] it all *1TS(1)*   30 eager *2TS(2)TH*] mad *1TS*   30 almost unholy, *1TS*] resistless *SG*

ashamed of having ceded herself to him. If her mother had not been beside her she would have screamed out aloud in her exasperating pain.

Mrs Ambrose lifted up her voice. "What are you looking at, child? ... My dear, I want a little word with you. Are you attending? When you pout your lip like that, Rosalys, I always know that you are in a bad frame of mind.... The vicar has been here; and he has made me a little unhappy."

"I should have thought he was too stupid to give anyone a pang! Why do they put such simpletons into the churches!"

"Well—he says that people are chattering about you and that young Durrant. And I must tell you that—that, from a marrying point of view, he is impossible. You know that. And I don't want him to make up to you. Now, Rosalys, my darling, tell me honestly—I feel I have not looked after you lately as I ought to have done—tell me honestly: Is he in love with you?"

"He is not, mother, to my certain knowledge."

"Are you with him?"

"No. That I swear."

V

Seven years and some months had passed since Rosalys spoke as above-written. And never a sound of Jim.

As she had mentally matured under the touch of the gliding seasons, Miss Ambrose had determined to act upon the hint Jim had thrown out to her as to the practical nullity of their marriage-contract if they simply kept in different hemispheres without a word. She had never written to him a line; and he had never written a line to her.

He might be dead for all that she knew: he possibly was dead. She had taken no steps to ascertain anything about him, though she had been aware for years that he was no longer in the Army-list. Dead or alive he was completely cut off from the county in which he and she

2 exasperating *PR(2)TH* [*added*]   5† attending *1TS*] sure—you are attending *2TS(2)* [sure *and line indicating transposition of* are *and* you *TH*]] —are you attending *2TS(1)*   9–10 pang! ... churches!" *1TS(2)TH*] pang." *1TS(1)*   23–4 As she ... Ambrose *1TS(2)TH*] She *1TS(1)*   24 Jim *1TS(2)TH*] he *1TS(1)* 29–30 him, though ... Army-list. *1TS(2)TH*] ... that his name was ... *SG*] him. *1TS(1)*   31 county *1TS, PR(2)TH*] country *2TS*

had lived, for his father had died a long time before this, his house and properties had been sold, and not a scion of the line of Durrant remained in that part of England.

5 Rosalys had readily imbibed his ideas of their mutual independence; and now, after the lapse of all these years, had acted upon them with the surprising literalness of her sex when they act upon advice at all.

Mrs Ambrose, who had distinguished herself no whit during her fifty years of life saving by the fact of having brought a singularly 10 beautiful girl into the world, had passed quietly out of it. Rosalys' uncle had succeeded his sister-in-law in the possession of the old house with its red tower, and the broad paths and garden-lands; he had been followed by an unsatisfactory son of his, last in the entail, and thus unexpectedly Rosalys Ambrose found herself sole mistress 15 of the spot of her birth.

People marvelled somewhat that she continued to call herself Miss Ambrose. Though a woman now getting on for thirty she was distinctly attractive both in face and in figure, and could confront the sunlight as well as the moonbeams still. In the manner of women who 20 are yet sure of their charms she was fond of representing herself as much older than she really was. Perhaps she would have been disappointed if her friends had not laughed and contradicted her, and told her that she was still lovely and looked like a girl. Lord Parkhurst, anyhow, was firmly of that contradictory opinion; and 25 perhaps she cared more for his views than for anyone else's at the present time.

That distinguished sailor had been but one of many suitors; but he stirred her heart as none of the others could do. It was not merely that

---

1 a long time *1TS(2)TH*] some years *1TS(1)*   2 properties *1TS(2)TH*] property *1TS(1)* [propert *undeleted*]   2† line *1TS*] house *2TS*   8† herself *1TS*] herself in *2TS*   10 beautiful *1TS* [*restored in 2TS*]] attractive *2TS(2)TH* [*deleted*]   10 Rosalys' *1TS(2)TH*] Her *1TS(1)*   12 paths *2TS(2)TH*] path *1TS* [*undeleted in 2TS*]   16–17 continued ... Ambrose. *PR(4)* [continued to *TH*]] called herself Miss Ambrose still. *1TS(2)* [still *restored PR(3)TH*]] ... Ambrose yet. *PR(2)* [yet *TH; deleted*]   18 distinctly *1TS*] remarkably *SG*   18–19 in figure ... still. *2TS(2)* [confront *TH;* still *restored PR(3)TH* and *PR(5)TH*]] ... moonbeams. *PR(2), PR(4)* [*deletions TH*]] ... could face the ... moon beams. still. *1TS(3)TH*] ... moon beams. *1TS(2)TH*] figure. *1TS(1)* [figure *undeleted*]   20 yet *PR(2)TH*] still *1TS*   21 really *2TS(2)TH* [*added*]   23 girl *1TS*] young girl *SG* 25 views *1TS(2)TH*] view *1TS(1)* [*undeleted*]   27† but he *1TS*] but he had *2TS(2)* [he *TH*]] but had *2TS(1)*

he was brave, and pleasing, and had returned from a late campaign in Egypt with a hero's reputation; but that his chivalrous feelings towards women, originating perhaps in the fact that he knew very little about them, were sufficient to gratify the most exacting of the sex.

His rigid notions of duty and honour, both towards them and from them, made the blood of Rosalys run cold when she thought of a certain little episode of her past life, notwithstanding that, or perhaps because, she loved him dearly.

"He is not the least bit of a flirt, like most sailors," said Miss Ambrose to her cousin and companion, Miss Jennings, on a particular afternoon in this eighth year of Jim Durrant's obliteration from her life. It was an afternoon with an immense event immediately ahead of it; no less an event than Rosalys' marriage with Lord Parkhurst, which was to take place on the very next day.

The local newspaper had duly announced the coming wedding in proper terms as "the approaching nuptials of the beautiful and wealthy Miss Ambrose of Ambrose Towers with a distinguished naval officer, the Lord Parkhurst." There followed an ornamental account of the future bridegroom's heroic conduct during the late war. "The handsome face and figure of Lord Parkhurst," wound up the honest paragraphist, "are not altogether unknown to us in this vicinity, as he has recently been visiting his uncle, Colonel Lacy, High Sheriff of the County. We wish all prosperity to the happy couple, who have doubtless a brilliant and cloudless future before them."

This was the way in which her acceptance of Durrant's views had worked themselves out. He had said; "After seven years of mutual oblivion we can marry again if we choose."

And she had chosen.

Rosalys almost wished that Lord Parkhurst had been a flirt, or at least had won experience as the victim of one, or many, of those precious creatures, and had not so implicitly trusted her. It would have brought things more nearly to a level.

"A flirt! I should think not," said Jane Jennings. "In fact, Rosalys, he is almost alarmingly strict in his ideas. It is a mistake to believe

1 and pleasing, *1TS(2)TH*] handsome, *1TS(1)*   1† late *1TS* [*not in 2TS+*]
1–2 campaign in Egypt *1TS(2)FHp&TH*] blockade *1TS(1)*   11 this eighth *1TS*]
the eighth *SG*   18 the Lord *1TS*] Lord *TD*   18 There *1TS(2)TH*] Then
1TS(1) [The *undeleted*]   27–8 of mutual oblivion *1TS(2)TH* [*added*]   30–2 or at
... creatures, *2TS(2)* [of those precious creatures, *TH*]] ... many, *1TS(2)TH* [*added*]

that so many women are angels, as he does. He is too simple. He is
bound to be disappointed some day."

Miss Ambrose sighed nervously. "Yes," she said.

"I don't mean by you to-morrow! God forbid!"

5   "No."

Miss Ambrose sighed again, and a silence followed, during which,
while recalling unutterable things of the past, Rosalys gazed absently
out of the window at the lake, that some men were dredging, the mud
left bare by draining down the water being imprinted with hundreds
10   of little footmarks of plovers feeding there. Eight or nine herons stood
further away, one or two composedly fishing, their grey figures
reflected with unblurred clearness in the mirror of the pool. Some
little water-hens waddled with a fussy gait across the sodden ground
in front of them, and a procession of wild geese came through the sky,
15   and passed on till they faded away into a row of black dots.

Suddenly the plovers rose into the air, uttering their customary
wails, and dispersing like a group of stars from a rocket; and the
herons drew up their flail-like legs, and flapped themselves away.
Something had disturbed them; a carriage, sweeping round to the
20   other side of the house.

"There's the door-bell!" Rosalys exclaimed, with a start. "That's
he, for certain! Is my hair untidy Jane? I've been rumpling it awfully,
leaning back on the cushions. And do see if my gown is all right at the
back—it never did fit well."

25   The butler flung open the folding-doors and announced in the voice

---

6–20 followed ... house. [*1TS(2)TH with later revisions*]] followed. *1TS(1)* +
7 while recalling *1TS(3)TH*] dreaming *1TS(2)TH*   8 lake, that *2TS(2)TH*] lake,
which *1TS(2)TH*   9 draining down *1TS(3)TH*] the draining off *1TS(2)TH*
[draining *undeleted*]   9 imprinted with *1TS(3)THp*] imprinted by *1TS(2)TH*
10 plovers feeding there *1TS(3)TH*] plovers, which rose uttering their wailing cries
1TS(2)TH   12 pool *PR(2)TH*] lake *1TS(2)TH*   13 sodden *1TS(3)TH*]
slushy *1TS(2)TH*   14 sky *2TS(2)TH*] air *1TS(2)TH*   16 uttering
1TS(3)TH] wheeling *1TS(2)TH* [*not continued*]   16–17 customary wails
1TS(4)TH] wailing cries *1TS(3)TH*   17–18 rocket; ... away. *2TS(2)* [themselves
TH]] ... flapped away. *1TS(5)TH*] ... their legs ... *1TS(4)TH*] rocket. *1TS(3)TH*
19 them; *1TS(6)TH*] them: the noise of *1TS(3)TH* [*restored:* the *readded and* noise of
stetted]] them: an approaching *1TS(4)TH* [*not continued*]   19 carriage, sweeping
round to *1TS(4)TH*] carriage on *1TS(3)TH*   21 "There's *2TS(2)TH*] "Good
gracious, there's *1TS* [here's *of* There's *undeleted in 2TS*]   21 Rosalys *2TS(2)TH*]
she *1TS*   21 exclaimed *1TS(2)TH*] exclaimed presently *1TS(1)*   22 for
certain *1TS*] it must be *SG*   22 untidy *1TS(2)FHp&TH*] all right *1TS(1)*
23 all right *1TS(2)FHp&TH*] in place *1TS(1)*

of a man who felt that it was quite time for this nonsense of calling to be put an end to by the more compact arrangement of the morrow: "Lord Parkhurst!"

A man of middle size, with a fair and pleasant face, and a short beard, entered the room. His blue eyes smiled rather more than his lips as he took the little hand of his hostess in his own with the air of one verging on proprietorship of the same, and said: "Now, darling; about what we have to settle before the morning! I have come entirely on business, as you perceive!"

Rosalys tenderly smiled up at him. Miss Jennings left the room, and Rosalys' sailor silently kissed and admired his betrothed, till he continued:

"Ah—my beautiful one! I have nothing to give you in return for the immeasurable gift you are about to bestow on me—excepting such love as no man ever felt before! I almost wish you were not quite so good and perfect and innocent as you are! And I wish you were a poorer woman—as poor as I—and had no lovely home such as this. To think you have kept yourself from all other men for such an unworthy fellow as me!"

Rosalys looked away from him along the green vistas of chestnuts and beeches stretching far down outside the windows.

"Oswald—I know how much you care for me: and that is why I—hope you won't be disappointed—after you have taken me to-morrow for good and all! I wonder if I shall hinder and hamper you in your profession. Perhaps you ought to marry a girl much younger than yourself—your nature is so young—not a maturing woman like me."

For all answer he smiled at her with the confiding, fearless gaze that she loved.

Lord Parkhurst stayed on through a paradisical hour till Miss Jennings came to tell them that tea was in the library. Presently they were reminded by the same faithful relative and dependent that on that evening of all evenings they had promised to drive across to the

7 said *1TS(2)FHp&TH*] archly said *1TS(1)* [said *undeleted*] 10 tenderly *PR(2)TH*] merely *1TS* 11 kissed and *1TS(2)TH* [*added*] 16 and innocent *2TS(2)TH* [*added*] 17 lovely *1TS(2)FHp&TH*] handsome *1TS(1)* 18 kept yourself from *1TS*] rejected *SG* 24–7 all! ... me." *2TS(2)* [maturing *TH*]] ... a woman ... *1TS(3)TH*] ... young. *1TS(2)TH*] all!" *1TS(1)* 28–30 the confiding ... Parkhurst *1TS(2)TH*] a confiding, fearless, gaze. He *1TS(1)* [confiding, fearless, gaze *undeleted*] 30 through a paradisical *1TS(2)TH*] for an *1TS(1)* 33 drive *1TS(2)FHp&TH*] trot *1TS(1)*

house of Colonel Lacy, Lord Parkhurst's uncle, and one of Rosalys'
near neighbours, and dine there quietly with two or three intimate
friends.

VI

5   When Rosalys entered Colonel Lacy's drawing-room before dinner,
the eyes of the few guests assembled there were naturally enough
fixed upon her.

"By Jove, she's better looking than ever—though she's not more
than a year or two under thirty!" whispered young Lacy to a man
10 standing in the shadow behind a high lamp.

The person addressed started, and did not answer for a moment.
Then he laughed and said forcedly,

"Yes, wonderful for her age, she certainly is."

As he spoke his hostess, a fat and genial lady, came blandly
15 towards him.

"Mr Durrant, I'm so sorry we've no lady for you to take in to-night.
One or two people have thrown us over. I want to introduce you to
Miss Ambrose. Isn't she lovely? O, how stupid I am! Of course you
grew up in this neighbourhood, and must have known all about her as
20 a girl."

Jim Durrant it was, in the flesh; once the soldier, now the "traveller
and explorer" of the little known interiors of Asiatic countries; to use
the words in which he described himself. His foreign-looking and
sun-dried face was rather pale and set as he walked last into the
25 dining-room with young Lacy. He had only arrived on that day at an
hotel in the nearest town, where he had been accidentally met and
recognized by that young man, and asked to dinner off-hand.

6 there *2TS(2)TH* [*added*]   9 or two *2TS(2)TH* [*added*]   12 said forcedly,
1TS(2)TH] said— *1TS(1)*   13 wonderful for her age, *1TS*] wonderfully handsome
SG   14 hostess ... lady, *1TS(3)TH*] ... fat & smilin *1TS(2)TH* [*not continued*]]
hostess *1TS(1)*   14 blandly *2TS(2)TH*] smilingly *1TS* [ly *undeleted in 2TS*]
19 grew ... about her *1TS(2)TH*] knew her *1TS(1)*   21–3 flesh ... himself.
[*1TS(3)TH with later revisions*]] ... now the adventurer explorer *1TS(2)TH* [*not
continued*]] flesh— *1TS(1)* +   22 of the *1TS(4)TH*] of *1TS(3)TH* [*of deleted and
readded*]   22† interiors *1TS(3)TH*] interior *2TS*   22–3 to use the words in which
2TS(2)TH] so *1TS(3)TH*   23–4 foreign-looking and sun-dried *1TS(3)TH*] now
foreign-looking ... *1TS(2)TH* [*added*]   24 was *2TS(2)TH* [*added*]   24 set as
he *2TS(2)TH*] set, who *1TS*   27 that young man *2TS(2)TH*] young Lacy *1TS*
[young *undeleted in 2TS*]

Smiling, and apparently unconscious, he sat down on the left side of his hostess, talking calmly to her and across the table to the one or two he knew. Rosalys heard his voice as the phantom of a dead sound mingling with the usual trivial words and light laughter of the rest, Lord Parkhurst's conversation about Egyptian finance, and Mrs 5 Lacy's platitudes about the Home-Rule question, as if she were living through a curiously incoherent dream.

Suddenly during the progress of the dinner Mrs Lacy looked across with a glance of solicitude towards the other end of the table, and said in a low voice: 10

"I am afraid Miss Ambrose is rather overstrained—as she may naturally be? She looks *so* white and tired. Do you think, Parkhurst, that she finds this room too hot? I will have the window opened at the top."

"She does look pale," Lord Parkhurst murmured, and as he spoke 15 glanced anxiously and tenderly towards his betrothed. "I think too, she has a little over-taxed herself—she don't usually get so white as this."

Rosalys felt his eyes upon her, looked across at him, and smiled strangely. 20

When dinner was ended Rosalys still seemed not quite herself, whereupon she was taken in hand by her good and fussy hostess; sal-volatile was brought, and she was given the most comfortable chair and the largest cushions the house afforded. It seemed to Rosalys as if hours had elapsed before the men joined the ladies and there 25 came that general moving of places like the shuffling of a pack of cards. She heard Jim's voice speaking close to her ear:

"I want to have a word with you."

"I can't!" she faltered.

"Did you get my letter?" 30

"No!" said she.

1 side *2TS(2)TH*] hand *1TS*   3 two *1TS*] two whom *SG*   3–4 his voice . . . mingling with *1TS(3)TH* [*altered in same line*]] his voice, *1TS(2)TH* [*added*]   4 of the rest *1TS(2)TH* [*added*]   8† during . . . dinner *1TS(2)TH* [*added*]] . . . of dinner *2TS*   9 glance of solicitude *1TS(3)TH*] kindly, fat smile of solicitude *1TS(2)* [*comma and* of solicitude *TH;* of *deleted and readded*]] kindly fat smile *1TS(1)* 9–10 table . . . voice: *1TS(2)TH*] table. *1TS(1)*   12 think, *1TS(2)FHp&TH*] think, Lord *1TS(1)*   15 pale . . . murmured, and *2TS(2)* [*comma after* pale *and* murmured, and *TH*]] pale." Lord Parkhurst, *1TS*   17 don't *1TS*] doesn't *TD* 19 Rosalys *1TS(2)TH*] She *1TS(1)*   21 ended *2TS(2)TH*] over *1TS* 22 in *1TS* [*not in 2TS*]

"I wonder how that was! Well—I'll be at the door of Ambrose Towers while the stable-clock is striking twelve to-night. Be there to meet me. I'll not detain you long. We must have an understanding."

"For God's sake how do you come here?"

5 "I saw in the newspapers that you were going to marry. What could I do otherwise than let you know I was alive?"

"O, you might have done it less cruelly!"

"Will you be at the door?"

"I *must*, I suppose! . . . Don't tell him here—before these people! It
10 will be such an agonising disturbance that—"

"Of course I shan't. Be there."

This was all they could say. Lord Parkhurst came forward, and observing to Durrant, "They are wanting you for bézique," sat down beside Rosalys.

15 She had intended to go home early: and went even earlier than she had planned. At half-past ten she found herself in her own hall, not knowing how she had got there, or when she had bidden adieu to Lord Parkhurst, or what she had said to him.

Jim's letter was lying on the table awaiting her.

20 As soon as she had got upstairs and slipped into her dressing-gown, had dispatched her maid, and ascertained that all the household had retired, she read her husband's note, which briefly informed her that he had led an adventurous life since they had parted, and had come back to see if she were living, when he suddenly heard that she was
25 going to be married. Then Rosalys sat down at her writing-table to begin somehow a letter to Lord Parkhurst. To write that was an imperative duty before she slept. It need not be said that awful indeed to her was its object, the letting Lord Parkhurst know that she had a

1 was! *1TS(2)TH*] is! *1TS(1)*   4 For God's sake *2TS(2)TH [added]*   7 O,
2TS(2)TH [added]   9–11 suppose! . . . there." *2TS(2)* [an agonising *TH*]] . . .
such a disturbance . . . *1TS(3)TH*] . . . here—it will . . . *1TS(2)TH*] suppose!" *1TS(1)*
13 observing *1TS(2)TH*] saying *1TS(1)*   13 bézique *1TS(2)FHp&TH*] cards
1TS(1)   20 she had *1TS, 2TS(2)TH*] she *2TS(1)*   20 got upstairs and *1TS(2)TH*
[added]   23–5 he had . . . married. *2TS(3)* [to see . . . living *restored;* when he . . .
married *TH*]] . . . back lately <*illegible*> *2TS(2)* [lately *and illegible words THp*]] . . .
back to see if she were living *1TS(3)TH*] . . . back to claim her. *1TS(2)TH*] he had
come back. *2TS(2)TH*] [had come back *undeleted*]   25 Rosalys *2TS(2)TH*] she *1TS*
26 begin somehow *1TS(3)TH*] write *1TS(2)FHp*] pen *1TS(1)*   26 To write that
1TS(2)TH] That *1TS(1)* [*see TN*]   27–323. 1 awful . . . day. *2TS(3)* [awful . . .
the *TH, except for* its object; the *p&i*]] its object the letting . . . day. was awful *2TS(2)*
[the *and* was awful *THp*]] its object was the awful one, to her, of letting . . . day. *1TS(2)*
[its object *TH*]] the duty was . . . *1TS(1)*

husband, and had seen him that day. But she could not shape a single line, and the visioned aspect that she would wear in his eyes as soon as he discovered this truth of her history, was so terrible to her that she burst into hysterical sobbing over the paper as she sat.

The clock crept on to twelve before Rosalys had written a word.   5
The labour seemed Herculean—insuperable. Why had she not told him face to face?

Twelve o'clock it was; and nothing done; and controlling herself as women can, when they must, she went down to the door. Softly opening it a little way she saw against the iron gate immediately   10
without it the form of her husband, Jim Durrant—upon the whole much the same form that she had known eight years ago.

"Here I am," said he.

"Yes," said she.

"Open this iron thing."   15
A momentary feeling of aversion caused her to hesitate.

"Do you hear—do you mean to say—Rosalys!" he began.

"No—no. Of course I will!" She opened the grille and he came up and touched her hand lightly.

"Kissing not allowed, I suppose," he observed, with mock   20
solemnity, "in view of the fact that you are to be married to-morrow?"

"You know better!" she said. "Of course I'm not going to commit bigamy! The wedding is not to be."

"Have you explained to him?"

"N-no—not yet. I was just writing it when—"   25
"Ha—you haven't! Good. Woman's way. Shall I give him a friendly call to-morrow morning?"

"O no, no—let me do it!" she implored. "I love him so well, and it will break his poor heart if it is not done gently! O God—if I could only die to-night, while he still believes in me! You don't know what   30
affection I have felt for him!" she continued miserably, not caring

1–2 But . . . line, and *1TS(4)TH*] She could . . . *1TS(3)TH*] Before she had written a line *1TS(2)* [written *TH*]] . . . had penned a line *1TS(1)* [*see TN*]   3† discovered this *1TS*] discovered the *2TS*   5 Rosalys *2TS(2)TH*] she *1TS*   8–9 controlling . . . down *2TS(3)TH*] she went down *2TS(2)* [down *TH*]] down she went *1TS* 11–12 Durrant . . . ago. *1TS(2)TH*] . . . form she . . . *SG*] Durrant. *1TS(1)*   20 Kissing *1TS(2)TH*] A kiss is *SG*] Kissing is *1TS(1)*   20 suppose *1TS(2)FHp&TH*] presume *1TS(1)*   20 mock *1TS*] a mock *SG*   24† explained *1TS*] explained it *2TS*   25† N-no—not *1TS*] N—no—not *PR*   26 Woman's way. *1TS(2)TH* [*added*]   27 friendly *2TS(2)TH* [*added*]   29 poor *2TS(2)TH* [*added; not in SG*]

what Jim thought. "He has been my whole world! And he—he believes me to be so good! He has all the old-fashioned ideas of marriage that people of your fast sets smile at! He knows nothing of any kind of former acquaintance between you and me. I ought not to
5 have done it—kept him in the dark! I tried not to. But I was so fearfully lonely! And now I've lost him!. . . If I could only have got at that register in that City church, how I would have torn out the leaf!" she added vehemently.

"That's a pleasant remark to make to a husband!"
10 "Well—that was my feeling; I may as well be honest! I didn't know you were coming back any more; and you yourself suggested that I might be able to re-marry!"

"You'd better do it—I shan't tell. And if anybody else did, the punishment is not heavy nowadays. The judges are beginning to
15 discountenance informers on previous marriages, if the new-assorted parties themselves are satisfied to forget them."

"Don't insult me so. You've not forgotten how to do that in all these years!"

There was a silence, in which she regarded with passive gloom the
20 familiar scene before her. The inquisitive jays, the pensive wood-doves, that lodged at their ease thereabout, as if knowing that their proprietor was a gunless woman, all slept calmly; and not a creature was conscious of the presence of these two but a little squirrel they had disturbed in a beech near the shady wall. Durrant remained
25 gazing at her; then he spoke, in a changed and richer voice:

"Rosalys!"

She looked vaguely at his face without answering.

3 your fast sets *1TS(3)TH*] your fast set *SG*] your new school *1TS(2)* [your *FHp*]]
the new school *1TS(1)*   6 have got *1TS(2)TH*] get *1TS(1)*   6–7 at that *2TS(2)TH*]
at the *1TS*   7 have torn *1TS(2)TH*] tear *1TS(1)*   8 she added vehemently.
2TS(2)TH [*added*]   10 that was … honest! *1TS(2)TH* [*added*]   13 else
1TS(2)TH [*added*]   15–16 new-assorted parties *1TS(3)TH*] new-assorted
couples *SG*] parties *1TS(2)FHp&TH*] pairs *1TS(1)*   16 satisfied to forget them."
1TS(2)TH] satisfied." *1TS(1)*   19–22 silence … calmly; [*1TS(2)TH with later
revisions*]] silence: *1TS(1)* +   19† regarded with passive gloom *1TS(4)TH*]
with passive gloom regarded *2TS*] passively regarded *1TS(3)TH*] drearily regarded
1TS(2)TH   20 scene before her. *1TS(3)TH*] scene. *1TS(2)TH*   21–2 as if
… calmly; *2TS(2)* [*calmly TH*]] … slept soundly; *1TS(5)TH*] … a woman …
1TS(4)TH [*altered in same line*]] … slept, *1TS(3)TH*] all slept, knowing … woman
1TS(2)TH   23 of the *1TS(2)TH*] of their *1TS(1)* [*only ir deleted*]   23 of these
two *1TS(2)TH*] there *1TS(1)*   24 near *1TS(2)TH*] by *1TS(1)*   24 shady
2TS(2)TH] red *1TS*

"How pretty you look in this star-light—much as you did when we used to meet out here nine or ten years ago!"

"Ah! But—"

The sentence was broken by his abrupt movement forward. He seized her firmly in his arms, and kissed her repeatedly before she was aware.   5

"Don't—don't!" she said, struggling.

"Why?"

"I don't like you—I don't like you!"

"What rot! Yes, you do! Come—damn you, dear—put up your face   10 as you used to! Now, I'm not going off in a huff—I'm determined I won't; nor shall you either!... Let me sit down in your hall, or somewhere, Rosalys! I've come a long way to-day, and I'm tired. And after eight years!"

"I don't know what to say to it—there's no light downstairs! The   15 servants may hear us too—it is not so very late!"

"We can whisper. And suppose they do? They must know to-morrow!"

She gasped a sigh, and preceded him in through the door; and the squirrel saw nothing more.   20

VII

It was three-hours-and-half later when they re-appeared. The lawn was as silent as when they had left it, though the sleep of things had weakened to a certain precarious slightness; and round the corner of the house a low line of light showed the dawn.   25

2† out *1TS* [*not in 2TS+*]   4–12 The sentence ... Let *PR*] '... Let *SG* [*ellipsis in SG; i.e. 4–12 (up to ellipsis) omitted*] +   5 repeatedly *PR(2)TH* [*added*] 10–11 Come ... to! *2TS(2)* [face *TH*]] ... your mouth as ... *1TS(3)TH*] ... you— put ... *1TS(2)TH* [*added*]   12–13 or somewhere, *1TS(2)TH* [*added*] 13 to-day, *1TS(2)TH* [*added*]   13–14 And after eight years! *1TS(3)TH*] After ... *1TS(2)TH* [*added*]   17 We can whisper. And *1TS(2)TH*] But *1TS(1)* 19–20 door ... more. *1TS*] door. ¶ 'Yes, they must!' she said. *SG* +   20 squirrel *1TS, PR(2)TH*] innocent squirrel *2TS(2)THp&i* [squirrel *undeleted*]   22 It was ... The [*PR(2) with 1TS(2)TH emendation*]] When they re-appeared the *SG* + 22 It was *PR(2)TH* [*added*]   22† three-hours-and-half *1TS(2)TH*] Three hours and a half *1TS(1), 2TS*   22 when *PR(2)TH* [*added*]   22 re-appeared. *2TS(2)TH*] re-emerged. *1TS* [re- *undeleted in 2TS*]   23–4† though ... slightness; *1TS(2)TH* [*added; see TN*]] ... weakened down to ... *2TS(2)* [weakened down *TH*]] ... had wakened to ... *2TS(1)*

"Now, good-bye, dear," said her husband, lightly. "You'll let him know at once?"

"Of course."

"And send to me directly after?"

5 "Yes."

"And now for my walk across the fields to the hotel. These boots are thin, but I know the old way well enough. By Jove, I wonder what Mélanie—"

"Who?"

10 "O—what Mélanie will think, I was going to say. It slipped out—I didn't mean to hurt your feelings at all."

"Mélanie—who is she?"

"Well—she's a French lady. You know, of course, Rosalys, that I thought you were perhaps dead—and—so this lady passes as Mrs

15 Durrant."

Rosalys started.

"In fact I found her in the East, and took pity upon her—that's all. Though if it had happened that you had not been living now I have got back, I should of course, have married her at once."

20 "Is—she, then, here with you at the hotel?"

"O no—I wouldn't bring her on here till I knew how things were."

"Then where is she?"

"I left her at my rooms in London. O, it will be all right—I shall see her safely back to Paris, and make a little provision for her. Nobody in

25 England knows anything of her existence."

"When—did you part from her?"

"Well, of course, at breakfast-time."

Rosalys bowed herself against the doorway. "O—O—what have I

4–5 "And send ... Yes." *1TS(2)TH* [*added*] 6–7 These boots ... but *2TS(3)TH*]
My boots are thin enough, but *2TS(2)TH* [*added*] 7 Jove *1TS(2)FHp&TH*] Gad
1TS(1) 8 Mélanie—" *1TS(1)* [*restored*]] Mélanie is doing at this—" *1TS(2)TH*
[*deleted*] 12 Mélanie— *1TS(2)TH* [*added*] 14 and—so *1TS(2)TH*] and
1TS(1) 15–17 Durrant. ... fact *1TS(2)TH*] Durrant. *1TS(1)* 17–18 her—
that's all. Though *1TS(2)TH*] her. *1TS(1)* 18 it had happened that *2TS(2)TH*
[*added*] 18–19 living ... back, *2TS(2)TH*] living, *1TS* 19† of course ...
once." *1TS(1)*] have married her at once, of course." *2TS(3)* [at once." *TH*]]
... her long ago, of course. *2TS(2)* [long ago, of course. *TH*]] ... her now at once."
2TS(1) [have married her *undeleted*]] of course, have married her now at once." *1TS(2)*
[now *TH*] 20 here *1TS(2)TH* [*added*] 21–3 were. ... "I *1TS(2)TH*]
were. I *1TS(1)* [*undeleted*] 23 rooms *1TS(2)FHp&TH*] hotel *1TS(1)*
28–327. 3 doorway. ... Jim *1TS(2)*] doorway, and Jim *SG +*

done! What a fool—what a weak fool!" she moaned. "Go away from me—go away!"

Jim was almost distressed when he saw the distortion of her agonized face. "Now why should you take on like this! There's nothing in it. People do these things. Living in a prim society here you don't know how the world goes on!"

"O, but to think it didn't occur to me that the sort of man—"

Jim, though anxious, seemed to awaken to something humorous in the situation, and vented a momentary chuckle. "Well, it is rather funny that I should have let it out. But still—"

"Don't make a deep wrong deeper by cruel levity! Go away!"

"You'll be in a better mood to-morrow, mark me, and then I'll tell you all my history. There—I'm gone! *Au revoir!*"

He disappeared under the trees. Rosalys, rousing herself, closed the gate and fastened the door, and sat down in one of the hall chairs, her teeth shut tight, and her little hands clenched. When she had passed this mood, and returned upstairs, she regarded the state of her room sadly, and bent again over her writing-table, murmuring "O, how weak, how weak was I!"

But in a few minutes she found herself nerved to an unexpected and passionate vigour of action; and began writing her letter to Lord Parkhurst with great rapidity. Sheet after sheet she filled, and, having read them over, she sealed up the letter and placed it on the mantelpiece to be given to a groom and dispatched by hand as soon as the morning was a little further advanced.

1 weak *1TS(2)TH* [*added*]   3 distressed *2TS(2)TH*] frightened *1TS*
4 agonized *1TS(2)TH* [*added*]   5–13 "Now ... "You'll *2TS(2)* [*see below for TH additions*]] "Now ... in it. Living ... "You'll *1TS(5)TH* [*see TN*]] "Now ... goes on. You'll *1TS(4)TH*] "But why ... in it. "Now you'll *1TS(3)TH*] "W<e> *1TS(2)TH* [*not continued*]] "Now you'll *1TS(1)* [*undeleted*] +   6 People do these things. *2TS(2)TH* [*added*]   6 here *1TS(4)TH*] like this *1TS(3)TH*   9 awaken to *2TS(2)TH*] see *1TS(5)TH*   12 cruel *2TS(2)TH*] mean *1TS(5)TH*   13–14 me ... There *1TS(2)TH*] me," he said soothingly. "There *1TS(1)* [There *undeleted*] 15 trees. *1TS(2)TH*] trees, and *1TS(1)*   15 Rosalys, rousing herself, *1TS(2)TH*] Rosalys *1TS(1)*   17 shut *1TS(2)TH*] closed *1TS(1)*   17 little *1TS(2)TH* [*added*] 17–18 had passed ... returned *2TS(3)TH* [*altered in same line*]] ... and gone *2TS(2)TH*] got *1TS*   18–19 regarded ... sadly, and *2TS(2)* [the state of *TH*]] regarded her ... *1TS(2)TH* [*added; not in SG*]   writing-table ... I!" *1TS*] writing-table and wept. *SG*   21 few minutes *1TS(2)TH*] minute *1TS(1)* [*undeleted*] 22 passionate *1TS(2)TH*] frigid *1TS(1)*   23 filled, and, *1TS(1)*, *2TS(2)TH*] filled, when, *1TS(2)TH*   24 over, she *1TS(2)TH*] over, and *1TS(1)*   24 letter and *1TS(2)TH*] letter she *1TS(1)*   26 morning *2TS(2)TH*] day *1TS*

With cold feet and a burning head she flung herself upon the bed just as she was, and waited for the day without the power to sleep. When she had lain nearly two hours, and the morning had crept in, and she could hear from the direction of the stables that the men were
5 astir, she rang for her maid, and taking the letter in her hand stood with it in an attitude of suspense as the woman entered. The latter looked full of intelligence.

"Are any of the men about?" asked Rosalys.

"O yes, ma'am. There've been such an accident in the meads this
10 past night—about half-a-mile down the river—and Jones ran up from the lodge to call for help quite early; and Benton and Peters went as soon as they were dressed. A gentleman drowned—yes—it's Mr James Durrant—the son of old Mr Durrant who died some years ago. He came home only yesterday, after having been heard nothing of for
15 years and years. He left Mrs Durrant, who they say is a French lady, somewhere in London, but they have telegraphed and found her, and she's coming. They say she's quite distracted. The poor gentleman left the Three Lions last night and went out to dinner, saying he would walk home, as it was a fine night and not very far: and it is
20 supposed he took the old short cut across the moor where there used to be a path when he was a lad at home, crossing the big river by a plank. There is only a rail now, and he must have tried to get across upon it, for it was broken in two, and his body found in the water-weeds just below."

25 "Is he—dead?"

"O yes. They had a great trouble to get him out. The men have just come in from carrying him to the hotel. It will be sad for his poor wife when she gets there!"

"His poor wife—yes."

30 "Travelling all the way from London on such a call!"

Rosalys had allowed the hand in which she held the letter to Lord

3–4 the morning ... and she *1TS(3)TH*] & the morning ... *1TS(2)TH* [*added*]
4 men *1TS(2)FHp&TH*] stable-men *1TS(1)* [-men *undeleted*]   5 taking the *1TS*]
taking her *SGa*   6 the woman *1TS(2)FHp&TH*] her maid *1TS(1)*   6 latter
1TS(2)FHp&TH] maid *1TS(1)*   9† O yes *1TS*] Yes *2TS*   9† There've *1TS*]
There have *PR*   10 —about ... river— *1TS(2)TH* [*added*]   13† old *1TS*]
the *2TS(2)TH* [*not in 2TS(1), SG*]   18 Lions *2TS(2)TH*] Crown *2TS(1)*]
Crowns *1TS*   26 They had ... out. *1TS(2)TH* [*added; see TN*]   27† come
in *1TS*] come *2TS*   29–30 "His poor ... call!" *1TS(2)TH* [*added; see TN*]] ...
such an errand!' *SG*   31 had allowed ... held *1TS(2)TH*] put *1TS(1)*

Parkhurst to drop to her side: she now put it in the pocket of her dressing-gown.

"I was wishing to send somewhere," she said. "But I think I will wait till later."

The house was astir betimes on account of the wedding, and 5 Rosalys' companion in particular, who was not sad because she was going to live on with the bride. When Miss Jennings saw her cousin's agitation she said she looked ill, and insisted upon sending for the doctor. He, who was the local practitioner, arrived at breakfast time; very proud to attend such an important lady, who mostly got 10 doctored in London. He said Rosalys certainly was not quite in her usual state of health; prescribed a tonic, and declared that she would be all right in an hour or two. He then informed her that he had been suddenly called up that morning to the case of which they had possibly heard—the drowning of Mr Durrant. 15

"And you could do nothing?" asked Rosalys.

"O no. He'd been under water too long for any human aid. Dead and stiff.... It was not so very far down from here.... Yes, I remember him quite as a boy. But he has had no relations hereabout for years past—old Durrant's property was sold to pay his debts, if 20 you recollect; and nobody expected to see the son again. I think he has lived in the East Indies a good deal. Much better for him if he had not come—poor fellow!"

When the doctor had left Rosalys went to the window, and remained for some time thinking. There was the lake from which the 25

---

1 to drop ... put it *1TS(2)TH* [*added*] 3 will *1TS, SGa*] shall *SG* 5 astir *1TS, PR(2)TH*] bestir *PR(1)* [stir *undeleted*] 5-7 wedding ... bride. *1TS(2)TH*] wedding. *1TS(1)* 7-8 cousin's agitation *2TS(2)TH*] cousin *1TS* [*undeleted in 2TS*] 10 such an *1TS(2)FH.?p*] such a *1TS(1)* [*undeleted*] 10 important *1TS(2)FHp&TH*] prominent *1TS(1)* 10-11 lady ... He *1TS(2)TH*] ... who usually got ... *SG*] lady; *1TS(1)* 11 Rosalys certainly *1TS*] that Rosalys *SG* 12 usual *1TS*] ordinary *SG* 14† up that morning to *1TS*] up that morning about *SG*] upon that morning in *2TS* 17-18 Dead ... here.... *1TS(3)TH* [*2nd ellipsis TH*]] Dead and stiff. *1TS(2)THp&i* [*added*] 19 hereabout *1TS(2)TH*] here *1TS(1)* [*undeleted*] 20 sold ... debts, *PR(2)TH*] sold, *1TS* 21 recollect *1TS(2)TH*] remember *1TS(1)* [re *undeleted*] 21 the son *1TS(2)TH*] him *1TS(1)* 21-2 I think ... deal. *1TS(2)TH* [*added*] 24 went to the window, and *1TS(2)THp&i* [*added*] 25-330. 3 There was ... Mélanie. *2TS* [had *(preceding* drowned*) TH*]] ... his life with ... *SG*] ... down to the ... his continuous life of caresses with ... *TD*] ... down the river that drowned ... *1TS(4)TH*] ... her, as an interlude in his intimate life with ... *1TS(3)TH* [*added*]] The lake was before her, & from the mud at the edge *1TS(2)TH* [*not continued; see TN*]

water had flowed down the river that had drowned Jim after visiting
her last night—as a mere interlude in his continuous life of caresses
with the Frenchwoman Mélanie. She turned, took from her dressing-
gown pocket the renunciatory letter to her intended husband Lord
5 Parkhurst, thrust it through the bars of the grate, and watched it till it
was entirely consumed.

The wedding had been fixed for an early hour in the afternoon, and
as the morning wore on Rosalys felt increasing strength, mental and
physical. The doctor's dose had been a powerful one: the image of
10 "Mélanie", too, had much to do with her recuperative mood; more
still, Rosalys' innate qualities; the nerve of the woman who nine years
earlier had gone to the city to be married as if it were a mere shopping
expedition; most of all, she loved Lord Parkhurst; he was the man
among all men she desired. Rosalys allowed things to take their
15 course.

Soon the dressing began; and she sat through it quite calmly. When
Lord Parkhurst rode across for a short visit that day he only noticed
that she seemed strung-up, nervous, and that the flush of love which
mantled her cheek died away to pale rather quickly.
20 On the way to church the road skirted the low-lying ground where
the river was, and about a dozen men were seen in the bright green
meadow, standing beside the deep central stream, and looking
intently at a broken rail.

"Who are those men?" said the bride.
25 "O—they are the coroner's jury, I think," said Miss Jennings;
"come to view the place where that unfortunate Mr Durrant lost his
life last night. It was curious that, by the merest accident, he should
have been at Mrs Lacy's dinner,—since they hardly know him at all."

3 turned, *1TS(2)TH* [*see TN*]] then *1TS(1)*   4 renunciatory *1TS(2)TH*
[*added*]   4–5 intended ... Parkhurst, *1TS(2)TH*] affianced husband, *1TS(1)*
[husband *undeleted*]   10 much *1TS(2)TH*] something *1TS(1)*   10 her
recuperative mood *1TS(2)TH*] it *1TS(1)*   13 Parkhurst; he *1TS(2)TH*]
Parkhurst; and a title was a handy thing, a very handy thing, for a woman with a big
house and park like hers. She honestly owned it to herself; but, in justice to her, it *1TS(1)*
[*deletion to end of 1st sentence FHp&TH*]   14 among all men she *2TS* [among *and* she
TH]] she of all men *1TS(2)TH*] she most *1TS(1)* [she *undeleted*]   14 Rosalys
1TS(2)TH] She *1TS(1)*   19 away to *1TS(2)TH*] away *1TS(1)*   20 On the
1TS(2)TH] On their *1TS(1)* [*only* ir *deleted*]   20–1 the road ... was, and *1TS(2)TH*
[*added*]   21 bright green *1TS(2)TH* [*added*]   26† where that *1TS*] where the *PR*
27–331. 2 last ... church. [*1TS(2)TH with later revisions*]] yesterday." *1TS(1)* +
27 last night *2TS(2)TH*] yesterday *1TS*   27 It was *1TS(3)TH* [*added*]
28 since *1TS(3)TH*] when *1TS(2)TH*   28† know *1TS*] knew *2TS*

"It was—I saw him there," said Rosalys.

They had reached the church. Ten minutes later she was kneeling against the altar-railings, with Lord Parkhurst on her right hand.

The wedding was by no means a gay one, and there were few people invited, Rosalys, for one thing, having hardly any relations. The newly united pair got away from the house very soon after the ceremony. When they drove off there was a group of people round the door, and some among the bystanders asked how far they were going that day.

"To Dover. They cross the Channel to-morrow, I believe."

To-morrow came, and those who had gathered together at the wedding went about their usual duties and amusements, Colonel Lacy among the rest. As he and his wife were returning home by the late afternoon train after a short journey up the line, he bought a copy of an evening paper, and glanced at the latest telegrams.

"My good God!" he cried.

"What?" said she, starting towards him.

He tried to read—then handed the paper; and she read for herself:

"D O V E R.—DEATH OF LORD PARKHURST, R.N.—

"We regret to announce that this distinguished nobleman and "heroic naval officer, who arrived with Lady Parkhurst last evening at "the Lord Chamberlain Hotel in this town, preparatory to starting on "their wedding-tour, entered his dressing-room very early this "morning, and shot himself through the head with a revolver. The "report was heard shortly after dawn, none of the inmates of the hotel "being astir at the time. No reason can be assigned for the rash act."

T H E   E N D.

2† They had reached the church. *1TS(2)TH* [*not in 2TS+*]   7–8 there was ... door, and *1TS(2)TH* [*added*]   10 to-morrow, I believe. *1TS(2)TH*] to-morrow. *1TS(1)*   14 late afternoon *1TS(2)TH*] evening *1TS(1)*   20–1 nobleman ... officer, *1TS(3)TH*] hero *1TS(2)THp* [*added as a possible alternative above the undeleted* nobleman *and later absorbed in* heroic]] nobleman, *1TS(1)*

Blue Jimmy: The Horse Stealer *and* The Unconquerable

INTRODUCTION

'The Spectre of the Real' is not Hardy's only collaborative work, though it is the only one he publicly acknowledged. As early as 1876 he had been sent for criticism a story by Evangeline Smith, the twenty-two-year-old sister of his long-time friend, Reginald Bosworth Smith. Hardy wrote comments on Smith's manuscript and in a covering letter made numerous suggestions, ranging from the desirability of omitting specific scenes to the necessity of writing 'in a clear round hand in a first MS'.[1] The story was apparently not published, though Smith did subsequently publish three novels. Hardy's tone when addressing her was (appropriately enough) that of the established author advising the novice—a tone not markedly different from that he used nearly twenty years later when writing to Agnes Grove, the woman who succeeded Florence Henniker as his literary protégée and, to a lesser extent, as the object of his romantic attentions.[2] The wife of Walter (later Sir Walter) Grove and the daughter of the archaeologist General Augustus Lane Fox Pitt-Rivers, Grove moved in the same aristocratic and fashionable circles as Henniker and also shared her predecessor's strong literary ambitions. At the time of her meeting with Hardy in 1895, however, she had published nothing of substance and was understandably flattered by his attentions, apparently never objecting to his condescension, even when it resulted in her being referred to as 'a good little pupil'[3]—something Henniker never was. Hardy and Grove did not embark on a formal collaborative venture—Hardy had perhaps learned his lesson with Henniker—but he did revise her drafts, help to place her work, and correct her proofs.[4] On occasion he even suggested essay topics of current interest, one of which she worked up and published in two parts as 'Our Children. What Children Should Be Told' (*Free Review* (July 1896)), a

---

[1] *CL* i. 46.   [2] See *Biography*, 365–6.   [3] 24 Mar. 1896 (*CL* ii. 117).
[4] See TH's letters to Grove in *CL* ii.

modestly liberal contribution to the contemporary debate on religious and sexual mores,[5] Hardy was most active as Grove's mentor from 1895 to 1900, but as late as 1907 he was reading proofs of her book, *The Social Fetich*, a light-hearted commentary on current manners. The proofs survive[6] and contain numerous Hardyan revisions—almost all adopted by Grove—from grammatical corrections to suggestions for toning down some class-determined and consequently snobbish remarks. By this time, however, more of his attention was being claimed by his most recent literary protégée, Florence Dugdale, the woman who in 1914 would become his second wife.

The daughter of Edward Dugdale, an Enfield schoolmaster, and his wife Emma, a former governess, Dugdale was herself a teacher, but by the early 1900s (when she was in her early twenties) she had begun contributing occasional articles, stories, and theatrical reviews to the local newspaper in the hope of becoming a professional writer, both for writing's sake and as a means of escape from her much disliked teaching.[7] When Dugdale and Hardy met in 1905 she had already published several pamphlet-length stories for the Society for Promoting Christian Knowledge—including *Little Lie-a-bed; and Other Stories* ([1903]), *Jack Deane's Reward* ([1905]), and *Jennie, Who Did Not Like Christmas* ([1905])—and was about to publish a volume of stories for Collins, *Old Time Tales* ([1906]). Several other books appeared shortly thereafter: *Tim's Sister* (SPCK, [1907]), *Cousin Christine* (Collins, [1907]), and *Country Life* (Collins, [1908]).[8] All are, however, children's stories of thoroughly conventional kinds, for the most part overtly didactic morality tales or sentimentalized sketches involving small creatures. Hardy appears to have had no part in the production of these works, though in a letter of 21 March 1907 he did advise Dugdale to insist on twenty-one guineas—rather than the offered eight pounds—for writing 21,000 words of children's fiction (presumably the stories which subsequently appeared in *Country Life*).[9]

Hardy's active involvement in Dugdale's career seems in fact only to have come to the fore in 1907, perhaps in part because the April closure of the British Museum Library for extensive renovation pre-

---

[5] Ibid. 101, 114–18, 120.   [6] Beinecke.

[7] See *Biography*, 444–6, and Robert Gittings and Jo Manton, *The Second Mrs Hardy* (London: Heinemann, 1979), 24 ff.

[8] *Eminent Women* (Collins, n.d.) was presumably also published during this period.

[9] *CL* iii. 249.

vented his continuing to offer her employment—some of which had probably been invented[10]—as his research assistant. On 8 July 1907 he recommended Dugdale to Maurice Macmillan as someone 'well qualified to be of assistance to your firm in the preparation of school books & supplementary readers', and the following day he wrote to Archibald Marshall, the editor of the *Daily Mail* books supplement, suggesting that she might be 'of use in one or other department of the paper', perhaps 'in reviewing books for the young'.[11]

Hardy's influence was almost certainly responsible for Reginald Smith's acceptance in September of her 'The Apotheosis of the Minx', published in the *Cornhill* the following May,[12] and it is highly probable that his participation extended beyond the mere placing of the story. Certainly the tale represents a departure from most of Dugdale's earlier fiction, not only in its being addressed to an adult audience but also in its distinctly Hardyan plot. Robert Engle, a young assistant-teacher with 'the soul of a poet' but entrapped by the sordid drudgery of the schoolroom, believes that he has found 'the embodiment of his most ecstatic vision' in Etty Clark, in reality a frivolous and ambitious dressmaker's assistant; she, unable to see 'the passion that consume[s] him', is frustrated by his restrained manner and vociferously upbraids him, shattering his illusions and ending their very short-lived relationship.[13] Etty subsequently marries a handsome and rising grocer's assistant, but dies during her first confinement; Engle, meeting the grieving widower, learns to his amazement that he had himself been the only man Etty ever loved, and promptly creates 'an ideal image . . . obscuring all her faults, annihilating all her sordidness, and winning his worship'.[14] Hearing a year later that her former husband is to remarry, Engle joyously claims the idealized Etty as his own and finds unutterable happiness in 'this dream of one who was his own creation'.[15] Though the bleak account of Engle's frustrations as a teacher, so strongly reminiscent of Dugdale's own experiences, suggests her authorship—as, indeed, does the insipid prose style, generously sprinkled with overblown romantic clichés—the story's emphasis on the search for the ideal and especially its contrapuntal ironic structure point to a not inconsiderable involvement on Hardy's part.

[10] As she herself acknowledged in a letter of 20 Mar. 1937 to Carroll Wilson (copy, Beinecke).
[11] *CL* iii. 261–2.　　[12] See TH to Smith, 26 Sept. 1907 (*CL* iii. 274).
[13] *Cornhill*, NS 24 (1908), 647, 644, 646.
[14] Ibid. 651.　　[15] Ibid. 653.

Much the same can be said of 'The Scholar's Wife', a Hawthornesque tale recalling 'Rappaccini's Daughter' in its Italian setting, use of archaic language for dialogue, and portrait of a learned scholar compounding deadly poisons, but distinctly Hardyan in its concluding ironic twist. The scholar, overhearing a declaration of love between his young wife Alis and her 'gay and light of foot' cousin Doria, resolves to poison all three of them when Doria returns from a brief journey; however, the expected absence 'of some days' extends to one of some months and Alis, hearing no tidings, sickens.[16] When at last Alis learns from her husband that Doria is about to return, her joy is so irrepressible that the scholar pities her and decides that he alone will die, though only 'if she so wills it'.[17] He shows her the lethal liquid he has created and she grasps the opportunity, poisoning his wine on the day of her cousin's return, only to hear that Doria has married; the bride and groom find Alis dead beside her husband, a phial on the floor at her feet. Hardy, recommending the story in July 1908 to H. Greenough Smith, editor of the *Strand Magazine*, wrote: 'it is somewhat lurid & sensational, but not too much so for the supposed date [the sixteenth century], & to my mind it is well told & striking.'[18] Dugdale's use of archaisms, unlike Hawthorne's in 'Rappaccini's Daughter', is in fact so stilted as to seem parodic ('Art wearied, good wife? ... a wife is a good gift verily, and I am neither hoar nor old, so we will have lavish time of bliss together yet'[19]) and it is evident that Hardy's literary judgement was obscured—or overruled—by his personal feelings for Dugdale. 'The Scholar's Wife' was rejected by Smith, but Hardy, undeterred, evidently sent it to Clement Shorter: it was almost certainly the 'rather good little story' recommended for the *Sphere* or the *Tatler* in August 1908.[20] This attempt to place the story was also unsuccessful, though it was eventually published—no doubt at Hardy's renewed instigation—in the *Pall Mall Magazine*, January 1909.

Hardy was also instrumental in placing Dugdale's 'Trafalgar! How Nelson's Death Inspired the Tailor'. Arguably the worst of her stories written for adults, 'Trafalgar!' briefly recounts how during a Ramblers' Society visit to the *Victory* a 'silent, sullen, puny and dull-faced' tailor is 'transfigured' when he—to the considerable astonishment of his neighbours—breaks into a moving rendition of 'The

---

[16] *Pall Mall Magazine*, 43 (1909), 79, 80.   [17] Ibid. 81.   [18] *CL* vii. 147.
[19] *Pall Mall Magazine*, 80.   [20] *CL* iii. 329.

Death of Nelson'.[21] The plot is not particularly Hardyan, but that Hardy introduced some revisions (as he presumably did to both 'The Apotheosis of the Minx' and 'The Scholar's Wife') is clear from a letter to Dugdale of September 1909: 'The sketch reads remarkably well. If you feel you do not like my supposed improvements, rub them out; though I *advise* you to recopy the story just as it now stands.'[22] Hardy went on to suggest that she send the story, accompanied by a letter of recommendation from him, to the *Daily Mail*, then (if unsuccessful) to the *Daily Chronicle*, then to the *Daily News*, 'or [to] any other you think of'. This list of alternatives suggests that Hardy had accurately estimated the story's minimal literary merit, and indeed Dugdale did not succeed in getting it accepted. A year later, however, when the anniversary of Trafalgar was again approaching, Hardy wrote in almost peremptory terms to James Milne, then on the staff of the *Daily Chronicle*:

I am sending you for the Daily Chronicle a little topical sketch that was forwarded to the paper a year ago by the author, for publication on Oct 21. I have just read it, & have come to the conclusion that its rejection on that occasion must have been owing to oversight or press of matter, for it is about the only thing left to say in print concerning Trafalgar Day, & it is, moreover, said well, & with real literary art. If you & the Editor tell me that the Daily Chronicle does not want literature I have, of course, no answer to make.[23]

Such a letter from an author of Hardy's standing—he had earlier that year been awarded the Order of Merit—was little short of coercive, and the story duly appeared on 21 October 1910.

The following February Dugdale's 'Blue Jimmy: The Horse Stealer' was published in the *Cornhill*. According to Gittings, the story had been 'entirely written by [Hardy], and passed off as [Dugdale's]',[24] and Purdy accepts the presence of Hardy's hand on the surviving *Cornhill* proofs[25] as a basis for including 'Blue Jimmy' among Hardy's uncollected works.[26] The actual situation, however, was by no means so straightforward. On 12 August 1910 Hardy— neglecting, perhaps deliberately, to mention Dugdale's earlier *Cornhill* contribution, 'The Apotheosis of the Minx'—had written to Smith:

[21] *Daily Chronicle*, 21 Oct. 1910, 4.   [22] *CL* iv. 45.
[23] 20 Sept. 1910 (*CL* iv. 117).
[24] Robert Gittings, *The Older Hardy* (London: Heinemann, 1978), 180.
[25] Adams.   [26] Purdy, 314.

At last I send the story—or rather record—I spoke about: "Blue Jimmy the horse-stealer". It seems interesting to me, &, if I may say so, worthy of the Cornhill, even if only from the novelty of its subject. I hope you will think the same. The writer has been at some pains to hunt up the particulars at the British Museum, & I gave her also a few traditional ones. I can guarantee the truth of the story—if truth has any virtue in such a case.[27]

The epigraph to 'Blue Jimmy', as the story's opening paragraph acknowledges, is in fact a quotation of Hardy's own allusion to the notorious horse-thief in 'A Trampwoman's Tragedy'—a ballad, amusingly enough, that Smith had declined in 1902 'on the ground of it not being a poem he could possibly print in a family periodical'.[28] As early as 1884, during his systematic reading of the 1826–30 files of the *Dorset County Chronicle and Somersetshire Gazette*,[29] Hardy had summarized in his 'Facts' notebook the 3 May 1827 report of the final trial and execution of James Clace (better known as Blue Jimmy):

Notorious Horse stealer—"Blue Jemmy" [*sic*]—at Ilchester (executed)—had stolen more than 100 horses. Came to Crown & anchor Misterton, with a horse. Landlord having heard his fame as a horsestealer went & looked at horse—was offered him at £25, afterw^ds £19—much less than value. Land^d did not buy, but privately cut 3 notches in mane of mare. Following day a handbill was left at house, offering reward for the recovery of a mare that had been stolen. Land^d pointed out direction in wh. the prisoner went. Finding himself pursued prisoner left horse concealed in a pit. . . . Prisoner had been brought to bar 19 times.[30]

A pencilled annotation points also to Hardy's local knowledge of Blue Jimmy's exploits: 'He stole a horse belonging to W. Keats's father: grazing in Bock^n Lane.' Since *Life* identifies William Keats as the tranter who 'had been the many years' neighbour of the Hardys, and did the haulage of building materials for Hardy's father, of whom he also rented a field for his horses',[31] it must be to this same incident that Hardy refers in one of his published notes to 'A Trampwoman's Tragedy':

[27] *CL* iv. 114.   [28] *Life*, 341; see *CL* iii. 58–9.

[29] See Michael Millgate, *Thomas Hardy: His Career as a Novelist* (London: The Bodley Head, 1971), 237.

[30] 'Facts' notebook, 64–5 (DCM); TH's ellipsis. The large number of notebook quotations on the same general subject suggests that TH considered including some kind of horse-stealing episode in a future work.

[31] *Life*, 94.

"Blue Jimmy" ... was a notorious horse-stealer of Wessex in those days, who appropriated more than a hundred horses before he was caught, among others one belonging to a neighbour of the writer's grandfather. He was hanged at the now demolished Ivel-chester or Ilchester jail ... that building formerly of so many sinister associations in the minds of the local peasantry ... Its site is now an innocent-looking green meadow.[32]

Hardy gave Dugdale a copy of *Time's Laughingstocks* in December 1909,[33] and it may well have been her reading of the ballad and its accompanying notes which led to the writing of 'Blue Jimmy'. The note just quoted is certainly echoed, with the kind of floral amplification so typical of Dugdale, in her description of the 'county gaol— till lately remembered, though now removed—on the edge of a wide expanse of meadow-land, spread at that season of the year with a carpet of butter-cups and daisies'. Dugdale's primary sources, however, were the newspaper accounts that, according to Hardy, she had 'been at some pains to hunt up ... at the British Museum',[34] specifically the 3 May 1827 *Dorset County Chronicle* paragraph summarized in Hardy's 'Facts' notebook and directly cited at the conclusion of 'Blue Jimmy', and the reports of the 1825 and 1827 Somerset Lent Assizes in the *Taunton Courier and Western Advertiser* and the *Dorset County Chronicle*. Although the basic details—names, dates, places, prices, and so forth—of Jimmy's theft and resale of a mare as given at his 28 March 1825 trial and reported two days later in the *Taunton Courier* are embellished by description and dialogue in the early scenes of 'Blue Jimmy', the fictionalized account directly incorporates many of the newspaper's phrases:

Witness [Wheller] asked Wilkins if he knew Prisoner; he said he knew him well, that he was a ... small farmer, and worth thousands. The ensuing day witness discovered that the mare was startish, and went in search of prisoner, whom he found at the Golden Heart, in Coombe St. Nicholas, and told him that he suspected he did not come honestly by the mare, and therefore requested to have back his money and his cart-horse. Prisoner said he was quite willing so to do, and called to the landlady for a pipe and some beer, and immediately brushed out at the back door ... (*Taunton Courier*)

Wilkins ... assured Wheller that he knew the seller well, and that he was a farmer worth thousands ...

[32] *Time's Laughingstocks* (Wessex Edition), 274; 'among others one belonging to a neighbour of the writer's grandfather' does not appear in the first (1909) edition.
[33] Purdy, 150.   [34] *CL* iv. 114.

Wheller did not suspect that anything was wrong till he found the next day that the animal was what he called "startish" ... He went in search of [Jimmy], and eventually found him at that ancient hostel "The Golden Heart" at Coombe St. Nicholas ...

[Wheller said, "I] suspect that you did not come honestly by that mare, and request to have back my money and cart-horse, when I'll return her." ...

["T]hat I'm quite willing to do. Here, landlady! A pipe and ale for this gentleman. ..."

Blue Jimmy went out at the back ... ('Blue Jimmy')

W. Yeo deposed to the mare having four black streaks down her right fore foot, and to her tail having been stringed in a particular manner. ... Was certain it was the same mare that he broke in for prosecutor, and never before saw a horse or mare so particularly marked. (*Taunton Courier*)

"She has four black streaks down her right fore-foot, and her tail is 'stringed' so"—here he described ... the particular manner in which the tail had been prepared ... [He] was certain it was the same mare ... He had broken it in for Mr Sheppard, and never before had known a mare so peculiarly marked. ('Blue Jimmy')

As Dugdale's narrative progresses it becomes increasingly dependent on its printed sources. Other details of the 28 March trial are taken almost verbatim from the 30 March *Taunton Courier*:

The prosecutor could not swear positively to the marks as described by the last witness.—The Learned Judge, in summing up, directed the Jury to consider whether the identity of the mare had been so indubitably proved as to warrant them in pronouncing the prisoner guilty, and suggested that the marks, described by the prisoner [*sic*] Yeo, might be found upon other horses. It was remarkable, his Lordship observed, that Wilkins, who was present when Wheller bought the horse, although the nephew of the latter, and living within half a mile of him, had not been brought into Court, to give evidence, when witnesses from so considerable a distance as Cornwall had been examined. (*Taunton Courier*)

Mr Sheppard, when cross-examined on the marks described by his assistant Yeo, declared he could not swear positively to any of them.

The learned Judge, in summing up, directed the jury to consider whether the identity of the mare had been so indubitably proved as to warrant them in pronouncing the prisoner guilty, and suggested that the marks described by the witness Yeo might be found upon many horses. "It was remarkable," his Lordship observed, "that Wilkins, who was present when Wheller bought the horse, although the nephew of the latter, and living within half a mile of him, had not been brought into court to give evidence, though witnesses from so considerable a distance as Cornwall had been examined." ('Blue Jimmy')

The degree of correspondence with an 11 April 1827 *Taunton Courier* paragraph—possibly also printed in the *Dorset County Chronicle* the following day[35]—is, if anything, still greater, as will emerge from a comparison of the following passage with pp. 352–4 below:

Last time [Mr Holcombe] saw his mare in the field from which he lost it, was on the 8th of October; on the 10th he missed it; did not see her again till the 21st when she was at Mr Oliver's, in Dorchester.—[Cross examined, Mr JEREMY.]—The field from which the mare was taken was adjoining the public road; never knew the mare to escape; it was not possible for her to leave the field unless she was taken out.—Elizabeth Mills, examined. Her husband keeps the Crown and Anchor, at Mosterton; prisoner came to her house on the 9th of October; he had two horses with him; prisoner arrived about four o'clock; he asked any person to put them in the stable; another person was with him; the other person put them in the stable himself; prisoner rode the mare; it was a bay one; her husband returned about nine at night.—[Cross-examined by Mr JEREMY.]—Prisoner bargained with her husband for the horses; Pierce, the constable, was there, while prisoner and her husband was talking; prisoner left next morning.—Mills, husband of last witness, examined. Reached home about nine o'clock on the 9th of October. Went with Pierce, the constable, into the stable, and saw a blood mare there, and also a poney mare. Constable and witness took two bridles and a saddle, belonging to the horses, into the house, having a mistrust that the horses were not honestly acquired. Prisoner asked for his horses next morning, and asked what he had to pay. Witness said, "Jemmy, I don't think you came by these horses *strait.*" "He [*sic*] replied, "I chopped her at Alphington Fair for a black cart horse." Prisoner spoke of the pedigree of the mare, and asked 25 sovereigns for it, and 12 for the poney. Witness offered 12 for the mare. Prisoner refused, paid his reckoning, and ordered his horses. While the saddle was being put on, witness cut two marks in the hair, under the mane. Prisoner then left the house. The other man went away before witness returned the

[35] The 'Blue Jimmy' narrator refers to the account of the execution as appearing 'in the same old *County Chronicle*', though in fact no newspaper has previously been mentioned. The reference may have been a TH addition based on the (possibly erroneous) assumption that Dugdale was working from the *Dorset County Chronicle*. Unfortunately no files of the 1827 *County Chronicle* appear to have survived.

night before. The poney was left. Witness saw the mare afterwards on the 22d, in Mr Holcombe's possession. Examined the mare, and found the private marks on her he had made under her mane. Witness [never] saw the prisoner between the time he first arrived at his house, and when he saw him in Tiverton prison.—[Cross-examined by Mr JEREMY.]—The morning after prisoner brought the horses to his house, prisoner asked for some beer, and said he was going to Bridport Fair.... A witness named Gillard, as he was going to church in the morning of the 8th (the morning before the robbery was committed) saw the prisoner in a lane about three miles from Fitzhead, sitting on the ground between two camps of gipsies.... The prisoner said nothing in his defence.—Verdict, *Guilty.* His Lordship in passing sentence of *Death,* entreated the prisoner to make the best use of the short time he would have to live in this world. He had been two years since brought before him, and in 1823 had been capitally convicted by his Learned Brother Hullock, for a similar offence, the full weight of the punishment awarded to his crime must now fall upon him, without the least chance of its mitigation.[36]

The almost word-for-word quotation, even to the point of the parenthetical 'Cross-examined by Mr Jeremy', leaves no doubt as to Dugdale's source.

In the story's concluding sections a debt to the *Dorset County Chronicle* is directly acknowledged and the borrowed material placed in quotation marks. The issue quoted was presumably that of 3 May 1827 (the date recorded in the 'Facts' notebook after the Blue Jemmy entry), but unfortunately no copy of it appears to have survived. The 2 May *Taunton Courier* account, however, sufficiently resembles both the 'Facts' entry and the 'Blue Jimmy' quotations as to suggest that the paragraph was essentially the same in the two papers. At the same time, the concluding reference to the execution of the sheep-stealer William Hazlett (actually Hewlett) in 'Blue Jimmy' suggests that the two papers may at least have differed in their use of italics, since in the *Taunton Courier* it is not Hewlett's seeming to imagine that his 'was a very hard case' which is italicized but the explanation of that feeling: '*He said that he had never, previous to the commission of the above offence, stolen more than four and twenty sheep!*' One can only speculate as to whether the paragraph did actually appear in a different form in the *Dorset County Chronicle,* whether Dugdale's transcription was inaccurate, or whether she—or Hardy—merely exercised a little poetic licence in order to conclude the story with a witty remark about

[36] The square brackets enclosing the references to Mr Jeremy's cross-examinations are in the newspaper text.

Hazlett's lack of gratitude for the privilege of being 'provided with a "new drop"' and of having 'for his fellow voyager into futurity that renowned Wessex horse-thief, Blue Jimmy'.

What is certain is that 'Blue Jimmy' is constituted more largely of plagiarized newspaper paragraphs than of original composition by either Dugdale or Hardy. On the other hand, some of the paragraphs—the second and fourth, for example—are distinctly Hardyan in style and, as Hardy himself acknowledged in his letter to Smith, he did supply some of the story's traditional details. The paragraph about Jimmy's 'repute for blueness' is probably Hardy's: included between the newspaper accounts of the final trial and of the execution, it is poorly integrated—hence, at least in part,[37] its omission from the published *Cornhill* text—and was almost certainly a later addition. Equally intrusive is the paragraph—relegated to a footnote in the published text—recording Jimmy's claim never to have stolen 'from people who were more honest than himself', but in this case there is direct evidence of authorship in that the passage is written in Hardy's hand on the surviving proofs. The *Cornhill* proof-reader (perhaps Smith himself) was presumably responsible for two corrections of typographical errors and one query as to word-usage, but all of the other markings on the proofs are Hardy's: for the most part they are minor stylistic revisions—'stories' is altered to 'reminiscences', 'going' to 'walking', and so forth—though there is also the occasional amplification, such as the passage just cited and the reference to the lack of any explanation for Wilkins's strange assurance that he knew Jimmy well.

Revisions of a similar kind in Hardy's hand can also be found on the surviving carbon typescript of an unpublished story entitled 'The Unconquerable'.[38] Hitherto overlooked by critics and biographers, the story is nominally Dugdale's (her name and Enfield address appear on the title-page), but it is distinctly Hardyan—more so, indeed, than any of her other fiction—in terms of both plot and style. As a tale of mistimings and missed opportunities centring upon the love of two friends for the same woman, 'The Unconquerable' resembles 'Fellow-Townsmen'. Fadelle's arrival at Gertrude's home a few hours after her engagement to Wingate, for example, can be com-

---

[37] The story was slightly abridged in order to conclude at the bottom of a page.
[38] DCM.

pared to Barnet's discovery of his wife's death only a few minutes before Lucy's marriage to Downe. Similarly, the widowed Gertrude's regret at declining Fadelle—implicit in her hint that in time she might 'feel her obligation [to her former husband] less strongly' and in the crucial unspoken word which seems to be 'on her lips and in her eyes' when she drives Fadelle to the station in her less than widow-like attire—recalls Lucy's resolution not to retract her refusal of Barnet 'for the present' but to allow herself 'to be induced to reconsider the case'.[39] In each instance, the decision to act comes too late: Gertrude, attempting to keep up with the departing carriage, evidently has 'something to say then that might never again be said', while Lucy, her note having missed Barnet, waits 'years and years' for a return that never takes place.[40]

The stories also share structural similarities—most notably, perhaps, the swings of fortune which appear to favour alternately first one friend and then the other but come to rest in the realization that these apparent triumphs are finally specious. Thus in 'The Unconquerable' Fadelle, after reading Wingate's incriminating letters, exults in fate's having at last 'taken up arms against her erstwhile favourite on [his] behalf' only to find himself unable to exploit his advantage, while in 'Fellow-Townsmen' Barnet, to all outward appearance the more fortunate of the two friends, is consistently shown to have the less enviable lot. The two stories are also similar in their development of that concluding ironic twist so common in Hardy's short fiction, although in 'The Unconquerable' the irony revolves less around the woman's recognition of her missed opportunity—the resolution of 'Fellow-Townsmen'—than around the victory of the dead friend. Fadelle realizes that Wingate had accurately 'gauged, weighed, and estimated his tendency to idealize', and that in failing to expose Wingate's falseness he is acting exactly as his friend calculated he would do: as the story's closing words point up, 'from the other side of the grave Wingate had played his last card and won'.

The surviving typescript of 'The Unconquerable' demonstrates that Hardy carefully worked over the story—possibly more than once, since the style of even the unrevised text is often Hardyan. He corrected typographical errors, revised punctuation and paragraphing, and pencilled in alternative readings, most of these being subsequently inked over, though some were erased and others

---

[39] *Wessex Tales*, 172.   [40] Ibid. 173.

altered. As with 'Blue Jimmy', Hardy's changes were predominantly stylistic, involving the restructuring of awkward sentences
(see, for example, p. 357. 14–22) or the elaboration of statements
originally simple: thus 'died' was altered to 'succumbed with appalling swiftness', 'said' to 'announced in the worn formula', 'friendly'
to 'cynically good-natured', and so forth. Hardy also introduced
clarifications and amplifications, most of them emphasizing Wingate's unconquerable will: for example, his terse revision (quoted
above) of the now illegible earlier version of the concluding clause.
Although several of the revisions stressed Fadelle's moral predica-
ment, most of these were subsequently rejected. Compare, for
example, these successive variations:

"He will not fail me". He repeated the words musingly. Yes, Wingate had
judged him well, he could not fail him. (original version)

"He will not fail me". He repeated the words musingly. They were almost
uncanny: for by wooing Geraldine he would be failing his former friend.
Yes, there it was again; the dead man's unconquerable hand. Wingate had
judged him well, he could not fail him. (first revised version)

"He will not fail me". He repeated the words: they were uncanny now. Yes,
Wingate had judged him well, he could not fail him; could not reveal. (final
revised version)

Similarly, the added sentence, 'Wingate had been working through
himself as if he were still alive', is only the beginning of an abandoned longer passage which continued: 'that which made another
thought of union with Geraldine impossible. Thus Fadelle's own
writing had opened a gulf between them, if he continued the man of
honour that he hoped [he would always be].'

    The exploration of a man's ability to wield power after death,
even to the point of determining his own posthumous image, is a
fascinating one, all the more so in view of the fact that as Hardy's
widow Dugdale would publish over her own name the biography of
her husband that had in fact been almost entirely written by him
during the early years of their marriage (see p. 217). In the
meantime Hardy continued to make unacknowledged contributions
to Dugdale's work, going so far as entirely to ghost-write several of
the poems included in her 'Descriptions' for E. J. Detmold's illustrations in Henry Frowde and Hodder & Stoughton's *The Book of
Baby Beasts* ([1911]), *The Book of Baby Birds* ([1912]), and *The Book of*

Baby Pets ([1913]).[41] 'The Yellow-Hammer' (*The Book of Baby Birds*) and 'The Lizard' (*The Book of Baby Pets*) survive in Hardy's holograph manuscript,[42] 'The Calf' (*The Book of Baby Beasts*) was attributed to him by Dugdale's sisters, and, as Purdy suggests, Hardy probably also 'had a hand in the revision of other poems in the book[s]'.[43]

It also seems significant that of the small group of surviving short-story outlines in Hardy's hand in the Dorset County Museum at least two were clearly written after he had met Dugdale, hence long after he had himself turned from fiction to poetry: one is scribbled on the verso of an automobile advertisement referring to the 1909 season, the other on an opened-out envelope postmarked 21 March 1916. The earlier outline, belonging to the period when Hardy was most active in Dugdale's career, also includes a note to see his 'Facts' notebook, thus suggesting, perhaps, that the outline was intended for someone else's use; indeed, one of the other two (undated) outlines for the same story concludes with a rather similar note, 'See Grove's Dictionary of Music. Article on "Barthélémon".'

The element of collaboration in the composition of Dugdale's stories for adults, then, would seem to be similar in kind—though perhaps not always in extent—to that involved in the writing of 'Spectre', with Hardy providing the central idea or plot outline to be worked up by his collaborator and then revising the resulting draft(s). Certainly this appears to have been the pattern with both 'Blue Jimmy' and 'The Unconquerable'.

The non-publication of the latter story is more than a little surprising in view not only of Hardy's extensive involvement in its composition but also of its considerable literary merit: it is certainly superior to any of Dugdale's other stories and even to several of Hardy's. If, as is probable, it is a late story, written after 'Blue Jimmy' (published in 1911) but while Dugdale was still living at Enfield (the address on the typescript), it may have been completed shortly before Emma Hardy's death in November 1912 and then put aside and lost sight of in the midst of more pressing concerns. This still would not explain its remaining unpublished during subsequent

[41] Purdy (317) states that this volume was published in 1915, but the Bodleian Library acquisition stamp is dated '14.5.1914' and the catalogue gives 1913 as the year of publication.

[42] Beinecke; TH's note on the MS of 'The Yellow-Hammer' indirectly acknowledges his authorship (see Purdy, 316).

[43] Purdy, 314, 316, 317.

years, although it is true that when Dugdale and Hardy married in 1913 the question of her writing became something of an issue. In a letter of 22 July 1914 Florence Hardy (as she now was) asked their mutual friend Lady Hoare, 'Ought I—in fairness to my husband—to give up my scribbling?', and four days later reopened the subject:

> With regard to my own writing I have a feeling, deep within in [*sic*], that my husband rather dislikes my being a scribbling woman. Personally I *love* writing, poor though the result be, but I do realize that I can find plenty of domestic work to do, & can also devote a great deal of time to him. It is a great problem.[44]

Certainly Hardy could not have been pleased to have her publishing—especially under the name of 'Mrs. Thomas Hardy'—such stories as the sentimental and crudely patriotic ' "Greater Love Hath No Man .."': The Story of a Village Ne'er-Do-Weel' (*Sunday Pictorial*, 13 June 1915). But there seems to be little that he could have found to object to in 'The Unconquerable'. Perhaps the story was simply misplaced; perhaps Dugdale hesitated on this occasion to put her name to something so largely the work of someone else; perhaps the conception and secret composition of Hardy's biography made the story's plot seem embarrassingly close to the bone. Alternatively, since only a carbon copy of the typescript has survived, it is just conceivable that the ribbon copy was in fact submitted to a magazine and that the story was rejected, accepted but never published, or even published anonymously, possibly under another title.

So far as can be determined, however, 'The Unconquerable' appears in print for the first time here, and 'Blue Jimmy' for the first time since its original publication in the *Cornhill*. Although, as this introduction has demonstrated, it can be argued that most of Dugdale's stories for adult readers are collaborative works, the only specific external evidence of Hardy's participation in any of them is the presence of his hand on the 'Blue Jimmy' proofs and the typescript of 'The Unconquerable'. It is on this basis that these stories have been included in the present collection, although they are, in any case, the most obviously Hardyan of 'her' works—always excepting, of course, *Early Life* and *Later Years*.

---

[44] Wiltshire Record Office.

BIBLIOGRAPHICAL DESCRIPTIONS OF 'BLUE JIMMY: THE HORSE STEALER'

Proofs

The *Cornhill* page proofs, accompanied by Dugdale's signed copy of the *Cornhill* issue in which the story was published, are now in the Frederick B. Adams collection. Each of the two proof-sheets, measuring approximately 23.5 cm. by 29.8 cm., is printed with two pages of text on the recto and two on the verso. The paper is cream in colour and 0.11 mm. thick.

With the exception of a wording query and two corrections of typographical errors in an unknown hand (presumably the *Cornhill* proof-reader's), all markings on the proofs are TH's.

Periodical Publication

Cornhill, NS 30 (Feb. 1911)
The text begins on p. 225 and concludes on p. 231. The title reads:
BLUE JIMMY: THE HORSE-STEALER.
'F. E. DUGDALE' appears at the conclusion of the text.

NOTE ON THE TEXT OF 'BLUE JIMMY: THE HORSE STEALER'

The copy-text is the *Cornhill* proofs (PR), as revised by TH. The only other surviving witness is the *Cornhill* printing itself (*C*), but its variants, consisting only of minor pointing and styling details and abridgements clearly introduced in order to conclude the story at the bottom of a page, are almost certainly attributable to a member of the magazine's staff and have therefore not been incorporated into the edited text, though they are recorded.

In the variants lists the source of lemmata not followed by sigla is PR.

BLUE JIMMY: THE HORSE STEALER

> Blue Jimmy stole full many a steed
> Ere his last fling he flung.

The name of "Blue Jimmy"—a passing allusion to whose career is quoted above from Mr Thomas Hardy's ballad "A
5 Trampwoman's Tragedy"—is now nearly forgotten even in the West of England. Yet he and his daring exploits were on the tongues of old rustics in that district down to twenty or thirty years ago, and there are still men and women living who can recall their fathers' reminiscences of him.

10 To revive the adventures of any notorious horse-thief may not at first sight seem edifying; but in the present case, if stories may be believed, the career of the delinquent discloses that curious feature we notice in the traditions of only some few of the craft—a mechanical persistence in a series of actions as if by no will or necessity of the
15 actor, but as if under some external or internal compulsion against which reason and a foresight of sure disaster were powerless to argue.

Jimmy is said to have been, in one account of him, "worth thousands," in another a "well-to-do" farmer, and in all a man who found or would have found no difficulty in making an honest income.
20 Yet this could not hinder him from indulging year after year in his hazardous pursuit, or recreation, as it would seem to have been, till he had reft more than a hundred horses from their owners, and planted them profitably on innocent purchasers.

This was in full view of the fact that in those days the sentence for
25 horse-stealing was, as readers will hardly need to be reminded, death without hope of mitigation. It is usually assumed that the merciless judicial sentence, however lacking in Christian loving-kindness towards the criminal, had at least the virtue always of being in the highest degree deterrent; yet at that date, when death was the penalty
30 for many of what we should now consider minor crimes, their frequency was extraordinary. This particular offence figures almost continually in the calendar at each assize, and usually there were

9 reminiscences *PR(2)THp*] stories *PR(1)*   16 sure *PR(2)THp* [*added*]

several instances at each town on a circuit. Jimmy must have known this well enough; but the imminent risk of his neck for a few pounds in each case did not deter him.

He stood nineteen times before my lord judge ere the final sentence came—no verdict being previously returned against him for the full 5 offence through lack of sufficient evidence.

Of this long string of trials we may pass over the details till we reach the eighteenth—a ticklish one for Jimmy—in which he escaped, by a hair's breadth only, the doom that overtook him on the nineteenth for good and all. What had happened was as follows:— 10

On a December day in 1822 a certain John Wheller, living near Chard, in Somerset, was standing at his door when Jimmy—whose real name was James Clace—blithely rode by on a valuable mare.

They "passed the time of day" to each other, and then, without much preface: 15

"A fine morning," says Jimmy cheerfully.

"'Tis so," says Mr Wheller.

"We shall have a dry Christmas," Jimmy continues.

"I think we shall so," answers Wheller.

Jimmy pulled rein. "Now do you happen to want a good mare that 20 I bought last week at Stratton Fair?" And he turned his eye on the flank of the animal.

"I don't know that I do."

"The fact is a friend of mine bought one for me at the same time without my knowledge and, as I don't want two, I must get rid of this 25 one at any sacrifice. You shall have her for fourteen pounds."

Wheller shook his head, but negotiation proceeded. Another man, one named Wilkins, a nephew of Wheller, happening to pass just then, assured Wheller that he knew the seller well, and that he was a farmer worth thousands who lived at Tiverton. Eventually the mare was 30 exchanged for a cart-horse of Wheller's and three pounds in money.

Curiously enough Wheller did not suspect that anything was wrong till he found the next day that the animal was what he called "startish"—and, having begun to reflect upon the transaction, he went to his nephew Wilkins, who also lived at Chard, half a mile from 35 Wheller, and asked him how he knew that the vendor of the mare was a farmer at Tiverton? The reply was vague and unsatisfying—in short

14–15 They...preface: [*not in C*]   37–350. 2 —in short...
explained— *PR(3)THp* [*added*]

the strange assurance of Wilkins, Wheller's own nephew, was never explained—and Wheller wished he had had nothing to do with the "man worth thousands." He went in search of him, and eventually found him at that ancient hostel "The Golden Heart" at Coombe St.
5 Nicholas, placidly smoking a long clay pipe in the parlour over a tankard of ale.

"I have been looking for you," said Mr Wheller with severe suddenness.

"To get another such bargain, no doubt," says Jimmy with the
10 bitter air of a man who has been a too generous fool in his dealings.

"Not at all. I suspect that you did not come honestly by that mare, and request to have back my money and cart-horse, when I'll return her."

"Good news for me!" says Jimmy, "for that I'm quite willing to do.
15 Here, landlady! A pipe and ale for this gentleman. I've sent my man out to bring round my gig; and you can go back to my farm with me, and have your horse this very afternoon, on your promising to bring mine to-morrow. Whilst you are drinking I'll see if my man is getting ready."

20 Blue Jimmy went out at the back, and Wheller saw him go up the stable-yard, half-regretting that he had suspected such a cheerful and open man of business. He smoked and drank and waited, but his friend did not come back; and then it occurred to him to ask the landlady where her customer, the farmer, lived.

25 "What farmer?" said the landlady.

"He who has gone out to the stables—I forget his name—to get his horse put-to."

"I don't know that he's a farmer. He's got no horse in our stables—he's quite a stranger here."

30 "But he keeps the market here every week?"

"I never saw him before in my life. And I'll trouble you to pay for your ale, and his likewise, as he didn't."

When Wheller reached the yard the "farmer" had vanished, and no trace of him was discoverable in the town.

35 This looked suspicious, yet after all it might have meant only that the man who sold him the mare did not wish to reopen the transaction. So Wheller went home to Chard, resolving to say nothing, but to dispose of the mare on the first opportunity. This he incontinently did to Mr Loveridge, a neighbour, at a somewhat low

price, rubbed his hands, and devoutly hoped that no more would be heard of the matter. And nothing was for some while.

We now take up the experience of Mr Loveridge with the animal. He had possessed her for some year or two when it was rumoured in Chard that a Mr Thomas Sheppard, of Stratton, in Cornwall, had been making inquiries about the mare.

Mr Loveridge felt uneasy, and spoke to Wheller, of whom he had bought her, who seemed innocence itself, and who certainly had not stolen her; and by and by another neighbour who had just heard of the matter came in with the information that handbills were in circulation in Cornwall when he was last there, offering a reward for a particular mare like Mr Loveridge's, which disappeared at Stratton Fair.

Loveridge felt more and more uncomfortable, and began to be troubled by bad dreams. He grew more and more sure, although he had no actual proof, that the horse in his possession was the missing one, until, valuable to him as his property was for hauling and riding, his conscience compelled him to write a letter to the said Mr Sheppard, the owner of the lost animal.

In a few days W. Yeo, an emissary of Mr Sheppard, appeared at Mr Loveridge's door. "What is the lost mare like?" said Mr Loveridge cautiously.

"She has four black streaks down her right fore-foot, and her tail is 'stringed' so"—here he described the shades, gave the particular manner in which the tail had been prepared for the fair, and, adding other descriptive details, was certain it was the same mare that had been brought to Chard. He had broken it in for Mr Sheppard, and never before had known a mare so peculiarly marked.

The end of the colloquy was that Mr Loveridge gave up the animal, and found himself the loser of the money he had paid for it. For being richer than his worthy neighbour Wheller who had sold it to him, he magnanimously made up their temporary quarrel on the declaration of Wheller that he did not know of the theft, and had honestly bought the horse. Together then they vowed vengeance against the thief, and with the assistance of Mr Sheppard he was ultimately found at Dorchester. He was committed for the crime, and proving to be no less a personage than the already notorious Blue Jimmy, tried at the Taunton Assizes on March 28, 1825, before Mr Justice Park.

During the trial all the crowd in court thought that this was to be the end of famous Blue Jimmy; but an odd feature in the evidence
5 against him was that the prosecutor, Mr Sheppard, when cross-examined on the marks described by his assistant Yeo, declared that he could not swear positively to any of them.

The learned Judge, in summing up, directed the jury to consider whether the identity of the mare had been so indubitably proved as to
10 warrant them in pronouncing the prisoner guilty, and suggested that the marks described by the witness Yeo might be found upon many horses. "It was remarkable," his Lordship observed, "that Wilkins, who was present when Wheller bought the horse, although the nephew of the latter, and living within half a mile of him, had not been
15 brought into court to give evidence, though witnesses from so considerable a distance as Cornwall had been examined."

In spite of this summing-up people in court were all expecting that Blue Jimmy would swing for his offences this time; yet the verdict was "Not Guilty," and we may well imagine the expression of integrity on
20 Blue Jimmy's countenance as he walked out of the dock, although, as later discoveries proved, he had, as a matter of fact, stolen the mare.

But the final scene for Blue Jimmy was not long in maturing itself. Almost exactly two years later he stood at the bar in the same assize court at Taunton, indicted for a similar offence. This time the loser
25 was one Mr Holcombe, of Fitzhead, and the interest in the trial was keener even than in the previous one.

Jimmy's first question had been, "Who is the judge?" and the answer came that it was Mr Justice Park, who had tried him before.

"Then I'm a dead man!" said Jimmy, and closed his lips, and
30 appeared to consider his defence no longer.

It was also a mare on this occasion, a bay one, and the evidence was opened by the prosecutor, Mr Holcombe, who stated that the last time he saw his mare in the field from which he had lost her was on the 8th of the preceding October; on the 10th he missed her; he did not see
35 her again till the 21st, when she was in a stall of Mr Oliver's, at the King's Arms, Dorchester.

Cross-examined by Mr Jeremy: The field from which the mare was stolen was adjoining the public road; he had never known the mare to

11 might *PR(2)THp*] might not *PR(1)*   23 later *PR(2)THp*] after *PR(1)*

escape; it was not possible for her to leave the field unless she was taken out.

Elizabeth Mills examined. Her husband kept the Crown and Anchor at Mosterton, Somerset; the prisoner came to her house about four o'clock on October 9. He had two horses with him. He asked for some person to put them in the stable; another man was in his company, and eventually the other man put them in the stable himself. The prisoner was riding the mare on his arrival; it was a bay one. Her husband returned about nine at night. (Cross-examined by Mr Jeremy.) Prisoner bargained with her husband for the horses; Pierce, the constable, was there while prisoner and her husband were talking; prisoner left next morning.

Robert Mills, husband of the last witness, examined. He reached home about nine o'clock on October 9. He went with Pierce the constable into the stable and saw a blood mare; also a pony mare. Constable and witness took two bridles and a saddle belonging to the horses into the house, having a mistrust that the animals were not honestly acquired. Prisoner called for his horses next morning, and asked what he had to pay. Witness, who now began to recognise him, said: "Jimmy, I don't think you came by these horses straight." He replied, "I don't know why you address me by the familiar name of Jimmy, since it is not mine. I chopped the mare at Alphington Fair for a black cart-horse." Prisoner spoke of the pedigree of the mare, and asked twenty-five guineas for it, and twelve for the pony. Witness offered twelve for the mare. Prisoner refused, paid his reckoning and ordered his horses. While the saddle was being put on, witness cut two marks in the hair under the mane. Prisoner then left the house. The other man had gone away before witness returned the night before. The pony was left. Witness saw the mare afterwards, on the 22nd, in Mr Holcombe's possession. He examined the mare and found the private marks he had made on her under the mane. He had never seen the prisoner between the time the latter put up at his house and when he saw him in Tiverton Prison. (Cross-examined by Mr Jeremy.) The morning after prisoner brought the horses to his house he asked for some beer, though he .was accustomed to wine, he remarked, and said that he was going to Bridport Fair to spend a score of bank-notes or so by way of killing time.

A witness named Gillard, as he was walking to church on the

38 walking *PR(2)THp*] going *PR(1)*

morning of the 8th (the morning before the robbery was committed)
saw the prisoner in a lane three miles from Fitzhead, sitting on the
ground between two camps of gipsies.

The prisoner said nothing in his defence, merely shaking his head
5 with a grim smile. The verdict was Guilty.

His Lordship, in passing sentence of death, entreated the prisoner
to make the best use of the short time he would have to live in this
world. The prisoner had been two years since brought before him and
in 1823 he had been convicted by his learned Brother Hullock for a
10 similar offence. The full weight of the punishment awarded to his
crime must now fall upon him, without the least hope of mitigation.

Such was horse-stealing in the 'twenties of the last century, and
such its punishment.

How Jimmy acquired his repute for blueness—whether the
15 appellative was suggested to some luminous mind by his clothes, or
by his complexion, or by his morals, has never been explained, and
never will be now by any historian.

About a month later, in the same old *County Chronicle*, one finds a
tepid and unemotional account of the end of him at Ilchester,
20 Somerset, where then stood the county gaol—till lately remembered,
though now removed—on the edge of a wide expanse of meadow-
land, spread at that season of the year with a carpet of butter-cups
and daisies. The account appears under the laconic heading,
"Execution, Wednesday, April 25, 1827: James Clace, better known
25 by the name of Blue Jimmy, suffered the extreme sentence of the law
upon the new drop at Ilchester ... Clace appears to have been a very
notorious character" (this is a cautious statement of the reporter's,
quite unlike the exuberant reporting of the present day: the culprit
was notorious indubitably). "He is said to have confessed to having
30 stolen an enormous number of horses, and he had been brought to the
bar nineteen times for that class of offence.... In early life he lived as
a postboy at Salisbury; afterwards he joined himself to some gipsies
for the humour of the thing, and at length began those practices which
brought him to an untimely end; aged 52."

35 A tradition was till lately current as to his hanging. When on the

8 two ... him *PR(1)*, *C*] brought before him two years ago [*suggested alteration in PR; see TN*]   11–17 him ... historian.] him. *C*   35–355. 4 A tradition ... one. *PR(3)THp* [*added; written over an extensive illegible erasure*]] ... When he was on ... *C* [*entire passage relegated to a footnote; see TN*]

gallows he stated blandly that he had followed the strict rule of never stealing horses from people who were more honest than himself, but only from skinflints, taskmasters, lawyers, and parsons. Otherwise he might have stolen a dozen where he had only stolen one.

The same newspaper paragraph briefly alludes to a young man who 5 was hanged side by side with Blue Jimmy, upon the "new drop":—

"William Hazlett—aged 25—for having stolen some sheep and some lambs. The miserable man, after being condemned, seemed to imagine that his *was a very hard case.*"

The *County Chronicle* prints the last few words in italics, appearing 10 to hold up its hands in horror at the ingratitude of the aforesaid William Hazlett. For was not he provided with a "new drop," and had he not for his fellow voyager into futurity that renowned Wessex horse-thief, Blue Jimmy, who doubtless "flung his last fling" more boldly than many of his betters? 15

5 newspaper *PR(2)THp* [*added; not in C*]

BIBLIOGRAPHICAL DESCRIPTION OF
'THE UNCONQUERABLE'

Typescript

The typescript, a carbon copy bearing numerous TH holograph corrections, was among the Max Gate papers at FEH's death and is now in the Dorset County Museum. It is comprised of twenty-two leaves, the title-leaf and twenty-one leaves of text numbered 1 to 20 (12 is used twice). The title-leaf reads:

THE UNCONQUERABLE. | [*rule 51.5 mm.*] | F. E. Dugdale, | River Front, | Enfield. Middx

The leaves are of two different kinds of paper. The title-leaf and the leaves numbered 17 through 20 are cream in colour and have no watermarks or chain lines. These leaves measure 26 cm. by 20.3 cm. and are 0.102 mm. thick. The paper of the remaining seventeen leaves is essentially the same shade of cream, but has artificially imposed chain lines and is watermarked: 'EXCELSIOR | SUPERFINE | BRITISH MAKE'. These leaves measure 26.07 cm. by 20.39 cm. and are 0.095 mm. thick. All the leaves are pierced at the top left corner and fastened with a metal pin.

NOTE ON THE TEXT OF 'THE UNCONQUERABLE'

The copy-text is the sole surviving textual witness, the typescript (TS), as corrected by TH. Dugdale's only revisions were introduced during the course of her typing. Marked '*TS(2)*', they are typed over erased earlier readings. In the variants lists the source of all variant readings not followed by sigla is the unrevised typescript.

THE UNCONQUERABLE

I

There were times when Philip Fadelle acknowledged to himself with a sense of amusement not untinged with bitterness that even death had scarce succeeded in tempering the force of that inflexible will which he had ever recognised as an essential part of the being of his friend Roger Wingate. From the time when they were schoolboys together it had been a goad to urge him into paths whither he would not, the more effective in that it was wielded with the semblance of good-fellowship. The compelling pressure on his arm had been so much the friendly grip of one whose mastery of circumstance has given him the right to hale his friend, by the hair if need be, into ways of prosperity, that now when these fingers were cold and relaxed the moral force remained as potent as ever.

Among other things he remembered that, when he had spoken or rather hinted, of his intention to ask Gertrude Norton to be his wife, this same good friend had revealed the fact that there would be rivalry between them, but in mitigation, he had dwelt insistingly, his hand meanwhile pressing Philip's shoulder somewhat more heavily than usual, upon the fact that Gertrude Norton had been framed by Nature, obviously, to be the wife of himself, the astute and rising young politician, rather than to be the divinity of the struggling man of letters. Upon this occasion, Fadelle was glad to remember, he had refused to grant the premisses, not that this was of great moment, seeing that some weeks later Roger Wingate was the accepted suitor of the girl whose gay looks and bounding spirits had seemed to merit some orbit of their own, instead of suffering eclipse by the luminous and self-sufficient personality of a too eminent husband.

4 scarce *TS(2)THp?&i*] not   6 were *TS(2)*] had [*not continued*]   8 the semblance *TS(2)*] a sem [*not continued*]   15 Norton *TS(2)THp&i*] Wingate   15 wife, *TS(2)TH*] wife that   18–19 meanwhile ... usual, *TS(2)THp&i*] pressing meanwhile, somewhat ... usual Philip's shoulder, [*only comma after* meanwhile *deleted*]   23 grant the premisses, not *TS(3)THp?&i*] accept, not *TS(2)* [not *undeleted*]] accept th [*not continued*]   26 orbit *TS(2)*] sphere   26 instead of suffering *TS(2)TH*] rather than

He remembered also, with less of gratitude, that if he had acted more promptly and had omitted to confide in his friend, all might have gone differently. When, at length, he had decided to go to her he had broken his journey to linger irresolutely a day or two in an old
5   Cathedral town, within the peaceful close and under the shadow of one of the most notable piles of Mediaeval architecture in England. His dallying had led to his arrival at the home of the woman he wished to make his wife a few hours after her engagement to Roger Wingate.

10   Had he been earlier, he fancied, he might have won her, for a gleam in her eyes seemed to reproach him. He found scant comfort from the recollection that it had always been Wingate's way to supersede him, even when they were at school together.

Five years after Roger Wingate's marriage, at a time when his
15   career had seemed secure against mischance, he had succumbed with appalling swiftness to a few days' illness and an operation from which he never rallied. It was difficult for those who had known him to contemplate the idea of the extinction of one so vital. The force which had emanated from him had seemed imperishable.

20   The news, revealed in course of time by the widow, that it had been Wingate's definitely expressed wish that some memoir of himself should be compiled by his friend was to Philip Fadelle another, perhaps the last, manifestation of that overpowering will. Though none else had contemplated Wingate's death, he himself had done so,
25   and in providing that his friend's hand should raise him a memorial lucent and rare, he had linked to this evidence of his friend's literary gift a sense of his own domination.

"Of course, had he lived longer, the biography would have been a work of importance; but as it is, with his letters—unique in their way,
30   I believe—something not unworthy might be done." Gertrude had hesitated at this point, and then, in a lower key, had given her tribute to that unseen power:

---

1 also *TS(2)TH*] too   4–5 broken . . . within *TS(4)TH*] . . . linger a . . . town, to loiter irresolutely in *TS(3)TH* [irresolutely *undeleted, marked for insertion after* linger]] . . . loiter in *TS(2)*] lingered a day or two <*illegible*> [*not continued*]   5 under *TS(2)TH*] in   6–7 architecture . . . arrival *TS(4)TH*] . . . England. The d *TS(3)TH* [*not continued; see TN*]] architecture, thus arriving [arriv *undeleted*] 14–16 Roger . . . swiftness to *TS(3)TH*] . . . he had died, after *TS(2)THp*] his marriage . . . Roger Wingate had died after [*see TN*]   24 none *TS(2)TH*] noone [*only second* o *deleted*]   29 letters— *TS(2)THp&i*] letters which are

"One feels, somehow, constrained to obey what one knows to have been his wish."

In this the man of letters had acquiesced, with a sigh that had a groan at its heart. He knew that the telling of that brief though redundant life might with safety be left in his hands, and he was prepared to offer what slight fame he had already garnered as incense to his dead comrade's memory.

"You have always been a most dear and generous friend to us both," she added, with a smile that had in it as much of tenderness (it seemed) for the living, as regret for the dead.

The memory of the past bloomed between them like some wan flower of which both inhaled the faint perfume; till Fadelle suddenly remembered that his friend had now been dead for nearly six months, and that the time would soon be at hand when he might make that proposal so long delayed. His face brightened and a shadow passed from his eyes: he spoke of the memoir with interest, even with pleasure. "It will be the last token that friendship can offer," he said almost with emotion, and to himself he added that it would be in the nature of a seal set upon Wingate's tomb.

As weeks passed and he gave himself wholeheartedly to the work he had undertaken he began to realize that here, under his hand, Wingate's character was developing into such complexities as hitherto he had not suspected! Besides those sterner qualities which had impelled him onward in his chosen career there were suggestions of mystery, definite shades, of romance it might be, almost incredible in one who had mastered the hard facts of life so unshrinkingly. More wonderful still was the presumption that this side of that forcible character had been revealed to no-one! Gertrude, so far as he could gather, had never seen it.

The biography, he judged, would do full justice to a personality almost unique in its qualities of ingenuous comradeship allied to a wellnigh overwhelming dominance: a rare enough combination.

The summer following Wingate's death had nearly passed when Fadelle decided to visit Gertrude, who had been living for some time with her mother in the country. He had refrained from accepting the

3 In *TS(2)THp&i*] To   7 comrade's *TS(3)TH*] friends [*sic*]   8 a most *TS(2)TH*] so   8† generous *Ed.*] generous a   12 till *TS(2)TH*] and 13 dead *TS(2)THp*] dear [dea *undeleted*]   29 gather, *TS(2)THp?&i*] judge, 31 almost unique *TS(2)TH*] unique almost [*undeleted*]   31–2 a wellnigh *TS(2)TH*] an almost   33 nearly *TS(2)TH*] almost

invitation, often and pressingly repeated, until he had almost finished the biography. Now that this had been accomplished for all practical purposes, and the anniversary of Roger Wingate's death had come and gone, the way seemed clear for the furtherance of his chief desire.

5　He was filled with a pleasing certainty as his train carried him on to his destination, and when he alighted at a little country station he accepted it as a good omen that she was there to meet him.

She had changed greatly. He remembered that after a few months of married life she had seemed subdued to that strong will, had been

10　absorbed into that overwhelming personality with which she had been mated. Now, as she sat in the dog-cart, waiting to drive her guest to her house, he noted with a leaping heart that the Gertrude of her maiden days had been reincarnated. In her bright face was all the arch vivacity of unfettered girlhood, and as they were carried swiftly

15　between green hedgerows he rejoiced to hear again the gay inconsequence that Roger had always tacitly suppressed.

Glancing at her charming profile he wondered, once again, if she had ever plumbed that hidden well of sentiment which he fancied he had discovered in the secret writings of his friend. Some day he might

20　ask,—but not yet.

"I have a heap of things to show you," she assured him triumphantly, "and ever so much to discuss. It is easier to talk, don't you think, than to write?"

"About what?"

25　"Oh, about the biography, of course."

His gaze fastened itself upon the bracken at the side of the lane down which they were passing and sought out the flecks of golden brown among the green.

"Ah, yes."

30　When he turned to her again there was something so unwidow-like in her grey tweed, in the small jaunty plume of her hat, and her business-like dog-skin gloves that a smile hovered where doubt had been.

"Ah, that biography! It will need days and days of discussion. Of

35　course it must be a tremendous thing."

"Of course it must, but do you know—" her eyes sought his with

2 this *TS(2)THp&i* [*added*]　　4 furtherance *TS(2)THp&i*] accomplishment
10 with *TS(2)THp*] to　　16 Roger *TS(2)TH*] Roger Wingate　　24 what
TS(2)TH [*added*]

laughing embarrassment, "sometimes I am afraid that it is going to be something of an obsession."

His glance held hers with amused assurance.

"I'm not quite sure that I have not found it something of that sort already."

Then mysteriously, a sense of loyalty to the dear husband and friend descended between them and froze their gaiety.

"Of course it must be great—powerful—like himself."

"Of course." He spoke dully and his mobile jaw grew rigid. Twice already, within one brief hour, he had met with an invisible rebuff; yet the hand that dealt it was one that he had thought bereft of power.

They passed a tiny lodge and swept up a drive.

"Here is the house; rather small; but a haven of rest for tired souls. It is rather sweet, isn't it?"

He thought it was, as he saw it nestling among the trees, grey walled and red roofed, and in front, walking on the wide gravel sweep before the door, as if to lend the final touch of domesticity, a mushroom-hatted and lace-shawled lady, Gertrude's mother, who turned at the sound of wheels to greet her visitor.

The days of his visit passed, and deliberate and continued observation confirmed Philip Fadelle in the assurance that to Gertrude Wingate the past thirteen months had brought a virtual renewal of blithe girlhood; but when she discussed with him the biography she became preternaturally solemn, and assumed a delightfully important manner as of one in whose small hands weighty affairs of state have been placed.

At such times the author noticed, with a sense of irritated amusement, that his work had sufficed to raise Wingate on to a loftier pedestal than he had, in his wife's estimation, previously occupied. She was pleased to be Fadelle's divinity, but there were moments when he told himself bitterly that in spirit she remained Wingate's slave.

This intuition, however, did not suffice to rob his holiday of any perceptible amount of charm, since Gertrude Wingate, as she rambled with him through woods and fields, betrayed the gaiety of a child who has escaped from the durance of a stern school. When she referred to her late husband it was in notes of eulogy rather than of regretful reminiscence.

3 His *TS(2)TH*] His amused 10–11 yet ... it *TS(2)THp&i*] and the hand [the hand *undeleted*] 29 occupied *TS(2)TH*] held

"This immaculate man has only just begun to live," Fadelle told himself with chagrin. "He was born in the first chapter of the biography."

Nevertheless he worked assiduously at his task: every stone set into
5 that destined memorial must be polished and repolished, even though it were with bleeding hands. There was something in Gertrude's bright friendship that sustained him. Often when she turned from the subject of the biography to discuss his other more personal work she unconsciously gained in vividness, and her eyes
10 beamed with a kindlier interest. She was quickly appreciative of subtle intangible moods, she was swift to catch a meaning, and was there, with him, in a moment, when women of a more pronounced intellectuality would have been labouring painfully behind.

The best minutes of the day to him were those when, after dinner,
15 they together paced up and down before the lighted windows of the house. As they turned again and again in their steady pacing, one luminous rectangle, which showed the calm figure of Gertrude's mother knitting beside a shaded lamp, was to them a link with civilization; for, on the other hand, the lawn sloped away to a
20 whispering darkness full of primeval mystery.

"You know, of course, that I took no part in the political life that Roger led," she said suddenly one evening when walking thus. "I might have understood, I suppose, all that there was; but I could never have really cared. I belong more to that." She thrust her hand
25 through the darkness and waved it at the shrouded woods and fields beyond.

"Listen!"

There was a fair in the village some distance away, hidden behind the woods. A hoarse murmur reached them faintly, and on the sky one
30 sullen patch betrayed the reflected light of the flaming naptha-lamps that hung on the booths, and the screaming merry-go-round.

They pierced, venturously, further into the darkness, walking some way down the avenue, while the ghostly branches waved blackly overhead. It was then, he afterwards felt, that he should have spoken
35 but, unlike his erstwhile friend and school-fellow, he let the decisive moment fall away. Together they returned to the house and the warm

10 was *TS(2)THp&i*] was so   14 minutes *TS(2)TH*] moments   16 one
TS(2)TH] that   17 which showed *TS(2)TH*] showing   22 evening when
walking thus. *TS(2)TH*] evening.   28 distance *TS(2)*] two miles

and lighted sanity of the drawingroom, to discuss a chapter dealing with a political crisis in which the inflexible will and insistent personality of Roger Wingate had not been found wanting.

It was, as Fadelle had imagined it would be, during one of those late evening strollings and communings that he asked Gertrude to be his wife. When she slowly and reluctantly gave a refusal she tempered it with explanations of an unsuspected character, so that the listener, peering bewilderedly at a totally strange aspect of Roger Wingate, almost missed the sense of his own loss.

"If there was one thing that he hated, one thing which always worried and upset him," she explained, "it was the idea, suggested to him in some way that I cannot understand, of my marrying again in the event of his early death. To him it seemed betrayal of the basest kind, utterly unforgiveable."

"I remember," she continued, "how he urged upon me the idea that the one who survived should remain faithful to the memory of the deceased. I—" here she flushed and lowered her eyes, "gave no actual pledge; but still—"

"Then I—" he returned with pale severity, "can say no more,—if you think you are in any way bound by an implied consent."

This strangely enough, she disclaimed, faltering and hesitating: she was not bound, in one sense, she believed, but a sense of loyalty stood as such a bond. Had her husband been less true, for that he was made of truth no-one could deny, it would have been quite simple, for she had given no pledge. It might even be, she hinted, that in time to come she would feel her obligation less strongly.

"It is the biography, partly, I believe," she uttered, laying her hand on his arm with a soft impulsiveness, "I don't think that I ever—I am almost ashamed to say it—I don't think I ever fully realized before I read what you have written, how strong, how true, how utterly loyal he was to me."

There was the cadence of tears in her voice as she urged this point of view upon him. He had raised in her a finer appreciation of Wingate's qualities, and this being so she could not repay loyalty with disloyalty: she felt that he would agree with her in that.

They stood together at the edge of the gravel sweep where it touched the darker line of the grass: beside them reared itself a tall

19 returned *TS(2)THp&i*] spoke   23 as such a bond *TS(2)TH*] in the way
27 the *TS(2)TH* [*added*]   31 was to me. *TS(2)THp&i*] was.

yew, stern against the sombre purple of the sky. He watched, and through his sense of this outward beauty there pierced the knowledge that he was conquered, overwhelmed by a far reaching power, and he knew how well his friend had gauged, weighed, and estimated his 5 tendency to idealize, and how well he had made use of it. Wingate had been working through himself as if he were still alive.

There seemed, under the circumstances, little that need be said, but as they moved slowly back to the opened and lighted porch Gertrude walked beside him, and, holding up her white skirt in one of 10 the pretty ways she had at her command, pleaded that nothing should be altered, and that he must always be her dear and close friend. Fadelle felt the groan he was too heartsick to utter aloud. Yes, all was to remain as before; had not Wingate willed it so?

II

15   It was not later than the next morning that he announced in the worn formula that pressing affairs demanded his quick return to Town. Mrs Norton, benignly presiding over the breakfast table, was puzzled and mildly reproachful: her daughter looked conscience-stricken, and her eyes, for an instant, grew wider and brighter as if with unshed 20 tears.

"Is there nothing I can say?" she asked softly when they were alone together. "Nothing that I can say to persuade you to remain with us a little longer?"

He feared not, unless—this with a poor smile,—she could induce 25 his publishers to wait upon him here, in the country, and the authorities of the British Museum to send him several parcels of books and papers.

"And the biography?" she asked without the least pretence of accepting the laboured joke.

30   That, he replied, was practically finished, and he proceeded to enlarge upon the subject with much deliberation, while Gertrude

---

5–6 Wingate ... alive. *TS(4)TH*] ... alive, that which made another thought of union with Gertrude impossible. Thus Fadelle's own writing had opened a gulf between them, if he continued the man of honour that he hoped <*illegible*> *TS(3)THp*] Wingate was working ... *TS(2)THp* [*added; see TN*]   15–16 announced ... that *TS(3)TH*] announced that *TS(2)THp*] said that [that *undeleted in 1st revision*] 24 poor *TS(2)TH* [*added*] listened with weary blankness. Her interest in the biography seemed to have passed.

"There is something," she said with sudden remembrance, "something that I have forgotten to tell you. I should have spoken about it before." She told him that she had discovered an 5 accumulation of papers and letters in an old bureau which had been sent down from her town house, together with other furniture. If he cared to look through them, he might be able to tell whether the letters were of any consequence. They were tied up carefully, dated and docketed, she thought, and a few minutes would doubtless serve 10 to determine their importance.

"I had no idea until a day or two ago that there were any letters there," she said. "The bureau was in a room where Roger kept old books that he never used, but evidently did not wish to destroy or give away; his school trunks, sets of games and other boyish treasures. 15 Indeed I did not know that he used the bureau at all for he always kept the room locked up."

They went together to a spare room and she showed him the letters and papers, all neatly ranged in various drawers and pigeon-holes.

"I would have gone through these myself," she said in a low tone; 20 "but just now it seems beyond me."

He threw an enquiring glance towards her and noticed her air of depression, and the weary look in her eyes. She left him when he had assured her that he could run through the letters more expeditiously without her aid. Taking a packet from the top drawer and slipping off 25 an elastic band he began to read.

He had been through quite half a dozen letters before the meaning of their so careful concealment in the bureau struck home to his puzzled senses. Here, he felt, his hand was on a clue which, followed up, would explain much of the hidden side of Wingate's character 30 that he had suspected but never clearly viewed. Reading on and on he drew deep breaths of bewilderment as packet after packet revealed a hitherto unknown Wingate, one to whom base trickery and unholy alliances had not been too mean weapons for gaining desired ends. No laudatory biography could have been written had these 35 circumstances been revealed before. He remembered bitterly one chapter that he had filled with an exposition of Wingate's loyalty to a

23 the *TS(2)THp*] a   24 run *TS(2)TH*] look   34 for gaining desired *TS(2)THp&i*] to gain her [gain *undeleted*]

party, which, as these letters showed, he had basely sold. There was no proof of any great, overwhelming temptation and sudden, pitiable fall, such as the heart of any understanding man might have forgiven. He had lied and cheated in a calm deliberate manner, using, as in all
5 other circumstances of his life, that unconquerable will, which it seemed had awed his accomplices into lasting silence.

Fadelle, in reading, wondered why Wingate should have piled together and preserved this mass of evidence now before him, for had these letters and papers, all damning records, been burnt, the high
10 integrity of his character would have remained undoubted. An ordinary man, with little of statecraft and nothing of Wingate's ability, would have taken this ordinary precaution. Nevertheless, people did such things as keep compromising papers, and, it was not out of accord with Wingate's character that he should have hurled his
15 own image from its pedestal thus violently. No gradual descent would have served that supreme wilfulness.

The last packet of letters gave the final blow, and Fadelle put his hand to his head mechanically, as if amazed at the dull numbing pain it had sustained. Up to this moment he had held that his friend had
20 carried, as a well of sweetening waters in the inviolable recesses of his heart, deep and unstained reverence for a domestic ideal, but these letters spoke of the deepest treachery, not to his party this time but to his wife.

He put them down and rested his aching head on his hands.
25 Gradually the dubious haze and confusion cleared away and a tiny ray of light, no more than a pin-point at first—pierced the darkness and grew and grew until his mind was illuminated by one vast idea. He, Philip Fadelle, had triumphed at last: his adversary, after long years of victory, had met with one finally decisive stroke, for Fate had
30 taken up arms against her erstwhile favourite on Fadelle's behalf.

One thing seemed plain enough to him: the biography could hardly be published now, at any rate not as he had written it. Gertrude would share the disillusionment, and not, so he dared to think, too

---

2 and *TS(2)THp&i*] and a   13 people . . . and, *TS(3)TH*] . . . things, and, *TS(2)TH* [*added*]   13–14 not out of accord *TS(2)TH*] in accordance [accord *undeleted*]   16 wilfulness. *TS(2)TH*] will. [wil *undeleted*]   26 ray *TS(2)*] pin point   28 last: *TS(1)*, *TS(3)TH*] last: loyalty was demanded no longer to this dead man; Gertrude was his to sue; *TS(2)THp*   29 finally decisive stroke, *TS(3)TH*] finally decisive stroke, working through Wingate's own <*word ending* eries> *TS(2)THp*] decisive stroke at last, [*only* at last *deleted*]

regretfully. There was no reason now for her keeping faith with the memory of one who had been so unfaithful to her as she must be made to know. Things grew clearer and clearer to him, and at length he was serenely contented. He seemed to be holding out a cynically good-natured hand to Wingate across the dividing stream. 5

"I've won at last, old friend. You made a good fight of it always; but now, like the sportsman you always were, you must confess yourself beaten."

Strange that even now, with that confuting pile of letters before him, he should still cherish the idea of Wingate's straightness. 10

A slight noise made him start, and he turned to see that Gertrude had entered the room. In her hand she held some unfolded pages. She had been looking in a writing case that had belonged to her husband, one that had been used only when he was travelling, and in it she had found a letter, unfinished. "Addressed to me," she said with a slight 15 tremor in her voice. "From the date I imagine that it was written while he was out of Town, during that last short holiday he took before his death. I remember that he was called back suddenly, and that is, probably, why this letter was never finished."

He asked, somewhat bewildered, if she wished him to read it. 20

"I thought you would like to, as he speaks very beautifully of you. I was greatly touched. It is like a message from the dead."

Fadelle's eyes lingered for a moment upon the letters spread before him on the bureau: there, too, was a message, but of a different cast. "Have you found anything there of importance?" asked Gertrude, her 25 glance following his.

Moved by a sudden impulse, strange even to himself, he answered hurriedly that there was nothing; he supposed that the letters had been put there so that they might, after an interval, be destroyed. Of their nature he said nothing, and Gertrude then left him. 30

When he was alone he wondered why he had failed to reveal that which must be made known at some time: the opportunity had presented itself so aptly, and yet he had omitted to make use of it. Wingate, he was sure, had never hesitated to grasp the slightest chance; and here was he, in the moment of victory, acknowledging his weakness.

With a sigh he gathered together the letters of the last packet and slipped around them their elastic band, having done which he took up
5 the written sheets which Gertrude had left.

"I have been wondering who would be the best man for this purpose, and I have come to the conclusion that there is only one of all my host of acquaintances in whom I am able to place implicit trust, and that one is Philip Fadelle. I am sorry that we have seen so little of him lately, but that has
10 not been my fault. Indeed, as years pass, I realize more fully the loyalty of his friendship; he has been the same from boyhood, your friend and my friend, and I am certain that if I call upon him now to do me this service he will not fail me. I am going to ask him—"

The letter ended abruptly, leaving Fadelle in ignorance concerning
15 the request that his dead friend would have made. With a steady hand he laid it on the top of the bureau. It was, indeed, a message from the dead, a supplication rather, an appeal, to which he could not but respond.

"He will not fail me." He repeated the words: they were uncanny
20 now. Yes, Wingate had judged him well, he could not fail him; could not reveal. Once more his glance fell upon the packets of betraying letters, ranged in drawer and pigeon-hole, and then he walked back to one of the windows. Below, in the sunlight, he saw the figure of Gertrude moving among the flaming torch-lilies and flaunting
25 golden-rod in the long garden at the side of the house. Some distance behind her, at the end of the kitchen garden, arose a thin blue column of smoke from a pile of burning weeds; the sight suggested to him a course of action and he went down.

As he drew near to her he saw in her eyes that she wished to know
30 how the letter had affected him, but of that he had determined he would not speak.

"I have looked through the letters in the bureau," he said steadily. "They relate mostly to private political matters, and were evidently meant to be destroyed. Perhaps it would be better for me to take them

away with me to look through them again more leisurely than I have
time to do now. If I find nothing in them that needs preserving I
suppose I have your permission to destroy them. I suppose that you
do not wish to read them?"

He waited in strained suspense for her answer, which came as he 5
had thought.

"No thank you. I would much rather not, if you do not think it
necessary. I think there can be nothing more depressing than reading
such letters, and I hope that I have seen the last of them."

As they sauntered in the garden she again approached, almost 10
shyly, the question of his departure, and it was evident that she
wished him to remain longer. These tentative advances were
disregarded by Fadelle. All that he wished now was to free himself as
quickly as possible from the burden of obligation to his dead friend,
which pressed upon his shoulders with ever increasing weight. 15

When the time arrived for him to go to the station and Gertrude
appeared, ready to drive him in her dogcart, it was clear, even to his
dulled bachelor perceptions, that her costume of thick cream serge
and hat to match had no suggestion of widowhood; and the light
tendrils of hair that blew across her brow were almost virginal in their 20
significance.

As they drove along he remarked dully that the bracken was taking
to itself deeper tints of brown and gold. A strange silence fell between
them, a silence that seemed ever at breaking point. He felt that at a
word from Gertrude the whole face of his mental world might have 25
changed for ever, but the word was not spoken, though he seemed to
see its shadow on her lips and in her eyes. At the same quiet wayside
station where she had met him upon his arrival the pony drew up,
and he found that there was the briefest possible space in which to
wait for the train; he wondered, even then, what the interval might 30
bring forth, but its sliding moments proved barren. Gertrude spoke of
the bright flowers of early autumn that were beginning to bloom in
the neat little station-garden, and she stooped and petted a serious
station-cat which strolled leisurely among the luggage. Then the
train rushed in. 35

5 strained *TS(2)THp&i*] tense   16 go to *TS(2)*] drive to   20 almost
TS(2)THp&i [*added*]   21 significance. *TS(2)THp&i*] suggestion.
28† his *Ed.*] her   28–9 arrival...up, and *TS(2)THp&i*] arrival,
30 train; *TS(3)THp*] train; yet *TS(2)THp*] train, and   30 the interval *TS(2)TH*]
that [th *undeleted*]   31 its *TS(2)TH*] the

Fadelle had made his farewell and taken his seat when she moved suddenly forward, her lips eagerly parted.

"Goodbye, Goodbye!" He leaned from the window as the train started, and his voice drowned what she might have said.

5   She took a few quick steps, not half a dozen in all, by the side of the moving carriage, and he knew that she had something to say then that might never again be said.

"Goodbye!" He dropped back in his seat and saw her left behind, the light dying out of her face as she stood still.

10   It was not until the train had pulsed and rattled onward for some miles, and he felt himself being carried to pastures unstained by memory, that he uttered to himself a comment which was to him the final token of the affair—that from the other side of the grave Wingate had played his last card and won.

13–14 that ... won. *TS(3) TH*] that Wingate ... *TS(2)*] ... won, <*illegible erasure approximately the length of one typed line*>

Editorial Apparatus

HOW I BUILT MYSELF A HOUSE

EXPLANATORY NOTES

18 2   *Euclid*: Athenian mathematician of the third century BC; his *Elements* is the basis for the most common type of geometry.

19 4   *tenth commandment*: 'Thou shalt not covet thy neighbour's house, thou shalt not covet thy neighbour's wife, nor his manservant, nor his maidservant, nor his ox, nor his ass, nor any thing that is thy neighbour's' (Exod. 20: 17).

20 39 *St George's Hospital*: a famous London hospital located at Hyde Park Corner.

22 15 *royal letters extraordinary kitchen-range*: for the widespread appropriation of royal allusions and images by Victorian advertisers, see John May, *Victoria Remembered: A Royal History 1817–1861* (London: Heinemann, 1983) and, for later in the century, Thomas Richards, 'The Image of Victoria in the Year of the Jubilee', *Victorian Studies*, 31 (autumn 1987), 7–32.

TEXTUAL NOTE

17 8   *showed*: the copy-text reads 'shewed'. As TH never used the 'e'-form, all instances of this verb (also at pp. 17. 10, 32, 19. 19, 22. 22) have been emended; cf. the editorial policy with respect to US spellings.

PUNCTUATION AND STYLING VARIANTS

Double quotation marks in the edited text are single in the copy-text.

17 8†   showed] shewed
    10† shown] shewn
    32† showed] shewed

18 21† hundred—"] ~'—
    22† what—"] ~'—

19 19† showing] shewing

22 22† show] shew

COMPOUND WORDS HYPHENATED AT END OF LINE
IN COPY-TEXT

17 8　　fishponds

20 33　　hooping-cough

22 11　　rain-water

DESTINY AND A BLUE CLOAK

EXPLANATORY NOTES

30 26　　*Cloton*: presumably based on Netherbury; all other place-names in the story are actual places.

33 10　　*Beaminster*: presumably TH's slip for Maiden Newton; the carrier has just arrived in Beaminster (see pp. 30. 10–13 and 32. 6–8).

34 15　　*Macaulay*: Thomas Babington Macaulay (1800–59, historian and essayist; *DNB*) vigorously supported the India Bill introduced by Sir Charles Wood in 1853. The bill embodied clauses originally introduced by Macaulay in 1833 for opening appointments to competition.

38 25　　*Bess*: presumably baby-talk for 'Bless'.

41 3　　*gloury*: Wright's *English Dialect Dictionary* defines 'glowery' as 'out of temper, cross, surly' and *OED* lists 'glour' as an alternative spelling of 'glower'. Although Dorset is not mentioned in Wright's entry, the word could have been local, or was perhaps an 'import' from Devon.

TEXTUAL NOTES

30 11　　*Maiden-Newton*: although the name is usually not hyphenated, the copy-text has been followed here and at p. 31. 21 (unhyphenated) and p. 32. 6 (hyphenated), since TH's practice with double place-names was inconsistent.

43 20　　*come;*: in all copies of *NYT* examined only the very beginning of the tail of the semi-colon can be seen, and it therefore looks like a colon. The context, of course, requires a semi-colon.

43 29　　*mantle-piece*: although now obsolete, the 'le' spelling was used in the nineteenth century and has therefore not been emended.

PUNCTUATION AND STYLING VARIANTS AND TYPOGRAPHICAL ERRORS

The edited text differs from the copy-text in not using periods after 'Mr' and 'Mrs'.

31 30† ploughed] plowed

32 29† said,ˏ ″it] ~,″ ˏ~

33 18† embedded] imbedded
19† waggon] wagon

34 15† honoured] honored
16† ardour] ardor
38† expect—″] ~″—

35 4† good-bye] good-by
9† neighbourhood] neighborhood
20† honour] honor
31† colour] color

36 36† shrivelled] shriveled

37 23† article] articl

38 2† murmuring] murmering

40 36† good-bye] good-by

42 2† behaviour] behavior
26† offence] offense

44 9† gaiety] gayety
34† why—″] ~″—

45 26† difficult task] difficulttask
36† incredulously] increduously

46 12† favour] favor

48 25† good-bye] good-by

COMPOUND WORDS HYPHENATED AT END OF LINE IN COPY-TEXT

33 15 high-road

42 7 church-restorers

45 24 postman

48 8 wedding-day

THE THIEVES WHO COULDN'T HELP SNEEZING

EXPLANATORY NOTES

63　21　*Can ... deep*: 'I can call spirits from the vasty deep' (Shakespeare, *I Henry IV*, v. 73 (III. i. 52)).

　　22　*tempest in a cupboard*: presumably an allusion to the proverbial expression 'a tempest in a teacup', derived from the title of William Bayle Bernard's popular farce, *A Storm in a Tea Cup* (1854).

COMPOUND WORD HYPHENATED AT END OF LINE IN COPY-TEXT

59　1　oak-trees

AN INDISCRETION IN THE LIFE OF AN HEIRESS

EXPLANATORY NOTES

87　3–6　*When ... Isabel*: Shakespeare, *Measure for Measure*, i. 365 (II. iv. 1–4).

　　7　*Tollamore Church*: presumably based on Stinsford Church; certainly the monument to Geraldine's ancestors shares all the features of the Grey monument in Stinsford (see *An Inventory of Historical Monuments in the County of Dorset* (London: Royal Commission on Historical Monuments, 1970), iii. 253 and plate 203).

90　19–24　*She ... all*: Browning, 'The Flight of the Duchess', st. VIII; TH omitted the four lines which follow 'tire'.

94　17–18　*But ... eye*: Tennyson, *In Memoriam*, sect. LXVIII; the *HW* reading 'I find' is in fact correct.

95　16　*dropping of the lives*: under a form of copyhold lease still widely used in nineteenth-century Dorset (though of feudal origin), many village tenancies were held 'on lives', the lease remaining in effect until the death of the longest lived of up to three persons, usually the current tenant, his wife, and eldest son; see Joan Brocklebank, *Affpuddle in the County of Dorset A.D. 987–1953* (Bournemouth: Horace G. Commin, 1968), 9–10. TH's birthplace was held on a lifehold tenancy and the system provides significant plot elements in several other works, most notably *The Woodlanders* and 'Netty Sargent's Copyhold'.

97 19–20 *Childe Harold's Pilgrimage*: Byron's poem; TH's marked copy (Halifax: Milner and Sowerby, 1865) is in DCM.

98 19–21 *Oh . . . provide*: Shakespeare, Sonnet 111; the only alteration of wording is 'deed' for 'deeds'. The *HW* epigraph is from Pope, 'The Rape of the Lock', III. 155.

102 20–3 *Ulysses . . . Melanthus . . . rest*: Melanthus, properly Melanthius, is the goatherd who sides with the suitors and insults Ulysses when the latter arrives in Ithaca disguised as a beggar. The quotation, from Chapman's translation of Homer's *Odyssey* (17. 313–14), describes Ulysses' reaction to his servant's abuse.

103 28–104 3 *So . . . end?*: Browning, 'Instans Tyrannus', sts. VI–VII.

109 6–11 *Hath . . . loved?*: Byron, *The Corsair*, III. viii. 3; in l. 10 the correct reading is 'despite thy crimes'.

33 *lack . . . idleness*: correctly, 'want of other idleness' (Shakespeare, *Twelfth Night*, iii. 392 (I. v. 64)).

112 27–8 *Come . . . society*: Thackeray, *The Book of Snobs*, 'Chapter Last' [XLV], eleventh paragraph.

29–30 *lay the foundation-stone*: this scene is based on a ceremony TH attended with Arthur Blomfield in 1865 and described in his notebook. As recorded in *Life* (50) the note reads:

> Blomfield handed her [the then Crown Princess of Germany] the trowel, and during the ceremony she got her glove daubed with the mortar. In her distress she handed the trowel back to him with an impatient whisper of 'Take it, take it!'

116 12–14 *And . . . known*: Shelley, 'The Revolt of Islam', IX. xxxi; TH omitted the two lines which precede 'what we have done'. This stanza is marked in TH's copy of *Queen Mab, and Other Poems* (Halifax: Milner and Sowerby, 1865; Adams).

117 11–14 *The . . . foes*: Browning, 'The Statue and the Bust', ll. 138–41; the text of the 1849 edn. of *Poems* (apparently TH's source) does not include 'we' in the final line. TH used this quotation in several other works, including *Desperate Remedies*, 'The Waiting Supper', and *Jude*.

120 16 *met on the previous Christmas*: Geraldine and Egbert in fact met at harvest-time; for a discussion of the inconsistency see pp. 74–5.

122 7–11 *He . . . relies*: Dryden, *The Works of Virgil, Aeneis*, v. 587–91; the quotation is accurate in wording except for the substitution of 'He' for 'And'. These lines are marked in TH's copy (London: T. Allman & Son, n.d.; DCM), an early gift from his mother.

123 15 *Correggio*: Italian painter (1494–1534); *Desperate Remedies* (1871 edn., ii. 163) also refers to his flesh shades. All of the artists mentioned in this paragraph were studied by TH himself during his early London years. TH's 'Schools of Painting' notebook, dated 12 May 1863, includes under *'School of Parma'* an entry for *'Antonio Allegri—da Correggio'*:

> b.1494. very original—poor—rose up, no one knows how— assumption of the Virgin, in the cathl. of Parma his great work in wh. he equalled M.A. & R. Mengs, in his estimate of Italian genius gives the 1st. place to Raphael, 2nd. Corregio [*sic*] 3rd. Titian—"An ideal beauty, with not so much of heaven as in Raphl. yet surpassing that of nature, but not too lofty for our love." great knowlge. of lights & shades. (*PN* 108–9)

16 *Angelico*: Italian painter (1387–1455), usually known as Fra Angelico. In his notebook TH wrote: 'best of the succeeding Florentine painters [i.e. after Masaccio] studied in his school . . . 1. B. Giovanni Angelico, a monk—remarkable beauty in his angels—' (*PN* 105).

17 *Murillo*: Bartolomé-Esteban Murillo, Spanish painter (bap. 1618, d. 1682). TH's notebook entry reads: 'the chief boast of Spain b 1613 his holy family in N.G. equals Da Vinci, Raphl. & Correggio in sweetness of col: & freedom of touch. often coarse, never mean. often incorrect, never weak in character. d 1682' (*PN* 111).

18 *Rubens*: Flemish painter, identified accurately and described by TH as *'Peter Paul Rubens* 1577—majesty & pomp—warmth of colour—deficient in soft and sublime inspiration consps: in Italian painters. Living life. voluptuousness—beauty of expression rather than form. d 1640' (*PN* 112).

18 *Turner*: Joseph Mallord William Turner, English painter (1775–1851; *DNB*).

19 *Romney . . . Reynolds . . . Lady Hamilton*: George Romney (1734–1802; *DNB*), like Sir Joshua Reynolds (1723–92; *DNB*) a very successful portrait-painter, was said to have had an affair with his beautiful model, Emma Hart, the future Lady Hamilton (née Amy Lyon, 1761?–1815; *DNB*), who later became Nelson's mistress. TH's notebook includes entries for both painters: '*Sir Joshua Reynolds* 1723. gt. power in portraits, correct taste—little imagination . . . Romney. 1746 [*sic*]. Lady Hamilton his chief model' (*PN* 113).

123 20–1   *Bonozzi Gozzoli*: correctly, Benozzo Gozzoli, Italian painter (1420–97). The immediate source for the misspelling was presumably TH's notebook entry (also incorrect in its date): '*Bonozzi Gozzoli*—studied under Angelico died 1478' (*PN* 105).

   21   *Raffaelle*: Italian painter and architect (1483–1520). TH's notebook entry reads: '*Raphael*—b. 1483. ideal beauty, loftiness, & volupts. . the rival of M. Angelo.—chief glory, his Transfiguration—in emulation of Michel Angelo's cold. by Sebastiano, in the chapel of St Peter' (*PN* 107).

124 25–7   *And . . . prosper*: Ps. 1: 3–4 (*Book of Common Prayer*).

125 24–6   *Towards . . . light*: Shelley, 'Epipsychidion', ll. 219–21; TH omitted the initial 'And' in the first line.

127   9   *Chevron Square*: perhaps Belgrave Square; the location is certainly Belgravia and the choice of name could have been suggested by the unusual lozenge shape and diagonal organization of this particular square.

   24   Messiah: Handel's oratorio. The words of the first chorus and aria referred to are:

> Lift up your heads, O ye gates; and be ye lift up, everlasting doors; and the King of Glory shall come in. Who is the King of Glory? The Lord strong and mighty, the Lord mighty in battle. . . .
>   Why do the nations so furiously rage together, and why do the people imagine a vain thing? The kings of the earth rise up, and the rulers take counsel together against the Lord, and against His Anointed.

130 9–10   *Bright . . . sky*: Shelley, 'Lines' ('When the lamp is shattered'), st. IV.

134 28–9   *Then . . . wise?*: Eccles. 2: 15; the verse in fact begins 'Then said I'.

136   1–5   *Time . . . childhood*: cf. TH's reflections on revisiting Hatfield. His 6 June 1866 note as recorded in *Life* (56) reads: 'Changed since my early visit. . . . Pied rabbits in the Park, descendants of those I knew. The once children are quite old inhabitants.'

137 21–3   *How . . . jealousy!*: Shakespeare, *The Merchant of Venice*, ii. 493–4 (III. ii. 108–10).

143 24–5   *Better . . . pay*: Eccles. 5: 5.

145   2–3   *Hence . . . tell*: Shakespeare, *Romeo and Juliet*, viii. 156 (II. ii. 188–9).

148 2–3 *How ... fair!*: Edmund Waller, 'Go, Lovely Rose!' The *HW* epigraph is from Shakespeare, *Romeo and Juliet*, viii. 174 (II. vi. 9–10).

150 33 *when he lived at the school*: Egbert never did live at the school; for a discussion of the inconsistency, see p. 75.

153 12–13 *A silence ... tears*: Shelley, 'The Revolt of Islam', VI. xxxi; 'A' is an alteration of 'In'. This stanza is marked in TH's copy of *Queen Mab, and Other Poems* (Halifax: Milner and Sowerby, 1865; Adams).

TEXTUAL NOTES

94 7 *subjunctive*: *NQM* reads 'subjective', evidently a compositorial misreading of 'subjunctive', TH's minims often being difficult to distinguish. The error was noticed (assuming that the setting-copy was uncorrected *NQM* proof) and altered for the *HW* text.

97 16 *continue. ¶*: the omission of a paragraph break in *NQM*—presumably an authorial oversight since it was TH's practice to separate different speakers in dialogue—has been emended.

36 *grandfather*: *NQM* reads 'father', but earlier in the chapter the narrator states that the house was built by Broadford's 'father's father'. The inconsistency could be the result of a compositorial error or of TH's own confusion in distancing Egbert—cf. Strong, Springrove, and TH himself—from his peasant ancestry by making Broadford Egbert's grandfather rather than father. The edited text follows the *HW* reading, presumably an editorial or compositorial correction.

111 29 *been*: the *NQM* reading 'being' may reflect the lost MS, but is more likely to be a compositorial error. The adopted *HW* reading, though awkward, is at least a possible one.

143 14 *Bretton*: in *HW* followed by a semi-colon with an insufficiently pressed down tail, which in some copies looks like a colon.

PUNCTUATION AND STYLING VARIANTS AND TYPOGRAPHICAL ERRORS

The edited text differs from *NQM* in using double quotation marks and from both *NQM* and *HW* in not including periods after 'Dr' and 'Mr'.

87 1 I] FIRST
3 ‚When] "~
4 words;] ~,

87 6   Isabel.ₐ] ~."
   8   backwards] backward
   8   forwards] forward
   9   children,] ~ₐ
   9   gallery,] ~ₐ
  12   bird,] ~ₐ
  14   schoolmaster;] school-master,
  18   forwards;] forward,
  20   she.] ~!
  22   neighbourhood] neighborhood
  23   pulpit-candles] ~ₐ~

88 1   westwards] westward
   4   discerned,] ~—
   7   female;] ~,
   8   cherubim] cherubs
  10   slab,] ~ₐ
  11   pediment,] ~ₐ
  12   schoolmaster] school-master

90 7   her,] ~—
  13   cherish. The] ~; the
  14   rallying-points] ~ₐ~
  14   defence] defense
  15   her;] ~,
  19   ₐShe] "~
  24   all.ₐ] ~."

91 5   neighbouring] neighboring
  12   hastily;] ~,
  15   schoolmaster] school-master
  16   schoolmaster.ₐ] school-master!
  17   Goodₐmorning] ~-~
  30   routine.ₐ] ~,
  34   clear,] ~ₐ
  34   subtly-curved] ~ₐ~

92 4   attire,] ~—
   7   beheld;] ~,
  10   but,] ~ₐ
  13   sentences,] ~ₐ
  18   thought, perhaps,] ~ₐ ~ₐ
  19   schoolmaster] school-master
  24†   persons' *HW*] person's *NQM*
  26   mean,] ~—

92 31   Everybody has.] Every body has,
    35   tempted,] ~.

93   1   speaking,] ~.
    17   was;] ~,
    18   experience,] ~.
    22   ages,] ~.
    22   particulars.] ~,
    27   tone:] ~,
    28   schoolmaster] school-master
    28   But,] ~.

94   2   beauty,] ~.
     3   endeavoured] endeavored
    12   aye] ay
    17   .But] "~
    17   about.] ~,
    18   eye..] ~."
    20   schoolmaster] school-master

95   2   and,] ~.
     4   Government] government
     4   in.] ~,
     6   farmhouse] farm-house
     6   backwards] backward
     7   forwards] forward
    16   father;] ~,
    17   Squire] squire
    25   farmhouse] farm-house
    28   inquiringly,] ~.
    30   enemy.] ~,
    32   Squire] squire
    32   neighbour] Neighbor
    35   Squire] squire

96   1   endeavoured] endeavored
     4   echoed.] ~,
    17   stayed] staid
    19   died,] ~.
    19   had.] ~,
    27   trees;] ~:
    33   anything] any thing

97 15   have—" he] ~—" He
    16   farther] further
    16† continue, ¶ HW] ~, .NQM

97	20	Pilgrimage,"] ~"—
	22	this;] ~,
	23	conversation.] ~,
	25	said. hastily,] ~, ~.
	30	Indeed,] ~!—
	33	said.] ~,
	35	house.] ~,
	36	Yes. His] ~; his
98	3	question.] ~,
	5	does,] ~.
	7	out.] ~,
	9	said.] ~,
	10	colour] color
	11	added.] ~,
	24	idealisation] idealization
	35	said;] ~,
99	4	Egbert.] ~,
	4	earnestly,] ~.
	7	truth.] ~,
	9	impressionable—] ~,
	10	gaol,] jail.
	11	father;] ~,
	15	anybody] any body
	24	eyes;] ~,
	29	love,] ~.
	30	her;] ~,
	4	ardour] ardor
	6	this,] ~.
	8	rencounter] recontre
	9	afterwards] afterward
	10	third] 3d
	11	twelfth] 12th
	12	twenty-eighth] 28th
	12	ninth] 9th
	13	seventeenth] 17th
	17	out of doors] ~-~-~
	25	patronise] patronize
	27	continued.] ~,
	29¹	voice.] ~,
	34	remained.] ~,
101	6	towards] toward

101	8	sometimes] somtimes
	10	neighbours] neighbors
	12	to-night.] ~,
	14	twelve,] ~—
	21	attachment,] ~.
	23	Allenville, too,] ~. ~.
	32	Egbert.] ~,
	33	speaking,] ~.
102	8	grey] gray
	9	towards her,] toward ~.
	12	her.] ~,
	15	do,] ~.
	21	Melanthus] Melanthius
	22	.Entertained] "entertained
	23	rest..] ~."
	27	leant] leaned
103	1	Yet, no,] ~. ~!
	1	murmured,] ~;
	7	defence] defense
	9	House.] ~,
	12	house,] ~.
	12	her;] ~,
	21	action,] ~.
	22	excused,] ~.
	26	favour] favor
	28	.So] "~
	29	man,] ~;
	30	break.] ~,
	32	Over head] Overhead
	33	underground mine:] under-ground ~,
104	1	labour] labor
	2	event.] ~;
	3	sudden—how] ~— How
	3	end?.] ~?"
	5	was. after all.] ~, ~ ~,
	9	encumbrance] incumbrance
	10	time!] ~,
	11	her,] ~.
	11	her;] ~,
	12	alarm,] ~.
	17	indoors] in-doors

104 18   creatures,] ~ˏ
   21   chairs,] ~ˏ
   31   again)ˏ] ~),
   31   learnt] learned
 32–3   look-out;] ~,
   33   and,] ~ˏ
   34   half-week] ~ˏ~
   36   advance,] ~ˏ

105 8   flushed,] ~ˏ
   13   spotˏ] ~,
   17   oratoryˏ] ~,
   23   him—] ~,
   24   blame—] ~,
   28   grass;] ~,
   29   corner,] ~ˏ
   31   you;] ~,
   31   inaudibly,] ~ˏ
   32   recognised] recognized
   34   result,] ~ˏ
   37   dressing-bell] ~ˏ~

106 1   wordˏ] ~,
   4   sympathising] sympathizing
   5²   toˏ] ~,
   7   figure,] ~ˏ
   9   saidˏ] ~,
  11   Oh] O
  14   churchyard] church-yard
  16   churchyard] church-yard
  16   porchˏ] ~,
  18   spoke.] ~:
  22   saidˏ] ~,
  25   answeredˏ] ~,
  26   Still,] ~ˏ
  32   toˏ] ~—
  33   booksˏ] ~,
  33   anything] any thing

107 3   Allenville!] ~,
   3   heˏ] ~,
   7   emotionˏ] ~,
  11   whilst] while
  17   labouring-men] laboring-men

107 17   bed,] ~;
     26   trifles;] ~,
     31   place.] ~,
     35   away; his] ~. His
108   1   great. When] ~: when
      1   gone.] ~,
      4   confidences,] ~.
      5   made;] ~:
     10   Squire] squire
     11   She,] ~.
     14   Egbert.] ~,
     15   you.—] ~?—
     16   harm?] ~.
     20   boy,] ~!
     27   said.] ~,
     30   it;] ~:
     31   honourable] honorable
     31   honour] honor
     33   high-born.] ~,
     34†   angel." HW] ~.. NQM
109   6   .Hath] "~
     10   Because,] ~.
     10   faults,] ~.
     11   loved?.] ~?"
     22   towards] toward
     22   upstairs] up stairs
     31   more,] ~;
     33   "lack] .~
     33   idleness,"] ~,.
     36   society,] ~;
110   5   moonlit] moon-lit
      6   door;] ~,
      9   upstairs] up stairs
     11   coming—] ~.
     12   I, indeed,] ~. ~.
     16   you,] ~—
     17   Egbert.—] ~?—
     17   me?] ~.
     18   own.] ~,
     25   likely,] ~.
     29   fine-lady] ~.~
     34   murmured.] ~,

110 36 everything] every thing

111 1   he.] ~,
     2   life,] ~;
    13   anybody] any body
    16   me,] ~—
    16   to,] ~.
    18   all—] ~,
    18   anybody,] any body.
    19   it,] ~.
    22   anything] any thing
    29   honour] honor
    31   weakness,] ~.

112 2   times;] ~,
     6   colours] colors
     6   afterwards] afterward
    13   'Yes'] .yes.
    15   'Yes.'] .yes..
    18   wood,] ~.
    21   afterwards] afterward
    27   .Come] "~
    27   organise] organize
    28   society..] ~."
    30   beacon.] ~,
    31   erect.] ~,
    31   brother,] ~.
    32   General] general
    32   school.children] ~-~

113 1   distance,] ~.
     1   towards] toward
     5   loud,] ~.
     5   soft,] ~.
     9   father,] ~—
     9   five-and-forty,] ~—
    10   house;] ~,
    12   bottle.] ~,
    13   enclosed] inclosed
    19   anything] any thing
    30   whispered.] ~,
    35   said. softly.] ~, ~,

114 1   eyes.] ~,
     1   added,] ~:

114 6   replied.] ~,
     6   tone,] ~—
     6-7 her. "The] ~—"the
     9   Westcombe. ¶] ~. ˄
     11 him.] ~,
     13 hours—so] ~! So
     15 miles—who] ~! Who
     15 thing!] ~?
     25 habits.] ~,
     26 reconciled. ¶] ~. ˄
     29 recognised] recognized
     33 occasion,] ~˄

115 2   side.] ~,
     6   another; what] ~: What
     7   father,] ~˄
     11 of,] ~—
     14 felt;] ~,
     17 determined.] ~,
     17 events.] ~,
     17 her,] ~;
     19 realise] realize
     24 for ever] forever
     33 pretence] pretense
     38 morning. ¶] ~. ˄

116 11 tale:] ~;
     12 ˄And] '~
     13 dead:] ~;
     14 known..] ~.'
     15 fellow.] ~,
     19 cannot] can not
     20 me,] ~˄
     21 favour] favor
     22 oh,] ~!
     22 it—] ~;
     26 neighbouring society.] neighboring ~?
     27 towards] toward
     27 picture,] ~˄
     28 ahead,] ~˄
     31 ˄"Good-bye] ¶ "Good-by
     32 said.] ~,
     33 Good-bye] Good-by
     33 answered;] ~,

116 35 and.] ~,
   35 it.] ~,

117 3 wondered.] ~,
   3 after.days.] ~-~,
   4 reality,] ~.
   5 keen.] ~,
   6 Yet,] ~.
   7 perhaps,] ~.
   7 womanlike,] woman-like.
   11 .The] "~
   14 foes..] ~."
   20 dinner,] ~.
   20 life;] ~,
   23 at;] ~—

118 7 thought,] ~.
   13 submissive,] ~.
   15 murmured,] ~:
   22 hand,] ~.
   23 that—.] ~—.
   24 wife, but] ~. But

119 2–3 school.children] ~-~
   6 Egbert,] ~.
   7 schoolmaster] school-master
   7 spoilt] spoiled
   9 half-past three,] ~.~ ~;
   12 candle-flame] ~.~
   14 labourers] laborers
   17 candlelight] candle-light
   19 downstairs,] down stairs.
   20 weakness.] ~,
   25 good.mornen] ~-~
   26 sir] Sir
   27 Brown's,] ~;
   31 heavens,] ~!
   33 gloom,] ~.

120 3 enough;] ~?
   3 forgetful,] ~.
   6 towards] toward
   8 reassured] re-assured
   10 said.] ~,
   10 ground.floor] ~-~

120 11 side, go] ~. Go
   14 taper,] ~ˌ
   15 glowworm] glow-worm
   16 loose,] ~ˌ
   19 said.] ~,
   19 softly.] ~,
   21 Half-an-hour] ~ˌ~ˌ~
   27 said,] ~;
   27 cannot] can not
   35[†] "'Suppose *HW*] ˌ"~ *NQM*
   36 him.] ~,
   38 goodness.] ~,

121 12 'Backbone of Society,'] ˌ~ ~ ~,ˌ
   12–13 'Tendency of Modern Thought,'] ˌ~ ~ ~ ~,ˌ
   14 Lord] lord
   14' with.] ~,
   14 man,] ~ˌ
   17 Tyrrell's;] ~—
   17 occasion';] ~,'
   24 cannot] can not
   25 ledge;] ~:
   27 amongst] among
   28 head.] ~,
   28 him,] ~ˌ
   30 precincts,] ~ˌ
   31 parting.] ~,
   37 grey] gray

122 2 half-past] ~ˌ~
   3 harbour.] harbor,
   5 II] SECOND
   7 ˌHe] "~
   11 relies.ˌ] ~."
   14 minuteness] minutiae
   15 few, comparatively,] ~ˌ ~ˌ
   18 mustˌ thenˌ] ~, ~,
   20 drive.] ~,
   24 merit,] ~ˌ

123 3 Afterwards] Afterward
   4 literature;] ~,
   5 awhile] a while
   12 picture galleries,] ~-/~ˌ

123 13   humour] humor
    16   shades; Angelico,] ~, ~ˍ
    1⁊   saints; Murillo,] ~, ~ˍ
    18   men;] ~,
    18   women;] ~,
    21   Raffaelle,] ~ˍ
    25   shineˍ] ~,
    28   though, unfortunately,] ~ˍ ~ˍ
    29   thisˍ he hopedˍ] ~, ~ ~,
    34   ardour] ardor
124 3   Tollamore House] TOLLAMORE HOUSE
    4–5   EGBERT,ˍ ¶ "How] ~,—~
     5   happened! and] ~? And
     5   silenceˍ] ~,
    12   hope;] ~,
    12   longˍ] ~,
    14   cannot] can not
    15   towards usˍ] toward ~,
  15–16   wrong. [*6 spaced asterisks on following line*]] ~....
    19   you.] ~!
    20   cannot] can not
    23   moment;] ~,
    24   Sunday,] ~ˍ
    25   watersideˍ] water-side,
    31   blankness] Blankness
    33   thoughtsˍ] ~,
    34   anything] any thing
    36   Good-bye] Good-by
    36   cannot] can not
    37   Good-bye, good-bye] Good-by, good-by
    38   "G. A.] ˍ~

125 1   P.S.ˍ] ~—
     3   honourably] honorably
     8   which,] ~ˍ
     8   sure,] ~ˍ
    15   learnt] learned
    19   towards] toward
    21   attempt,] ~ˍ
    24   ˍTowards] "Toward
    26   light..] ~."
    30   warm,] ~ˍ
    33   newly-painted] ~ˍ~

126 7   her, Geraldine,] ∼: ∼ˌ
     17   her,] ∼ˌ
     20   her,] ∼ˌ

127 6   out.] ∼!
     9   streets,] ∼ˌ
     9   neighbourhood] neighborhood
     10   town-house] ∼ˌ∼
     14   her,] ∼ˌ
     19   passed,] ∼ˌ
     20   evening,] ∼ˌ
     33   ticket-office] ∼ˌ∼

     35–128 1   said, "but] ∼. "But
128 4   place,] ∼ˌ
     9   space,] ∼ˌ
     14   thought;] ∼,
     23   ¶ Never,] ˌ∼ˌ
     24   harmonies,] ∼ˌ
     30   libretto.] ∼,
     32   chorus.] ∼,
     34   towards] toward
     35   him.] ∼,

129 1   together.] ∼?
     11   morning.] ∼,
     15   place,] ∼!
     17   anything] any thing
     18   hand,] ∼ˌ
     20   somewhat.] ∼,
     21   nearer.] ∼,
     22   love!] ∼.
     26   realised] realized
     27   said;] ∼,
     32   Mine,] ∼ˌ
     33   now.] ∼,

130 2   front.door] ∼-∼
     6   and,] ∼ˌ
     7   doorway,] ∼ˌ
     9   ˌBright] "∼
     10   sky..] ∼."
     12   mantel-clock.] ∼ˌ∼,
     13   half-past] ∼ˌ∼
     14   street.] ∼,

130 20   everything] every thing
    23   front.door] ~-~
    27   named.] ~,
131 4   initials,—] ~.—
     4   open.] ~,
     6   handwriting:—] ~:.
    12   learnt] learned
    13   is;] ~—
    13   ask,] ~—
    14   exact.] ~—
    14   say.] ~,
    14   not] Not
    14   cannot] can not
    17   habit,] ~.
    20   knowledge?. A] ~?—a
    20   wisdom?. None] ~?—none
    23   worse.] ~,
    24   practised] practiced
    29   heartfelt] heart-felt
    32   anything] any thing
    33   and,] ~.
    34   meaning.] ~:
    35   position.] ~,
    35   but,] ~.
    36   cannot] can not
    39   "G. A.] .~
132 1   still;] ~:
     2   direction.] ~,
     3   towards] toward
     4   Road,] ~;
     8   afterwards] afterward
    11   towards] toward
    11   and,] ~.
    15   rooms.] ~,
    22   them, at least,] ~. ~ ~.
    24   Squire] squire
    24   patronised] patronized
    25   review.] ~,
    25   note:—] ~:.
    26   —,] ~.
    27   exercised,] ~.
    30   paragraph:—] ~:.

132 34   towards] toward
   34   there˄] ~,
   35   door,] ~˄
133 1   her,] ~!
    2   contained:—] ~:˄
    3   Twelve o'clock] *Twelve o'clock*
    4   learnt] learned
  10   for ever] forever
  14   "G. A.] ˄~
  16   stillness˄] ~,
  18   from; and,] ~, ~˄
  23   downstairs] down stairs
  24   towards] toward
  25   behaviour] behavior
  26   juncture,] ~˄
  33   bell˄] ~,
  35   footman˄] ~,
134 1   spoken˄] ~,
    2   downstairs] down stairs
    3   creature,] ~˄
    5   recognised] recognized
  13   cannot] can not
  13   said˄] ~,
  14   me˄] ~,
  14   cannot] can not
  16   Oh,] O˄
  18   cannot] can not
  19†   know." HW] ~.˄ NQM
  21   labour] labor
  24   go!] ~.
  28   ˄Then] "~
  28   "As] ˄~
  29   I˄ then˄] ~, ~,
  32   realisation] realization
135 4   success˄] ~,
  15   present,] ~˄
  16   distinction;] ~,
  17   course. ¶] ~. ˄
  26   haymaking] hay-making
  27   out˄of˄doors] ~-~-~
  27   spot,] ~˄
  32   mind;] ~,

134 33   Vale,] vale.ᵥ
     33   smelt] smelled

136 10   whilst] while
     16   grey] gray
     16   towards] toward
     16   and.ᵥ] ~,
     17   there.ᵥ towards] ~, toward
     20   towards] toward
     20   Park] park
     24   expected,] ~—
     28   church-bells] ~.ᵥ~
     29   shepherd.ᵥ] ~,
     30   Practising] Practicing
     31   Miss's] miss's
     34   shabby,] ~.ᵥ
     35   spot,] ~.ᵥ
     36   appletrees] apple-trees
     38   front.ᵥdoor] ~-~

137 8   Fairland.ᵥ] ~,
     10   neighbourhood] neighborhood
     11   17th] seventeenth
     17   loth] loath
     18   district;] ~,
     21   .ᵥHow] "~
     21   air,] ~.ᵥ
     22   despair.ᵥ] ~,
     23   jealousy!.ᵥ] ~!"
     27   Squire's lawn,] squire's ~.ᵥ
     28   bridesmaids] bride-maids
     32   he, too,] ~.ᵥ ~.ᵥ
     33   churchyard] church-yard

138 5   chancel-arch] ~.ᵥ~
     10   neighbouring] neighboring
     11   chancel.ᵥ] ~,
     15   altar-railing] ~.ᵥ~
     16   don't.] ~!
     19   to.ᵥday] ~-~
     20   way." ¶] ~."ᵥ
     21   towards] toward
     24   but.ᵥ] ~,
     24   design.ᵥ] ~,

138 25   afterwards] afterward
    26   Good.evening] ~-~
    26   said.] ~,
    29   and,] ~.
    31   anything] any thing
    34   door.] ~,
    34   head,] ~.
    35   hand,] ~.

139 1   said.] ~,
    4   out-do] outdo
    5   tone, ¶] ~: .
    13   that?] ~,
    13   answered.] ~,
    19   cannot] can not
    21   Indeed!] ~?
    26   floor;] ~,
    31   anything] any thing
    33   day,] ~.

140 2   afterwards understand.] afterward ~:
    12   not,] ~—
    13   anything] any thing
    24   further,] ~.
    25   more. Now] ~: now
    28   good-bye] good-by
    30   door,] ~.
    31   path,] ~.
    33   churchyard] church-yard
    35   recognised] recognized

141 2   made.up] ~-~
    5   now!] ~?
    6   suppose.] ~,
    6   Egbert.] ~,
    7   towards] toward
    12   half-reservations] ~.~
    13   wishes,] ~!
    14   this!] ~?
    15   towards] toward
    16   endeavour] endeavor
    19   Fairland.] ~,
    19   awhile] a while
    20   mind.] ~,

141 21   meditating,] ~ͺ
     28   flush,] ~ͺ
     34   marriage] Marriage
     37   boring,] ~ͺ

142   2   towards] toward
     13   it:] ~;
     14   Geraldine. ¶] ~. ͺ
   15–16   front.door] ~-~
     21   cried.] ~,
     24   house,] ~ͺ
     24   question,] ~ͺ
     25   front.room] ~-~
     26   you!] ~,
     35   perhaps, after all,] ~ͺ ~ ~ͺ

143   2   gaiety] gayety
      3   eyes—] ~;
      8   now.] ~,
     10   behaviour] behavior
     11   learnt afterwards] learned afterward
     11   Ah!] ~,
     12   did?] ~!
     14   Bretton—] ~;
     15   concert—] ~:
     16   then,] ~ͺ
     17   longer!] ~,
     17   labour] labor
     18   night.] ~,
     18   horrible—] ~,
     23   Geraldine!] ~,
     24   mind,] ~.
     25   vow,] ~ͺ
     27   again,] ~ͺ
     28   noiselessly,] ~ͺ
     31   do?. Oh] ~?—oh
     32   father—no] ~— No
     32   cannot] can not
     32   now—] ~;
     34   that,] ~;
     35   Yes.] ~?

144   1   wife,] ~ͺ
      3   Egbert!] ~,

144   7   came ...] ~.
      8   replied.] ~,
     12   excitement. ¶] ~. ͵
     16   cannot] can not
     18   no;] ~,
     20   yes; not] ~. Not
     21   man—] ~;
     26   cupboard;] ~:
     27   now.] ~—
     28   anybody] any body
     31   burnt] burned

145   2   ͵Hence] ″~
      2   cell;] ~,
      3   tell..] ~.″
      5   neighbour] neighbor
     15   his.] ~,
     19   and,] ~͵
     20   towards] toward
     29   license. ͵] ~. ¶
     29   done,] ~͵
     30   mantelpiece] mantel-piece
     33   cannot] can not
     34† to — HW] ~— *NQM*
     36   Undoubtedly;] ~,
     36   anybody] any body

146   1   paying;] ~—
      3   No;] ~,
      5   surrogate.] ~,
      6   towards] toward
      8   cognisance] cognizance
      8   things,] ~͵
     12   document,] ~͵
     13   inn.] ~,
     17   him,] ~͵
     24   hat,] ~͵
     24   well;] ~,
     30   waiting. ͵] ~. ¶
     30   gaily] gayly
     30   breathlessly.] ~,
     31   and,] ~͵
     34   gathered;] ~,

147 1 cannot] can not
     1 murmured.] ~,
    11 and,] ~ˌ
    11 future,] ~ˌ
    14 hastily-married] ~ˌ~
    24 And,] ~ˌ
    25 off.] ~,
    30 turnpike‸road] ~-~
    30 fly,] ~ˌ
    34 seaport] sea-port

148 8 headed.] ~,
    11 unadvisable] inadvisable
    14 neighbourhood] neighborhood
    18 neighbouring] neighboring
    24 particulars.] Particulars:
    26 Fairland,] ~ˌ

149 1 said.] ~,
     3 darling;] ~,
     5 Yes;] ~,
     8 everything] every thing
    10 wonder,] ~—
    15 myself.] ~,
    17 anything] any thing
    19 fell,] ~—
    21 first;] ~,
    25 them;] ~,
    32 said.] ~,
    35 oak‸trees] ~-~
    37 humoured] humored
    37 everything] every thing

150 2 up.] ~,
     3 moonlit] moon-lit
     7 leant] leaned
     9 himself;] ~:
    10 it;] ~,
    22 her,] ~ˌ
    23 honeymoon] honey-moon
    26 am—] ~;
    26 return,] ~—
    27 answered; and] ~. And
    28 towards] toward

150 32   wife‸] ~,
   32   demarcation] demarkation
   36   down,] ~‸
   38   neighbourhood] neighborhood

151 11   thought‸] ~,
   12   him;] ~:
   14   them,] ~‸
   15   man,] ~‸
   17   absence,] ~‸
   19   favourable] favorable
   28   home‸] ~,
   32   out‸ and,] ~, ~‸

152 4   Egbert‸] ~,
    6   fainted,] ~‸
   11   after‸years] ~-~
   18   danger,] ~‸
   20   behaviour] behavior
   20   hand,] ~‸
   21   said‸] ~,
   23   turned,] ~‸
   24   saying‸] ~,
   24   low‸] ~,
   25   sir] Sir
   29   whispered‸] ~,
   29   cannot] can not
   32   Anything] Any thing
   32   said‸] ~,
   33   anything] any thing

153 4   said‸] ~,
    9   fulness] fullness
   11   breathing:] ~—
   12   ‸A] "~
   13   tears‸‸] ~."
   29   Egbert;] ~,
   32   head;] ~—
   35   behaviour] behavior

154 6   downstairs,] down‸stairs‸
   10   fainting-fit] ~‸~
   12   flown;] ~,
   13   wandered;] ~,
   13   towards] toward

154 22   Everything] Every thing
    24   anxious.] ~,
    25   death] Death

COMPOUND WORDS HYPHENATED AT END OF LINE IN COPY-TEXT

90 14   rallying-points
97 26   grandfather
102 29   ill-treat
106 16   churchyard
107 17   labouring-men
108 23   threshing-machine
109 13   bandy-legged
132 23   drawing-room
136 36   appletrees
139 1–2   half-whispered
144 31   daylight
150 14   summer-house
152 10   man-servant
154 10   fainting-fit

OUR EXPLOITS AT WEST POLEY

EXPLANATORY NOTES

169 14–15   *Carlyle . . . do*: On Heroes, Hero-Worship, and the Heroic in History, Lecture VI, 'The Hero as King. Cromwell. Napoleon: Modern Revolutionism'. The 1841 first edn. (352) reads: 'Virtue, *Vir-tus*, manhood, *hero*-hood, is not fairspoken immaculate regularity; it is first of all, what the Germans well name it, *Tugend* (*Taugend*, *dow*-ing or *Dough*tiness), Courage and the Faculty to *do*.'

173 3–4   *nether . . . shore*: in classical mythology the Styx is one of the rivers forming the expanse of water which had to be crossed by the souls of the dead before reaching the kingdom of Hades.

178 7   *mill-tail*: 'The water which runs away from a mill-wheel' (*OED*).

179 34   *Yesterday afternoon*: earlier two days are said to have passed before the boys visit East Poley; the inconsistency is presumably an authorial oversight (see pp. 157–8).

182 29 *Jeremy Bentham*: political philosopher (1748–1832; *DNB*) who
believed that utility was the touchstone of morality and that the
greatest increase of happiness for the largest number of people
should be the guiding principle of conduct.

   38   *Hamlet to the Ghost:*
                           Remember thee?
                Ay, thou poor ghost, while memory holds a seat
                In this distracted globe. Remember thee?
                Yea, from the table of my memory
                I'll wipe away all trivial fond records,
                All saws of books, all forms, all pressures past,
                That youth and observation copied there;
                And thy commandment all alone shall live
                Within the book and volume of my brain,
                Unmix'd with baser matter: yes, yes, by heaven.
                    Shakespeare, *Hamlet*, ix. 180 (I. v. 95–104)

185 17 Hi ... horum: schoolboy Latin; the nominative and genitive plur-
als of *hic* ('this').

187 8–9 *When ... hands*: yet another example of expired lifehold (see
explanatory note to p. 95. 16); cf. also the widow's desire to stay in
the family-built house and Broadford's similar wish in 'Indiscretion'.

191 6   *discovered by Steve*: in chapter I it is Leonard who discovers the
second hole; the inconsistency is perhaps unintentional but see the
discussion of Leonard as an unreliable narrator deliberately
minimizing his responsibility in Pamela Dalziel, 'A Critical Edition of Thomas Hardy's Uncollected Stories', D.Phil. thesis
(University of Oxford, 1989), 363 ff.

195 30–2 *Flaminius ... escape*: Flaminius was killed and his army destroyed by Hannibal's ambush at Lake Trasimene in 217 BC; the
quotation is from Livy, 22. 5.

202 30–1 *place in another mill*: in chapter II Job's new situation is said to be
on a farm, not necessarily a contradiction since Job, preferring to
complete his apprenticeship, could have turned down the farmer
when he found mill-work. In the final chapter, however, he is again
said to be with the farmer. The inconsistency is presumably an
authorial oversight.

205 31 *farmer*: presumably a (compositorial?) error, since there is no reference to any of the farmers accompanying Leonard, the baker, and
the shoemaker. Perhaps the original MS passage was abridged and
the reading should in fact be 'former'.

206 9   *discovered by Steve*: see note to p. 191. 6.

207 18   *meanfully*: perhaps a compositorial misreading of 'meanly' but more probably a TH invention meaning with malevolent intent.

209 11–12   *Romans ... Samnites*: described by Livy, 9. 5–6; like the East Poleyites, the Romans did not accept their defeat gracefully and war was resumed in 316 BC, five years after the surrender.

211 24   *situation with the farmer*: see note to p. 202. 30–1.

    32   *Coleridge or an Emerson*: Samuel Taylor Coleridge, poet, critic, and philosopher (1772–1834; *DNB*); Ralph Waldo Emerson, American poet, essayist, and philosopher (1803–82).

212 37   *liever*: dialect for 'More willingly, rather' (Wright's *English Dialect Dictionary*; also listed in *OED*). Cf. William Barnes's definition of 'lief': 'as willingly, or soon' (*A Glossary of the Dorset Dialect with a Grammar of its Word Shapening and Wording* (London: Trübner, 1886)). TH uses 'liefer' in 'The Wedding Morning'.

TEXTUAL NOTES

170 19   *Mendip*: *H* reads 'Mondip', presumably a compositorial error owing to the difficulty of distinguishing TH's vowels, especially as appearing within unfamiliar English place-names.

    21   *Cheddar*: *H* reads 'Chuddar'; see preceding note.

171 32   *unobserved*: in *H* the first 'e' failed to print. Also not printed is the 'v' in 'above' (p. 172. 17).

    38   *original*: in *H* followed by a comma, presumably added by a compositor blindly following some kind of house style. Since the *H* pointing obscures the meaning of the sentence it has been emended. For the same reason commas have been removed after 'there' (p. 172. 3), 'beautiful' (p. 174. 24), 'Now' (p. 180. 3), 'eleven-fifteen' (p. 184. 27), 'endeavouring' (p. 186. 20), 'thus' (p. 186. 21), 'moved' (p. 187. 11), 'Then' (p. 190. 13), 'attempt' (p. 192. 28), 'small' (p. 213. 7), and 'doubt' (p. 213. 33), and those after 'ways' (p. 192. 28) and 'farmers (p. 203. 17) have been emended to a colon and a semi-colon, respectively.

172 10   *Somersetshire*: *H* reads 'the Somersetshire'; perhaps Somersetshire was used adjectivally in the MS and the compositor omitted a word or, more probably, in his unfamiliarity with the use of English county-names he added the redundant article.

174 2   *Channel*: *H* reads 'channel', probably a compositorial error owing to the difficulty of distinguishing TH's upper- from his lower-case 'c' (see *CL* i. xv).

174 27   *frills*: an emendation of the *H* reading 'pills', which makes no sense
         in a description of ornaments resembling lace and coats of mail.
         TH's 'fr' could easily have been mistaken for 'p'; cf. FEH's 'primly'
         for 'firmly' in 'Old Mrs Chundle' (see TN for p. 229. 22).

175 8   *day*: possibly a compositorial misreading of 'date'; however, as 'at
         an early day' is not an impossible construction and might be
         authorial, the copy-text reading has been retained.

176 33   *loach, sticklebacks*: *H* reads 'leach, stickbacks', presumably com-
         positorial misreadings of the unfamiliar fish-names.

178 26   *shan't*: *H* reads 'sha'n't'; since TH never used this form it has been
         emended (cf. the editorial policy with respect to single quotation
         marks and periods after abbreviations).

180 21   *quite*: in *H* preceded by 'being', which perhaps indicates that the
         MS's original final clause was deleted; as the sentence stands,
         however, the participle is redundant and has therefore been
         omitted.

181 28   *Man who had Failed*: the omission of 'had' in *H* may reflect the MS
         (cf. 'Man who has Failed' (p. 170. 3)) but is more likely to be a
         compositorial error.

187 22   *and then,*: *H* reads 'and, then'; the comma (probably a composito-
         rial addition) has been moved as required by the context.

188 36   *this*: in *H* followed by a semi-colon, presumably a compositorial
         error as the context requires a colon.

190 14   *came*: the *H* reading 'come' may reflect the MS but is probably a
         compositorial error since TH's vowels are often difficult to distin-
         guish and the sentence requires a verb in the past tense.

     27 *why*: in *H* not followed by any punctuation mark but the context
         clearly requires a colon.

191 7   *closed*: *H* reads 'close', a possible but not probable MS reading.

     38 *thousand*: the absence of any punctuation mark in *H* may be
         authorial since TH's pointing was rhetorical and often incon-
         sistent, particularly in hastily written manuscripts. Usually no
         attempt has been made to 'correct' unconventional usage (cf.
         pp. 189. 2–4, 196. 6, 24–5), but in this case the sentence was too
         awkward and potentially disruptive to be left unemended.

197 20   *said. ¶* : the absence of a paragraph break in *H* may reflect the MS
         but is in any case an unintentional error requiring emendation.

212 15 *the*: perhaps a compositorial error for 'that', but the use of the definite article in this context was not uncommon during the nineteenth century; cf. 'at the moment' in *Little Dorrit* (Oxford: Clarendon, 1979), 796.

37 *liever*: *H* reads 'never', presumably an example of *lectio familior*. J. C. Maxwell was the first to suggest that the compositor misread the dialect word; see 'Hardy's "Our Exploits at West Poley": A Correction', *Notes and Queries*, ns 6 (1959), 113.

PUNCTUATION AND STYLING VARIANTS AND TYPOGRAPHICAL ERRORS

The edited text differs from the copy-text in not using periods after 'Mr' and 'Mrs'.

170 19[†] he.] ~,

171 16[†] neighbourhood] neighborhood
    38[†] original.] ~,

172 3[†] there.] ~,

174 2[†] Channel] channel
     6[†] labours] labors
    24[†] beautiful.] ~,
    26–7[†] flesh-coloured] flesh-colored

176 29[†] labour] labor

178 17[†] neighbour] neighbor
    26[†] shan't] sha'n't
    32[†] labourers] laborers
    36[†] day..] ~."

179 6[†] than] then

180 3[†] Now.] ~,

183 9[†] screamed] sereamed

184 27[†] eleven-fifteen.] ~,

185 8[†] we—"] ~"—

186 20–1[†] endeavouring. thus.] endeavoring, ~,
    27[†] hedge] hegde

187 11[†] moved.] ~,
    22[†] and. then,] ~, ~.

188 36[†] this:] ~;

189 39[†] neighbours] neighbors

190 13[†] Then.] ~,
   27[†] why:] ~.

191 2[†] cauldron] caldron
   32[†] stones."] ~..
   38[†] thousand–] ~.

192 28[†] attempt. in two ways:] ~, ~ ~ ~,

194 7[†] endeavoured] endeavored

195 8[†] .What] "~

197 20[†] said. ¶] ~. .
   23[†] anxiety.] ~,

199 26[†] I'd—"] ~"—

201 19[†] labours] labors
   38[†] neighbours] neighbors

203 17[†] farmers;] ~,
   31[†] "Did] .~

204 14[†] neighbours] neighbors

207 1[†] labour] labor
   5[†] vigour] vigor
   27[†] labour] labor

208 39[†] labour] labor

209 3[†] more.] ~,

211 31[†] favouring] favoring

213 7[†] small.] ~,
   33[†] doubt.] ~,
   34[†] labours] labors

COMPOUND WORDS HYPHENATED AT END OF LINE IN COPY-TEXT

169 3 farmhouse

170 17 hypercritical

171 12 gravel-pits

172 9 limestone

174 23 watercourse

175 6 recrossed

179 5 preoccupied
   18 homesteads

OLD MRS CHUNDLE

EXPLANATORY NOTES

228   3   *Corvsgate*: from 'Corfgetes', the Saxon name for Corfe Castle.

229 32   *Enckworth*: Wessex name for Encombe.

230   4   *Anglebury*: Wessex name for Wareham.

         7   *Kingscreech*: presumably based on Gillingham; see pp. 224–5.

231 13   *lumpering*: from the dialect verb 'to lumper', also used in *Jude* (275),
             The Dynasts, Part First (67), and 'The Bride-Night Fire'; in the 1912
             Wessex Edition of *Wessex Poems* (96) TH glossed 'lumpered'
             'stumbled'.

       14   *plock*: a dialect word meaning 'block' (William Barnes, *A Glossary
             of the Dorset Dialect with a Grammar of its Word Shapening and Wording*
             (London: Trübner, 1886), 88).

232 10   *jimcracks*: an alternative spelling of 'gimcracks'; 'jim-cracks'
             appears in *Two on a Tower* (277) and 'jimcrack' (used as an adjec-
             tive) in *Under the Greenwood Tree* (11) and *A Pair of Blue Eyes* (205,
             256).

       13   *Creech Barrow*: a 200-m. tumulus in the Purbeck Hills, 6 km. west of
             Corfe Castle.

234 21 *en*: a dialect word defined according to context as 'it' or 'him' in TH's glosses for *Select Poems of William Barnes* (London: Henry Frowde, 1908).

236 12 *Peter at the cock-crow*: 'And Peter remembered the word of Jesus, which said unto him, Before the cock crow, thou shalt deny me thrice. And he went out, and wept bitterly' (Matt. 26: 75; also described in the other gospels).

TEXTUAL NOTES

228 9 *eat,*: in MS the alteration of the original question mark and closing quotation marks to a comma suggests that 'my good woman'— and perhaps also 'he said'—was not in the draft from which TH was copying.

14 *he. ¶*: TH's failure to introduce the paragraph break necessitated by the added dialogue in the MS interlineation was presumably an oversight.

22 *ye,*: the alteration of the period to a comma in MS suggests that the sentence ended at this point in the draft from which TH was copying. Similar alterations of periods to commas occur after 'halfpence' (p. 229. 23), 'Chundle' (p. 230. 15), 'pleasure' (p. 231. 25), 'good' (p. 232. 9), 'Ay' (p. 232. 28), 'cease' (p. 233. 11), and 'man' (p. 235. 3).

28 *here."*: in MS the quotation marks slightly precede the period, but they appear to be a later addition and the (presumably unintended) order has been emended. Similar instances occur at p. 229. 22 ('firmly. "Why'), 32 ('Enckworth."'), and 34 ('true."'). Neither the authorial additions of the quotation marks nor the editorial emendations of the order are recorded in the listing of variants.

229 22 *firmly*: misread as 'primly' by FEH (typescript sent to Curtis Brown, fo. 3; David Holmes collection) and hitherto uncorrected.

23 *three halfpence*: the words are not separated in MS; since the 'h' is written over the descender of a 'p', TH probably started to write 'threepence'.

230 7 *Kingscreech*: MS reads 'Kingcreech', though 'Kingscreech' is also used once (p. 231, 34); the latter spelling has been chosen largely for euphonic reasons, but see also p. 224.

232 29 *nothing,*: in MS followed by the undeleted first half of the original closing quotation marks; the second half is absorbed into the added 'I'.

233 20   *interruption;*: the alteration of the period to a semi-colon in MS suggests that the sentence ended at this point in the draft from which TH was copying.

    36   *consideration—"*: the dash was probably a later addition as MS reads 'consideration"—'. The spacing of the punctuation after 'consider' (p. 234. 4) is similar. Neither is recorded in the listing of variants.

234   5–6   *have made!"*: in MS written above the last line of text, presumably in order to avoid carrying the sentence over to the next page.

    19   *you*: the 'y' is written over a 'w' in MS.

235 13   *week.*: the period looks like a dash in MS, but since TH was obviously writing at a considerable speed and his stops are occasionally elongated (cf. fo. 4. 25), the more logical punctuation has been adopted.

    19   *How*: in MS followed by a deleted ascender, presumably the beginning of 'M'.

236   6   *peoples's.'*: the paragraph initially ended at this point; the first half of the original closing quotation marks remains undeleted in MS (the second half is absorbed into the added 'S' of 'She'). The following sentence and paragraph relating to Mrs Chundle's will are therefore later additions which TH apparently thought of including only after he had written out the first lines of the concluding paragraph.

    7   *It*: in MS written over an erasure, apparently 'wet' (the expected next word in the deleted lines from the concluding paragraph).

   10   *framed*: in MS the 'f' is written over an 's', presumably the beginning of 'sampler'.

PUNCTUATION AND STYLING VARIANTS AND TRANSCRIPTIONAL ERRORS

Ampersands in the copy-text have been expanded in the edited text.

228   9   eat,] ~?"
    9†   said. *Ed.*] ~ˌ *MS*
   11†   shouted. *Ed.*] ~ˌ *MS*
   14†   he. ¶ *Ed.*] ~. ˌ *MS*
   17†   it?ˌ But *Ed.*] ~?—But *MS(3)* ˈ ~?—but *MS(2)*] ~?—or *MS(1)*
   19†   here." *Ed.*] ~.ˌ *MS*
   22   ye,] ~.

229 11   b'lieve!] ~.
   13†   'Tis *Ed.*] 'tis *MS*

229 22 more!] ~.
  23† three halfpence, *Ed.*] threehalfpence, *MS(2)*] threehalfpence. *MS(1)*

230 4 marketing;] ~:
  14† name—a *Ed.*] ~—A *MS(2)*] ~. A *MS(1)*
  15 Chundle,] ~.
  24† deception!" *Ed.*] ~!ₐ *MS(2)*] ~.ₐ *MS(1)*
  27 me!] ~.

231 25 pleasure,] ~.

232 7† nonsense. *Ed.*] ~ₐ *MS*
  9 good,] ~.
  28 Ay,] ~.
  30† kind-hearted *Ed.*] ~ₐ~ *MS*

233 11 cease,] ~.
  19 brethren] bretheren
  20 interruption;] ~.
  27† miracle. *Ed.*] ~ₐ *MS*
  37† himself. *Ed.*] ~ₐ *MS*

234 25† me?" *Ed.*] ~?ₐ *MS*
  26† course. *Ed.*] ~ₐ *MS*
  30† alone. *Ed.*] ~ₐ *MS*
  33† ha!" *Ed.*] ~!ₐ *MS*

235 3 man,] ~.
  5† out. *Ed.*] ~ₐ *MS*
  10† re-erect *Ed.*] re-eret *MS*
  20† whisper. *Ed.*] ~ₐ *MS*

COMPOUND WORD HYPHENATED AT END OF LINE IN
COPY-TEXT

233 26–7 pulpit-floor

THE DOCTOR'S LEGEND

EXPLANATORY NOTES

248 3 *mansion*: presumably Came House, Joseph Damer's residence before he purchased Milton Abbey.

  9–10 *one whom . . . soften*: Horace Walpole's 20 Aug. 1776 letter to Sir Horace Mann; see p. 242, n. 29.

253 3   *necrophobist*: not listed in *OED*; a 'necrophobe' is 'one who has a horror of death or of dead bodies'.

253 14   *an Abbey and its estates*: Milton Abbas.

258 13–14   *like Herod . . . remains*: 'And immediately the angel of the Lord smote him, because he gave not God the glory: and he was eaten of worms, and gave up the ghost' (Acts 12: 23); the Herod in question is Herod Agrippa I (d. AD 44 at the age of 34), grandson of Herod the Great.

20–8   *Isaiah . . . saith the Lord*: the words are quoted accurately except that 'him' replaces 'them' in 'I will rise up against them'; the omitted verses indicated by the ellipsis are 13–21.

TEXTUAL NOTES

248 9–10   *'one . . . soften'*: the edited text agrees with the copy-text in printing single quotation marks. In MS the double quotation marks have erroneously been altered—apparently by TH—to single.

13   *dirty*: followed in MS by an illegible deletion, perhaps 't' or '&'.

19   *it,*: the shape and spacing of the comma in MS suggest that it was a TH addition; the evidence, however, seems too tenuous to justify an entry in the list of variants. Other commas which appear to be TH's include those following 'nevertheless', 'afterwards' (p. 249. 4), 'be' (p. 249. 6), 'her' (p. 249. 13), 'child' (p. 249. 20), 'shoulder' (p. 249. 21), 'scene' (p. 249. 28), 'mother' (p. 250. 19), 'celebrated', 'rejoicing' (p. 251. 6), 'bells' (p. 251. 7), 'general', 'charitable' (p. 251. 12), 'dusk' (p. 251. 17), 'quivering' (p. 252. 9), 'spring' (p. 252. 12), 'concerned' (p. 252. 13), 'slabs' (p. 253. 21), 'married' (p. 254. 5), 'turnings' (p. 254. 23), 'associations' (p. 254. 33), 'centuries' (p. 255. 11), 'been' (p. 255. 19), 'bones' (p. 256. 3), 'peer' (p. 256. 9), 'son' (p. 256. 10), 'each-other' (p. 256. 12), 'grave' (p. 258. 23), 'ground' (p. 258. 26), 'hearers' (p. 259. 3). The apostrophe in 'shan't' (p. 256. 34) and the semi-colons after 'large' (p. 248. 18) and 'home' (p. 249. 31) also appear to be TH additions.

248 24   *villagers*: in MS the 'v' looks like a capital, but EH often made her initial 'v' very large; cf. 'view' (fo. 1. 19), 'violent' (fo. 4. 1), and 'viols' (fo. 16. 10). Other ambiguous instances where the lower-case 'v' has been chosen are 'villagers' (pp. 252. 8, 255. 4) and 'village' (pp. 253. 5, 254. 19, 28, 255. 1).

249 1   *this*: followed by a deleted 'I' in MS; its location just to the left of
         the caret suggests that TH originally intended to add only 'It
         seems that'.

    19   *Squire,*: although the comma actually follows the deleted 'victim'
         (*MS(3)TH*) and is not enclosed in the circle around the retained
         'now', it is clearly undeleted and was presumably intended to be
         included.

250 14 *deep.*: followed by a redundant period in MS. Other redundant
         punctuation includes commas after 'and' (p. 251. 24) and 'dis-
         turbed' (p. 256. 6), periods after 'wall' (p. 251. 27) and 'accom-
         plishments' (p. 257. 16), an apostrophe after 'Lady' (p. 252. 8),
         and a semi-colon after 'hearts' (p. 254. 13).

    20³ *the*: perhaps an EH correction since it is written slightly above the
         line.

    28   *'Death's Head'*: EH mistakenly used single quotation marks; the
         edited text therefore follows the copy-text.

    28   *since . . . hair,*: in MS added slightly above the line in the space after
         'skull.', and perhaps originally intended to conclude the sentence.

251 25 *deary!'*: originally the end of the sentence; the 's' of the following
         'she' remains capitalized in MS.

252 1   *it*: a deleted 's' and downstroke above the line in MS suggest that
         TH started to write 'she' and then changed his mind.

    28   *knights*: in MS the 'k' looks like a capital, but EH tended to make
         this letter very large; cf. 'gamekeepers' (fo. 2. 7), 'nick-named' (fo.
         5. 8), and 'monkish' (fo. 8. 21). Lower case has also been used for
         the ambiguous 'k' in 'knightly' (p. 253. 6).

253 3   *at which*: in MS the beginning of a downstroke above the 'a' is
         deleted.

    7   *another*: EH first wrote 'inother', then altered it to 'another' and
         added 'in' above the line.

254 7   *peers*: TH deleted EH's 'peers' and wrote 'peers' above it, pre-
         sumably because EH's 'p' is unclear. TH also rewrote 'peer'
         (p. 255. 8) and redrew the dash after 'was' (p. 258. 5) and the
         commas after 'ball-room' (p. 255. 30) and 'aforesaid' (p. 256. 16).

    32   *conventual*: in *IN* the 't' failed to print.

256 12 *each-other*: the hyphenated form also appears in the MS of *The
         Woodlanders*, fo. 23 (DCM).

256 20   *the other*: separated in MS by a vertical line, perhaps to avoid ambiguity (the words are written quite close together). The redundant dash after 'other' has not been included in the edited text; TH, focusing on the end-of-sentence revision, presumably neglected to delete it.

   25   *would*: in MS followed by a deleted 'b', presumably the beginning of 'be'.

259 1   *Here*: in the space marking the paragraph indentation TH wrote '[Blank line]' above ' ¶ Here~~with~~'.

PUNCTUATION AND STYLING VARIANTS AND TYPOGRAPHICAL ERRORS

The edited text follows *IN* in expanding the MS's ampersands and doubling its single quotation marks.

248   2   half-a-dozen] ~ˌ~ˌ~ *IN*
     9   'one *MS(2)TH*] "~ *MS(1)*
  10–11   soften'. ¶ "This *MS(2)TH*] ~.' ¶ "~ *IN*] ~". ˌˌ~ *MS(1)*
   14   fore-lock *MS(2)TH*] forelock *IN*
   15   Honour *MS(2)TH*] Honor *IN*] honour *MS(1)*
   15   Squire', *MS(2)TH*] ~,' *IN*] squire", *MS(1)*
   20   though] tho *IN*
   20   well-watched] ~ˌ~ *IN*
   21   gamekeepers *MS(2)EH*] game-keepers *MS(1)*
   21   dependants] dependents *IN*
   23   enclosed] inclosed *IN*
   25   grounds. *MS(2)TH*] ~, *MS(1)*
   28   occasion,] ~ˌ *IN*

249   2   afterwards *MS(2)TH*] afterward *IN*
   3¹†   the *IN*] The *MS*
   4   afterwards] afterward *IN*
   6   and, *MS(2)TH*] &ˌ *MS(1)*
   9¹†   as *IN*] As *MS*
   12   endeavoured] endeavored *IN*
   24   that, *MS(2)TH*] ~ˌ *MS(1)*
   28   and, *MS(2)TH*] &ˌ *MS(1)*
   29   gardeners *MS(2)EH?*] gardiners *MS(1)*
   29   near, *MS(2)TH*] ~: *MS(1)*
   30   squire] Squire *IN*

250   4   condition:] ~; *IN*
   4   distressed,] ~ˌ *IN*

250 5   when.] ~, *IN*
    8   recognised] recognized *IN*
    9† scare-crow *Ed.*] scarecrow *IN*] scarce-crow *MS*
    9   appeared,] ~. *IN*
    13 impunity. And *MS(3)TH*] ~; and *IN*
    14 become. *MS(2)TH*] ~, *MS(1)*
    15 and, *MS(2)TH*] &. *MS(1)*
    15 villagers, *MS(2)TH*] ~. *MS(1)*
    16 ruffian.] ~, *IN*
    17 mansion.] ~, *IN*
    22 idiotized *MS(2)TH*] idiotised *MS(1)*
    23 day.] ~, *IN*
    25¹ Head *MS(2)TH*] head *MS(1)*
    25² Death's Head *MS(2)TH*] death's head *MS(1)*
    27–8 nick-named] nicknamed *IN*
    28 Head *MS(2)TH*] head *MS(1)*
    30 gone.] ~, *IN*
    31 distance. *MS(2)EH*] ~, *MS(1)*
    32 cheeks] checks *IN*

251 1   had, *MS(2)TH*] ~. *MS(1)*
    2   indeed, *MS(2)TH*] ~. *MS(1)*
    3   Squire *MS(2)EH*] squire *MS(1)*
    8   woman. *MS(2)TH*] ~, *MS(1)*, *IN*
    10 Squire, *MS(2)TH*] ~. *IN*] squire, *MS(1)*
    11 newly-wedded] ~.~ *IN*
    13 endeavouring] endeavoring *IN*
    14 particular *MS(2)TH*] particlar *IN*
    14 Autumn. *MS(2)TH*] autumn. *IN*] Autumn, *MS(1)*
    15 parish-visiting] ~.~ *IN*
    17 churchyard-wall] ~.~ *IN*
    19 widow.] ~, *IN*
    19 girl.] ~, *IN*
    24† and. *IN*] &, *MS*
    25 her.] ~, *IN*
    25† she *IN*] She *MS*
    28† "The *IN*] .~ *MS*

252 5   death-like] deathlike *IN*
    5   and, *MS(2)TH*] &. *MS(1)*
    10 prostrate] prostate *IN*
    15 However.] ~, *IN*
    16 and, *MS(2)TH*] &. *MS(1)*
    16 friends,] ~. *IN*

252 18   before-mentioned] ~.~ *IN*
    22   Uncle] uncle *IN*
    23   time,] ~. *IN*
    24   nephew.] ~, *IN*
    26   necessity, *MS(2)EH*] ~. *MS(1)*
    28   County] county *IN*
    28   knights] Knights *IN*

253 6   knightly] Knightly *IN*
    7   of] of of *IN*
   11   though] tho *IN*
   13   country-seat] ~.~ *IN*
   15   wealthy *MS(2)TH*] weathy *IN*
   19   Archbishop] archbishop *IN*
   20   fish-ponds] ~.~ *IN*
   20   abbey-church] ~.~ *IN*
   20   Abbots'] abbots' *IN*
 24–5[†]   shoulder. ¶ "'We've *IN*] ~. ¶ .''~ *MS(2)TH*] ~. . .''~ *MS(1)*
   26   unrivalled] unrivaled *IN*
   26   Ha] ha *IN*
  27[†]   don't *IN*] dont *MS*
  27[†]   Abbeys,' *Ed.*] abbeys.' *IN*] Abbeys''. *MS*
  27[†]   'They *IN*] .~ *MS*
  31[†]   Yes.'*IN*] ~.'' *MS*
   32   mitred Abbots] mitered abbots *IN*

254 1   monks—] ~, *IN*
    1   money. ... Yes.] ~— ~, *IN*
    2   Ho-ho] Ho, ho *IN*
   3[†]   men,' *IN*] ~'', *MS*
    4   'despite *MS(2)EH?*] .~ *MS(1)*
    5   up,] ~. *IN*
    7   this,] ~. *IN*
    8   reasons.] ~, *IN*
    9   legend;] ~, *IN*
   10   neighbours] neighbors *IN*
   12   honoured] honored *IN*
   13   though *MS(2)TH*] tho *IN*
   13   honoured *MS(2)TH*] honored *IN*
   15   beauty. nevertheless.] ~, ~, *IN*
   17   all.] ~, *IN*
   21   died;] ~, *IN*
   23   Though] Tho *IN*
   23   cells,] ~. *IN*

254 24   (as *MS(2)TH*] ‿~ *MS(1)*
    25   become). *MS(2)TH*] ~‿. *MS(1)*
    25   Abbot's] Abbots' *IN*
    27   Earl] earl *IN*
    27   Earls] earls *IN*
    28   Moreover‿] ~, *IN*
    29   lawn,] ~; *IN*
    31   Church] church *IN*

255 2   new,] ~‿ *IN*
     2   and, *MS(2)TH*] ~‿ *MS(1)*
     5   Abbey-Church] Abbey‿church *IN*
    10   waggons] wagons *IN*
    15   "It *MS(2)TH?*] ‿~ *MS(1)*
    17   down‿] ~, *IN*
    20   levelled] leveled *IN*
    20   Abbots] abbots *IN*
    23†   "Of *IN*] ‿~ *MS*
    31   card-parlour *MS(2)TH*] card‿parlor *IN*
    32   mitred] mitered *IN*

256 1†   "'Put *IN*] ‿."~ *MS*
     1   hole, *MS(2)TH?*] ~. *MS(1)*
     2   time,] ~. *IN*
     3†   lord,' *IN*] ~", *MS*
     6   looked *MS(2)TH*] look *IN*
     7   room. ‿ *MS(2)TH*] ~. ¶ *MS(1)*
     9†   "'Curse *IN*] ‿."~ *MS*
    10   More, *MS(2)TH?*] ~? *MS(1)*
    11   find!] ~. *IN*
    12   each-other] ~‿~ *IN*
    16†   accomplished *IN*] accomplised *MS*
    20   Angel *MS(2)TH*] angel *MS(1)*
    20†   other‿ *IN*] ~— *MS*
    22†   vogue). Might *Ed.*] ~)‿ might *IN*] ~)‿ Might *MS(2)TH*
    29   lady, *MS(2)TH?*] ~. *MS(1)*
    30   she;] ~. *IN*
    33-4 he. 'And] ~, 'and *IN*
    34   shan't] sha'n't *IN*

257 1†   won't *IN*] wont *MS*
    1-2   them ... *MS(2)TH*] ~— *IN*] ~, *MS(1)*
     2   least.... So] ~—so *IN*
     2†   let's *IN*] lets *MS*

257 4 man.ˌ *MS(2)TH*] ~, *IN*
    4† the *IN*] The *MS*
    4 though] tho *IN*
    5 character; *MS(2)TH*] ~: *MS(1)*
    9 acquaintance; *MS(2)TH*] ~: *MS(1)*
   10 skull.ˌ] ~, *IN*
   10 model.ˌ] ~, *IN*
   12 being.ˌ as usual.ˌ] ~, ~ ~, *IN*
   19 modelling *MS(2)TH*] modeling *IN*
   20 death's-head] ~.ˌ~ *IN*
   25 hand;] ~, *IN*
   27 before!' *MS(2)TH*] ~", *MS(1)*
   27 cried.ˌ] ~, *IN*
   27† accents. *Ed.*] ~; *IN*] ~.ˌ *MS*
   27 Where] where *IN*
   30 pistol.ˌ] ~, *IN*

258 1 charming; *MS(2)TH*] ~, *MS(1)*, *IN*
    4 persons— *MS(2)TH*] ~, *MS(1)*
    4 though] tho *IN*
    6 mother.ˌ] ~, *IN*
    8 Death's-Head', *MS(2)TH*] ~.ˌ~,' *IN*] death's-head", *MS(1)*
  11²† the *IN*] The *MS(1)*
   14 be.ˌ] be, *IN*
   17 neighbourhood] neighborhood *IN*
   20 text,] ~.ˌ *IN*
   20 XIV.] xiv, *IN*
   21 10–23:— *MS(2)TH*] ~:.ˌ *IN*] 10.23:.ˌ *MS(1)*
   28† Lord.' *IN*] ~". *MS*

259 1¹ the *IN*] The *MS*

COMPOUND WORDS HYPHENATED AT END OF LINE IN COPY-TEXT

253 32 underground

256 16 aforesaid

THE SPECTRE OF THE REAL

EXPLANATORY NOTES

299 2 *waning age*: Shakespeare, *The Taming of the Shrew*, iii. 140 (Ind., ii. 63).

15 *floor-stones of the Apocalyptic City*: an allusion to the new Jerusalem, as described in Rev. 21. TH's original revision, 'stones of the Apocalyptic City', in fact more closely corresponds to the biblical account: 'the foundations of the wall of the city were garnished with all manner of precious stones.... [T]he street of the city was pure gold ... '(vv. 19, 21).

300 23 *Harmony*: 'A collation of passages on the same subject from different writings, arranged so as to exhibit their agreement and account for their discrepancies; now chiefly used of a work showing the correspondences between the four Gospels and the chronological succession of the events recorded in them' (*OED*).

301 14 *Paladins*: the Twelve Peers or famous warriors of Charlemagne's court.

303 19–21 *Prince's ... Beloved*: in the Song of Solomon (7: 12) the prince's daughter says to her beloved, 'let us see if the vine flourish, whether the tender grape appear, and the pomegranates bud forth: there will I give thee my loves'.

304 1 *Qualms ... pelf*: unidentified.

307 9–10 *From ... him*: the biblical passage describing Absalom in fact reads, 'from the sole of his foot even to the crown of his head there was no blemish in him' (2 Sam. 14: 25).

317 1–2 *late campaign in Egypt*: presumably either the bombardment of Alexandria in July 1882, immediately preceding the British occupation of Egypt, or the capture of the Suez canal in August.

321 6 *Home-Rule question*: on 8 April 1886 Gladstone brought in his first bill for establishing Home Rule for Ireland.

TEXTUAL NOTES

299 title An ... Narrative: the use of upper- and lower-case letters follows 1TS; in all subsequent editions the title appears in full capitals. In 2TS TH corrected 'NARRAVITE' in pencil and then ink.

7–11 *into the ... play.*: added on a separate piece of paper pasted on to the original leaf of 1TS, which was cut in two and then cropped at the top and bottom to make it the same size as the other leaves. The new text is therefore an insertion rather than a replacement: the earlier version written in the left margin (see note to p. 300. 3–8) was mostly cut away, as was the original typed half-line—presumably 'into the moonlight.'—before 'She moved'.

300   1   *though*: written over an illegible pencil erasure in 1TS.

     3   *making*: in 1TS there is an illegible pencil erasure above the line.

     3–8 *making . . . windows*: in 1TS there is a pencil erasure in the margin to the left of this passage. The first few words are not legible, but are clearly part of an earlier version of p. 299. 7–11, since the final words read 'to a contract that causes a slight sinking in the poetry'. Presumably TH decided the addition was not sufficiently legible in the margin and therefore wrote it out again—perhaps making additional revisions—before inserting it in the body of the text.

     10   *out*: in 1TS followed by FH's pencil comma which TH deleted and then readded in ink. When revising 2TS he reverted to his original decision and again deleted it.

     15   *experiences*: initially followed in 2TS by a period and then a comma; TH altered the former to a comma and deleted the latter with the caret indicating the addition of 'since'.

     26   *that*: added above the line by FH in pencil and then inked over by TH. FH usually wrote her corrections in the margin (see following note); those added above the line—another 'that' (p. 308. 14), 'rooms' (p. 326. 23), 'the woman' and 'latter' (p. 328. 6)—were perhaps meant to be definite, the others tentative.

     29   *an officer*: in 1TS FH deleted 'n officer' and wrote 'soldier/' in pencil in the margin; TH deleted 'an officer' in ink, erased FH's revision, and wrote 'a soldier' above the line (he later reverted to the original reading). Sigla ending '*FHp&TH*', apart from those listed in the preceding note, indicate a repetition of this sequence.

301   1   *here*),: the location of the comma inside the closing parentheses in 1TS may be authorial, in that it was left uncorrected in both typescripts and FH and TH often placed punctuation inside closing brackets (see FH to TH, 25 Oct. 1913, 1 Nov. 1914, 28 Nov. 1914 (DCM) and *CL* i. xvi). The edited text follows PR, however, in emending the 1TS sequence, perhaps a reflection of pre-copy-text revisions: the presence of dashes as well as parentheses after 'death' and 'here,' suggests that in MS FH or TH first wrote 'death—you' and 'here,—I'; later, when the brackets were added, s/he neglected to delete the redundant dashes.

301 5   *at the*: the deleted 'either' above the line in 1TS may have been the beginning of an emendation which TH abandoned, but its position slightly to the right suggests that it was intended to be an insertion between these two words, expanding the revised reading. Presumably it was deleted almost immediately once TH decided not to introduce an alternative object of Jim's sneer.

     22   *complete*: followed in 1TS by a pencil mark which does not, however, appear to be a period.

302 19 *upon.*: followed in 2TS by a redundant period. Other redundant punctuation in 2TS includes: commas after 'Beloved' (p. 303. 21), 'tender-hearted' (p. 304. 16), 'her' (p. 322. 19), and 'thin' (p. 326. 7); periods after, 'Parkhurst!"' (p. 319. 3), 'me!' (p. 323. 30), 're-appeared' (p. 325. 22), and 'on!"' (p. 327. 7); and quotation marks before 'There's' (p. 318. 21). Redundant punctuation in 1TS includes: a comma after 'you' (p. 313. 11), a period after 'moonbeams' (p. 316. 19), and an exclamation mark after suppose?' (p. 323. 20*).

304 1   "*Qualms ... pelf*": set off from the body of the text in 1TS, but ink lines (presumably TH's) indicate that it is to follow on without a break.

305 3   *afloat,*: a period beneath the comma in 1TS suggests that TH considered, if only briefly, concluding the sentence at this point.

    12–13 *father-in-law*: the 'w' did not print in *TD*; other unprinted characters include the 'r' of 'room' (p. 319. 10) and the hyphen in 'to-morrow' (p. 327. 13).

306 13 *circumstances,*: the deletion of the comma in 2TS was presumably influenced by the typist's omission of the comma after 'hope'. The pointing of 1TS has therefore been retained.

307 18 *luncheon*: 'in a' is deleted above the line in 1TS; TH probably thought of writing a phrase similar to that added in 2TS and then changed his mind.

308 4   *country-house*: first typed in 2TS and then emended by the typist to agree with the 1TS reading. When revising 2TS TH apparently decided he preferred the 2TS typist's original reading.

     22   *this,*: the edited text follows 2TS in adding the comma, since the context clearly requires one.

309 26 *paused,*: the 1TS comma is retained, since TH's deletion of it in PR was presumably influenced by the non-authoritative comma after 'brutally'.

309 28   *"I am*: TH probably intended these words to begin a new paragraph as they did in the earlier 1TS version. Although 'changed:' is written only slightly above the line and no pilcrow has been added, dialogue is almost always set off from narrative elsewhere in the typescript.

310 27   *She*: beginning beneath the 'e' in 1TS there is an ink erasure of which all that is legible is 'She'.

28*   *gentlemanly*: in 2TS TH wrote and deleted a 'g' above the line before choosing 'kindly' as his revised reading.

312 14–17   *view . . . on*: to the left of this passage in the margin of 1TS is an ink erasure which is an abandoned attempt to reintroduce FH's description of the butterflies after 'centuries' (eventually inserted at p. 313. 21–3). A few of the words can still be made out: '<She paused> over the <*illegible*> a copper-coloured butterfly <*illegible*> of <*illegible*> in the hedge with a little blue companion.'

18   *"Are*: in 1TS the typed opening quotation marks have been erased, as has an illegible deleted ink addition above the line.

313 25   *church*: the edited text follows 2TS in using a small 'c', since the capital in 1TS was probably a typing error—or, indeed, a misreading of TH's hand if, as the context suggests, the sentence was added by him in MS. For the difficulty of distinguishing between TH's lower- and upper-case 'c', see *CL* i. xv.

314 6   *event*: in 1TS the word begins with a downstroke; TH presumably started to write 'that'.

20   *perched*: it is impossible to know precisely when TH deleted 'inquiringly' in 1TS. He may only have noticed the redundancy after finishing the sentence, but it is probable that after writing 'perched inquiringly on the yew hedge,' he decided to emphasize the robin's inquisitiveness more strongly and therefore deleted 'inquiringly' before continuing.

315 16   *honestly*: followed in 1TS by an ink punctuation mark which looks somewhat like a comma, though it was presumably intended to be a period—as, indeed, the 2TS typist assumed.

24   *Ambrose*: followed in 1TS by a deleted caret.

30   *Army-list*: in 1TS the punctuation mark after 'Army' may be a period rather than a hyphen, in which case 'list' was (if only fractionally) a later addition.

316 19   *moonbeams*: 1TS reads 'moon beams', but as 'moon' is squeezed into the right margin and the line encircling 'beams' may indicate that the words were to be run together, the edited text follows TH's normal practice in using the unhyphenated compound.

318 6 *followed,*: the edited text follows 2TS in adding the comma; the absence of punctuation in 1TS is presumably an oversight, as TH would have been concentrating on the lengthy addition overleaf (from 'during which' to the end of the following paragraph).

8 *dredging,*: the 1TS pointing has been retained, since TH's emendation of it in PR was presumably influenced by the compositor's addition of commas after 'mud' and 'water'.

319 15 *I almost*: 1TS reads 'I.almost'.

25 *profession*: in 2TS followed by an added question mark which is probably TH's, but since it is a correction of the typist's '½' it has not been incorporated in the edited text. To conclude with the unconventional—but presumably authorial—1TS pointing better indicates Rosalys's musing, in which she is addressing herself as much as Parkhurst.

25 *Perhaps*: preceded in 1TS by a deleted 'Y', presumably the beginning of 'You'.

321 21 *herself,*: in 2TS TH redrew only the tail of the extremely faint typed semi-colon; his failure to redraw the upper dot suggests that he was in fact revising the pointing—as, indeed, the *TD* compositor assumed.

322 26 *write*: in 1TS written over an illegible erasure beginning with a capital letter.

323 1–2 *But . . . line, and*: a caret between the typed 'a' and 'line' in 1TS suggests that there may have been another stage of revision (the addition of 'single') before 'She could not shape a' and 'line, and' were written. The spacing and ink flow, however, suggest that the addition was made all at the same time, in which case the caret was a false start.

324 21 *lodged*: written over an illegible erasure in 1TS.

325 24 *weakened*: written over an illegible erasure in 1TS.

326 6–11 *"And now ... all."*: in the left margin of 2TS TH marked these paragraphs with a wavy line and wrote in pencil, 'N.B. Don't omit the accents of the French name'.

17 *"In*: in 1TS TH decided to include a paragraph break only after writing the opening quotation marks; he deleted the original set with a pilcrow and then restarted the sentence.

18 *living*: followed by a technically erased comma in 1TS; however, as the remainder of the line was erased and then retyped the erasure was presumably unintentional—as, indeed, the 2TS typist assumed.

326 19 *of course*: the phrase has been restored to its 1TS position; in 2TS it was omitted by the typist and then readded at the end of the sentence by TH.

23 *in London*: TH wrote and then deleted 'where w' above the line in 2TS.

327 5 *on*: 1TS reads 'o̶n̶ on'; TH presumably either corrected his dittography or deleted the first (somewhat illegible) 'on' immediately after writing it and then rewrote the word.

8–12 *"O . . . away!"*: in 1TS all of this passage up to 'make' was added in pencil by TH and then inked over. The rest of the line is written over an illegible ink erasure which was presumably also first added in pencil. The entire passage is enclosed by an ink line, an erased portion of which, if continued, would have excluded the first paragraph. It is therefore possible that the first paragraph was an afterthought, but as the amount of white space after the typed text would have been unusually large if the addition had begun with the second paragraph, the erased line was probably a slip of the pen.

13 *"You'll*: in addition to marking the 'y' of the typed 'you'll' for capitalization, TH concluded his lengthy addition '"You'll be in, &c.' to avoid possible confusion.

328 10 *night—*: a dash was also present in 1TS(1), but was deleted in pencil, presumably by FH.

18 *Lions*: the edited text incorporates the 2TS emendation even though it is a revision of the unauthoritative 'Crown', since the 2TS typist's error was so obvious it would not have prevented TH from restoring the 1TS reading 'Crowns' if that had been his preference.

26 *They . . . out.*: although marked for insertion after 'yes.' in 1TS, the addition was added below the first line of the paragraph and was no doubt originally intended to follow 'hotel.'.

30 *Travelling all the way*: written over an illegible erasure in 1TS.

329 8 *agitation*: in 2TS the first 'a' was initially written in pencil; TH presumably intended the addition to be tentative and then changed his mind.

25–330. 3 *There . . . Mélanie*: the first, incomplete version of the addition remains undeleted on fo. 35ᵛ of 1TS. TH apparently intended to reintroduce FH's 'description of the pool, & the bird tracks' at this point, and then decided to revise p. 318. 6–20 instead.

330 3 *turned*: preceded by and partially superimposed upon an illegible erasure in 1TS.

330 21   *bright green*: at first glance there appears to be a hyphen between
these words in 1TS, but it is in fact only the cross-stroke of the 't'.

26   *Mr*: followed in 2TS by an ink period. Although the period may
have been added by TH—he very occasionally wrote 'Mr.' or
'Mrs.' (see following note)—it is extremely unlikely that he would
have altered the typist's 'Mr', since he clearly considered 'Mr.'
incorrect.

28   *Mrs*: even though the 1TS period is undoubtedly TH's it has been
omitted, not because TH preferred the abbreviation without it (no
attempt to impose consistency on the text has been made elsewhere), but because it seemed pedantic to include it when its
removal would have been considered automatic if the copy-text
had been a printed document.

331 18   *herself*: to the left of the space between the paragraphs in 2TS TH
wrote 'white line'.

19–26   *"DOVER.... act. "*: quotation marks have been added before
'DOVER' as the presence of concluding ones after 'act.' suggests
that the omission was an oversight. The edited text also follows
2TS in continuing to use double quotation marks even though
those added to the beginning of each line in 1TS are single. TH
may have resorted to this somewhat archaic device in order to
emphasize that the passage is intended to be a quotation from the
newspaper and not part of the dialogue, as the use of only opening
and closing quotation marks might have suggested. If so, his purpose is also achieved by the use of double quotation marks before
each line (cf. the pointing in PR).

PUNCTUATION AND STYLING VARIANTS AND TYPOGRAPHICAL ERRORS

Holograph ampersands in the copy-text have been expanded in the edited
text. Differences in the spacing of contractions (e.g. 'I'll' and 'I 'll', 'didn't'
and 'did n't') and in the use of single and double quotation marks and periods
after 'Mr' and 'Mrs' have not been individually recorded: *SG*a introduces
spaces in contractions; *SG* and *SG*a use single quotation marks; and all texts
except 1TS and 2TS include periods after 'Mr' and 'Mrs'.

299 4†   stable-clock *2TS(2)TH*] ~.~ *1TS*

4   quarter-to-ten *1TS(2)TH*] ~.~.~ *1TS(1)*, *SG*

5   entrance-hall *1TS(2)TH*] ~.~ *1TS(1)*

6   wrought-iron *1TS(2)TH*, *2TS(2)TH*] ~.~ *2TS(1)*

10†   beheld; *2TS(2)TH*] ~, *SG*] ~. *1TS(2)TH*

12–13   cedar-tree *1TS(2)TH*] ~.~ *1TS(1)*

299 13 funereal *1TS(2)TH, PR(2)TH*] funeral *PR(1)*
    14 Grand *1TS(2)TH*] grand *1TS(1)*
    14 Walk *1TS(2)TH, 2TS(2)TH*] walk *1TS(1), 2TS(1)*
    15* precious-stones *1TS(2)TH*] ∼ₐ∼ *1TS(1)* [*not in 2TS(2)+*]
    15 City *2TS(3)TH*] city *2TS(2)TH* [*not in 1TS*]
    16 daytime, *1TS(3)TH*] ∼— *1TS(2)TH* [*dash deleted p&i*]

300 1† tower; *PR(2)TH*] ∼, *2TS(2)TH, SG*] ∼— *1TS(2)TH*] ∼.
        1TS(1)
     1 than *1TS(3)TH, SG*] then *2TS*
     3 face, *1TS(2)TH*] ∼ₐ *1TS(1)*
     5 servants' *1TS, 2TS(2)TH?*] servant's *2TS(1)*
     6 house,ₐ *1TS(2)TH, 2TS(2)TH*] ∼,— *1TS(1), 2TS(1)*
     7 terrace, *1TS(2)TH*] ∼ₐ *1TS(1)*
     9 lake, *1TS(2)TH*] ∼ₐ *1TS(1)*
    10† out.ₐ *1TS(1), 1TS(3)TH, 2TS(2)TH*] ∼, *1TS(2)FHp, 1TS(4)TH*
    11 sunk-fence *1TS*] ∼ₐ∼ *2TS*
    12 leapt *1TS, PR*] lept *2TS*
    13 half-light *1TS(2)TH*] ∼ₐ∼ *1TS(1)*
    13 under-lip *1TS*] underlip *PR*] under-/lip *2TS*
    15 guessed, *1TS*] ∼ₐ *2TS*
    16† assurance, *PR(2)TH*] ∼ₐ *2TS(2)TH* [*not in 1TS*]
    17 arm.ₐ *1TS(2)TH, 2TS(2)TH*] ∼, *1TS(1), 2TS(1), SG*
    18 only.ₐ *1TS(2)TH*] ∼, *1TS(1)*
    20 again." *1TS*] ∼," *PR*] ∼", *2TS*
    21 Oh? *1TS*] ∼! *SGa*
    21† new. *2TS(2)TH*] ∼! *1TS*
    25 not. *1TS, SG*] ∼ₐ *TD*
    26† Jim. *2TS*] ∼ₐ *1TS*
    29 Line *1TS(2)TH*] line *1TS(1)*

301 1 death.ₐ *1TS(2)TH*] ∼— *1TS(1)*
     1 life-interest *1TS, 2TS(2)TH*] ∼ₐ∼ *2TS(1)*
     1† here), *PR*] ∼)ₐ *SG*] ∼,) *1TS(2)TH*] ∼,—) *1TS(1)*
     5 lady: ¶ *1TS(2)TH*] ∼: ₐ *2TS*
     7 one; *1TS(4)TH*] ∼— *SG*
    10 dear.ₐ *1TS(2)FHp, TD*] ∼, *1TS(1), 2TS*
    10 *I* had *1TS, PR*] *I*had *2TS*
    11 moment!" *1TS(2)TH, PR*] ∼!' *2TS(2)TH?*] ∼.ₐ *2TS(1)*] ∼."
        1TS(1)
    13 Certainly.ₐ *1TS*] ∼, *SG*
    13† went.ₐ *2TS(2)TH*] ∼, *1TS, SG*
    14 Crusaders *1TS(2)TH*] crusaders *1TS(1)*
    15 aquiline *1TS, PR*] aquline *2TS*

301 15† nose, *2TS(2)TH*] ∼, *1TS*
    16   motionless, *1TS(2)TH*] ∼, *1TS(1)*, *PR*
    17   ardour *1TS*] ardor *SGa*
    20   it; *1TS(2)TH*] ∼, *1TS(1)*
    22† complete. *2TS*] ∼, *1TS(1)*

302 2   weeks? *1TS, 2TS(2)TH*] ∼. *2TS(1)*, *SGa*
     8   condition? *1TS, SG*] ∼! *PR*
     8   me! *1TS(2)TH*] ∼. *1TS(1)*
    10   silently; *2TS(2)TH*] ∼, *PR* [*not in 1TS*]
    13† really— *2TS(2)TH*] ∼, *1TS*
    13   Jim, *1TS*] ∼, *SG*
    14   unendurable *1TS, 2TS(2)TH*] unindurable *2TS(1)*
    15   wife, *1TS*] ∼, *SG*
    16   but, *1TS*] ∼, *SG*
    16† course, *2TS(2)TH*] ∼, *1TS, SG*
    17   indeed, *1TS*] ∼, *SG*
    18   too *1TS, PR*] tto *2TS*
    18   her; *1TS(2)TH*] ∼, *1TS(1)*
    18   and, besides, *1TS(2)TH*] ∼, ∼, *1TS(1)*
    20   do?" *1TS, PR*] ∼"? *2TS*
    20   Rosalys, *1TS, SG*] ∼, *2TS*
    21   arguments. *1TS(2)FHp*] ∼, *1TS(1)*
    21   concealment, *1TS(2)TH*] ∼, *1TS(1)*
    22   privately! *1TS(2)TH*] ∼. *1TS(1)*
    23   of— *1TS(2)TH*] ∼, *1TS(1)*
    23   meetings, *1TS(2)TH*] ∼, *1TS(1)*, *SG*
    24   Therefore, *1TS*] ∼, *SG*
    27   silky, *1TS*] ∼, *SG*
    29   said, *1TS(2)TH*] ∼, *1TS(1)*
    30   obstinate, *1TS, SG*] ∼, *PR*
    30   Jim! *1TS, 2TS(2)TH*] ∼. *2TS(2)*

303 1   me?" , *1TS*] ∼.' ¶ *SGa*] ∼?" ¶ *PR*
     2   with *1TS, PR*] witth *2TS*
     3† now! *2TS(2)TH*] ∼, *1TS*
     4   little *1TS, 2TS(2)TH*] littke *2TS(1)*
     5   marble. *1TS*] ∼! *SGa*
     7   Good-bye—good-bye *1TS*] Good-by—good-by *SGa*
     9   lake, *1TS(2)TH*] ∼, *1TS(1)*
    10   house, *1TS(2)TH*] ∼, *1TS(1)*
    11† sky, *2TS(2)TH*] ∼, *1TS*
    19* Princess *1TS(2)TH*] princess *1TS(1)* [*not in 2TS(2)+*]

303 20 fountains, *1TS(2)TH*] ∼‸ *1TS(1)* [*not in 2TS(2)+*]
   21 lover-prince, *1TS(2)TH*] ∼‸ *1TS(1)* [*not in 2TS(2)+*]
   24 hotly‸pink *1TS(2)TH*] ∼-∼ *1TS(1)*

304   1 Qualms *1TS*] qualms *SG*
    1 pelf‸ *1TS*] ∼, *SG*
    3 seemed; *1TS(2)TH*] ∼, *1TS(1)*
    8† commonplace *2TS(2)TH*] common-place *1TS*
    9 colour *1TS*] color *SGa*
  10† veil, *2TS(2)TH*] ∼‸ *1TS*
  11 day: *1TS(2)TH*] ∼; *SG*
  12 eyes: *1TS(2)TH*] ∼; *2TS*
  12 hansom‸ *1TS*] ∼, *SG*
  13 Embankment. ¶ *1TS(2)TH*] ∼. ‸ *1TS(1)*
  14 pre-occupation *1TS*] preoccupation *SG*
  15 chestnut-horse *1TS(2)TH*] ∼‸∼ *1TS(1)*
  16 tender-hearted, *1TS(2)FHp*] ∼‸ *1TS(1)*
  18† alighted‸ *1TS(1)*, *2TS(2)TH*] ∼, *1TS(2)TH*
  18 man, *1TS(2)TH*] ∼‸ *1TS(1)*
  20 foot‸ *1TS*] ∼, *SG*
  20 called, *1TS(2)TH*] ∼‸ *1TS(1)*
  21† whiskers, *2TS(2)TH*] ∼‸ *1TS*
  21 recognized *1TS, 2TS(2)TH, SGa*] recognised *2TS(1)*, *PR*
  24 half-respectful *1TS(2)TH*] ∼‸∼ *1TS(1)*
  24 half-friendly *1TS(2)TH, 2TS(2)TH*] ∼‸∼ *1TS(1), 2TS(1)*
  25 frightened *1TS, 2TS(2)TH*] frightedned *2TS(1)*
  26 land-agencies *1TS(2)TH*] ∼‸∼ *1TS(1)*
  26 lived, *1TS(2)FHp*] ∼‸ *1TS(1)*.
  27 city *1TS*] City *PR*

305   2 uncle‸ *1TS(2)TH*] ∼, *SGa*
    2† Lacy." *PR*] ∼". *1TS(2)TH*
    3 afloat," *1TS(3)TH, PR*] ∼", *2TS*] ∼. " *1TS(2)TH*
    4† we're *2TS*] We're *1TS*
    4 Terrace; *1TS(2)TH*] ∼. *2TS*] ∼, *1TS(1)*
    4† otherwise, *Ed.*] Otherwise‸ *2TS*] Otherwise, *1TS*
    5 Ambrose? *1TS*] ∼! *TD*
    6 now, *1TS*] ∼‸ *SG*
    7† well, *2TS*] we‸ll *1TS*
    7† it's *PR*] its *1TS*
    9 Yes? *1TS*] ∼! *SG*
    9 Hi! *1TS, 2TS(2)TH*] ∼' *2TS(1)*
    9 And *1TS*] and *2TS*
  10 much‸ *1TS*] ∼, *PR*

305 10   Ambrose. "And *1TS(2)TH*] ~ˏ "and *1TS(1)*
    11   Mamma *1TS*] mamma *TD*
    11   Durrant *1TS(2)TH*] Durant *1TS(1)*
    15   blooming̩ˏ *1TS*] ~, *SG*
    15–16   well-dressed *1TS*] ~ˏ~ *SG*
    17   vehicle̩ˏ *1TS*] ~, *SG*
    17   city-wards *1TS*] City-wards *PR*
    20   "You *1TS, PR*] ˏ~ *2TS*
    22   brave, *1TS*] ~ˏ *2TS*
    25   carts, *1TS(2)TH*] ~ˏ *1TS(1)*
    25   foot-passengers *1TS, 2TS(2)TH*] ~ˏ~ *2TS(1)*
    25   imminent *1TS, 2TS(2)TH*] eminent *2TS(1)*
    26   amid *1TS, PR*] amind *2TS*
    27   Rosalys' *1TS*] Rosalys's *SGa*
    29   neighbourhood *1TS*] neighborhood *SGa*
    29†   meat-market *2TS(2)TH*] ~ˏ~ *1TS*

306 1   butcher *1TS(2)*] buthcer *1TS(1)*
     2   men.... *1TS(2)TH*] ~. *1TS(1)*
     5   here *1TS(2)FHp&TH*] Here *1TS(1)*
     5   woman! *1TS(2)TH*] ~. *1TS(1)*
     9   Jimmy̩ˏ *1TS*] ~, *PR*
     9   darling; *1TS(2)TH*] ~, *1TS(1)*
    10   said̩ˏ *1TS*] ~, *PR*
    10†   porch, *2TS(2)TH*] ~ˏ *1TS*
    11   pre-occupation *1TS*] preoccupation *SG*
    12†   did," *PR*] ~", *2TS(2)TH*] ~". *1TS(2)FHp*] ~"ˏ *1TS(1)*
    13   hope, *1TS*] ~ˏ *2TS*
    13   circumstances, *1TS*] ~ˏ *2TS(2)TH*
    13   it's *1TS(2)FHp, PR*] its *1TS(1), 2TS*
    14   Rosalys; *1TS(2)TH*] ~, *1TS(1)*
    14   solemn! *1TS(2)TH*] ~. *1TS(1)*
    16   her. ¶ *1TS(2)TH*] ~. ˏ *1TS(1)*
    20   errand: a *1TS(2)TH, TD*] ~; ~ *2TS*] ~. A *1TS(1)*
    20   bonnet, *1TS, TD*] ~ˏ *2TS*
    20–1   on to *1TS*] onto *SGa*
    21   short̩ˏ *1TS*] ~, *PR*] ~- *2TS(2)*] ~; *2TS(1)*
    22   nerve *1TS, 2TS(2)TH*] nerver *2TS(1)*
    23   ordeal: *1TS*] ~; *2TS*
    24   black: *1TS*] ~; *2TS(2)TH*] ~, *2TS(1)*
    24   man, *1TS*] ~ˏ *2TS*
    25   chest, *1TS(2)TH*] ~ˏ *1TS(1)*
    31   singular *1TS, 2TS(2)TH*] sungular *2TS(1)*

307 1 loveliness *1TS, 2TS(2)TH*] lovliness *2TS(1)*
   3† vestry. *2TS(2)TH*] ~, *1TS*
   3 altar *1TS, 2TS(2)TH*] alter *2TS(1)*
   7 forward,ʌ *1TS(2)TH*] ~ₐ *SGa*] ~,— *1TS(1)*
   8 moment, *1TS, SGa*] ~ₐ *SG*
   8 too, *1TS(2)TH, SGa*] ~ₐ *SG*
   9 From *1TS, SGa*] from *SG*
  12 fancied, *1TS, 2TS(2)TH*] ~ₐ *2TS(1)*
  12 east-wind *1TS*] ~ₐ~ *TD*
  13 tooth-ache *1TS*] toothache *SG*
  13† severe, *2TS(2)TH*] ~ₐ *1TS*
  17 Embankment *1TS(2)TH*] embankment *1TS(1)*
  22 *You 1TS*] You *2TS*
  23 sudden! *1TS(2)TH*] ~. *1TS(1)*
  23 know!" ¶ *1TS(2)TH*] ~!"ₐ *1TS(1)*
  24 changed. *1TS*] ~, *SG*
  24 gaze, *1TS(2)TH*] ~ₐ *1TS(1)*
  25 low, *1TS(2)TH, 2TS(2)TH*] ~ₐ *PR*] ~; *2TS(1)*] ~: *1TS(1)*
  25 throat: *1TS(2)TH, SGa*] ~— *TD*
  26 O. *1TS(2)TH, SG*] ~, *TD*] Oh! *1TS(1)*
  26 dear. *1TS(2)FHp, SG*] ~, *1TS(1), 2TS, SGa*
  26 darling! *1TS(2)TH*] ~, *1TS(1)*

308 3 Durrant, *1TS(2)TH, 2TS(2)TH*] ~ₐ *2TS(1)*] Durant, *1TS(1)*
   4† country-house. *PR*] ~ₐ~. *TD*] ~-~ₐ *2TS(3)TH* [*not in 1TS*]
   7 frequently *1TS, PR*] frewuently *2TS*
  10 suburban *1TS, PR*] subarban *2TS*
  11* coffee-houses *SG*] ~ₐ~ *SGa* [*not in earlier editions*]
  12 lose *1TS, 2TS(2)TH*] loe *2TS(1)*
  21 fervour *PR(2)TH*] fervor *SGa* [*not in earlier editions*]
  22† this, *2TS*] ~ₐ *1TS*

309 2 involved: *1TS*] ~; *2TS*
   7 pre-occupied *1TS*] preoccupied *SG*
   8 utterance. *1TS(2)TH, 2TS(2)TH*] ~, *2TS(1)*] ~. *1TS(1)*
  12 vulgar! *1TS*] ~. *2TS*
  12 do! *1TS, 2TS(2)TH*] ~. *2TS(1)*
  15 man! *1TS(2)TH*] ~. *1TS(1)*
  17 refuge *1TS, PR*] refuse *2TS*
  18 "Unfortunately *1TS, TD*] ₐ~ *PR*
  18 murmured. *1TS, SG*] ~ₐ *TD*
  20 bound *1TS, PR*] bonnd *2TS*
  21 soon! *1TS*] ~. *2TS*
  21 Are *1TS(2)TH*] are *1TS(1)*

309 21   angry? *1TS, SGa*] ~. *SG*
　　22   Don't. for God's sake. *1TS, SGa*] ~, ~ ~ ~, *SG*
　　24   Gardens; *1TS(2)TH, SGa*] ~, *SG*] gardens: *1TS(1)*
　　25   Rosalys!" . *1TS*] ~!" ¶ *PR*
　　26   brutally. *1TS*] ~, *PR*
　　26   paused, *1TS(2)TH*] ~. *PR(2)TH* ~. *1TS(1)*
　　27   changed: ¶ *1TS(2)TH, PR*] ~. ¶ *TD*] ~: . *2TS*
　　28†   cross! *2TS(2)TH*] ~. *1TS*
　　31   .Jim *1TS, TD*] "~ *PR*
　　31   under-lip *1TS*] underlip *2TS*
　　31   firmly.curved *1TS, SG*] ~-~ *PR*
　　32   lid, *1TS(2)TH*] ~. *1TS(1)*
　　33   loveliness *1TS, 2TS(2)TH*] lovliness *2TS(1)*

310 2   from *1TS, PR*] fron *2TS*
　　3†   his *2TS*] hir *1TS*
　　5   Good-bye *1TS*] Good-by *SGa*
　　5   meet? *1TS(2)TH*] ~. *1TS(1)*
　　9   again, *1TS(2)TH*] ~— *1TS(1)*
　　13   last. The *1TS(2)TH*] ~; the *1TS(1)*
　　15   good-bye *1TS*] good-by *SGa*
　　15   she. *1TS(2)TH, PR*] ~. *2TS*
　　17   you." *1TS(2)TH, PR*] ~". *2TS*] ~.. *1TS(1)*
　　18   *you* *1TS(2)TH*] you *1TS(1)*
　　18†   cried, *2TS(2)TH*] ~. *1TS*
　　23†   You *2TS(2)TH*] You *1TS*
　　26   them,— *1TS*] ~.— *TD*
　　28   realized *1TS, 2TS(2)TH, SGa*] realised *2TS(1), PR*
　　29   good-feeling *1TS(2)TH*] ~.~ *1TS(1)*

311 7   self; *1TS(2)TH*] ~, *1TS(1)*
　　7   subdued, *1TS(2)FHp*] ~. *1TS(1)*
　　11   discontinued, *1TS*] ~; *2TS(2)TH*] ~. *2TS(1)*
　　13   shrubberies *1TS, PR*] shubberies *2TS*
　　14†   yew-hedges *2TS(2)TH*] ~.~ *1TS, TD*
　　16   side, *1TS(2)TH*] ~. *1TS(1)*
　　24   Rosalys. *1TS(3)TH*] ~, *1TS(2)TH*] ~. *1TS(1)*
　　25†   tête-à-tête *2TS(2)TH*] *tête-à-tête PR*] tete-a-tete *1TS(1), 2TS(1)*]
　　　　　tete-a-tête *1TS(2)TH?*

312 2   plans; how *1TS(2)TH*] ~. How *1TS(1)*
　　2†   write, *2TS(2)TH*] ~. *1TS*
　　2   on." *1TS, PR*] ~". *2TS*
　　3   down, *1TS*] ~. *SG*

312 3 arbour *1TS(2)TH*] arbor *1TS(1), SGa*

3 logs, *1TS*] ~, *SG*

5 crevices; here *1TS(2)TH*] ~. Here *1TS(1)*

6 strips; above *1TS(2)TH*] ~. Above *1TS(1)*

10 foreground *1TS, TD*] fore-ground *PR*

12 interlacing *1TS, PR(2)TH*] inter-lacing *PR(1)*

13 rustic˷shelter *1TS, PR(2)TH*] ~-~ *PR(1)*

14–15 brick˷house˷ *1TS*] ~˷~, *TD*] ~-~, *PR*

16 be, *1TS, 2TS(2)TH*] ~˷ *2TS(1)*

17† years, *PR*] ~. *1TS*

18† "Are *1TS(1), 2TS*] ˷~ *1TS(2)TH*

19† complaint. *2TS*] ~˷ *1TS(2)TH*

21 Besides, *1TS(2)TH*] ~˷ *1TS(1)*

24 answered˷ *1TS(2)TH?p*] ~, *1TS(1)*

24–5 log˷roof *1TS*] ~-~ *PR*

29 figure, *1TS(2)TH*] ~˷ *1TS(1)*

313 4 arbour *1TS(2)TH*] arbor *1TS(1), SGa*

10† arm˷ *2TS(2)TH*] ~, *1TS*

11† you!"˷ *PR*] ~!", *2TS(2)TH*] ~˷", *2TS(1)*] ~,!" *1TS(2)FHp&TH*

12† again!˷ *PR*] ~!" *1TS*

14 not! *1TS*] ~? *PR*

15† understanding! ... *2TS(2)TH*] ~! ˷ *1TS, PR*

15 Indeed˷ *1TS(2)TH*] ~, *2TS*

16† you'll *2TS*] You'll *1TS*

16† you, *2TS(2)TH*] ~˷ *1TS*

17† mean! *PR(2)TH*] ~. *1TS*

22 copper-coloured *1TS(3)TH*] copper-colored *SGa*

25† church *2TS*] Church *1TS*

28 shall *1TS, 2TS(2)*] shal *2TS(1)*

30 obliviousness *1TS*] oblivousness *SGa*

314 6† nature—" *Ed.*] ~." *2TS(2)TH*] ~." *2TS(1)*] ~."— *1TS(3)TH*

7† yours! *PR(2)TH*] ~. *1TS(3)TH*

11 gown˷ *1TS(2)TH*] ~, *PR*

13 cried. *1TS(2)*] ~˷ *1TS(1)*

13† Oh, *PR(2)TH*] ~! *1TS*

13 colour *1TS*] color *SGa*

14 got, *1TS, 2TS(2)TH*] ~˷ *2TS(1)*

14 child! *1TS, PR(2)TH*] ~. *2TS*

15 Yes. *1TS, 2TS(2)TH*] ~, *2TS(1)*

16 discussion, *1TS, 2TS(2)TH*] ~˷ *2TS(1)*

16 mamma *1TS, TD*] Mamma *2TS*

20 larch˷tree *1TS(3)TH, SGa*] ~-/~ *SG*

314 24   good-bye *1TS*] good-by *SGa*
   28   paralysed *1TS*] paralyzed *SGa*
   30   unholy, *1TS(2)TH*] ∼ˏ *1TS(1)* [*not in SG*]

315 7†   here; *2TS(2)TH*] ∼ˏ *1TS*
   9   anyone *1TS*] any one *SG*
  10   churches! *1TS(2)TH*] ∼? *PR*] ∼? *2TS*
  12   that, *1TS(2)TH*] ∼ˏ *1TS(1)*
  13   view, *1TS(2)TH*] ∼ˏ *1TS(1)*
  13   that. *1TS(2)TH?*] ∼, *1TS(1)*
  16†   honestly: *PR(2)TH*] ∼. *1TS(2)*] ∼ˏ *1TS(1)*
  22†   above-written *2TS(2)TH*] ∼ˏ∼ *1TS*
  25   marriage-contract *1TS(2)TH, 2TS(2)TH*] ∼ˏ∼ *1TS(1), 2TS(1), TD*
  28   knew: *1TS*] ∼; *2TS*
  28   dead. *1TS(2)*] ∼ˏ *1TS(1)*
  30   Army-list *1TS(2)TH*] Army List *TD*

316 2   sold, *1TS(2)TH*] ∼ˏ *1TS(1)*
  10   Rosalys' *1TS(2)TH*] Rosalys's *SG*
  15   birth. *1TS(2)*] ∼ˏ *1TS(1)*
  17   thirty. *1TS, SGa*] ∼, *SG*
  19†   moonbeams *PR*] moon-beams *2TS*] moonˏbeams *1TS(2)TH*
  20†   charms. *PR(2)TH*] ∼, *1TS*
  25   anyone *1TS*] any one *SG*

317 2   Egypt *1TS(2)FHp&TH, 2TS(2)TH*] Egypy *2TS(1)*
  3   women, *1TS(2)FHp*] ∼ˏ *1TS(1)*
  4   them,ˏ *1TS(3)TH*] ∼,— *1TS(2)FHp*] ∼ˏ— *1TS(1)*
  5   honour *1TS*] honor *SGa*
  9   sailors," *1TS, 2TS(2)TH*] ∼ˏ *2TS(1)*
  13   than *1TS, PR*] that *2TS*
  13   Rosalys' *1TS*] Rosalys's *SG*
  17   Ambrose. of Ambrose Towers. *1TS*] ∼, ∼ ∼ ∼, *PR*
  18   Parkhurst." *1TS(2)TH, PR*] ∼". *2TS*] ∼.ˏ *1TS(1)*
  19   heroic *1TS, 2TS(2)TH*] herioic *2TS(1)*
  23   County *1TS*] county *TD*
  26   way. *1TS(2)TH, 2TS(2)TH*] ∼, *1TS(1), 2TS(1)*
  27   said; *1TS*] ∼: *PR*
  31   many, *1TS(2)TH, PR(2)TH*] ∼ˏ *2TS(2)TH*

318 2   day." ¶ *1TS, 2TS(2)TH*] ∼." ˏ *2TS(1)*
  4   to-morrow! *1TS(2)TH*] ∼. *1TS(1)*
  5†   No." ¶ *2TS(2)TH*] ∼." ˏ *1TS*

318 6   again, *1TS(2)TH*] ~. *1TS(1)*
     6†   followed, *2TS*] ~. *1TS(2)TH*] ~. *1TS(1)*
     6   which, *1TS(2)TH, 2TS(2)TH*] ~. *2TS(1)*
     8   dredging, *1TS(2)TH*] ~; *PR(2)TH*
     8   mud. *1TS(2)TH*] ~, *PR*
     9   water. *1TS(2)TH*] ~, *PR*
    15   dots. ¶ *1TS(3)TH*] ~. . *1TS(2)TH*
    17   wails, *1TS(4)TH, 2TS(2)TH*] ~. *2TS(1)*
    18   away. . *1TS(4)TH*] ~. ¶ *2TS*
    19   carriage, *1TS(4)TH*] ~. *2TS*
    21*   ¶ "Good *1TS(2)TH*] . .~ *1TS(1)* [*not in 2TS(2)+*]
    21*   presently, *1TS(2)TH*] ~. *1TS(1)* [*not in 2TS+*]
    22†   certain! *2TS(2)TH*] ~. *1TS(2)*] ~. *1TS(1)*
    22   untidy. *1TS(2)FHp&TH*] ~, *PR*
    24   well." *1TS(2)*] ~.. *1TS(1)*
    25   folding-doors. *1TS(2)TH, 2TS(2)TH*] ~-~, *SGa*] ~.~, *TD*]
          ~.~. *1TS(1), 2TS(1)*

319 2²   the *1TS(2)FHp*] th- *1TS(1)*
     2   morrow: *1TS, SGa*] ~— *TD*
     3   Parkhurst!". *1TS, PR*] ~!". *2TS(2)TH*] ~.". *2TS(1)*
     7   said: *1TS, PR*] ~; *2TS*
     9   perceive!" *1TS(2)TH*] ~." *PR*] ~.. *1TS(1)*
    11   Rosalys' *1TS*] Rosalys's *SG*
    11   betrothed, *1TS, 2TS(2)TH*] ~. *2TS(1)*
    12   continued: *1TS, SGa*] ~— *TD*
    15   before! *1TS, TD*] ~? *PR*
    16   good. and perfect. *1TS*] ~, ~ ~, *PR*
    22   me: *1TS*] ~; *TD*
    25   profession. *1TS(2)TH*] ~? *2TS(2)TH*] ~½ *2TS(1)*
    26†   me." *PR*] ~.. *1TS(3)TH*
    27†   fearless. *2TS*] ~, *1TS*
    30   paradisical *1TS(2)TH*] paradisiacal *SG*] paradisaical *SGa*
    32   dependent *1TS*] dependant *SG*

320 1   Rosalys' *1TS*] Rosalys's *SG*
     1   neighbours *1TS*] neighbors *SGa*
     5   Rosalys entered *1TS, PR(2)TH*] Rosaly sentered *PR(1)*
     8   ever— *1TS(2)TH*] ~! *1TS(1)*
    12   forcedly,. *1TS(2)TH*] ~:— *SGa*] ~.— *TD*] ~:. *2TS*
    13*   handsome. *SG*] ~, *SGa* [*not in earlier editions*]
    15   him. *1TS(2)TH*] ~~— *1TS(1)*
    18   O, *1TS(2)FHp*] Oh, *SG*] O. *1TS(1)*
    18   Of *1TS(2)TH*] of *1TS(1)*

320 19   neighbourhood *1TS(2)TH*] neighborhood *SGa*

    21   "traveller *1TS(4)TH*] ˏ~ *1TS(3)TH*

    22   explorer" *1TS(4)TH, 2TS(2)TH*] exploere" *2TS(1)*] explorer.ˏ *1TS(3)TH*

    22   little.ˏknown *1TS(3)TH, SGa*] ~.ˏ~ *SG*

    22   countries; *1TS(3)TH, SGa*] ~, *SG*

    23†   himself. His *2TS(2)TH*] ~; his *1TS(3)TH*

    27   recognized *1TS, SGa*] recognised *2TS*

    27*   Lacy, *1TS(2)TH*] ~.ˏ *1TS(1)* [*not in 2TS(2)+*]

    27†   off-hand. ¶ *2TS(2)TH, SGa*] offhand. ¶ *SG*] off-hand. ˏ *1TS*

321 1   Smiling, *1TS(2)TH, SG*] ~.ˏ *1TS(1), 2TS, SGa*

    3†   sound.ˏ *2TS(2)TH*] ~; *1TS(3)TH*

    4   rest, *1TS(2)TH*] ~— *TD*

    6   Home-Rule *1TS(2)TH*] ~.ˏ~ *1TS(1), TD*

    6   question, *1TS*] ~— *TD*

    10   voice: *1TS(2)TH, SGa*] ~— *TD*

    12   be? *1TS*] ~. *SGa*

    15†   does *2TS(2)TH*] *does 1TS*

    15†   spoke.ˏ *2TS(2)TH*] ~, *1TS*

    16   towards *1TS, SG*] toward *PR*

    16   think.ˏ *1TS*] ~, *PR*

    17   over-taxed *1TS, SGa*] overtaxed *SG*

    18   this." *1TS, PR*] ~". *2TS*

    19   smiled *1TS(2)FHp&TH*] smile *1TS(1)*

    21*   over.ˏ *1TS(2)TH*] ~, *1TS(1)* [*not in 2TS(2)+*]

    21†   herself, *1TS(1), 2TS(2)TH*] ~; *1TS(2)TH*

    22   she was *1TS, PR(2)TH*] shew as *PR(1)*

    25   ladies.ˏ *1TS(2)TH*] ~, *1TS(1), 2TS(2)TH*] ·~— *2TS(1)*

    27   speaking *1TS, PR*] speakingc *2TS*

    27†   ear: *2TS(2)TH, SGa*] ~— *TD*] ~. *1TS*

    31   No!" *1TS*] ~," *PR*] ~", *2TS*

    31   she. *1TS(2)*] ~½ *1TS(1)*

322 2   stable-clock *1TS, 2TS(2)TH*] ~.ˏ~ *2TS(1)*

    4†   how *PR*] How *1TS*

    7   O *2TS(2)TH*] Oh *SG* [*not in 1TS*]

    7†   you *PR*] You *1TS*

    7   cruelly! *1TS, 2TS(2)TH*] ~. *2TS(1)*

    9†   *must 2TS(2)TH*] must *1TS*

    9   suppose! ... *1TS(2)TH, 2TS(2)TH*] ~...... *2TS(1)*] ~! ˏ *1TS(1)*

    9†   people! It *2TS(2)TH*] ~—it *1TS(3)TH*

    10   agonising *2TS(2)TH*] agonizing *SGa* [*not in 1TS*]

322 11 "Of *1TS(2)TH, SGa*] ‚~ *SG*

11 shan't *1TS(2)TH, SG*] sha'n't *TD, SGa*

12 say. *1TS(2)*]] ~‚ *1TS(1)*

12† forward, *2TS(2)TH*] ~‚ *1TS*

13 Durrant, *1TS, SGa*] ~‚ *SG*

13 bézique *1TS(2)FHp&TH, PR(2)TH*] bezique *2TS, PR(1)*

15 early: *1TS*] ~, *PR*

16† half-past *2TS(2)TH*] ~‚~ *1TS*

18 him. *1TS, 2TS(2)TH?*] ~‚ *2TS(1)*

21 dispatched *1TS*] despatched *SG*

22 retired, *1TS(2)TH*] ~‚ *1TS(1)*

24 living, *2TS(3)TH*] ~. *2TS(1)*] ~‚ *1TS(3)TH*

25† married. *PR*] ~‚ *2TS(3)TH* [*not in 1TS*]

25 writing-table *1TS(2)TH*] ~‚~ *1TS(1)*

27 duty‚ *1TS(2)FHp*] ~, *1TS(1), 2TS*

28 object, *2TS(3)TH*] ~— *TD* [*not in 1TS*]

323 1 him *1TS, PR*] himm *2TS*

1† she *2TS*] She *1TS(3)TH*

2 line, *1TS(3)TH*] ~; *TD*

2 eyes‚ *1TS, SG*] ~, *PR, SGa*

3 history, *1TS*] ~‚ *SG*

4 hysterical *1TS, 2TS(2)TH*] histerical *2TS(1)*

6 labour *1TS*] labor *SGa*

8 was; *1TS*] ~, *PR*

9 can, *2TS(3)TH, SGa*] ~‚ *SG* [*not in 1TS*]

13 am," *1TS, PR*] ~", *2TS*

13 said‚he. *1TS(2)FHp*] ~.~‚ *1TS(1)*

16 hesitate. ¶ *1TS(2)TH*] ~. ‚ *1TS(1)*

17 began. *1TS, 2TS(2)TH?*] ~‚ *2TS(1)*

18 no. *1TS, PR*] ~, *2TS*

18 will! *1TS(2)TH*] ~. *1TS(1)*

19 lightly. ¶ *1*TS(2)TH] ~. ‚ *1TS(1)*

20† suppose, *2TS(2)TH*] ~? *1TS(3)TH*] ~! *1TS(2)FHp*

20 observed, *1TS(2)FHp*] ~‚ *1TS(1)*

21† solemnity, *1TS(1), 2TS(2)TH*] ~; *1TS(2)TH*

21† to-morrow? *2TS(2)TH*] ~. *1TS*

22 better! *1TS*] ~, *2TS(2)TH*] ~‚ *2TS(1)*

22 said. *1TS, SGa*] ~, *SG*

23 bigamy!‚ *1TS(2)TH?*] ~!" *1TS(1)*

26 haven't! *1TS(2)TH, PR(2)TH*] ~. *1TS(1), PR(1)*

28 O‚ *1TS*] Oh, *SG*] O, *TD*

28 "I *1TS, SGa*] ‚I *SG*

323 29   O.ₐ *1TS, SG*] ~, *TD*

324 2   good! *1TS(2)TH*] ~. *1TS(1)*

     2   all *1TS, PR*] al *2TS*

     3†   at! *2TS(2)TH*] ~. *1TS*

     5†   dark! *2TS(2)TH*] ~. *1TS*

     5   to. *1TS(1), 1TS(3)TH*] ~! *1TS(2)TH*

     6†   him! ... *2TS(2)TH*] ~.ₐ *2TS(1)*] ~!ₐ *1TS*

    10†   honest! *2TS(2)TH*] ~. *1TS(2)TH*

    13   shan't *1TS*] sha'n't *SGa*

    13†   tell *2TS*] tel *1TS*

    13   And *1TS(2)FHp&TH*] and *1TS(1)*

    15   new-assorted *1TS(2)TH, 2TS(2)TH*] ~ₐ~ *2TS(1)*

    16   them." *1TS(2)TH, PR*] ~". *2TS*

    21   thereabout *1TS(2)TH*] thereabouts *2TS*

    22   calmly; [soundly; *1TS(4)TH*]] calmly, *2TS(2)TH*] soundly.ₐ
        2TS(1)

    23†   they *2TS*] thay *1TS*

    25   voice: *1TS, SGa*] ~— *TD*

325 1   star-light *1TS, SGa*] starlight *SG*

    12   ... Let *1TS(2)TH*] ₐ~ *1TS(1)*

    13   way.ₐ *1TS(1), 1TS(3)TH*] ~, *1TS(2)TH*

    14†   after *2TS*] After *1TS(2)TH*

    15   downstairs! *1TS(2)TH*] ~. *1TS(1)*

    16   us.ₐ *1TS*] ~, *PR*

    16   too—it *1TS(3)TH*] ~! It *1TS(2)TH*] ~. It *1TS(1)*

    16   late! *1TS*] ~. *2TS*

    17–18   to-morrow *1TS*] ~. *PR*] ~.ₐ *2TS*

    19   sigh, *1TS*] ~.ₐ *SG*

    22†   three-hours-and-half *Ed.*] ~.ₐ~.ₐ~.ₐa.ₐhalf *TD*] Three.ₐ~.ₐ~.ₐa.ₐ
        half *1TS(1), 2TS*] Three-hours-and-half *1TS(2)TH* [*not in SG*]

    24   slightness; *1TS(2)TH, SGa*] ~, *SG*

    24   and *1TS(2)FHp&TH*] ane *1TS(1)*

326 1   Now *1TS(2)TH*] Noc *1TS(1)*

     1   good-bye *1TS*] good-by *SGa*

     1   husband, *1TS*] ~.ₐ *SG*

     2   once? *1TS(2)TH*] ~. *1TS(1)*

     5   Yes." *1TS(2)TH, PR*] ~". *2TS*

     6   "And *1TS, PR*] ,~ *2TS*

     6   hotel. *1TS, 2TS(2)TH*] ~, *2TS(1)*

     8†   Mélanie—" *1TS(3)TH, 2TS(2)TH*] Melanie—" *2TS(1)*]
        Mélanie—ₐ *1TS(2), 1TS(4)TH*] Melanie—ₐ *1TS(1)*

326 10[†] O *PR(2)TH, SGa*] Oh *1TS, SG*
    10 Mélanie *1TS(2), 2TS(2)TH*] Melanie *1TS(1), 2TS(1)*
    10 out— *1TS*] ~. *PR*
    12 Mélanie *1TS(2), 2TS(2)TH*] Melanie *2TS(1)*
    12[†] who *PR*] Who *1TS*
    13 ",Well *1TS(2)TH*] "—Well *1TS(1)*
    14 so, *1TS(3)TH*] ~— *1TS(2)TH*
    16 started. ¶ *1TS(3)TH*] ~. , *1TS(2)TH*
    17 fact, *1TS(2)TH*] ~, *SGa*
    17 East, *1TS(2)TH*] ~, *1TS(1)*
    18[†] if *2TS*] If *1TS*
    20[†] then, *2TS(2)TH*] ~, *1TS*
    21 O, *1TS*] Oh, *SG*] Oh, *SGa*] O, *TD*
    23 O *1TS*] Oh *SG*
    24 Paris, *1TS, 2TS(2)TH, SG*] ~; *PR, SGa*] ~, *2TS(1)*
    26 When— *1TS(1), 1TS(3)TH*] ~, *1TS(2)FHp*
    27 breakfast-time *1TS(2)TH*] ~,~ *1TS(1)*
    28 doorway. *1TS*] ~, *SG*] ~, *SGa*
    28 O—O *1TS(2)TH*] Oh—oh *1TS(1)* [*not in SG*]

327 1[†] done! What *2TS(2)TH*] ~? ~ *PR*] ~—what *1TS(1)* [*not in SG*]
    1 fool— *1TS*] ~, *2TS(2)TH*] ~, *2TS(1)* [*not in SG*]
    1 fool! *1TS, PR*] ~? *2TS* [*not in SG*]
    4 agonized *1TS(3)TH, 2TS(2)TH, SGa*] agonised *1TS(2)TH,*
       2TS(1), SG
    7[†] on!", *PR*] ~!". *2TS(2)TH*] ~,". *2TS(1)*] ~.", *1*TS(3)TH
    8 O *1TS(5)TH*] Oh *SG*
    9 humorous *1TS(5)TH, PR*] humourous *2TS*
    12 levity! *1TS(5)TH*] ~. *PR*
    13 to-morrow, *1TS(2)TH*] ~— *1TS(1)*
    13 me, *1TS(2)TH*] ~; *2TS(2)TH*] ~, *1TS(1), 2TS(1)*
    14[†] revoir! *2TS*] revoir! *PR*] revoir! *1TS*
    15 trees *1TS(2)FHp&TH*] tress *1TS(1)*
    15 Rosalys, *1TS(2)TH, 2TS(2)TH*] ~, *2TS(1)*
    15 herself, *1TS(2)TH, 2TS(2)TH*] ~, *2TS(1)*
    16 door, *1TS(2)TH*] ~, *1TS(1)*
    18[†] upstairs, *2TS(2)TH*] ~, *1TS*
    19 writing-table *1TS(2)TH, 2TS(2)TH*] ~,~ *1TS(1), 2TS(1)*
    19 O, *1TS(2)TH, TD*] ~, *2TS*] Oh, *1TS(1)* [*not in SG*]
    21 ¶ But *1TS(2)TH*] , ~ *1TS(1)*
    22 vigour *1TS*] vigor *SGa*
    22 action; *1TS*] ~, *TD*
    23[†] and, *2TS(2)TH*] ~, *1TS(1), PR*] when, *1TS(2)TH*

327 25	mantelpiece *1TS, PR*] mantlepiece *2TS*
　　25	dispatched *1TS*] despatched *SG*

328 3	in, *1TS(2)TH, SGa*] ~ˏ *SG*
　　4†	ˏmen *2TS*] -men *1TS(2)FH&TH*
　　5	astir, *1TS(2)FHp*] ~ˏ *1TS(1)*
　　5	andˏ *1TS, SGa*] ~, *SG*
　　5	handˏ *1TS, SGa*] ~, *SG*
　　9	O *1TS(2)TH?p*] Oh *1TS(1)* [*not in 2TS+*]
　　9	meads *1TS*] Meads *PR*
　　10	half-a-mile *1TS(2)TH, SGa*] ~ˏ~ˏ~ *SG*
　　19†	home, *2TS(2)TH*] ~ˏ *1TS*
　　19	far: *1TS*] ~; *2TS*
　　26	Oˏ *1TS*] Ohˏ *SG*] Oh, *SGa*] O, *TD*
　　27	hotel *1TS, TD*] Hotel *2TS*
　　28	there! *1TS(2)*] ~. *2TS*] ~½ *1TS(1)*
　　29	yes." *1TS(2)TH, PR*] ~". *2TS*

329 6†	Rosalys' *2TS*] Rosalys's *SG*] Rosalysˏ *1TS(2)TH*
　　6	in *1TS(2)TH, 2TS(2)TH*] is *2TS(1)*
　　9	practitioner, *1TS(2)TH*] ~ˏ *1TS(1)*
　　9	breakfastˏtime *1TS, SGa*] ~-~ *SG*
　　12	health; *1TS, SGa*] ~, *SG*
　　12	tonic, *1TS*] ~ˏ *SGa*
　　17	Oˏ *1TS*] Ohˏ *SG*] Oh, *SGa*] O, *TD*
　　18†	stiff. ... *2TS(2)TH*] ~!.... *1TS(3)TH*] ~. ˏ *1TS(2)TH*
　　19	hereabout *1TS(2)TH, 2TS(2)TH*] here about *2TS(1)*
　　23	fellow! *1TS*] ~. *2TS*
　　24†	leftˏ *2TS(2)TH*] ~, *1TS, PR*

330 2†	night— *2TS(2)TH*] ~, *1TS(4)TH*
　　3	Mélanie *1TS(3)TH, 2TS(2)TH*] Melanie *2TS(1)*
　　4	husbandˏ *1TS(2)TH, 2TS(2)TH*] ~, *1TS(1), 2TS(1), PR*
　　5	Parkhurst, *1TS(2)TH, 2TS(2)TH*] ~ˏ *2TS(1)*
　　9	one: *1TS(2)TH*] ~; *TD*] ~ˏ *1TS(1)*
　　10†	"Mélanie", *2TS(2)TH*] ˏ~ˏ, *SG*] "~," *PR, SGa*] "Melanie"ˏ *1TS, 2TS(1)*
　　11	Rosalys' *1TS*] Rosalys's *SG*
　　11	qualities; *1TS, SGa*] ~, *SG*
　　12	city *1TS, SG*] City *PR*
　　13	all, *1TS(2)FHp&TH*] ~; *1TS(1)*
　　14	desired. *1TS, 2TS(2)TH?*] ~ˏ *2TS(1)*
　　21	brightˏgreen *1TS(2)TH*] ~-~ *2TS*
　　22	stream *1TS, PR*] atream *2TS*

330 23   rail. ¶ *1TS(2)TH*] ~. ‸ *1TS(1)*
     25†   O *PR(2)TH*] Oh *1TS, SG*
     25†   think, *2TS(2)TH*] ~‸ *1TS*
     25   Jennings; *1TS, SGa*] ~, *SG*
     26   Mr‸ *1TS*] ~. *2TS(2)*
     27†   curious *2TS*] Curious *1TS(2)TH*
     28†   Mrs‸ *2TS*] ~. *1TS(2)TH, PR*
     28†   dinner,— *2TS(2)TH*] ~‸— *1TS(2)TH, TD*
     28   all." *1TS(2)TH, PR*] ~". *2TS*

331 3   altar-railings *1TS, PR*] ~‸~ *SG*] alter-railings *2TS*
     5   relations. *1TS(2)*] ~‸ *1TS(1)*
     8   door, *1TS(2)TH, PR(2)TH*] ~‸ *2TS*
     8   bystanders *1TS, SG*] by-standers *TD*] by-/standers *PR*
     10   believe." *1TS(2)TH, PR*] ~". *2TS*
     11†   To-morrow *2TS*] TO-morrow *1TS*
     15   telegrams *1TS, PR*] telgrams *2TS*
     16†   good *2TS*] Good *1TS*
     18   herself: *1TS*] ~— *TD*
     19†   "D O V E R. *Ed.*] "DOVER. *PR*] ‸D O V E R. *1TS, 2TS(2)TH*]
         ‸D O V E R‸ *2TS(1)*
     19†   PARKHURST, *2TS(2)TH*] ~. *1TS*
     19   R.N.— *1TS*] ~‸ *PR*
     20†   ‸"We *Ed.*] ¶ "~ *2TS*] ‸'~ *1TS(2)TH*] ‸‸~ *1TS(1)*
     20–6†   [" *before each line in edited text and 2TS; nothing in 1TS(1) and PR,*
         ' in 1TS(2)TH]

COMPOUND WORDS HYPHENATED AT END OF LINE IN COPY-TEXT

301   1   life-interest
     24   downstairs

309   4   overmuch
     31   under-lip

312   3   overlooked

321 23   sal-volatile

323 27   to-morrow

325 15   downstairs

BLUE JIMMY: THE HORSE STEALER

EXPLANATORY NOTES

348 1–2 *Blue ... flung*: TH, 'A Trampwoman's Tragedy', stanza X; in the first line the correct reading is 'stole right many'.

3 *"Blue Jimmy"*: the popular name of the notorious horse thief James Clace (d. 1827 at the age of 52). For the historical basis of the narrative—including all of its named characters—see pp. 337 ff.

349 11–12 *near Chard*: according to the 30 Mar. 1825 *Taunton Courier*, Wheller lived at Coombe St Nicholas.

21 *Stratton Fair*: according to the 30 Mar. 1825 *Taunton Courier*, Clace told Wheller he bought the mare 'near Tiverton'.

28 *happening ... then*: according to the 30 Mar. 1825 *Taunton Courier*, Wilkins was with Clace when the latter first spoke to Wheller.

351 35–6 *he ... Dorchester*: according to the 30 Mar. 1824 *Taunton Courier*, Clace was already in Dorchester Gaol when Loveridge wrote to Sheppard.

353 24 *twenty-five guineas*: according to the 11 Apr. 1827 *Taunton Courier*, the price asked was twenty-five sovereigns.

354 18 County Chronicle: the *Dorset County Chronicle and Somersetshire Gazette*, see p. 340, n. 35.

355 7 *Hazlett*: the 2 May 1827 *Taunton Courier* records the name as 'Hewlett'.

14 *"flung his last fling"*: an allusion to the epigraph.

TEXTUAL NOTE

354 8 *two years since*: circled and queried in PR. The unidentified proof-reader—presumably a member of the *Cornhill* staff—suggested instead 'two years ago', which was written in the margin beside a question mark and marked for insertion after 'him'.

PUNCTUATION AND STYLING VARIANTS AND TYPOGRAPHICAL ERRORS

The edited text differs from the copy-text in using double quotation marks and not including periods after 'Mr'.

348 title   HORSE.STEALER] ~-~ *C*

349 2   imminent *PR(2)*] immenent *PR(1)*

10   follows:—] ~:ᴧ *C*

25   knowledge.] ~, *C*

349 32 enough.] ~, *C*
    37† unsatisfying.— *C*] ~,— *PR(2)THp*] ~,ᴬ *PR(1)*
    37 short.] ~, *C*

350 1 Wilkins, *PR(3)THp*] ~— *PR(2)THp* [*not in PR(1)*]

351 9 by and by] ~.~.~ *C*
    12 Loveridge's, *PR(2)THp*] ~ᴬ *PR(1)*
    16 proof, *PR(2)THp*] ~ᴬ *PR(1)*
    23† fore-foot *C*] four-foot *PR*

352 27 judge] Judge *C*

354 22 butter-cups] buttercups *C*

355 6 drop":— ¶] ~":ᴬ ᴬ *C*
    11 to hold *PR(2)*] t ohold *PR(1)*
    13 fellow.voyager] ~-~ *C*

COMPOUND WORDS HYPHENATED AT END OF LINE IN
COPY-TEXT

348 5 Trampwoman's

349 34 transaction

353 9 Cross-examined

THE UNCONQUERABLE

TEXTUAL NOTES

358 6 *in England*: in TS first added in pencil, then erased and written in
        ink. This phrase and an illegible pencil erasure beneath 'dallying'
        presumably formed part of TH's first revision.

    14–15 *Roger ... he*: in TS TH first pencilled 'Roger Wingate's' above
        the typed 'his' and 'he' above 'Roger Wingate'; he later erased
        these revisions, added an ink ' 's' to the typed 'Roger Wingate'
        which was then marked for insertion before 'marriage', deleted the
        typed 'his', and began the revision of the final clause with 'he'.

360 34 ¶ *"Ah*: although no paragraph indentation occurs in TS, the pre-
        ceding short line clearly indicates that a break was intended. Four
        other new paragraphs also begin at the left margin in TS: at
        pp. 367. 20, 21, 27, and 368. 19. For all except the third of these TH
        added a pilcrow to avoid confusion.

362 2   *born*: in TS two letters, evidently the beginning of an abandoned
         revision, were written above 'bo' and then erased.

     19 *hand,*: in TS the comma looks like an addition at first glance, but it
         was in fact drawn over a faint typed comma.

363 8   *at a*: in TS followed by an erased typed 't', evidently the beginning
         of 'totally', for which there was insufficient space in the line. Other
         line-end erasures and deletions dictated by insufficient space in-
         clude: 'ac' after 'he' (p. 360. 6), 'i' after 'reared' (p. 363. 37), and
         's' after 'white' (p. 364. 9).

364 5–6 *Wingate … alive.*: the first two versions of this addition were
         written in pencil in the top margin of TS and then erased, pre-
         sumably after the final version had been added to the body of the
         text.

365 18 *showed*: typed over an illegible erasure.

PUNCTUATION AND STYLING VARIANTS AND
TYPOGRAPHICAL ERRORS

357 12 relaxed *TS(2)TH*] r laxed
     23 moment, *TS(2)TH*] ~ˏ
     26[†] luminous *Ed.*] luminious

358 3   decided *TS(2)THp*] decide
     15[†] against *Ed.*] agȧnst
     16[†] days' *Ed.*] ~ˏ
     19 emanated *TS(2)THp&i*] emenated
     22 Fadelle *TS(2)THp*] Fadell
     24 he. *TS(2)THp*] ~,
     26 rare, *TS(2)THp*] ~ˏ
     27 gift. *TS(2)THp*] ~,
     28 course, *TS(2)THp*] ~ˏ
     28 longer, *TS(2)THp*] ~ˏ
     29 importance; *TS(2)THp*] ~,
     30 believe— *TS(2)THp&i*] ~,
     31 point, *TS(2)THp*] ~ˏ
     32 power: *TS(2)THp*] ~.

359 1[†] wish. *Ed.*] ~ˏ
     3   acquiesced, *TS(2)THp*] ~ˏ
     6   garnered *TS(2)THp*] garn red
     7[*] friend's *TS(2)THp*] friends
     9[†] both," *Ed.*] ~",

359 9–10   (it seemed) *TS(2)THp&i*] ‿~ ~,
    12   perfume; *TS(2)TH*] ~,
    17†   offer," *Ed.*] ~",
    23   suspected *TS(2)THp*] suspedted
    31   comradeship‿ *TS(2)TH*] ~,
    34   Gertrude, *TS(2)TH*] ~‿

360 2   accomplished‿ *TS(2)*] ~,
    5   his *TS(2)TH*] hid
    15†   green hedgerows *Ed.*] green-/hedgerows
    16†   suppressed *Ed.*] supressed
    17†   charming *Ed.*] charmimg
    19†   writings *Ed.*] writing s
    30   again *TS(2)TH*] afain
    36   must, *TS(2)*] ~"

361 1†   sometimes *Ed.*] Sometimes
    4†   ‿"I'm *Ed.*] " "~
    5†   already. *Ed.*] ~‿
    8†   himself. *Ed.*] ~‿
    9†   course." *Ed.*] ~".
    9   rigid. *TS(2)TH*] ~‿
    10   hour, *TS(2)TH*] ~‿
    10   rebuff; *TS(2)THp*] ~,
    13   small; *TS(2)THp*] ~,
    18†   lace-shawled *Ed.*] ~‿~
    20   passed, *TS(2)THp*] ~‿
    21   to *TS(3)TH*] t *TS(2)*] tl
    23   girlhood; *TS(2)THp*] ~,
    24   solemn, *TS(2)THp*] ~‿
    30   divinity, *TS(2)THp*] ~‿

362 1†   live, *Ed.*] ~.
    6   hands. ‿ *TS(2)THp&i*] ~. ¶
    9   unconsciously *TS(2)THp&i*] unconsc
    9   vividness, *TS(2)THp*] ~‿
    10   interest. *TS(2)THp*] ~‿
    14   when, *TS(2)THp*] ~‿
    15   they‿ together‿ *TS(2)THp*] ~, ~,
    16   pacing, *TS(2)THp*] ~‿
    18   mother‿ *TS(2)THp*] ~,
    19   civilization; for, *TS(2)TH*] ~, ~‿
    23   was; *TS(2)THp*] ~,
    29   faintly, *TS(2)THp*] ~‿

362 30   naptha-lamps *TS(2)THp*] ~.~
    31   booths, *TS(2)THp*] ~.
    35   erstwhile *TS(2)TH*] erewhile
    36   house. *TS(2)*] ~,

363 1   drawingroom, *TS(2)TH*] ~.
     7   an *TS(2)THp&i*] a
     8   Wingate, *TS(2)THp*] ~.
    11   it *TS(2)THp*] It
    14† utterly *Ed.*] uttcly
    18   pledge; *TS(2)THp*] ~,
    19   more,— *TS(2)THp*] ~,.
    21   disclaimed *TS(2)THp&i*] declained   [*alteration of* n *to* m *pencil only*]
    34   qualities, *TS(2)THp*] ~.
    36   edge *TS(2)THp*] ddge
    37   reared *TS(2)TH*] rsared

364 1   purple *TS(2)THp&i*] purpoe
     4† gauged *Ed.*] guaged
     4   weighed, *TS(2)THp*] ~.
    12* heart-/sick *TS(2)THp*] ~./~
    18† conscience-stricken, *Ed.*] conscience-striken, *TS(2)THp*] ~.~.
    19† instant *Ed.*] instand
    22† together. *Ed.*] ~,

365 13† said. *Ed.*] ~,
    14   used, *TS(2)THp*] ~.
    15   away; *TS(2)THp*] ~:
    20   tone; *TS(2)THp*] ~,
    25   Taking *TS(2)TH*] Taling
    32   breaths *TS(2)THp&i*] breats
    32   bewilderment *TS(2)THp&i*] bewildermnet
    35   had *TS(2)THp&i*] hd

366 3   any *TS(2)TH*] ay
     9   burnt, *TS(2)THp*] ~.
    11   statecraft *TS(2)THp*] statescraft
    11   nothing *TS(2)THp&i*] nothig
    12   ability, *TS(2)TH*] ~.
    16   served *TS(2)THp*] se rved
    19   held *TS(2)THp*] hrld
    20   carried, *TS(2)THp*] ~.
    25† away and *Ed.*] awayand
    29   victory, *TS(2)THp*] ~.

367 3 him, *TS(2)THp*] ~.
6 always; *TS(2)THp*] ~,
7 were, *TS(2)THp*] ~.
11 start, *TS(2)THp*] ~.
16 voice. *TS(2)THp*] ~,
18 suddenly, *TS(2)THp*] ~.
19† finished *Ed.*] finsihed
25 importance?" *TS(2)THp*] ~.
27 himself, *TS(2)THp*] ~.
30 nothing, *TS(2)THp*] ~.
33 aptly, *TS(2)THp*] ~.

368 1 chance; *TS(2)THp*] ~,
6 purpose, *TS(2)THp*] ~.
10 fault *TS(2)THp&i*] falt
19† me." *Ed.*] ~".
22 pigeon-hole *TS(2)THp*] ~.~
25 golden-rod *TS(2)TH*] ~.~
28 action. *TS(2)THp*] ~,
32 steadily. *TS(2)THp*] ~,
33 matters, *TS(2)THp*] ~.

369 5 answer, *TS(2)THp*] ~.
5 came. *TS(2)THp&i*] ~,
8 depressing *TS(2)TH*] depressin
18 bachelor *TS(2)THp&i*] batchelor
19 widowhood; *TS(2)THp*] ~,
26 spoken, *TS(2)TH*] ~.
33 station-garden *TS(2)TH*] ~.~
34 station-cat *TS(2)TH*] ~.~

COMPOUND WORDS HYPHENATED AT END OF LINE IN COPY-TEXT

360 30 unwidow-like

362 35 school-fellow

364 12 heartsick

366 11 statecraft